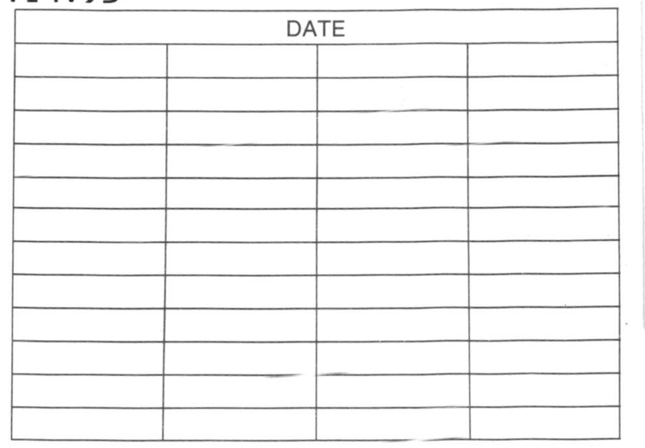

ALSO BY HELEN BRYAN

The Sisterhood

War Brides

Martha Washington: First Lady of Liberty

Planning Applications and Appeals

The Valley

Book One of the Valley Trilogy

HELEN BRYAN

LAKE UNION PUBLISHING

This is a work of fiction. Names, characters, organizations, places, events, and incidents are either products of the author's imagination or are used fictitiously.

Published by Lake Union Publishing, Seattle

www.apub.com

ISBN-13: 9781503936157
ISBN-10: 1503936155

Cover design by Shasti O'Leary-Soudant

Printed in the United States of America

With love for Roger Low

For Michelle, Niels, Bo, and Poppy Bryan-Low

For Cassell Bryan-Low and Jonny and Jake Horsman

PROLOGUE

London, 1754

On a sunny afternoon in late July, the brigantine *Betsy Wisdom*, packed with passengers bound for Virginia, hove out with the tide from the Billingsgate docks into the teeming river traffic on the Thames, nudging between ferrymen's skiffs, lightermen's boats, and the velvet-draped barges of wealthy folk, toward Blackwall. She passed the homes of merchants and noblemen that rose grandly above the river and squalid clusters of dwellings hugging the river's edge. Gliding past the Custom House, she left behind London's teeming, dirty streets; its cutpurses, prostitutes, and beggars; its lawyers in the Temple; its statesmen at Whitehall; its surgeons and barbers and poets; its guildhalls, markets, courts, and theaters. The church steeples of London grew smaller in the distance, the peal of their bells growing fainter and fainter. The towers of Eastbury Manor rose over the Dagenham marshes and gleamed in the setting sun as the *Betsy Wisdom* passed, heading toward Kent and the Thames Estuary, beyond which lay the open sea.

At the mouth of the estuary, sails were raised, catching a northeasterly wind that sent the ship briefly into the North Sea before she tacked south.

But the summer breeze was fitful, and there was barely enough wind to send the ship into the Channel. The calm start reassured the passengers, but the sailors knew the dangers ahead. After Plymouth, when the ship turned south and west into the Atlantic, they kept an apprehensive watch on the horizon. To a man, they were uneasy that the *Betsy Wisdom* sailed alone, instead of in a convoy of ships. A single ship was easy prey for pirates. Moslem corsairs prowling the north coast of Africa from Tunis and Algiers were no less feared than the Christian pirates hovering off Malta. All would pounce on English, French, and Spanish ships; seize the cargo; and sell the passengers and crew in the slave markets of North Africa. White slaves fetched a premium.

Even if they eluded pirates, August weather was famously unpredictable—the sea appeared as gentle as the English waters they had recently left, but out in the Atlantic, a ferocious storm could strike with terrifying suddenness. But the *Betsy Wisdom*'s captain was impatient to make the return voyage before winter made Atlantic crossings even more perilous. The return voyage would convey so valuable a cargo of tobacco back to England that the captain was willing to take risks for a share of the profits. There was an insatiable appetite for tobacco in Europe.

When they approached the Canaries, three schooners appeared on the horizon and the watch raised the alarm, but the schooners sailed into the distance. The captain judged by their position that they were Guineamen with a cargo of slaves from West Africa, not pirates.

The sailors' relief was short-lived. In the space of an afternoon, the sun dulled, then vanished behind gray clouds. The sea grew rough. The gentle blue swell became rising gray waves tipped with white foam. The wind blew harder. The sailors hurried to reef the sails, knowing what would come. By nightfall a fierce gale lashed and tore at the reefed sails, and larger and larger waves battered the *Betsy Wisdom*, now plunging up and down through high mountains and deep caverns of angry water, her timbers creaking and groaning above the howling wind until it seemed certain they would burst apart. But pitching and shuddering, waves crashing over the bow, the ship miraculously stayed intact and held its course, driven on by the only force stronger than the elements—human greed.

The terrified passengers suffered and prayed. A peer's daughter and her lady companion had the luxury of being wretchedly seasick in the privacy of a tiny, damp cubicle of a cabin, where the two women struggled to brace themselves together in a narrow wooden bunk to keep from being thrown about like rag dolls with the violent pitch and heave of the ship. They clutched handkerchiefs soaked in lavender water to their foreheads and tried to recite psalms to comfort each other.

Below, in the dark, rat-infested hold, transported criminals and poor families were packed tightly together, ankle deep in fetid water that soaked their meager belongings. They were seasick, frightened of drowning, and as helpless against the fury of the sea as they had been powerless against the authorities and the wealthy on dry land. Death crept in among them in the form of scurvy and dysentery. Children were its first, easiest victims, least able to withstand the wet, overcrowded, unsanitary conditions—the rotten beef and moldy biscuits, putrid drinking water, the constant vomiting and diarrhea, cramps and dizziness, mouth sores, and lice. But as terrible days and terrible nights became indistinguishable, sated Death turned its eyes from the children to the adults, waiting for a final moment of weakness and despair, for the will to live to give way, to seize its larger prey. The dead were flung overboard without winding sheet or ceremony. The living were left to repent of their journey, to mourn the corpses of their unburied children sinking to the ocean floor to feed the fish, to long for the hardships they had left behind. But the *Betsy Wisdom* sailed on, seemingly into the jaws of hell, leaving the dead in its wake and carrying the living to a dearly bought, uncertain fate in the New World.

For those who survived, the journey would take eight weeks.

CHAPTER 1
ST. JAMES'S PALACE

London, January 1751

It was the first official drawing room of the New Year, and the fashionable and would-be fashionable of London were assembled at St. James's Palace to pass a dank winter's evening in a throng of company. The only requirement for attendance was the correct formal attire—a wide mantua dress with whalebone hoops for the ladies, while men were obliged to wear wigs, embroidered suits, fine stockings, swords, and the ceremonial flat hats that were carried under the arm as emphasis that no man covered his head in the presence of the monarch. This well-dressed crowd jostled and squeezed into the great drawing room at St. James's Palace and spilled over into card rooms, the dancing room, and the room with refreshments.

They had come to pay their respects to the king, some desperate to get close enough to the throne to be noticed, to court a favor or seek a job or preferment for themselves or a relative. They had come to meet their acquaintance, hear the latest gossip about the crown prince, to see lovers or mistresses, dance, drink punch, play cards. They were looking to seize any advantage, to cultivate relations with influential patrons, to find amusement where it could be found.

Noticeable on this particular evening was a group of excited and nervous young girls in the first flush of elegance, with ribbons, hothouse flowers, and new gowns, waiting with their male relatives or female sponsors to be presented at court and formally received by King George II and his daughter Princess Amelia.

The Honorable Sophia Grafton was one of them, on the arm of her father, Viscount Grafton, and her godmother, Lady Burnham, on her other side. Presentation was general notice to all the world that a young woman was officially suitable to be received in company and foreign courts, but everyone present knew that it signaled that she was of an age to be married.

Four months past her sixteenth birthday, Sophia was naturally interested in being marriageable, though only in a general sort of way. To Sophia's mind, marriage itself was a distant, dull, and probably inevitable prospect, inextricably bound up with duty and bearing children. It seemed to her far less interesting than the immediate prospects open to a girl out in fashionable society. Mainly, being out meant she could attend balls, something she had looked forward to for years. Balls offered the prospect of romance in a general sort of way that had nothing to do with actual marriage duty but everything to do with pretty gowns, music, and ballrooms crowded with young men eager to dance with her. While some young women of Sophia's rank in life looked forward to being married, because some wives often enjoyed the freedom to do as they pleased once they had produced an heir, Sophia had observed a wife's freedom depended upon her husband's whim. A man had the power to curtail his wife's freedom as much as he pleased. Lord Grafton was an indulgent father, and Sophia, not being interested in any young man in particular, was in no hurry to exchange such a benevolent parent for the uncertain temper of a husband.

Once satisfied that Sophia had finally acquired the decorum and good sense he had been at such pains to instill in her, it was true Lord Grafton allowed her a great deal of freedom. His friends had warned him that sixteen was a difficult age, when girls were all too ready to fancy themselves in love. Lord Grafton believed, however, that the difficult stage of Sophia's upbringing, turbulent though it had been for a time, was now over. Pretty Sophia had a practical turn of mind and a quick wit. She was not fond of reading novels and had never evinced the least romantic sensibility or inclination to pine for a dashing hero. If her heart was set on balls, at her age that was only to be expected. Dancing was a harmless pastime, and Lord Grafton stood ready to allow it.

To Sophia, this evening's presentation meant a final escape from the tedium of the schoolroom, the nursery, and her strict governess. To wear a beautiful gown and dance in company, be admired and eat late suppers, had been her object for four years, the most desirable thing imaginable. Waiting impatiently for the line to move forward, she heard the tantalizing strains of music from the dancing room and longed for the girl ahead of her to move along more quickly. Sophia felt the gates of paradise were about to swing open to receive her, and she chaffed at the delay.

Her eyes sparkled as she drank in the glorious panoply of the company that she was part of tonight—the flash of jewels; the heavy scents of perfumes and powders that masked stronger odors; the elegant little black velvet patches and the towering headdresses of the most fashionable ladies; the feathers; the sea of fine fabrics stretched over wide hoop skirts; bodices cut and artfully boned so they barely contained swelling bosoms; the colorful sashes, waistcoats, and decorations worn by the men; the occasional dash of regimentals; the livery of the footmen; the wigs; the ruffles; the fans furled and unfurled to deliver secret coded messages between lovers; glitter and pomp everywhere!

Sophia felt herself happily in looks tonight and, observing the other girls and the fashionable ladies, saw that her own dress was much the prettiest. There had been a battle with her godmother over her gown. Upright Lady Burnham, dressed tonight in ancient black silk, though with the requisite wide skirts and lace ruffles at the elbow, had become a convert to the Evangelicals since the death of her husband. With fervor unusual in her class, she had embraced Bible readings, missionary societies, and good works among the poor. She disapproved of anything frivolous, a category that included girls being out, fine gowns, presentations, pleasure gardens, plays, balls, and almost anything else that diverted their attention from the workings of the Spirit, the attainment of salvation, or charitable deeds. She had worked hard to achieve some sort of religious awakening in Sophia, though so far with no discernible result.

Yet despite her dislike of frivolous pastimes and her preoccupation with her goddaughter's spiritual welfare, Lady Burnham had felt duty bound to accompany Sophia tonight, in place of her dead mother, because Lord Grafton absolutely insisted that his daughter, the last of the Grafton line, make her formal entrance into fashionable society. Though Lady Burnham saw no necessity for this, she had conceded that rank had its due and put aside her reservations. She reasoned that once Sophia was out, her father would concentrate his efforts to have her suitably and swiftly married, and once married, retirement to the country would remove Sophia from the gaudy temptations of the fashionable world and set her feet in the more easily trodden paths of virtue in Sussex. Lady Burnham had been brought up in the country and was firmly of the opinion that righteousness was more effectively pursued there than in London.

And Lady Burnham knew from her experience what was required in the way of formal dress and deportment if a female were to have the *entrée* to the drawing room and the royal presence. She had been a lady-in-waiting to the late Queen Caroline and, after her death, to the royal princesses for several years, and thus was in a position to coach Sophia in preparation. In return, she had insisted on the power to veto any gown that she deemed too risqué. To Sophia's dismay, Lady Burnham refused to countenance the fashionable low décolletage that exposed almost the entire bosom and insisted the Venetian red brocade embellished with black lace and black ribbons Sophia had set her heart on was unsuitable for a young girl.

Obliged to relinquish the Venetian red, Sophia had tried to wheedle permission to use face paint as part of the bargain. Rouge and a kind of white paste on the face were the mark of a lady of fashion, and if Sophia thought the modesty of her décolletage unfashionably schoolgirlish, makeup would lend her an air of sophistication. Predictably, the request had prompted one of Lady Burnham's lectures. "Paint!" Lady Burnham had been horrified. "Truly poisoned vanity. Many a beauty has died for her red-and-white complexion. Only reflect, Sophia, that Jezebel was a *painted* harlot! And consider her end, eaten by dogs. Your mother never painted. Take a lesson and be satisfied with the coloring God has given you."

Sophia flushed rebelliously. "Oh, bother Jezebel! That was a long time ago! And one never hears of beautiful ladies being eaten by dogs nowadays," she had muttered defiantly. On the morning of her presentation, she sent her maid to buy powder, rouge, and whitener for her skin. She had heard that face paint was sometimes poisonous—that powder was made of lead, that arsenic brightened the complexion—but she was anxious to look as pretty as possible on this momentous occasion and reasoned that surely a little wouldn't be dangerous. She thought her father would be so astonished and delighted by her transformation that it would stifle any objections Lady Burnham was minded to voice. She hid the intriguing little pots her maid had obtained from a well-known barber.

That evening after her hair was arranged and all that remained to be done was to put on her gown and her mother's jewels, she had sent her maid away. She collected the pots from under her handkerchiefs, pulled the candles close to her looking glass, and dabbed white all over her face and neck and the top of her chest where it would show above her new gown. Then she took the pad of Spanish wool and rubbed rouge on her cheeks and fixed a small heart-shaped black velvet patch next to her mouth. Lady Burnham had warned her that these cunning little patches were a mark of deception, that their purpose was to hide pockmarks. But Sophia thought they were the height of enchanting sophistication and next to a mouth said "Kiss me!"

She stepped back to observe the effect of her efforts, thinking her father would be so amazed at her transformation that his delight would silence Lady Burnham. And the young men would notice and all want to be introduced and dance with her . . .

"Oh! Oh dear!" she murmured. An odd being stared back at her. Her cheeks, normally a smooth, healthy pink, miraculously unpitted by a mild case of smallpox suffered in childhood, stood out like hectic red apples in a porcelain-white face. To be lovely required a fair complexion, of course, but . . . ought she to look so very white? Her brown eyes, with their long lashes and heavy, level brows, had become dark holes. She had prepared to remedy this by using a trick she had heard was employed by the great beauties, who shaved off their eyebrows, applied paint over the spot, and glued on false brows made of mouse skin, arched at an attractive angle. She had a razor at the ready and little strips of mouse skin laid out on a handkerchief when she paused to wonder, would dead mouse really improve things? Looking at the hairy rodent skin, she shuddered. Perhaps it wouldn't. She put down the razor.

She considered her reflection again, struggling to see a resemblance to the fashionable young ladies she had admired riding in the park and the dazzling courtesans in their jewels and carriages, who drew admiring looks wherever they went, though they made Lady Burnham sniff and look pointedly in the other direction. It was said they all painted. Why didn't she resemble them now? She struggled to persuade herself that she did, until sense prevailed and she unwillingly concluded she looked feverish and hard, like the women who called from the shadows to men in the streets. Suddenly her father's delighted approval seemed less certain, and as for Lady Burnham . . . She had sighed and scrubbed her face clean at her washstand, emptied the paint pots into her commode, and tossed the mouse eyebrows into the fire.

At least she and Lady Burnham had reached a pleasing compromise over her presentation gown. After much debate, one near tantrum, wheedling, and negotiations that would have astonished Lord Grafton, Lady Burnham had allowed Sophia's second choice of fabrics and colors, though she still thought them ostentatious.

Now, standing in line, she couldn't resist another satisfied inventory of her new finery, just to be sure it looked as pleasing as she had thought when choosing it. Her gown had required many yards of delicious pale-blue Spitalfields silk shot with silver threads that shimmered in the candlelight. It had been enormously expensive—Lady Burnham had thrown up her hands in disbelief, hearing the price—but the cost did not signify, Sophia thought happily. Her clothing allowance was generous, and the color was most becoming. She smoothed the yellow silk underskirt that contrasted so beautifully with the blue of her gown, admired the deep lace ruffles caught with large bows at her elbows, and adjusted the pearl necklace that had been her mother's. She shook her head a little to feel the pleasant weight of the sapphire and diamond eardrops that had also been her mother's tremble against her jaw. Her hair had been carefully dressed to show them off, and she checked again that the new Chinese painted ivory fan was still attached to the fine gold chain at her waist.

"Compose yourself! Stop preening!" whispered Lady Burnham. "You're not a parrot." Sophia sighed and tried to emulate her godmother's calm dignity. But oh she *did* love her gown!

Choosing the right gown had been the easy part, compared with other preparations for her presentation. Sophia had had lessons in dancing, etiquette, and deportment. She had learned the correct way to address everyone from bishops and ambassadors to the royal family and knew who took precedence over whom. She could converse, slowly but correctly, in French and Italian. She had been required to read the newspapers to familiarize herself with the important topics of the day. Lord Grafton greatly disliked ill-informed, empty-headed women, ignorant of contemporary affairs and with no flair for conversation.

And crucially, Sophia had mastered the art of wearing her new grown-up clothes.

Mantua gowns presented a challenge. They had outrageously wide hooped skirts, which required careful management to pass through company in a crowded room and were very heavy on account of the quantity of fabric necessary to make them. It was essential not to move too quickly, or there was a danger of being unbalanced by the dress. Negotiating stairs was difficult. Practicing at home in her dress and new high-heeled slippers had cost her several tumbles down the staircase, but Sophia had picked herself up and persevered. She learned how to maneuver the hooped skirts sideways through narrow doors; how to take tiny, elegant steps so the hoops didn't sway like a church bell rung by a drunken sacristan; and, when traveling in a chair or carriage, how to settle her vast skirts gracefully around her. "You are a butterfly folding its wings," her dancing master had instructed, "not a cow settling in the mud."

She had learned to curtsey elegantly. Though Sophia expected a curtsey would be the least of her problems, Lady Burnham insisted she practice in her new dress, over and over. "You're certain to be up and down all evening," she warned. "It's surprisingly tiring."

Sophia also learned how women dealt with emergencies of a personal nature in public. This involved pissing discreetly into a chamber pot hidden beneath her gown so no one noticed or, if necessary, into a small bourdaloue jug gripped between her thighs. Sophia hoped it wouldn't come to that. She had practiced while wearing her nightdress, but it was remarkably difficult. It would be dreadful if she missed, not at all elegant if a puddle spread from under her skirt. To avoid the possibility, she had drunk nothing since breakfast, and if she drank nothing until she returned home, she hoped she could last.

Then there was the matter of her new high-heeled slippers with their crystal buckles. Very pretty, catching a flash of light now and then when a satin-slippered toe peeked from under her gown, but they required a stately step. For most of her life, Sophia had been quick on her feet. Now she had to remind herself to move slowly.

As the line ahead of them edged forward, Sophia was mentally reviewing all the things she must and must not do. It was nearly their turn. She would have had butterflies in her stomach had she not been laced into her new gown almost too tightly to breathe.

"At last, you are next," whispered Lord Grafton. Sophia flashed him an anxious look, he patted her hand, and they were announced: "Viscount Grafton, Lady Burnham, and the Honorable Sophia Grafton." Sophia said a little prayer she wouldn't do something wrong, trip and find herself on the floor, or be publicly rebuked by an irritated king, who, she had been warned, was a stickler for etiquette, easily bored, and quite brusque in his manner. She lifted her chin as if she were going into battle. Up the steps they went, and there ahead of them on a dais sat the king and Princess Amelia.

At a signal from the chamberlain, Sophia took five careful steps forward from between her father and Lady Burnham. At the correct distance from the royal personages, she made a slow curtsey. The king looked decidedly grim and muttered something that might have been a pleasantry or might have been a wish they would all go home. Princess Amelia smiled and beckoned her closer. Sophia advanced and knelt, careful of her skirt.

Milestone though it was, the presentation was very short, over as soon as Sophia had been kissed on the forehead by the princess, who had murmured something kind about the pleasure of seeing Lord

Grafton's daughter at court at last. Then to her consternation, the king barked a question at her in his guttural German accent. It had sounded something like "Ha! They tell me the ladies are all writing boetry these days. Troublesome. Do you care for boets and boetry, Miss Grafton?" Sophia thought there was something accusatory in his tone and swiftly racked her brains to think what *boetry* might be.

It was not permissible to say "What?" or "I beg your pardon" to the king.

Fortunately her father had anticipated that she might be asked an incomprehensible question and, whatever it was, had advised her to answer, "If it please Your Majesty, yes, but only as my father thinks proper for me." The king had seemed satisfied with that reply and nodded. Relieved, Sophia rose from her knees, curtseyed the requisite three times, and backed carefully away from the royal presence to her place between her father and godmother.

As soon as they left the presentation room, Lady Burnham considered her duty done. She sent a footman to find her servant in the servants' hall to call for her chair, kissed Sophia good night, and went home to bed.

Sophia tugged her father's arm, in a frenzy of impatience to reach the dancing room. The doors were open, and she could hear the enticing strains of a French dance and see that it was quite crowded. Oh, how she longed to dance! She had paid attention to her dancing master's every word. She had practiced and practiced the minuet, the allemande, and the quadrille and had marshalled her tutors, her governess, the housekeeper, and the maids to help her practice the figures of the *contredanse*, with the result that the household staff could now perform it rather skillfully. She had even practiced dancing in her court dress.

But their progress through the crush of people was slowed by Lord Grafton's many acquaintances, as this or that friend stopped to bow a greeting, be introduced to Sophia, and exchange a few words about matters of state or Lord Grafton's recent retirement and mention how affected the king had been to lose his special diplomatic emissary and adviser. All swept Sophia with an appraising look. "So this is the young lady who does the honors of your house, sir! We hear such charming reports of your dinners. You do your father great credit, my dear."

Sophia curtseyed and thanked them, earnestly wishing her father would stop chatting. "Papa, pray be brief! The dancing will be at an end!" she whispered urgently. When they finally reached the dancing room, a society hostess, glittering with diamonds, caught sight of the viscount and, exclaiming what a long time it had been since she had had the pleasure of meeting him at a ball, held out a hand to be kissed.

As Lord Grafton made the introduction, Sophia curtseyed yet again, feeling her gown grow heavier each time she bent her knees. The hostess beamed, offering to take Sophia under her wing so that Lord Grafton might be free to see his friends or play cards. She begged leave to introduce her nephew, a tall young captain in the guards. Lord Grafton gave permission, and the captain swept a happy Sophia away to dance, and inquiring looks followed the couple as they took their places in the set.

Lord Grafton suppressed a smile as he moved away, knowing that no one excites more interest at a ball than a pretty new face. He could see that the hostess was already whispering to her friend and pointing Sophia out. Her pedigree would be established among the company within the space of a few dances. This suited him perfectly. Sophia was officially marriageable, and he was confident it would not be long before the House of Grafton would be restored as he had hoped and dreamed it would be.

The news that the girl in the shimmering gown was Viscount Grafton's daughter was soon circulating through the ballroom. This made Sophia a very interesting presence indeed. The family was an old and prominent one, and Lord Grafton was a person of both wealth and influence, who had served the king as a trusted adviser on foreign affairs for many years. His formidable intellect and diplomatic finesse had made him an invaluable envoy and negotiator, and despite his recent retirement, people continued to seek his patronage and advice.

A handsome man of sixty, Lord Grafton was courteous and obliging to all and especially gallant to women, though at the same time, a little formal and distant with the ladies. An element of tragedy added to his air of distinction, as it was well-known that his heart went to the grave the day he buried his beautiful young wife, Lady Catherine, dead of childbed fever a few years after their marriage.

Sophia was the only child of the marriage, and as heiress to the whole Grafton estate, she was more charming by the hour as speculation grew about the size of her dowry. She had no lack of partners; at the far end of the room, young men had besieged the society hostess, begging to be introduced.

Only a cluster of older ladies, playing whist at a strategically placed table in the card room from which they could watch the dancing, eavesdrop on men's conversations, and recall how much gayer drawing rooms had been in dear, departed Queen Caroline's day, were surprised to learn the identity of the belle of the evening. They raised their eyebrows in astonishment and craned their necks to see if she had grown up to resemble her mother.

All in this circle of elderly aristocrats were intimate friends of Lady Burnham, and they regretted that they were now deprived of her company at evening parties because her Evangelicals believed dancing, music, and cards were snares set by the Devil. But in her younger days, when Lady Burnham had still been a high Anglican, she had enjoyed attending drawing rooms and evening parties with her husband. Then the women had seen a great deal of each other, and Lady Burnham's friends had been witness to her efforts to do her duty as godmother to Lord Grafton's motherless child. She had spared no effort, but little Sophia had been a horrid child—unmanageable, dirty, impertinent, and spoiled. No sooner had she learned to walk than servants' gossip reported her nursemaids called their charge "the very Devil." There had been shocking stories about the child's behavior abroad, the ladies recalled. It had reflected badly on Lord Grafton, but had not affected his standing with the king. The king, who was not particularly fond of his own offspring, had merely commented that all children were troublesome fools who should be whipped regularly.

"The girl must have undergone a marvelous transformation," remarked one of the whist players dryly. "The young gentlemen passing behind us praise her in the most flattering terms. An angel of light has descended from heaven, apparently. Such sweetness in her smile, such charming manners, such good breeding in her countenance, so graceful, all loveliness. Her like has never before been seen in St. James's."

Her friend triumphantly finessed the trick being played. "Hmm. I suppose her fortune plays no part in their raptures? If you recall her godmother's accounts of her, it was a narrow thing. If she's turned out well, it's down to that breeding in her countenance. She *is* a Grafton. Though the last of the line." The other ladies nodded sagely, acknowledging the power of superior breeding such as theirs to bestow distinction and loveliness. As the next trick was dealt, they turned to the interesting topic of the advantageous matches Sophia might make, comparing the fortunes and pedigrees of various eligible young men.

"Though Miss Grafton's marriage is contingent on some very strict conditions, I understand," one reminded them.

"Quite true. If a man is accustomed to London and Bath, fond of the shooting in Scotland, the races, and visiting, he will find his freedom curtailed."

"An older man may be more amenable than a young one."

"And I understand that the Grafton estate has not been so very profitable as it once was. Lord Grafton has lived at considerable expense, you know, just as his grandfather did."

"That may not signify, because they say there's been a significant addition to Lord Grafton's fortune, a tobacco plantation in Virginia . . . Ha! I have the trump, the trick is mine, and I thank you!"

"Yes, a gift from the king. Who can say whether His Majesty felt some recompense due for the expenditure Lord Grafton has been put to in his service or whether it was distress at losing one of the few advisers who dared to speak plainly to him? I daresay his skills as a diplomat have been as much in play dealing with the king as with the French and the Austrians. Most exhausting for him. It's said he is quite worn-out with the traveling. I hear that he was surprised when he was informed of the plantation, but he could hardly refuse."

"But what was His Majesty's purpose, I wonder. A valuable gift, of course; Virginia tobacco is the foundation of many a *new* fortune. But surely the king cannot intend that Lord Grafton remove himself to Virginia!"

"No, one can hardly imagine Lord Grafton, of all people, going to live among the Negroes and savages and those colonial tobacco planters we sometimes see in London, who flaunt their fortunes in ill-fitting new breeches—this one boasting loudly of the number of his slaves and his acres of tobacco and that one how many pounds of tobacco were required to pay for his wife's gowns, all of them bleating that their London factors and merchants are thieves and swindlers who ought to be hung."

"Colonial manners! Atrocious! I beg you will not speak of them! No, one cannot imagine Lord Grafton in Virginia for a moment."

"I hear he proposes to have it managed, and the income is to be settled on the girl when she marries. How curious that his conditions for her marriage are so restrictive as to prevent her and her husband from going to Virginia to visit the property. They say he fears a disconnection of the family and the estate if they were to be long absent. Really, it is quite wonderful how keenly Lord Grafton feels his attachment to the estate now. He all but abandoned it when he first inherited."

"He'll have much to do to eliminate the fortune hunters. You know what happens when a girl is rich. She's handsome enough, resembles her mother in looks if not in sweetness. I daresay she's improved in manners or even her father would not venture to bring her to a drawing room. Conditions or not, it's not to be supposed there'll be any lack of candidates for her hand, and she'll find herself married before she knows it. It's her duty. Her godmother will have drummed that into her—dear Lady Burnham is a great one for duty."

"Quite so," murmured her friend, rolling her eyes slightly.

"It's only to be hoped that, unlike her poor mother, the girl will be capable of breeding a large family, as Lord Grafton evidently hopes. She is the last of the Graftons."

"Yes, a sad loss to the nation when old families die out. And the Graftons are *very* old. Everything depends upon Miss Grafton now. Looking at it in that light, one quite understands Lord Grafton's conditions. Thank you, my turn to deal?"

CHAPTER 2
THE GRAFTONS

The Graftons were an old family, with the kind of pedigree that in certain circles of society, not to mention in the view of Lord Grafton, outweighed even the matter of their wealth. They had begun as ambitious Norman knights with a fearsome reputation for bravery and a shrewdly calculated willingness to serve those powerful enough to reward them well. They had owned large estates in Sussex since the eleventh century, when William the Conqueror rewarded the services of his loyal baron, and possibly illegitimate son, Hugh de Graftonne, with a fiefdom confiscated from Saxon landowners. Hugh built a fortified castle on the south coast, had worn out several wives by the siring of his many children, and, ruthlessly ambitious, was said to have rendered any service to the king, including the murder of some disaffected nobles who plotted against William. Hugh's fortunes flourished.

Over the following centuries, the de Graftonnes multiplied and prospered, anglicizing the name to Grafton. In due course they moved inland, where they built a handsome manor house and amassed a fortune from the wool trade and, it was whispered, an even greater fortune from smuggling on the Sussex coast. As their wealth grew, so did the family's political influence. They acquired a reputation for cleverness among their supporters, for scheming and ruthlessness among their detractors. By the time of the Tudors, they had proved clever or scheming enough to render invaluable service to the Crown, though such service was rendered shrewdly, in a manner that kept their heads attached to their necks. The Grafton title was elevated to viscount.

But by the middle of the seventeenth century, the once-numerous family had diminished. There had been much intermarriage between cousins, and there were fewer and fewer surviving offspring. The great plague had taken Graftons young and old to the grave, and nearly an entire generation of young Grafton Cavaliers perished bearing Royalist arms in the English Civil War. Foreign adventures in pestilent tropical climes had claimed some of the next generation before they had married, while others had failed to beget sons. The Grafton line gradually dwindled, all but dying out. The present Viscount Grafton was the last of the male line, and his only child, Sophia, was the last of the Grafton blood.

As the youngest of three sons, Peregrine Grafton had not expected to inherit the title but to go into the church. He and two older brothers were educated at Winchester from a young age at his father's behest. Afterward, he attended Oxford, while his eldest brother returned to Sussex to take up the reins of the estate upon succeeding to the title on their father's death. That brother had died in a hunting accident, unmarried.

The second brother did not live to inherit. According to his father's plan, he should have gone into the navy. But having no taste for a naval life, and given to indolence and pleasure, from a young age he had drifted into a life of gaming and dissolution that had left him dead of consumption and syphilis at the age of twenty-four.

The title of Viscount Grafton descended to Peregrine.

Until the demise of his brothers, Peregrine had followed his intellectual interests, making a grand tour of Europe as his father and grandfather had done. Traditionally, in a family of three sons, the eldest inherited, the second went into the military, and the third to the church. Though Peregrine was not particularly religious, the church as an institution was interesting and powerful, and theology had its own intellectual appeal, so he had no objection to taking holy orders as his father had intended. But he had been in no hurry. Blessed with the Grafton intelligence—some wags even said the last of the Grafton intelligence—coupled with the canny Grafton ability to use it well, he was a courteous, convivial young man, well-read, fluent in five languages, the sort of man who made himself agreeable and quickly at home in any foreign city. He was also possessed of a natural diplomatic cunning that was a legacy from his more scheming ancestors. It was a characteristic that would have assisted his swift rise in the church hierarchy to an archbishopric had his elder brothers not predeceased him.

Having watched his elder brother's descent into a life of degradation, Peregrine had always eschewed vicious habits. He had been a brilliant scholar at Oxford and, on his return from his grand tour, was preparing to read divinity there when he learned his second brother had died and he had inherited. The new Lord Grafton regretfully left his Oxford college and went home to Sussex to shoulder the responsibilities of the title and the estate.

Clever though he was, he was unprepared for that task. He was unusual among the landed nobility in that the prospect of a private gentleman's life in the country held little appeal for him. He had no understanding of running an estate or making it profitable. In truth, it bored him, though he did at first attempt some interesting innovations on the estate. One and all, his experiments and schemes were costly failures. Conceding he had no head for business, young Lord Grafton wisely consigned management of his property to his steward's capable hands and took himself to London.

There he joined the ranks of the *beau monde* for a time, but a vapid existence of leisure passed in late mornings, late dinners, and gentlemen's clubs left him bored and restless. He cast about for some interesting pastime suitable for a young man of his rank. He was fond of visiting the law courts and watching trials and legal proceedings, and decided life at the Bar would suit him very well. He was eating his dinners at the Temple and had set his sights on rising to become Lord Chief Justice of the King's Bench when an old family friend, Lord Burnham, thought Lord Grafton might put his talents to better use and recommended him as a promising protégé to the British ambassador to Paris.

It was a testing time for the British diplomatic mission. English relations with France were perpetually under strain, but young Lord Grafton embraced the challenge. Urbane, charming, quick-witted enough to master any complicated brief very quickly, he could talk round awkward issues to English advantage. He found the diplomatic life perfectly suited to his abilities, and appointments to various other diplomatic missions followed, until he had achieved the distinction of being a sort of diplomatic emissary-at-large, dispatched whenever and wherever a delicate situation required special finesse to resolve matters in England's interests without disrupting diplomatic relationships.

In the tradition of his ancestors who had served the Tudors, Lord Grafton made himself indispensable to the House of Hanover. It was no easy task. German-born George II was a difficult personality, a moody and irascible monarch with a dogged interest in foreign policy. After the death of his Queen Caroline, he belatedly realized he had lost one of his cleverest and most sensible advisers and became increasingly reliant on Lord Grafton, whose views on foreign policy issues mirrored, the king believed, the king's own perceptions. Within a few years Lord Grafton had partially filled the void left by the queen's death to become the king's most trusted source of advice on diplomatic matters. Since Lord Grafton's duties obliged him to be often abroad, and to be readily available to the king when in England, he rented a palatial house near

St. James's and rarely visited his Sussex estate, saying in jest that it went along better without him.

However, as the years passed, there came a nagging awareness that he had neglected his hereditary obligations. In short, he had been far too busy to think of marriage, as the last of the Graftons ought to have done. Above all he had failed to beget a legitimate heir.

In his youth he had dutifully met an endless succession of wellborn girls ranging in age from twelve to twenty, but none appealed to him. He could not bear silly females; his wife must be capable of conversation. He also had an eye for beauty and grace. Finding a bride who combined the attributes of birth, beauty, elegance, virtue, and good sense with that of a sound education was a time-consuming business. Had he persisted, eventually he might have found such a paragon, but it must be said that he did not seek for her as hard as he might have done.

As a young man, he had made the agreeable discovery that he was attractive to women. This had led to a succession of liaisons with beautiful ladies at foreign courts and cities, which occupied any attention he could spare from his work. It said much for his skill in diplomacy that these affairs were conducted discreetly, without scandal and usually concluded in such a way that both parties remained on amiable terms afterward. Lord Grafton was never in one place for long. This would have been an obstacle to any long-standing relationship, had not most of the ladies concerned been married already or achieved a status as courtesans that they were unwilling to relinquish in favor of a man who was absent more often than not.

Things had continued in this pleasant way until he was in late middle age and still a bachelor. Then Lord Burnham's widow, an upright, devout lady-in-waiting to Princess Amelia, scandalized by Lord Grafton's unsettled womanizing, introduced him to her young cousin and ward. Catherine Vassey was a penniless orphan of sixteen, recently come to court from the charitable school for aristocratic orphans, where she had been educated. Lady Burnham had arranged an appointment at court for Catherine as assistant lady-in-waiting, and Catherine's sweet ways and virtuous behavior had quickly won Lady Burnham's approval. Lord Grafton, accustomed to great beauties, scarcely noticed the shy young woman in her shabby gown, beyond supposing she was a pretty child.

Despite her modest demeanor and threadbare clothes, Catherine found herself the object of men's attention. Life at her charitable school had been very plain and scrimped, divided between lessons and church. She had hoped that life at court would provide a few enjoyments, and at first this had promised to be the case. She discovered that young men constantly put themselves in her way, sent her gifts and sonnets, and made her laugh by their extravagant claims they were languishing in love for her. However, Lady Burnham warned her that young girls of no fortune must beware of fashionable young men, whose sweet words were more certain to lead a girl to ruin than to the altar. Catherine sighed. But she obeyed Lady Burnham, was deaf to protestations of love, and returned the poems and sonnets and gifts men sent her. She tried not to envy the other assistants to the royal ladies-in-waiting, girls who wore pretty clothes, ate sweetmeats, read novels, giggled together in the garden, and danced with these same young men. Dutifully Catherine followed Lady Burnham to church and spent her evenings reading aloud from a book of sermons while the older woman stitched at her embroidery frame in her small grace-and-favor apartments, a dull little oasis in St. James's Palace.

Catherine's behavior provoked the young gallants who pursued her. One night, after drinking too much wine, they competed to mock her as a false paragon of virtue and ended by wagering among themselves as to who would be first to have his way with her. A purse of sovereigns contributed by all sealed the wager.

Catherine was crossing a dark courtyard one night, believing she was obeying an unusually late summons from one of the royal princesses. Waiting in the shadows were three masked fellows who had sent the false message. They stepped out of the shadows and attacked her, pulling and tearing her clothing, laughing that they would have their sport and then split the purse three ways.

Lord Grafton had been nearby, waiting to dine with the king. While he waited he paced a long corridor that opened onto the courtyard, lost in thought as he mulled over a problem they were to discuss at dinner. His ruminations were interrupted by a girl's screams. He hurried toward the sound and saw three men who had pushed a young woman up against a wall. Fury lent Lord Grafton strength. He flung the attackers aside and shouted for help, and footmen and guards came running, just as the villains were trying to draw their swords. They were too drunk to resist arrest, and when their masks were ripped away to reveal their identities, they sniveled that it had only been a jest. It was then Lord Grafton realized the distraught girl clutching her torn gown, with her hair disheveled and a bruise on her cheek, was Lady Burnham's ward. Lord Grafton ordered the guards to lock the men up, as roughly as possible, he added.

He put his coat around Catherine's shoulders and handed her his handkerchief to dry her tears. Struggling to recover her dignity, Catherine hiccupped, "You must think it strange to find me about the palace at this hour, but truly, sir, I was told the princess had summoned me. Alas, it was a trick. I have always obeyed Lady Burnham and paid the young men no attention, and for that they torment me. And they would have . . . you prevented their succeeding, sir. I am only distressed, not harmed."

Lord Grafton swore to see the young men flogged.

Trying to hold her ruined dress together, Catherine shook her head. "Sir, pray do not! It will only cause a scandal, and I dare not risk losing my position at court. I thank you for your help, but I shall manage. I only need to mend this rent in my gown before Lady Burnham sees it." Her lip quivered. "And persuade one of the other girls to lend me a little of her face powder to hide the bruises. I shall be more on my guard now. I must keep my place at court. I have nowhere else to go." Catherine broke down and wept.

Lord Grafton promised that he would say nothing publicly, as Catherine wished. Privately, he vowed to see the young men exiled indefinitely to a dreary, remote outpost in Ireland under the guise of a royal appointment. He had the ear of the king and knew how such things might be arranged. He would do it tonight. By tomorrow morning, the miscreants would find themselves on board a ship bound for Ireland.

Reassuring Catherine that all would be well, he escorted her back to Lady Burnham's apartments. Along the way, he noticed what he had not before, that Catherine was not just pretty, she was beautiful. By the time they reached her door, a plan had taken shape in his mind. Catherine was a gentlewoman, educated and young enough to bear children. But save for Lady Burnham, she had no powerful friend at court. As the night's outrage had proved, she was in need of protection beyond what Lady Burnham could provide. He ought to have been married long since. He decided that the next day, when she had had time to recover herself, he would ask Catherine to be his wife.

The next afternoon, he called upon Lady Burnham, asked to speak to her privately, and, as soon as they had shut the door of the sitting room, asked for Catherine's hand. Lady Burnham gave permission at once. Catherine was summoned to the sitting room and informed of Lord Grafton's wish. She was astonished that so powerful and wealthy a man, whom she hardly knew, suddenly wished to marry her, but Lady Burnham approved and Catherine was in the habit of obeying.

They married quickly, and Catherine was transformed from poor relation to viscountess. Overnight she became mistress of a large and handsome London house and a vast Sussex estate. She was told to command whatever she wished, was deferred to by all around her, given jewels belonging to the Grafton family and a carriage of her own, and urged to order new clothes without delay, since it was important she at once make a good appearance as Lady Grafton. Catherine felt she had ventured into a fairy tale. She proceeded cautiously, anxious to please a husband she scarcely knew and of whom she was a little in awe.

Catherine was sensible beyond her years. She had learned at an early age that the world was a hard place for a poor orphan and was grateful for the security of her new position, valuing her husband's kindness to her beyond his fortune or her jewels. Though she cared little for the admiration she attracted, she wanted to make an elegant appearance to please him. She begged Lady Burnham to help her choose new clothes and advise her about how she was to conduct herself in her new position.

Lady Burnham was ready with advice on everything from clothes to what was expected of Viscountess Grafton, emphasizing that Catherine's position carried duties and responsibilities beyond merely looking nice for her husband. Within a year of her marriage, Catherine became patroness of the new Foundling Hospital in London, had established a school for the village children on the Grafton Sussex estate, and made a large contribution to the poor relief of that parish.

This too pleased Lord Grafton. Though he did not live in the country, he took his responsibilities to the Grafton estate tenants seriously, and he automatically expected his wife to share in this, as well as observing a tradition of *noblesse oblige* in relation to the poor and less fortunate. He also felt it was a point of family honor. He found enjoyment watching Catherine bloom from the shabby ward of Lady Burnham to the shyly gracious and elegant Lady Grafton, celebrated for her charity as much as for her beauty. He congratulated himself that he had chosen well—his young wife was everything that Lady Grafton ought to be. Initial satisfaction with his choice gradually deepened into something else as he became aware of an unexpected contentment in her companionship, an appreciation of her sensible conversation, her thoughtful attention to his wishes, and her delight and gratitude when he surprised her with pretty gifts. A marriage so hastily concluded for reasons of convenience to both parties, and the disparity in the ages of husband and wife, might have precluded any real understanding, but as the couple became better acquainted, their attachment grew.

Lord Grafton hardly recognized himself—he had never imagined the world would revolve around one woman. It did. Catherine was secure and happy, and Lord Grafton parted with his heart for the first time in his life.

All that remained to complete the couple's happiness were children, and Catherine prayed for the son she knew her husband wanted desperately. And at first it appeared her prayers would be answered. In the space of four years, she conceived nine times. But their hopes were repeatedly dashed, as Catherine miscarried one infant after another and sadly observed the poor children who thrived in the Foundling Hospital. Finally, she carried a tenth child to term, and a midwife highly recommended by the wives of Lord Grafton's acquaintance was engaged to attend Catherine's lying-in. When her birth pangs began, she assured her anxious husband that all would be well.

After a long and difficult labor, Catherine gave birth to a daughter. Catherine kissed and cuddled the swaddled baby and asked that she be named Sophia after her own mother. "An older sister for our sons," she told her husband when he tiptoed in for a first look at his daughter. Catherine had been washed and put into a clean gown with lace at the sleeves and neck, and she lay pale and tired but smiling beneath a silk comforter. Lord Grafton kissed her, thinking she had never looked more beautiful, and concealed his disappointment at the baby's sex.

A day after the birth, Catherine complained to the midwife of a bad pain in her abdomen. The midwife said briskly that women must expect to suffer as God ordained, this was common with new mothers, and Catherine resigned herself. By the following day, she was feverish. By nighttime, she was shaking with chills despite her fever. Her head hurt, and her fever climbed. Her sheets were soaked with a foul-smelling discharge. She had no strength to hold the baby. In a fog of pain,

Catherine drifted in and out of consciousness and no longer recognized her husband.

Within a week Catherine was dead.

"Childbed fever," said the midwife, barely pausing to wipe her hands on her dirty apron after removing the soiled sheet. "God's will be done." She left to attend other mothers, to deliver other infants. She would neither change her apron nor wash her bloodstained hands. Of the mothers and infants, some would live despite her, and many, like Catherine, would die. Sophia was one of the fortunate babies who did not.

Lord Grafton could scarcely grasp his sudden, unbearable descent into widowerhood. He expected every minute to see Catherine smiling at him from the doorway, the sofa, across the table, from the bed. Sometimes from the corner of his eye, he thought he glimpsed her, felt her presence in the room, her hand on his shoulder, but she would vanish before he could be sure. The palatial house that once suited him so comfortably was empty and cold without Catherine. The nursery and schoolroom apartments on an upper floor rang with the crying of his motherless infant, uncomforted by her two wet nurses.

He would travel again on the king's work, he decided. The house where he had been happy was intolerable. He would have it shut up, live there only briefly between postings when it was necessary to be in London.

Lady Burnham, who had had no children of her own destined to live past infancy, mourned Catherine as if she had been her own daughter and found a new outlet for her maternal feelings in Sophia, to whom she stood as godmother. In tears, she made a solemn vow at the baptismal font that Sophia would grow up in the image of her mother—modest, virtuous, devout, and devoted to her duty. She urged Lord Grafton to bear his sorrow like a Christian and not to repine. It was God's will.

Undone by grief, Lord Grafton ceased all pretense of believing in God. His hopes for a son and a large family of children had died with his beloved Catherine. He would not contemplate remarrying. It compounded his grief that this meant the Grafton line ended with Sophia.

Unless he could find a way to prevent it.

Preventing such a calamity soon became an obsession to distract him from his grief. When Sophia was still in her cradle, he instructed his solicitors to devise a scheme to continue the line through his daughter, to restore the connection between the family and the estate that had been nearly severed in his own lifetime and to ensure that Sophia, a Grafton by blood, would become mistress of the ancestral home and progenitress of a new Grafton dynasty. He hoped that he would live to see a grandson and Grafton heir settled in the old nursery in Sussex.

By the time Sophia had cut her first tooth on a silver-and-coral teething stick, the plan had been drawn up. Lord Grafton had ordered the solicitors to leave no stone unturned, to leave nothing to chance. This resulted in an elaborate document arranging matters so that Sophia's marriage would reestablish the Graftons in their Sussex family seat. Sophia's husband must agree to take the Grafton name to ensure that Sophia's children would bear it, Graftons by both blood and name. It would also be written into the marriage articles that the couple and their children would live at Grafton Manor for nine months of every year, as Lord Grafton's own experience had taught him that living elsewhere loosened the ties that ought to bind the owner to the estate. This was reinforced by a legal provision restricting the use of Sophia's dowry and the Grafton fortune in such a way that her husband and the Grafton heirs thereafter must comply with his conditions or forfeit any right to the income of the estate.

From that time on, Lord Grafton began to pin all his hopes and expectations on Sophia's marriage, which he expected would take place seventeen or eighteen years hence. As Lady Burnham had vowed at Sophia's baptism, he intended Sophia would grow up like Catherine in every way, a model of female excellence, a gem in the Grafton crown. She would be educated, elegant, trained in the gracious arts, instructed in the responsibilities of her rank, and devoted to her home, her family, and those who depended on her charity. Having done as much as he could to map out this future for a one-year-old child on whose small shoulders rested the continuance of the Grafton family, the grieving widower sought oblivion in his work.

CHAPTER 3
HOYDEN

True to his vow never to remarry, Lord Grafton resisted all attempts to match him with a second wife. No woman could compare with Catherine. He remained devoted to her memory, and his daughter was the sole object of his affections. During Sophia's early years, Lord Grafton found solace and a welcome distraction in his work and gradually became more absorbed than he realized. He had an academic's tendency to single-minded concentration at the best of times, and his first fervent intention of raising Sophia to be a paragon among women lost some of its intensity. Though Lady Burnham was eager to have Sophia live with her, Lord Grafton refused to part with the child, insisting Sophia accompany him when he traveled on the king's business. He was blind to the inconvenience a child and its entourage caused his hosts, as a wet nurse, nurse, nursery maid, and nursery footman joined the secretaries, footmen, coachmen, pages, valet, and cooks who accompanied him on his postings.

Sophia's early upbringing was not at all what Lady Burnham thought suitable for a small child, and unsurprisingly, things did not go quite as Lady Burnham had intended at the baptismal font. Instead of the regular hours, simple food, and calm surroundings of the nursery, Sophia grew up accustomed to the bustle of travel, the sight of new places—sprawling cities and minarets, cathedrals and onion-shaped domes of eastern churches, snow-capped mountains, and castles and palaces where she and her father were ceremoniously lodged and entertained in luxury. She learned French from a succession of nursemaids, and a coarse Italian dialect, including some shocking epithets and oaths, from her father's valet. She was allowed to stay up till all hours because she had tantrums when put to bed. She often tore her clothes and took off and threw away her shoes because she preferred to go barefoot. She disliked having her hair combed. She acquired a taste for late dinners, rich puddings and cake, and learned that no matter how naughty her behavior, the servants would ply her with sweets and cover up her misdeeds, lest they be dismissed from their posts.

When Lord Grafton returned to London between postings, Lady Burnham was scandalized by her goddaughter's behavior, disorderly dress, tangled hair, and free speech and was alarmed by the late hours she was permitted to keep, but she struggled to persuade Lord Grafton of the harm that was being done. Lord Grafton was a fond father, but he inhabited a largely male world, far removed from the domestic concerns and realities of child raising that would have been the province of a wife. He was an extremely busy man, usually immersed in his work and a busy schedule, surrounded by secretaries and clerks vying for his attention. When he had time to bestow on his daughter, he found Sophia a pretty, delightfully precocious child who resembled her mother in looks and made him laugh indulgently with her impish little sallies and pranks. He never noticed her bare, dirty toes under her dress or her sticky, grubby little hands. After half an hour he would chuck her under the chin and send the little angel back to her nurse, thinking there had never been a more enchanting child.

Lady Burnham, who spent as much time with her goddaughter as possible when Lord Grafton returned home to London, saw a small, willful monster of impertinence, a grinning little caricature of Catherine, more uncivilized with every visit. She referred acerbically to her goddaughter as Miss Sauce and complained to her friends that distance made it impossible for her to correct the woeful upbringing of dear Catherine's child.

Of the two, Lady Burnham's was the accurate picture. Sophia had discovered early on that she could outrun her nurse and do as she pleased until one of the footmen retrieved her. She was never stopped or reprimanded, never denied her own way in everything. Her father, whom she adored, could easily have rectified her behavior. His disapproval and even a scolding would have done wonders in the early years.

While he was involved in tense negotiations with the French, trying to avert the war between the European powers over the matter of the succession to the Hapsburg throne and simultaneously reach an accord between the French and English over territorial boundaries in the American colonies, Sophia had ridden a pony into the palace at Versailles early one morning before the court was awake. The page who opened a side door for her whispered she must whip the pony to a canter, then pull on the reins, and she would have a thrilling ride. Whipped to a frenzy, the animal had cantered full tilt up and down corridors and through gilded salons, its hooves sliding out of control on the polished floors until it crashed into something or someone. It kicked footmen, trampled maids, knocked over the fat Duchesse de Montjoie on her way to early Mass in the royal chapel, and left a mess and a trail of broken mirrors and smashed priceless porcelain and a shattered Italian marquetry cabinet that was a favorite piece of the king's, before being cornered and led away.

A laughing Sophia pointed at Henri, the thirteen-year-old page especially assigned the job of keeping watch over her. "He told me to do it! I want to do it again!" she cried. The unfortunate Henri was given the sound thrashing that no one dared give Sophia.

In St. Petersburg, Sophia had stolen a valuable jeweled box from the nobleman's palace where Lord Grafton and his entourage were lodged and exchanged it for a dancing bear cub held on a chain by a boy her age. She and the boy then coaxed the cub into the coach house and shut it in the nobleman's pride and joy, his splendid gilded carriage that had been painted inside with an intensely pornographic rendition of Leda and the Swan by a specially commissioned Florentine artist. Sophia fed the cub *bonbons* through the window for an afternoon until she grew bored and went off in search of some cake the cook had promised her. The cub chewed the velvet seats and the gilding to pieces, clawed the painted insides to shreds, broke the side panel, and escaped into the city, dragging its chain.

In Spain, Sophia disappeared for an entire day, leaving the frantic servants responsible for her searching high and low in a lather of fear. She was eventually discovered to have gone off with some Gypsies and was found singing bawdy songs on a tabletop and dancing for coins in a tavern while the Gypsies fiddled. She bit the footman who had to drag her bodily away.

Lord Grafton's servants and secretaries had to work harder and harder to conceal Sophia's misdeeds from their employer. However, Sophia's escapades became the talk of London, and the gossip reached Lady Burnham's ears.

The episode with the Gypsies was the last straw. She wrote a stern letter to Lord Grafton, repeating what she had heard, warning that Sophia was fast becoming an ignorant, coarse, unmanageable hoyden whose behavior, if left unchecked, would cause her to end her days in disgrace, an object of ridicule, pity, or shame, at best shunned by respectable society and at worst on the streets or in the almshouse. Catherine would have been shocked and distressed. It was Lord Grafton's duty to ensure his daughter's respectability. At ten years of age, Sophia should not be always on the move, nor allowed to bend the household staff to her will. She was in need of more education and guidance than the desultory attentions of a traveling tutor and a lax nursemaid. He must rectify things before she reached a point of no return. If he failed to attend to Sophia's education as a gentlewoman, she would never be a gentleman's wife.

"Sophia cost Catherine her life. Do not allow that sacrifice to have been made in vain. It is your duty to Catherine to see she turns out as she ought," Lady Burnham finished.

"There!" she exclaimed as she impressed the Burnham arms into the hot wax sealing the letter, satisfied she had done what she ought to have done long ago. Satisfyingly soon she had a reply from an alarmed Lord Grafton. He protested that he was shocked; he had not had the slightest idea of Sophia's misbehavior. He intended to return with her to London as soon as his present business allowed, and he would put in place the necessary measures for Sophia's education and to correct any defects in her behavior. He promised to adopt any special measures Lady Burnham thought efficacious.

Lady Burnham breathed a sigh of relief. Better late than never. Her views on a gentlewoman's education were firmly old-fashioned. She had been brought up in the country and educated at home. She deplored the modern fashionable tendency to send girls to boarding schools and dispense with teaching wellborn girls the old-fashioned practical skills of housewifery. She believed that those skills, a close acquaintance with the *Book of Common Prayer*, good manners, sound morals, and decorum in dress were the foundations of a woman's happiness and respectability and all the preparation necessary for a girl to become a wife and mother and fulfill her purpose as mistress of a Christian household. She fondly imagined Sophia's education would closely resemble her own. She did not for a moment imagine Lord Grafton felt differently.

Lord Grafton thought altogether differently. Once he turned his attention from his work to the proper education of a daughter he had continued to think of as an infant in caps for far too long, he was startled to realize how his daughter had grown. According to his plan, she was within a few years of marriage and becoming mistress of the Grafton estate and matriarch of a new generation of Graftons. Though there had been a series of tutors who traveled with his household, they had been much put-upon, and Sophia had learned little beyond the ability to read and write and do simple sums, and that little only because she was occasionally bored in the intervals between mischiefs.

And now that he belatedly attended to the sort of child Sophia was, he suddenly appreciated how unfit she was for her role. Save for her good looks, which promised to blossom into beauty, Sophia could hardly have been less like Catherine. There was a great deal to be done, quickly. A very great deal, if Lady Burnham's list was to be believed—education, deportment, regulated behavior, manners, feminine grace, discretion, an understanding of her charitable obligations and duties toward the poor and toward the villagers who had served the Grafton family and estate for generations. As Lord Grafton saw with dismay, at present Sophia hardly promised to be a companion of sense and understanding to her husband, a conscientious mistress of her household, a mother capable of guiding her children well, or a benefactress to those who depended on her largesse.

He sighed and wished for the thousandth time that Catherine had lived to oversee Sophia's upbringing. Lady Burnham was the best of women, but her blunt religious sensibilities meant that in some respects she was lacking. She would not teach Sophia grace and elegance, which he believed were indispensable for a woman. And acquainted as he now was with accounts of Sophia's past misdeeds and bad behavior, he himself was at sea over where to begin to correct the oversights and mismanagement of her earlier years.

He decided to begin with Sophia's education. Education he understood.

Lord Grafton could not conceive of an education that did not comprehend Latin, mathematics, history, logic, an understanding of the solar system, music, and philosophy, and because none of the schools for young ladies met his standards, he hired tutors from his college at Oxford. This was going overboard somewhat, in Lady Burnham's eyes. A girl had no need whatsoever of Latin, mathematics, and logic, and surely a competent governess could manage the rest, but Lord Grafton was adamant. However, what she most deplored was the lack of religious instruction.

Lady Burnham had always been devout, but in later life she had come to the view that the established Church of England had become complacent in a world rife with evil. The Evangelicals had a more robust approach to combatting the works of the Devil and had made a deep impression. She was a fervent convert, had taken to reading her Bible with a new zeal and a conviction that it was necessary to be born again to achieve everlasting salvation. Never a woman to shirk from what she believed to be her duty, she felt it was incumbent upon her to foster a similar awareness of conscience, sin, salvation, and duty in her goddaughter.

She regarded Lord Grafton as an obstacle on this point. He was sadly lax in matters of religion, and not just regarding the established church. He was an admirer of John Locke and held distressingly broad-minded views; in fact, she suspected he was that deplorable thing, a freethinker. His opinion was that dissidents and Quakers, Catholics, and even heathen Jews and Hindus should be allowed to practice their faiths undisturbed. He failed to observe the Sabbath, reading what he pleased instead of restricting himself to Bible study or sermons, and thought nothing of traveling, visiting, or working on his official papers then. All this was anathema to Lady Burnham, but worst of all, he absolutely declined to engage a religious tutor despite Lady Burnham's recommending several divines for the post. She saw it would be necessary to take Sophia's religious and moral instruction in hand herself.

As for Sophia, she had returned to London little suspecting what was in store. She was at first incredulous, then furious to learn of the changes in her situation. Instead of romping at will through palaces and foreign courts of Europe where she was petted and indulged, she would be confined to the nursery and schoolroom in the London house. There were to be early dinners, fixed bedtimes, and a full timetable of lessons. Her outings were limited to chaperoned walks or rides in the park and trips to church.

"I am to *stay behind? No! I will not!*" she shrieked, outraged to hear that she would no longer accompany her father on his foreign postings. She hated on sight the experienced governess with sharp eyes hired on her godmother's recommendation, whom Lady Burnham herself would supervise in the course of regular visits to the household.

Determined to compensate for the lack of religious instruction, Lady Burnham decreed Sophia would accompany her to church twice on Sundays, to sessions of hymn-singing and Bible reading with the Evangelicals, to meetings of her Evangelical missionary and antislavery societies, and on her charitable rounds to the Foundling Hospital where Catherine had been patroness.

"No! No, no, no, no," screamed Sophia until she was hoarse. But for once no one took any notice.

Between Lady Burnham, the governess, and the tutors, Sophia was required to rise early, dress neatly, and attend prayers—Lord Grafton gave way on this at Lady Burnham's insistence—then lessons in the schoolroom, followed by music, embroidery, sketching, and, again at Lady Burnham's particular insistence, afternoon lessons from the Grafton housekeeper. To the annoyance of his excellent French cook, Lord Grafton had been obliged to bring the country housekeeper, Mrs. Betts, to London for the sole purpose of teaching Sophia the kind of old-fashioned domestic arts that young gentlewomen, even wealthy ones, had been obliged to master in Lady Burnham's day—cookery and the best ways to rid tapestry of moths to the care of invalids and the raising of poultry. This seemed so unnecessary that Sophia was too incredulous to even protest. The Grafton servants were numerous, and it was unlikely Sophia would ever be required to lift a finger. Even Lord Grafton wondered about the usefulness of such a program, but Lady Burnham brooked no resistance, insisting this was knowledge suitable for all women no matter how great their station in life. It was the old-fashioned way.

Sophia rebelled. She was insufferably rude to everyone. She threw inkpots at her tutors when they reprimanded her, stuck out her tongue at Mrs. Betts, and called Lady Burnham Old Lady Tittle-Tattle behind her back. She dragged her feet noisily into church, refused to sing hymns, and scowled and fidgeted through the sermon, kicking the pew in front of her. Her father was obliged to double the tutors' stipends to keep them from leaving, give Mrs. Betts a generous honorarium, and regularly placate Lady Burnham by speaking of their duty to Catherine.

The phlegmatic governess was unmovable as a pillar of stone whatever Sophia did, and Lady Burnham and Mrs. Betts held firm, though Lady Burnham, now in her seventies, found encounters with her goddaughter increasingly exhausting. By the time Sophia was twelve, the tutors had changed several times, all of them assuring Lord Grafton as they left that Sophia was clever enough when in a humor to attend to her lessons, but as that was rarely the case, she had made little progress in her studies. Her behavior was too appalling to be borne any longer.

Lord Grafton was perplexed. Surely Sophia was not getting worse?

Matters came to a head as Sophia was approaching thirteen. Lord Grafton returned home exhausted from a taxing mission where the conflicting demands of the king, the Austrians, and the Poles had proved impossible to resolve. Feeling battered by an especially rough Channel crossing, and soaked and chilled from a hard rain that lashed the carriage from Gravesend, he arrived home wanting nothing so much as a restoring supper before the fire in his library, a bottle of claret, and a book. Instead he was met by domestic uproar. A short-tempered Mrs. Betts asked to speak to him, so put out by Miss Sophia's rudeness that she was giving notice at once unless Lord Grafton sent her home to Sussex. The latest group of tutors followed her into the library and announced, to a man, they would leave at the end of their term. There was a querulous note from Lady Burnham informing him that she was unequal to the task of dragging an unwilling Sophia to church any longer, and begging to be excused from any dealings with the child for the time being.

In short, Sophia was utterly horrid, incorrigible, and spoiled, and looked likely to remain so.

Lord Grafton was rarely angry. He viewed anger as the last resort of a weak man and ineffectual as a means to an end. However, it was not a good night. His mission had ended badly, he felt the beginnings of a cold, and confronted with a host of problems caused by a willful and intransigent child who seemed worse each time he returned to London, he lost his temper.

He called Sophia into his library, and there was a stormy interview. For the first time in his life, Lord Grafton railed and shouted at his daughter, told her he was ashamed of her, she was a reproach to the blessed memory of her mother and a disgrace to the name of Grafton. She would never be allowed in society until she acquired an education and manners worthy of her name and until her father could be confident that she would comport herself in a becoming and ladylike manner. She was as ungovernable, ill-mannered, and ignorant as a child of four, and unless she changed her ways, like a child of four she would spend the rest of her days in the nursery.

His reaction caught Sophia off guard. She was shocked speechless at first by the threat she would remain in the nursery when she reached an age to be out. She was Miss Grafton! Of course she would go about in society when she was old enough! It was unthinkable that she would not!

Then, as the import of his words sank in, she regarded her father with alarm. He had always been affectionate, and when she had been reprimanded by her tutors or the governess, he had always found a way to excuse her shortcomings while chiding mildly that she really ought to do better. She had never experienced his anger, and the reference to her mother shook her completely. Few things had the power to affect Sophia, but she knew that her mother, Catherine, had been a saint—beautiful, good, and beloved by all—and that giving birth to Sophia had killed her. This knowledge lay guiltily on her heart. Now her father, who had always doted on her, had grown suddenly stern and unkind. And what if he truly meant she must stay in the nursery?

This was terrible, terrible!

She attempted a saucy answer, but her lip trembled and she burst into tears. Everything and everyone was against her, she sobbed. She hated staying behind in London, she hated the governess, and she hated the tutors. They all hated her. She hated bossy Mrs. Betts and her stupid housewifery. This was all horrid Lady Burnham's fault, talebearing, interfering Lady Tittle-Tattle! Horrid, ugly old witch!

Lord Grafton's eyes were rudely opened to the common perception of Sophia, and he was appalled. How had his sweet Catherine given birth to such a vile-tempered creature? Lady Burnham was right—the girl was unmarriageable, she could not be inflicted on any man's family, and she was unfit to raise children. The Grafton line would die out. The list of her faults was long, that she had forgotten herself and been impertinent to Lady Burnham was terrible, but to learn that she had been rude to Mrs. Betts! Rudeness to an old and faithful servant was, in Lord Grafton's eyes, mean-spirited and unworthy of any woman of rank. This to him was the very worst of Sophia's sins.

What in God's name was he to do now? He rubbed his eyes and tried to think. When the storm finally subsided and Sophia was sniffing forlornly into her handkerchief, he fell back on the negotiating skill for which he was famed.

Maintaining his stern tone, he said that perhaps it was not too late for amendment. *If* Sophia could persuade her tutors to stay, *if* he was pleased with their reports of her progress, *if* Mrs. Betts confirmed that Sophia's manner toward her showed the respect and courtesy that were Mrs. Betts's due, *if* she apologized to Mrs. Betts and applied herself profitably to the lessons of housewifery, and above all *if* her manners toward Lady Burnham were what they ought to be, she might look forward to her first ball when she turned thirty. He would not lift a finger to help her; it must all be her doing. And proof would depend entirely on the accounts of the tutor, Mrs. Betts, and all.

"But they're all against me and . . . Thirty! Oh, how *unfair*!" Sophia wailed. She burst into tears again and buried her face in her handkerchief.

Lord Grafton, who never raised his voice, roared, "Silence! I am not yet done. My daughter will find it not only her duty but to her advantage to heed my wishes."

"Why, Papa?" Sophia muttered sullenly through her sobs.

"Because when my daughter proves by her obedient behavior that she is worthy of her father's love and confidence and has learned to conduct herself in a manner befitting her station in life, then she shall have a yearly allowance for her clothes when she turns sixteen."

"What?" said Sophia mid-sniff. Had she heard correctly?

Lord Grafton repeated what he had said about the allowance, but told her she must gain it by her own efforts. He reminded her that in little more than three years' time, she would be the age her mother was when she married. At sixteen, Catherine had been well educated, celebrated for her virtue, decorous behavior, courtesy, and attention to her duty. She had been elegant and modest, with charming manners. A woman who was everything a woman ought to be, an ornament to her sex and the Grafton family. That was what he wished Sophia to be as well.

Overwhelmed by the ideal of perfection, Sophia sighed. "Oh. Yes, quite, Papa. Of course. But about balls, Papa, surely there's no need to wait until I'm thirty . . ."

"There will be no further talk of balls! Never speak again of balls!" He was furious that Sophia had a head full of nonsense when he'd been speaking seriously to her of Catherine's example. He sent her back to the nursery in disgrace.

Upstairs after the interview in the library, Sophia kicked everything in reach and raged and screamed she hated, hated, *hated* detestable Lady Burnham! This was all her doing! But resentment was exhausting, and when the flames of anger eventually burned themselves out, she couldn't help comparing what would be gained from doing as her father wished with nothing to be gained from continuing as she was. The promise of a dress allowance was sweet, but above all she wanted her father to love her again. And it seemed that the only way that would happen was if she became more like her mother. How was she to resemble a dead saint? Her father had set her a hopeless task. Confused, sulky, and angry, Sophia began to feel very miserable. And bored. Lessons were at an end, as the tutors were busy packing their valises and preparing to return to Oxford. Her governess confirmed that she would be stuck in the nursery and schoolroom with nothing to do but look out the window.

It occurred to Sophia that she might as well try to do as her father wished. She waited until the tutors were on the verge of leaving, steeled herself for the humiliation, and through clenched teeth mumbled a speech of apology, promising to attend to her lessons if they agreed to stay. The tutors were surprised. They hadn't much confidence that Sophia's behavior or attention would improve, but in the event that Sophia apologized, Lord Grafton had offered a large increase in their pay if they agreed to stay. For such a large sum, they could put up with her rudeness and impertinence a little longer.

To their surprise, the rudeness was less and less in evidence as time passed. Sophia checked her tendency to impertinent answers. When she was admonished for her behavior or poor work or lack of attention, she no longer aped the admonition in a high voice; she apologized. She even applied herself to her lessons. Formerly blotted and carelessly scrawled exercise books gradually became models of neatness. The tutors were astonished.

Her performance on the hated pianoforte improved, because she gritted her teeth and practiced each day. To her surprise, the governess put down her sewing one day to listen and nodded approval. "You play very pleasantly when you've a mind to. Your application to practice has much improved your proficiency. I shall speak of it to Lord Grafton when he's next home."

"Oh! Will you?" Sophia was startled by praise from such an unexpected quarter but knew it would do her cause no harm. She decided it would be politic to be more accommodating to her governess. She set herself to learn a piano sonata her father particularly liked.

It was a struggle, but as Lord Grafton had shrewdly judged, the prospect of new clothes was a most persuasive argument with a young girl. Surprised to find how well her efforts to improve were rewarded with praise and assurances her father would be pleased by this or that, Sophia seized every opportunity to shine.

Mrs. Betts, who had endured hours of Sophia's unwilling presence in the kitchen to no good purpose, was surprised when the annual delivery of quinces from the home farm in Sussex was shortly followed by the appearance of Sophia in the kitchen, all smiles, sweetly asking to be provided with an apron to help preserve the quinces in honey. "Lord Grafton is particularly fond of preserved quinces," said Sophia by way of explanation. Mrs. Betts rolled her eyes at the cook and set Sophia before a basket of rock-hard quinces that needed peeling. "Oh!" exclaimed Sophia faintly, picking up a hard quince in one hand and the small peeling knife in the other. "How, exactly, does one peel?" She felt sure this was the kitchen maid's job, and had fancied herself merely stirring the pot as the honey bubbled, but she thought better of saying so and, to the astonishment of the kitchen staff, set to work without a complaint.

At her next lesson, Sophia demanded to learn her father's favorite dish, a fricassee of duck in a chafing dish. Mrs. Betts protested it was a difficult dish to master, and the cook suggested they attempt a plain baked apple instead, but Sophia was determined. The work of the kitchen came to a halt while a duck was sent for, killed, singed and plucked, scalded, soaked in boiled milk, rubbed with herbs, roasted, cut up, and finally flamed in a chafing dish with brandy and a sauce made using onions and the liver. As Sophia insisted on carrying out each step in the process herself, it took the better part of a day. When the dish was finished, she flushed with pleasure when Mrs. Betts and the cook praised the results, though the duck was so tough the cook secretly fed it to the cat later.

Mrs. Betts longed to be back in Sussex. Lord Grafton, for the most part, made only brief visits to his estate. Despite this, his orders were that the house be kept up and the London house supplied with game and fruit from the home farm. Other than maintaining the manor house in good order and packing produce in straw, Mrs. Betts and the other servants had little to do and enjoyed a good deal of leisure. Sophia's newfound enthusiasm for cookery and sudden appearances in the kitchen always created a mess, saddling Mrs. Betts, the cook, and the scullery maids with much more work. Mrs. Betts disapproved of the gentry dabbling in the housekeeping and heartily wished Lady Burnham had not insisted Sophia learn something for which she had absolutely no need.

But Mrs. Betts had to admit there had been a change for the better. Sophia had not been rude in many weeks. In fact, she had painstakingly said, "Please, Mrs. Betts," and "Thank you, Mrs. Betts," and "Do you advise lavender or pomander as best for keeping moths from the linen chest, Mrs. Betts?"

Just one person remained to be reconciled, and Sophia had to think long and hard about the clothing allowance before she could gather sufficient resolve to ask Lady Burnham to resume their excursions to church and Evangelical meetings. When she finally did, she was obliged to endure a long, pointed lecture about what awaited selfish, ungrateful, and disobedient children on Judgment Day, followed by another about girls who did not attend to their duty but thought only of clothes and balls and amusements, before Lady Burnham judged Sophia properly remorseful and mindful of her sinful nature.

At church Sophia appeared to listen to entire sermons without squirming. Dragging her feet only a little, she accompanied Lady Burnham on visits to the Foundling Hospital where her mother had been a benefactress and helped dole out soup and clothing. She attended Evangelical hymn singings and lecture meetings where she listened to long speeches about missions to the heathens and the abolition of African slavery, during which she struggled not to fall asleep.

In her efforts to win over Lady Burnham, Sophia even went so far as asking Lord Grafton for pocket money to buy warm stockings for the orphans and Bibles for the heathens. Bemused by this newfound compassion and piety, Lord Grafton gave it to her, albeit not without worrying his unorthodox methods might have gone too far, sending her into the arms of the Evangelicals along with her godmother. However, on reflection he decided that once in possession of a clothing allowance, Sophia would lose interest in the Evangelicals.

He could hardly have chosen a better incentive or timed it more perfectly. Within a year Sophia's mentors were cautiously telling Lord Grafton that though there was still room for improvement, a different Sophia was emerging, like a butterfly from its chrysalis, mostly attentive to her lessons, civil to those about her, and able to quote Bible verses at length. The tutors said nothing more about leaving. Mrs. Betts didn't have the heart to give notice, and Lady Burnham was heard to say to the governess that perhaps there was hope after all, provided the child's head wasn't addled by reading too many of the godless books her father and her tutors thought necessary.

When younger, Sophia was so careless in her dress that Lady Burnham would ask tartly if she had put on her clothes with a pitchfork. But a girl of fourteen begins to think of looking well. Sophia was growing taller, and her childish form filling out, so that her dresses had to be let down in the hem and let out around her shoulders and bosom. No new ones were ordered—by Lord Grafton's express instructions to the governess and Lady Burnham—and the old ones grew shabby and too tight. When she and her governess walked in the St. James's Gardens with the daughters of Lord Grafton's acquaintance, or when Lady Burnham took her to church, Sophia was painfully conscious of her unbecoming schoolgirl's gowns. She observed the dresses, hats, and ribbons of other young ladies with envious eyes, and imagined they looked at her with scorn. She pulled her cloak tight around her and tucked her chin into her collar so all that was visible was her plain bonnet. She pinned her hopes on the promised dress allowance and tried harder to be good.

When her father returned to London between postings, Sophia hovered outside the library to overhear what the governess, the tutors, and the housekeeper said about her progress. She thought there were murmurs of approval, but the door was very thick.

On her fifteenth birthday, Lord Grafton told her that he proposed to hire another tutor.

"Oh no! Not Greek!" Sophia's heart sank. Lord Grafton often spoke of his own knowledge of ancient Greek and regretted that few women of his acquaintance were familiar with the classics.

"I had in mind a dancing master, though if you would prefer a Greek tutor instead, naturally I could—"

"Oh! No, please, Papa, a dancing master! Let us not think of Greek!" she begged. Later she wondered why there should be a dancing master if she were not to attend balls until she was old and decrepit at thirty, when it would be too late to wear anything but matronly gowns in plain colors, and probably no one would ask her to dance. Looking in the mirror, she thought she would do much better at balls now, in a pretty gown. Once she would have importuned. Now she dared not say so out loud.

When her anxiously awaited sixteenth birthday dawned, Lord Grafton traveled home to London. After a long meeting that morning with the tutors and Mrs. Betts, Lord Grafton called Sophia into the library. Sophia, nearly expiring with anxiety to know whether she had performed her part of the bargain, observed with dismay that her father looked solemn. In fact, Lord Grafton was so pleased that he was plotting Sophia's next step to the altar.

"Oh, Papa, truly I have tried my best. Please say whether I have done as well as you wished!"

To her relief, he said that he had had excellent reports of her improvement in her conduct, her studies, and, above all, her manners and behavior that gratified him immensely. He smiled wryly and said that according to Lady Burnham, her soul was awakening to the possibility of a true conversion experience. He told her he was proud of her, that she had earned her reward, and named a generous sum that she might spend each year.

Sophia gasped at the size of it.

"Your mother had that same allowance settled on her after our marriage."

Sophia threw herself into his arms. "Oh, Papa! Thank you!"

Then her imagination ran riot. A moment later she was dancing ecstatically round the study, imagining India shawls and China fans, hats with stuffed birds, bright silks, jewels, patches and powder, ribbons, dancing slippers. She was sweeping an imaginary train behind her while fluttering an imaginary fan, watched admiringly by an imaginary crowd whispering that was Lady Catherine Grafton's daughter, that she promised to be as great a beauty as her mother . . .

Sophia was abruptly called to order by Lord Grafton and stopped mid-whirl. He repeated what he had just said. He had told the king he wished to retire on the grounds that his health was no longer equal to the constant traveling. And if Sophia was to be out, that required him to be in residence in London.

Sophia could scarcely believe her ears. "Out!" And tentatively, "It would be very hard to be out, yet not allowed balls, Papa."

He nodded. "It would. Therefore"—he smiled—"I have changed my mind."

"I may attend *balls*? Oh, Papa! When?"

"Your presentation at court must take place first. But I must be satisfied of several things, Sophia. You must always bear in mind that a girl who is out is no longer a child but old enough to be married. In society, people will watch closely how Miss Grafton looks and conducts herself publicly, and believe me, they will be quick to note any misstep. Be guided by your godmother. Yes, I know she is constantly lecturing you, but she knows what is right. And," he added sternly, "never again refer to Lady Burnham as Lady Tittle-Tattle. Such rudeness is unbecoming."

Sophia flushed and nodded.

"And when you are out, it will not be long before you enter into a whole new sphere of life, as you are likely to be soon married. We will delay presentation just a little longer, so you are better prepared."

"What do you mean, Papa?" Sophia wished with all her heart there was no need for further delay.

"Your position will oblige you to receive and entertain many sorts of company, and you must learn to do so with ease. There will be no time to learn once you are engaged." It was the kind of thing mothers taught their daughters by example over time, but there was no mother and little time, so being a man, he had arrived at what struck him as an eminently practical solution. "You will be my hostess at an official dinner in two weeks."

"Oh . . . will I?" Sophia faltered. Eager as she was to be grown-up, this sudden promotion from the schoolroom to presiding in the drawing room and at the dinner table was unexpected. And daunting. What must she do exactly? She frowned.

"Let us look on the bright side. I imagine you will require a new gown for the occasion? Two weeks should be time enough to acquire one. Need I remind you already of your allowance?" Lord Grafton smiled.

Sophia's doubtful expression brightened at once. "My allowance! Oh yes, Papa. And not only for the dinner. Indeed I require all new gowns—I have none that fit. I will order some at once." *Three. Or four . . . perhaps five.* How the haughty young ladies of fashion would envy *her* now!

"My dear girl, your allowance is a generous one, but before you make the fortunes of every shop owner in Cheapside, you must consult your godmother as to what is appropriate to your age and station in life, and learn to keep your accounts."

"Must I?" Sophia cried. Lady Burnham with her widow's weeds, plain black caps, and her only jewelry a mourning ring with a lock of her late husband's hair! If Sophia was grown-up, surely her godmother need not be hovering round with her everlasting lectures and sermons.

Lord Grafton was firm. Lady Burnham would know what was proper for the occasion. And Lady Burnham would explain how to behave at his dinner. Therefore, Lady Burnham must be applied to. Sophia longed to stamp her foot and refuse, but just in time, it occurred to her that foot stamping was likely to jeopardize future balls and other agreeable prospects. Also, she had no idea what was required of her at the dinner and realized she would have to ask someone. She swallowed and said, "By all means, Papa, if you think it best."

Later that morning, a polite note of entreaty to accompany Sophia shopping was sent off with a footman to Lady Burnham. He brought a reply back immediately: Lady Burnham was at Miss Grafton's disposal and would call for her in the carriage in the afternoon.

Lord Grafton had had to persuade Lady Burnham on the matter of Sophia's dress allowance. She disapproved of bribing a young girl into good behavior and thought it unwise for Sophia to have free rein with either a large sum of money or the choice of her clothes.

Lord Grafton had countered with it being a means of teaching Sophia to manage her personal expenditure, to avoid the pitfalls of having money at her disposal, and to acquire the art of dressing with refinement and restraint, which Catherine had so quickly mastered. His insistence that it would teach Sophia to keep her accounts met with Lady Burnham's approval. He produced a small morocco-leather book with a gold pencil attached on a golden chain. Sophia would have a large amount settled on her at marriage, and she must learn to regulate expenditure. Many a woman of fashion had ruined herself and shamed her husband by getting into debt with careless spending on jewels and gambling. That must not be said of a Grafton. Nor must it be said that the Honorable Miss Grafton made herself ridiculous. "If the child has her way, she will look like a peacock! People will stare and point. And worse, the cartoonists and satirists will mock her in the papers, as they often attempt to do with public men like myself. When they cannot attack and satirize the man, as you know, dear Lady Burnham, they make a target of wives and daughters." And if Sophia became a satirical target, it would hardly enhance her marriage prospects. With no mother to guide Sophia's taste, Lady Burnham's advice would be invaluable.

Lady Burnham retorted that her advice was the last thing Sophia would wish for or accept.

Lord Grafton privately thought this was true, but if Sophia were to choose her first grown-up clothes without guidance, the result didn't bear thinking of. He shuddered at the thought that a Grafton daughter would be exposed to public notice or ridicule. While many ladies of his acquaintance would gladly have accepted the charge of guiding Sophia's first forays into fashion, he preferred Lady Burnham to undertake the task because she could be counted upon to err on the side of restraint and not be persuaded into excess. Ever the courtier, he remarked smoothly, "And it depends of course, dear Lady Burnham, on the *manner* in which the advice is given. Sometimes, you know, a light hand on the reins is all the direction a thoroughbred requires."

Lady Burnham sighed and gave in.

When she called for Sophia for their first visit to the warehouses of Cheapside, her dour presence failed to dampen Sophia's exuberance. As they passed the shop windows of bonnets and ribbons, India shawls and laces, gloves, bracelets, and perfumes, Sophia felt the thrilling power of her dress allowance.

Her determination to spend it did not go unnoticed by the merchants, who sent the clerks hurrying to fetch their most costly and enticing wares for the young lady's examination. "Oh, but look, Lady Burnham! Look at this! And this!" Sophia cried again and again. Lady Burnham held her tongue while the merchants bowed obsequiously and hurried to display their goods. Sophia was in raptures. She gasped. She wanted everything! She glanced at Lady Burnham and her elation dimmed. Lady Burnham was unmoved by the display, and Sophia braced herself for a lecture about the vanities of the world. But to her surprise, no lecture was forthcoming.

For the first time in her life, Sophia ventured to ask her godmother's opinion.

"Dear Lady Burnham . . . what do you think of the fabrics? Are they not marvelous? Which would make the most elegant gowns? Do you like the red? Is striped silk suitable for underskirts? But then the silver cloth is so . . . Oh, it is all so lovely! I cannot decide! Why do you not speak? How I should love to buy it all and be thought the most fashionable girl in London!"

Her godmother patted Sophia's hand. "What does an old woman know of fashion? All vanity in a godless world. I leave you to choose, my dear. Whatever pleases you."

Sophia looked at her godmother suspiciously. Lady Burnham had never been slow to offer her opinion before. Sophia prodded, "This purple satin is exquisite!" Hopefully, she held up a length of shiny material of a violent hue and enormous cost. It seemed wonderfully vibrant after her dull schoolgirl's frocks.

Lady Burnham took a moment to consider. While she did not approve of some of Lord Grafton's methods of raising his daughter, she felt duty bound to supply the guidance for which he asked. If she failed to, who would? Inwardly she shuddered at the prospect of Sophia's toilette if left to her own devices. But if she were clever about it, Sophia might listen. And Lady Burnham knew in her heart that long ago, in her younger days, she had been fond of a pretty gown herself. She was not given to jewels or powder or extravagance but had her small vanities. She had always been particular about the quality of fabrics, despite choosing only plain dark colors. Her caps and handkerchiefs were trimmed with Venetian lace. Even her widow's weeds fit perfectly to enhance her height and dignity. Striving not to sound Evangelical, she tried another line of persuasion.

"Your dear mother had excellent taste. She was fondest of . . . of simplicity, nothing excessive. I remember coming with her to this very warehouse when she was first married. Your father wished her to dress handsomely, because he is very particular about women's appearance, you know. She was anxious to please him and asked me to help her choose. She feared displeasing him by looking excessive or ridiculous."

Interesting as this was, Sophia was distracted by a clerk unrolling yet another bolt of fabric. The hopeful clerks hovered, arms full, pressing satins, silks, muslins, striped and plain, patterned and iridescent, upon Sophia. They held up gold and silver lace, feathers and glittering buckles and Chinese fans. There were heaped displays of ribbons and trimmings. Sophia turned wildly from one thing to another. "I thought perhaps with orange-and-red ribbon roses and a cloth of gold underskirt, I am certain to be noticed. I daresay my mother would have found it pretty."

"It would never have occurred to Catherine to invite attention by dressing like a mountebank!" said Lady Burnham tartly, and stopped herself. A light hand on the reins. She took a deep breath. "In your mother's case, the simpler the gown, the more her beauty shone in contrast," said Lady Burnham slyly. "Let us not make a hasty choice. Before making a selection, one first attends to quality . . ." Lady Burnham warmed to her subject, leaned forward, and took charge, putting aside her Evangelical objections to finery. It was the perfect opportunity to give Sophia a lesson in good taste and economy, and she knew she would not get many chances. There would be little to encourage a girl of Sophia's wealth and position to consider either. For the moment Sophia was listening, prepared to be guided with her mother as an example.

To the merchants' chagrin, Lady Burnham inspected the fabrics with a sharp eye, pointing out what distinguished cheap from good materials, advising what choices would make Sophia's allowance go further, something which a woman of sense and elegance would always consider "no matter how much money was at her disposal," said Lady Burnham severely. What was suitable for day, afternoon, and evening, holding up this swatch and that to see what color was becoming to Sophia's complexion, and above all, what was appropriate for a young lady of sixteen if she wished her resemblance to her mother to be remarked upon. This was unanswerable. Sophia sighed and said no more as Lady Burnham directed the clerks to remove most of the piled-up goods and leave a few chosen items on a table nearby.

"Now, tell me, child, who will attend the dinner?"

"Only some merchants. Dutchmen, I believe. Papa mentioned negotiations, a trading treaty. Does it signify?"

"Hmmm. It does indeed. In Holland and the Low Countries, fine without ostentation is the fashion. Godly people, the Dutch. For such an occasion, I think . . . that is, your mother would have selected this, and this . . ." Lady Burnham, enjoying herself just a little now, made a brisk selection from the approved items of blue damask and, scrutinizing the lace with a practiced eye, held up some white and some cream-colored Belgian lace against the blue dress fabric. "This," she pronounced, pointing to the cream lace, telling the clerk to mind what he was about when cutting it. She then suggested some plain and some flowered muslins she said were suitable for morning calls and afternoon gowns, and some black serge for a new riding habit. All were to be wrapped and delivered next day to her own dressmaker.

There were kid gloves and silk stockings and flat kid slippers with laces and finally, yielding to Sophia's urgent desire to have one pretty thing of her own choosing, some high-heeled red satin shoes with small paste buckles that Sophia thought were the most beautiful things she had ever seen and passionately desired. Crowing with the joy of possessing them, Sophia resigned herself to the fact nothing else was striking or colorful enough to match her ideas of finery.

She intended to place an order or two of her own when Lady Burnham's back was turned, but her godmother gave Sophia no time to order more, insisting that she was now very tired after an entire afternoon's shopping and they mustn't keep the carriage waiting any longer. Dragging her feet all the way to the carriage, Sophia obeyed but silently vowed never to ask Lady Burnham again. As they arrived home, Lady Burnham handed Sophia a small book of blank pages. "Now you are receiving an allowance, you must keep your accounts, my dear. From now on, write down each item of expenditure. Your father expects it, and it is easiest if done at once. There are the receipts." She pressed the slips of paper into Sophia's hand.

Once upstairs in her dressing room, Sophia groaned as she put the slips and the little account book down on her writing desk. There seemed to be lessons every way she turned, but she decided to obey Lady Burnham in case her father asked to see her accounts book. She was rather startled to see how much her new gowns and other things added up to. Still, it did not signify greatly; after she calculated, she found that there was still a considerable portion of her allowance left to spend. And she would receive it every year.

Happily, she needn't worry about expense, she thought, and went to try on her new red satin shoes. She spent an hour before her looking glass, admiring how they looked. Now *there* was finery!

On the night of the dinner, Sophia again stood before her looking glass while her maid shook out the folds of her first grown-up evening gown, delivered from the dressmaker that morning, and slipped it over her head. Sophia was not particularly pleased with it. She thought all her good behavior might have earned her something prettier than plain dark-blue damask with a godly high neckline! As the maid laced it up, she exclaimed how well it fit her mistress and admired the fine lace on the petticoat and sleeves, saying it showed off handsomely against the blue. The maid tied a simple lace fichu at Sophia's neck instead of the paste pendant and earrings Sophia had coveted, then, as Lady Burnham had urged was appropriate for her age, brushed and tied back Sophia's hair with a velvet bow.

Sophia had longed to send for a hairdresser to have it arranged elaborately, curled and powdered and decorated with feathers and pearls, but had reluctantly taken her godmother's advice when Lady Burnham had advised her that it was a fashion faux pas if the formality of the dressed hair exceeded the formality of the dress.

Sophia examined the effect in her looking glass, turning her head this way and that. She sighed. She looked well enough, she supposed, though hardly dazzling. And she was worried about the part she was to play tonight, which she understood was a test set by her father. She had first thought all that was required of her was to look pretty and smile at the dinner. But no, there had been no end of things she must do and remember; she had had so much advice about her duties as hostess that she now dreaded the evening.

Lord Grafton's ideas as to what characterized a good hostess had been formed in lively diplomatic salons across Europe, where a good hostess made it a point to be well-informed of matters that involved her guests. With that in mind, he had lectured her about the Dutch and the importance of their trade negotiations with England and the terms of the treaty until Sophia had clapped her hand over her mouth to hide her gleeful smile. "Papa, if I understand you aright, the dinner is intended to charm the Dutch envoys and obscure how greatly this treaty benefits England at the expense of the Dutch!"

Lord Grafton had roared with laughter that Sophia had seen so quickly to the heart of the matter. "Yes, my dear, and your presence at dinner will distract their attention from that fact."

Lady Burnham and Mrs. Betts had lectured her about the hostess's obligation to oversee the comfort of her guests and ensure the dinner went forward smoothly, to cover awkward pauses in the conversation, to signal the servants if anything was wanted. Lady Burnham had made her practice her curtsey over and over, and stressed she must give her hand and speak a few words of welcome to each member of the party. When dinner was announced she was expected to lead the way into the dining room on her father's arm, and afterward she must retire and leave the gentlemen to their port and brandy, as it was the custom for the men to pass round a piss pot under the table to relieve themselves. She must wait in the drawing room to pour out their coffee at the end of the evening.

The little gilt clock in Sophia's room chimed the hour of doom when she was to appear in the drawing room. She was so nervous she could not remember a word of anyone's advice. She would do everything wrong and embarrass her father, it would be a horrible evening, and it would put an end to any chance of dancing at a ball. She stepped into her red shoes and descended the stairs as slowly as she could, partly because walking in her new shoes required care and also because the knot of panic in her stomach grew tighter with each step.

The footman waiting to open the door had known her since she was a child, and he had helped conceal her exploits. Now she gave him an agonized look and he smiled encouragingly. "Don't worry. You'll do very well tonight, Miss Sophia," he whispered. Then he flung open the door and Sophia heard herself announced.

Before her, the drawing room was ablaze with candles and crowded with men in dark, sober clothing that set off dazzling white collars and neatly trimmed beards. Interrupting the buzz of conversation, Lord Grafton stepped forward and said, "*Heren, mag ik mijn dochter, Sophia, aan u voorstellen?* Gentlemen, may I present to you my daughter, Sophia?" Everyone stopped talking and turned to look at Sophia. In silence, all the dark-clad company bowed.

Sophia froze. "Oh!" she whimpered, tempted to bolt back upstairs to the safety of the schoolroom. Just in time, she caught her father's eye. She took a deep breath and curtseyed. It was nearly always appropriate and polite for a woman to curtsey, and besides—Lady Burnham had smiled, giving this bit of advice—a curtsey allowed time for a woman to think what to do next, and Sophia would find that it was often useful to have an instant for composure.

Tonight Sophia's composing thought was *Thank heaven I have a dark gown! How odd anything else would have appeared in this company!*

Looking up from her curtsey, she was startled to see men regarding her with admiration, and made an interesting discovery. In the blink of an eye, something had changed. She had been a child when she bowed her head and sank. She had risen a young lady—Miss Grafton, the same age her mother had been when she married. In the space of a curtsey, the child Sophia had flown. That knowledge brought a frisson of fear and excitement, but it propelled her forward. She extended her hand to the first Dutch merchant and stammered that she hoped that he and his party found themselves comfortable in their lodgings. Politely, she turned to the next guests and inquired nervously about their impressions of London. To the next she wished them better weather than the heavy rain they had at present.

She made her way unhurriedly through the room, and smiling triumphantly up at her father as dinner was announced, she took his arm to lead the guests to the dining room as if she had done it all her life.

Once seated, Sophia was too busy watching the guests like a hawk to eat. To the chagrin of the butler, she kept signaling the servants to fill wineglasses or pass another course, though her directions were unnecessary; Lord Grafton's well-trained footmen were accustomed to the smooth running of dinners. She was alert to lulls in the conversation because Lady Burnham had told her a good hostess did not allow the company to lapse into tedious silence. She must keep everyone talking.

"How am I to do that, Lady Burnham? What am I to say?" Sophia had wailed, aghast at being obliged to lead the conversation with a host of men.

"Just ask a general question, my dear, such as how they find London or to tell you of their cities. They are Dutchmen. Mention tulips, if necessary, but always let the gentlemen do the talking. You needn't actually say much yourself, only suggest a subject. Gentlemen are generally happiest to hear themselves speak. It never really signifies what a woman says in company."

Sophia was in a quandary. Lady Burnham's view that women should say as little as possible accorded perfectly with her desire not to have to say anything but was at odds with her father's view that ignorance was unbecoming in a woman and that she must prepare for conversation in company just as carefully as she dressed. By way of example he had explained the background to the trade agreement England was hoping to ratify with Holland. Sophia had actually found it rather interesting.

"Very well. I could discuss Papa's trade negotiations. He has explained it all to me, only in my opinion, it sounds as if the English merchants will come off to greater advantage than the Dutch, though the Dutch do not realize it, because the terms of the treaty are worded so as to—"

Lady Burnham shook her head. "Absolutely not! Say nothing of treaties or terms! Leave opinions to the men," she said firmly.

So at dinner, though much was said on the subject of the treaty, Sophia decided it was safest to follow Lady Burnham's advice. She kept her opinions to herself, smiled politely, and turned from the man on her right to the man on her left and let them harangue her on the benefits Holland would gain from the new trade agreement. Sophia thought they were entirely mistaken but managed to hold her tongue. Lord Grafton kept a good table, and he was supplied by an excellent wine merchant—and the atmosphere grew more and more convivial. Sophia tried to look interested while the men launched into enthusiastic descriptions of Amsterdam and Delft, and she suppressed her yawns through an endless procession of dishes—oysters, crayfish in cream, roast mutton, venison, veal tongue, and carp and roasted pigeons and peas *à la française* and a magnificent iced pudding topped with sugar swans.

By that time, Sophia had broached every topic, including tulips, and was racking her brains to think of another when she saw her father give a small nod as port and Madeira and nuts were placed on the table. Thankfully, she rose and left the gentlemen to their wine. There was only coffee in the drawing room to be got through, and she could go to bed.

When taking their leave at the end of the evening, the Dutch merchants complimented Lord Grafton on his charming young hostess who had delighted them all with her smiles and gracious attention. The young hostess herself was exhausted and glad to be relieved of her responsibilities and unlaced from her new gown. She took a glass of Madeira and some plain cake and fell into bed, thanking heaven the evening was behind her.

The next morning at breakfast her father repeated the guests' compliments and added some of his own. He ended by saying that her mother would have been proud of her, as he was. This, Sophia knew, was praise indeed, and she blushed with happiness as she buttered her bread. "Thank you, dear Papa. But I am so glad that it is over."

Lord Grafton shook his head. "Not so, my dear. You are grown up now and have acquitted yourself so well you shall act as my hostess from now on."

"How delightful!" Sophia said faintly. Her heart sank. Then she brightened. "I daresay I shall require many new gowns."

CHAPTER 4
THE HONORABLE SOPHIA GRAFTON

1751

Lord Grafton watched, gratified and rather surprised to observe the success of his methods as Sophia grew out of her youthful awkwardness into her new role and its responsibilities. Acting as her father's hostess, she gained in poise and confidence, which in turn reinforced her newfound good behavior. She became at ease and gracious in company, her manners more polished, exemplary. He was pleased with her appearance too. She looked just as a young woman of the Grafton family ought: her clothes were elegant but demure; she was always charmingly dressed but neat and modest. No one would point out the Honorable Miss Grafton as faddish or frivolous, awkward or uncivil, or, as often happened with fashionable females, lampoon her taste in gowns or hats in cartoons in the papers.

So charming and poised a young hostess ensured his dinners were much talked about in London. As for Sophia, she made the agreeable discovery that her new grown-up role allowed her to give orders about dinners and flowers and a great many other things, and giving orders suited her. She had new gowns too, as many as she wished, though her father insisted she submit to Lady Burnham's preference for high necklines and restrained taste, saying this was appropriate for her age and rank. She got in the habit of keeping her accounts, though there was little point in doing so; she could spend what she liked.

Sophia spent a good deal of time in front of her mirror, looking at herself from different angles. While she believed she resembled the portrait of her mother that hung in the drawing room, she wondered if she would ever be admired as her mother had been. She thought that taken as a whole, she looked well enough—she had a small, neat waist and was tall enough for elegance, her brown hair was luxuriant, her nose was small, and her complexion was clear. Though she was sure she would look considerably better if she were allowed to have her way with her toilette. She felt certain that cloth of gold cut low over her bosom, her face and décolletage powdered white, her full lips painted into a tiny rosebud, and a heart-shaped velvet patch on her cheek would mark her out as one of the great beauties of society and attract universal admiration. But she would never, never be able to persuade Lady Burnham.

Lord Grafton decided Sophia was now prepared to make her entrance into society. He gave her the happy news that her presentation at court would take place after Christmas. Once she was out, she might appear in public at balls and dance as much as she pleased. Lord Grafton was easy in his mind about her Season—it was only a brief period of enjoyment with other young people, in the interval between the schoolroom and her responsibilities as a wife and mother in the country. Let her dance with anyone she liked, he thought indulgently. It would not do any harm. He did not think Sophia was missish or romantic like many young girls and was confident that she would never forget herself and fall in love, as the novels would have it, without his approval and permission. He and Lady Burnham had between them made sure she understood where her duty lay in the future.

While Sophia was absorbed in preparations for this momentous event, Lord Grafton turned his attention to a short list of possible matches for her. In aristocratic families, perpetuating the family line ranked as the foremost duty of the younger generation, and marriages were dynastic alliances between families and generally arranged or agreed upon when the participants were young. If a girl was not married when she left the schoolroom but was allowed a Season, the purpose was to introduce men from suitable families to form such an alliance. A wellborn girl was usually engaged before the end of her Season and married soon thereafter. In drawing up his list, Lord Grafton was doing exactly what was expected of him.

Lord Grafton believed that the conditions he had laid down for Sophia's husband presented no obstacle. Aside from her fortune, he fondly believed Sophia would be sought for herself—she was everything Miss Grafton ought to be. That she was handsome was beyond a doubt. There was no trace of the former hoyden. She combined pleasing, well-bred manners with a lively wit that amused him and exasperated her godmother. She would grace any house, and her husband would not find her dull company. True, she had an imperious streak and vastly enjoyed being in charge of things, but Lord Grafton believed that would be a useful quality later when ordering her family and her parish concerns and overseeing the upbringing and education of her children.

Lady Burnham, who was far more concerned about moral characteristics than outward appearances or cleverness, had tried to instill good principles and the sense of *noblesse oblige* that ought to be part of a great lady's character. She had acquainted Sophia with her duties as patroness of her village in the country. Naturally, the Grafton family contributed to the parish poor relief, they had built an almshouse and seen to improvements in the tenants' cottages, and Catherine had founded a school in the village. Sophia must prepare to involve herself similarly.

Sophia questioned her godmother minutely about her future role in the village. How gratifying, thought Lady Burnham, that Sophia was beginning to feel a sense of her responsibilities toward the villagers who had served the Grafton family for centuries. In fact, Sophia was charmed by the prospect of a new sphere of influence. She imagined the Grafton tenants curtseying or doffing hats, herself giving orders for the improvement of the school, presiding over prize days attired in a fetching hat and pelisse, being deferred to by the teacher, and graciously distributing sweets and Bibles to the children. She would be universally loved, as her mother had been.

For Sophia this rosy picture was a more distant future prospect than what Lord Grafton anticipated. He had given much thought to the sort of man he wished Sophia to marry and was prepared with a list of possible alliances. He had decided upon two criteria. First, Sophia's husband must be fit to be the paterfamilias of a new Grafton dynasty. This had little to do with rank or fortune. Sophia need not marry to acquire a title or, indeed, distinction in name. The Graftons predated not only the House of Hanover and the Stuarts but the Tudors and even the Plantagenets, and the antiquity of Sophia's pedigree outweighed any later title. Whomever she married, Sophia would always be a Grafton and a viscount's daughter. As to fortune, she need not marry for that. Her own fortune was considerable enough for any man, and the Grafton estate was a prize.

No, the most important qualification for Lord Grafton was that Sophia's husband be a gentleman, of unblemished character, in sound health, and, above all, free of vice. Lord Grafton was a man of the world, and he knew very well that many of the eligible bachelors presently hovering round Sophia did not conform to his idea of the Grafton patriarch at all. Though the general view in society was that to marry one of these young men would be to marry well, his inquiries revealed that many of them had very bad habits, losing fortunes at gaming and the horses, given to brothels and whoring, keeping mistresses. This often led to their being afflicted with the French pox or the Spanish disease, which, by either name, covered their bodies with sores and pustules, made their nether regions burn with pain, and caused them to piss slime. Lord Grafton knew that children born to such fathers were sometimes blind or disfigured with their fathers' saddle noses, while their wives were often afflicted too. Just as the pustules could be powdered over, title and fortune could blind ambitious parents of marriageable daughters to disease but not outweigh its later consequences. He would never marry Sophia to a man likely to breed idiots or gamble away the Grafton property and, above all, one who would infect her with the pox. On that point he was determined.

The second point on which he must be satisfied was that the man be capable of making Sophia happy. Though her husband ought to be, first, a man of sense and a natural *gravitas*, Lord Grafton was far from being a domestic tyrant. Sophia's happiness was dear to him. He did not, of course, go so far as to believe she should marry for love. Such an idea rarely crossed the minds of fathers in Lord Grafton's rank of life. But he wanted to be satisfied the man was fond of Sophia and capable of engaging her affection and respect in return.

Had Lord Grafton been the sort of man to examine his scheme closely, he might have concluded that perhaps he was trying to arrange matters so that Sophia and her husband might live out the long, happy, child-filled marriage denied to him and Catherine. But as he was not that introspective, he was simply persuaded his plan was for the best advancement of the family.

He had approached the matter in a rational way. After making his inquiries about this man and that, he drew up a list of suitable candidates and decided he would arrange a series of dinners and *soirées* so Sophia could meet them over the course of an evening or two. Such gatherings would be necessary, as he suspected many of the men he thought suitable were either not to be met at balls or, if they were, might well be past dancing. And in any case, a ball offered few opportunities for the sort of acquaintance that might establish a man's character and allow Sophia to decide who pleased her most. When she had settled on her preference, Lord Grafton would open negotiations with the man's family, and in due course, the matter would be turned over to the lawyers to draw up the marriage articles and settlements. Sophia was certain to be engaged by summer and probably married by autumn.

In little more than a twelvemonth, the grandson of his dreams might be lying in his cradle in the old nursery in Sussex.

Guided by such benevolent and rational motives, it never occurred to Lord Grafton that it might be difficult for a suitor to please both father and daughter, no matter how kindly the father or how dutiful the daughter, or that the dignity, morals, and *gravitas* he thought essential might not be the attributes that would appeal to a girl of sixteen, especially one whose marriage would oblige her to relinquish the heady pleasures of London for a domestic life in the country.

Lord Grafton arranged the first of the dinners that were to introduce possible husbands and turned to another pressing matter. His decision to retire had brought an unexpected reward for his years of service when the king made a gift to him of a large patent of undeveloped land in Virginia Colony. London was abuzz with news of it and the great tobacco fortune it would bring Lord Grafton. While Lord Grafton would have welcomed anything in the shape of a fortune, he knew better than anyone that the king was often devious and difficult. The plantation struck Lord Grafton as less a mark of royal gratitude than a ploy in England's strategic interests.

When he learned that his plantation was in the unsettled southwestern part of Virginia Colony, he shrewdly guessed the king's motive was less to reward his services than to extend a buffer zone of British settlement on the boundary of Virginia as a bulwark against French encroachment from their domain on the Mississippi and Ohio. The same policy, he reflected wryly, as that of William the Conqueror, who had given knights like Hugh de Graftonne land to erect fortified castles to defend the English coast.

But Lord Grafton's plantation became the subject of speculation and gossip in fashionable society. His Virginia estate was a thousand acres, according to one rumor; no, it was five hundred thousand acres, according to another; while yet another school of thought insisted it was a million acres. The tobacco itself, let alone lumber and perhaps mines and wheat, from it would double, no, triple the Grafton fortune. Lord Grafton laughed when he heard these rumors, because having seen the deeds and map of the patent, he himself was uncertain how large it was, perhaps ten or fifteen thousand acres of land, but it had been drawn up quickly on the orders of the king, and the land did not as yet grow anything, had not even been surveyed, and depended on rivers and mountains to delineate its boundaries.

It all appeared to him somewhat vague, and the patent was so far away it might as well have been on the moon. He laughed aside any suggestion he would take up residence in Virginia. Tobacco was a young man's business, and at his age, he had no desire to cross the ocean and live on a plantation in the Virginia wilderness, by all accounts a wild and untamed place of dark forests teeming with savage beasts and Indians. The very thought made him shudder—he found himself rather bored in the country on the rare occasions when it was absolutely necessary that he pay a short visit to his Sussex property.

But as he could hardly decline the royal gift, his friends gradually persuaded him that he must do something with it. He could put the land to use in one of two ways: either a resident manager could grow and ship the tobacco or the entire estate could be rented out to a planter in the colony who would remit a share of the profits. It was suggested that the latter plan was likely to be more profitable and less trouble for Lord Grafton.

He was advised to send an agent to Virginia to assess the property and draw up a plan for its cultivation. His solicitors made inquiries and recommended a Mr. George Barker, who had lately returned to England after selling his own tobacco plantation in Virginia, where he had cleared and tamed thousands of acres in the southern part of the colony and made a fortune. He had returned to England and was recently married. Mr. Barker was at first reluctant to leave his new wife, but for a substantial sum, he finally agreed to return to Virginia and report on the state of the property, put it in good order, and plant the first crop of tobacco.

When Mr. Barker's first report arrived with the breakfast post one morning in late April, Sophia was yawning over her tea after a ball the previous evening where she had danced holes in her slippers, and she struggled to pay attention as Lord Grafton read it aloud. Mr. Barker assured him that the bulk of the land lay in a river valley that promised to produce tobacco as fine as any in Virginia, particularly of the Orinoco variety that was preferred in Europe. That the plantation would bring Lord Grafton a fortune was beyond a doubt. However, he emphasized that a substantial investment was required.

The land needed clearing before it could be cultivated, and there were many things that would have to be ordered from England—farm implements, nails, bricks, and tools—though fortunately these could be sent by raft from Yorktown or a landing on the James River. The Grafton patent, though in an unsettled part of Virginia a considerable distance from the coast, was fortunately positioned so that it could be reached by river, thanks to a recent discovery of a waterway that cut through a mountain pass. This meant shipments from England and tobacco could be transported by water unless river levels were unusually low. Sending it overland by wagon was possible on a river trail but much more expensive. Therefore they should build a river landing as well.

He also advised building a good house of brick immediately. Mr. Barker could not remain in Virginia beyond the time necessary to see the first crop of tobacco harvested and the income assured, and after that the plantation should be rented to another planter for a share in what promised to be great profits. Since Virginians attached great importance to their houses, a fine brick house of six or eight rooms in the colonial style, with all the necessary outbuildings, was required to attract a planter to live so far from the settled part of the colony. Such a house would add immeasurably to the value of the plantation if it were sold in the future.

Brick, he wrote, was costly, but it was an unavoidable expense. The finest homes in Virginia were all of brick, not wood. Lord Grafton fumed, "But surely there is a ready supply of wood in Virginia! Surely a house of wood is good enough for a colonial tobacco farmer!"

"I suppose we must allow Mr. Barker to judge, Papa," sighed Sophia, who was beginning to find the Virginia business tedious.

"Bless me, Barker's even given the place a name!" Lord Grafton exclaimed. The letter continued saying that in the way of Virginia, it had been necessary to do so at once, in order that letters and, eventually, the supplies from England might be directed to it. Mr. Barker had taken the liberty of calling the Grafton land Wildwood Plantation, suitable, he thought, as it lay in heavily forested country, so Lord Grafton should address his future letters to the plantation by name and add, "Lying west beyond Amelia County on the forked branch of the river between Frog Mountain and Little Frog Mountain."

"Frog Mountain? And *Little* Frog Mountain! Wildwood? What charming, rustic names!" Sophia buttered her toast and poured herself another cup of tea.

Lord Grafton smiled. "Rustic certainly. Hardly charming. Virginia Colony sounds an altogether peculiar place." Then his smile faded as he read Sophia the next part of Mr. Barker's letter. Mr. Barker regretted he had not included in his initial estimate of the costs of developing the property that additional cash would be required to purchase slaves to clear and plow the land, then plant and harvest the tobacco and complete the building work.

"Slaves, Papa?"

"According to Mr. Barker, tobacco cannot be grown without them."

"But, Papa, don't you recall that Lady Burnham says Christians should abhor commerce in human beings? There was a Quaker lady who spoke about it at one of the societies. And really, though speakers usually made me close my eyes and pray for the time when we could leave, she made it sound so wicked I had to listen. Why not have farm tenants and laborers as we do in Sussex?"

"My dear, we do not grow tobacco in Sussex. Matters of business and tobacco are beyond Lady Burnham's understanding, excellent though that is in all other respects. It is more expedient to have slaves grow the tobacco than laborers."

"But, Papa, if slavery is objectionable but a matter of expediency, Lady Burnham says that a true Christian must turn resolutely from an expedient evil to the right course of action, no matter how difficult or inconvenient. She says—"

"Sophia, for all that your ideas echo the Evangelicals and Quakers, you argue like a Jesuit! I must blame myself if you do. Never fear. I'll give strict orders the slaves are to be as well treated as our own servants. It is in the order of things that some are born to serve, whether as servants or slaves." Lord Grafton spoke sharply, which was unlike him, but he was alarmed by the increased investment Mr. Barker requested. The cost, the cost! He'd had no idea how expensive slaves were. Several dozen able-bodied men were required before anything could be done, according to Mr. Barker, and able-bodied male slaves commanded a high price, as all the landowners needed them. There was nothing for it; the loan would have to be increased to buy them, the estate mortgaged more heavily.

Again, Lord Grafton was assured that the financial burden would be short-lived. According to established practice, when the first crop of

Wildwood tobacco was shipped to England, his factors would advance him money against future crops, and he could repay the loan immediately. But it was imperative Lord Grafton remit the money at once, because without it, Wildwood was worthless, and to delay would be to miss growing seasons. The price of Virginia tobacco was rising. With enough slaves and good management, he would realize a great profit very quickly.

Lord Grafton sent for his solicitors. They agreed Mr. Barker must purchase the slaves and that the tobacco, especially the lucrative Orinoco variety Mr. Barker said grew well there, would quickly pay off the debt. The solicitors understood very well the position Lord Grafton was in. In common with many ancient landowning families, Lord Grafton was what would be called land rich and cash poor. Although the Grafton fortune was great, much of it was tied up in the land, and perhaps to a greater extent than he realized, the lifestyle to which the Graftons were accustomed and that he had kept up since inheriting the title had for generations been increasingly maintained on credit. Though the Grafton credit was understood to be sound, the solicitors explained in the most tactful terms that it would be expedient for Lord Grafton to seize the opportunity to augment the family fortune with ready income. However, they insisted Lord Grafton needn't feel the slightest alarm; it was normal practice to use English property as security when funds were needed for some purpose connected with the American colonies.

Lord Grafton sighed and shook his head. "The business puzzles me." The terms of the loan and the interest on it seemed to him quite staggering, but the solicitors insisted this was always so when a large sum of money was needed immediately. The actual debt would be discharged within a year or eighteen months, and he need think nothing more of it.

Lord Grafton finally gave in, and the necessary papers were drawn up for him to sign. He then made the legal and beneficial title of the plantation over to Sophia, the income to be settled on her marriage or at the age of twenty-one, whichever came first. The lawyers congratulated him on the increase to his daughter's dowry and marriage settlements.

The business done, Lord Grafton returned his attention to Sophia, whose matrimonial prospects had now become a topic of widespread speculation. There had quickly collected round her an admiring circle of eligible London beaux who professed their devotion, sent her poems, paid her compliments, and vied to dance with her. There had been approaches from suitors, but few matched Lord Grafton's idea of what Sophia's husband should be, and of those few of whom he spoke warmly, "too old" and "too dull" were Sophia's verdicts. Usually that meant "They do not dance."

Sophia had always understood the conditions attached to her marriage, and it had never occurred to her to question her father's plan. She had been born into the knowledge that rank had its duties. But on the other hand, the life of a wealthy young lady in London, with no cares or responsibilities, save that of choosing gowns and dancing partners and being charming to her father's friends, was very sweet. Duty was not an enticing prospect when weighed against balls and *soirées*, pleasure gardens and theaters, and she saw no reason to hasten to the altar and cut short a very agreeable existence.

Sophia privately likened her foppish admirers to a flock of peacocks and would have no more considered one of them as a possible husband than her father would have done, but she was an acknowledged belle among them. They were amusing company and most danced well, which could be said for none of the suitors her father was beginning to push her way. She was puzzled that someone as clever, urbane, and popular as her father could light on such stolid, unprepossessing men as he recommended to her attention. His select dinners to introduce his list of candidates were something of a trial as she labored to make conversation with one middle-aged dullard after another.

Then suddenly, she was on the verge of losing her heart altogether to a dark-haired, blue- eyed, dashingly robust Irish peer who was neither peacock nor dullard but exceedingly handsome, with a charming word for all he met. Somehow all eyes were drawn to him when he strode into a room. He enlivened any company he joined, was on cordial terms with the younger men while duly respectful of the elder. His winning countenance and his manner of gazing into a woman's eyes that somehow said, "Ah, to find such beauty! I am captivated! We understand each other completely," set the hearts of ladies young and old fluttering. He was fond of dancing, and he chose Sophia as his partner so often that people had begun to comment on his attentions, saying that her beauty and his gallant appearance complemented each other. He always had something unexpected and novel to say that made her laugh and a ready compliment loaded with meaning that made her blush. And one night during a lull in the dancing, he had pulled her into a conservatory among a display of orange trees in bloom, crushed her in his arms, and kissed her very slowly, insistently, and agreeably, leaving Sophia overpowered by the heady scent of orange blossoms combined with shivery sensations from the tickle of his mustache on her lips and throat and just behind her ear. It had been the most delicious, thrilling experience of her life, and she willed him to go on and on kissing her, but they were disturbed by a couple wishing to pluck a few sprigs of orange blossom for the girl's nosegay. Reluctantly, Sophia returned to the dance.

Afterward, she relived those moments in the conservatory over and over, growing light-headed as she recalled what the kissing had felt like and aching to experience more. That there *was* more, she knew, but she had never considered the marital bed in any light except that of a very distant future and her duty. Suddenly it seemed infinitely alluring, and visions of being secluded in the country with the Irish peer as her husband became the stuff of her daydreams, the most agreeable thing imaginable.

Lord Grafton was startled out of his complacent confidence that Sophia would never forget herself and develop a preference for any young man before he sanctioned it. Now Sophia kept finding reasons to praise the Irish peer, to enumerate the ways he was superior to all other men, and pressed Lord Grafton to say whether he had ever seen the Irish peer's equal. She blushed when she spoke of him, and she spoke of him constantly. Lord Grafton, who had not previously deigned to notice the man beyond common civility to a man who danced often with his daughter, made his inquiries and was horrified.

While an Irish title might be dubious at the best of times, Lord Grafton learned that in this case there was no title at all. The young man was an imposter and a rogue. He kept a string of racehorses and one expensive actress, by what means no one knew for sure, because there was no more fortune than there was a title. He was a *habitué* of the gaming establishments, a frequent loser at cards, and in debt to a host of tradesmen. It was rumored he had a share in several brothels in Shepherd Market and was already married to an Irish wife.

Alarmed to learn Sophia had become attracted to such a character without his realizing, Lord Grafton told her sternly exactly why she must not think further of this man. He did not mince his words. Though the young man may have appeared the kind of dashing hero beloved of novelists, he was a fortune hunter and a scoundrel who would leave her penniless, ruined, and wretched, probably with many children and a disease. He gave her all the facts he had collected and told her to judge for herself if she had not had a lucky escape.

Sophia wept a little, dried her eyes, and reminded her father that she never read novels. But she didn't protest. She felt the compliment of his appeal to her reason and judgment strongly enough that she could agree that he was right without resentment or defiance, though not without sadness. The Irish peer, or whatever he was, would not be thought of any longer, she assured him. Lord Grafton patted her shoulder, thankful for such a display of good sense.

Still, the heady moments in the conservatory, the kisses and the sensations they aroused, burned in her memory. Sophia now began to consider the approved candidates for her hand in a new light, imagining what it would be like to kiss them. Unlikely to be as exciting as kissing the Irish peer, she thought, but to be sure, she put it to the test by kissing the most likely of them. But none of her experiments produced the same interesting sensations, and some of the men were shocked by her forwardness. This was most discouraging, and she soon gave up the experiment. It was too disagreeable to contemplate, marrying a man she did not want to kiss or who did not want to kiss her. To the surprise of everyone interested in the subject, her first Season passed without an engagement.

Lady Burnham was even more dismayed than Lord Grafton. She deplored Sophia's attachment to amusements, dancing, and pretty clothes instead of spiritual matters. She privately thought allowing a girl to be out was like exhibiting a prize heifer to the bull pen, and in Sophia's case, a prize heifer with a golden dowry bell round her neck. But anything to get her goddaughter married and away from London and its temptations, anything to fix Sophia's attention on her home, husband, and family, as a woman's ought to be. Not to mention that once married and living in the country, Sophia would be in a position to direct the religious life of her village and parish in Sussex away from high Anglicism. Lady Burnham had in mind a book of Evangelical sermons she proposed to give Sophia as a wedding gift for this very purpose.

As she tirelessly reminded Lord Grafton, engagements had been managed very differently in the old days, when Lady Burnham was a girl, and parents took the lead in introducing suitable young people to each other, quietly, at home, and marriages were arranged, so to speak, behind the scenes.

Sophia held opinions of her own about men in a way that would have been considered ill-bred in Lady Burnham's day, and Lady Burnham observed it was entirely unnecessary for her father to encourage her. Lord Grafton only laughed when he heard this. After the efforts made with her education, he would have been surprised if Sophia had

had no opinions to form about men or anything else. This exasperated Lady Burnham. What about the favorable opinion she had formed of the Irish peer? What if Sophia took it into her head to like another unsuitable man? Would her father encourage her opinion then? She could be quite stubborn. Lord Grafton brushed her worries aside. He had added to his list of candidates.

But Sophia liked none of them. As Sophia's second Season drew to a close, Lady Burnham reminded Sophia that she had been put on earth for a serious purpose. Much was hinted and much was said to Sophia on the subject of little Graftons and her duty. "Duty over inclination" became Lady Burnham's constant refrain.

But Sophia heard the call of duty only faintly and from a great distance. Believing they were steering Sophia to her destiny, Lord Grafton and Lady Burnham, with their selection of boring suitors and talk of duty, were in fact discouraging Sophia from marrying at all. The more she considered the matter, the less appealing was the prospect of being confined to the country to breed with a middle-aged man she scarcely knew. She was not fond of the country, which she remembered as being extremely muddy, all cowpats and tangled hedgerows and rain. She was aware of Lady Burnham's intention that she would influence the life of her Sussex parish away from the Anglican tradition, but Sophia was not the least inclined to interfere with the work of the parish vicar, much less turn them Evangelical!

Despite approaches from families wishing to discuss a Grafton alliance for a third or fourth son, Sophia's second Season ended like the first, with no engagement.

As Sophia prepared for her third Season with the assistance of a new dressmaker, Lady Burnham lost patience and warned her that a marriageable girl lost her luster after being out too many Seasons. "You've been too much indulged. You cannot be forever gadding about on schemes of pleasure or to the dressmaker. You should respect your father's wish to see you settled before he dies. Within the last twelvemonth, you have declined three perfectly acceptable men, agreeable to your father, and indeed to me, who is no careless judge of these things. They were amenable to all the conditions, would have made sound husbands. If your father gives a man permission to propose, you ought to—"

"I know, but oh, dear Lady Burnham! Papa is so particular that he eliminates all but the men no other woman would marry, for very good reason. Of the three you mention, one was so pompous I couldn't listen to him for five minutes without laughing, and no woman can wish for a lifetime of hilarity. One was old, at least thirty-eight, and his favorite topic of conversation was the attention he devotes night and day to the maintenance of his health. He might as well have been ninety. The last one was fat, which outweighed the fact he is an earl's son. I could imagine none of them as a companion, let alone a bedfellow!"

"Bedfellow!" Lady Burnham threw up her hands.

"Well, husband then, married people . . . one must consider the bedfellow part, you know. Oh, don't say it's indelicate, Lady Burnham. I know you understand me, you mustn't pretend not to! I will never marry a man Papa doesn't approve, yet I alone can decide on the man I can accept. I'll be mired in the country with him, so I must like him very much indeed and therefore shall wait until such a man appears."

Sophia tried not to think of the Irish peer as she said this. She kissed her godmother and departed to choose some new fans from a consignment just delivered to her favorite haberdasher. Sophia's sentiments left Lady Burnham shaking her head and wondering how things had been allowed to go so far. Love or liking or whatever one wished to call it could come perfectly well after marriage, just as it had done for Lord Grafton and Catherine and for Lady Burnham and her husband. In Lady Burnham's day, a girl obeyed her parents, married as they decreed, and usually everything turned out well enough after the first baby came. If things failed to do so, Lady Burnham counseled, the knowledge of having done one's duty was a great consolation.

However, Sophia was never going to be that biddable, Lady Burnham concluded gloomily. But Sophia's views on *bedfellows* prompted an idea that might move matters forward. Though she could hardly advance this particular argument to Lord Grafton, in her experience young men were often more vigorously lusty in the country—she fancied it had to do with the hunting, outdoor pursuits, and fresh air. Surprisingly good teeth and often smelling of horse, if she remembered correctly. Perhaps that was the sort of young man Sophia would like. London men could be such fops, painting, scenting, and powdering as much as the women.

She invited Lord Grafton to drink tea with her, and when he was seated, cup in hand and cake before him on the tea table, she turned the conversation to Sophia and said she believed Lord Grafton's conditions were posing something of a problem, while the pool of Sophia's admirers was shrinking as each Season passed.

"It seems to me that there are, in London, no men whom you think suitable and Sophia finds appealing. Might it be as well to have a change of scene before another Irishman appears? Would it be wise to take her away from London for a time?"

"Abroad?" asked Lord Grafton, dismayed. It would never answer his purpose for Sophia to marry a foreigner.

"Certainly not abroad! I meant Sussex. She has paid only a few short visits there. At the moment she rather sees it as a form of exile. Were she to know it better, become acquainted with the ways of the countryside, the neighbors, and the tenants on the estate, to understand her position and sphere of influence, what good she might do there, it might be a good thing. It is a beautiful estate, and she has not seen it in four years. And one never knows, now that she is old enough to go about in society, perhaps there is a young man among the county families who would . . . er, please her better than the London men do. That would help her to see Sussex in a new light.

"If so, he is likely to make a husband of good character, or at least will have had fewer opportunities to acquire a bad one than in London. As long as he is a gentleman, and she likes him, rank and fortune are not the first considerations. Her son, so long as he is a Grafton, will inherit the title. And I believe you have some neighbors in Sussex with unmarried sons of the right age?"

Lord Grafton put down his cup and pondered the suggestion. He did not feel any great enthusiasm for a long holiday in the country, and it was certainly not something that would have occurred to him. But as he thought about it, the picture Lady Burnham painted of the kind of man Sophia could meet in the country was exactly what he was looking for. A man of robust English country stock, the kind who preferred Sussex to London, was fond of his family, his dogs, and his horses, and whose worst vice was hunting whenever the opportunity presented itself. A man who would father a large family and devote himself to his wife, his children, and the estate. Solid and settled. Just what the future head of the Grafton family ought to be. And yes, he knew there were young unmarried men among the county families of his acquaintance.

Lord Grafton promised to consider a visit to his country estate when an opportunity presented itself. Lady Burnham was satisfied. "I am glad we think alike on such an important matter. You have borne with my plain speaking in regard to your daughter, but I loved Catherine and I love Sophia and am as anxious as you to see her respectably settled. And more than that, it will be better when she enters into a life where she must set a Christian example and consider what good she might do in the world instead of concentrating on a life of pleasures and fine gowns. Now, if you will forgive me, I must retire to my bed. Talking tires one extremely, I find. I am so often tired these days."

A week later Lord Grafton and Sophia were interrupted at one of the dinners for prospective husbands. Sophia was smiling politely while praying for the evening to be over when a message came from Lady Burnham's maid. Lady Burnham had fallen unconscious, and though revived, she could no longer move her right arm or leg. The servants had sent for a doctor, but the maid feared for her mistress's life and begged them to come at once. Lord Grafton and Sophia made their apologies, left their guests, and rushed to Lady Burnham's apartments at St. James's Palace, where they found the formidable old lady covered with a shawl on her favorite sofa, looking small, frail, and white, her mouth twisted. Her maid was in tears. Lady Burnham made a slight motion with her left hand and said something unintelligible.

"My mistress means her prayer book on the table. She could never bear to part with it after Lady Catherine, your mother, died, but only yesterday she bade me remember that you were to have it on her death, miss," sobbed the maid. Sophia picked it up, and Lady Burnham managed a nod. Inside was inscribed Catherine Vassey, and below that an inscription from Lady Burnham to Dearest Sophia, bidding her remember that the surest path to peace of mind and heart lay in choosing duty over inclination and the path of righteousness. "Duty over inclination" was underscored.

When Sophia looked up, Lady Burnham's eyes were closed. "Dear Lady Burnham, you have been as a mother to me!" Sophia kissed her and dissolved into floods of tears, remorseful for the times she had been rude or resented Lady Burnham's interference. The doctor arrived but could do nothing. Within the hour, Lady Burnham was no more.

Lady Burnham had divided her fortune between the Evangelicals "for the propagation of the gospel and for the relief of the poor" and the Society for the Abolition of the African Trade in Slaves to the Americas, save for a small legacy to her maid and a smaller one to Sophia to remember her by, together with the prayer book that had belonged to Catherine.

Sophia was surprised how keenly she missed her godmother, while Lord Grafton felt quite undone by his old friend's death. At her funeral, heedless of a cold January drizzle, he lingered at the graveside as dusk fell, pondering the impermanence of life, thinking of Catherine. Wet and chilled to the bone, he took a final leave of the woman who had introduced them and always devoted herself to their daughter. He was a long time returning home in his wet clothes, and by the next morning, he was feverish with a sore throat and a severe cold that kept him bedridden for weeks and afterward left him weak with a wracking cough and a lethargy he could not shake off. His gout was often troublesome, and his fever came and went. He found himself disinclined to move from the bath chair in his library for days on end.

Too unwell to escort Sophia about in London or keep late hours, he engaged a respectable officer's widow, Mrs. Grey, to act as Sophia's companion and chaperone. When Sophia grew worried, he protested that he was in his seventh decade, when a bad cold naturally took longer to vanquish. But Sophia insisted on summoning an eminent physician. The physician examined him, shook his head, diagnosed asthenia, and ordered a change of air.

That decided Lord Grafton to act on Lady Burnham's advice to visit the country without further delay. He told Sophia that they would close up the house in St. James's and go to Sussex for the spring and summer. He was sorry to interrupt her enjoyments, but Sophia assured him they must do anything that would restore his health. Lord Grafton was touched by her concern and assured her that every family in the county would visit and extend invitations. Mrs. Grey would accompany them so that Sophia's social life would not be curtailed for want of a chaperone.

He wrote to his Sussex acquaintances, inquiring in a roundabout way as to the health of their families, to discover which had unmarried sons. He would call on them and reestablish old family conncctions. He would have his neighbors to dinner. There would be a little hunting before the season ended. Sophia was fond of hunting. He would do everything in his power to introduce Sophia to as many men as possible in Sussex. She couldn't marry anyone unless she met him first.

Trunks were packed. Mrs. Betts oversaw shrouding of the drawing room furniture and portraits in dust sheets, and the servants were put on board wages until Lord Grafton returned in the autumn. Then Mrs. Betts went on ahead to open the house in Sussex. Sophia and Mrs. Grey attended a last *soirée*, where Sophia's absence from London for the next few months was roundly deplored by her many beaux. The next day, they departed for the country.

CHAPTER 5

A BELLE'S LIFE IN THE COUNTRY

Sussex, 1753

Lord Grafton had not previously enjoyed his short visits to Sussex so much that he had been tempted to lengthen them. While he was alive to his obligations as a landowner and ensured that his steward took the necessary steps to safeguard the welfare of the Grafton tenants and oversee the proper cultivation of the estate, the country and the landowners that made up his circle of society there were dull compared with London and his cosmopolitan friends. He therefore went to the country resigned to finding this extended visit tedious, though he acknowledged it was necessary. He would have visited the wilds of Africa if it would get Sophia suitably married.

But once in his ancestral home, he found it soothing to be back there. He was perhaps more tired than he'd realized, no longer in want of excitement and stimulation as he had been in his younger days. Now that he acknowledged feeling the effects of age, he was more pleased than before to note things that signaled permanence and a reassuring sense of continuity—the fourteenth-century chapel, the Tudor linen fold paneling in the library with its centuries of books, the wide staircase carved with garlands and fruit, the ancestral portraits, the rooms that held the scent of generations of log fires, furniture well-rubbed with beeswax, mingled with the aromas of orange and spice and lavender from bowls of *potpourri* to sweeten the air and drive away disease.

The weather turned uncommonly mild in mid-March. Primroses bloomed everywhere, and the leaded windows, with views of the gardens and the deer park beyond, were thrown open. The house filled with spring sunshine and great vases of blossoming *prunus*. Mrs. Betts gave orders left and right to the gardener for asparagus, strawberries, and forced rhubarb from the greenhouse and rejoiced in a bountiful supply of ducks and chickens from the poultry yard.

Fresh air, wholesome food, peace, and quiet worked their restorative magic after the crowds, dirt, and bustle of London, and within a few weeks, Sophia was pleased to observe how much her father's health had improved. Color had returned to his face, and the wracking cough that had troubled him since Lady Burnham's funeral had almost disappeared.

The fine weather showed off Sussex at its best. Orchards and hedgerows were in bloom, fields newly planted. The Downs, dotted with sheep and new lambs, rose gently in the distance. Lord Grafton took Sophia for a gallop across the Downs to show her the curious figure of the Long Man cut into the chalk hill by ancient hands, pointing out the sweeping views of the countryside, the home farm, and the boundaries of the Grafton estate in the distance. He recalled the pleasures of his youth, the hunting and balls and the pheasant shoots. To the delight of his gamekeeper, he gave orders for the pheasant guns to be oiled in readiness for September.

Within a week of their arrival at Grafton Manor, old acquaintances from neighboring estates paid calls on Lord Grafton and Sophia. Lord

Grafton felt well enough to accept and return their invitations to dinner. Their neighbors held evening parties in their honor, and there was a subscription ball organized at a country tavern, where Sophia had danced and practiced her wiles on the young men of the county. As her father had predicted, she was soon caught up in a steady round of engagements—the dances and hunts, picnics, dinners, and private theatricals that kept the young people of the county entertained.

Sophia found the country holiday more agreeable than she expected. The weather was often fine enough that mud was no inconvenience. She had had some pretty frocks made up in what the London dressmaker assured her was a simple mode suitable for mornings in the country, and some fetching wide-brimmed hats with ribbons for out-of-doors.

And Sophia discovered a new realm to command. When not gadding about the countryside, she amused herself ordering elaborate French or Italian dishes that she thought might pique her father's appetite or choosing which fruits from the hothouse would be eaten at dinner. Flowers were her new passion. She took an interest in the pink rosebushes the gardener planted on her orders. She chose which flowers were to be cut for display in the house and arranged them to her liking. She sent to London for watercolors and brushes and a great deal of expensive sketching paper and, with her new friends the young Misses Hawkhurst, who were their nearest neighbors at Hawkhurst Castle, took up painting wildflowers. She called on her new acquaintances in the neighborhood, behaved charmingly, and was much approved of. The fashion papers arrived with the post, and on the rare rainy days, she amused herself planning the gowns she would order when they returned to town in the autumn.

Mrs. Betts made a pointed reference to the villagers waiting to learn if Miss Sophia would be as kind a mistress as her mother had been. In a benevolent frame of mind, Sophia took the hint and accompanied Mrs. Betts when the housekeeper delivered the traditional covered baskets of baby's things for new mothers, or soup, port, and custard for the elderly or ill tenants. Prompted by Lord Grafton, Sophia made an official visit to the village school to hear the children recite and afterward could be counted on to have a supply of sweets in her pocket if the village children happened to meet her out walking or painting. She basked in her importance and popularity and thought earnestly about what improvements could be made to the school.

The villagers agreed it was good to have the family in residence again. Miss Sophia with her flower painting and sweets meant well, and the children were fond of her. They liked her better when Mrs. Betts reported many children had fallen ill with a high fever and spots and it was Sophia who sent at once for the local apothecary to determine if this was the dreaded smallpox. The apothecary diagnosed measles, and Sophia made apple water and a refreshing rhubarb jelly with her own hands and swept into the village houses with Mrs. Betts, carrying the baskets to distribute these treats to the little sufferers herself. The villagers, who depended on the goodwill and help of the Grafton family in times of crisis, began to see a resemblance to Lady Catherine that they hadn't noticed before.

For Sophia these were well-intentioned, diverting novelties to while away the time until they returned to London. For Lord Grafton it signaled that she was settling into her future role. She, in turn, was unaware he expected that when he returned to London in the autumn, he would return alone.

Within a month of their arrival, Lord Grafton had been amused to entertain many nervous young men seeking his permission to court Sophia, leading him to observe that his daughter had attracted country suitors as quickly as rose gardens attracted bees. He hoped she would like one of them, because he began to understand why Lady Burnham had thought Sophia needed to meet a different type of man. There was something appealing about these strapping, straightforward sons of the local families, who loved the land and the country and for whom his conditions for Sophia's marriage posed no obstacles as they had seemed to do in London. On the contrary, his country neighbors entirely approved of his stipulations as sound and wise.

And by mid-June his hopes were rising. Sophia seemed to be growing fond of young John Hawkhurst, the heir at neighboring Hawkhurst Castle. John found an excuse to pay a call on Lord Grafton almost every morning, bringing messages from his father, uncles, or gamekeeper, some fine strawberries of which the Hawkhurst gardener had a surplus, or some fat pigeons he had shot in the grain. The two men would discuss the business of their respective estates for a quarter of an hour, and usually Sophia would appear as if by accident, pretty as a picture in one of her new morning gowns. Sophia would feign surprise at seeing him, make a delighted speech of thanks for whatever John had brought that day, and order refreshments, which were always accepted, though to Lord Grafton's amusement the seedcake went almost untasted and the glass of Lord Grafton's excellent Madeira undrunk by either John or Sophia. Did Lord Grafton imagine it, or did Sophia blush in John's presence?

This was a welcome development. Perhaps the age and *gravitas* he had thought necessary in Sophia's husband could be dispensed with at the outset. John would acquire both in time. In fact, Lord Grafton was prepared to relax many of his qualifications he had previously insisted upon for Sophia's husband. He was growing more anxious to hurry things along.

The truth was that after an encouraging return to health in the spring, by June he no longer felt quite as well as he had. His cough had returned, though he put it down to having gotten his feet wet with dew in an early morning walk across the fields to look at some badger setts in the deer park. He was a little more breathless, a little more tired in the daytime, sometimes feverish at night, and increasingly reluctant to accept invitations. Dinners exhausted him. He hoped these were no more than the reminders of mortality that, unwelcome though they were, must be expected at his age. But even so, they reminded him of his transient place in the long Grafton line, that he would not live forever. He hoped the longed-for grandson would become a reality as soon as possible.

Midsummer Night approached, and he had reason to believe that things would be settled between Sophia and John then.

John had called on Lord Grafton the previous afternoon while Sophia was out riding with his sisters and stammered out the usual request for permission to speak to Sophia the following night. John had told Lord Grafton he had been waiting for that evening to propose, because Midsummer Night was his birthday, and what occasion could be more proper for the heir to ask the woman he loved to marry him? And he did love Sophia, he said firmly, very much indeed. Lord Grafton liked the certainty with which he said it and was touched by the way John had carefully planned the timing and setting for his proposal.

For generations it had been the Hawkhursts' custom to mark the longest night of the year with a Midsummer Ball for the surrounding county families, and John's choice of the evening to propose struck Lord Grafton as fitting, romantic, and certain to have an effect on Sophia. In fact, it was this sensitivity to tradition that made an alliance between the Graftons and the Hawkhursts so desirable in Lord Grafton's eyes. He approved what the Hawkhursts represented—continuity and a solid connection to age-old customs—and he had grown fond of John.

To London eyes, the castle might appear rather shabby—the Tudor rose medallions worn, the gardens a little overgrown, the fountain no longer splashing but full of ducks—while the castle itself, once a fortification against a French invasion after the Crusades, had become incorporated into a sprawling country house, a testament to fifteen generations of Hawkhursts who had lived there and added this or that new wing.

Although there was no title, the Hawkhurst estate was a fine one, and nearly as old as that of the Graftons, the Hawkhursts having owned the property since the Crusades. The marriage of Sophia and John would unite two distinguished old families and merge two fine estates for their descendants. Lord Grafton thought John seemed the sort of man to have a large family of children, a robust and hearty fellow.

As to the conditions attached to Sophia's hand, John assured Lord Grafton these had been discussed with his father. Though he was the Hawkhurst heir, his father wished for John's happiness more than anything and was willing for John to relinquish the Hawkhurst name so long as John's heir would inherit the combined estates. John explained all this to Lord Grafton in a forthright manner, saying he wished all such matters to be clear and agreeable to both their families. This was a sentiment Lord Grafton approved as much as the honesty in John's straightforward gaze. Permission to ask Sophia was warmly given, and Lord Grafton heartily wished John success.

As the young man left, Lord Grafton congratulated himself that he had followed Lady Burnham's advice. His imagination leaped ahead. No need for a long engagement. Young people never wanted that. The wedding could take place in the family chapel immediately after the harvest in August. There would be a grand wedding breakfast for all the county, a party in the servants' hall and another in the village. He would send to his London wine merchants for champagne and port to drink to the couple's health.

There would be another great celebration when their first child was christened. When that happy day came, he magnanimously decided he would not insist on particular names. He would not hope for Peregrine. Provided the boy's last name was Grafton, Sophia and John might christen the baby what they pleased. In a burst of generosity, he decided he would even suggest Frederick, the name of John's father and grandfather, in compliment to the Hawkhursts. Lord Grafton saw himself looking on beside the vicar as the ancient words were read. He supposed the pretty Hawkhurst sisters would stand as godmothers. Lord Grafton rubbed his hands with glee, seeing in his mind's eye the gathering round the twelfth-century baptismal font in the family chapel, the young godmothers passing the baby back and forth between them and Sophia, John standing proudly behind his wife. Lord Grafton smiled, supposing that Sophia would commission an elegant new gown and bonnet for the occasion. No doubt that christening would be the first of many.

The afternoon of the ball, he consulted the almanac, which told him there would be a full moon on Midsummer Night. When Sophia was dressed and came to take her leave of him, he thought she must have taken special care dressing for the evening. She looked particularly fetching in a pink muslin gown trimmed with silk roses, which had arrived from the London dressmaker. Her curls were gathered up in jeweled combs to tumble down her shoulders, her mother's pearls at her throat. *All for John's benefit,* Lord Grafton thought with satisfaction as he leaned from the library window to wave off the carriage containing Sophia and Mrs. Grey.

Settling back into his chair to think of the young lovers, Lord Grafton recalled his youth, when he and his brothers had attended Midsummer Balls at the castle. He doubted much had changed since then. Between dances, lovers would find their way into the walled gardens, and he supposed that was where John would propose. The air would be sweet with sun-warmed lavender and new-mown hay in the surrounding fields. He fancied there would still be Chinese lanterns hung outdoors. On such a warm night as this, music would spill from the tall open windows. Inside there would be the timeless scenes typical of country balls—portly gentlemen would be playing quadrille and whist in the library, the long mahogany table in the dining room laden with cold ham and chicken, *epergnes* of fruit, and punch, ready for the supper interval. In the long gallery where the dancing took place, matrons would fan themselves on the sidelines, while clusters of girls giggled and whispered together, waiting to be asked to dance, surreptitiously eyed by the young men before they rushed to choose a partner. The same portraits of Hawkhurst ancestors would look down at the young people, as if to ask, "Who will be the heir's choice? Who will become one of the family?"

Lord Grafton congratulated himself that tonight he knew the answer.

These reflections were a soothing reminder that life would go on, whatever the state of his health. He looked forward to breakfast, when Sophia would ask for his blessing. Preparing for bed at his usual early hour, it was all he could do not to confide in his valet that Miss Sophia was soon to be married.

Three hours after leaving home, Sophia was part of just such a scene as her father remembered. She curtseyed to John, her fifth partner of the evening, as couples were taking their places for a dance called the allemande. Everyone in the room was watching Sophia and John from the corner of his or her eyes. It was plain that John was in love with Sophia, but it was harder for the watchers to gauge Sophia's feelings. Sophia seemed uncharacteristically reserved. Her eyes were modestly cast down, and her fan was raised to hide her face, but her demeanor was put down to the emotion of the moment, the understandable agitation a girl feels when she senses a proposal in the air. The general expectation was that their engagement would be announced before the night was over.

In fact, Sophia raised her fan to hide a grimace. She thought John a perfectly amiable if tongue-tied young man and liked him a great deal for his kind attention in visiting her father so often. She had seen the pleasure Lord Grafton took in these frequent visits and was ready in her thanks to John for the steady flow of fruit and game that piqued her father's flagging appetite. But until tonight it had not occurred to her that John's frequent calls were anything to do with her. She was uncomfortably aware that he was gazing at her with a strangely soulful expression. It made her think of a disconsolate cow. She had twice refused his invitation to step outside and see the lanterns, and hoped nothing more would come of it. She wished John would turn his attention to his sweet-faced cousin Polly, who hung on his every word and plainly adored him. And just at the moment, Sophia wished someone else were her partner for the allemande.

As soon as Sophia had arrived at the ball, John had abandoned Polly and elbowed ahead of Sophia's other beaux to claim the allemande because she had once remarked it was her favorite dance. She had seen the distress on Polly's face and understood that Polly wished with all her fifteen-year-old heart Sophia and her father had stayed in London where they belonged. Sophia sighed and lowered her fan. She tried to smile at John in a way that wouldn't be taken as encouragement. Polly was a sweet girl. When the dance ended, she would contrive to send John back to her. Meanwhile, she hoped she would get through the dance without injury. Dancing with John was like dancing with a cart horse.

John was a hearty, florid, good-hearted young man, every inch the country squire, well liked by the tenants, happiest when hunting or shooting pheasant, affectionate to his sisters, a steady hand with a horse, and a head for farming when it was not full of Sophia. But he had no aptitude at all for dancing. The allemande was particularly problematic, as the male dancer was required to perform a series of little leaps and hops followed by heel clicking midair. With the best of intentions, John would leap heavily and hop at will rather than in time to the music, and for the next quarter of an hour, Sophia was on the alert as she danced, trying to swish her hem out of the way of his large feet.

When the music ended, Sophia was relieved to find her train still attached to her gown. John had landed on it several times. The warm night and the dancing had left her thirsty and longing for a cool glass of punch, but John clutched her hand in a firm grip and dragged her out through the French windows, saying in a loud voice that she absolutely must see the lanterns. Those near enough to hear smiled knowingly at each other. Sophia couldn't pull away without making a scene, and resigned herself.

Leading Sophia into the physic garden, John stopped and breathlessly launched into his proposal, a declaration she had bewitched him out of his senses, he loved her, and she would make him the happiest of men by consenting to be his wife and mistress of Hawkhurst Castle. He kept talking, marshalling every argument at his command, from the fact Lord Grafton approved to the nearness of their properties and that it would make his family almost as happy as it made him, before again declaring his love and his intention to do anything in his power to make her happy. His rush of eloquence was finally exhausted, and John looked at her beseechingly, waiting for her answer.

For a moment Sophia wavered. She was not immune to the charm of a moonlit walled garden or sun-warmed lavender. The Hawkhursts were kind. It would make her father happy. It would make John and everyone happy. She was tired of pressure to marry men who all seemed old and dull, and when she returned to London, she could only expect another procession of old and dull men would be introduced by her ever-hopeful father until she gave in and married one of them. She would have to marry eventually—she couldn't shirk that particular duty forever. John couldn't dance, but at least he was young, and she thought of her father's joy upon seeing the grandchild he spoke of constantly.

But then she imagined kissing John. Despite the moonlight she felt no impulse to try the experiment. *Let him kiss Polly,* she thought. Her answer must be no.

Sophia knew what to say. She thanked John for the honor of his proposal but feared that her feelings were not such as he would look for in a wife. She wished him well very sincerely and prevented his trying to argue her out of her refusal by insisting they return to the ball. She said his cousin Polly, now sitting disconsolately in the corner, needed someone to take her in to supper.

At supper no engagement was announced. The Hawkhurst girls raised their eyebrows at each other in surprise, and guests drew their own conclusions from John's glum expression. Only Polly, who had been taken in to supper by John, went home from the ball in happier spirits than those in which she had begun the evening.

CHAPTER 6

SHADOWS IN SUSSEX

As the maid laced her gown the next morning, Sophia's heart sank recalling her father's high spirits of the previous day. She dreaded facing him at breakfast. She suspected Lord Grafton had not only given John permission to propose but had actively encouraged him to believe he would be accepted. Now she would deliver disappointing news, and her father would be irritable for the rest of the morning. *If only Papa wouldn't meddle. There's bound to be a man I'll like enough to marry, that Papa and I'll* both *like enough for me to marry, eventually,* she thought as she descended the stairs. *I ought to be grateful Papa hasn't positively insisted on anyone. I'm not ready to give up London just yet.* She entered the sunny breakfast parlor, kissed her father, and took her seat, determined to be extra dutiful to make up for last night's refusal.

Smiling sweetly, Sophia poured out his tea and made her confession as quickly as possible to get it over with.

Lord Grafton put his head in his hands.

Sophia tried to mitigate the damage, saying, "Dear Papa, John is the same as the other young men here, pleasant in a country-bred sort of way, but rather dull. Their only reading is the almanac. They talk mainly of their land, the crops, their dogs, their horses, their pheasants, and their hunting. They are nice enough to ride and hunt and dance with, but none would be interesting enough to while away a long winter in the country. And, dear Papa, I flatter myself that I am indispensable to your comfort in London. What would you do for a hostess, without me? Pray let us speak of something else. I see the letters at your place. News of Wildwood and the tobacco?" She buttered her toast energetically.

"A fat packet from Mr. Barker and a letter, no, two letters from the solicitors," Lord Grafton said gloomily, picking up his paper knife. What did "interesting" matter? Certainly he had never considered whether Catherine was "interesting," and he had never wondered if Catherine had found him so. It had been a marriage of convenience, like most marriages; they had both understood that quite well, yet they had been happy. Why would the same formula not work for Sophia? He opened up the first solicitors' letter.

His expression of gloom deepened as he read. It was brief, informing him that a further large advance of capital had been added to the mortgage on the Grafton estate and sent to Mr. Barker, as they were expecting to hear every day that the first shipment of tobacco had arrived.

When Sophia asked if the letter contained anything troubling, Lord Grafton said it was merely a business matter and turned to Mr. Barker's packet. "Let us see what Barker has to say for himself. I expect this and the solicitors' letters crossed in the post. I daresay these are the particulars of his first sale." At least there was good news from another quarter this morning, he thought as he cut open the fat envelope.

But there was nothing about tobacco or accounts from Mr. Barker. Instead he wrote to inform Lord Grafton that the new house at Wildwood was finished. He had enclosed sketches of the house and gardens and hoped Lord Grafton approved of his design for the formal garden and avenue of trees he had laid out. "Handsome enough as new houses in Virginia go, I daresay. Perhaps not unlike a small manor," Lord Grafton said, passing the sketches to Sophia. "As it should be, considering the cost. Brick is inordinately expensive. But where is the tobacco!"

"Perhaps that news comes by separate letter, Papa. I daresay he has sent the accounts directly to the solicitors so as not to trouble you. You know how you dislike business matters," Sophia said soothingly, grateful they had something to discuss other than her marriage prospects. She took the sketch. The drawing showed a plain two-story building, five windows wide, with chimneys at either end, and a porch with a portico and broad steps. It was flanked with box bushes, and behind the house a walled garden was sketched. Another plan showed the outbuildings some distance from the house—kitchen, barns, stables, tobacco shed, smokehouse, and some pretty little cottages labeled "slave quarters."

"The new house looks well enough, Papa, very neat and, I daresay, comfortable. And the slave quarters appear to be a tidy little village. It all seems just as you ordered. Is there a tenant?"

Lord Grafton continued with Mr. Barker's letter to find out and exclaimed in surprise. There was no tenant yet, because the property must be furnished and equipped. To that end he required Lord Grafton to authorize a further sum of money on a long list of goods that must be purchased in England and shipped.

"Everything needed in Virginia—furniture, fabrics, even glass for the windows—must be obtained here! There's no mention of tobacco, only of more confounded expenditure! It is inexplicable!" Lord Grafton expostulated angrily. "And why the Devil had the fellow taken so much care over the garden arrangements while the house is not yet for a tenant and his family?"

Sophia, of course, had no answer.

Fuming, Lord Grafton opened the second letter from his solicitors, who had echoed the same note of urgency in their letters for the past half year. They had had the same request for funds for the furnishing of the property, but the interest on the loan was rapidly becoming unsustainable . . . What he read next brought on a violent fit of coughing. He raised his handkerchief to his lips and quickly left the breakfast table, waving Sophia to finish her breakfast.

These distressing letters drained him. The situation on the Virginia plantation had become unmanageable; the debt was spiraling out of control. He felt himself trapped and ill again. His fits of coughing spattered his handkerchief with blood, though he hid this from Sophia. Worry and a recurring pain in his back kept him awake at night, made him uncharacteristically short-tempered during the day. What would become of Sophia if anything happened to him? They had no family. Ought he to appoint a guardian? Or should he hope that John might renew his suit, and this time, be accepted?

But John had ceased his daily calls and Sophia no longer rode or sketched or visited with the Hawkhurst girls.

For Sophia the charms of Sussex were beginning to pale. Her father was out of sorts. She felt she had exhausted the enjoyments in the country, and relations with the Hawkhurst girls had become strained. She began to count the days until they could return to London and bore patiently with her father's irritability, believing he too was tiring of the country, though there would be little point returning to a hot, dirty city in August.

She proposed a house party. "Perhaps the house is dull for you, Papa? We've had no one visit in weeks. I'll write to invite a party for the shooting in September. You gave orders for the guns to be oiled, and the gamekeeper says he's never seen the pheasant so plentiful."

"I beg you, do not write to invite anyone! At my age it's too fatiguing to be always entertaining people—their constant chatter is exhausting. You must allow me to feel unequal to company if it suits me to do so!"

It was not like Lord Grafton. He was a sociable man with a large circle of interesting friends and normally very fond of company. "As you wish, Papa," she said soothingly. *We shall be back in London soon enough,* Sophia thought as her father pushed back his chair and walked impatiently out of the breakfast room.

By mid-August Sophia was worried that her father had grown uncharacteristically lethargic, and his complexion was pale. He had always been a lover of books and particular about his wine. Now orders from his London bookseller piled up on the library table, with their pages uncut, and wine went into his cellar untasted. Though August was very warm, he spent the day in his bath chair under a blanket, insisting he was not ill, merely had a touch of rheumatism. There were regular letters from the solicitors that he only half read.

Sophia gave up accepting invitations so as to keep him company in the evenings, playing whist or chess to try and distract him from his ailments. Behind his bedroom door, she could hear him coughing at night. He complained the pain in his back grew worse every day.

Over Lord Grafton's protest that he hated fuss, Sophia finally insisted on summoning the local apothecary, who diagnosed dyspepsia and advised he should be nursed back to health through careful attention to diet and some powders he supplied at great expense. Sophia embraced her new role as nurse. She measured out the correct dose of the powders morning and evening and took herself down to the kitchen, donned an apron, and asked Mrs. Betts for her best recipes to revive invalids—beef tea, rice milk, custards, arrowroot jelly. She had the gardener point out where elecampane and comfrey grew, and brewed a syrup Mrs. Betts recommended as particularly efficacious in the case of a bad and lingering cough.

He hardly touched any of it, complaining everything was bitter. Sophia brought cordials to mask the taste and preserves to build up his strength, saw that the bedroom was aired and his pillows plumped. He grew no better. By mid-September Sophia was frightened by how thin, pinched, and diminished he looked, how rarely he stirred from the fire he insisted be lit, though the September days were sunny and mellow. His cheeks were brightly flushed in his pale face. There was no question of his walking about the fields after pheasant. There was no longer talk of when they would return to town. He no longer protested that he was not the least bit ill.

Throughout this time, Mrs. Grey hovered, anxious to be of use, until barely able to mask her irritation Sophia sent Mrs. Grey on a holiday to visit her sister in Scotland and wrote to their London friends, asking them to recommend doctors and surgeons. The doctors and surgeons arrived with tonics and leeches and razors. They dosed him and bled him until Lord Grafton could scarcely move. They spoke of scrofula and the "king's evil" and advised Jesuit's bark and, much richer, departed for town, leaving the patient enfeebled by their attentions. Sophia tried to follow all the instructions given. She obtained this medicine and that tonic, nursed him devotedly, read to him, fed him the little he could eat, and prayed while he slept.

As autumn set in and the days grew shorter, Sophia felt a dark cloud enveloping the manor house and overwhelming her spirits. It rained, leaves fell, the weather turned cold. Flowers in the garden had become brown stalks. The candles were lit earlier and earlier in the afternoons, and Sophia gave orders for fires to be kept burning in all the rooms to drive away a pervasive chill that had settled on the old house. She hugged a shawl round her shoulders when she took a little exercise, walking up and down the cold corridors while her father napped. The prayer book that had belonged to her mother was now her greatest comfort as she watched by Lord Grafton's side. The bedroom filled with a heavy silence broken only by the crackle of the fire, the rasp of his breathing, and Sophia's reading the psalms when he was awake. Lord Grafton was not a religious man, but he had always found the psalms to his taste. On the pillow, his sleeping head was skull-like.

Sophia could no longer hope or pretend her father would recover. Before her eyes, he was slipping away beyond the power of soups and cordials, leeches and prayers. He was in constant pain, and she sent for the apothecary again and begged him for anything that would give her father some ease. The apothecary supplied her with pills and powders and, finally, laudanum. Sophia and Mrs. Betts took turns sitting with him through the night and giving him the laudanum when he roused and moaned. Mrs. Grey returned from Scotland but kept out of the way. The vicar called, anxious to give Lord Grafton the last rites and reminding Sophia that resignation to the will of God was a Christian duty.

Sophia wanted to scream and shake the man out of his moral complacency. Lord Grafton had always dismissed the vicar as a sanctimonious fool but had refused to replace him, saying the vicar's family had had the living for generations and the vicar had three small children and a wife to support. "Let him be. Vicars are all much the same. He'll do as well as another," Lord Grafton had said.

But Death was creeping closer and closer no matter how hard she tried to keep it at bay. Sophia was torn—ought she to allow him to die as a Christian? She finally permitted her father to be given the last rites, though the laudanum had rendered him almost insensible of anything that was happening. When it was done, she felt she had signed her father's death warrant.

One night in November, Sophia looked up from reading evensong out loud to him—her father was trying to say something. "Papa? Is there anything I can do for you?"

She leaned closer and heard, "Catherine, Catherine, are you there?" A look of peace settled on his face, and she realized that her father was dead.

Throughout the funeral service in the cold Grafton chapel, Sophia maintained a steely composure in front of the servants, the farmers, and the village, their country neighbors, and those friends who had made a hasty trip from London. But as he was interred in the family mausoleum beside her mother, and the chapel bell tolled, Sophia was overcome with grief, and she and Mrs. Betts wept in each other's arms.

She tried to read her Bible, to practice submission to God's will as Lady Burnham had often said she must, but they were empty words and failed to banish the melancholy thought that she had no one and the world was a sorrowful place. She often thought that if only she had married John and presented her father with the longed-for grandson before he died, it would seem a little less sorrowful; she would have had a husband and baby for comfort. But she had not wanted John; she had only thought of their returning to London. Regret and guilt took away her appetite, and she slept badly. She avoided the neighbors who paid condolence calls, and took long, solitary walks through the woods in the snow or frozen mud.

Christmas came and went, then Easter. Mrs. Grey's well-intentioned efforts at consolation were more irritating than comforting. Sophia struggled to be polite but tried to avoid her company. One day slipped into another, bleak and empty of purpose. She would return from her solitary rambles chilled to the bone, feeling insubstantial in a sad house filled with the ghosts of Grafton ancestors. They berated her silently, reminded her that her father had died unhappy and she might have prevented that.

Sophia answered letters of condolence, including a stiff and formal one from the Hawkhurst sisters, who added at the bottom of theirs that John and his cousin Polly were to marry in June. There were many letters from her father's lawyers. These always began with commiseration, followed by a request to discuss the will, stressing that they awaited her instructions about whether to relinquish the London house and ending with incomprehensible urgency about the need to do something or other. Sophia never finished them. She tossed them all into a drawer in the library, thinking wearily that she couldn't trouble about the London house now. She didn't feel capable of deciding anything.

The days grew longer and the trees were in bud, the Downs were green, and ewes and their lambs dotted the hillsides as they had done the previous spring. Primroses and bluebells sprang up in the wood, but she felt no joy. Hoping to tempt her, the gardener brought the first strawberries and asparagus from the hothouse. Sophia thought they had no taste, though Mrs. Grey praised them.

She tried to take an interest in the village as she ought. She visited the village school and heard boys' recitations, praised examples of the girls' sewing. On Prize Day she handed out Bibles to the best students and watched the girls dance the Maypole. She had given orders for a lavish Prize Day tea with ham and plenty of cake in the gardens, where the roses and peonies had been coaxed into early bloom by the gardener. The sun shone and the children laughed and shouted, and the tenant farmers doffed their caps to her, while their wives in their Sunday best whispered that the poor young mistress was such a sad figure in her mourning on this sunny afternoon and it was a pity she hadn't married the young Hawkhurst squire. "Why did she refuse him?" they asked each other over their teacups. A husband and some young ones of her own was what she needed. They'd lighten her heart more than all her great fortune. Because she was all alone in the world now.

CHAPTER 7
DEBT

1754

Spring gave way to a wet and dreary English summer. On a melancholy June day, Lord Grafton's lawyers made an uncomfortable journey to Sussex in a heavy downpour. The old butler opened the door to two solemn men under dripping umbrellas who asked to see Miss Grafton. The butler informed them loftily that Miss Grafton was in mourning and not receiving visitors.

"She'll see us, or see the bailiffs," said the older lawyer sharply.

The butler showed them into the library and sent for his mistress.

When Sophia, dull eyed and pale in her mourning dress, had shaken their hands and sat down, the butler murmured he would send Mrs. Betts with Madeira and biscuits, and withdrew. The solicitors drank and ate and paid their condolences. Then the two men fell silent, staring uncomfortably at the floor and their wet shoes.

Sophia sensed something was amiss. "To what do I owe the honor of this visit? I do not think you would have come so far, and in such dirty weather, to merely discuss the London house or repeat the commiserations in your letters. Pray, speak plainly."

The elder lawyer sighed. "Miss Grafton, our many letters have gone unanswered. We regret the inconvenience but felt we had no choice but to wait on you in person and insist on a discussion of certain matters of urgency that require me to speak more plainly than you will wish to hear."

"Matters of urgency? I am in mourning, sir. Can they not wait?"

"Miss Grafton, they cannot. I will explain. The first of these is that we have let the London house go."

"By what authority? I gave you no leave!" Sophia was indignant. "I have not yet decided when I shall return to London, and I wish to keep the London establishment for the present."

"It was too great a drain on the estate to retain the lease. I regret being the bearer of distressing and unwelcome news, Miss Grafton, but as you know the estate was heavily mortgaged by your father three years ago in the expectation of having a good tobacco crop within a year or at most two. It was necessary to raise a substantial sum very quickly, which was only possible at an exorbitant rate of interest, something normally we would not have countenanced, but in the circumstances there seemed no reason not to do so at the time.

"Mr. Barker's assessment was that a fortune would be quickly realized. Unfortunately, we now believe Mr. Barker misled us as to when we could expect the first tobacco. No tobacco has yet been shipped, and despite our inquiries, Mr. Barker is unable or unwilling to tell us when we might expect it. In fact, we cannot ascertain whether any has even been planted, though the factors in London have showed us bills of the expenditures—the very great expenditures—that Mr. Barker has incurred on your father's behalf, ordering goods and equipment that were shipped to Virginia for Wildwood. Your father was put to a great deal of extra expenditure here, and was also obliged to remit a good part of the family's income for the past three years to Virginia. The income from the estate is not—has not been for some time—what Lord Grafton believed it to be, but the expectation was that once the Virginia estate was profitable, that would supply the shortfall from the English one. That was in part what prompted us to advise as we did.

"But as you may not have realized, Miss Grafton, Lord Grafton's expenses were always considerable, keeping up the house in London as well as the estate here in the manner of his father and grandfather. The burden of debt on the estate has been unsustainable. In short, both the debt and the interest on it have mounted alarmingly, and unless something is done, the Grafton estate and manor will be seized and sold. Forgive me for burdening you with business at such a time, but unless we act, Miss Grafton, I fear you are in danger of being left a pauper."

The solicitor's words came from a distance, meaningless noise. Sophia's attention drifted. She looked out the window at the rain and the sodden lawn and box garden, the wet roses bent almost to the ground. *The roses need tying up. I must remind the gardener,* she thought.

Pauper? Of whom were they speaking?

"I do not have the pleasure of understanding you, sir," she said. "Lord Grafton acted on your advice."

The solicitors' faces grew red. "Ahem! Indeed. But regrettably, this was a case where the circumstances were impossible to predict. It seemed at the time that Lord Grafton's manner of living required something be done to make the Virginia estate profitable, and something must be done now because payments on the debt are seriously in arrears, incurring ever more debt on debt. In our opinion the soundest course of action would be if the estate were sold outright to pay back the entire debt, to prevent it mounting any higher. At least that would leave you with a small balance from the sale. With careful investment it could supply you with a modest income."

"Sold! The Grafton estate sold! Nonsense. That is unthinkable!"

The solicitor wiped his brow. "There is a second possibility, a most fortunate occurrence. A gentleman of considerable means has presented himself, desirous of renting a large property in the neighborhood for his family. We believe that the manor house and grounds could be let to him, and the agricultural land on the estate could be let to the local farmers or even some of the surrounding estates. This might yield enough to pay the interest until the tobacco revenues come, provided the first shipment arrives by the end of the summer. If not, the estate will be seized and sold by the creditors. But let us not give up hope entirely. It is just possible that a communication from Mr. Barker has gone astray, informing us that the Grafton tobacco will soon land. Still, I fear that we must be prepared in case it does not.

"The prospective tenant has no use for the dower house and has graciously agreed that you may move into it while he is in occupation here." The lawyer waved a hand to take in the paneled library, the minstrels' gallery, the drawing room, library, pantries, bedrooms, paintings, and furniture collected by generations of Graftons. "You will have no income from this arrangement, as it will merely service the debt, but there is the legacy left you by Lady Burnham—it would allow you to live there quietly. As you are in mourning, it will attract no notice that you do not live in the grand style you did formerly when your father was alive."

Attract no notice? Everyone in Sussex would know within a week. Sophia's eyes flashed with outrage. "I . . . *I* have *permission* to move to the dower house?"

"Forgive me, Miss Grafton, but I beg you to understand that the debt grows, and as things unfortunately stand at the moment, there is no time to lose. This tenant is the only one who is agreeable to the terms we offered as well as being agreeable to your staying at the dower house. He is, ahem, in trade, but there can be no objection, as he is very liberal as to the terms and exceedingly anxious to be seen by the world as . . . established in such a house as this."

Agreeable? Sophia felt as if an invisible hand were tightening her stays like a vise, tighter . . . tighter, squeezing the life out of her. "And when . . . when does this remarkable tenant wish to . . . ?" She could not bring herself to say it.

"By the end of July, next month, in fact."

Move to the old dower house? Sophia's head spun, trying to imagine it. Impossible! Who could live there? Her father had shown it to her on one of their rides the previous year. It had been a handsome small house once, but now was overgrown with vines, chilly and damp inside, in the shade of some large yew trees that made it dark, and had been uninhabited for a long time. The paint and paper inside were peeling and moldy, the floorboards warped. Worst of all, it had a view of the manor.

She struggled to get her breath. "How could I manage there . . . and the servants!"

"The new tenants are desirous of keeping the servants on. But with Lady Burnham's legacy, you could perhaps manage *one* if the wages were small," said the younger solicitor. "Perhaps a young maid of all work. Your neighbors and friends are bound to send presents of game and fruit, and I daresay the tenant will have no objection to your taking firewood."

The manor let! The London house gone! No servants! Lord Grafton's daughter turned out of her home and reduced to counting candles in patched gowns, thin porridge, scavenging firewood, and, worst of all, the charity of her neighbors! Sophia felt faint with outrage and disbelief.

At the sight of her stricken face, the clerk leaned forward and, meaning to be comforting, reminded her that the Virginia property in her dowry was untouched by the mortgage on the English estate, and though it was behind in coming to profitability, it had a great deal of money invested in it and was sure to yield a steady income eventually. He hinted that Miss Grafton had had no lack of suitors and there was the likelihood she would marry and remove to her husband's home before the year of mourning was out, which, in the circumstances, no one was likely to censure her for doing. In fact, they had understood from Lord Grafton that the Hawkhurst heir had made an offer for her hand and been refused . . . if the solicitors were to approach the Hawkhursts, the family might be persuaded that Sophia had had a change of heart.

Sophia glared at them. This impertinence was worse than anything. Did they imagine she would go begging to marry John Hawkhurst? How dare they! And in any case, it was too late. "John Hawkhurst is recently married to his cousin," she said icily, "regarded as a most suitable match by all his friends. I wish them joy. If that is all, I bid you good day."

The lawyer and his clerk hemmed uncomfortably, exchanged a glance, and changed the subject. "Miss Grafton, I must beg you will allow us a few moments yet. We must speak of the letter from your guardian."

"Guardian? I have no guardian, sir."

"Ah," said the solicitors, hastening to explain that she did. The previous summer, when he began to realize he was seriously ill, her father had appointed a boyhood friend, Thomas de Bouldin, with whom he had once shared lessons, as her guardian until she turned twenty-one or married. The de Bouldin fortune had been lost at the gaming tables by Thomas's elder brother, and Thomas had gone to seek his fortune in Virginia and never returned to England. Lord Grafton discovered that Thomas had indeed prospered there, acquiring a large plantation and a house in Williamsburg, becoming sufficiently prominent to be elected a member of the governing body of the colony. Lord Grafton wrote to Thomas, seeking his advice about his Virginia property, and though Thomas had not seen the property, he was certain what Mr. Barker had said about necessary investment had been correct and that Lord Grafton had done well to make the investment. In his next letter, Lord Grafton, who by now was very unwell, asked Thomas to consent to act as his daughter's guardian in the event Lord Grafton's fears about his health were realized. Lord Grafton wrote that he had reason to think that the Virginia property would comprise the only valuable portion of Sophia's dowry, and since Thomas lived in Virginia, he was best placed to act as her guardian and adviser. For the sake of their old acquaintance, Lord Grafton had begged Thomas de Bouldin to agree.

"We have corresponded with Mr. de Bouldin since your father's death, and he has sent this letter to be passed on to you." The younger man handed a sealed letter to Sophia. Sophia opened it. It contained the usual condolences on Lord Grafton's death, his agreement to act as Sophia's guardian, and his opinion that the solicitors were right, that the English property should be let to pay off the mounting debt for the Virginia estate. It also contained an invitation. As Sophia was unmarried and had no relations in England, Thomas de Bouldin suggested she should make her home with him and his wife in Virginia, as he was certain her father would have wished.

Wordlessly Sophia handed the letter to the older solicitor and nodded for him to read it. She no longer comprehended anything. She felt numb, overwhelmed by misfortune and sudden ruin. *I never thought to rejoice in Papa's death, but thanks be to God he does not know what he has done!* she thought bitterly.

"Why did my father never mention Thomas de Bouldin?"

"He decided against telling you because he hoped you were soon to become engaged and, as a married woman, would have no need for a guardian. Letters between Virginia and England can take months. And it seems that while waiting for a response from Mr. de Bouldin, Lord Grafton grew too ill to consider what he ought to do."

Sophia remembered the laudanum and knew he was right.

"But if Lord Grafton appointed Thomas de Bouldin as his daughter's guardian, he believed that she could confidently regard him as her friend," urged the older man.

"What you mean to say, sir, is that I must choose between the dower house and going to Virginia to make my home?" The solicitors nodded, their expressions solemn and commiserating, their faces long.

They look like human sheep, Sophia thought, hating them. *Stupid, stupid sheep.*

She couldn't go to the dower house. She *couldn't.* She took a deep breath and said defiantly, "Well then. I daresay it would be an adventure to go to Virginia, and that is what I will do. I will accept Thomas de Bouldin's invitation, but only to pay him a visit. After that I shall live at Wildwood Plantation. I shall . . . I shall . . . learn how the tobacco is managed. And manage it I will, with Mr. Barker's help, until the English debt is paid. When that is done, I will sell Wildwood and return."

The solicitors were startled. They protested that ladies did not understand such things, until the expression on Sophia's face warned them it would be wise to say nothing more on that matter. Instead they mumbled that they were, of course, at her service to assist with the necessary arrangements. "There is a ship, the *Betsy Wisdom,* sailing in mid-July," began one. "It goes to Yorktown. And there is a fast packet to Virginia leaving from London this week. We may be in time to send Thomas de Bouldin a message to expect you on the *Betsy Wisdom.* That leaves only a few weeks to prepare, but we advise making haste to avoid the necessity for an autumn crossing. Shall we book passage for you?"

"It will be necessary to arrange two passages, sir. My companion, Mrs. Grey, will go with me, of course. And . . . I suppose I must make my preparations for the journey. Perhaps you will be good enough to take a commission to my dressmaker? Things I will require for traveling." Sophia rose and walked to her desk, took a sheet of paper, and made a hasty list.

The solicitors took it and promised to have the deeds to the Virginia property conveyed to her at once so that she might take them to Virginia to hand over to Thomas de Bouldin. Sophia nodded her thanks, and the solicitors bowed themselves out.

On the journey back to London, they agreed that Miss Grafton couldn't be expected to know any more about growing tobacco than the solicitor's cat would. But they were anxious for her to be gone, lest their part in the loss of the Grafton fortune became known, and in any case, with a tobacco plantation as dowry, she would soon find a husband in the colony and remain there. That would be for the best, and they agreed that in the interest of seeing Miss Grafton on her way as soon as possible, they would absorb the expenditure on the sea passage and settle the dressmaker's account. There was no Grafton money left for either.

Sophia was shaken from her mourning torpor. There was much to be done, and the days passed in a rush. She gave orders to have the house thoroughly aired and cleaned, directed which of the books, the silver, and the stores of wine should be locked away in the cellar against her return in several years' time. She wrote notes of farewell to the families of the county and received visitors come to bid her good-bye. The new clothes needed for the expedition arrived and were packed into the traveling trunk before Sophia so much as looked at them. Finally, she carefully rolled the deeds to Wildwood with the accompanying map, wrapped them in oilskin, and packed them in a leather pouch in a compartment of her trunk.

After a sad farewell to the servants and a melancholy hour spent by her parents' grave in the family churchyard, Sophia and Mrs. Grey departed. As the coach rattled north to London between hedgerows and fields ripening in the sun, through the little villages with their greens and ponds and churches on the Grafton and then the Hawkhurst estates, Sophia told herself she must stifle all regrets. Marriage to John would have changed nothing, and as John's wife, she could not have gone to Virginia to see the debt repaid. She would return in only a few years and resume her life here, where she belonged.

On board the *Betsy Wisdom* two days later, Sophia remained on deck while Mrs. Grey settled their things in the tiny cabin that would scarcely hold the two ladies and their sea trunks. It had been shockingly expensive to procure. She could not understand how the solicitors had neglected to engage a private cabin.

She had been so busy with her preparations to leave that she had had no leisure to think of anything else for the past five weeks. Now she stood at the rail of the ship, with nothing to do but watch the bustling scene below on the Billingsgate dock, where porters and sailors, prostitutes and hawkers mingled with the passengers looking for this or that ship.

She was calculating how much was left of Lady Burnham's legacy after she paid for the cabin when her thoughts were interrupted by a noisy group of disreputable-looking men approaching the gangplank. Surrounded by constables, they were evidently waiting for the horde of bedraggled women and dirty children with bundles and babies, pushing their way across the crowded docks. Constables began directing and shoving this turbulent mass of humanity up the gangplank of the *Betsy Wisdom*, some of the men cursing, some of the women weeping, some shouting for their children, many of the babies crying. Sophia asked a passing sailor why these people were traveling to Virginia. The sailor nodded. "Oh, miss, them's criminals, you see, murderers and debtors. If they don't get hung or clapped into prison, they gets transported, has to be sold like slaves there to pay their passage," he said and hurried on.

Debtors! Sophia was chilled by the word. Debtors went to prison. Was she, the Honorable Miss Grafton, a debtor no better than the dirty, ragged people belowdecks? Her eyes filled with hopeless tears.

The sailors shouted something about the tide, the captain shouted back orders, sailors ran here and there, and the ship slipped its moorings to be carried downriver to the sea. Sophia remained on deck, watching London recede in the distance until its church spires and the dome of St. Paul's disappeared as the Thames wound its way east. The sound of church bells across the water grew fainter and fainter. They passed the

Barking level and the chimneys of Eastbury Manor House silhouetted against the evening sky.

What if she were never to see England again! She hugged her shawl tightly round her shoulders for comfort. "It's only for a time. The tobacco will pay, everyone says so. I *will* come home again," she muttered over and over as the tears flowed down her cheeks. "I will," she swore to the darkening sky. "I will," she promised the flock of starlings overhead flying home to roost. "I will," she shouted over the seagulls swooping and cawing in the ship's wake. "I swear it. You'll see! You'll see!"

The seagulls' shrill cries floated back mockingly on the breeze, "We'll see, we'll see, we'll see."

CHAPTER 8
THE DRUMHELLERS

London, July 1754

In the bowels of the assizes court, the bewigged judge peered over his spectacles at the prisoners and ordered flogging for the lucky few. Molly Drumheller fought down the nausea of another pregnancy and nursed the baby under a ragged shawl, listening while one prisoner after another was tried for theft or forgery or murder. Any faint hope Molly had was long evaporated. She shuddered each time the judge's gavel fell as he pronounced a verdict. Time after time he donned his black cap and sentenced this prisoner or that "to be hung by the neck until dead, and may God have mercy on your soul." His voice was a monotone, as if he found this a tedious demand on his time. He wanted to be done and eat his dinner.

Not for the first time, Molly marveled that her family had been brought so low. They had had a little farm once, a piece of land from her father's great farm, with a low-beamed cottage built snug against the clean winds that swept in from the sea over the flat Suffolk coast. There had been geese and chickens pecking among the apple trees, a dovecote, a pig, and two cows in the shed. Rufus's newly built forge had thrived, so they had a laborer to help on the farm and two apprentices at the forge. The boys had been fat, happy babies. It was a distant golden dream now.

When her father died, how swiftly their lives had been undone. She and Rufus had been cheated out of it all by her half brother, angry their father had given this good piece of land to a daughter of his second marriage, the girl who'd lowered the family by marrying the blacksmith's son. He had gone to court to contest the will and won. He took the property for himself and married another local landowner's daughter soon after.

The loss of her dowry land and the forge had ruined Molly and Rufus, driven them to London with two children, to live in a single room in a narrow, dark street running with filth, crammed with poor families, maimed and starving veterans of the war with France, pick-pockets, rogues, and the most desperate class of prostitutes, the older ones, living on gin, disfigured by rotting noses, barely able to wheedle their wares in the shadows. Molly felt stifled, missed the dunes and the fish from the sea and the hard East Anglia wind that blew everything clean. In London she drew in dirt and foul smells and misery with every breath.

Desperate to feed his family, Rufus had tried to emulate the pick-pockets, but a pickpocket gang had beaten him senseless, breaking his nose and leaving him with a scarred face that gave him a criminal appearance. Somehow he had managed to apprentice the boys to a baker. It had seemed like a small stroke of luck at the time.

Now Molly looked up at the courtroom window set high in the ceiling, barred against escape. Beneath it the court clerk bent his nose almost to the paper to record proceedings in the little light that penetrated.

The clerk shouted out the next names on the docket, and a scruffy man and two boys, one no taller than his elbow, stood in the dock.

"Is your name Rufus Drumheller?"

"Yes, Your Worship."

The boys sniveled and hung their heads. In the front row of the courtroom that stank of unwashed bodies, Molly rocked back and forth, weeping now with quiet despair, praying the sentence would be flogging. As the clerk called the next name on the docket, a fat man in a baker's apron scowled at the man and two boys in the dock.

The clerk snapped, "Toby Drumheller? Which of you is Toby Drumheller? Answer, boy!"

Rufus gave the taller boy a shake.

"Yes, Your Worship," the boy mumbled truculently, looking at his feet.

"And are you Jack Drumheller?"

The littler boy nodded and sobbed, "Yes."

The boys were terrified. As well they should have been.

The clerk read out the charges against them—theft and arson. The boys had been apprenticed to the baker, who was glaring at them. They were charged with stealing bread and starting a fire that burned the bakery to the ground. The baker rose and came forward to give his evidence, angry testimony that the boys were incorrigible, dirty, dishonest, and disobedient, with faults that could not be corrected by beatings—in short, the worst apprentices it had been his misfortune to take on, which he had only done out of pity for a poor family. And this was how he had been repaid—his business burned to the ground, his family's livelihood destroyed! The baker insisted Rufus Drumheller had taken umbrage at the necessary correction meted out to his good-for-nothing sons and sworn revenge.

Rufus Drumheller, the boys' father, stood in the dock and vehemently denied encouraging his sons to burn the bakery. He protested that the baker had half starved the lads until, driven by the hunger pangs of growing boys, they had snatched a loaf from the oven. They had not foreseen the accident that happened next, that live coals would fall upon the floor and set the bakery alight. They were young and hungry but meant no harm.

The baker shouted angrily they were all thieves and liars.

The judge snorted and silenced both parties.

"Goodmen, ye of the jury! You have heard what the honest baker has suffered. You have heard what these dishonest prisoners can say for themselves. Have an eye to your oath and your duty and do that which God shall put in your minds to the discharge of your consciences."

The jury nodded among themselves and returned a verdict in minutes. "Guilty!"

Molly wailed aloud, and both boys burst into tears. Rufus Drumheller's face crumpled with despair.

The judge reached for the black cap waiting by his hand. "Guilty. I sentence you, Rufus Drumheller, you, Toby Drumheller, and you, Jack Drumheller, to be hung by the neck until dead, and may God have mercy on your—"

The clerk tugged the judge's arm.

The interrupted judge gave him an irritated look. "What is it?"

The clerk leaned up and murmured in the judge's ear.

Leaving his black cap on, the judge resumed, "I sentence you to be hung by the neck until dead . . . but in mercy, this court offers you the alternative of transportation to Virginia, where you will pay for your passage by selling your indentured labor and expiate your crimes through hard work."

The boys collapsed against their father, who put an arm round their shoulders to steady them. He looked over the dock at his wife. She nodded frantically, eyes wide. *Anything, Rufus.*

"Well? Your answer!" the judge demanded.

"Please, Your Worship . . . transportation. Thank you, Your Worship."

The judge shrugged. The wretches rarely opted for hanging, though the judge privately thought a quick dispatch more merciful. Virginia Colony was a fierce place, rife with cannibalism and wild savages, wilder animals. But so long as the criminals were off London's streets, it was nothing to him. "Clerk, prepare the docket for passage, to go as soon as possible."

"Please, Your Worship, my wife, the boys' mother . . ." Rufus pointed.

The judge frowned down at the wretched female with her infant, sitting below him. The colony needed all the laborers it could get, and if the woman stayed behind, she would only breed more criminals. Let her go breed them in Virginia. "Transport her as well," he ordered. "*Her* name," he demanded.

"Molly Drumheller, Your Worship."

"A ship this very evening, my lord," murmured the clerk, scribbling furiously. "The *Betsy Wisdom*, bound for Yorktown." The clerk gave a satisfied little smirk. He received a bounty for every prisoner he persuaded the judge to send to Virginia. The five Drumhellers would be indentured as servants there until they had paid the cost of their passage, and he would be the better for ten shillings.

Warned to be quick about it, Molly dried her eyes and scurried off to gather the family's pitiful belongings and make her way to the Thames. There, in the bustle and confusion of the quayside, she grew frantic, clutching the baby and her bundles as she pushed past the guards, looking for her husband and sons. The ships had their names on the side, but Molly couldn't read, so she asked timidly at first and then grew bolder, fearing she would miss them altogether and be left behind, until a sailor pointed, and to her relief she saw her husband and sons in a throng of prisoners, surrounded by constables. A ship loomed over them, and sailors bustled about on the decks over their heads, shouting orders as they prepared to sail. The wind whipped around them, the river ran gray and choppy, and the ship creaked and strained at the mooring ropes. Molly looked up at the prow, terrified. She was slightly reassured to see the figure of a woman on the deck, a lady of quality by the looks of her. Perhaps all would be well after all if such as she was prepared to trust themselves to this ship. Rufus and the boys had escaped with their lives, which was the main thing.

The gangplank was lowered, and sailors pushed and shoved the crowd of prisoners and their families onboard and into a fetid hold. More and more people were crammed in, and the Drumhellers found themselves squeezed into a tiny, dark corner with two narrow wooden shelves for berths.

"The privy?" asked Molly in a whisper, pulling her shawl tighter around her shoulders. She was four months pregnant and needed the privy constantly.

"There!" said the sailor, pointing behind her to a ragged piece of old sail, screening a hole from which the sea was visible below. There was more shouting and the sound of feet on the deck above.

"Prepare to cast off!"

The people crowded into the hold exchanged apprehensive looks, but it was too late for second thoughts, even had anyone there had the option of having them.

"Aye, aye." The hatch slammed down over their heads.

"Are we sailing yet?" asked Toby, wide-eyed. "When will we get to Virginia? Will we see savages?"

"I'm hungry," whimpered Jack.

"Shh," said Molly, an arm round her son's thin shoulders.

The sailor reappeared and doled out rounds of hard bread, pointed out a barrel of water and a dipper, and disappeared back up the hatch. The Drumhellers huddled together tightly on their two narrow bunks and tried to chew their hard biscuits.

"Well . . . ," said Rufus and Molly to each other apprehensively as the ship began to roll gently. The baby whimpered, and Molly put it to her breast. Toby and Jack put their heads in her lap.

"I'm glad they didn't 'ang us," murmured Toby sleepily. Jack said nothing. His dirty thumb had found its way into his mouth, and his jaw moved rhythmically as he sucked and sucked. Molly stroked his head.

"It'll be all right, Moll," whispered Rufus. "Seven years, we can work and then make ourselves a new life. They say there's land for the taking. I'll build a house, snug as anything. We'll have our own farm again, I promise, with a cow or even two, like before. Think of churning your own butter again, eh? We'll plant an orchard too, and you shall keep your poultry. Geese even, though they're noisy devils. A goose for Christmas, eh? The boys'll grow fat, perhaps you'll grow fat too, eh, Moll, for all you're such a dainty little thing and—"

"I'd never grow fat, Rufus!"

Rufus laughed. "You will if you're breeding. We'll have a daughter or two yet. You'll see, Virginia's not as bad as they say."

"Ha!" barked a man from the next bunk. "Who says Virginia's not so bad? What I hear, nothing to choose between wild beasts big as houses and savage devils in the forests who'll cut your throat, tear your scalp from your head, and eat your brains. Folks who'll buy white men like slaves, starve and beat you, and work you till you lays down to die like a dog long before seven years is gone."

Molly stopped listening and rested her head on her husband's shoulder. She sank into an exhausted sleep. When she woke, the ship was lurching up and down and she could hear people vomiting and children crying. She clutched the boys, who slept on, and tried not to be sick herself. Somewhere a woman began to pray.

One day turned hellishly into another in the dim, crowded hold. They felt the ship rise and fall, up and down and up and down, and people lost all track of time. The constant motion made people seasick, and the packed hold stank of vomit. The sailors threw down dry biscuits and cold pease porridge that not many people could eat. Everyone was thirsty, but there was no small beer that even the poorest would have drunk at home on dry land, and the water had a foul taste.

Crowded together as they were, Molly thought the boys were feverish and then thought it was she who was feverish. She felt constantly sick. The baby cried fitfully from hunger as she tried to nurse it. Then one day she woke from her nauseous sleep, reached for the baby, and it was gone. A woman said it had gone to a better place. Molly lay back, dizzy and dry-eyed, listening to her husband talk of farms and cows and the New World, pastures and forests and rivers . . . her mouth was dry, so dry.

She dreamed of a dark forest, where wild beasts crept toward her through the shadows as she turned this way and that, seeking an escape, a place to hide . . . A beast big as a house had seized her around the waist and was sinking his fangs into her abdomen . . . tearing her to pieces. Yet she was too tired to resist. Finally the pain was greater than the need to sleep. "Molly! Molly! Wake up!" she heard someone shouting.

She woke briefly and groaned. The pain was no dream. Her husband was holding a bloody cloth and looked bewildered. Two women were shoving him aside and bending over, lifting her skirts. "Miscarried, poor thing . . . Poor little bit of a baby."

"Here, give us a strip of your petticoat. Nell, struth, mop this blood." Faces swayed back and forth in the dimness. Above her a lantern swayed dizzily too. Why was all the world tilting? Then she remembered. They were on a ship. She and Rufus and the boys, they were going somewhere . . . Virginia. A bit of land. Their own cow. Chickens in the orchard, the boys plump and well, fresh, fresh air . . .

"Rufus . . ."

"It'll be all right, Moll!"

"Mother!"

The beast hovered, waiting. She felt its presence.

"Aye, she looks bad."

"Hush, Nell!"

"Mother!" A boy was crying, faintly, in the distance. Who was he? Molly struggled to remember her sons' names. She opened her eyes.

Toby. Rufus was saying something about land, and Jack's mouth was open, but their voices were far away, drowned out by the ringing in her ears. She was thirsty. She tried to ask for a drink. Something was carrying her away. She was in the courtroom again, the judge scowling down at her as the beast's fangs sank deep. "Mercy, Your Worship," gasped Molly, "have mercy on my boys," and she slipped out of the beast's clutches into darkness.

CHAPTER 9
VIRGINIA COLONY

September 1754

The seas calmed as they approached the Caribbean before turning north to Virginia. Sophia's seasickness vanished and her melancholy lifted. She wrapped herself in a pretty India shawl and, leaving Mrs. Grey, who still felt poorly, went up on deck. The sky was warm and blue, the breeze fresh and the sea gentle, a clear, delicious aquamarine in the sun. She allowed her hair to blow free in the breeze, invigorated by the sunlight and the warmth. After the terrors of the crossing, being alive under a blue sky left her euphoric. She had enjoyed traveling with her father when she was a child, and here was an adventure, with much to look forward to. Virginia was certain to be interesting, and she was eager to meet her father's old friend and his wife. She was curious to see Wildwood, her new home. Judging by Mr. Barker's drawings, the house was handsome enough, though she was in some doubts that the gardens could look quite as he had drawn them, with a profusion of roses and a walkway lined with tall box bushes. Surely they had not matured so quickly. The gardener in Sussex had insisted roses grew in their own good time. Though perhaps Virginia soil was uncommonly fertile.

She was full of plans. She would learn everything about tobacco—how it was grown and transported to England and, above all, how quickly it would be possible to sell enough to pay off the debt and return to England. She was filled with a sense of purpose and energy for the task ahead of her, and was prepared to be pleased with Wildwood, no matter the state of the rose garden.

When the *Betsy Wisdom* docked at Yorktown early on a warm September morning, the sunny coast was cheerful and welcoming. The only unpleasant note was the horrible stench that rose from the open hold when the transportees were let out. The transportees looked hardly human, more like pale gray worms, thin and blinking in the light and as filthy as could be imagined. Mrs. Grey clung to Sophia's arm as they disembarked, complaining that she still felt the motion of the ship. In the bustling port, a man who seemed to be the sheriff and members of the militia appeared to surround the passengers from belowdecks, calling out the names on the ship's manifest and shoving them into order to be auctioned as indentured servants. Sophia thought they looked unpromising.

A black slave in ill-fitting livery pushed past them, inquiring loudly, "Graf'n? Graf'n?" When Sophia asked if he meant Grafton, he said he expected he did, if she was "Miss Sophy," and pointed to a carriage with the de Bouldin arms on the door that he said would take the ladies home to Williamsburg, where "Massa" was attending the House of Burgesses. Approaching the coach, the ladies were startled to see that the coachman's head was enclosed in something that resembled a birdcage fixed round his neck with a lock. It looked hideously heavy and uncomfortable, especially as the flies from the horses' backs crawled over his head and face, and he was unable to wave them away. "How can the poor fellow eat or sleep?" whispered a shocked Mrs. Grey to Sophia.

The trunks were loaded onto a wagon, which set off ahead of them, throwing up a cloud of warm dust. Sophia and Mrs. Grey struggled to arrange themselves for the journey inside the carriage. Up close it was in very poor repair, with the veneer peeling off, hard seats, and missing the leather curtains to keep out the hot sun. They jolted off and were soon enveloped in dust that threatened to choke them all during the bone-shaking journey to Williamsburg. Mrs. Grey was sick again from the motion of the coach.

Late in the afternoon there was a shout, "Ladies, here we be!" and mercifully, they stopped. Sophia and Mrs. Grey stepped down in front of a handsome brick house flanked with box bushes, but the grand impression did not last long. Inside, the house was, like the coach, in a terrible state. Housekeeping at the de Bouldin home was badly neglected—everything was dusty, the floors unpolished, the plaster cornicing damaged by water, the Turkish carpets chewed by mice, and fireplaces overflowing with old ashes. An unpleasant smell, as if something were rotting or chamber pots had not been emptied, permeated the house. The bedrooms to which the ladies were shown had sagging curtains at the windows and cobwebs full of dead flies in the ceiling corners. They overlooked a derelict kitchen garden and some hovels Sophia thought were kennels but proved to be the slave quarters.

Both ladies were overwhelmed with dismay.

"I daresay poor Mistress de Bouldin is too indisposed to direct her housekeeping," murmured Mrs. Grey, finally.

"We must wash off the dust," said Sophia. She pulled the bell rope several times, and eventually a barefoot Negro girl in a ragged shift appeared to ask what they wanted. Sophia asked what her name was and was surprised to find it was Venus. "Well then, Venus, please bring us hot water and soap at once." Venus shuffled off and nearly an hour later reappeared with a pitcher of lukewarm water and a minuscule sliver of yellow soap. When Sophia said they would dine in their room, as they were very tired, Venus simply shrugged and disappeared. The two ladies fell asleep supperless.

They did not meet Thomas de Bouldin until the next day at breakfast, a dispiriting meal of weak tea and coarse yellow bread that did little to lift their spirits, but the encounter dashed Sophia's expectations altogether. Her hand was gripped and shaken by a very large red-faced man with a loud voice, who was bursting out of a stained waistcoat and dirty breeches, and who stank of brandy despite the early hour. Any hope that this bluffness hid a kind heart was soon disappointed. After perfunctory condolences about Sophia's father, he informed the two ladies that they would leave for his plantation in the southern part of the colony as soon as Publick Times were over.

"Publick Times . . . what is that? And when will they be over?" asked Sophia.

Thomas fished a fly out of the butter that was melting in the heat. "House of Burgesses sits in Publick Times. I'm a burgess. We're elected to do our duty and make laws, govern the colony with the governor's help. Damned inconvenient being a member sometimes, but elected is elected." He grinned slyly. "A hogshead of whiskey on election day and the deed is done."

"And how long must the members attend?"

"Another month I expect. Then we'll leave."

"As you please, sir. We will be ready," Sophia assented, and Thomas fell to his breakfast, obviously disinclined to further conversation, though Sophia thought it polite to make an effort. Over the noise of his eating, she asked, "Pray, sir, what does your coachman wear on his head? It looks like a birdcage!"

"Bah, niggers are the Devil. The fool tried to run away. Didn't get far, the militia gave him a whipping he won't soon forget. Then I had the cage soldered on, that'll teach him to try it again! A firm hand, necessary, you know. Otherwise they'll murder us in our beds." Wishing the ladies an abrupt "Good day," he left. Mrs. Grey and Sophia looked at each other in horror.

Thomas's manners did not improve on closer acquaintance, but Sophia observed that people in Williamsburg did not seem to find him strange or uncouth. As a burgess, he was invited everywhere, and as his ward, she was included in those invitations. Mrs. Grey always went with Sophia, and though in the past Sophia had often found Mrs. Grey's meekness irritating, here she was grateful for the older woman's genteel companionship. Despite the hospitality at the beautiful houses in Williamsburg and on the surrounding plantations, Sophia sensed something raw and uncomfortable in the air. The presence of slaves was menacing, an evil miasma that permeated everything as if the wickedness of owning another human sucked the good from the soul of both the owned and the owner.

Sophia complained to Mrs. Grey in private, "These people claim to be Christians, but how can they reconcile their consciences? Instead of servants they insist the slaves are chattels, like horses and cows, only thinking what steps must be taken to prevent the slaves from rebelling and burning their owners' houses over their heads. If there are indeed slaves on my plantation, I vow to set them free." However, both women quickly learned not to express these sentiments among their new acquaintance. They spoke instead of London fashions and attended to the Williamsburg gossip of marriages, scandals, runaway slaves, the dancing master lately arrived from Italy, and when the French along the Ohio would be driven back.

Then one evening at a ball, Mrs. Grey was introduced to a tobacco planter whose wife had recently died, leaving him with six young children. He had indulged in the briefest possible period of mourning and hastened to Williamsburg to find a new wife. After dancing all night with Mrs. Grey, he proposed. She seized her chance. By the following morning, Mrs. Grey had packed her things and, without waiting for the banns to be read, accepted the remainder of her wages, kissed

Sophia farewell, and left Williamsburg with him for his plantation in the northern part of the colony.

In England a swift departure to marry a man on the strength of a night's acquaintance would have appeared shockingly rash. And for a newly widowed man to act so precipitously seemed like indecent haste. But after a short time in Virginia, Sophia had seen that what the English would have considered refined sentiments were often brushed aside in the interest of practicality. It was not considered unusual or unseemly for marriage to be contracted at such short notice. Women, particularly women not in the first flush of youth, were often content to dispense with a period of wooing, and the realities of plantation life often meant the men had little time for such things even if they were so inclined.

A plantation that depends on slavery! I wonder how she will like that! Sophia thought, furious at being abandoned but helpless to do anything about it. Mrs. Grey's departure left Sophia feeling exposed and uneasy. Thomas drank a great deal, and a group of young Negro women seemed to have no purpose other than as his concubines—they certainly did no work in the house. Sophia took care to lock her bedroom door and decided that once in the country, she would stay close to Anne de Bouldin for the whole of her visit, which would be as short as she could make it. But poor Anne, she thought. Was she aware of Thomas's depravity?

The prospect of visiting the de Bouldins began to oppress Sophia, but she could think of no way to remain in Williamsburg, and she felt obliged to pay Anne a visit out of courtesy. To add to her woes, after paying Mrs. Grey, she had very little money now, and was wondering if she might contrive to sell some of her jewelry. She had obtained enough information to know that Wildwood was far away, in the southwest of the colony, but fortunately the de Bouldin plantation lay in that direction. Traveling with Thomas as far as his plantation would take her part of the way, though she had no idea how much farther her own property was.

Meanwhile, the Virginians were charmed with Sophia. A viscount's daughter who was also a beautiful young heiress fresh from England was a novelty. They sympathized with the loss of her father and took her under their wing. The Williamsburg ladies invited her to drink tea almost every day, and when she was asked to dinner at the surrounding plantations, she was offered a bed for the night and sent back to Thomas's house the next day in the family carriage. Sophia was struck by the contrast in the gracious homes where she visited and the squalor of Thomas's house, but she supposed she would find his plantation house as handsome as the homes where she dined.

Sophia began to look forward to seeing her own plantation. Wildwood was known to be a very large estate and was as interesting a topic of conversation to the ladies as Sophia herself, perhaps more so, as they found her manners rather stiff and formal, though her English clothes were enviably pretty.

They were rather shocked that Sophia proposed living there alone, and exchanged significant looks that said such an attractive young woman with her own plantation would not be single long.

As for Sophia, much as she appreciated the friendliness and easy hospitality, she couldn't help finding Virginians' manners a little rough, their speech more blunt, and their plantation ways cruder than she was accustomed to in England. To Sophia's amusement, they questioned her relentlessly and not very subtly.

"And is Wildwood on a river, Miss Grafton?"

"Yes. The map shows a river runs through it, but I can't tell you which one, as the map does not give its name. The agent says the plantation produces Orinoco tobacco, which I am told is the best kind. Do you agree?"

The ladies nodded. They were the wives and daughters of tobacco planters. Orinoco fetched the highest price.

"And on the river as Wildwood is, I suppose you have a landing?" Many of the plantations had river frontage on the James. Sophia had been amazed to see with her own eyes the ships sailing up the James to unload the plantation orders and take away the tobacco.

"I don't know yet. I suppose it must."

"If not, you must have one built at once, my dear. So large an estate—what a quantity of tobacco it must yield! How large *are* your shipments now, Miss Grafton?"

"I do not yet know. Naturally I've left all that to the agent." Wildwood's first tobacco had undoubtedly shipped by now, but to prevent the ladies pressing the point in a thinly disguised attempt to calculate her income, Sophia changed the subject. "Perhaps you can advise me about furnishing my house."

The ladies nodded and leaned closer, flattered to be asked for advice by so grand a visitor.

"I do not yet know whether Mr. Barker has furnished it."

"Oh, depend upon it, my dear, he will not have done. Men think all that's necessary is a bed for them to sleep in and a table and chair for their meals. Men know nothing of furnishing a house!" The ladies nodded vigorously in agreement.

Sophia sighed. "Neither do I, I fear. Furnishing houses is far outside my experience. I've no idea how it is done. Of course my father ordered his books and his wine, but I don't recollect anything else. Our houses in London and in Sussex simply had the family belongings, and the housekeeper saw to the rest if anything was needed. But here people seem to order everything new from England, and I do not know what that ought to be."

Accustomed to London merchants and the availability of everything imaginable, Sophia had been astonished to learn that in Virginia so much had to come from England—wallpaper, window glass, furniture, plows and carriages, and great casks of rum, wine, and Madeira. "If you would be so kind, help me draw up a list of the most necessary things."

She had no money now, but she would soon. She took out her little morocco pocket account book with its gold pencil and noted down names of the best London merchants for knives and forks and glassware, candle branches and knife boxes and tea chests, the best purveyors of fashionable fabrics for bed hangings and curtains and paints. She asked about delftware tea bowls. She noted their recommendation about which London merchants supplied Virginia ladies with clothes, shoes, and bonnets and could be trusted to pack the items properly for the ocean voyage and which were so careless that orders arrived ruined by seawater. Frowning slightly, Sophia added coarse linen and woolen material to the list, for slave clothing. Did Sophia know that it was necessary to order pins and needles, sewing cotton, and embroidery thread? She did not, and added them to the list. After keeping her accounts since the age of sixteen Sophia could see all this was going to be exorbitantly expensive.

Everyone assured her she would have a constant stream of company, that long visits among the plantation owners were usual. She could expect to visit and be visited almost as soon as she arrived. Sophia smiled and said she would be delighted to see her new friends at Wildwood as soon as she was settled enough to assure their comfort.

The women accepted readily. They were eager with their promises to visit and were already calculating which of their unmarried or widowed brothers or cousins would be prevailed on to accompany them.

Constantly in the back of Sophia's mind was the nagging worry that she had almost no money. Once she reached Wildwood, of course Mr. Barker could supply her with funds, but until then she would have to think of a plan to travel the rest of the way from the de Bouldins' plantation. She wondered if any of her Williamsburg acquaintance might lend her money—but decided that she really knew no one well enough to make such a request. She could not get used to the fact that she of all people should be in want of money, if only temporarily. It was a most distressing position in which to find herself. But she would have to manage somehow. Lord Grafton's daughter could not go begging.

She consulted her morocco accounts book. While her father was alive, Sophia had always obeyed his rule that she record her expenditures.

But when her father was alive, the expenses she dutifully recorded were almost meaningless since there was money enough for anything her heart desired. When she reached Wildwood and was again in possession of money, she resolved to practice more careful economy.

Publick Times were nearly over, tonight was the final ball of the season, and Thomas was impatient to be gone. Sophia sighed and opened her trunk to retrieve a ball dress. At the bottom of her trunk, she discovered her maid in Sussex had packed the gown she had worn to her first ball. After her presentation at St. James's Palace it had been altered to take smaller hoops than the mantua required, and her maid had thought the gown particularly becoming on Sophia. She pulled it out and gave it a shake. The silver threads in the fabric were a little less bright than they had once been, but it reminded her of her first ball and happier times, and in defiance of everything that had happened, she decided to wear it tonight. And she'd wear her mother's pearls and eardrops, just as she had then. She might be destitute, but pride dictated she mustn't look it.

She sat before her mirror in her lace-trimmed shift and began to dress her hair herself. Having no lady's maid and unable to afford the hairdresser, it was a task she'd been obliged to master. She hoped that when she was done, Venus would be in earshot of the bell, to come and lace her tightly enough to get into the gown.

She vowed that when she reached Wildwood, her first order of business would be to engage a proper lady's maid. Virginia ladies she knew all had female slaves as their personal maids, trained to sew and dress hair and starch caps, but she would insist on a decent Englishwoman.

She turned her head this way and that to see the result of her hairdressing in the mirror and sighed. How perverse that her hair looked very becoming. It mattered not a whit.

CHAPTER 10
THE BIRTHNIGHT BALL

October 1754

Autumn had begun its transformation in Williamsburg. Late October sun slanted gold through the changing leaves—red, yellow, and copper—though the weather was still warm. The day had been fine and promised a balmy evening. All that day, Williamsburg's streets had been uncharacteristically empty, save for slaves going about their business, servants delivering notes, and hairdressers and their assistants bustling from house to house, family to family with curling tongs and cases of powders and patches. Otherwise people stayed home to breakfast late, wait for the hairdresser to call, and then begin their toilettes in preparation for the highlight of the Williamsburg social year—the Birthnight Ball, the annual celebration of the king's official birthday.

Virginians boasted Williamsburg celebrated the occasion with as much pomp as London. The occasion also marked the end of this autumn session of Publick Times, when the Virginia burgesses and the

Governor's Council met to transact the colony's affairs. It was a social time as well as a civic one. The twice-yearly Publick Times were set to coincide with the end of the tobacco harvest in the fall and the end of the planting season in the spring. With the main work of the plantation finished for the season, planters and their families from all over the colony flocked to Williamsburg for a holiday. Those who had no house of their own in town stayed with friends, or otherwise filled the inns and taverns and lodgings until they were bursting at the seams.

At dusk, slaves in livery appeared in the streets, lighting torches along the route to the Governor's Palace, and the sounds of an orchestra tuning up drifted from the open windows of the mansion.

Across Williamsburg, girls preened before their looking glasses, added hair ribbons and powder, and speculated about the romantic possibilities of the evening.

Typical of many households, chaos reigned in the Fitzwilliam lodgings above a tavern, where the seven Fitzwilliam daughters crowded in front of one mirror, arguing over laces and stockings and rosettes and fans, all appealing to their mother about who had first rights to which disputed accessories. Their father soon gave up trying to read the newspaper, abandoning his armchair to seek refuge with other husbands and fathers downstairs. The men gathered around a bowl of strong punch and waited for the females of their families to send word they were ready. Over their punch, the men shook their heads and grumbled about the high cost of daughters—clothes, flounces, furbelows, gewgaws, and trinkets, all ordered from London and costing a small fortune; mantua makers and hairdressers in Williamsburg, who charged another fortune for their services; and, if that weren't enough to ruin them all, a poxy Italian dancing master who had come prancing into town to add to the cost of the season.

"A dancing master!" Mr. Fitzwilliam snorted. "What's dancing but a matter of two feet, step this way, step that way. Any fool can do it. No dancing master in our day!" There was a chorus of agreement.

At last, when no more dressing could be done, the first carriages and sedan chairs appeared in the torchlit streets, immediately joined by others carrying the cream of Virginia society to the Governor's Palace. Among the throng, no one was looking forward to the ball tonight more than twenty-two-year-old Colonel George Washington, lately promoted to the command of the Virginia militia. He had a fine new linen shirt, velvet waistcoat, and dancing pumps ordered from England. Unaccountably, the pumps were the wrong size—too small for his large feet, though he had sent the most careful measurements to his English factors. But there was no help for it now; he would dance anyway and ignore his pinched feet. Colonel Washington loved dancing almost as much as he loved foxhunting, and there were pretty girls aplenty to dance with. He might find a wife among them, a girl who would bring money and slaves to Mount Vernon, only she must be a pretty one—he liked a pretty face—and good-tempered, a sweet voice over the breakfast table. And besides courting, he had another task ahead of him tonight. He had to find a way back into the governor's favor after accidentally inflaming England's smoldering dispute with France about American territory west of the Ohio. Dispatched on a sensitive diplomatic mission to the Ohio to parley with the French encroaching on English territory, Colonel Washington had betrayed his inexperience, panicked, and led the charge when his Indian guides fired at a small French encampment before the parley could get under way. A highborn French envoy had been killed—some said tomahawked by Washington's Indian guides, some said by a mistaken shot. But the mission had been a disaster, triggering precisely the political crisis England wished to avoid. The governor was livid. Colonel Washington thanked a merciful providence the governor had not been angry enough to withhold an invitation to the Birthnight Ball.

Though officially in disgrace, the tall young colonel was a hero in the colony. The French and their Indian allies were much hated. The French encouraged the Indians to raid English settlements in the distant northern and western borders of the colony, burning cabins and barns and crops, slaughtering livestock, sometimes taking women and children prisoner for ransom or for slaves, sometime murdering whole families outright and taking scalps for the bounty the French would pay for each one. Most colonists ardently wished Colonel Washington had shot more Frenchmen when he had the chance.

Tonight as he threaded his chestnut hunter between the carriages and chairs, people waved and cheered as he passed. Washington gallantly swept off his hat in acknowledgment and bowed from the saddle to the ladies.

An outrageously elegant young man riding in a sedan chair carried by two shabby white fellows in ragged coats craned his neck to see the passing hero. Colonel Washington's stirrup scraped the sedan chair. The young man settled back with a smile and touched the black patch that decorated his lightly rouged cheek.

At the end of Palace Street stood the governor's mansion, and the pretty cupola on the roof, known as the lanthorn, glowed against the twilight. In front of the palace, coachmen eased into the throng pushing for position in the circular drive. Men in velvet breeches, embroidered waistcoats, and powdered hair sprang out to hand their women down the carriage steps. The ladies held their skirts and trains high to avoid the dust, revealing silk stockings and backless high-heeled satin and damask slippers sparkling with diamante buckles.

The men carrying sedan chairs jostled among the carriage wheels and snorting horses, and the young man who had watched Colonel Washington narrowly avoided being trampled as he alighted and straightened his clothes. He tossed a coin each to the two sad-eyed men who had carried his chair and made a quick motion with his wrist, as if tossing down a drink. He knew the two men were indentured to an evil-natured tavern owner, notorious even in a colony where bondage servants were treated harshly. Whatever the law said about a master's obligations, the tavern owner famously worked his bondservants until they dropped, beat them on the slightest provocation, fed them slops, and made them sleep in the stables, sharing the straw of his dogs and horses, even in the coldest winter.

"Come on, Rufus," said one to the other. "A glass of rum before the old devil misses us. Ease those stripes on your back, man."

"No," said the other, wincing and pocketing the coin. "I'll save it for the boys. If I don't buy them out of this bloody indenture, they'll never last another five years. They treat Jacky worse than a slave. He pisses his pallet in the night, and for punishment his devil of a mistress makes him piss in a jar and drink it. And as for Toby, he's a hothead, he is, already been whipped twice for insolence, and they've a heavy hand with a whip here. He's an angry one. I fear he'll be hung for killing his master before he's done . . . To see my own treated so and be helpless to stop it! I can't bear much more, I tell you. At least poor Molly was spared knowing."

The other man sidled closer. "Don't think of running away, Rufus," he muttered. "You know what'll happen. They'll find you, you'll get a beating so fierce you'll wish you'd died, and then the magistrates will bind you twenty more years and smile. What would become of the boys then? You're their only hope, man. Endure it for their sakes. We've only seven years, then we'll lay claim to some land and work hard, and grow rich with the fattest of 'em."

None of the festive crowd crying greetings to each other took any notice of the two ragged fellows carrying their empty sedan chair back in the direction of the inn. The governor's guests swept up the walk in a cloud of violet-scented hair powder, across the main hall with its royal coat of arms, and ascended the wide staircase to the first floor, where a smiling Governor Dinwiddie and his wife, Lady Rachel, welcomed their guests beneath portraits of King George II and Queen Caroline in their state robes.

Against a swell of conversation, a slave orchestra struck up in the ballroom. Liveried footmen passed among the guests with trays of punch, cordials, Madeira, and port. Couples formed on the sidelines, impatient for Governor and Lady Dinwiddie to open the ball and anxious not to lose a dancing minute. A little apart from them, Colonel Washington stood at the window with his hands clasped behind his back, seemingly absorbed in the view of the formal gardens and late roses blooming between neatly laid brick walkways and rows of lanterns strung between the trees in the park. But his large foot in its painfully tight dancing pump tapped to the music, and from the corner of his eye, he watched a pretty newcomer in a blue-and-silver gown. He looked for an acquaintance to introduce them, so he might ask her to dance.

The young man from the sedan chair entered the ballroom, noted the colonel's whereabouts, then turned with a fixed smile as the first delighted squeals of "Are you waiting for us, Signor Valentino? Here we are!" Rotund and beaming, Mrs. Fitzwilliam and her cluster of large, unmarried daughters bore down triumphantly on the dancing master ahead of the other ladies.

At the other end of the room, a group of men rolled their eyes scornfully. They didn't care for the flamboyant newcomer. Signor Valentino cut an exotic figure even in a society not given to restraint in dress, and where clothing spoke volumes about the wearer's wealth and position. They weren't sure what the Italian's clothes said about him. He sported brocade coats trimmed with gilded lace, flourishing satin ribbons tied in extravagant bows. Even the buckles on his shoes were larger and more sparklingly ornate than the buckles habitually seen in the colony. The Virginia squires had slave valets and footmen from the plantation, but Signor Valentino traveled with two attendants from his own country. His valet, Teobaldo, kept the signor in perfect order. No matter what time of day or night, Signor Valentino's hair was immaculately dressed and powdered, his linen and stockings spotless and fresh, and his shoes free from any speck of dirt. His manners were charming, his bows graceful, and his attitude deferential yet so decided that somehow, no one contradicted him. He took perfumed snuff from enameled snuffboxes and flourished a handkerchief that was three-quarters lace.

Even the musician Signor Francesco, who accompanied the dancing master during the lessons, played with a foppish air and hand flourishes. And that was another source of irritation. The planters took umbrage that anyone considered Williamsburg's slave musicians inferior to orchestras in Europe. "A minuet's a minuet, wherever it's played!" the men muttered, wishing they could send Signor Valentino and his waistcoats, buckles, valet, musician, and exorbitant bills to the Devil.

Arriving on a ship from Genoa in late August, the tall young man, whose penetrating dark eyes under dark brows contrasted splendidly with his immaculately powdered hair, had taken rooms in a tavern, where he set himself up as a dancing master, lately acquainted with the manners and personalities of the highest circles of English society. He promised that his pupils, both girls and boys, would acquire the refined deportment, the graceful distinction, of the aristocratic youth of London.

The country planters arriving for Publick Times were unpersuaded this was necessary. Their children were good enough as they stood. But the men were overruled. Signor Valentino had charmed the ladies of Williamsburg, who, like Mrs. Fitzwilliam, had taken Signor Valentino to their collective bosom. Publick Times offered young people a chance to meet and socialize before returning to the isolation of distant family plantations, and like young people everywhere, they loved balls and welcomed a chance to flirt and court and show off their English clothes. Colonial mothers could see the advantages where their marriageable children were concerned. Even a plain girl could look fetching in an evening dress by candlelight, but if she were to catch a husband, she couldn't sit on the sidelines like a dullard. She must be able to dance. And heaven knew, their rowdy boys stood to benefit from some polish. Dancing lessons were the answer, and dancing lessons their children would have.

Among the women, rumor had swiftly worked in Signor Valentino's favor. Apparently Signor Valentino had a letter of introduction from a Gentleman of the Bedchamber confirming him as a person of exceptional morals and refinement, well regarded in London, a model of propriety entrusted to instruct the children of the highest nobility in the social arts. Many a father took a more jaundiced view of the dancing master, protesting that the Italian was more likely to be a debauched and diseased libertine seeking a rich Virginia wife and swearing that he would not be coaxed into the expense of dancing lessons after all the laces, gowns, slippers, bonnets, gloves, fans, and folderols ordered from London. However, most fathers were eventually wheedled and cajoled into agreeing, and the young people of Williamsburg were enrolled by their mothers.

Signor Valentino was an exacting teacher, and his students showed a marked improvement. He was strict about ballroom etiquette and deportment. Even the older ladies who sat on the sidelines of the dance commended Signor Valentino's elegant breeding and exemplary behavior. Far from showing signs of debauchery, he was a model of circumspection and courtesy. He never got drunk and crashed into the furniture, spat on the floor, or otherwise forgot himself. His waistcoats bore no stains from his dinner. He refused to take snuff when ladies were present. His complexion was unspotted by smallpox. He kissed the air over the hands of married ladies but even the most sharp-eyed chaperones saw nothing to complain of in his behavior toward the girls in his charge. He had no favorites and was scrupulously correct, even stern, with the young ladies despite their attempts to flirt.

But what particularly recommended this model of decorum to the older matrons was his attention to them at balls. Regardless of her age, every female in the room longed to dance with Signor Valentino. He never forgot the steps, kept perfect time to the music, never lurched tipsily in the wrong direction, never trod on flounces or ladies' feet. Alas for the young married women and single girls who hinted and sighed in vain to dance in public with Signor Valentino, the dancing master only chose partners from the cluster of older matrons whose husbands were either dead or otherwise occupied at the gaming tables. To their delight, ladies who had not danced in years found themselves dancing once more, with a man who made them feel young and desirable again. And since he confined his attentions to the older matrons, Signor Valentino avoided scandal. No hotheaded husband of a pretty young wife, no lovelorn swain, took offense at his attentions to a lady and challenged him to a duel.

Having approved of him, the ladies who ruled Williamsburg society saw to it that Signor Valentino was invited everywhere. *Italian* dancing masters, they told the men firmly, had been taken up by all the best society in London, *quite* the thing nowadays! After all, it wasn't as if he were *French*.

Mrs. Fitzwilliam spoke for them all when she exclaimed, "Oh no! If he were French, no one would have anything to do with him. Mr. Fitzwilliam says if there's one thing he wishes beyond seeing the girls settled with husbands, it's the chance to shoot a Frenchman!"

Tonight Signor Valentino bowed to the other ladies arriving to swell the little crowd made by Mrs. Fitzwilliam and her daughters, and after he paid extravagant compliments to each of them, to his relief, the musicians struck up a minuet. The governor and Lady Rachel made their way to the center of the ballroom to open the ball, and people were invited to take their partners for the first dance. Signor Valentino bowed with a flourish of his lace handkerchief, extended his hand to seventy-two-year-old Grandmother Burwell, and begged for the honor. Granny Burwell hobbled off delightedly, ribbons fluttering on her widow's cap, exclaiming, "We'll show the young people how it ought to be done!"

As the dancing continued, the ballroom grew hot, despite the French windows open to the garden. The matrons sat chatting under the sconces and fanned themselves, sipping punch and raspberry shrub while keeping an eye on their daughters' dancing partners. In a few days, they would be home again, confined in the country through the winter, not to meet until next spring's Publick Times.

The matrons remarked on the changing leaves: the colors had never been so beautiful. They agreed they felt the first hint of autumn chill on the mornings lately. Occasionally there was a pause in their conversation. A melancholy shadow always hung over their last gathering of the season. Every year, illness and death claimed some of their number, and while they depended on the tobacco, their husbands complained it was harder to make the tobacco pay than it used to be. The inspectors who certified the tobacco were scoundrels, claiming that more and more of the planters' tobacco was poor quality than was the case, even burning it at the warehouses to prevent its being shipped. All the while the shippers and insurers took their usual cut of the sale price, and London merchants could send exorbitant bills to be paid by the planters' London factors, leading to debts that would have to be paid off when next year's tobacco was sold. And since the Virginia planters ordered everything from farm equipment to bricks to furniture to seeds to clothes and carriages from England, these debts mounted alarmingly. Some landowners were either in financial difficulties or had been altogether ruined by debts that compounded while their incomes fell. Some had been driven to destitution; one prominent member of the colony had taken his own life as a result. And to add to the financial woes and insecurities, they constantly feared a slave insurrection that would see them and their families murdered and their homes burned. No, the ladies were not free of worries.

But determined to make the most of their last evening together, they did their best to banish sad thoughts. They watched the dancers and speculated on likely matches among the young people. Engagements were often made and announced on the final night.

While waiting to hear whether their predictions would be confirmed, the ladies had plenty to say on the subject of the younger generation. They discussed the shocking deterioration in young people's manners, morals, and behavior since their day. They exchanged gossip about which young College of William & Mary hotheads had fought a duel over a particular girl and debated whether she was a bold minx who had encouraged them. They speculated on how many acres of land a certain young man would inherit, what families had a peculiar streak in their bloodline, which widower needed a stepmother for his children, what girl ought to accept him because she was nearly twenty and an old maid, how much money or how many slaves a certain girl was expected to have as a dowry, whether such and such a young man was likely to be a reliable husband, and whether another girl would make a capable plantation mistress or looked like a poor breeder.

While taking part in the general chatter, Mrs. Fitzwilliam was trying to keep an eye on her daughters and their partners dancing a lively allemande. She smiled as her fourteen-year-old, Millicent, twirled round one of the young Carters, who tried to snatch a kiss. A match? Fourteen was young to marry, perhaps, but if it were a Carter, she wouldn't stand in Millie's way. Then she frowned at sixteen-year-old Nancy, who was dancing with Colonel Washington and smiling up at him, Mrs. Fitzwilliam thought, rather too adoringly. Hero or not, the young colonel hadn't a penny to bless himself, no property but an unprofitable estate on the Potomac, leased from his brother's widow, and no slaves to work it. With so many sisters, Nancy's dowry wouldn't be big enough to make a difference. Nancy could do better elsewhere. Mrs. Fitzwilliam caught her daughter's eye and shook her head ever so slightly.

Her friend Mrs. Randolph nudged her hard in the ribs. "Here comes Signor Valentino!" Fluttering her fan, Mrs. Randolph whispered, "I hope he won't forget it's my turn!" Signor Valentino handed a breathless Granny Burwell back to her seat, bowed with a flourish, and offered his arm to Mrs. Randolph, who rose, beaming with relief, to sweep triumphantly off, followed by envious looks over the fans.

As he handed Mrs. Randolph into the line of dancers, Signor Valentino touched his lace handkerchief to his sweating forehead. It seemed that every woman in Williamsburg had crowded into the overheated ballroom, and the stiff skirts of the ladies' fashionable sacques made it difficult to move on the crowded dance floor and nearly impossible to move off it, as those not dancing pushed forward to watch the elegant performance of the dancing master and his happy partner of the moment. He had not paused for breath since the dancing began.

And he knew that Colonel Washington was observing him as closely as any of the ladies, trying to copy Signor Valentino's turns and flourishing bows. It seemed ridiculous. Signor Valentino's first impression of the colonel, with his big feet and backwoodsman's ruddy complexion, was that he was a bumpkin, but up close, his gaze watching Signor Valentino was too steady and penetrating for comfort. Between the bows and turns of the minuet, the dancing master began to wonder if he had somehow given himself away.

He and his two companions were constantly on edge now, always on their guard. For none of them were Italian, and Signor Valentino was no more a dancing master than his companions were musicians or valets. Their youthful high spirits had at first made the role highly diverting, and he had assumed such an identity as if it were a great joke. Now France and England were almost at war again, and impoverished young Frenchman Henri de Marechal was a government spy in Williamsburg and certain to be hung along with his companions if discovered. It had become a strain to keep their guard up and maintain their disguise.

The person responsible for their being in Virginia was the enchanting Marquise de Pompadour, Louis XV's influential mistress and confidante.

At Versailles, Madame de Pompadour had been much taken with Henri de Marechal, the natural son of the penniless Comte de Marechal, who owned a crumbling château on the Loire on a rundown estate good for little but hunting. The countess and her children remained in the country while the count held a minor position at court, where he had taken a mistress. The mistress had died and left him with Henri. The count took his paternal duties seriously, arranging for Henri to be educated at court along with two bastard sons of a cardinal. All three boys occupied a somewhat precarious social position on the fringes of court life and clung together like brothers. The count encouraged the friendship between the three and even allowed the cardinal's sons to join Henri in the country at the gatekeeper's lodge during their holidays. Though he was very fond of Henri, the count had a legitimate heir as well as other sons and a daughter, all of whom must be provided for, so he was not in a position to advance Henri in life. He had done what he could, giving the child the benefit of his aristocratic surname, had him appointed a page and, with the help of the cardinal, who was grateful for the time his sons spent with Henri in the country, had made arrangements for him to enter the church in due course, though only at a second-rate provincial abbey.

At court Henri caught Madame de Pompadour's eye. He was good-looking, well mannered, and surprisingly gallant for a boy in his teens. That he was rather infatuated with her was touching, and she frequently asked him to perform some task for her. She also pointed out Henri to Louis XV, saying it was a pity that such a promising boy was destined to a dull monastic life among rustics. Amused by her interest, the king said that he knew the boy's father and promised to see what might be done for him, but shortly thereafter, Henri left court. An unexpected legacy provided the count with sufficient funds to send Henri to Italy to complete his education and obtain introductions to powerful figures in the church in Rome. But in Italy Henri had employed his time and money very differently, in less-worthy pursuits, and lived the life of a young gallant until his funds ran out. He did not return to France until the count was on his deathbed. By then Henri was twenty-three, as charming and quick-witted and penniless as ever, with a veneer of

Continental culture laid over the French education he had received from his Jesuit tutor at court.

His reappearance revived Madame de Pompadour's indulgent notice. Once again, she determined to do something for him.

One night after Henri's return, Madame de Pompadour observed over supper with the king that he seemed vexed by the news from the American colonies. The king was indeed vexed. It seemed likely that the dispute between France and England over territory on the borders of Virginia Colony in America might lead to a new, financially draining war only a few years after the last war with England. France had very little information about English intentions, he fumed. Were they not as tired of their everlasting wars as France was?

Madame de Pompadour nibbled an ortolan and wondered aloud if the French agents among the Indians in the western part of Virginia Colony were too far from the center of command in Williamsburg. Intelligence from Williamsburg itself would surely be more useful.

The king agreed it would be expedient to know whether England intended to dispatch their regular army to the colony, which would indicate another costly European war with England was inevitable, or whether they would rely on their colonial militias, in which case it would be a matter of skirmishes, irritating but contained in America. Colonel Washington, who commanded the Virginia militia, was very young and had no formal military training. Judging by his bungled attempt to parley with the French about withdrawing from the Ohio Valley that had ended in chaos and a massacre of the French party, he seemed thoroughly incompetent to lead anything. He might be easily defeated or simply written off as more likely to shoot himself in the extremities and save France the trouble. But if England bypassed the colonial officers, this raised more alarming possibilities. The king asked if Madame perhaps had a plan to infiltrate the colony to obtain better intelligence. Madame de Pompadour agreed that she had, a scheme that would place an informant in the midst of their enemies. She would explain . . . The king listened to what she had to say, considered, and nodded. Then he laughed.

Henri was duly summoned to an audience with the king and informed he would receive a reward large enough to allow him to abandon the church if he undertook a mission for France. Was he willing to become a spy in Virginia Colony?

A startled Henri caught Madame's eye, bowed deeply, and declared he was entirely at His Majesty's service. He had no idea of how he was to become a spy, but the reward was enough to persuade him to go almost anywhere and do almost anything.

He learned that he was to prepare to spend some months in Williamsburg. He would be accompanied by his two boyhood friends, Thierry and François Charbonneau, the cardinal's sons who had shared his lessons. They too had little provision for the future and were as gleeful as Henri at the prospect of the reward and what promised to be a novel adventure.

The three young men were to travel in disguise, Henri as Signor Valentino, a dancing master; Thierry as Signor Teobaldo, Henri's valet; and François, who would be given a swift training in dance music, would become Signor Francesco, the musical accompanist. Valet and musician. These disguises were Madame Pompadour's idea. She reasoned that a dancing master could easily ingratiate himself with the ladies, and an Italian identity would provide the necessary cover for his French accent. Henri's charm and good manners would open doors so that he'd become an intimate of the colonists' drawing rooms, where he would be in a position to overhear the colony's gossip. He could then compile information about the local militia and whether English regular troops were expected in the colony to march to the Ohio, who was to command them, and whether reinforcements should be sent north from the garrison in La Nouvelle-Orléans.

He must also provide information about Colonel Washington, who should have been a nonentity, as he was neither wealthy nor wellborn, yet by whatever strange standards the Virginians judged young men, his name kept cropping up in dispatches.

None of the three young Frenchmen had any material prospects whatsoever in France. All three were natural sons with no prospects of any fortune. Henri had no expectations of anything except a dull life in the church. The best the other two could hope for was that at some distant time in the future, they would be able to marry a tolerably wellborn girl, with a modest dowry, who would produce a legitimate heir. The prospect of a legitimate son of one's own was compelling, as if it would somehow regularize their precarious position in society. Virginia promised to be a splendid adventure, and the reward at the end would set them up for life. They set off in high spirits to be outfitted in Italy at royal expense, anticipating how they would spend their rewards. Henri thought his reward would be sufficient to purchase an estate with a modest château, where he could indulge his fondness for hunting, gambling, and women.

A month later they sailed for Virginia from Genoa, each with a trunk of new clothes in the latest styles and a large purse of guineas somewhat diminished by a riotous month passed in the brothels and taverns of Genoa. They tested each other on the information that would prove they had spent time in London—the names of the royal family, the parks and pleasure gardens, the weather, the best playhouses, and the latest gossip. Lighthearted François, who had been obliged to learn music, practiced imaginary minuets, fingers drumming on the ship's rail with an exaggerated flourish, rolling his eyes and making droll faces. Thierry and Henri practiced their dance steps on deck, arguing about whose turn it was to be Hortense, as they called the lady partner, after one of Thierry's conquests. They argued about whether it would be customary to wear a sword as a formality in Virginia, as they understood it usually was in England. They made crude jokes about the sword getting in the way of Hortense's feet and laughed uproariously. They engaged in mock three-way swordfights. They were young, and they would soon be rich.

That they would be isolated among the enemy, their nearest place of safety the French settlement and garrison far to the west in Louisiana, had been a matter of no concern. At the time.

But by October, the adventure had worn thin. Compared with France, the colony was a rude and uncivilized backwater, the people boorish and uncultivated. All three Frenchmen were heartily sick of Virginia and tired of pretending to be Italian. Since it had been thought safer for Thierry and François to keep a low profile, as befitted the dancing master's servants, the two of them had led a dull and sober existence. Worst of all, they had had to avoid the local girls, lest they betray themselves in a moment of passion.

"Hortense!" they muttered plaintively.

They longed for France, were impatient to leave for Louisiana. Meanwhile at the Birthnight Ball, Henri pretended to drink to the English king's health, "God save the king!" quite loudly, and congratulated himself that the plan had worked. As Madame de Pompadour anticipated, Henri had indeed been well placed to hear Williamsburg gossip, and he had paid close attention. People were remarkably unguarded in what they said, and he had managed to compile a detailed report on the governor, British plans, sketches and maps of the region, the general incompetence of the Virginia militia, and the fact that British troops were expected to arrive soon. But Colonel Washington's name was often mentioned favorably.

Henri tried to decide for his report whether the dancing Colonel Washington looked like a possible commander of anything or whether he was just a very tall young man with a weather-beaten face whose expression suggested that his shoes pinched. Then he caught Washington's name again as a group of planters passed by from the card tables on their way to the dining room for refreshments. Henri excused himself from the chattering ladies, touched his face delicately with his handkerchief, and casually followed the men into the dining room.

The dining room was even hotter than the ballroom, full of red-faced men taking a break from cards and dice, drinking heavily, and talking at the top of their voices. Henri patted the sweat from his face again. Light from a multitude of candles blazed from sconces on the walls, and huge silver candelabras illuminated vast tables spread with food-game pies, devilled crabs, terrapin soup, Virginia ham, syllabubs, marzipan fancies, cakes, crystallized fruits, and a magnificent centerpiece of pineapples imported from the Caribbean, surrounded by grapes, pears, and peaches from the palace garden. Henri was starving and making his way toward the table when a bellow of "Signor Valentino!" stopped him in his tracks.

Stout, red-faced Squire Fitzwilliam detached himself from a group of men talking loudly above the din and shouldered his way unsteadily through the throng to Henri. He slapped Henri on the back.

"Come, come, some refreshments, signor! Leave the ladies, God bless 'em, for a moment!" He beckoned a liveried slave carrying a tray of tall cups and took two. Ignoring Henri's protests, he forced a cool glass into Henri's hand and pulled him into the noisy circle of men. Henri hesitated. Virginians were inordinately fond of their filthy home-brewed spirits that left one feeling kicked by a horse. He tried to avoid them. But he was hot and thirsty after dancing all night, and without meaning to, he drank it all down in one go, choking on raw whiskey, whose taste was barely masked by the flavor of some herb. The drink left a gritty residue of what he thought at first was sand in his mouth. Trying to spit it discreetly into his handkerchief, he found it was coarse sugar.

"That's the way, have another julep, har, har, har!" Squire Fitzwilliam beckoned over another slave with a tray. The squire's friends laughed and agreed the ladies were thirsty work. In vain, Henri tried to refuse as another glass was pressed into his hand and he was pulled to join the knot of men. The planters were discussing Colonel Washington.

To hide the fact he was listening intently, Henri lifted his second glass and, unwisely, drank.

"All Washington did was rid the world of a few poxy Frenchmen. Send 'em all to the Devil, I say. They won't keep him in the cold for long. It would antagonize old Fairfax."

His brain fogging from alcohol, Henri struggled to recall what the Fairfaxes had to do with Colonel Washington. The Fairfaxes were a powerful family. Lord Fairfax was the only English peer to live in America, an eccentric old man who owned five million acres of Virginia Colony in addition to his English estates. A friend to Washington?

"Aye, and they say the old man prefers Washington to his own nephew, George William Fairfax."

"Doesn't like George William's wife, Sally Cary, she was. Calls her 'the barren cow.' Determined she'll not be the next Lady Fairfax."

"So Colonel Washington, he has a powerful patron in this Englosh . . . *English* lord?" Henri asked.

The men nodded. Lord Fairfax had considerable influence in Virginia but still hadn't managed to get his protégé a regular commission in the British army. There was a chorus of agreement that the governor would come round and Washington would soon be back in favor. He was already at the ball.

"Washington swears he'll resign unless his British commission comes through. Wants a proper red coat, with officer's insignia, quite right too."

"Aye, but don't know that he'll get one—*colonials*, you know," another man said bitterly. "They look down their noses at us."

"Dinwiddie won't be so rash as to lose him. Washington knows the wilderness from the Blue Ridge to the Ohio like the back of his hand. They need him if they're to mop up the French bastards."

An unfortunate third julep had followed Henri's second while he struggled to understand the connection between Colonel Washington, Lord Fairfax, and the colonial administration. Now the spirits choked him, and he spluttered into his lace handkerchief. The squire pounded him heavily on the back. "There's Colonel Washington now, courting, by the looks of it," he said pointedly as the tall young man passed near them and scooped up two silver cups of syllabub from a tray.

A heavyset red-faced man with coarse features had edged over to join their group, and Mr. Fitzwilliam turned to him and changed the subject. "Ah, here's the man we're waiting for! Thomas de Bouldin at last! Let's get on with it, Thomas. The raffle tickets you promised, if you please!"

The red-faced man grinned slyly as his companions pulled out their purses. Henri had seen him at the gaming tables and had heard him spoken of as a burgess. He understood from the gossip that a rich wife had brought him a handsome plantation that lay a week's ride to the south, but Henri wondered what woman could have borne to marry such an unpleasant specimen of humanity. He had small, sharp eyes; a red-veined nose; and a fleshy, wet lower lip. Up close he reeked of alcohol, and his teeth, bared in an unpleasant smirk, were rotten. Stepping back involuntarily, Henri wondered if what he'd heard was true, that Virginians had such bad teeth because they ate hot bread at every meal.

Thomas de Bouldin belched and doled out tickets as money—sterling and Virginia scrip—was eagerly held out to him.

"Thomas, the signor must have a ticket." The other men laughed and nudged Henri.

The room seemed to be tilting. Henri murmured faintly that he desired nothing in the world so much as to buy a raffle ticket and again patted his hot forehead with his handkerchief. He was dizzy from the whiskey.

"Well, well, signor . . . *Virginia* spirits too strong for an *Italian* stomach?" Thomas de Bouldin sneered but reached back into his pocket. "Wish I had your poxy Italian gift for making money. Only one raffle ticket, sir? A pound buys six. Surely you've that to spare, considering how these gentlemen"—he gestured at the circle of men—"have swollen your purse paying for dancing lessons?"

The circle of men nodded. "Aye, that we have," said one. "Sell him a brace of tickets, Thomas!"

Henri was abruptly distracted from the business of overpriced raffle tickets. Through the open doors of the dining room, he saw Colonel Washington hand a syllabub to a girl whose face caught his eye. The girl was somewhere between pretty and beautiful, with an arresting intelligent face, lively eyes, and a fine little nose she wrinkled as she talked animatedly to Colonel Washington. She was slender and elegant in a pale-blue silk gown over a yellow silk petticoat, her hair arranged rather higher than it was generally worn in the colony, powdered, and threaded with pearls. Henri, accustomed to the elegant toilettes of the ladies at Versailles, recognized at once that she was the most beautifully dressed female in a room of sturdy colonial girls in their ill-fitting English-made gowns.

Henri was disconcerted by a feeling there was something familiar about her, though if she was English, that was unlikely. Still, it was impossible to recall every girl. Henri, attention on Colonel Washington, the girl, and the syllabub she was spooning into her pretty mouth, murmured, "*Si!* Do me the honor . . . half a dozen raffle tickets." Yes, he was certain he knew her, and despite his befuddled state, he felt a frisson of alarm that she would be equally certain to recognize him.

Thomas de Bouldin hemmed loudly. Recalled to the business of the moment, Henri stopped staring and fumbled in his haste to extract money from his purse. The fat man snatched the sovereign and handed him six greasy stubs of paper in return. "A prize worth having," Thomas de Bouldin said, closing his purse with satisfaction. The others nodded.

"Pray, what is the prize?" asked Henri, looking over the man's shoulder to see where the girl and Colonel Washington had gone.

The fat man leered. "My nigger wench Venus." The man sniffed his fingers suggestively, and the other men laughed and nudged each other.

"Fourteen, a ripe little thing. Promises to be a good breeder. Got her with child myself to be sure, only raffling her because, you know." He nodded at the gaming tables in the next room. "The raffle winner gets two slaves. A bargain! I'll deliver the wench to the winner at the spring session if she's spawned by then; if not, then next fall." He laughed loudly, fingered the money, belched, and turned away toward the card tables, licking his lips.

Henri's jaw dropped.

Squire Fitzwilliam misinterpreted Henri's shocked expression. He nodded after the broad departing back. "I know, sad thing, this gambling fever. The planter's curse. De Bouldin married well too, wife an heiress. Had one of the biggest patents in the colony, after the Custises and the Parkes and King Carter. But he's lost most of it—the money his wife brought him, the silver, her jewelry, one field slave after another until there aren't enough left to make the tobacco pay. Wagers anything he gets his hands on, loses it all eventually. They say he's in debt to moneylenders here, his English debts mount and mount. The interest alone on what he owes is mounting, bound to ruin him soon. Burgess or not, he'll be thrown into the debtors' cell at the jail."

Another man shook his head. "His London factors won't advance him a penny more against the next crop. Villains, they complain the quality is poor and pay less every year. A pox on 'em all!" Squire Fitzwilliam explained how Thomas de Bouldin had kept one step ahead of his creditors. "For the last fifteen years, he's kept his young slave women, raises money breeding with them, sells the offspring when they're weaned."

Henri was appalled. "He sells his *children*?"

"My good sir, they're slaves! You know, the child follows the mother—a slave woman's child is a slave. That's the law. Good thing for us, eh, when nature increases our property. Takes them to the slave market when they're four, best age to train 'em," said Mr. Fitzwilliam. "Bought one of his myself last year. My girls needed a new maid. Plus, they're mulattos. Light skinned look well in a house. But Thomas is lusty, wearing his breeders out, so he's taken to breeding with the ones he's sired. No children with his wife, but she's been ill a long time. They say she's dying, expect he'll remarry soon."

Drunk as he was, Henri was agog with shock—*his own daughters?*

"Some think Anne de Bouldin's being helped to the grave," said one man in a low voice. "There's a new heiress in the picture. His ward, they say . . ." He nodded at Colonel Washington's companion. "Lately come from England."

"Charming! Won't stay single long in Williamsburg."

"An orphan, only child. King gave her father one of the biggest patents in the colonies, but it's far away to the south. Among the Indians. Not well settled. They say she's set her heart on living there, but she'll be scalped before she takes possession. Hasn't been surveyed that far south. Young Colonel Washington seems to be putting himself forward for that job. Ha-ha-ha! Wants a rich wife, he does!"

"You'd think old Lord Fairfax would seize the chance and marry her himself."

"Not him, hates women. Jilted once—at the church door, I hear. You mark my words, Washington's the man, or Thomas'll have her when his wife dies."

Henri suppressed a shudder at the thought of any woman at the mercy of Thomas de Bouldin, especially such a pretty one. He felt contaminated by the greasy scraps of paper in his waistcoat pocket. The man was a monster.

"De Bouldin had better look to it then. Colonel Washington danced with her five times tonight."

"Marry her and he could forget that wreck of an estate on the Potomac. Hardly the best tobacco land . . ."

Then the talk turned from Washington to the colony's favorite topic, tobacco and the iniquity of their London factors, as the men settled into a long discussion of falling prices.

Henri bowed and withdrew. He returned unsteadily to the ballroom and his dancing duties. He groaned inwardly as he realized it was Mrs. Fitzwilliam's turn, and she was looking at him with hope and breathless expectation.

Mrs. Fitzwilliam was indeed breathless. She never wore stays on the plantation and had been tightly laced tonight in order to get into her best gown. She could scarcely draw breath as Signor Valentino led her to the center of the dance floor, where she smiled triumphantly back at the circle of ladies, and Henri watched Colonel Washington taking his place for the next dance at the end of the set. The colonel's partner was the girl in blue.

Drunk, and loathing Virginians who bred with their slaves and daughters and probably their cattle and pigs as well, with their vile whiskey and their antagonism to France, Henri felt disgusted by everyone present, and his irritation soon manifested itself in his dancing. He threw caution to the winds and began leading poor Mrs. Fitzwilliam through an uninhibited dance of his own on-the-spot improvising. Hoping it would give her apoplexy, he informed her that it was the latest, the *very* latest Italian quadrille, straight from Venice and danced in all the best society in Europe. Having left discretion and his manners in the dining room and keeping more or less in time to the music and the figure of the dance, he capered this way and that, bounding and prancing with abandon, completely carried away, waving a lace handkerchief over his head in exaggerated flourishes.

"Wh . . . wh . . . what do they call this dance, Signore Valentino?" panted Mrs. Fitzwilliam, trying to keep up.

"Peacocks a-courting in springtime, milady," he smirked archly over his shoulder, twirling and bowing dizzily so that the tails of his coat flopped over his head. "The male peacock intends to attract the attention of the female! Dazzle her, in fact! Pray, have I succeeded? Are you dazzled, *cara* signora?"

"D . . . d . . . azzled . . . yes, upon my word, quite dazzled . . ." Gasp. "Is . . . is p . . . p . . . peacocks a"—gasp—"courting much danced in"—gasp—"London?"

"Oh, indeed! But only in the most select gatherings, signora!" Signor Valentino gave her an arch smile. "At St. James's. In honor of the royal birthday, I have waited until tonight, to dance it with the only woman in Williamsburg who could do it justice! You, dear lady!"

"Oh!" Mrs. Fitzwilliam puffed, gratified but hoping her stays wouldn't burst.

"Princess Amelia's favorite dance!" he declared, and improvised further by springing sideways to the left, giving a little kick, then springing to the right as the set of dancers changed places, giving another little kick sideways and a flourish of his handkerchief as the circles of men and women moved on to new partners. Having by some miracle avoided falling over, he straightened up to find himself face-to-face with his next partner, the girl who had begun the dance with Colonel Washington.

"You!" she exclaimed, startled but not missing a step of the dance. Drunk as he was, Henri thought at first she was impressed by his command of the dance. "Whatever *are* you doing here?" she hissed, but before Henri could think of an answer, she spun away and danced round the man on her left.

He mumbled that she must be confused.

The next steps brought them shoulder to shoulder, and almost face-to-face. "Do explain!" she exclaimed. Her brown eyes, brimming with tears of merriment, looked directly into his over her fan. "You are making *quite* a spectacle of yourself! Are you mad?" The corners of her eyes crinkled, and she raised her fan again as laughter shook her shoulders. She spun gracefully again and danced round the man on her right. Henri's head swam from all the bobbing and spinning. Then she was back again, preparing to dance around him. She sashayed behind him, looking back at him over her fan. "Peacocks!" she hissed in his ear.

"*Courting!* Especially in that colorful coat! *Signore Valentino.* Pray, when does the male peacock fan out his tail and squawk? I can scarcely wait!"

Then she disappeared down the set. Even Henri registered the startled looks on the faces of the other dancers, who were gawking at him.

Thankfully the musicians stopped playing, and Henri handed puce-faced Mrs. Fitzwilliam over to her friends. As she sank into a chair, gasping for breath and fanning herself, her clutch of sturdy daughters besieged Henri, all eager to know more of Princess Amelia's favorite dance. Henri, mumbling apologies, bowed himself out of their grasp, begging they would excuse him.

The night was wearing on, the band struck up a livelier air, and the younger people sprang to take their places. Virginians preferred English country dances to the minuet, and most were tapping their toes and clapping in time. Henri made his escape from the ballroom as the young people began flinging each other about. He wandered from room to room, not entirely steady on his feet, searching for the girl but unable to see her anywhere.

Finally he spied her elaborately dressed hair among the heads of the crowd and pushed his way toward her. He was in time to see her dropping a farewell curtsey to the governor and Lady Rebecca and their two daughters, the youngest of whom, being only fourteen, threw her arms impulsively round the departing guest and kissed her. Lady Rebecca held out her hands to her departing guest. Whoever she was, the girl was clearly a favorite. Then to Henri's horror, a swaying Thomas de Bouldin appeared by her side, harrumphed loudly, held out his arm, and led her away. Liveried footmen bowed as they passed.

Henri hurried outside and watched Thomas hand the girl into a carriage driven by a slave coachman in an odd-shaped hat that looked like a large birdcage. Why would the coachman's head be encased in a birdcage? He rubbed his eyes. The carriage rocked as Thomas de Bouldin heaved himself in and slammed the carriage door shut. The coachman with the caged head cracked his whip, and away it rolled down the drive, leaving Henri gazing after it. *"Nom de Dieu!"* he whispered.

Two men strode out of the shadows into the light of the burning torches. One of them was Colonel Washington, in conversation with one of the governor's aides but watching the girl with Thomas de Bouldin. The three men acknowledged one another with a slight bow, and Colonel Washington indicated politely that the intoxicated Henri should precede him. Henri lurched unsteadily up the steps and back into the palace.

The sky behind them lit up with a loud bang as a volley of fireworks filled the sky with a shower of light. The Birthnight Ball was officially over.

CHAPTER 11
AFTER THE BALL

In the days that followed, Henri was plagued by his inability to place the girl who recognized him. Had she mistaken him for someone else? Would she betray him? He looked for her everywhere but was wary of asking too openly about her. Williamsburg emptied of visitors, and the streets were filled with departing carriages, slave wagons, men on horseback, and ladies' cries of "Farewell!" from carriages and parlor windows. The golden autumn days turned sharply cold, with a hard frost in the mornings. In the space of a week, a raw wind had stripped the blazing trees of leaves and sent the remaining inhabitants of the town home to their firesides. The streets smelled of wood smoke, and news reached Williamsburg that the tense standoff between the British and the French on the northern Ohio border had escalated into war.

A regiment of uniformed British troops disembarked in Virginia under the command of General Braddock to take over from Colonel Washington's chaotic Virginia militia and lead an expedition to the Ohio. War made Henri's already precarious position here even more dangerous. He became aware that Governor Dinwiddie's aide, who had been speaking with Colonel Washington the night of the ball, was now watching him closely and asking pointed questions about Henri's valet and musician.

It added to his anxieties when Henri learned that to the west, the Blue Ridge Mountains now lay under a blanket of early snow. They were trapped in Williamsburg until the promised Indian guides arrived to escort them to the French garrison on the Mississippi. Henri's report was finished. There was little more news to be had, and he and Thierry and François were anxious to deliver the report, board a ship in La Nouvelle-Orléans, and go home to their reward. But day after day passed with no sign of the guides.

While they waited, the three Frenchmen struggled to maintain their Italian disguise, a pastime that was no longer entertaining. Henri paid calls on the ladies, behaved charmingly, drank tea and Madeira, listened to fireside gossip, and talked openly of his need to depart for England as soon as the weather allowed, fretting that he was urgently awaited in London to prepare young ladies for the spring Season.

Was it his imagination, or were the Williamsburg ladies cooling toward their darling?

The streets were full of red coats, and the inhabitants of Williamsburg continued to complain about the British snub to their local militia. Colonel Washington had experience on the frontier and General Braddock did not. They speculated when and how General Braddock would attack to teach the French a lesson. At night Henri recorded everything he had heard and, piecing together what he now knew of the geography involved, surmised General Braddock would have to wait until spring, when warmer weather made the mountains passable, before he could get his men to the Ohio and attack. So far as Henri could gather from the local gossip, moving a large, heavily supplied army across the mountain wilderness would prove arduous enough that the British were unlikely to engage the French before midsummer. Meanwhile, week succeeded week without the promised guides appearing.

In mid-December, an itinerant tinker passed through Williamsburg with a dilapidated mule cart filled with odds and ends of pewter and tin goods, most so broken and battered as to be unusable. He managed to find Henri at his lodging, and under the guise of trying to sell him a twisted candelabra, cadged a coin from him and slipped a dirty scrap of paper into Henri's hand, and then he left Williamsburg, complaining loudly that there was no business for an honest man in the town.

The piece of paper contained a cryptic message that a party of Indians and their interpreter would collect Henri's report and deliver it to Louisiana. The Indians could travel faster without white men unused to the wilderness in winter. Henri and his companions must wait in Williamsburg, then sail for Europe in the spring.

Henri was furious and knew that unless he delivered the report in person, he had no leverage to guarantee their return home.

Meanwhile, Thierry and François's disguises as Signors Teodoro and Francesco were slipping, dangerously. Bored with their roles, wanting a Hortense very badly indeed, they took to passing their evenings in the taverns. Drink loosened their tongues, making them careless in their remarks about the British troops. Then Thierry got entangled with a local girl, a barmaid in her father's tavern. Late one night, a drunken Thierry stood in the street beneath Nancy's window and serenaded her with a bawdy French song at the top of his voice. Three passing British soldiers cursed the French for devils and beat Thierry unconscious. The next morning Henri explained to anyone who would listen that his Italian valet's fondness for the French song was only accounted for by the extreme bawdiness of French lyrics, but following that incident, the atmosphere in Williamsburg cooled further toward the three Italians. It was only a matter of time until one of them again betrayed the fact they were French. They had to leave Williamsburg. Soon.

By the time Thierry recovered enough to sit on a horse, Henri had gathered as much information as he could in the course of his social calls about what lay west of Williamsburg. He had even extracted directions to La Nouvelle-Orléans, which lay to the southwest, where the unimaginably vast Mississippi River emptied into the Gulf of Mexico. He gathered there were two routes, one known as the "way west" that went through a gap in a vast mountain range to Kentuckee, where, it was said, he would eventually find the Mississippi if he traveled west long enough. Or there was another route taken by settlers and long hunters that followed rivers and buffalo trails through passes in lesser mountain chains to the Tinassi River in the southwest. The Tinassi or perhaps another river flowed west into the Mississippi River. The garrison near La Nouvelle-Orléans was on the Mississippi. Henri had little information about the distances except that they were great, and there were Indians. He had heard terrible tales of hostilities on the borders of the colony where there had been savage Indian attacks on English settlements, where Indians had sworn to avenge relatives killed by whites by wiping their tears with settlers' scalps.

He gathered the trip would be dangerous and hard, had no idea whether it was possible for three men to negotiate a safe passage with the Indians since they had no wish to fight or seize Indian land, and such directions as he had as to how to reach Louisiana seemed vague and uncertain. Added to that, undertaking a journey into the wilderness in midwinter was perilous but remaining in Williamsburg had become more dangerous. And Henri's funds were dwindling. There were no dancing lessons to be given now, and their lodgings were very expensive.

With the last of his money, Henri bribed one of the tavern's slaves to obtain rough clothing, muskets, ammunition, and long hunting knives for the three of them. They would go disguised as long hunters. Henri committed the material he had collected to memory and burned his laboriously compiled report, destroying anything that might be used in evidence against them if they were caught. They abandoned their expensive clothes for the innkeeper in lieu of paying their bill, and before daybreak on Christmas Day, while Williamsburg slept off its riotous Christmas Eve dinners, they stole five horses from the livery stable, one for each of the Frenchmen and two packhorses. They pulled their hats low over their faces and led their loaded packhorses into a bleak, black morning, heading south. It was snowing lightly, and Henri hoped it would cover their tracks so that when their absence was discovered, no one would know which direction they had taken.

Beyond town, a man suddenly leaped from behind a tree, waving a musket and crying, "Halt!" Henri's startled horse reared, and Henri swore as his hat fell off and he struggled to unsheathe his hunting knife. The man lowered the musket, and Henri recognized one of the wretches who carried sedan chairs around Williamsburg.

"Idiot! Are you mad?" Henri raged, but nevertheless felt for his purse and threw the ragamuffin highwayman a few coins. "Now, out of the way!"

Just then a boy crept from the shadows behind the tree. "Please, Your Honor," said the boy, scurrying to pick up coins, then Henri's hat. He handed the hat up. "Don't hurt Father. Only we overheard people at the tavern talking about you, saying you wasn't Italian. They said if they arrested you and you were French, they'd hang you. Father kept an eye, thought you'd leave. Please don't kill us, Your Honor, take us with you. Our masters are so hard, my brother is ill, and they beat us so."

Another, smaller shadow appeared by his side, echoing, "Please."

The highwayman put an arm around each boy, and all three stood in the horses' way, blocking the narrow road. "We'll work, sir, turn our hands to anything. I can shoe horses. You'll need a smith, wherever you're going. Take us with you, or kill us now. Our indenture is a living hell and will be doubly so if they catch us. I stole my master's musket, and if you won't take us, I'll shoot the boys and then myself."

"Children! Impossible," muttered Thierry angrily.

"Please, Your Honor, Father tried to stop my master beating us," piped up the smaller child bravely, sneezing, "and the justices called him a troublemaker and increased our term to ten years. It will kill us, and Father too. Please, sir." The child was very thin, and his teeth chattered.

Henri swore furiously, but he was in a dilemma. He couldn't leave them behind to point out the direction they had taken to the militia, but he could hardly murder three such miserable specimens of humanity. They would have to take the wretches along until he could leave them to fend for themselves. Henri ordered the man to mount one of the packhorses and, reaching down, swept the younger child onto the saddle in front of him. He told a reluctant François to take the older boy pillion. Feeling the small boy shake with cold, Henri swept his cloak over both of them, and they rode on, Thierry's protests echoing in his ears.

They traveled slowly, heads bent against a bitter wind on a road of frozen mud ruts that made it hard going for the horses. After ten slow, stumbling days, they were lost in a blinding snowstorm, unable to tell if they were on the road or not. They tried to make a camp to sit out the bad weather, but they struggled to construct a shelter and build a fire and would surely have perished from hunger and exposure had not four Cherokee braves and a shifty-eyed Huguenot interpreter loomed out of the swirling snow. In the course of trying to ask them directions, Henri discovered they were en route to Williamsburg to collect his report.

The interpreter angrily demanded to know why the Frenchmen had attempted the journey; it should have been left to the Indians, who had been promised guns and rum to deliver Henri's speaking papers. Henri retorted they had no speaking papers, and he and his two French companions had each committed different elements of the report to memory and must deliver the information in person. The man Rufus was a blacksmith, needed for the horses, and his two boys were servants.

The Indians received this information in hostile silence. Nothing had been said to them about guiding anyone but the interpreter. Henri promised that the commander at the French garrison would reward the Indians with extra guns, blankets, and a keg of brandy for their trouble. The interpreter relayed this information to the Cherokees, and after a discussion in which the braves expressed their dissatisfaction, the interpreter shrugged a surly agreement.

They forced Henri's party to travel quickly through a snow-laden landscape. The way narrowed through the hills, and the trees were stark against a leaden sky. Unaccustomed as Henri and his companions were to living outdoors in such weather, riding in sleet, wet, and cold, and sleeping on the ground, they fell sick and were coughing and feverish. With a pounding head, aching in every limb, struggling to breathe, and a throat so sore he could no longer swallow, Henri shivered and tried to rally Thierry, who slumped coughing in his saddle. Burning with fever, Rufus wrapped a blanket round his boys and clutched them tight to keep them from slipping off the stumbling packhorse. François was knocked from his horse by a low-hanging branch and lay too weak to get up. Henri ordered the interpreter to halt, saying they would be no use to the French or the Indians if they were dead. They had to stop, get warm, and recover their strength.

The Indians demanded they leave François and the Drumhellers behind, saying they were too weak to make the journey and would soon die. Henri thought the Indians were right, the Drumhellers all looked on the point of death, but he refused to abandon them or François. He insisted he, François, and Thierry all had different information to pass on. There was another argument between the interpreter and the Indians, in a mixture of French and Cherokee. It sounded like the Indians wanted to torture the information out of them, but the sly interpreter, anxious for his own payment from the garrison commander, wanted to keep them alive.

After another heated exchange with the interpreter, the interpreter insisting the whites were worth more guns alive than dead, the Cherokees agreed to halt. They set about building a cramped, windowless shelter called a winter house. The whole party crawled inside for warmth and huddled on top of each other under buffalo skins, racked by chills and fevers, and almost stifled by a smoky fire. Outside the weather was relentless—it snowed and froze, thawed a little, and snowed again. Day and night were painful, indistinguishable. Inside the winter house, the fever-ridden Drumhellers and the Frenchmen lost track of time. They feebly chewed shreds of rock-hard dried meat, sucked handfuls of snow, and coughed and coughed.

François was the worst of all, his cheeks hot and red in his stretched face, coughing like he was drowning. "Help me, Henri," he gasped in the dark, over and over. "Mother of God, help me breathe! Such a pain in my chest!" But Henri was too ill himself to do more than try and hold François as he shuddered and coughed and struggled for breath. One morning, Henri felt something wet on his hand—the fire blazed up to show François's mouth and chin covered in dark blood.

François was wild-eyed, insisting Death was outside, trying to get in past the pelt at the narrow opening. "See, Death is there," cried François, terrified, pointing at the flapping pelt. Henri mumbled it was only the wind, but François wept feebly and begged them not to let Death in. In intervals between ranting and a restless sleep, François grew calmer, believing he was a boy again in France. To humor his friend, a feverish Henri described the fields and forests around his father's château, where the boys had spent their summers together in the gatekeeper's lodge, where the gatekeeper's wife fed them well and clucked over the state of their trousers and shoes, how the gatekeeper would take them fishing early in the morning when mist lay thick on the fields, before the chapel bell rang for matins. They remembered how the wild boar charged the hunting dogs, how the wounded hounds had their entrails stuffed back into their stomachs and the stomachs were sewn together with thick thread. How later they had competed to bed the village girls.

"Yes," whispered François. "We'll be there again, won't we, Henri? It will be summer soon? And Hortense . . ."

"Of course. We must not forget Hortense."

Henri held his friend's hand through a final night, drifting in and out of sleep, while Thierry begged his brother to live. Toward the end, François insisted Henri was the priest, and his pleas for absolution penetrated Henri's dreams. Thierry shook Henri awake. "You must."

Henri struggled groggily to recall the words, and finally croaked, *"Dominus noster Jesus Christus te absolvat, et ego auctoritate ipsius te absolvo ab omni vinculo excommunicationis suspensioni et interdicti in quantum possum et tu indiges. Deinde, ego te absolvo a peccatis tuis in nomine Patris, et Filii, et Spiritus Sancti. Amen."*

François whispered, "Amen," closed his eyes, and died.

During the night François's corpse grew cold and rigid beside Henri, who knew they ought to bury him, but the ground was frozen, and in any case, he and Thierry were too weak to dig it. In the morning Henri and Thierry dragged themselves shivering from their buffalo hides to push and pull the corpse outside the winter house. They had no strength to do more. Wild animals came in the night, and next morning the body was gone.

Drifting in and out of his fevered sleep, Henri overheard the interpreter and Indians speaking half in French, half in Cherokee. Partially awake, he listened, absorbing enough to follow the conversation, the talk of trails and war parties; the cowardice of whites; the value of men's, women's, and children's scalps; hunting; and the habits of the animals and snakes and spirits and shape-changers that inhabited the region, until he dozed again. When he did, he was visited by the girl in Williamsburg. "Who are you?" he muttered. "A peacock!" She laughed, pirouetting with a swish of silken skirts that turned into a peacock's tail, before she soared into the air like the witch in a fairy tale.

Henri surrendered to the mercy of other dreams: of graceful Madame de Pompadour; of Italy and the taste of oranges; of gilded palaces, horses, and hunting dogs; and of his rare visits to his father's château with its moth-eaten tapestries, its great fireplaces with roast venison turning on a spit, round loaves of bread, cheese, flasks of wine, and his place among the lesser company where it was nevertheless warm and he could eat his fill as he watched his half brothers dining on either side of his father at the far end of the room. He smelled the tantalizing aromas of well-basted meat, took a mouthful of rough wine, felt his mouth close on the pastry of a sugared tart . . .

Reality was the worse when he awoke. Virginia was hell—its bestial inhabitants, the impenetrable forests, the frozen rivers, the bitter cold, and the smoky taste of pemmican, hard as leather to chew. When he slept again, the girl at the Governor's Palace returned to taunt him, "*Quite* mad!" she said as clearly as if she were there. "Mad, mad, mad." Her laugh echoed as she retreated. He would try to reach out to catch her, but each time, his hands closed on air.

CHAPTER 12
AN UNEXPECTED ENCOUNTER

Thanks to his youth and a strong constitution, Henri began to recover in spite of everything. He was weak but knew he was more alive than dead. Now he had to rebuild his strength, make sure Thierry rebuilt his too. They drank a bitter tea the Indians brewed from bark and ate dried corn soaked in melted snow and boiled to mush, and the occasional lean rabbit the Indians trapped. Henri forced himself to stand and then walk outside. Surprisingly, Rufus and his sons hadn't died, but they lay like a collection of bones loosely connected in their skins. He forced the tea and boiled corn mush into their weakly protesting mouths and urged them to sit and then stand.

Finally Henri tired of playing nursemaid and said he was sorry for them but he had enough to do saving himself and Thierry. He wasn't responsible for them. "Get well or die," he told them bluntly. That made Rufus drink the tea and force the boys to do the same. "You must stand and walk about," Henri ordered. He tried to rally Thierry's spirits, telling him they had survived and they only had to keep going until they reached Louisiana. Then it was only a matter of a voyage to France, and in a few months, they would be in possession of their reward.

Thierry's response to this encouragement was to groan, "Go to the Devil," and close his eyes.

Henri had no idea how much time had passed while they were ill nor where they were, other than camped by a frozen river somewhere far to the west of Williamsburg. One morning he was woken by the distinct sound of rushing water. The ice had melted, and that must mean spring.

The strong constitution that had pulled him through his illness reasserted itself as he gained strength. Every day he walked a little farther from the camp, marking the arrival of spring, irritated that the others made so little effort to do the same. Outside the winter house, the weather had changed and the wilderness had taken on a green tint in the hills that rose and fell beyond the river. The river was swollen with melted snow, and water rushed noisily over the rocks. The sunshine was warm on his skin. Thierry and the Drumhellers huddled inside until midday, when the sun was strongest, and then they would crawl outside to warm themselves.

Impatient with them, Henri took to wandering along the bank for a little longer each day, trying to plan how he and Thierry could slip away from their guides and set out for La Nouvelle-Orléans on their own. One of many drawbacks to this plan was that the Indian guides had appropriated the muskets they had taken from Williamsburg, and the only weapon Henri had now was a hunting knife.

One morning Henri left camp before dawn, telling the interpreter he was going to catch fish. He was ravenously hungry and sick of chewing pemmican. The Indians shrugged. They did not think he would catch fish with a knife. He would come back. If not, he would die or be captured.

The rising sun slanted through the trees as Henri retraced their route upriver, wondering if they had passed a plantation with horses. If so, he and Thierry could leave the others, steal the horses, and try to ride west by the sun. Rufus and his boys would have to be left behind. The sun grew hotter on his back, and he kept his eyes open for mountain lions, snakes who might also be warming themselves, and Indians. He kept walking briskly as the sun grew warmer, taking pleasure in the exercise and a return of vigor. Finally he grew hot and began to itch. He felt something crawling under his shirt. He came to a place where the bank flattened out on the opposite side of the river and rocks had dammed a pool on his side.

After living in his clothes for months Henri doubted his own father would recognize him now, a lice-ridden backwoodsman in a sort of jerkin and leggings made from badly cured animal skins. His hair was matted, his beard had grown, and he could feel things crawling on his skin and in his hair and beard. He decided to have a bath and get rid of them. He stripped off his clothes, turned them inside out, and threw them over a branch on the fallen tree so his garments could air in the sun and get rid of whatever crawled inside. Then he picked his way across the wet stones and gasped as he plunged into the pool of icy water.

He submerged himself and scrubbed all over with handfuls of river sand until he could bear the cold no longer. Shivering, he climbed out and stretched to let the sun dry him, remembering fastidious Signor Valentino who had been shaved every morning and smelled of violet snuff. Dry, he eyed the stinking garments he had worn for months and shuddered. He put his hat on, grabbed his clothes, shook them hard to dislodge the vermin still inside, and was giving them a final hard slap against the tree when a crackle of underbrush on the opposite bank signaled something was approaching. Henri clutched his clothes and slipped behind a rock, certain it was a war party. He had overheard the Huguenot interpreter talking about the ways Indian women tortured prisoners, scraping their skin off with sharp shells or burning them alive. Agreeing, the guides laughed scornfully that whites cried like babies when that happened. Indians never betrayed fear or pain if they suffered tortures.

His only chance was that they would pass without having seen or heard him. He held his breath.

But Indians would make no noise, so it must be an animal, and a large one, judging by the crashing undergrowth. A panther or mountain lion headed for the large, flat rock on the opposite bank? Or worse, a bear, irritable with hunger after its winter hibernation, coming to the river after fish? Or the most ferocious of all, a female bear with a cub to protect? Henri was armed only with a hunting knife and knew he lacked the strength or skill to kill an angry bear with it. He narrowed his eyes on the spot where the noise came from, praying it was only a thirsty deer.

On the opposite bank just across the shallows from Henri, a large brown figure was visible in the bushes, approaching the flat rock jutting into the river. Henri's hiding place was close enough that he knew the bear would soon get his scent. He clutched the hunting knife and looked for the cub. He knew he couldn't outrun the bear—they could travel as fast as a galloping horse and climb trees after their prey. Then his jaw dropped. He rubbed his eyes. The large brown animal had a human head. And behind it, a pink hat tied with broad ribbons appeared above the underbrush in the animal's wake.

Then two figures emerged into the sunshine on the opposite bank. One was a light-skinned slave in a brown dress, obviously pregnant and carrying a basket. Behind her was a slim white girl in a flowered muslin frock, laden with another basket and a quilt. The brim of the pink hat hid the girl's face, and below it, brown curls tumbled over a shawl round her shoulders. Henri was too much a Frenchman not to notice it was a rather fine India shawl.

"That rock looks dry, Venus. We can stop here and breakfast and wait until they've left. Don't worry, they haven't followed us. Those fellows are anxious to get Thomas to Williamsburg. He'll go without you this time. And next time . . . I'll think of something before the next time." Both set down their burdens. The girl in the pink hat unfolded the quilt and spread it on the rock in a patch of sunlight. Henri squinted and leaned incautiously from his hiding place to get a better look.

The high, clear voice was English, and he had heard it before.

The pregnant slave sank to her knees with a sigh. "Maybe they gone like you say, Miss Sophy, but I'se afraid. 'Cause they come back one day, and he take me and the baby away, sell us. It's what Massa do, sells all the girl slaves and their childs. Unless he keep 'em, do it all over again."

"I know, Venus. He's an evil man. If I can find a way to take you to my plantation, I swear I will. Then I'll set you free."

"Don't know nothing 'bout being free, Miss Sophy. What I do then? Where I go so they don't catch me and take me back to Massa? I go to your plantation wif you. I can stay and work for you. Work hard. Seth would too if you take him." Venus sighed and opened her basket and laid out ham, bread, cheese, butter, and slices of cake on the quilt. "Miss Sophy, I'se hungry."

The girl in the pink hat settled herself on the blanket, opened her basket, and took out a sheaf of paper and a small box with paints and brushes. "Eat, Venus, help yourself. I'll sketch something." She removed a rectangular box from her basket and drew water from the river into a small pitcher, then sighed and lifted her face to the sun. For a moment Henri thought he was dreaming again. Beneath the extravagant hat was a sadder and thinner face, but one fixed in Henri's mind. The mystery girl from the governor's ball.

She dabbled a paintbrush in the water and took a sheet of paper and looked across the river, saying, "I'll draw that willow with its branches in the water and that big rock behind it."

Henri rose from his hiding place, grinning.

Sophia looked up to see a cadaverous, bearded wild man with a deranged smile, naked except for a hat held over his privates, an armload of clothes, and a large unsheathed knife. She screamed. Her paint box went flying as she sprang to her feet, while the slave dropped the biscuit she was buttering and shrieked, "Miss Sophy, we be killed! Oh missus, oh missus . . ."

Henri hastily repositioned his bundle of clothes to preserve as much modesty as possible in the circumstances. With the hand holding the knife, he shifted the hat and bowed to the girl on the opposite bank as graciously as if they were in the gardens at Versailles. He tried adopting his best Signor Valentino manner, but found it was necessary to bellow to make himself heard over the screaming slave.

"My compliments, madame! I fear I have alarmed you. Pray tell your maid not to scream so loudly. I beg you will pardon my . . . dishabille. Hardly dressed for the company of ladies, I know, but I never expected to encounter a lady and her maid taking refreshments in such a lonely and dangerous spot. There are warring Indians and cougars and, er, bears about. Deadly reptiles. Allow me to advise you to return home at once . . . though before you do so, might you spare a morsel of your repast? I confess I am hungry." Henri took a tentative step into the river, and Venus's screams rose to a new pitch.

"Venus, don't scream! It spoils my aim." The girl had pulled something from the housewife at her waist and leveled the object at Henri. She was holding a small pistol. Henri stopped.

"Perhaps then your guardian or your . . . er . . . husband is nearby for your protection?" Henri was now midthigh in cold water. He remembered Thomas de Bouldin. Had he somehow arrived at the accursed man's plantation? What if de Bouldin suddenly appeared, searching for the girl, and found him standing naked in the river a short distance from her? What if de Bouldin's wife had now died and the girl had married him?

"I am not married yet, thank God."

This impassioned statement left Henri at something of a loss. "Indeed, that so charming a lady as yourself . . . all loveliness as you . . . not married . . . er . . . your affections yet unengaged." Henri floundered, losing the thread of the kind of flowery long-winded nonsense the ladies of Williamsburg had believed was the latest thing in Anglo-Italian gallantry. His feet had lost all feeling. His legs were getting numb, and he needed to get out of the water before his male appendages were frozen beyond repair.

He shifted a little to keep his circulation going, smirked, and tried again. "Your sentiments, dear madame . . . er . . . the most modest in a female . . . and . . . er . . . yet it may in time prove susceptible to persuasion by a man worthy of such a model of female worthiness . . . er . . . we must hope such sentiments are not entirely hopeless of change . . ." His glib nothings deserted him entirely, so he waved the hand with the knife in a Signor Valentino–like flourish, and bowed again.

The girl squinted. "What twaddle! I never in my life heard anything so stupid," she said, lowering the pistol. "So it's you. Signor Valentino, lately of Williamsburg, last seen prancing like a peahen, no, *peacock*, on hot coals, in cloth of gold, lace about your person, flapping around your neck and wrists like"—she gave an unladylike snicker—"the feathers of a molting swan. Your present attire is equally . . . unusual." She shaded her eyes with her hand. "That must be an entire raccoon you're wearing on your head. How very cold it must be, standing in the water up to your . . . your . . ." She dissolved in giggles.

"Ah. Yes. I can explain." Henri used the hand holding the knife to reposition his bundle of clothes, noting that the coonskin hat smelled very rank indeed in the sun. How, precisely, was he to explain?

She cut him short. "And, *signor*, unless I am very much mistaken, you are my childhood tormentor Henri de Marechal. Don't you remember me? Chambord? And then Versailles? You persuaded me to gallop your pony through the Hall of Mirrors, hoping I would be punished. Instead I had a thrilling ride, and you—"

"What?" said Henri, shifting from foot to foot. "Chambord? I don't think there were English girls at Chambord, a few whores perhaps. The ladies of the court didn't usually . . . and Versailles? I don't recall . . . Oh no! Aaaaah! *Mon Dieu!* Not *you*!" he exclaimed in a tone of anguish. It all came back to him, the five-year-old child with her fine clothes in tatters, bare feet, and a dirty face looking up at him adoringly, a hideous little girl who had ruined his one chance to experience a royal hunt. The ugly little monkey, he had called her under his breath. He could still remember wanting to choke her. "*Mademoiselle Singe! Quelle horreur!* The Devil has sent you!"

"So you do remember me!"

Henri shuddered. He would much rather not. He had hated her with a passion and had done his best to make her life a misery. With no success whatever. He hated her still.

Gratified by some service Henri's father rendered at court, the king had invited him and his obliging son Henri to join a week's hunt in the forest of Chambord in honor of the English envoy, Viscount Grafton. When Henri's father expressed their thanks but regretted the de Marechals kept only workhorses that were not suitable for such an occasion, the king waved these objections aside and said both the viscount and Henri must choose horses from the royal stable. Henri adored hunting, and to be invited to take part in a grand venery at thirteen years old was unheard of. And oh, to have a fine mount instead of his old pony! How he would fly at a gallop through the forest to the call of the horns and the barking of the dogs! Henri was almost sick with excitement at the prospect as they set off with the court to Chambord, the royal hunting lodge in the Loire Valley, surrounded by dark, mysterious forests full of game.

Chambord! Henri was too excited to sleep, waiting impatiently for the final preparations to be completed on the first day of the hunt. He and his father were dressing by candlelight in the predawn darkness when Henri's father was summoned by the king's chamberlain. Left on his own, Henri was unable to eat breakfast and hopped about in the thrilling melee of baying hounds, handlers, prancing horses and grooms, torches, and hunting horns, waiting for the signal to mount and wishing his father would hurry back. Then his father reappeared, looking grave. He interrupted Henri's exclamation that he would remember this as the best day of his life and told him he would have to stay behind.

Henri had stared at him, aghast. "Impossible, Father, my horse is saddled! No, no!"

His father sighed and said, "Remember, you are only a page and at court by His Majesty's indulgence. It is because he has formed a good opinion of you that he commands you to stay behind and keep watch on the English emissary's daughter. The child is a little English savage, but her mother is dead and she is the apple of her father's eye. They say Lord Grafton takes the child with him everywhere, and the king has just been informed he insisted on bringing her to Chambord. The king is furious, of course—the English have no sense of decorum, no sense of etiquette, no sense of anything civilized, but there's nothing to be done. The child's been nothing but trouble, keeps running off from her nurse, who is too fat to run after her. The footmen have fished her out of the fountains many times, the grooms discovered her in the stables under the hooves of the king's favorite hunter, where she sent the horse into a frantic state and was nearly trampled, and yesterday at Chambord, as she is fond of puppies, she slipped into the kennels and let loose a valuable litter bred for stag hunting. They have scattered into the forest, probably eaten by boars. I need not tell you how angry the loss of these dogs made the king, but he is determined to agree to this treaty and keep France out of another war. We have reached a delicate point in negotiations. If anything befalls the wretched girl, it would upset everything. His Majesty assured Lord Grafton his favorite and most trustworthy page would ensure her safety.

"Therefore you must stay behind and keep watch on her while we're gone. Make sure she does not drown, get trampled by the horses, or fall into the pigsties to be eaten by the pigs. In short, you are not to leave her side. Keep her safe, whatever it takes."

"But, Father, to miss the *hunt* to play nursemaid for a *girl*," he protested, sick with dismay.

"Shh! Here is Mademoiselle Sophia," his father said as the fat nurse waddled up to hand over her charge. *The sooner the better,* the nurse's expression said.

"Mademoiselle, I present my son Henri. He is to have the honor of being your friend and guardian while your papa is gone to hunt." Sophia squinted up at Henri and grinned. Henri looked down at her with loathing. She slipped a sticky hand into his. Henri snatched his away.

The king, the English envoy, and their entourage emerged from the château, and the signal to mount sounded. Harnesses jingled, the hounds strained under the keepers' whips. Draughts of brandy were handed up to the mounted hunting party, and the beaters set off. A horn sounded the blast to begin the hunt.

Henri directed a look of pure anguish at his father. His father said sharply, "Henri, this is a mark of the king's favor. I depend on that. You depend on that! Now do what you must to keep the child safe until her father returns." With those parting words, Henri's father mounted and joined the throng behind the royal party. The horns sounded again, and the hunt rode off toward the dark forest, leaving Henri gazing forlornly after it. Seething with the injustice of life, and close to tears, he watched them disappear, the horns and cries of the hunting dogs growing fainter and fainter in the dark, enticing depths of the forest.

He scowled down at the loathsome child and told her in French that she was ugly as a monkey. He would call her Miss Monkey—*Mademoiselle Singe*. She didn't speak French. She beamed up at him. While he had no choice but to keep her out of trouble, he swore to make her as miserable as possible in the process. He would treat her as sternly as the kennel masters treated the dogs. He refused to speak to her in English and addressed her, coldly, only in French. Seething, he fed her with bonbons on which he had spat, and let her ride his pony, which he prodded with a sharp stick to make it gallop and buck so that she tumbled to the ground.

But the child was impervious to Henri's ill treatment. No matter how horrid Henri was, it failed to dent her stubborn adoration. He found it was extremely difficult to make her cry.

Even after they had returned to Versailles from Chambord and Henri expected to be released from nursemaid duties, she had stuck to him like a shadow. This had irritated Henri to distraction, but he dared not show it, because Madame de Pompadour was amused. Henri had gritted his teeth and longed for Lord Grafton's mission to end. He tried very hard to get her into trouble—he had indeed set her on his pony and sent her cantering down Versailles's grand mirrored hall, but despite the havoc and mess and broken glass, she did not get the beating Henri had hoped for such an exploit. Henri had, at the hands of his furious father.

When the day of their departure for England came, Sophia had clung to Henri, demanding in much-improved French, "Henri, when I grow up to be a beautiful lady like Madame, will you come to England and marry me?"

Madame de Pompadour had actually laughed and chucked the nasty child under her chin, and the king smiled and said, "I think, Henri, you cannot refuse such an advantageous match. It is settled, is it not? I congratulate you."

Despising all adults, a seething Henri had no choice but to acquiesce graciously. He replied with a courtier's bow and even held out his arm to escort the child to her waiting carriage as if she were a departing princess. To his disgust, Sophia threw her arms around his neck and kissed him. He longed to strangle her. *Please, please, go back to England, you spawn of Satan,* he prayed silently as the carriage door slammed. Sophia leaned so far out the carriage window to wave and blow him good-bye kisses that she nearly fell out. "May your ship sink in the Channel," Henri muttered as he waved back.

Now, in the wilds of nowhere, he was rather glad to see her again. "Of course, *Mademoiselle Singe*! Delightful to see you again. Turn your back!" Henri exclaimed.

"Why?"

"Because I am coming to you. Or look, if you like!" he said carelessly. A woman had never complained before. Holding his clothes over his head, he waded on, and he managed to reach the other side with his clothes dry. Sophia had turned aside modestly, but he heard Venus gasp.

"Don't look, Venus!"

"My dear *Mademoiselle Singe*, allow me to explain the curious position in which I find myself . . . ," he began, dressing hastily, thinking that his hat smelled more rancid than ever. Then he was distracted by the picnic, still spread out and uneaten. "Oh, Sophia, my little monkey, is that ham? Is that . . . cake? I've eaten nothing but dried leather for months, I am starving!"

Sophia turned her head back to look at him. "I might have known what you were really after with your 'delightful to see you.' The Honorable Sophia Grafton, if you please! I beg you will notice I am quite grown-up. You may address me as Miss Grafton, not Sophia, certainly not Miss Monkey. Then perhaps I'll allow you a morsel . . ."

"Oh, quite grown-up, indeed! I noticed that at once. Miss Graf . . . Sophy, please!" Henri sank to his knees and fell on the biscuits and ham.

"No, you didn't. You didn't recognize me at the ball!"

"I saw an elegant miss in some rather fine pearls. How was I to recognize a she-devil of five with muddy skirts?" Henri retorted with as much acerbity as a crammed mouth allowed.

She smiled with a touch of her former liveliness. "You promised to come to England and marry me. In front of the king. You proved false. So typical of a Frenchman. My godmother thought the French an untrustworthy race, and she was right."

"Mmm. Ham! Delicious, I'll just eat the rest if I may . . . my *dear* Sophia, you were practically an infant. The king and Madame may have thought you were sweet, but they were deceived. Persistent, you were always persistent when you wanted something, used to getting your way, quite a spoiled, nasty child."

"I was nothing of the sort! I adored you. I did everything you told me to do. Though you were not particularly kind, and I had many bruises. But I had adventures with you, and that was far more interesting than life with Nurse. After we left, I missed you terribly, you know. It had been such fun. And then, there you were, whirling round the governor's ballroom in Williamsburg like your coattails were on fire, waving your handkerchief as if to put it out, bounding in circles round poor Mrs. Fitzwilliam." She collapsed into giggles.

"I'm not to be held responsible. Some gentlemen forced me to drink a fearsome concoction called *julerp*. Horrible!"

"*That* was obvious." Sophia gave a final hiccup of laughter. "But what madness possessed you to come to Virginia? England is almost at war with France over some territory or other in the colonies. Though in Williamsburg, the talk was all of the *Italian* dancing master . . . Aha! I wonder . . ."

Henri shrugged, mouth too full of bread and ham to answer. He tried to think of a plausible explanation.

"How very odd to see you in Williamsburg, Sophy, let alone here in the wilderness. But I suppose your father was posted to Virginia?" he asked. He was puzzled that no one had mentioned Lord Grafton's name while he had been in Williamsburg, though he had listened attentively to every scrap of gossip.

Having finished the ham and bread and two brandied peaches, he delved back into the basket.

Her smile faded. "Oh, Henri, if only you *had* come to England and married me. It would have been worth your while. There is a very large estate in England, and I am my father's only heir. Though, I confess there is . . . just at the moment . . . a difficulty with the English inheritance."

"Oh. What a pity."

"Yes, but I also have a property settled on me here. Wildwood Plantation, part of my dowry and untouched by the English difficulties. Perhaps you should reconsider marrying me," Sophia said lightly.

Henri stopped eating and weighed up the possibility. Lord Grafton was an important man, highly placed in the English aristocracy, and wealthy. If Sophia was his only heir, marrying her for her fortune might have been preferable to this present adventure. It wasn't as if she had grown up ugly, and though he detested her, as a Frenchman he knew that actually liking a wife-to-be wasn't absolutely necessary provided her dowry was adequate. If he asked for Sophia's hand now, saying he wished to honor his engagement, would Lord Grafton be likely to consent? Overlook the fact he was French? Use his influence to get Sophia's fiancé out of the colony and back to France? Would Sophia assist him in such a farce? Would she understand that it was a farce? Would Lord Grafton believe it? On the whole, he thought the answer to everything would be a resounding no.

"Fruitcake? . . . How delicious . . . ," he exclaimed.

Sophia's eyes narrowed. "I still don't understand what you were doing in Williamsburg pretending to be an Italian . . . no, perhaps I do. It was the talk of Williamsburg, whether there would be a war with France, whether British forces would attack the French on the Ohio." She considered. "Henri, is it possible you . . . were you spying for France?"

Henri shrugged and tried to think of a way to deny this convincingly.

"Spying! Of course you were, otherwise you'd never have assumed such a strange disguise. Dancing master indeed! I'm surprised you weren't discovered and hung. Though I daresay you would hardly look worse a-hanging than you do now. Or smell worse as a corpse." She wrinkled her nose and sniffed. "Your hat is quite . . . Ugh!"

Henri tossed the hat into the bushes. "Well, you must tell me, why you are in Virginia and at the ball with that *cochon* of a planter. They say he's married, but I gathered his wife was likely to die, and he may be looking to marry again. But . . . surely *you* don't find him appealing enough to be his mistress. And I cannot imagine that your father likes him," murmured Henri, attacking the fruitcake.

She placed a hand on his arm. "Don't eat so fast, you'll be sick. My father died last year, and I am trapped in hell with Thomas de Bouldin, whom he appointed as my guardian. You must help me get away from him, and Venus too. Poor Venus is carrying Thomas's child. You of all people have cunning enough to rescue us."

Henri made a noise with his mouth full that might have been an expression of curiosity about how Sophia had found herself in this desperate situation, or a demur that his powers of cunning were sufficient to do anything about it.

"Oh? How terrible! You must tell me everything," he said, finishing the fruitcake.

CHAPTER 13
SOPHIA'S STORY

"Thomas has made me a prisoner, and I fear for my life."

"Sophy, surely you exaggerate? As I remember, you were your father's darling. He would not have made such a dangerous character your guardian."

Sophia sighed. "My father knew Thomas when they were boys, but Thomas went to Virginia to make his fortune, and my father had no idea what he had become. Everything changed with my father's death, but the seeds were sown when my father retired from the king's service and the king rewarded him with a large patent of land here in Virginia.

"Then my father appointed an agent experienced in growing tobacco, who visited the patent nearly four years ago and reported that it would grow a fortune's worth of the best tobacco, but it required investment to clear land, plant crops, and build a house. On the advice of his lawyers, my father borrowed heavily against our English estate to provide the investment needed to turn it into a tobacco plantation called Wildwood.

"After Papa's death, I learned that he had borrowed and borrowed again, at a very high rate of interest, and secured the loan against our English property at a time when income from that property was declining. Papa, I fear, tended to ignore such things, and his manner of living had always been very lavish. It would have been inconceivable to him that a Grafton should economize, and in any case, he believed the tobacco would solve everything. Inexplicably, by the time of my father's death, no tobacco had been shipped to our English factors, who were waiting to receive it. All this time the debt was slowly crippling the estate. Papa had never spoken to me of financial matters, and I was in mourning and knew nothing of it until last summer, when our family solicitors informed me that the Grafton estate would have to be let."

"But why not sell this Wildwood?"

"Wildwood had been made part of my dowry, and it was untouched by the debt. That's why Papa made Thomas my guardian. He thought Thomas in Virginia would be best placed of all his friends to advise me regarding plantation matters. I accepted Thomas's invitation to visit him, but my purpose in coming was to take possession of Wildwood and see that tobacco pays off the debts on our English estate. Before it is too late."

"You, a tobacco planter?" snorted Henri, choking back laughter. "A *woman*? Especially a grand English miss?"

Sophia tossed her head. "And why not? I will learn because I must. But Wildwood is still far away, and by accepting Thomas's invitation, I accomplished two things. I felt it proper to pay Anne de Bouldin a visit, as she was an invalid. And doing so has brought me part of the way from Williamsburg."

"And where is Wildwood?" asked Henri.

"Somewhere to the south and west. But I don't know how I'm to reach it. I left England with little money, and most of that was spent in Williamsburg. I can hardly strike out alone"—Sophia pointed to the river and the forest—"there. At the ball I met Colonel Washington, who seemed such a gentleman that I had resolved to confide in him and ask his advice and perhaps his help. Then I recognized you—*il Signor Valentino* everyone spoke of—despite your peculiar disguise. I decided to ask you instead. I would have had to think of some excuse for accepting the protection of the dancing master—you know what everyone would think—but before I could do so, Thomas insisted we leave the ball, saying we had an early start for his plantation next morning.

"There was no time to send you a message. I looked back as we left Williamsburg, fearing I had lost a chance to escape. That feeling deepened as we drove on. To my relief, Thomas rode ahead on horseback and I was alone in the uncomfortable carriage. The Negro women followed in an open cart, some of them noticeably pregnant. Such a week followed, of rough roads, taverns full of fleas, a few miserable farms. Still, the country is pretty enough, and at the end of our journey, I expected to see a fine hospitable house with whitewashed outbuildings and neat fields such as the plantation homes I had visited near Williamsburg. But we turned into an overgrown drive that ended before a ramshackle building, part brick, part wood. Beyond it were dilapidated outbuildings, and then fields and a forest beyond. There was an overwhelming air of gloom and ruin.

"My bedroom had odds and ends of furniture that had been handsome once, but the bed hangings and curtains were frayed and dirty, the candlesticks tarnished, and the basin and ewer cracked. I heard mice almost under my feet. The dust made me sneeze. As an invited guest, it was not the welcome I expected, but I reminded myself Madame de Bouldin was very ill.

"I told Thomas I hoped to make myself useful during my visit and help care for his wife, but he retorted that was his privilege as her husband. He allowed me a brief glance into Anne's room, and all I could see was a white face on the pillow. Thomas said that she was asleep most of the time. Despite the bad impression I had formed of Thomas's character, I was touched when I saw how solicitous he was for his poor, suffering wife, how he insisted on administering her medicine himself, morning and evening."

"Did he indeed?" said Henri, recalling the gossip about Thomas de Bouldin's wife in the governor's dining room and suddenly alert.

"I began to wish I could cut my visit short and go to my new home. The atmosphere in the house was oppressive with dirt, silence, and illness. The household slaves were sullen, inclined to do nothing unless threatened with a beating. I persuaded Venus to wash the curtains and bed hangings in exchange for a warm shawl and a petticoat. The poor girl had only a rough shift and was glad to have something warm. Thomas's slaves generally have to wrap themselves in whatever rags they find to keep off the cold.

"The days passed, and I realized I had no way of leaving until Thomas next attended the House of Burgesses, but I learned Publick Times would not take place until early spring. By then I rather understood that Wildwood lay farther to the south and west, and Thomas would be traveling north and east to Williamsburg. Anne's condition remained unchanged, Thomas did not encourage me to interrupt her rest, and he himself was always absent between breakfast and dinner, which was a blessing. I stayed by the fire in my room and read or sewed, waiting for the winter to pass so I could leave. The solicitors had given me the deeds to my property and the map showing its location, intending I should hand them over to Thomas for safekeeping, but of course I did not. I first hoped Thomas might have neighbors, that I would meet someone who might help me, but we are so deep in the country that Thomas has no near neighbors. Even the local militia has to be assembled from miles away, and unusually for Virginia, where every plantation house seems always full of company, no one had visited Thomas.

"After Christmas there was a thaw, and Thomas announced that he was called away on plantation business and would be gone for a fortnight. I again offered to take over Anne's care. He agreed, provided I could be counted on to give her medicine. Everything depended on her medicine. He told me several times how many spoonfuls must be mixed with water morning and evening when she had her tea. I promised to administer it faithfully. All she would eat, if she ate at all, he warned me, was a special gruel the cook made for her."

"And this medicine, did you give it to her?"

"I tried, but she refused it. The morning after he left, I carried up the tea tray with the medicine to Anne's room and dismissed the slave lighting the fire, saying I would care for the mistress myself. When I drew open her curtains, I saw that she lay in squalor. The curtains and coverlet on her bed, once fine chintz, were dirtier and more ragged than those in my bedroom, and the four-poster bed had a broken leg and was propped on a barrel. She looked at the tray, then gazed into my eyes as I helped her to sit up against her pillows. She placed a thin hand on my cheek and whispered, 'Miss Grafton. You have a kind face. Do not give me my medicine yet. Let me have my tea first.'

"I feared what would happen if she failed to have her medicine, but did as she asked. She smiled faintly and patted the bed for me to sit down. I helped her to drink a little and eat a bite or two of gruel before she fell back on the pillows. She looked frail, but she might have been beautiful once.

"She asked if I would read to her, saying it had been a long time since she had had the pleasure of hearing her favorite psalms. She had a Bible on her dressing table, and I read as she sipped her tea, thinking she would soon sleep again. But when I looked up, she seemed more alert than before, staring into the fire that crackled cheerfully. 'Have your medicine in the last of the tea now,' I said, lifting the pot, but she waved her hand and whispered, 'No! It makes me sleep. I am always asleep, and when I am not, I only feel myself getting weaker and weaker. Save for a little gruel now and then, I can eat nothing. Always asleep. Thomas . . . the medicine . . . he insists I need it . . . but . . .'

"She looked as gray, thin, and haggard as any beggar on the streets of London, but the gruel Thomas insisted she have was colorless and nasty. I thought it odd Thomas did not order her to have better care but hoped it was only because men did not understand how invalids should be cared for. Remembering how our housekeeper looked after my father in his illness, I made her nourishing food with my own hands, milk toast and broth and custard, and she began to improve even though she continued to refuse her medicine.

"At Anne's request, I read her psalms, then sat with my workbasket while she slept. When she woke, we would talk, and she asked me who I was and how I came to be in Virginia. I told her about my father and how he had known Thomas when they were boys, and about my old merry life in England when I had no cares. Anne seemed to enjoy listening. I thought her improvement remarkable."

"And did you expect Thomas would be grateful?" Henri laughed harshly.

"Of course! So I took the liberty of telling the head overseer, Mackland, that I would act for the mistress, and from now on the house slaves—the young maid Venus; a middle-aged woman named Saskia, who seemed to be housekeeper and cook; her child, Cully, who waited at table; and St. Peter, the poor coachman—would remain in the house and be given their orders by me. The overseer, who stank of spirits, sneered, 'You ain't mistress yet, and if I says they work in the fields, that's where they go.' But I assumed a haughty air and warned him that Thomas would punish his insolence if I complained. He believed me and sullenly said I could do as I pleased.

"It was a relief to have a useful occupation, nursing Anne, and the house slaves were glad of their respite from field work. I set them to work cleaning, dusting and polishing the floors, beating carpets, airing beds, scrubbing the larder. They grumbled and were as insubordinate as they dared be, but instead of threatening to have them beaten, I promised that they would have a chicken for their dinner and a glass of rum if all was done well. They worked with a better will after that, and I felt that if I could but effect Anne's recovery and clean and tidy the house,

I could leave for Wildwood with a clear conscience. I had begun to feel great sympathy for Anne.

"But one day she wished to walk a little. I called Venus to help support her. Between us we walked her up and down the hall, until Anne's arm touched Venus's stomach and she felt it swollen beneath Venus's shift. Angrily she demanded to know if Thomas was the father. Venus's eyes widened in fear, and she nodded. 'Missus, I didn't want him to!'

"Anne's voice took on a hard tone I had not heard before. 'Slattern! You seduced him! And after my kindness to you as a child, this is your gratitude. He would not have touched you otherwise. I should have you whipped senseless. Leave us!'

"This was cruel and coarse and shocking, and when I helped Anne back to bed, she must have seen from my expression that I found it so. She grumbled that the female slaves were fornicating animals who were always eager for a chance to seduce the master and men were just men. It was the female slaves' fault if Thomas got them with child. He usually sold the children when they were six, unless a child was very pretty. It was very trying to see children with Thomas's features; if she had her way, they would be sold much sooner, but men had no consideration for the feelings of mere wives. Saskia's son, Cully, was one of his, not yet sold because he was lame and no good for field work, but he was learning to serve at table. Mulatto house slaves were in demand, and if well trained, Cully would fetch a good price when the time came. She spoke with the resignation of a betrayed wife, but with none of the outrage a Christian should feel. And this from a woman who listened to psalms by the hour!

"Anne merely shrugged at my shock, said it was the way of Virginia; slaves were valuable property, like a good horse. She had brought many in her own dowry, including four-year-old Venus, who had just been weaned and taken from her mother. 'How do you suppose we would have our plantations, if not for the slaves?' she demanded. Negroes were savage and evil by nature and born to serve white masters and mistresses. Anne insisted she had done her duty Christianizing them, and explained they must patiently bear the yoke of servitude set upon them by God. She even read them the Bible on Sundays.

"Oh, Henri, slavery makes monsters of the owners and hypocrites of their Christian beliefs. I am ashamed to say that I had never considered the matter seriously, at least not in relation to myself or to Wildwood. And I fear that Mr. Barker has bought slaves for Wildwood. I do not wish to become one of the monsters, so I must free them."

"Fine sentiments, Sophy, but who will grow your tobacco? You face a difficult choice."

"I must not let it be so. My godmother believed that those who traffic in African slaves are doomed to hell. I never understood that until I came to Virginia," said Sophia bitterly.

"And after you took such care of Anne, was Thomas grateful?" asked Henri. He felt too full and sleepy to be discussing Sophia's problems any longer. He closed his eyes.

"I'll tell you how grateful. The next afternoon Thomas arrived with two strangers, rough men, one of whom was obviously ill. Thomas shouted for Cully and ordered him to show the men to an upstairs bedroom. Then he went straight up to Anne's room and I anticipated his happiness at seeing Anne better. Half an hour later, he stormed out in a fury, shouting for me, and demanded to know why I had disobeyed his orders about the medicine. I assured him she had improved without it. His face turned purple with rage, and I thought he would either strike me or fall down in a fit of apoplexy. He swore a vile oath that Anne would now take a large enough dose to make up for all she had missed. He rushed upstairs to her room again, and I heard a faint cry, then it was silent. When Thomas came out, he locked her door and pocketed the key. I never saw Anne again.

"I learned from Saskia that Thomas was heavily in debt to the men who accompanied him home. The slaves believed the men were slave traders and were all terrified that Thomas intended selling them to pay the debt. No one was more frightened than poor Saskia, who has always feared Cully would be sold and thinks that only his limp has saved him. But the slaves' worst fears were prevented for the moment because the man who was ill grew a great deal worse. I went in once or twice with basins of gruel, wishing it were in my power to poison him rather than give him nourishment, but I must leave life and death in God's hands. His eyes were red, and he was shivering and moaning with fever and pain in his limbs, and it gave me satisfaction to think that perhaps God had seen fit to make him suffer for the evil he does. The man who was not ill watched Thomas like a hawk, and stayed close to him.

"Cully was ordered to take food up to the man who was ill and reported the man was covered in red spots. I feared smallpox, but Thomas said it was only measles, the man's children had had them when they left. He muttered he wished it had been smallpox and that both his visitors were dead of it.

"I don't know whether Anne caught the measles or her weakened constitution gave way or whether something worse happened to her, but within a fortnight of Thomas's return, she died. She was buried beyond the orchard with little ceremony and no clergyman present, just Thomas and two male slaves who dug the grave. I stayed behind and said a prayer for her soul at the graveside."

Henri's eyes flew open. "Sophy, Thomas sounds like a murderer. He poisoned his wife."

"Yes, now I believe he is. And when I returned to my room, the leather pouch with the deeds and the map was missing. I knew at once that Thomas had taken it, and I was afraid. If I had been anxious to leave before, I was desperate now, but I had to find the map and deeds and some means of travel.

"That same week Thomas returned from his rounds of the plantation in an expansive mood because several of his slave women had given birth. He was usually so moody and irascible on account of his two visitors that I decided to seize my chance while he was refreshing himself with a glass of rum in the disordered den he calls his library. I went to the study door and with vile hypocrisy congratulated him on the increase in his slaves. Then I smiled and said I was longing to visit my property. 'No need,' he said, I could not inherit it until I was twenty-one. Almost another year. Unless, he said slyly, I were to marry. He admitted he had the deeds, had taken them from my room for protection. 'Had to keep them safe, risk of fire, you know. Black devils would burn us in our beds if I didn't keep a strong hold.'

"I sighed, assumed an expression of extreme stupidity, and made my eyes as wide as possible, like this—do wake up, Henri, and attend—and said that I had tried to read the documents but the deeds were so long. I found them incomprehensible, and I could make no sense of the map. How was I to understand maps of Virginia? Oh, it was all so confusing! Could he show me?

"He laughed at my ignorance. 'A pretty girl has no need to trouble her head about such things when there's a man to help her.'

"'Oh, Thomas, I daresay you are clever enough to read the map. Do explain where my plantation is,' I simpered. 'Is it far?'

"'I'll show you.' He helped himself to another glass of rum, pulled me closer, and opened a small leather trunk filled with papers. Thomas took out one, and I saw it was his marriage license. He looked at it thoughtfully for a moment, smiled, and muttered he had no more need of *that* one. He said that a Virginia girl would be ashamed to be unmarried at my age. I had better find a husband. He laughed heartily as if this were a great joke. I spotted my pouch. 'But is my property near to yours?' I asked.

"'No. Stand close, and I'll help you find it on the map,' he leered, spreading my documents on the desk. 'And perhaps help you to a husband as well.'

"I desperately needed the information he could give me, but it was horrible to feel myself pressed to his side, so I tried to divert his attention and his hands from me to the papers by uttering all sorts of nonsense about what wonderful heads men have for business! Though Thomas has less cause for vanity than any man alive, he was vain enough to puff himself up even larger than he is and apply himself to an explanation.

"He held up the documents he calls the *letters patent*. 'This is the grant from His Majesty to your father, a good deal of explanation about your father's service to the Crown and so on. You needn't trouble to read it. And these are the conveyance of title and a description of the property. You needn't bother with them either.'

"He smoothed out the last one, an expanse of heavy parchment marked with lines and bumps and odd notations. 'And this is the map. Your property is here, in the southernmost part of the colony, that patent marked with a broken line and the Grafton arms. Williamsburg's there.' Thomas pointed out 'W'burg' in the east on the other side of the map, then drew his finger west. 'We're here. That black line is the Fluvanna, boundary of my plantation on the south. Hmmm?' His pointing finger wandered to my bodice, and I tried to squirm away and still see the map. His breathing grew heavy as he traced a greasy finger along the Fluvanna and down a route with more black lines to the Grafton arms. Fending him off was distracting, but I gathered something about the New River and mountains and a valley between Frog Mountain and another called Little Frog Mountain.

"Trying to sound as stupid as possible, I giggled that Frog Mountain was a curious name and asked, 'And is it near? I should love to see mountains in the shape of frogs!' I had to edge away again from a hand that was no longer occupied with pointing. He traced along the map again, and I fear I paid attention with only half a mind because he was breathing down my neck. I think he was showing me where rivers connect and something about a trail overland, and somewhere there's a trading post, called a station, along the way because there are hunters and settlers traveling west. I said it didn't seem far, and Thomas said it might take a few weeks on horseback and something about it being surprising that His Majesty made a grant in that part of the colony. He wouldn't have believed it if he hadn't seen the map and the patent. He said that of course he hadn't seen it in person, not with the Indian raids on settlements in the western part of the colony.

"'Oh? Is there a difficulty?' I asked.

"'Deep in Indian territory, you know. The Crown's been anxious to keep settlers off the Indian lands in that part of the colony. I daresay there's been a treaty with the Indians if you've a grant there. England's eager enough to make treaties with the murdering savages. I say let 'em be damned, the land belongs to those who make it profit. Had some savages as slaves once, but too hard to make them work. They died. Easier to drive the blacks,' he droned on, trying to lean on me, and at that point I stepped back, unable to endure his foul breath any longer. 'But what a vast, pretty property, worth a fortune!' He licked his lips and leered down at me. 'They say the fellow Barker named it Wild Copse. Plenty of timber, I imagine. They want Virginia timber in England. Valuable. Wish I had more.'

"'The name is Wildwood, actually. Oh, how I long to see it!'

"'If you're a good girl, I'll take you. I expect the house needs a woman's touch, hmmm?' He edged closer, but I managed to slip out of reach. Repellant though he is, I dared not discourage him entirely. Thomas was my only means of getting there, though this is not an appealing prospect. So I pretended to be coy, squealing, 'Ooooh. Sir!' in what I hoped was an encouragingly coquettish manner, and fled. Thomas roared with laughter and let me go.

"The next day he cornered me and bluntly proposed, saying if I was so anxious to see my plantation, I should have my first glimpse of it as his wife. We would be married. I protested that Anne was hardly cold in her grave. He smirked and told me to consider my reputation—did I think now that Anne was dead I could remain in the house with him without scandal unless we were married? Married we would be, he said, as soon as he returned from the spring session of Publick Times. He would have the banns posted in Williamsburg.

"I pretended to agree, begging to go with him so that we might be married at the church there, since there was no church anywhere near Thomas's plantation. If I could only reach Williamsburg, I planned to throw myself on the governor's mercy. But Thomas's expression grew sly, and he told me that in Virginia it was the custom for girls to be married from home, and I must stay behind to plan my wedding. He moved to kiss me, and again I slipped out of reach and ran.

"The man who had arrived so poorly recovered, and I heard Thomas telling him, 'Congratulate me, sir. I'm to marry again, wife-to-be's rich. So you'll have your money.'

"Then the second man caught measles. The first watched Thomas as his friend had done, with a pistol to hand. Thomas grew angry and impatient and at last insisted the three of them leave today for Williamsburg, though the second man looked like death and was so ill he could scarcely sit a horse. Thomas will be back next month, with a clergyman to marry us. Thank God you are here! Take me and Venus to my plantation before he does. We dare not go alone. Henri? Are you listening?"

CHAPTER 14
RESCUERS

Henri forced his eyes open. "Sophy . . . what a terrible story! But I cannot help you. My companion and I must get to La Nouvelle-Orléans the moment he's well enough. It's urgent, and illness delayed us too long as it is. Thierry's waiting for me downriver with some Indian guides and an interpreter. I'm meant to be hunting or catching fish. We need food."

"Surely you won't leave me here after everything I've told you," Sophia exclaimed indignantly. "You couldn't!"

Henri felt very tired, as well as uncomfortably full. His stomach hurt. The sun was low behind the trees, and he would have to travel in the dark to return to camp. It would be a dangerous trip. He wasn't in the mood to argue. "I'll come back for you as soon as . . . er . . . as soon as I've completed my business in La Nouvelle-Orléans. I swear it."

"How long will that take?"

"Not long, Sophy, a week, perhaps two. Before Thomas returns from Williamsburg. Of course I won't let that man marry you. I give you my word," he promised.

Sophia sighed and looked at him gratefully. Henri could always tell what a woman was thinking, and he was relieved that she believed him. Henri had only a vague grasp of Virginia geography and he was quite certain it would take many weeks just to reach La Nouvelle-Orléans, and once he reached it, he and Thierry were sailing for home as soon as possible. The fact he was lying bothered him, but it was hardly the first time he had lied to a woman. It was often necessary to lie to women.

"Oh, Henri!" she breathed. "I knew I could depend on you! At least I can supply you for your journey. We've food—hams in the smokehouse and dried fruit left from last autumn, a cheese I made myself. It won't take us long to fetch them. Thomas and his friends are gone, so I can give you a horse. The only part of his plantation Thomas cares about is the stables and the horses he races or sells. They're the only thing treated well on this plantation."

"Cheese? And a horse?" Really, this was forgiving of the poor girl, whom he would, alas, leave to her fate. Henri was desperate for better food than pemmican, but it was terribly late. "Kind of you, Sophy, but I must—"

"And I think there's a whole fruitcake in the larder."

"I'll need to be quick," he said. Perhaps his stomach didn't hurt that badly. He stood and offered his hand to pull Sophia up.

She smiled up at him as she took it. "Naturally! The sooner you leave, the sooner you'll return for me. And Venus, of course."

"And Venus." It was unimaginable that he would take a pregnant slave! He smiled at the absurdity of it.

"Come along, Venus," said Sophia, retrieving her paint box and quilt.

Henri followed Sophia and Venus along an overgrown path from the river through a patch of woods. Through the trees he could see cleared fields and a ramshackle house surrounded by outbuildings. Slaves were at work in the fields, breaking up the earth and digging up a large stump. An overseer sat on another stump and watched them, a whip by his side, pistols in his belt, and a jug of the kind used for home-brewed spirits at his feet. The overseer spat, then took a long drink and tightened his hold on the whip. "You there, Seth," he called menacingly, "dig harder."

A large slave straightened up. "Ground still hard, massa." But he swung his hoe more vigorously than before.

"And you, Nott," the overseer bellowed at another slave who had also straightened up and was rubbing his back. "Don't you slack off neither, 'less you want a taste of the whip."

Sophia put up a hand and stopped Henri before they emerged from the trees. "Stay out of sight. That's Mackland, the head overseer," she said in a low voice. "He's a vicious brute who put the cage on St. Peter's head and, like Thomas, preys on the Negro women and girls. Thomas does not mind who fathers new slaves," she said angrily. "And they say that when Mackland cannot lay hands on a slave to his liking, an animal serves him equally well." She shuddered. "He's unpredictable and dangerous, especially when he's drunk. And he hates Seth, keeps urging Thomas to sell him. I think he's afraid of Seth."

Behind them, Venus hissed something that could have been agreement or a curse. Henri turned quickly to see Venus's eyes blazing with hate. Quickly she smoothed her face into a blank expression once again.

"Over there," said Sophia in a low voice, "is the barn where the wagons and cows are kept. And then the stables." She pointed to a dilapidated building surrounded by a mucky farmyard and a pigsty. A female slave made her way from the house to what looked to Henri like the chicken coop, in a sea of mud. "The slave quarters," murmured Sophia. "The overseers have the key and lock everyone in at night, except for any unfortunate women they fancy. I keep Venus with me at night, and we secure the door with a chest."

Mackland was shouting something in the direction of the house. "Lazer! *Lazer!* Git out here! Seth needin' to feel the whip again, Nott too. Tobacco don't get planted before he gets back, de Bouldin lowers our wages."

"No, massa, we workin'," protested the slaves, but there was a shout from inside the house, and then a younger man ambled out with his hat on crooked and groping for the coiled whip at his belt. He seemed unsteady on his feet.

"That's the other overseer, Lazer. They make free with Thomas's rum when he's away, then water it before he comes back. Thomas knows, but their harsh treatment of the slaves ensures the work is done, so he turns a blind eye," said Sophia.

Lazer might have been drunk, but he swung his arm hard, and there was a crack of rawhide and a cry from Seth, who fell to the ground, arms held up to protect his head. There was another crack, then another. The man Lazer coiled his whip. He hitched up his trousers and gave Seth a couple of hard kicks. He turned and swung the whip at Nott, then ambled back into the house. There was a rattle of leg irons, and the slave Meshack, whom Henri could now see was shackled to Seth, helped him up.

"Oh, Seth. Seth," muttered Venus. Henri turned to look at her and stepped back. Her eyes were narrowed, fixed on Lazer. "The Devil take him away down to hell where he belong. He die hard. I sees it happen . . . ," whispered Venus. "He open his eyes, he see Death coming for him, Devil close behind. I know. I sees it all."

Sophia murmured, "Hush, Venus. Soon, it'll be dark. That's when they lock the slaves in and go back to their drinking."

The sun was setting, and the two overseers were cracking their whips to herd the shuffling slaves back to their chicken-coop cabins. Chains clinked. "Git in!" Mackland ordered, slammed the door and locked it, then ambled into the house.

Sophia pulled Henri into the barn. "I'll come back as quickly as I can. Give me those filthy clothes to burn. I'll bring you some of Thomas's things."

"But, Sophy, those men, how will you manage?" muttered Henri, stripping off his clothes. Poor Sophy was doing everything she could to help him, and in return he was about to abandon her to a murderer and two drunken brutes. He felt guilty, of course, but what could he do?

"With this." She reached into the embroidered housewife she wore at her waist and withdrew a small, beautifully worked weapon. "A lady's pocket pistol," she said coolly. "My father obtained it in Spain and brought it home as a curiosity. See, it has this little dagger that extends on the end. The dagger can be tipped with poison from this vial fitted just here. Moorish. Pretty, isn't it?"

Henri stopped undressing. "Is it loaded?"

"Of course it's loaded! As you nearly discovered today before I recognized you. It would be small protection otherwise. I obtained a good store of shot in Williamsburg and have practiced until my aim is true. I made sure Mackland and Lazer know that I keep it with me all the time. Now give me the rest of your things!"

Sophia and Venus disappeared. Naked and cold, Henri dove into some hay to keep warm until Sophia came back.

But it was dark; the hay was warm and soft. He was comfortable for the first time in months. He dozed off and dreamed he was back in France, and the girl by his side was calling him . . . he rolled over grinning, to embrace her, when he heard his name called again, imperiously. He woke with a start, unable to remember where he was, and surrounded by strange people. Then he realized it was Sophia holding a lantern and a bundle of clothes. "Finally, Henri! You slept so soundly I thought perhaps you had died. Put these on," she ordered.

Rubbing sleep from his eyes, Henri reached for the shirt she held out, then turned away for modesty's sake and pulled on some breeches. "I was afraid you had forgotten me . . . Ahhh!" He savored the feel of clean linen and broadcloth against his skin. Thomas's breeches were too large, but they could be held up with a length of rope lying nearby.

"What time is it?" he asked, trying to make the rope serve as a belt. "And the food—you didn't forget the cake?"

"I never forget things. But it's nearly ten," said Sophia briskly. "Later than I planned, but the preparations took more time than I had expected. Let us go now."

"What?" Breeches hoisted, Henri turned and realized that Sophia was wearing a riding habit. By her side Venus wore a traveling cloak. Seth and Nott and Meshack loomed behind her. Henri could smell agitation and fear and desperation.

"What preparations? Why are you dressed for hunting, Sophy?"

"Not hunting, riding. Because we're going with you."

"What?"

"We're all going to Wildwood. I took the chest of papers from Thomas's study. There's a map, and we can follow it. Nothing could be easier."

"Impossible, Sophy! The overseers will follow us."

"I've dealt with the overseers. I poured Anne's old medicine into a bottle of rum, which I left in plain view on the sideboard. I think the reason she slept all the time was that the medicine contained opiates. Markham and Lazer drank it and are insensible on the dining parlor floor. Venus and I tied them tightly and gave Meshack, Seth, and Nott their boots, weapons, and whips. We unlocked the slave quarters, and Nott sawed the shackles off the men and removed the cage from Peter's head. The slaves are free to go."

"Coming with me?" he shouted in disbelief. "*You freed Thomas's slaves?* What in God's name are you thinking? Mackland and Lazer will get loose eventually and bring the militia!"

Sophia was defiant. "I doubt they will, not soon. We tied them too tightly. If they finally work themselves free, they'll believe it was the rum and their own carelessness that allowed the slaves to tie them up and escape. We'll be far away, and they'll think more of saving themselves from Thomas than coming after us, especially if they think we've gone south through the Indians' territory, which is where my property lies. As a child Mackland saw his parents scalped. He's more afraid of Indians than of Thomas, and Lazer won't go alone. And they'll have no weapons—I've taken all the guns, gunpowder, and ammunition in the house and given some to the slaves. Some I kept for us. By the time Thomas returns a month from now, the overseers will have vanished. He'll alert the militia, but there are very few of the militia here, and Anne complained they're lazy and good-for-nothing at the best of times.

"Most of the slaves will go to Florida, to the Spanish. The slaves from Charleston told them about a place in Spanish Florida, Fort Mosay—or something like that—where they can be free if they turn Catholic and serve in the Spanish army. They plan to go through the swamp in the east part of the colony. Slave patrols don't like to follow, because there are escaped slaves who've have taken husbands and wives among the Indians there, and there are alligators and snakes and sands that suck a man down. I hope Thomas's slaves will be safe."

"Sophy, this is madness!"

Sophia shook her head. "No, it isn't! I haven't finished explaining my plan. Venus is too near her time to make such a hard journey, so she'll come with me. Seth won't abandon Venus, Meshack is Seth's half brother, and Nott is related to both of them, a cousin, I think. The rest of the family were sold away, and they wish to stay together. I've left my jewelry for Thomas in payment for the things I've taken, the horses and wagons and slaves, and written a bill of sale showing they're mine now. I've brought a copy for me, left one on Thomas's desk, and I forged his signature on both. Rather well, I think. So it all looks perfectly legal. I've promised to free everyone as soon as there's time to do the manumission papers, and if they'll stay and work for me, I'll give them land. Seth, Meshack, and Nott agreed.

"The men harnessed all the mules to the wagons, and we're taking the cows and a calf and the pigs, and a horse for each of us from the stable. The other slaves took the remaining horses and drove the rest of the livestock into the forest, because they can't take them into the swamp. We divided the cornmeal and what was in the smokehouse and the blankets and quilts. There's a trading post and ferry downriver on the way to my property—it's marked on the map—so I've brought some silver plate, candlesticks, and other things to barter, in case we need more supplies before we get there. I've thought of everything, and my jewelry is very valuable and more than fair payment. Come on."

Henri stared at her, speechless.

"I wasn't taken in by your promises, Henri. You've no intention of coming back for me, and it would likely take you months to get to La Nouvelle-Orléans and back. If I was anxious to escape before, it is now impossible for any of us to stay. We'll have to travel through the wilderness, and there are Indians, and it will be dangerous, so you must and will let us join your party. You have guides, and the more of us there are, the safer we'll be. When we reach my plantation, I'll make it worth your while by supplying you and your friend with horses and whatever you need for your journey to Louisiana."

Four horses were saddled and waiting. "Henri, you, I, Meshack, and Venus will ride. Nott and Seth will drive the wagons."

"I refuse to lead this . . . this *cavalcade*, this . . . this *grande procession*!" Henri spluttered indignantly. "Runaways. Wagons . . . cows. Don't imagine you can lead everyone into the wilderness like Moses. You are not Moses, and you won't get far. Thomas will follow you with the militia, the slaves will be caught, whipped or hung or buried alive—have that on your conscience—and woman or not, you'll be put in the stocks or prison or whipped yourself, and your Wildwood will be confiscated. You know how barbaric these people are—helping runaways is worse than murder. Impossible. I won't help you escape. You have no idea how dangerous the wilderness is, the animals, the Indians . . ." He stopped, out of breath. Sophia was aiming her pocket pistol at him.

"I'll shoot you if I have to. In the knee. You'll not be able to get away from us then. And it may fester so that your leg must be amputated.

Fortunately I brought a saw. It will be difficult to reach Louisiana on one leg. I tell you, Henri, we are all of us desperate, and we *will* go tonight, and we're going with you." Sophia's eyes narrowed, and she held the pistol steady.

The slave behind her murmured. "Tie him up, Miss Sophy?" Seth unwound a length of rope.

Henri weighed his choices. The militia would not be feckless; they would soon catch up, and he wouldn't be able to help Sophia and her runaways then. Best not to be tied up, so he could escape when the time came. He shrugged and surrendered. "As you wish, Sophy. I agree. There are some Cherokee guides with us. When we get there, we'll make the next part of the plan, perhaps negotiate with one of them to take you to Wildwood."

Nott helped Sophia mount, and Seth boosted a nervous Venus onto the broad back of a farm horse and said, "Don't worry none. This horse big but he good, steady, and slow. I choose him for you. You be safe riding him. You got to kick him a little to make him go." Seth and Nott each climbed onto a loaded wagon hitched to a pair of mules, and Meshack, armed with a loaded musket, rode another large farm horse behind the cows. The animals were restless, as if they too were anxious to be gone. The mules shook their harnesses, while the cows tied to wagons lowed urgently and pulled against the ropes. The horses, even the steady, slow one bearing Venus, seemed alert, shaking their heads and whinnying.

Sophia's horse, a highly strung hunter, shook his head and back-stepped and pawed the ground. "Whatever's the matter with them?" exclaimed Sophia, turning her mount in a circle. "Whoa there! What's set them off? Is there a wild animal?"

"Do you smell smoke?" asked Henri, sniffing.

"We must have left the smokehouse door open when we took the hams, and the fire's flared up. Whoa!" cried Sophia.

Behind them a woman panted in the darkness, "Miss Sophia, Miss Sophia! Wait for us, we coming with you! Venus need me to help when the baby born. Miss Sophia, don't leave us behind!"

"Saskia?" cried Sophia, peering into the darkness. "I thought you'd gone with the others."

"Mama and me goin' with you!" called a young voice.

"Others lef' us behind. Won't take Cully, 'cause he can't walk right. They say he too young to go to the swamps, it be too hard. Can't stay here neither. Massa Thomas come back, say we help the people escape, sell us away to different folks if he don't whip us to death 'cause ain't nobody else lef' to whip. Can't stay here. Miss Sophia, please!"

Henri protested it was impossible. He was damned if he'd take another woman and child, but Sophia ignored him. "Of course, Saskia. Cully, hop up with Seth. Venus, Saskia can ride pillion with you." Meshack helped Saskia up behind Venus, and Cully scrambled aboard the wagon the mules were straining to pull now.

Nott had to hang on to the bridle of the plow horse. "What's wrong wi' you?" Nott demanded of the horse. It whinnied and set off the other animals. The mules rolled their eyes and brayed as the horses neighed and cows bellowed and strained, pulling hard on the ropes that tied them to the loaded wagons. And it was smoky.

Even Venus's farm horse was trying to trot away. "Seth," she cried. Seth jumped down to grab the bridle and lead the big farm horse in a circle.

"What's that sound?" growled Henri.

They turned to look back. Inside the house, light flickered here and there, and Sophia gasped, "Impossible! Lazer and Mackland can't have freed themselves! But they've got free, see, they've lanterns . . ." The glow flickering in the house grew brighter, lighting more windows on the upper floors. There was the unmistakable sound of snapping and crackling.

As they watched, at first not grasping that it was impossible the overseers had brought lanterns to every room in the house, a yellow tongue of flame licked the roof. "It's not lanterns, it's fire!" Henri shouted.

"But the overseers are where we left them!" Sophia cried. But the fire had spread rapidly. There was a crash inside the house, sparks flew from the windows and roof and blew in all directions, and a blast of heat forced everyone to turn their faces away.

"Let's go before someone sees it," said Henri, tugging the harness of the mules hitched to the first wagon, turning them round toward the river. "Come on."

"They're trapped!" Sophia cried. "The overseers! No, no! They'll burn to death!" There was a breeze that sent a tongue of flame leaping out of several windows, shattering glass, and sparks rained down. Sophia's horse let out a scream of terror, kicked viciously at the horse behind him, and reared, desperate to throw off its rider and flee. Sophia struggled to keep her seat, but the horse reared higher.

Henri left the mules and grabbed Sophia's bridle, tugging her horse away hard. "Come on! The house must have been a tinderbox to catch so fast," he shouted, pulling the hunter toward the river. The breeze blew more sparks over them, and the fire became an inferno. The animals jostled to run faster.

Sophia shrieked, "We can't leave them to die! We can't!" But Henri wasn't listening and wasn't allowing her to stop; no one was going to save the overseers.

Behind her, Saskia gasped and coughed as the smoke enveloped them. "Wasn't you, Miss Sophy, was Peter set the fire, set it good too. He swear when they put the cage on his head, he get a chance, he kill them. They done other things, bad things you don't know, never thought of. Evil men, Miss Sophy. Evil. Let them burn, leave them to the Devil."

"That's right! They burn to the Devil," shouted Venus. "Like I saw it. Wish Massa burn too. But he die soon, I know it. I see his face all dark, go black as me, then he fall down in the street. He dead. Burn inside. Devil come take him. I be glad."

Henri kept his grip tight on Sophia's bridle so the hunter wouldn't bolt into the dark forest, and a quarter of an hour later, they were driving the last of the livestock down the path to the river. There the procession turned for a last look back. The house was a flaming skeleton, and the slave quarters and the barn where Henri had slept were now alight. It would all burn.

"But I tied them up," Sophia wept, hysterical now. "If I hadn't . . ."

Henri stopped their horses, leaned over, and shook Sophia hard. "Sophy, you drugged them also. If you hadn't, neither you nor the slaves could have got away. You didn't intend for them to die, but you can hardly blame the slaves if they did. Now we must hurry, because someone is bound to see the fire and sound the alarm. The river," Henri said, tugging her horse. "The trail beside it leads back to our camp, and we can reach it by morning if we hurry these animals on."

Sophia hung her head. "What have I done?" she moaned to herself. She imagined the unconscious men as fire surrounded them. In the space of a few moments, she had become a murderess. She had never intended such a thing, was beside herself with shock, but she was carried along, part of the mass of wagons and animals and people crowding on the path toward the river, Henri still leading her horse.

He looked back at her and snapped, "Sophy, you have led these people into danger, and you are responsible for getting them to your plantation. Tears and female hysterics are a weakness neither you nor they can afford. Think of that instead of the overseers." He let go of her horse's bridle.

Sophia felt as if she had been slapped. She sniffed and rode in silence for a few moments. Finally she wiped the back of her sleeve across her wet eyes and muttered, "Yes, you're right." What had begun as a daring escape adventure had suddenly become deadly. To stave off fear, she had to concentrate, as Henri said, on getting everyone to her plantation. They rode in silence for a few more minutes, then Sophia asked, "How many are in your party? The more of us the better, I suppose."

"Two Frenchmen came to Virginia with me, but one died this winter after we set out for La Nouvelle-Orléans. One is back at camp. At Williamsburg, an Englishman and his two sons joined us—they were indentured and ran away. We have Cherokee guides who are anxious to be rid of us and go to war, and an interpreter."

"Is there a war among the Indians? Do you think we'll be attacked?"

"I don't know. I've heard Indians never attack in the dark, so I hope we'll be safe till morning."

"Do you think it's true?"

"I don't know."

"Oh!" This was a new worry. Reports of distant Indian attacks on the frontier were one thing, Sophia realized; to contemplate the possibility of an attack upon oneself was very different. She looked fearfully around her, her mind now distracted from the overseers. What was lurking in the forest beside them?

"You said there was a map showing where your property is. Did you bring it?" he asked.

"Of course, Henri, what do you take me for? I brought Thomas's entire trunk of documents."

Henri looked around and groaned. The wagons were piled with things, creaked loudly, and moved slowly. On them Seth and Nott were armed with muskets and whips taken from the overseers. Meshack was armed with a blunderbuss and brought up the rear, driving the cows ahead of him. Henri led the way. "Sophy, stay behind me; keep your eyes open and your pistol ready."

The spring night grew cold as Henri's wary party traveled down the river path. Through the trees, stars were visible, and the spring moon hung low in the sky, bright enough so that when the trail emerged from the forest, they could see their way, but it made the shadows blacker. Where the trail snaked into the shadows, the wagon wheels caught on tree roots or became stuck in gullies, and they halted many times for Meshack and Nott to coax the mules back or forward or cut branches to give the wheels of the heavy wagons some purchase. More than once a mountain lion screamed in the distance and the animals became agitated. They could travel no faster than the cows, and their progress was noisy. Henri knew that any Indians within miles had been alerted to their presence.

He heard faint sounds in the underbrush—a crackle as a twig snapped, a slight rustle disturbing the bushes, as if something were stalking them in the darkness. He tried to reason apprehension away, telling himself Indians would have made no sound.

Behind him, Sophia heard the sounds too. She kept one hand on the loaded pistol while trying to control her horse with the other. It kept spooking at the unfamiliar terrain and night noises. Cully was asleep under a pile of quilts, and Meshack and Venus and Saskia talked among themselves at the rear until they too fell silent as a dawn mist rose from the river. In the gray half-light, their surroundings had an air of unreality.

Henri was disoriented, unable to recognize landmarks or the terrain he had traveled the previous day. He must have gone farther upriver than he realized, because he thought they should be nearing the camp by now. He twisted in his saddle, looking for something familiar.

It grew lighter. The only sounds were the rattling and creaking of the wagons, an occasional crack of Meshack's whip to move the cows along, the rush of the river, and birdcalls. The crackle of underbrush or dead leaves had ceased. Whatever had followed them in the night was gone. Or waiting. Henri halted and looked around. The sun had risen, and light slanted through the trees. Everything looked safer, but Henri sensed it wasn't.

"What is it?" asked Sophia, pulling up beside him.

"Our camp. I'm sure we're close. I remember that." He pointed to an odd-shaped boulder with a tree growing out of it that lay half in, half out of the river. "But I can't smell a campfire."

Henri kicked his horse forward. Around the next bend was the clearing, but there was no camp. Where the winter house had stood was a pile of charred remains. There was no sign of the guides, the horses, or anyone. Then he saw the body on the ground. It was the interpreter—facedown with his head split open by a hatchet, in a mess of blood and brains.

Where was Thierry? Henri had heard grisly accounts from people who had been taken prisoner and escaped, of beatings and starvation—but they were the lucky ones. Less fortunate captives were tortured, burned alive, or killed slowly by having their skin scraped off with sharpened shells.

Sophia and the rest had nearly reached the clearing. He shouted to keep their weapons ready, the camp had been attacked. There was a faint cry from the forest, "Henri!"

He dismounted and shouted, "Thierry! Mother of God! Where are you? Where?"

"Ici!"

Henri plunged into the trees, finally locating Thierry, who had crawled into a space under a fallen tree and was trapped by a foot caught in a root. Henri, Meshack, and Nott managed to free his foot, and Henri dragged Thierry out. Thierry spat dirt from his mouth and choked, "I thought you'd left for good. Thank God you came back, or I'd have died! Yesterday, after you'd gone, I was relieving myself behind this tree when the devils came out of the forest. They took the guides prisoner, killed the interpreter, burned the winter house, and took the horses and left. It must have been Creeks. I managed to crawl under the tree just in time, thinking they would find me, praying they would kill me before they took my scalp . . . The Englishman and his sons left camp too when I did . . . I don't know, perhaps they are dead or prisoners . . ." Thierry slumped down onto the ground, shaking like a leaf. "God curse Virginia," he said and put his head in his hands.

"Henri!" called Sophia. "Look!"

First Rufus, then his two thin boys crawled out of the woods. Toby was white and shaking uncontrollably, and Jack's face was contorted as if he wanted to cry but couldn't. "Steady, lads," said Rufus, standing and putting an arm around each boy's shoulders. He was shaking too, and his voice cracked. "We're safe. We went . . ." He pointed toward the trees. "A white fawn. Toby and Jack followed it into the forest. That's where we were when we heard screaming . . . then—" He gestured toward the interpreter's body. "We hid in the bushes, sure they'd find us and kill us too, but it was the guides and the horses they wanted . . . We watched. They killed the interpreter . . . Fast . . . ," he said. "So fast. He was begging them not to." Weakly, he slumped to the ground beside Thierry, blank eyed.

"Henri, we must stop and rest the animals. Bury . . . him." Sophia's voice cracked as she gestured to the interpreter's body.

Nott helped her down, tethered the horses, and let them graze. Henri left Meshack and Rufus on watch. He set the boys to work milking the cows. Seth untied a wooden bucket and said, "Go on then, milk the cows. Take your brother till we done." Jack took Toby, who was still in a daze, by the hand and pulled him to the cows. Except for the lowing of the animals, it was quiet. Seth, Nott, and Henri dug a grave and buried the interpreter, and they all stood over the grave for a moment while Henri mumbled a paternoster.

Sophia watched the Drumheller boys milking the cows, told Venus to rest and Saskia to build a fire. Sophia rummaged in one of the wagons and returned with a teapot, a canister, a silver spoon, and a selection of porcelain cups. "We must have breakfast," she said.

"Breakfast?" repeated Henri incredulously.

"Everyone's too fatigued to move. Your friends are more dead than alive after what's happened. Tea, at least."

"Tea?" Henri exploded. "This isn't a *fête champêtre*! The war party will come back. Or another war party. The woods are crawling with Indians at war with each other."

"Henri, look around you! We're in the wilderness! We've no idea where the war party went, and there's as good a chance Indians will find us whether we go or stay."

Henri saw the others agreed with Sophia. Saskia and Venus were determinedly making up a campfire and heating a stone to bake corn cakes. Cully limped to fill the pot in the river and set it to boil on the fire. Henri watched, openmouthed, as Sophia unlocked the canister and sat down calmly to wait for the water to boil. "Jack, if you would bring the milk . . ."

Henri stalked off.

Sophia spooned tea into the pot, waited for it to brew, and filled the cups. She sipped hers. She made a second pot, filled cups again, and ate the corn cakes Saskia handed her. When she finished, she rose, rinsed and dried the cups, stored the tea things carefully in their basket, locked the tea canister, and put the basket back on the wagon.

"Now we'll see the map," she called to him, retrieving it from its pouch.

Henri returned fuming, unrolled the map and spread it out. He weighed down the corners with rocks and stared at it. It was crudely drawn in heavy ink, with a compass sketched in the upper right-hand corner. The main landmarks were lines of mounds running north to south, which Henri judged were mountains, and a few roughly sketched cabins with smoking chimneys dotted here and there. There were black lines that looked like rivers, with little tendrils of lines branching off that might be creeks.

"Sophy, do you know where we are?" growled Henri, still irritated by the tea and annoyed that he had to ask her help with the map because she was the only one with any idea where they might be on it.

Sophia bent over the map. “Here’s what Thomas showed me. I think we’re somewhere about here.” She pointed to a heavy black line running east to west. “See, the James River begins at the coast, then see it says ‘fluv-a river,’ the James becomes the Fluvanna. Thomas’s property is somewhere along that river, whatever it’s called”—she traced with her finger—“and it goes west through the mountains. Those bumps there must be the mountains, with a line snaking between them? Then the river line appears to stop, but I think Thomas said the map doesn’t show Beaver . . . no, Otter Pass. Otter Pass is where the river cuts through the mountains and joins another river on the other side. This one? Probably. Follow it down, there’s a little drawing of a cabin, where it says ‘c station.’ It’s a trading post, Thomas said, and beyond that you follow the river to ‘fr. m,’ that means Frog Mountain, and ‘lit fr. mt’ is Little Frog Mountain, and Wildwood Plantation is there, in that valley,” said Sophia, tapping her finger on the dotted line around the coat of arms. “Though it doesn’t say ‘Wildwood,’ because it wasn’t named when the map was drawn up. In fact, the house wasn’t built, but the patent is that area inside that broken line with the Grafton arms. The river goes right through it. It doesn’t look far. Taking us there won’t delay you, and I can give you horses and supplies.”

“How many days of traveling?”

“According to Thomas, perhaps a fortnight,” she said. Henri was about to protest he couldn’t waste an entire fortnight when he saw a black line that must be a river marked “tinassi” in tiny letters to the south of Sophia’s land. That changed things. It meant he could go southeast instead of due west, and the Tinassi would take him to the Mississippi without crossing through the mountains. So perhaps it would make sense to go by way of Sophia’s plantation, especially with the promise of horses and supplies.

Then he was struck by an ominous detail. “Those little triangles on the map? I think they represent Indian villages, even on your land, it appears. The Indians hate settlers, Sophy.” Henri thought it was typical

English arrogance or stupidity to have a grand *manoir* so deep in the frontier wilderness. In Williamsburg he had heard enough lurid stories of Indian attacks on the frontier settlers to believe it likely they would find the Grafton agent dead and the plantation in ruins, the mansion burned. But even if it was, he was still leaving her, the Negroes, and the Englishman and his sons there.

"Mr. Barker never mentioned any disputes with Indians about boundaries, though Colonel Washington told me the Grafton patent has never been surveyed. But I don't suppose it signifies. The map of the patent shows quite clearly what's mine."

"It might signify," said Henri grimly. Had Sophia not heard the stories about settler families slaughtered and scalped on the frontier? Did she have any idea of the risks she was taking? It would serve her right if she got scalped, he thought. The sooner he and Thierry left Sophia and her troubles behind, the better.

CHAPTER 15
WILDERNESS

After a wakeful, anxious night with the men leaping up with their weapons at every rustle in the trees, they set off at first light, Henri at the front of the procession, Thierry at the end, Venus and Saskia riding beside the wagon with Cully. They could go no faster than the cows could be driven, and by the day's end, they were all on edge, looking over their shoulders, certain they'd seen or heard pursuers.

Sophia rode beside Henri, and they discussed how much time they had before Thomas's burned plantation was discovered. Henri had been in the colony longer than Sophia and knew more about the local militias and the patrollers, and the fear of runaway slaves, than she did. He thought it likely someone, even a distant neighbor, would have seen the fire in the night and raised the alarm. When it was discovered the house and outbuildings had been burned to the ground, along with two dead bodies and the slaves gone, they would hunt the runaways down with a vengeance, if necessary hiring slave trackers who specialized in running slaves to earth, and offering large rewards for their capture by anyone.

Virginians lived in constant terror of a slave revolt on a large scale and pursued runaways to prevent them joining with other disaffected slaves. When caught, as they usually were, slaves were punished severely as an example to the others.

Sophia and Henri had no idea whether it was possible to tell who a burned body had been. Would they know the corpses were those of the overseers? Would they think one of them was Sophia? If a burned plantation and dead bodies didn't set the militia in pursuit, nothing would, especially if it appeared an Englishwoman had been murdered.

But after a week of looking over their shoulders, Henri guessed the militia must have gone east and south, following Thomas's slaves to the swamps. Until they caught up with them, they wouldn't know Saskia, Cully, Venus, Seth, and Meshack weren't with the other slaves. If he believed Sophia was still alive, Thomas might guess she had taken the slaves to Wildwood and send a slave tracker after them then. The slave trackers were often Indians or half-bloods who could track runaway slaves into the wilderness where the militia feared to go.

"But by then we'll be at Wildwood, and safe," Sophia said hopefully. "Mr. Barker and the slaves he bought, though I intend to free them, will help us if the militia comes."

Her naïveté irritated Henri. "Unless Wildwood is a moated fortress, Sophy, nothing will help you if the militia comes."

But with no one apparently in pursuit, the tension among the travelers slackened a little. Accustomed to unpredictable and usually cold English springs, Sophia found the weather delightfully warm. The river widened into a broad stretch, and she pointed out picturesque scenery to Henri and wished there were time to retrieve her paint box or at least sketch some of the wildflowers. Rufus fished with Henri and Thierry, and Saskia cooked their catch over a campfire. From time to time they found patches of intensely fragrant wild strawberries. They halted to pick them, and Cully, Jack, and Toby competed to see who could find and eat the most, and complained later their stomachs hurt. Sophia insisted on her tea every night even though the Frenchmen made fun of it.

Despite Henri's warning they weren't out of danger, Sophia's spirits rose, and she began to enjoy the expedition, the campfires at night, sleeping under the stars, insisting to Henri and Thierry that it was rather agreeable living like Gypsies for a week or so. She thought they were nearly there, perhaps a few days away from Wildwood. It was a relief, and little by little they all relaxed.

Seth fell asleep on his watch one night.

Their bucolic idyll was shattered next morning. They were woken before daybreak by a terrified shriek from Cully and bloodcurdling screams from Saskia. The men leaped up, reaching for their weapons. In the half-light, two braves with painted faces stood silently by the wagon where Cully slept, staring at the child and fingering the quilts he slept on. Henri ordered Thierry and the others to put the muskets down and stopped Saskia from attacking them with an iron pan, muttering he knew a little Cherokee. The safest thing to do was calm down and make breakfast. The braves were more curious than hostile, and he would invite them to eat.

Saskia did as he said and set corn cakes to bake, hardly watching what she was doing because she wouldn't take her eyes off her son. She was ready to launch herself like a panther at them if they touched Cully. Until the food was ready, the braves ambled around, picking up the group's belongings to look at them before losing interest and putting them down.

Henri asked if they had seen any Chickasaw or Creeks. They shook their heads, boasting of how many they would kill when they did. Next Henri asked if they knew where Otter Pass was, which would take them to the New River. They had never heard of Otter Pass and paid no attention to white names for rivers. Still, they knew of a river pass in the mountains. Was it far away? The Indians shrugged. "How many days' travel?" The Indians shook their heads. They had no idea how many days. After some negotiations, they agreed to guide the whites there in exchange for one of the muskets and some ammunition.

The river was meandering, and Henri hoped the guides would know a direct route overland to the mountains and the pass, but he was disappointed. The guides gestured at the wagons and cows and indicated no, it was impossible to get them up steep inclines or through the trees and undergrowth. They were forced to stay on the buffalo trail while the braves stalked ahead of the slow-moving party, disappearing for long periods of time. Henri knew they were scouting for their enemies. When they reappeared, the braves continued to hover over Cully, asking over and over how many beaver pelts he was worth. Like Saskia, Henri kept an eye on the child. Indians kidnapped children, to use as slaves or sometimes to take the place of a dead Indian child. He made sure they saw Cully was lame.

He and Sophia ended each day staring at Sophia's map, trying to calculate from its markings where they might be and how far they had traveled along the river. It had been two weeks since they left Thomas's plantation, and they were still following the Fluvanna among low hills. "Shouldn't we have reached Otter Pass by now?" asked Sophia anxiously. "I didn't think it would be this far." Henri hadn't thought so either.

A worried Saskia interrupted them. "Cully hot as fire, won't move. His eyes hurt, they all red. He so sick I feared he got the smallpox."

Sophia got up and went to have a look. Cully's eyes were indeed very red and swollen, and he was miserable, coughing and shivering, insisting he was cold despite the fact the weather was hot by late morning. He wanted his mother to pile the quilts on top of him.

"Let's hope it's measles," said Sophia. "Those men Thomas brought home had measles. Cully took them food, spent time in their room. He must have caught the measles like the second man did." She inspected his arms and chest. "Cully has little spots, but do you think they look poxy?" She sighed. "I hope it's just measles. Don't worry, Saskia. If it's measles, Cully will be well soon. I've had measles. All the children in our village in England had them too. Keep him under the quilts, and he'll be fine."

The wagons moved on slowly while a flotilla of rafts had passed them, crowded with buffalo hunters and settlers, their families, livestock, and household effects. The travelers called out that they were headed to Kentuckee.

"We need a raft," Henri said, looking after them as they disappeared downriver with enviable speed. "Several rafts."

After three weeks they still hadn't reached the mountains or the pass through them. The expedition had lost its charms for Sophia, and her companions were tired and grumbling. Cully's spots were fading, and Venus was so large that she could scarcely move. She could no longer ride pillion on horseback, so she sat by Seth on the wagon.

"Girl, you be tellin' me how to drive these mules again?" he said with a grin every morning as he helped her up.

"Can't tell you nothing you don't already know, Seth," she answered pertly. The wagon jolted her, and she sometimes had to clutch Seth to keep from tumbling off. It jolted so much that Seth often had to put an arm around Venus, to help her stay on her seat. They both smiled at nothing.

When they stopped, Venus kept wanting Saskia to feel her belly to see if the baby was coming. Saskia kept saying not yet, not yet. Finally Saskia thought that the baby had moved down, and at intervals Venus would exclaim, "Yes! I can feel something! It coming now!" Saskia lost patience and slapped her, snapping that Venus should save her breath for when the baby really started coming. She'd see then! Thereafter Venus just moaned softly every now and then, when Saskia was close enough to hear. Saskia ignored her. This went on until the intervals between moans got shorter and her moans got louder, and finally even Saskia could tell the baby really was coming.

Sophia insisted they stop. Though she knew nothing of childbirth, she felt sure Venus shouldn't give birth in a wagon jolting over rocks and tree trunks. This led to a blazing row with Henri, who knew nothing about childbirth either but saw no reason to stop. Rufus and Meshack backed away, staying out of the argument, as Sophia shouted imperiously, "I say we will stop!"

Henri roared they would certainly not stop, it was only a baby, and Venus, frightened now, began to cry. Seth and Nott settled the matter in Sophia's favor by simply unhitching the mules from the wagons, and Seth led the mules away to a good patch of grass.

One of the wagons was unloaded enough to make room for a bed among the remaining goods. Saskia made Seth cut armloads of branches, piling them up and covering them with a quilt to make a birthing bed, then she and a nervous Sophia helped Venus up to lie on it. By nightfall Venus was screaming, and Henri and Thierry were muttering curses on women having babies.

The birth unsettled all the men, especially Seth. The two braves disappeared. Rufus fiddled with the mules' harnesses and paced back and forth as far from the wagon as he could. Toby and Jack stuck their fingers in their ears and tried to stay as far away as possible. Cully wanted to go with Jack and Toby, but Saskia made him stay where she could see him. He made agonized faces at her every time Venus screamed, and begged his mother to make Venus stop.

Finally, after a day and a night, the baby, a little girl, was born. Sophia was drained by the experience and deeply thankful Saskia knew what to do. Sophia was shaken to realize how useless she'd been. She'd grown quite faint when the baby was actually coming out, grateful when Saskia sent her for a bucket of hot water and a wadded-up handkerchief.

In the dawn light, a proud Venus was propped up to feed the baby, and Saskia pulled the quilt from under Venus to soak in the river, where it dramatically turned the water red. All the men looked shocked and averted their eyes. "Hunh!" Saskia muttered contemptuously, pounding the quilt on a rock. Afterward she boiled it and draped it conspicuously across a large branch in the sun to dry. It hung like a birthing flag, the bloodstains still faintly visible, large and impossible to ignore. It made the men uneasy.

Venus insisted they baptize the baby Susan before they went on. Sophia volunteered to stand as godmother. "What's that?" asked Venus.

Sophia tried to think how to explain and finally said, "It's rather like an aunt, a special aunt. If anything happens to the mother, a godmother promises to look after the baby."

Venus was alarmed. In her fifteen years, what "happened" to slave mothers was that their children got sold away, or they got sold away themselves, without their children. Venus was still too young to contemplate death as a possibility—she'd only done that while in labor, but that was over now.

"That mean you take Susan away?" Venus asked suspiciously.

Saskia murmured, "You free now, girl. Baby free too. Nobody take her away."

Henri was prepared to do anything to get them moving again and conducted a hasty baptism with river water and a few Latin words, with Sophia prompting what she could remember about renouncing the Devil and all his works on Susan's behalf. The braves returned, sullen and uncommunicative, and they set off, with Venus and Susan propped on a fresh bed of leaves and branches covered with the dry quilt, wedged in the back of Seth's wagon between a spinning wheel and a churn.

The next morning just before dawn, Saskia got up to build the fire for breakfast and went to shake Cully awake to fetch her some sticks for kindling. But Cully's quilts were no longer in the wagon, and she soon realized her son was gone, as were the braves, several sacks of their cornmeal, and two of the horses. She let out a wail that woke everyone. "My boy!" shrilled a distraught Saskia. "They take my boy! Cully gone!"

She called him and called him, but there was no answer. The others searched the bushes and by the river, but there was no sign of the child.

Saskia was inconsolable, sobbing by the wagon. "I should have kept better watch over him! I thought if he can't walk right, nobody want him, not the slave traders, not the Indians, nobody buy him, nobody take him away from me. It's why I done the bad thing, so he be safe! Just so he be safe with his mama watchin' over him! Now he gone! It's my fault, doing something so bad! 'Cause this happen!"

Sophia was on her knees by Saskia. "What bad thing? Oh, Saskia, I can't imagine you'd do a bad thing to Cully. You love Cully."

Saskia collapsed onto Sophia's shoulder. "I cut his leg when he a baby, so he can't walk good and Massa can't sell him." She sobbed hopelessly. "Didn't want to hurt him, he my baby, it was so I can keep him. Poor baby, he cry, his eyes say, *Mama, why you hurt me?* And I crying too 'cause he hurt and bleedin' and I done it to keep him! But he taken away anyhow! Oh, my Cully!"

"Dear God in heaven," whispered Sophia, putting her arms round Saskia's shaking shoulders. "Henri? Can't we look for him?"

Henri shrugged. "But where? We've no idea in which direction the braves took Cully . . . But, Saskia, Indians often ransom people they kidnap."

"What's ransom?" sobbed Saskia.

"It's giving the Indians something in exchange for them giving Cully back to us. If they wanted Cully so badly, he'll be alive, Saskia."

"An' scared and crying for his mama! We don't know where they taken Cully. How we ransom him if we don't know that? Oh, Miss Sophia, I thought my child be safe!"

Sophia tried to comfort her, said they would pray Cully was safe and they would find a way to get him back.

"We need an Indian go-between," Henri muttered.

"And where do you propose to find one?" snapped Sophia.

They set off again. Now the Frenchmen had to walk. They now had only one plodding farm horse, which they all agreed Saskia should ride, with Jack and Toby pillion behind her, and the mules to pull the wagons. There was Sophia's hunter, but it had a nasty temperament, biting everyone but Sophia. Thierry had tried to ride it, but it had thrown him, kicked him twice, and bitten his shoulder so hard he was in pain for days. Rufus and Nott took turns walking and driving the second wagon, and the Frenchmen took turns with Meshack in guarding the rear. The loss of the cornmeal depleted their food stocks, and hunger and the muggy heat sapped them of energy.

The landscape changed. Trees were in full leaf, but hills and then mountains rose beyond them on either side of the river, which looked slow and sluggish. In fact, as Henri discovered when trying to catch some fish, it ran deep in places and had a fierce current. Then one after the other, Toby, then Jack, then Rufus fell ill with measles. Venus got out to walk because Rufus was in such a bad way he could no longer stand, and the boys couldn't stay on the horse. He was propped in the place vacated by Venus and the baby on the back of the wagon, and the boys squeezed beside him. All three Drumhellers were still weak from their winter ordeal, and the measles brought them to Death's door. It was hot, the river reflected the sun, and the Drumhellers were feverish skeletons. When they reached a grove of trees and a flat place on the riverbank, Sophia insisted that they stop and rest in the shade until they recovered.

But when they were still alive after another five days, Henri insisted they had to move on. Their food stocks were dangerously low, and they had to try and reach the trading post. If the Drumhellers lived, they lived; if they died, they died. Sophia reluctantly agreed he was right.

A week later, the river was passing through low hills, and beyond them in the distance they could see mountains. Sophia's courage was ebbing. She was hungry, footsore because her horse had thrown a shoe and she had to walk, and her nose was peeling with sunburn. She had grasped the extent of her ignorance about the wilderness, and she suspected they were lost. It had looked easy on the map, but she began to doubt the map was reliable. The trees grew thick on both sides of the river, hanging over the trail in places so they had to push through low branches. It felt like the landscape was slowly swallowing them up.

Now the trail went in and out of the forest, and wild animals stalked them among the trees. The men took turns guarding the cows and mules at night when the forest rustled and echoed with coyote howls, boars fighting, and deer coughing in the distance. Sometimes they saw the eyes of prowling red wolves reflecting the large campfire they kept burning all night. Thierry shot a bobcat feasting on a calf it had killed. They dismembered the calf's remains and cooked them over the campfire. They couldn't waste the food. They learned to use burning pine knots to keep predators away. Sometimes a raft carrying long hunters and the occasional settler with a family and a pile of household possessions went past on the river. "If only we had a raft," mused Sophia longingly.

"You'd need a fleet of rafts," retorted Henri.

Little by little they had all come to depend on Henri. He kept a clear head when the riverbank became rocks and the buffalo trail turned and disappeared into the woods. He and Thierry would follow it up hills and ridges too steep and difficult for the wagons and plot a way that could be cut through the lower part of the forest to rejoin the trail on the river when the bank widened again. When that was not possible, they cut branches to give the wagons traction enough as they whipped the mules up the steep parts. Away from the river, Sophia became hopelessly disoriented, but Henri seemed to have a sixth sense for direction.

If Henri was good at holding their direction, Thierry was the best hunter among them. To supplement the dwindling stock of cornmeal, he shot possums and squirrels with the muskets, or at least wounded them enough to be finished off by hand—the muskets weren't very accurate at the best of times.

Sophia was alarmed to overhear Thierry urging Henri in French that they should board the next passing raft. She tried to keep her fear at bay that they might never find Wildwood in this implacable wilderness. But if Henri and Thierry left, they would certainly die. She had to keep the two Frenchmen with her until they reached Wildwood.

The next evening when they stopped, Sophia said she was going down to the river. "Fishing? You never catch anything when you fish," said Henri.

"No, I want a bath," she called back. "I'll wager I'll catch more than fish," Sophia muttered to herself. Lady Burnham would be scandalized, but needs must.

Sophia spotted a fallen tree in the river, damming a pool next to the bank. That would do. Behind her, Henri was calling something about snakes. Sophia tried not to think about snakes. She quickly stripped and left her clothes on a bush, then walked into water up to her waist, trying not to imagine what might be in the squishy mud under her toes. She splashed as loudly as possible, so he would know where she was, then when she was sure he must be watching because the calling stopped abruptly, she immersed herself and paddled a little back and forth. She arched her back to wet her hair, and, after more noisy splashing, finally rose, dripping, and walked slowly back to her clothes.

That night as she and Venus made supper, Sophia noticed Henri was looking at her in a new way, though at the same time he was uncharacteristically subdued and preoccupied. As if he were thinking. *Very well, let him think about it.* In fact, Sophia took to having a bath whenever there was an opportunity.

The river narrowed between hills, running deep and fast, and Henri hoped they had finally reached Otter Pass, but they had no way of knowing for sure. The buffalo trail seemed to disappear, then Thierry discovered it winding through the trees above the river, where it became a rocky path that was steep for the wagons. They had no choice. They cut branches to put under the wagon wheels, and Seth and Nott whipped the mules forward mercilessly. Two of the cows fell down a sudden drop-off, broke their legs, and had to be killed. They cooked and ate as much of the fresh meat as possible, but the cows were skinny, and the meat was tough and stringy. What they couldn't eat soon went putrid in the heat.

They had gone into the forest, and sometimes they thought they were on the trail and sometimes it was impossible to be sure. Were they in the foothills of the mountains they should have reached? Perhaps they had missed Otter Pass and taken some other way into the mountains? Unless the river was ahead of them, Henri feared they were lost.

"Listen," said Sophia, one weary evening. She was crouched by the fire Meshack had built next to a spring running out of a rock. She was spooning the last pinch of tea into the teapot she insisted on unpacking every evening, waiting for the iron pot of water to boil. She clung doggedly to her ritual because it was the last vestige of her former civilized life. "There's a noise in the distance, it sounds like water. Can you hear it?"

Henri walked off and returned half an hour later to say excitedly, "Sophy, you were right. It's ahead, it's much bigger, and it's rushing over the rocks. The trail picks up again. Thank God for buffalo."

"Please, God, it's the river, the right river, and it won't be much farther to the trading post. Thomas said there was a mill. We'll trade something for flour or cornmeal." She tried to sound firm and positive. "We've plenty of silver things." Her teeth felt loose in their sockets from hunger. She poured water on the tea, then measured a small amount of the remaining cornmeal into the pot, calculating how much water she could add to stretch it as far as possible. Too runny and the batter wouldn't bake into cakes. She divided the mush carefully into one corn cake per person and set them to bake on the hot stones.

Henri cautioned they mustn't count on finding the trading post standing; it could have been attacked.

"But we haven't seen any Indians, Henri. Not since the braves took Cully."

"I know. It's very strange. Indian towns are marked on the map."

Finally they emerged from the forest, but now it was hard to be certain the river went west, because it meandered back and forth in a way not shown on the map. Judging by the sun, they were not taking a direct route, and it was costing them time. Everyone was dispirited except for Venus. She'd fashioned a sling to carry Susan and crooned in a low voice to the baby as she walked along. She sang about what a fine morning it was, about little babies being rocked to sleep by their mothers who were free of Massa now and going to have a cabin of their own to live in. She sang quietly, so grieving Saskia couldn't hear.

Rufus drove the wagon since he wasn't strong enough to walk for long, so Seth walked with Venus. "You a good walker, Venus. Everybody else tired to death, but you singing. Do my heart good to hear you. Don't even look tired."

"How I look then?" asked Venus softly, her eyes cast down.

"Fine. You looking fine, like you always do. Pretty as morning. Susan pretty too. For a baby, that is, she pretty. She take after you."

"Don't want her taking after nobody else!" said Venus sharply.

"No. I don't spect so."

"Susan's my child. Just mine!"

"She yours, but I can carry her a while. Rest your arms."

Venus thought for a minute, then said, "You got to hold her up on your shoulder, like this. You get tired, I'll take her back." She relinquished the baby.

"How could I get tired? Baby don't weigh nothin'! She feel kind of good. Warm little thing."

"She look mighty little on your big shoulder."

On and on they plodded wearily, animals and people. Had they lost their way and missed the trading post? Or were they nearly there? They stopped asking each other, and concentrated on moving ahead Only Venus and Seth, absorbed in their courting, forgot they were hungry.

CHAPTER 16

MALINDA

At first, the smell was intermittent whiffs of something nasty made worse by the hot day, but as they went farther, the foul, sickly odor grew stronger and stronger, so pervasive that they covered their noses. Sophia choked. "Ugh! Horrid! Is that what they call polecat?"

"Ain't polecat," said Saskia. "'Less it dead."

"And the size of a buffalo," said Henri.

Sophia clutched a wadded lace handkerchief to her nose and wished she had some lavender water.

They looked to see if it was something trapped in the river that had died—occasionally there were pools dammed up by felled trees or rocks—but there was nothing.

"Whatever it is, it's dreadful," Sophia said through the handkerchief. "Can we go any faster to get away from it?"

They couldn't. The faster they went, the worse the cloying, horribly sweetish smell became.

Venus squashed her face into Seth's shoulder, muttering, "Whoo! What stink that bad?"

"Look," said Seth, pointing above them. Above the trees, buzzards were circling against the sky ahead of them. "Whatever it is, reckon we find it 'fore long."

And they found it in a small clearing where the trail flattened out and a creek ran into the river. The cabin built halfway into the riverbank was hardly recognizable as any kind of habitation; it looked more like a log extension of an animal burrow, but there was a chimney made of rocks, a greased-paper window, and a door of roughly sawed timbers that hung open. Beyond the cabin were some fields still full of tree stumps where a half-grown crop had been burned. There were big black buzzards everywhere, and everything was quiet except for the buzzing of flies and the buzzards' flapping wings.

There were two dead cows and a calf lying in the mud. The cows' heads had been split, and the carcasses were grotesquely swollen in the heat and heaving with flies. Buzzards were ripping at the flesh, and judging by the state of the cows and a few white bones sticking through the blanket of flies, they'd been doing it for a while. Farther along, half in, half out of the creek were mounds black with flies and hooves at the end of rigid legs. Mules, two or three, though it was hard to tell exactly, as the dead animals had swelled up and burst, and there were more buzzards gathered round feasting on the carcasses.

Henri and Thierry buried their noses in the crook of their arms and walked over to investigate yet another fly-covered hump lying a short distance away from the cabin. It was surrounded by more busily pecking buzzards. The interrupted buzzards flapped away a short distance, squawking and hovering angrily. The lump was wearing ragged trousers and patched boots, toes turned in. He held a hoe—had it been a weapon?

Where the head had been was a bare skull with empty eye sockets and a few hairs still attached to a strip of skin at the base. The buzzards picked vigorously, working their beaks inside the skull to get at the brains. "Scalped," said Henri. "Indians."

"Dear God in heaven," whispered Sophia through her handkerchief.

Rufus was sick over the side of the wagon.

Inside the hovel, there was a cry. "Somebody alive there," said Saskia. No one was in a hurry to see, but the high-pitched cry came again, and Henri walked over, pushed the door, and went in. After a minute he came back looking shocked and saying the women would have to see to it. Clutching her handkerchief over her nose, Sophia went in and paused at the door, unable to see in the dim light from the door. Saskia followed.

Venus looked up at Seth. "I ain't going," she said firmly. "No tellin' what happen in there. I don't want to see it."

There was a whimpering noise and a different smell, not like outside, but unmistakably blood. The whimpering was a woman's moaning, "Water, Malinda, I need a dipper of water."

Inside it was dark, and Sophia groped for Saskia's shoulder. "Where is she, Saskia? I can't see anything."

"Oh, Miss Sophy," breathed Saskia. "There."

As their eyes adjusted after the brightness outdoors, they could make out a shape against what would have been a wall if it had not been a hole dug into the bank. It was a bed, with someone in it. A woman was half sitting, holding something to her chest with both hands.

"What happened?" Sophia blinked, trying to see. "Is she hurt in the chest?"

"No," said Saskia, who had moved closer.

The shape on the bed said querulously, "William? Is that you? Where you been at? I was calling for you. Are Indians come? You feared they'd come . . . I heard screaming but couldn't do nothing . . . the baby came hard, like Mother said. I want Mother. She knows what to do. Mother, is that you? You didn't want me to marry William, but now the baby's here. It's a boy. He was crying, but I fed him. He's quiet now. Sleeping." She held up a finger to her lips. "I want to sleep too, but it hurts . . . Mother?"

"She's confused, poor thing," said Sophia. There was a sharp intake of breath from Saskia. "Oh, Miss Sophy! Worse!"

The thing the woman held to her chest was a baby. It looked at first like she had nursed it to sleep. Then Saskia and Sophia saw the baby was attached to a cord that ran between the woman's legs, as fresh blood oozed to join the dried blood that surrounded her. The woman was shivering, staring with wide eyes focused on something the other two could not see. Sophia said, "We're not William or your mother, but we've come to help you." She turned her head and hissed, "Saskia, what must we do?" The baby stirred a little. "Thank God the baby's alive! I'll take it. You see what can be done for her."

Saskia shook her head. "Don't know how to help this. It's her innards, what inside her with the baby should have come out, but it didn't." She shooed the flies crawling over the baby and the woman. "Oh, Jesus, that baby . . ."

With her eyes now adjusted to the darkness, Sophia saw it wasn't the baby moving; it was the flies that covered it. She batted away flies and saw the baby was waxen and dead. Sophia's stomach heaved, and she fought down the vomit rising in her throat.

The woman started to sing a lullaby, rocking the baby as if they weren't there.

"And she bad, gon' die too. Cain't do nothing for her," Saskia whispered in Sophia's ear.

"How do you know? Oh, Saskia, please try!"

"Don't know what I can do—I can try and pull out what's inside, watched another slave woman do that at Massa's, but spect it might kill her quicker than if she just die if I don't. Before, the pulling made a lot of blood come. Girl who had the baby died. Massa whup us bad."

The woman looked back up at them, seeing and not seeing.

"What's your name?" asked Sophia.

"Lavinia . . . but you know William calls me Lavinny, Mother. I hurt. I hurt so bad, even with the baby born. Help me, Mother."

"I'm not your mother. I'm . . . I'm Sophia. We'll help you, Lavinia . . . Lavinny, let me . . . let me take the baby." She held out her arms.

Lavinia shifted the baby away from her protectively. "No, Mother! William wants a son. I have to show him, Mother. Tell William to come. He'll be happy when he sees the baby. And water . . . thirsty . . . I told Malinda go to the spring, but she hasn't come back. Bad girl."

"Malinda?" Sophia mouthed to Saskia. Whoever Malinda was, she was probably lying dead outside.

Sophia tried again. "I'll show William the baby, Lavinny. He's . . . waiting outside. He asked me to bring the baby out, while . . . while Saskia makes you comfortable." But she couldn't take the baby, because it was still attached to something black that went from the baby to between Lavinia's legs. Sophia looked desperately at Saskia.

"I needs a knife," Saskia ordered.

Sophia went to the door. "A knife. At once." Henri had fetched a spade from the wagon, and he came over and handed her his hunting knife.

Saskia took the knife and sliced through the black umbilical cord. Then Sophia reached out her arms, and after a second's hesitation, Lavinia let her take the little fly-covered corpse that Sophia realized was starting to decompose. "Does it . . . does he have a name?"

"John," moaned Lavinia. "Johnny. Show William, promise you'll show William, Mother."

"I need water. That bucket got water?" Saskia demanded.

Sophia reached the gourd dipper into the bucket and shook her head. "Empty!"

"Got to try and cool her head. She hot as fire," said Saskia, looking around. "Give me your handkerchief so I got something to wet, and get me some water."

Sophia handed the handkerchief to her. There was no way to muffle the smell of death. She had to bury the baby. "Get one of the men to fetch some water, Saskia."

"Mother," cried Lavinia, moaning again. "Where's Malinda? I forgot Malinda. Is she at the spring? Tell her that her brother's born."

"Here, Ma," said a small voice. "I told you, I can't bring no water 'cause Pa tied me. Can't reach the bucket."

Saskia and Sophia turned to look. A child with tangled hair and a ragged dress stared at them from the corner where she was tethered by a rope around her waist to a stake driven into the dirt floor. "I've been good," said the small voice. "Didn't make any noise, like Pa said. Is there johnnycake now? I et all them's on the plate. Pa said he'd make more if I was quiet." The child held up a battered pewter plate. "But he didn't."

"Malinda," gasped the woman on the bed. "Malinda."

Saskia took the bucket, went to the doorway, and shouted for Nott. "I needs water, fast as you can. You got to go up the creek to get it. Don't want it where that dead mule lyin' in it, you hear me?"

Sophia laid the fly-covered baby on the floor and tried to stop her hands from shaking so she could untie Malinda. "How old are you, Malinda?" she asked.

The child held up five fingers. "Ma said this many. She and Pa said I had to be quiet so the baby could come. But Ma wasn't quiet. Indians wasn't quiet. Pa said they didn't know about the baby, so he went to tell them. I couldn't go to the spring for Ma 'cause I's tied up."

Untied, Malinda wanted to go to her mother, but Saskia was busy over the bed, and whatever she was doing made Lavinia groan and beg her to stop. Sophia scooped up the dead baby in one arm and dragged Malinda with the other. Outside, Thierry and Henri had just finished digging a grave, an open trench where they laid what was left of William. Toby and Jack were staring down at the corpse with horrified fascination. Sophia wished they'd covered William with earth before Malinda saw him. She called Venus to give Susan back to Seth and come and help with Malinda, keep her from running back inside. When Venus protested, Sophia snapped an order so imperiously that Venus relinquished Susan and sulkily obeyed.

"We need another grave," said Sophia, and Henri looked at the baby in her arms and stuck his shovel back in the earth.

When Nott brought Saskia's bucket of clean water, some impulse made Sophia stop him before he took it in, wet her fingers, and make a sign of the cross on the baby's forehead. "In the name of the Father, the Son, and the Holy Ghost, I baptize thee . . . John."

Sophia reached under her skirt and ripped off a piece of her ragged petticoat to make a little shroud to wrap the dead baby. When the baby's small grave was ready, she laid the little white bundle in, then told Henri to dig another. She gestured with her head toward the hovel, whispering Saskia thought the baby's mother wouldn't live long. Then Henri shoveled earth and put rocks on the two graves, and Sophia called Malinda to come over and kneel down beside her while she recited the Twenty-third Psalm and the Lord's Prayer.

"Ma'll want me," interrupted the child, and she ran away back to her mother before Sophia had climbed to her feet. Henri tried to say they had to leave, and Sophia turned and said fiercely they had to wait. The woman's grave, with the tiny one between it and William's, lay open, pitiless and expectant.

Sophia hoped Saskia had finished what she had to do and that Lavinia would recognize her daughter and call Malinda her dearest dear one last time. She could do nothing except promise Lavinia they would take care of Malinda.

"We must take Malinda with us," Sophia said.

"I'll see if there's any food we can take," said Thierry. "Wish we'd been here before the buzzards."

Sophia's stomach heaved at the thought of food. She stumbled back inside the fetid cabin. Lavinia was covered now with a ragged, blood-stained quilt, and the air was heavy with the smell of hot, fresh blood. Her breath sounded harsh, and she jerked uncontrollably. Saskia was wiping her brow, and Malinda clutched her mother's hand. "Ma," she cried. "Ma!"

"Take Malinda, Mother!" the dying woman cried, her teeth chattering uncontrollably. "Malinda's a good girl, Mother. She's quiet."

"I will," said Sophia. "I'll take care of her."

Malinda cried desperately, "Ma! Don't want to go with nobody! I want to stay with you!"

"And Johnny . . . does William know, did he . . . see . . . Johnny . . ."

"Yes," said Sophia. "He's with his son now."

"Is William happy?"

"So happy. He . . . he'll see you . . . soon."

"Good," Lavinia sighed. She closed her eyes, and little by little, her body ceased its violent shaking. In a few minutes, her chest no longer rose and fell.

Saskia felt for breath, listened for a heartbeat. She pulled the bloodstained quilt over Lavinia's face. "She dead. Nothing I could do. I try, but she so hot, fever got a hold, and then she bleed so bad when I pull it out. It go rotten inside her."

"Ma! Ma!" screamed Malinda, pulling the quilt away. Sophia gently detached Malinda from her mother and pulled the quilt back over the dead face.

"Malinda. You must be a brave girl now and tell your mother goodbye. She's . . . gone away. She's going . . . up to heaven with your father and Jonny. But she can't go to heaven until she's buried. My mother and father are in heaven too. They'll take care of everyone. And you're going to come with me and live at my house. That's what your mother wanted you to do."

Malinda took a last long look at the covered corpse, drew a long, sobbing breath, and let Sophia pull her away from the bed and outside. She watched while they buried her mother wrapped in the bloodstained quilt, watched while they piled rocks on the third grave. She stared up at Sophia with dark, fathomless eyes and said nothing. Malinda would never speak again.

CHAPTER 17
GIDEON WOLFPAW VANN IN LOVE

When I went down to the river, the oldest catfish swam out from under a rock to greet me by my Tsalagi name. He said that a war party had killed some settlers, that one day the whites would send soldiers to take revenge, and that a party of swine eaters with animals and wagons and women and children were coming on the Great Path, not on the water. They were in a bad way, hungry and sick and might not live, but if they did, they would reach the Caradoc brothers' trading post before the next moon. They would ask me to guide them, and I should agree. I asked where they were going, but the catfish swam away. There was a warning in the air. In the direction the swine eaters were coming from, danger was approaching like the mist and fog that sometimes hides the mountains and settles over the river. I set my fishing lines and thought about this.

I am a beloved man among my people, the son of a white man, a long hunter with red hair, and a Tsalagi beloved woman who could interpret dreams so accurately from a young age she was allowed to sit in the council house. I am a man of two worlds, which gives me special powers. Like my mother, I can hear and sometimes see spirits. She taught me the healing powers of plants and how to commune with animals. I learned to hunt and endure pain and performed the initiation rites of a young brave at the proper age, but I was never a warrior. Instead I learned from the shamans' sacred prayers, songs, and formulas for hunting game, for asking forgiveness of the deer before killing it, for healing wounds, for making the corn grow, for protection in battle. I know the ceremonies and dances to perform for the Great Whirlwind and the Yellow Rattlesnake. I understand how to be silent and attend, and in this way, knowledge comes.

But because my father was white I understand there are evils that come from the whites against which no spell or sacred songs will protect us. My mother told me of one such, something that made our people fall ill and die, long ago when she was a girl. The shamans said it was an evil that came from the spotted frogs that we had offended in some way. They performed incantations to drive the evil away, and people ate the foul flesh of buzzards to repel the illness, and the water cure was tried when people grew fiery hot and swollen with spots. Still the people died, from one town to the next, there echoed death and mourning songs for the old and the children, and even for strong young braves and girls.

This came from the whites. I fear what else may come from them.

More and more whites come into the valley now, sometimes on foot, sometimes in canoes and rafts. Sometimes alone, sometimes only men who want pelts, sometimes with their women and children, and then they want land. I am often asked to guide them toward Kentuckee where our enemies the Chickasaw and Shawnee live. I show them how to pass safely among the tribes, what animals are clean and unclean to eat, how they must behave to avoid offending the spirits of everything.

I tell them they are safe with me only if they do as I say. They believe this too, because it is known that no whites have been killed or taken prisoner when they are with me. Some believe the Shawnee will not attack the companions of a beloved man who speaks with the spirit world. I do not believe this. No one would credit the Chickasaw or Shawnee with restraint, especially in the spring, when their young men are restless and eager for war.

Birds and animals and fish speak with me, also the mountains and sky and waters and plants; all have their own language. They warn of danger and enemies, and this allows me to avoid ambushes and attacks. So in this way, I can lead the whites by a safe path.

But the more of them there are, the more they quarrel among themselves. If they are men, long hunters, they want furs, bear oil, salt, lye, and hides for which they offer rusty guns and ammunition, beads and shiny trinkets, and the poisoned drink the whites are fond of, that steals a man's senses and gives him anger and weakness.

The catfish warned me long ago that their firewater is poison to the Tsalagi, that the spirits of those who taste it will long for it always, that they shrivel and wander away into darkness. I refuse it. And with my bow and arrows and traps, I have no need of their guns. I do not need their coins either—our people have fields for the crops and buffalo and courage, all that is needed. But if I guide white men, who cannot find the safe way alone, they give me their coins.

And now I have a use for the coins.

Old Caradoc has a daughter, Caitlin, with eyes the color of the sky and the same lilting manner of speaking as her father and uncles. Their voices are rough as rocks, but when Caitlin speaks, her voice is like shallow running water over stones. It pleases me to hear her laugh aloud at her father's jokes or sing as she goes about her work, drawing water or cooking or tending their cows and chickens. From the first time I laid eyes on her, when she was only a child, I knew she was the girl I had seen in the flames and smoke when I was a boy, and I wanted her for my wife. I learned a song, a charm that will gain the affections of a woman, though I do not know if a love charm will work on a white woman.

I intended to sing it and see, but the catfish advised me to wait and learn the ways of her people first. So for seven years I have watched and learned and been their friend. In this time I have brought the Caradocs many gifts of game, as a brave does for a woman he wishes to be his wife. Until now these gifts have been passenger pigeons and fish and squirrels, but once last year, I killed a bear just at the end of summer when it was fat before its winter sleep, and this year, I have brought deer.

Caradoc thanks me for the game and gives no sign he knows why I have brought it. But Caitlin has grown taller and smiles for me in a new way when she thanks me for the game. She has fifteen summers now. When I come near, she looks down, then up at me, and then down again, and her cheeks grow pink as sunrise.

I told the catfish I have sung my song for her in the forest. The time I waited for has come. After the catfish swam away, I gave the fish I had caught to the women planting corn and squash. A fish in each hill of corn makes it grow tall. I took dried buffalo meat and a new basket my grandmother wove and set off for the trading post, paddling my canoe upriver. The great river is slow; it has not rained for many days, and I go fast. I arrive as the sun is low in the sky on the third day. The bag of coins is heavy in my hand.

Old Caradoc values these coins greatly. He and his brothers are Welshmen whose name, they tell me, means "those who travel across the endless water." They say their god led them here eight years ago, because they had done evil things in their land, luring ships on the water into the coast where great rocks ground the ships to pieces. When this happened, the people there seized the goods that were floating in the water and exchanged them for coins, until the Caradocs had many coins, and the people in the ships died, though they were not the Caradocs' enemies.

This was wrongful, and these deaths were to be avenged by the Caradocs' deaths, just as there must be blood revenge when a clan member is killed. Soldiers of their people took them prisoners, and in prison, as they awaited death, a beloved man of the whites admonished them strongly for their evil ways, their treachery against their own people. The brothers promised their beloved man to live rightly if he helped them escape their captivity. He did, and they fled in the night with all the coins they could carry, found great water, and crossed it with their women and children. They came to this place on rafts loaded with many possessions purchased with their coins and built log dwellings on the riverbank. Soon after this, their women and children died with two of the brothers, when their boat was pulled down in the Suck when they tried to go upriver against the current. All the children drowned except for Caitlin, who was rescued by her father.

Now the Caradocs have a ferry, and they have spread over much land, with their home and fields, their animals, and a storehouse for the trading post. More rafts bring goods for the Caradoc brothers to trade to long hunters and settlers. Barrels of wheat flour and firewater, nails and horseshoes and plowshares, blocks of sugar, barrels of molasses and salt herring. Sometimes they have things that Caitlin asks her father to obtain for her, bolts of cloth and cooking pots. In exchange, the traders take furs and dried salt from the salt lick, tanned deer hides, buffalo hides, beaver pelts, lumber, dried corn and beans, and baskets our women weave from reeds.

Though ignorant on the whole, the whites have some interesting and useful things. Last year, the rafts brought a great wheel in pieces and a round stone. The mules dragged these to the place where a creek falls out of the mountain, a little way from the Caradocs' cabin, and the brothers built another log house there for this great paddled wheel, which they fitted together. Among our people, grinding corn is women's work, but this wheel and stone turned by the waterfall quickly grinds as much dried corn as twenty women. Old Caradoc and his brothers barter the ground corn for pelts and dried fish and baskets our people have, and also exchange it for whatever passing whites have. They call this grinding thing a mill.

They also sell rafts and flatboats the two younger brothers make. These are not good rafts; they are heavy and hard to steer, unlike a canoe. Often they leak and must be mended with pitch, or they sink, and these can only go downriver with the current. Then they are broken up. Anyone going upriver must go on the buffalo trail, and there are fur traders and long hunters with their pelts who come this way because they say as Englishmen they dare not go by way of the French territory and city to the south.

For a higher price, because the current is strong and they must unmake the raft and return by land, the Caradocs will take people and their belongings down the river. If the travelers have coins, they pay with coins. Otherwise Old Caradoc demands a chicken, a cooking pot, a spinning wheel, even a calf once, in payment. People complain but must give what he asks.

In this way the Caradocs have many things and made themselves comfortable. But since her mother and aunts died the year after their arrival, Caitlin has been left to shoulder all the work of tending to the cows, pigs, and chickens, as well as their garden. That first year, I found her crying at harvest time because deer had eaten most of the crops her mother and aunts had planted. They were very hungry then. I brought dried corn and deer jerky so they survived, and in the spring, I showed her how our women plant corn, beans, and squash together, so that the beans can climb the corn and the deer will not step into the winding squash vines. I also told her to bury fish among the vegetables, and secretly I said a charm to make their food grow. I brought her peach stones and told her where to plant them behind the cabin. Caitlin's harvest was good that next year, and I showed her how to dry pumpkin slices and beans and wild plums on nets in the sun so they would last the winter. I showed her how to make venison jerky and where strawberries and hickory nuts and persimmons grew and explained the way my grandmother makes bread from ground chestnuts and dried beans. Caitlin is always pleased when I tell her these things, and she now asks my advice very often.

In the Caradocs' cabin, there are beds to sleep in and a wooden churn to make butter. Caitlin does not wash clothes in the river. She has a pool made of metal, large enough to hold a man, that she fills with hot water and scrubs clothes with the soap she makes. And there is a strange tall thing that gives back a reflection, like still water. It is surrounded by decorations of leaves and vines, and the water surface has a line across a corner where it is broken. Caitlin is proud of it, and the fact that they have plates to eat from, made of pewter. She saves the ashes from the fire to scrub her pots and make her soap and rubs their table with wax from the bees. She makes blankets with small pieces of cloth from old clothes and scraps from her precious material that she stitches together. She says her mother and aunts taught her to make them. These have a pleasing look, and when I praised one and said that even my grandmother would admire such work, she insisted I take it to her as a gift.

Because Caradoc and his brothers were born far away beside the great endless water where they fished, they believed this meant they understood water, understood boats. But they learned white men do not understand the river. There are two dangerous places once past the Caradocs' trading post. The first is the shoals, where the loud water warns a raft or a flatboat will quickly break up against the rocks unless it is steered carefully in the safe waters. But beyond that, the place where the river narrows between the mountains is the deepest, most dangerous place of all, as the Caradocs learned.

The white men call it the Suck, where the river's secret strength suddenly pulls men and boats down. No one sees the whirlpool until it is too late. Any canoe or raft that crosses that water disturbs the spirits of the drowned who wait below the surface, trapped forever by the powerful god of water, who keeps them prisoner, choking and drowning continually, unless these dead spirits can pull down a living being to take their place. Otherwise they must suffer forever under the water and not go on to the Darkening Land. The dead spirits do not reveal their suffering. Instead the river god makes music above the water, and the dead appear happy, feasting and dancing below the water. It is possible to cross the Suck safely in only a few places, but those who try to cross this Suck must beware of hearing music.

Only a few careless young warriors have heard the music and escaped to describe how their fellow braves were carried away in the jaws of a giant fish or how they themselves were whirled round and round toward the bottom, where a great crowd of men and women called their names with open mouths and reached their hands up to clutch them just as the braves were caught by a current that pulled them up and outward and finally carried them to shore.

I showed the three remaining Caradoc brothers how to navigate the dangerous shoals, how to steer a raft so evil spirits below the Suck are not disturbed.

The sun is low in the sky when I pull the canoe up on the bank. It is a good time to fish, and before I go to the cabin, I fill the basket with river fish I have caught. While I do this, I hear the Caradoc brothers on their fiddles. They have built them from polished pine and strung them with long horsehairs. It makes a sound like rushing wind when they play them together in the evening.

They nod to me and keep playing when I reach the cabin. I sit and listen, and they fiddle for a while. They like visitors because visitors will listen to them. They play harder, until I feel sure the wind will blow us all away. Caitlin's presence fills the air. She glances my way and smiles. She is listening to the music while she sews, sitting on the seat her father and uncles hung on ropes for her from a beam overhead. She taps her foot in time to the music, sometimes hums a little.

When the men stop playing, I say, "I bring you news that travelers will come that way soon," and point up the Great Path.

I hand Caitlin the basket of fish, still cool from the water. Her teeth are small and white as river pearls when she smiles. "Oh, the beautiful basket! And so many fish! Thank you, Gideon." Caitlin likes these trout. She rolls them in cornmeal and fries them in bear grease. This is a good way to eat them. I know she will ask me to stay and eat with them, and from the way she looks at me, I can tell that she no longer sees Gideon her father's friend but Gideon the brave. I take care to walk very tall and upright before her. She watches and then lowers her eyes, and her face becomes red. For the first time, Old Caradoc notices. He looks at both of us with surprise, then at me, then his eyes narrow.

The Caradocs wipe their fiddles and bows with rags greasy with bear fat and put them away. Caitlin's father says, "Was a party of flatheads two days ago, traded some salt for blankets. Grieving. Many of their people are dead. We thought there must have been a battle, but they said no, an evil spell had taken them. Maybe you saw the Choctaw."

I shake my head. Choctaw. They bind the heads of their children to make them flat. I do not like this news. They are enemies and should be farther west. But that is not who is coming, or the other thing approaching, I do not understand. I must watch and do what I can.

But I am a man, and I want a wife, and I have come to get one, so I will think on this later. Now I tell them something they will like to hear. "Whites and slaves traveling here on the Great Path with wagons and horses. I think that they will need rafts." I do not call them "swine eaters," though it is a name the older people—even the old catfish—give the whites and their black slaves. It is not a good name. Tsalagi do not eat swine or wild pigs; they are unclean food, like owls or foxes.

"The Great Path? Not many long hunters'll risk the Great Path this time of year. Too dangerous."

"Yes." There are fallen trees on the Great Path. It is the Choctaw who prepared a trap. But the trap will not work . . . I cannot tell why. Again I feel a warning, but at the moment I am thinking of other things, and the warning goes away. "They will ask you to build them a raft. I will go with them. They will need a guide, and I know the river's ways. Depending how far they wish to go, perhaps I will be away a long time," I add, watching Caitlin carefully.

Caitlin looks at me and bites her lip, and then quickly drops her eyes back down at her sewing. Soon she says, "Of course you will stay to supper, Gideon?" and, without waiting for my answer, puts down her sewing and goes inside. I hear her bustling about the hearth.

"I want Caitlin," I say. Old Caradoc gapes at me in surprise. "For my wife."

"My Caitlin?" He frowns. "No!"

"Caitlin," I repeat. I take out the pouch of coins and give it to him. Its weight surprises him. He opens the string and takes out the biggest, a large yellow coin. Now instead of gaping at me, he gapes at the coin. "A doubloon!" exclaims a brother, craning for a look. He grabs the pouch, and it spills more coins. He sweeps them up greedily. Then Old Caradoc looks at me with anger in his eyes. I sense he would like to kill me, so that he could keep the coins without giving up his daughter. "You can't buy a godly Christian woman! Especially Caitlin!"

Whites believe everything is for buying with coins, I think scornfully. "I do not wish to buy her. I give you these coins you value, because I value her. I have no need for coins." But Old Caradoc is a little afraid of me and my connection with the spirits, and he is thinking what to say next. I know his wish to kill me has left him, and he does not want to offend me. To many of the tribes, whites are enemies, seizers of land, to be taken prisoner and ransomed or given to the women to torture and kill. Old Caradoc and his brothers believe it is because I am known as their friend that their trading post has not been attacked.

Though the Caradocs are greedy and wish always to own more and more coins and other things, I do not think any of the tribes will attack them, because many people of our tribe and other tribes bring their corn to be ground here by the stones turned by the water wheel. I have seen that the Caradocs are careful to deal fairly, give right measures of ground corn and salt, and they do not secretly keep some back for themselves or cheat those who bring them furs and hides, as some white traders do.

They say this is according to the command of their god, who let them live. They must do no more wrongful things, give right measures, must not pretend furs are ruined or thin when they are not. They obey their god's laws to deal honestly in business. This protects them from blood revenge for their wrong deeds when they were foolish young men. They say that their brothers who drowned forgot their vow; they cheated some Indian hunters out of a load of buffalo hides and brought bad luck upon themselves, drowning soon after with their families. Old Caradoc and the last two brothers believe they will die too if they break their vow.

"Caitlin will be safe with me," I say, knowing he will be afraid for her if she leaves him. "We will live downriver among my mother's clan, in our town beyond Frog Mountain. My grandmother agrees, and the rest of the clan have finally accepted this is my wish." I do not say all would have preferred me to take a girl of our tribe. A child belongs to its mother's clan, and a mother's brother, not its father, is responsible for teaching a boy what he must know. My mother was of the Wolf Clan, the people protectors; my sons and daughters will belong to no clan, and Caitlin has no brother. Still, I will teach the Tsalagi in them as much as I can, and perhaps my old uncle, my mother's brother, will do the rest for my sons.

Old Caradoc tests a coin between his teeth, but he is no longer thinking of coins. He screws his face to show he is thinking. "Hmmm. Settlers coming into the wilderness, more every month, looking for land, bringing their women and children. The lads and I are thinking of another trading post farther down the river, before it reaches the Tinassi. That way we'd get the rafts from the Talequo River too. And we'd need a partner there because the three of us are wanted here. Caitlin, she's helped me since she was a little thing, knows a thing or two about running a trading post. Then we'd need a spot with a flat bank, deep enough for a jetty . . ." He strokes his chin and looks at me sideways. "What if you were to build a cabin on the river instead of in your town? We've seen a place just suited for a trading post, at the big bend in the river. It's got a bank that would do for a landing."

I nod. Caradoc means the place where the river widens and flows toward the sinking sun, the Darkening Land. And he is right, I think; there are many rafts and flatboats and traders on the river trail now. The whites are slowly learning the dangers of the shoals and the Suck and manage to avoid them, or at least avoid drowning.

"Repairs," says Caradoc, understanding my thoughts. "A forge, even. They say there's iron there, in the mountains. And settlers need pots. Horseshoes. Hammers and nails, barrel hoops and such. They'll trade pelts and potash. Soon as you've built a jetty, we'll supply you. And you can barter the goods for deer hides and beaver pelts. That salt lick there that draws the animals—you can send us salt." He rubs his hands. "We could get mules to pull the rafts with the salt and pelts back here, can't pole. And you could set up a mill, like ours. Folks have to get their corn ground." He waits.

I say this is true, and that I would build the cabin where he wished.

He nods and grunts and reluctantly says, "I'll allow you to ask her, but only if a parson marries you, proper. Not some heathenish ceremony. We're God-fearing folk, Gideon." Old Caradoc has a tattered Bible. Caitlin once took it down to show me where her ancestors' names and her father's name and her uncles' and aunts' names were written. She showed me her name and the date of her birth, and her mother's name, that was also Caitlin. The Caradocs were surprised when I could read it as well as Caitlin, but they approve of me because I can. I told them that my father, the long hunter with red hair, owned a Bible too. He taught me to read it before he went away. My mother said the book held a different kind of power and I should learn it.

I nod. By "parson," Caradoc means John Baptist, a shaman of the whites who also uses this book. He has built a home of branches and hides on the island downriver where the mound builders once lived. It was a sacred place, where meetings between tribes took place, and even in times of war, nothing and no one was killed there. The spirits of the villagers are there, and no one troubles John Baptist. He has a hairy face like a buffalo, and sometimes has trances and visions. Other times he comes to drink firewater with the Caradocs, and then the Caradocs get out their fiddles and all sing their holy songs. He too has a Bible, and the Caradocs say he can make a man and woman husband and wife, though I do not believe he can do this. Only the man and woman who are willing can. He also performs a ceremony thrusting people into the river as if to drown them—though he does not drown them. It is like the water is a cure for illness. Whites say this pleases their god, and Caitlin was thrust in the river too. She wished me to undergo this ceremony as well, but I laughed and refused.

"Done!" says Old Caradoc, and he claps me on the back in a friendly way. "Go ask her tonight."

Caitlin says the food is ready and we must eat. The fish are laid on a blue-and-white dish with willow trees. She had added cress from the spring behind the cabin where there is a little house to keep her cheese and butter cool. There is a clay pot of this butter she had churned and some of the bread whites like, from ground corn mixed with white flour the whites prize so highly, instead of ground chestnuts or beans. It is curious bread, very soft, a women's bread, not a warrior's. But it is not bad to eat, with butter and the cooked mayhaws Caitlin calls "confit."

Caitlin has tied back her hair with a ribbon she had not been wearing earlier.

After we eat, the brothers take their whiskey jug back to the porch. I stay inside and drink a dipper of spring water from the bucket while Caitlin washes her platter and scours her plates with ashes and river sand.

"Come," I say when she is done, "we can walk." Caitlin takes a shawl and wraps it around her shoulders. We walk away from the cabin to the mill. We sit on the bank in the dusk with fireflies' small specks of light around us, watching the mill wheel turn and listening to the song rushing water makes. I tell her that I asked her father to let her be my wife and what her father said.

"Oh, Gideon!" she exclaims. Dark as it is, I can see a look of surprise cross her face, and her eyes widen. "Marry you!" Then she smiles as if she cannot help it. "But, Gideon, you have to ask me if I am willing. The girl who passed through last year, with her husband and a baby, she told me exactly what must be done. When a man wants to marry a girl, she must be asked with sweet words. Courted. Then they marry with a wedding, with flowers when they take their vows."

The girl with the husband and baby had been happy to find Caitlin. There had been no other women in the party she and her husband came with. In our tribe the unmarried girls are friends, are always together. But there are no other girls here for Caitlin, no friends, and my grandmother says it must be lonely. Caitlin was very happy to have a companion. There was a storm, and the men had to repair the rafts before they could continue. The two girls sat together laughing and whispering by the fire for several days, and Caitlin rocked the baby while its mother talked constantly, as if she had not been able to say anything for a long time. When the weather calmed, both girls cried as the raft carried the new friend and the baby away.

Now Caitlin smooths her hair and looks away, as if something very interesting is happening in the dark. She waits. I smile inside and wait too. Finally Caitlin sighs.

"You might think of *something* in all the world to say, Gideon! Unless you only want me for a business partner. And that would likely be Father's idea! For instance," she says, "a young man might say how pretty a girl was looking with a ribbon in her hair. Or that she has a pretty smile . . . or a light hand with the bread making . . . or . . . or that she sings like an angel. Gideon!"

Then I speak. I tell her that I know all these things are true, but there is more. "Your soul has entered my soul forever," I say. "We will be companions all our lives, we will shelter each other from the rain and warm each other in the cold, we will share one blanket and one life and one heart, and I want no other woman."

"Oh!" Caitlin catches her breath. Then she turns to me and puts her hand on my chest. "Oh, Gideon! Yes, yes I will marry you!" Her touch is fire on my heart.

The next day, I leave early, telling Caitlin I will return for her when I finish building the cabin where her father wishes her to have the trading post. Caitlin says she is happy and weeps when she says it. She wishes me to hurry, though we say good-bye for a long time. I will hurry.

CHAPTER 18

ANOTHER PROPOSAL

Henri scouted ahead of the others, climbing up the hills on either side of the river, hoping to see a curl of chimney smoke or some other sign of the trading post, but it was impossible to see through the trees. There were felled trees across the trail, and Henri feared this was Indians slowing them down for an attack. Every tree on the path meant they had to halt while the men cut it up, the three women armed and keeping watch over the men and the four children. Though they saw no Indians, they sensed their presence when the wind blew a certain way, bringing an eerie noise like keening or singing. But like an echo, it was impossible to tell from what direction it came or to judge how far away it was.

Hot weather had brought out mosquitoes and midges from brackish inlets along the river to add to their torments. It made them all irritable. Sophia had loaded the wagons with everything she could lay her hands on when they left. She insisted she had only brought a few essentials because her house was unfurnished. Thus they were encumbered with Sophia's traveling trunk, sewing boxes, writing boxes, dishes, a churn, various pots, a huge copper preserving pan, and Sophia's teapot. There were bedding and chamber pots and an embroidery frame, some lanterns, and the last of Anne de Bouldin's stock of candles. There were also Thomas's small chest of papers, a plow, a miscellaneous collection of tools with broken handles, all the ammunition from the overseers' stores, and two sacks of tobacco seeds.

When Henri jeered she would hang for a thief, Sophia protested hotly that she had left her valuable jewels in exchange for what she had taken, and anyway, there would be no one to notice the missing goods for a month. Or use them. The slaves would be gone, Anne was dead, and she doubted any other woman would be desperate enough for a husband to marry Thomas. Lacking a wife, Thomas himself was too slovenly to miss household things, such as cooking pots and bedding or the churn and copper preserving pot, though she conceded he would miss tools, guns, wagons, and horses. He would certainly have missed the chest with his papers and the Grafton property deeds in it. But her jewelry was worth far more than what she had taken. Her pearls alone . . .

Henri snorted and said her reasoning made no sense since the house had burned down and destroyed her jewelry with it.

Sophia swiftly changed tack. "Then even less reason to trouble my conscience. Had I lacked the foresight to take so many useful things, they would have burned too and been lost. That is what people will believe happened when they see the house was burned, that everything inside was destroyed. And I will need them," said Sophia airily. "The ladies in Williamsburg were quite certain that Mr. Barker will not have supplied the house. I planned well, and my intentions of paying for what I took were good."

When the trail grew rougher and the wagons slowed to a crawl as they bumped along, Henri demanded she leave the wagons, but she refused, backed up by Rufus and the Negroes, who were more knowledgeable about the realities of survival. They insisted they would need the plow, saws, axes, and other farm equipment even if Sophia didn't. Saskia was adamant they needed the quilts and pots and dishes, and Sophia pointed out they could hardly leave the muskets, gunpowder, and ammunition. Eventually Henri tired of arguing. The trip could hardly get worse or progress slower.

But it did. One of the mules died, and shoe or no shoe, they had hitched Sophia's horse to the wagon. The hunter was now too dispirited to resist or bite. Its ribs showed, and it had no energy to kick anyone. The cows were scrawny and had stopped giving milk. They had to stop when there was anything like pasturage and let the animals graze on whatever they could find. A wagon wheel broke, and it had taken a long time to unload the wagon and several attempts before the repair was done well enough so the reloaded wagon didn't unbalance.

Crossing a creek, Seth spotted a snapping turtle and caught it, and Saskia made a thin turtle stew. Then Thierry found some mushrooms that he insisted were chanterelles. He had cooked them up into a ragout with a possum Henri had snared, and everyone except Malinda was so hungry he or she had eaten it. Malinda screwed up her nose and shook her head, refusing to touch it. Everyone else was violently ill.

Malinda huddled by herself, sucking her thumb until they recovered. She was such a solemn, quiet little thing they often forgot she was there. She hadn't spoken a word since her mother died, just trudged on silently with the rest, showing more stamina than seemed normal for so young a child. Sophia made a pallet for Malinda to sleep on next to her, and if Sophia woke at night, she saw that, though Malinda lay quietly, her eyes were often wide open. Jack had taken a liking to Malinda and would hop and caper and make faces, trying to coax her to smile. He showed her how to make stones skip on the river and picked her up when she tumbled down the riverbank into the water. Malinda stayed silent and solemn, but she watched Jack's every move and walked as close to him as she could.

Then Jack had wandered off into the forest and disappeared. Toby had to be stopped from going into the forest after his brother, and Rufus had been frantic. They searched as far as they dared into the forest and called and shouted his name until "Jack, Jack, Jack" echoed back at them. Malinda cried silently and shook with distress. Thierry demanded they leave Rufus and Toby behind to look for him while the rest pressed on. Sophia had drawn her pistol and said they were staying until they found Jack—and later Jack wandered back out of the forest, looking dazed and talking about a small white deer that had come up to him and then trotted so playfully by his side that he followed it a long way into the trees and into a clearing with a spring of sweet water. He had drunk, and when he looked up, the deer had vanished.

Jack was unable to tell them how he had found his way back from the spring through the forest. Sophia recalled a story she had heard in Williamsburg about an English child, Virginia Dare, who disappeared, turned into a white deer. Saskia and Venus looked at one another and muttered about the spirits.

Thierry complained that if he'd been told about the deer, he could have shot it and they could have had venison. Lavinia and William had had no food beyond a barrel of weevily meal, and they'd tried to cook it, but the musty taste and the insects made corn cakes inedible. And Malinda was one more mouth to feed.

When Henri and Thierry weren't sparring with each other, Henri tried hard to keep Thierry's spirits up, thinking ahead to Wildwood, wondering how long they could afford to enjoy Sophia's hospitality before taking their new horses and supplies and getting on to Louisiana. They would have plenty to eat.

Listening to them, Sophia decided to play a mischievous game, describing out loud and in lingering detail the dinners she intended to see prepared for them before they left.

They would fall silent as she described roast capon, haunch of mutton with peas, larded pheasant, roast venison, fricasseed ducks, damson tarts, sauces of cream and brandy, melting pastry and spices, beef and lobster and puddings. In fact, she invented dishes she had never made—her cooking skills as taught by Mrs. Betts were sound but rudimentary—but her inventive litany of food kept the Frenchmen quiet.

Though salivating at her words, Thierry and Henri thought it was further proof that the English nobility lacked all sense of *amour propre* and dignity. The Frenchmen were shocked that a highborn girl was obliged to acquaint herself with domestic matters such as cooking; that was why there were chefs. They rolled their eyes and shrugged off Sophia's explanation that it was considered essential by her godmother's generation. No wellborn Frenchwoman of any generation would have set a foot in the kitchen.

But they were helpless to stop listening, and Sophia hoped hunger and greed would keep the two men with her until she reached her destination.

Greedy Henri hung on every word of Sophia's gluttonous recitals, asked for details, licked his lips, groaned with longing, and murmured, "Oh, Sophy!" Thierry said Henri sounded like a man in love. Henri retorted that he was merely hungry, that Sophia was the most disagreeable, bossy woman he had ever encountered, so unfeminine she was hardly a woman at all.

But ever since Sophia had taken to evening baths, Henri's head had been at war with his loins. He was powerless to stop spying on her or ignore the surge of desire when he did, try as he might to argue himself out of his feelings, reminding himself that she was the last woman in the world he would willingly choose. She wasn't sweet and pliable, as a woman should be, as Frenchwomen were. She had a steely masculine determination to reach her property, too much to say for herself, and a habit of giving orders to everyone, as if they were her serfs. The only reason she excited him now was because it had been so long since he'd had a woman. He hadn't dared risk it in Williamsburg.

His lust for Sophia, irrational as it was, was also unsatisfied, so gradually it had become an obsession. Henri always followed furtively as she made her way to find a bathing place. He was acutely aware of her presence whenever she was near, in or out of the water. It aroused him, never mind her disordered hair or her torn dress.

And he acknowledged her fortitude. Sophia never complained of hunger, blistered feet, or insect bites. She simply soldiered on, walking now like the rest. She refused to let Thierry kill her horse for food, threatening to shoot him or anyone who tried.

Thierry, Rufus, his sons, and the Negroes complained at length about anything. There was plenty to complain about. Their supply of cornmeal was nearly gone, and while sometimes they were lucky catching fish, sometimes they were not. They had the cured hams from Thomas's smokehouse, but they were hard and inedible as iron in their present state. Sophia and Saskia insisted cooking them required several days and involved cauldrons, soaking, and an oven with a large, steady fire. In desperation, Henri suggested they improvise an oven, but both women doubted they could cook it that way, and if not soaked and cooked properly, the ham would be wasted. And time would be wasted too. They could not afford to delay reaching the trading post. Without pasturage, the livestock were skin and bones from merely grazing along the trail. Surrounded by forest though they were, game was oddly elusive, and after Thierry's disastrous experiment with mushrooms, they stopped foraging for plants that might or might not be edible.

Hunger distracted Henri from worrying about what kind of trap the Indians had set that was taking so ominously long to spring and even interrupted his lustful musings on Sophia and her dinners. And above all, where the Devil *were* they? He kept looking and looking for something, anything, that tallied with the landmarks on the map.

The long, hot days blended into one another.

One evening as the light was fading, he and Sophia sat on a rock that was still hot from the sun, cooling their feet in the river, with the map spread out between them. It had become a nightly ritual, trying to plot distances, get their bearings, trying to relate what they had seen that day to landmarks on the map. The little ritual was meaningless, but they did it for no better reason than it kept a faint hope alive that they would eventually reach the trading post.

Henri stared gloomily at the map, with its bumps and crosses and lines that were marked as rivers that confusingly had one name in one place and another name farther along. There was the Tinassi that was also called the Talequo and the Clinches and the N'lichuky. There was a "shols" marked with a big skull and crossbones, and then there was the unnamed one that forked off between "fr. m" and "lit fr. mt." That was where the Grafton coat of arms was surrounded by a dotted line, with a black line of the forked river running through it. And neither he nor Sophia had the faintest idea where they were.

Henri slapped at midges that hummed in clouds by the river and got in his hair and eyes. He felt listless with heat and hunger. They all did. Even Thierry found it too much effort to complain. Venus feared her milk was drying up and Susan would starve. Saskia, formerly a large woman, was a shadow of her former self, her skin hanging in folds. Jack's and Toby's stomachs were distended, though their arms and legs were thin, and Rufus looked like a human skeleton. Sophia's cheekbones were sharp in her thin face.

"Henri, what if we're lost and I've led everyone off to die in the wilderness? I keep thinking of Lavinia and William, the poor baby. And Malinda. What if we hadn't come?" Her lower lip quivered.

Henri had seen Sophia in many states, but he had never seen her cry. Without thinking, he put his arm around her shoulders, protectively. "It's just farther than it looks on the map. Don't worry, Sophy, it'll be all right in the end. I know we're going more south than any other direction, and we haven't left the river. We're bound to reach the trading post eventually, get some supplies and a raft, find a guide who can negotiate with the Indians, perhaps even find where Cully's been taken and get him back. We'll reach your plantation eventually. Thierry and I'll have that magnificent dinner you promised and a good rest before we set off. This adventure will make a lively story at Versailles."

Sophia sighed. "I've been thinking."

"What?"

"Should something happen to me—Indians or I fall in the river and drown or . . . you know, things might happen to any of us."

"Don't be morbid!"

"If it did, I'm not twenty-one yet, and if the militia catches up with us, they'll take me back, Thomas will force me to marry him so he can claim my land and the slaves Mr. Barker bought, and he'll drag Venus and the others back in chains. I'll die before I let that happen. I swear I will never own slaves, and I swear to prevent any being returned to such a miserable condition. The Negroes have agreed to work for me in exchange for land of their own. Those Mr. Barker has bought I shall likewise set free and hope they'll stay on the same terms."

"But the law won't allow freed slaves in Virginia."

"Perhaps not, but we've hardly seen a soul besides ourselves and the travelers on the river. Look how long it's taking us to get there. Papa always said his patent looked suspiciously like it was meant to be on the very edge of the colony, because of the French. Wildwood may be so distant there will be no one to enforce that law. And I have a plan."

"But if the militia catches us, they'll return the slaves to Thomas. You can't prevent it."

"Ah, but there is a way. What if you had a piece of paper saying you won them in a gambling debt?"

Henri thought about it. "Ah . . . I do have something like that." He had kept the lottery ticket Thomas had sold him in his now-empty purse, and he recalled that Thomas had named Venus as the raffle prize.

"Good. If necessary, you can say Venus and Susan belong to you, and I can make a promissory note saying you've won Seth and the others in a game. Thomas is known to be a desperate gambler; the militia is likely to believe it."

"Hmm, Sophy. Who knew women were so clever?"

"That's only part of the plan."

"And the rest?"

"After making sure Thomas can't take those who were his slaves, I have to make sure he can't touch mine or take possession of my land by marrying me. And there's only one way to prevent that, which is . . ."

"No more talk of killing yourself, Sophy! It's a sin."

"I was talking of something else. If I'm already married and my property is my husband's, Thomas couldn't take it. I want you to marry me, Henri."

"What?" Henri's arm was still around Sophia's shoulders, but his hand, with a mind of its own, was hovering over her gaping bodice. He took his arm away and sat up straight to frown at her. "*What* did you say?"

"Marry me. What belongs to a woman belongs to her husband. If I'm already married to you, everything that is mine would belong to you. That's the law. Wildwood and the slaves Mr. Barker bought would be legally yours. You're more likely to survive than I. And you *did* promise to marry me all those years ago, before the king."

"*Non, merci!* I don't want you or your plantation! I will not pretend to own slaves. I will return to France like a civilized man and have nothing more to do with this American hell. With my reward from the king, I will buy an estate with French peasants to work the land, find a girl with a dowry to marry, have French children, go hunting, and go to Paris when I am bored. I will live as a Frenchman should, do my duty, get an heir, then spend the rest of my days enjoying life. My dear girl, only think, you and I are unsuited for each other at the best of times, let alone now, and were you to offer me all Virginia Colony and its tobacco in it, you could not induce me to remain here. When I promised to marry you long ago, kindly remember it was a promise extracted from me forcibly and given unwillingly. You were bossy even then, maneuvering me into an impossible corner before the king and Madame. But they aren't here now. *Non, non, non!*"

"Do stop saying *non* through your nose in that nasty French way! And stop dwelling on childish nonsense! This would merely be an arrangement, a formality. It need not interfere with your plans."

Henri sighed, assumed a long-suffering male expression, and began to explain the flaws in her plan, slowly and patiently, as if talking to a child.

"Sophy, *ma chère*, even if I wanted to marry you, which I don't, there's no one to marry us in these backwoods. I am a Catholic and can only be married by a priest or it isn't valid, and you, being English, are a Protestant heretic. Even if there were a priest, how would we manage an annulment or even a divorce? Hm? It is expensive and nearly impossible to obtain a divorce. Even when it is possible, it involves many years and private laws and permission from the pope, I think, and God knows what else. I suppose there's always an annulment, but even that isn't simple, and I think one must petition an ecclesiastical court, and—"

"Oh, bother all that sort of thing. We needn't worry ourselves with divorce or annulment." Sophia batted away such trifles with a wave of her hand. "And this is hardly the time to be troubled by your Catholic conscience, which, permit me to observe, appears to have left you in peace until now." She hitched her tattered skirts higher above her knees and splashed water on her thighs, her long, slender thighs, bending over so that her breasts were visible thanks to the gaping bodice.

Henri tried to ignore this distraction, but it proved so difficult he could barely gasp, "Pray, explain how marrying you would leave me free to also marry a Frenchwoman?"

"It's quite simple. Our marriage would be valid enough in Virginia to serve my purposes, while invalid in France for all the reasons you set out. So when you're in France, you could ignore it with a perfectly clear conscience. Rather a happy and convenient solution, don't you think?"

"What?" This logic was too tortuous and Machiavellian to follow, and quite startling coming from a woman. Besides, Henri was mesmerized by the fact another button of Sophia's bodice had slipped open, and she was sloshing water on her neck to cool it. Drops were running down her chest, and now her bodice was wet . . .

"Really, Henri, it's perfectly simple and logical. If we find a clergyman to marry us, we will marry, and I think we merely need the clergyman to sign a license to prove we've been married. Or we could just handfast each other—a custom I understand is much in favor among the Scottish peasants in the Borders, where there is a scarcity of clergymen—and declare ourselves married. I have Thomas and Anne's marriage license in Thomas's chest with my deeds. I can copy it and forge a license. A license proving we're married will put me and all I own beyond Thomas's power once and for all."

"What?" Bigamy *and* forgery! Henri stared at Sophia, torn between admiration and astonishment.

"You needn't look at me like that. Don't imagine for a moment I seriously want to marry *you*, Henri, no woman of sense would, but if anything happens to me, at least the license means you inherit my property, not Thomas. Inconvenient for you if I die and you're in France, but still, I imagine you will think of something since the property is quite valuable . . . Henri, are you listening! Goodness, how hot it is this evening!" She splashed more water on her arms and neck, careless that her skirt had slipped up higher and higher as she dangled her foot in the water.

"Mmm." Henri no longer had the slightest interest in theoretical discussion. He leaned closer, though Sophia, getting herself wet, didn't seem to notice.

"Since you can never be your father's legitimate heir, I should think there is a considerable advantage for you having a *manoir*—the house looks handsome enough even for a Frenchman—and a huge plantation, more riches for you. I have no wish to marry a Virginian and stay here any more than you do. I want to return to England, and if I marry, marry a good English husband. All I want is to be safe from Thomas while I'm here, and since my stay is likely to last several years, I want a home that's as pleasant as a home in this dreadful place can be.

"You can have the plantation once I've paid off the debt on my English property. After that I will want nothing more to do with Wildwood—it's brought nothing but trouble. Meanwhile you can return to France and find a sweet little French wife who'll say *oui* a dozen times a day. I've no incentive to pursue you to France and accuse you of bigamy, have I? I'll send you word when I'm back in England and you can either rent it to a tenant and keep the profits or sell it. I don't care."

Henri tried to focus on which of the two crimes Sophia was proposing was the more serious. Bigamy, he thought on balance. But was the arrangement bigamy? Or not? Technically, perhaps it wasn't. He reasoned that, as a Catholic, unless they found a Catholic priest in the wilderness, a marriage performed by anyone else would be invalid in the eyes of the Church. Back in France he could probably ignore it with a clear conscience. He would never mention it himself, and when the time came to claim Sophia's plantation as his own, he would simply wave the marriage license and claim that the first wife named on it had died of smallpox.

His conscience had never troubled him overmuch, and it didn't trouble him now. He couldn't see that he had anything to lose. And . . . he grinned. "What a devious, scheming thing is woman. Why not? If there is a way to marry you, I agree to marry you. However, there's a price to pay . . . ," he said, drawing a finger along the top of her bodice.

"What?" Sophia's eyes were large and innocent.

"That you behave in a conjugal fashion. A husband's rights."

"Ah, so that's your bargain, is it? Very well. Provided we're married, however we're married, of course you shall bed me."

Henri needed no further encouragement and bent to rip open the last of the fastenings on her bodice and roll her onto her back when Sophia spun out of his grasp and nimbly sprang to her feet. "Not until we're married, Henri!"

As she moved away, she smiled as she shook her skirts down, smoothed her hair, and refastened her bodice as best she could.

Henri lay on the rock and watched her go. He ground his teeth. He might have to wait for his wedding night, but then he'd prove to Sophia who had the upper hand. Oh yes, as her husband he would have the power. Tease him, would she? He'd give her a taste of the marriage bed, then when she wanted more, as she would, women always did, he would make her beg and beg. He relished the thought.

CHAPTER 19
WEDDINGS ON THE RIVER

June 1755

A permanent mist hung over the river, and it had been raining ever since Sophia and Henri and their ragged, footsore, and starving party had dragged their broken wagons and emaciated animals out of the woods at the Caradocs' trading post two weeks earlier. At the post, a pretty blue-eyed girl in a homespun dress and apron seemed to be in charge. The three men she introduced as her father and uncles just stared at the newcomers and scratched their heads, surprised anyone could have made it along the buffalo road without being attacked by Indians. Packhorse traders braved the journey only with a large armed guard.

The girl, Caitlin, had taken the travelers in hand at once, directing the men where to unhitch the wagon, where to take the animals to graze, where they'd find fodder; shepherding the women, boys, and Malinda inside; and murmuring, "Poor things." She had admired the baby and hugged Malinda, given the children milk sweetened with a little honey, and later fed everyone soup and cornmeal dumplings, but only a little, as she insisted too much would make them sick. Jack and Toby cried and begged for more and tried to snatch some jerky, but Caitlin smacked their hands and said they could have more when their stomachs were accustomed to food again. She brewed a pot of tea made from sprigs of new pine needles and mixed it with more honey. She had ointment for their sore and bleeding feet, made of bear oil and pounded senna root. Afterward she distributed quilts, and the whole party fell asleep on the porch overlooking the river, too overcome with fatigue to stir. Malinda snuggled up to Sophia and for once shut her eyes.

The baby Susan arrived listless and dull eyed, and Venus was terrified she would die. Venus's milk had almost stopped, and the baby no longer cried from hunger. At the trading post, Saskia quickly made up a teat with a clean rag, some milk, and sorghum for Susan to suck, and after an anxious few days, Venus found that having food again meant her milk came back. Within a week, food and rest meant everyone had recovered strength, and the animals too were livelier, the cows giving a little milk. Susan's feeble whimper to be fed became a healthy howl of hunger. They would hear Venus's sleepy voice as she picked up the baby, able to nurse her again, "Everything fine now, Susan. We all right. Mama feed you now, hush, baby."

Caradoc Station was a little settlement all its own, a haven of civilization and order after their journey. There was a big clearing on the river with a large two-story cabin of split logs and a wide porch round three sides. Bales of hides were stacked at one end. Inside, the main room was divided in half, with one side packed with barrels of salt, cornmeal, and sorghum syrup; rolls of homespun; iron pots; sides of bacon; blankets; baskets; tools; and horseshoes. The other side had a vast stone fireplace and walls lined with shelves holding a Bible, Caitlin's cooking pots, pewter plates, and a collection of mismatched china platters and dishes. There was a big wooden table with benches on either side, and a large clay pot on the table that Caitlin kept filled with wildflowers or blossoming branches that she thought looked pretty. Against one wall was a food cupboard with doors carved with a twisted lattice and hearts.

A gristmill had been built by a creek that ran down a hill into the river and powered the mill wheel. There were barns and a pigsty, a poultry run, a storehouse, and a sort of boat-building yard where a raft was half completed. Beyond that a field of a tall grassy-looking crop was growing. The Caradocs pointed it out proudly, said it had been the damnedest luck, some seeds traded by raft people for an iron pot and one of the Caradocs' chickens were sorghum. Boiled up, it made a sweet syrup; they'd been selling it ever since, made whiskey with it too.

The women helped Caitlin with her chores; the two boys minded the livestock and were set to weeding in the vegetable garden; Malinda was given the job of feeding chickens, gathering eggs, and sweeping the floor; while the men unloaded and repaired the wagons and helped the Caradocs with the raft. Thierry declined to help with the building, muttering it was a job for peasants; gentlemen went hunting. He came back with a steady supply of rabbits and possums and passenger pigeon squabs that Caitlin roasted on a spit.

A heavy mist seemed to hang permanently over the river that widened at the point. Beyond the clearing and the fields, and on the opposite bank, it was so thickly forested that Sophia understood why Mr. Barker had named the Grafton estate Wildwood. Sophia and Henri had showed the Caradocs the map and asked if they knew of Wildwood and how much farther down the river it was.

The Caradocs said it was about ten days' travel downriver and that when Caitlin and Gideon got married, they would be traveling that way, so why not wait for the wedding. The more people traveling together, the better. Did Sophia and Henri want a raft? It was faster and safer to travel on the river, provided you knew how to navigate around the dangerous spots, but Gideon could show them. They traced the broken line delineating the Grafton property and whistled when they saw the amount of land on both sides of the river. "Looks like you got a stretch of the river too! First time I heard of that!" exclaimed Caitlin's father.

They knew the Grafton agent, Mr. Barker, because he had stopped at the trading post the first time four years ago, with slaves and a white overseer, saying he was bound for the Grafton plantation. Since then he'd returned several times to meet rafts bringing goods and farm equipment he'd ordered. Sometimes there was a letter from his wife. These letters made him agitated. He would read them over and over and answer right away, so it could be sent by the next raft going in that direction to begin the long journey back to England. At the same time he would write a letter to his agents in England. Later, when he had partaken of the Caradocs' whiskey, he would complain what an expensive business a young wife and a baby were, but he supposed there was nothing for it except send his agent orders she be supplied with what she needed.

"Bought supplies here too, he did. Meal. Gunpowder. Salt pork. And whiskey. To keep out the cold! And keep it out he did!" All the Caradoc brothers laughed heartily.

Sophia traded a handsome pair of Anne's branched silver candlesticks for them to build two rafts to transport her party and goods.

But the youngest Caradoc scratched his head over the patent and said he thought there was a muddle somewhere. It was all very well for the English king to grant land and rivers, but according to the map, the Grafton property was also in Indian territory. It might belong to Sophia on paper, but it might not be as straightforward as that. There were frequent attacks on would-be settlers. Hadn't Mr. Barker written that they had fought off Indians several times?

Sophia was indignant. Of course her land was in Virginia. A patent from the king was a patent from the king. That outweighed everything. The king would hardly have given her father French property. As for it being Indian territory, Mr. Barker had mentioned treaties in a letter to her father.

"Very well, missy," said the uncle.

"Worse than our Caitlin," he muttered to Caitlin's father.

Meanwhile Sophia and Caitlin had become friends, and Caitlin confided she was engaged to Gideon Vann—a "mixed blood," she and the Caradocs called him—and said the couple planned to set up a trading post and mill downriver. She happily told Sophia all about Gideon, how he'd gone hunting and left deer and once even a bear outside the door of the trading post. "You know, Sophy, that meant he wanted to marry me, only I didn't know it then. I was only thirteen the first time he left game. Just think, Gideon's wanted to marry me for three years! Oh, Sophy, wait till you meet him! You'll say he's the finest man in all the world!"

Sophia asked the Caradocs to point out on her map where Caitlin and Gideon's trading post was to be. The youngest Caradoc brother traced with his finger to the edge of the Grafton patent and looked at her challengingly. It seemed that the new trading post on the river was actually on Grafton land. "It looks like it's on the edge of my . . . but of course there's no difficulty, my property or not," Sophia hastily assured the Caradocs, whose expressions, suddenly, were daring her to say otherwise. "It's a relief to know Caitlin and Gideon will be neighbors."

When Gideon arrived for the wedding, Sophia assumed he must know Wildwood, but he shrugged and said he hadn't seen her house.

He told Caitlin's father his cabin and landing were ready for Caitlin now. He said it was a good location, two valleys west of where his own tribe lived. There was good hunting in the valley, and fish in the river; the trading post and the fields that would be planted around it would not interfere with the tribes who hunted there. It would be a convenient place for Indians to trade their pelts and furs.

When the Caradocs explained how Sophia had come to own the valley, Gideon was incredulous and bemused that a man living far away across a great water believed he could "give" away a valley he had never seen, as if it were a blanket or a gun or a pelt. Gideon also saw that Caitlin's father regretted not asking a higher price for building the rafts.

He felt the warning in the air again. But Caitlin liked Sophia and begged him to agree they could all travel together since Gideon knew the river and they didn't. Gideon was glad Caitlin had a woman friend. Gideon had agreed to take Henri and Thierry on to the Mississippi after he had taken Caitlin to her new cabin.

They were waiting for John Baptist to arrive to conduct the wedding. "I wish he'd hurry!" Caitlin confided to Sophia, as day after day went by with no sign of the clergyman. The Caradocs explained that John Baptist was ordained, not by the English church, but an unspecified dissenting sect. They were used to Dissenters, they said. There were many in Wales. Sophia said a man of God was a man of God, however ordained. Satisfied with this response, the Caradocs nodded and agreed that was as true in Virginia as it was in Wales.

Sophia suggested to Henri that John Baptist might as well marry them when he married Caitlin and Gideon, and bother the banns and any irregularity about his ordination. It would do for their purposes. Henri shrugged and agreed. More time passed with no sign of John Baptist, and an irritated Henri volunteered to go and fetch him, but the Caradocs shrugged and said he'd come in his own good time. The next afternoon a loud bass voice singing hymns in the mist announced his arrival.

The wedding was fixed on two days later. Caitlin confided to Sophia she wished she had more time to prepare the wedding breakfast, but "wait any longer and John Baptist will have drunk so much whiskey he'll be seeing little red-and-green dragons. I'm not having dragons when I marry Gideon! And to think, now you'll be marrying Henri! The nicest thing in all the world, Sophy, that we are married together!"

Sophia observed the wedding preparations with a jaundiced eye. All she wanted was to endure whatever ceremony these people called a wedding. She felt surprisingly glum and even regretted her rash bargain. On the one hand, as a child she had been mesmerized by Henri, who was such a novelty that she would do anything he ordered her to do.

Though he hadn't been very nice, she hadn't minded because he had provided excitement. He still exerted a powerful effect on her, and she had to admit to herself that of all the men she'd met, he was the only one, other than the Irish peer, who seemed likely to prove exciting as a bedfellow. But she didn't love Henri, she knew. It would be unwise to love him. While Henri had his good points—he hadn't murdered the Drumhellers, he had been largely responsible for getting everyone to Caradoc Station in one piece, he had a sense of direction—Henri didn't love her, wasn't fond of her even, and she doubted he would make any woman a reliable husband. She vaguely suspected Frenchmen never did. Lady Burnham had often expressed her disapproval of French morals.

However, they would be husband and wife only briefly, then Henri and Thierry would leave, and that would be that. Going to Louisiana with him and Thierry was out of the question, let alone going to France. But for all that, Sophia was insatiably curious about what a wedding night with Henri would be like. She would just have to enjoy wifehood while it lasted.

Such reflections and reasoning depressed her spirits, especially seeing Caitlin's happiness. Sophia told herself she mustn't let her own circumstances blight the younger girl's wedding. She would enter into the spirit of the wedding for Caitlin's sake.

They had to prepare one of their precious hams for the wedding breakfast, so she and Saskia scrubbed, then soaked the biggest one in Caitlin's big iron pot and left it cooking for an entire day and night, filling the cabin with a rich, festive aroma. Caitlin, sleeves rolled to her elbows, went into a flurry of mixing and baking with Malinda as her helper. Following Caitlin's instructions, Malinda sifted flour to remove insects, and hacked lumps from a hard gray loaf of sugar, then energetically pounded the lumps fine with a mallet. She stirred and mixed and measured and, by the end of the day, was covered in a dusting of flour but looked very pleased with herself when Caitlin said she'd never had such a little helper in all the world.

By sunrise the morning of the wedding, the ham stood cooling on Caitlin's blue-and-white willow-pattern platter while Saskia spooned sorghum over to glaze it. A dish of dried apples, soaked back to fullness and then fried in the rich fat from the ham, waited beside it. Saskia had also made an Indian pudding with cornmeal, milk, and eggs, sweetened with honey. Malinda was helping Venus, turning the spit while Venus basted a pair of wild turkeys with bear grease, Susan asleep in her lap. There was a crock of blackberry shrub and another of muscadine wine that Caitlin had made the previous autumn "so the ladies can refresh themselves," according to the Caradoc men. The men had something much stronger from the Caradocs' still.

Caitlin had spent the better part of the previous day making a special raised pie with suet pastry, filled with smoked venison and pigeon, from an old recipe of her mother's written on a scrap of paper tucked in the Caradoc Bible. Using dried wild grapes and some precious wheat flour bartered the previous month by a family from Pennsylvania, Caitlin had also baked small cakes she called *bara brith* that she told Sophia proudly were a Welsh specialty. The morning of the wedding, she brought a cheese and a round of butter from the springhouse, washed the salt off the butter, and decorated it with wild strawberries.

"There!" she said proudly, covering her feast with muslin against the flies.

After a hasty meal, the four women cleared the breakfast things and swept and tidied the room thoroughly. The men were banished to the porch, where they sheltered from the rain with the whiskey jug. The Caradocs settled down with their fiddles to serenade the brides while the women and Malinda decorated the cabin. Caitlin and Sophia had gone out in the rain as soon as they were awake that morning to gather armfuls of hawthorn and wild trumpet vine and magnolias, and with these they turned the cabin's central room into a green, blossoming, sweet-smelling bower. Caitlin tucked a blossom behind Malinda's ear and told her to sit quietly while she and Sophia dressed.

The men began with Caitlin's favorite hymn, "Guide Me, O Thou Great Jehovah." Inside, Caitlin sang harmony to that and then other hymns in Welsh and English as she worked.

Thierry had tramped off, refusing to have anything to do with the wedding, and Gideon had declared drawing water was women's work and gone fishing, but the other men formed a bucket brigade to pass bucket after bucket of water up the slope from the river to the cabin. The girls had heated it in the iron cauldron where the ham had soaked and took turns to have a bath in the washing tub. Malinda wanted a bath too, so they let her have one. Then all three washed one another's hair with rainwater from the barrel Caitlin kept for that purpose.

Meanwhile, the hymn-singing on the porch got louder as the jug went round, though Henri passed up his chance at the jug with a shudder. "Do you think John Baptist will be too drunk to marry us?" Sophia asked Caitlin as they combed each other's damp hair in the cracked looking glass.

Caitlin sighed. "I hope not! Let's hurry and dress, though. Oh, Sophy, what are you doing?"

Sophia had had her trunk carried in from the wagon and was searching inside for something clean to wear. She had taken care to supply herself well for her Virginia adventure, and most of these new clothes were unworn. At Thomas's plantation she'd had no need for finery and had alternated two of her oldest day dresses. But her riding habit was in a sorry state after months of mud, dust, rain, and being snagged and torn in the forest; she thought she owed it to Caitlin to look a little fresher on the day of their wedding. Although she had forgotten about her appearance while they were traveling, she wanted to look her best for Henri so he would remember her looking that way when he left.

She looked up to see Caitlin and Malinda gawping at the trunk's contents.

"Oh, Sophy! How fine!" exclaimed Caitlin, stroking a lace-trimmed shift with a tentative finger.

Sophia blushed, suddenly ashamed of having so many pretty clothes when Caitlin possessed only two brown homespun dresses and some rough shifts. "I'm . . . I'm making a *trousseau* for you and me."

"A trussy? What's that, in all the world?" laughed Caitlin.

"You'll see."

Sophia dug down among her things to find two unworn plain traveling dresses with long hooded jackets, called Brunswicks. They were made of fine, light wool. She put one of gray trimmed with black ribbon to one side of the kitchen table for her and the other one of blue trimmed with tartan ribbon to the other side for Caitlin. To each dress she added a pair of wooden pattens she had worn when walking in the muddy fields of her Sussex home, and several pairs of woolen stockings and ribbon garters.

Caitlin's eyes grew bigger as Sophia shook out the two new morning gowns, made simply because the London dressmaker judged that would do in the colony. She selected one of fine sprigged muslin with blue flowers and lace-trimmed sleeves that Sophia thought would make Caitlin a pretty wedding dress. The blue flowers matched Caitlin's eyes. She chose the red-and-white patterned one for herself and then put two more of the dresses on each pile. She rummaged around and divided the rest of the trunk's contents: there were white kerchiefs, caps with ribbons, and a soft India shawl for each of them, as well as lace-trimmed shifts and petticoats, a nightdress and dressing gown, cambric handkerchiefs, silk stockings, and backless beaded silk slippers with buckles and high heels. They would be a little too big for Caitlin, but they were extremely pretty, and Caitlin's shoes were smaller versions of the clumsy footwear worn by her father and uncles. Sophia left the stays at the bottom of the trunk. No need to lace themselves up in the wilderness.

Caitlin stroked a shawl wistfully. "Oh, what grand and fine things you have! I never dreamed there were such pretty clothes in all the world. Fit for a queen, these are."

Sophia smiled and put the pile with the blue-flowered muslin dress on top into Caitlin's arms. "These are yours. Your *trousseau.* It means clothes for starting married life. And the dress on top is to get married in."

"Mine! No! Never in all the world!" Caitlin exclaimed, her arms full. "I never dreamed to have such things!" She burst into tears. Putting her new clothes carefully down, she threw her arms around Sophia, hugging her hard. "Oh, Sophy! You're so kind! Thank you! Thank you."

"Dear Caitlin, only think how good and kind you've been to us. Now stop crying or Gideon will see your red eyes and think you're unhappy and you've changed your mind. Besides, you don't want your nose snuffling on your wedding day. Try this shift first, then the petticoat, and then we'll see if Saskia needs to take it up . . . Yes, the dress is too long. You'll trip. Hold still while we pin it."

Malinda gazed entranced at the pretty clothes. Sophia gave her a kiss and fished out a lace-trimmed cap. She had never liked caps. Her hair was long and heavy, and when she piled it up, she thought a cap on top made her look like she was wearing a bird's nest. She put the cap on Malinda instead and pulled the child's hair, damp and curly from her bath, out from the sides so that the curls showed. Then she took a plain linen shift and said, "Caitlin, help me turn this into a gown for Malinda."

With the help of a sash, the two of them pulled and twisted and draped and hitched the shift into a sort of long dress for the child. The center of this fuss, Malinda stood very, very still, almost afraid to breathe lest she break the spell.

"It's dragging on the ground, though. Can you walk, Malinda? No? Sophy, we have to hitch it up in front with these ribbons." Finally Malinda's bare toes peeked from under the bottom.

"No running," Caitlin said. "You'll trip."

"Not even with Jack," said Sophia. "But how sweet you look. You shall stand up with us, darling!" she exclaimed, thinking she hadn't noticed before that once she was cleaned up, Malinda was quite a pretty child, with a little cat's nose and wide brown eyes. In the cap, which was very large on her small head, and Sophia's shift hitched up around her middle, Malinda resembled a little bundle of laundry. She flushed with pleasure at being admired and sat down to watch the others get ready.

The brides' dresses were hung from a peg in the wall. Since Caitlin was shorter than Sophia, the sewing box had also been unearthed from the wagon, and Saskia was stitching quickly, shortening the hems of Caitlin's new dresses before they dragged in the dirt. Outside, festivities on the porch had accelerated. Having exhausted their repertoire of hymns, the musicians progressed to love ballads and reels. Caitlin's father and her youngest uncle began dancing a jig with Toby and Jack, singing lustily, while their brother fiddled and John Baptist banged the whiskey jug on the floor to keep time and joined the others in the chorus:

You must make me a Holland shirt,
Blow, blow, blow, winds, blow,
Without a stitch of needlework,
Blow, ye winds that arise, blow, blow.

You must wash it in yonder spring,
Blow, blow, blow, ye winds, blow,
Where there's never a drop of water in,
Blow, ye winds that arise, blow, blow.

"Now, while Saskia takes up your dress, I'll write the licenses," said Sophia. In addition to her trunk and the sewing box, she had retrieved her writing box and Thomas's small trunk with his papers. She took out

Thomas and Anne's marriage license and carefully copied out the wording for her and Caitlin. She wondered if anyone reading the licenses would notice they weren't authentic, but she'd seen no sign of anyone who could remotely be described as the authorities since Williamsburg. She didn't count John Baptist.

"In England, marriages are recorded in the parish register, but since there's no parish here, that's not possible. So I've written these for us. If they're ever needed."

Caitlin peered over Sophia's shoulder as Sophia shook river sand on to dry the ink. Then Sophia held it up and read out loud, "'Be it known that this day, twenty-sixth of June the year of our Lord 1755, Caitlin Caradoc, sixteen, Spinster, having the consent of her Father, entered into the Holy State of Matrimony and is married to Gideon Vann, Cherokee, according to God's Holy Ordinance at Caradoc Station on the New River in the Colony of Virginia by the Reverend John Baptist.' The bride and groom have to sign. Just there."

"Oh, Sophy!" Caitlin gazed admiringly at the license and carefully signed at the bottom where Sophia had written "Bride."

Then Sophia wrote her own and read it to Caitlin. "'Be it known that this day, twenty-sixth of June the year of our lord 1755, the Honorable Sophia Grafton, twenty, Spinster, daughter of the late Viscount Grafton of Sussex, entered into the Holy State of Matrimony and is married according to God's Holy Ordinance to Henri de Marechal at Caradoc Station in the Colony of Virginia by the Reverend John Baptist.'

"They sound quite official, don't they?" Sophia congratulated herself. "I think they have to be signed by John Baptist too." But could John Baptist write? *No,* she decided, *I'll just forge his signature. He'll be too drunk to write and too drunk to notice I've forged his name.*

"Licenses! It's a comfort you're here, Sophy. You know about so many things, more than Tad, seeing everything's done right. I'm so glad that we're going together when your rafts are ready. It's like having an older sister. I didn't realize Gideon's cabin, where we'll have our trading post, is on the edge of your land. How do you suppose you tell whose land is whose?"

"Oh. I've no idea. At home I believe there were hedgerows and stone walls," Sophia said vaguely. She tried to recall what Colonel Washington had explained about surveying and boundaries and finally decided something must mark off her property from that owned by Gideon's people or Mr. Barker would have mentioned it. "Bother the boundaries! The main thing is, we'll be neighbors. You and I'll be company for each other. We'll visit each other all the time."

Sophia wiped the pen, thinking it truly was a relief that Caitlin and Gideon would be nearby. What on earth would she do if they ever decided to leave and settle elsewhere? Malinda was sweet and really quite quick in understanding what was wanted of her, but hardly company. It occurred to Sophia that one day she would take Malinda back to England with her and explain that she had adopted Malinda and let it be known that any man who courted her must take Malinda too. The prospect of an English husband in the future suddenly gave her qualms about today's marriage to Henri. Either the marriage to Henri was a sham and she would have immorality and deceit on her conscience, or if by some chance it was valid, in the future she would be guilty of bigamy. But she told herself this was no time to have qualms, there was nothing else she could do.

Outside, things grew nosier. They were singing the same song over and over. Rufus had taken his turn at the jug and was joining in on *"Blow, blow, blow."* Jack had been sent to feed the animals and was back, shooting pebbles with a slingshot Caitlin's father had made him. Nott, Seth, and Meshack were slumped at the end of the porch, watching Jack aim at the chickens pecking in Caitlin's vegetable patch and talking in low voices about whether they'd been wise to go south with the whites instead of east to the swamps with their friends.

"Big snakes in them swamps," muttered Seth. "I hates snakes worse'n the Devil. Venus afeard of snakes too. 'Sides, we free now. Miss

Sophy say so, give us a paper says so. If she give us some her land like she promise, I thinkin' me an Venus, we can have us a cabin, plant a garden, get some chickens. Maybe a cow."

"Sounds fine. You reckon Miss Sophy keep her promise 'bout land? She say she will, but can't trust what white folks say."

"She gettin' married, Nott. Don't matter can you trust Miss Sophy. She got to do what Mist' Henri say."

"Them two get married, they be one mind 'tween the two of them, and if you been watchin', Meshack, you know that mind Miss Sophy's. Besides, Mas' Henri a Frenchermen, Mas' Terry too, and half crazy trying to get him to go on west. He half crazy to go."

"How come he gettin' married then? What Miss Sophy want with him if he gone? What good that do her? They's some strange white folks."

"Don't know the answer there, but I think when she say she give us land, she do it so we stay and work for her."

"Hunh! We work for her all right! She make us be slaves again."

"Don't think she'll do that, Nott. She like tellin' folks what to do, but . . ."

"But they'll be slaves there. If they be slaves, they be an overseer. Then when we get there, what happen? Overseer make us work? We slaves again, that's what. Or we not slaves no more, but they are? We get land, build our own cabin, slaves don't? Don't like it. Trouble coming."

"Maybe Miss Sophy free everybody, Meshack."

"Ha, nothin' like *that* gon' happen. We shoulda gone to the swamp, snakes or not. One day the patrollers coming. I know it. They find us. Always do," said Meshack. "You seen what happen then. This time, the patrollers come, I swear I kill them or I die tryin', but won't be no slave again."

"Amen," said Seth.

"Yeah. Amen," said Nott.

The men were interrupted. The cabin door opened, and Caitlin, in her new dress and with her hair up in some pretty paste combs Sophia had insisted she wear, shouted to make herself heard over the music and the banging whiskey jug. "*Tad!* Uncle Geraint, Uncle Owen, we're ready for the wedding!"

"Awww."

Caitlin's father halted with one foot raised mid-jig. "Caitlin! *Cariad!* The image of your poor drowned mam the day we married!" He wiped his eyes. "By rights we should be settin' you on a horse. We need a horse." He looked around him, as if a horse might suddenly materialize on the porch.

Caitlin rolled her eyes at Sophia. "Tad says in Wales the bride has to ride off as fast as she can and be caught by the groom—they did that with my mam, but I'd rather not in my fine new dress. It's raining. Besides, if I rode away, Gideon might decide to leave instead of catching me. I'd rather just marry him now."

Her father looked about him. "We'd have to saddle the horse, though . . . We'll use the broomstick. Where's the broomstick?"

"Priodas coes ysgub," her uncles chorused, stamping their feet.

"Broomstick!" roared John Baptist. He winked suggestively at the brides and raised the jug to his lips.

Caitlin sighed. "There's no doing without the broomstick at a Welsh wedding."

"Whatever for?"

"Mam and Tad had one; everybody does in Wales. I explained to Gideon, my uncles hold my broom crossways and Gideon and I have to hold hands and jump over it. In Wales, I think it makes the marriage lawful, or did in the olden days. You and Henri better jump too, to keep the peace. Tad says in Wales people think that's enough to be married, but for Gideon and me, he insisted on John Baptist too. A girl who came through last year told me about what happened when she got married—a clergyman has to say the words 'I pronounce you man and wife' or it isn't real."

"Is John Baptist a real clergyman?" asked Sophia, not that she cared deeply. He would do for her purposes.

"He says he is, an English one too, but he got disgraced and came here to live on that little island downriver. He won't say what it was he did."

Caitlin then turned to deal with a loud argument between the three Caradoc men about how high the broom had to be. They were pulled up by a sharp "Tad!" from Caitlin, who snatched the broom away and flung it in the corner. "Not until *after* John Baptist marries us. Then we'll do it the Welsh way. Come inside, all of you, and look. We've decorated it up so fine and pretty. Come along now, John Baptist, up with you. I want you to stand there, in front of the fireplace." She pulled the bearded old man firmly by the arm to the fireplace and handed him the family Bible to hold. Then she ordered her swaying uncles to stand either side of him. "Hold him still, and hold yourselves still while you're about it!" she commanded. "Now Sophy, you and Henri stand on this side, and Gideon and me will stand just here, and Tad will stand up with me because . . . because when he and Mam got married, their parents stood up with them, and Mam isn't . . . Tad, don't you dare go crying about Mam and spoil my day!" Caitlin brushed away a tear and muttered, "I don't know why I'm crying!

"Rufus, you and Jack and Toby stand there, behind Sophy and Henri and Gideon and me getting married. Boys, no giggling and shoving! Jack, you and Toby stand here and stop shoving. Venus, stand here with Susan, Saskia here, and Seth and Nott and Meshack, line up beside Venus and Saskia. Malinda, you come stand up with Sophia and me. Little steps, Malinda, or that dress will come unhitched! Now I want everyone to be quiet and respectful—Jack and Toby, *stop that*!"

Seth cleared his throat and interrupted, "Miss Caitlin, me and Venus, we like to be married too, after you folks finished. They says slaves cain't get married for real, but Miss Sophia say we ain't slaves no more. Why can't us get married?"

Venus gasped, "Oh, Seth!"

Sophia turned around. "You're not slaves anymore, Seth, none of you. Of course you can be married too."

"With us," said Henri firmly, ignoring mutterings from John Baptist. "Move over, Sophy, let Venus and Seth join the circle."

Saskia reached out and took Susan from Venus, saying, "Give me that baby 'fo' it get dropped on its head in all this marryin'." Venus relinquished the baby and beamed up at Seth.

John Baptist cleared his throat and looked up at the ceiling. He swayed slightly and bellowed, "If everyone's finally ready! Let the couples join hands!"

The three couples did.

"Let us pray. Er . . . Lord in heaven, we're standing before the throne of grace because these people want to marry. Caitlin here is marrying Gideon, Sophia here is marrying Henry, and Venus here is marrying Seth. Dear Lord, we know there hasn't been any banns read, but, all-seeing God, you know who your children are, everyone knows about it, and ain't no objections. No need for banns. No need to repeat everything over and over neither. Now, one at a time.

"Caitlin Caradoc, do you marry Gideon Vann for your husband and promise to be his wife in er . . . health and sickness and wealth—not likely to be much wealth hereabouts in this part of Virginia, though the Caradocs can't complain—but poor too if that's what God sends you, for better and worse till, er, the cold hand of Death rends you apart? And you'll obey him and . . . have his children and sew his clothes and tend his garden and keep the fire up? Feed the livestock and at night you'll—"

"Yes!" exclaimed Caitlin. "Yes! I will!"

"Good. And Gideon Vann, do you want Caitlin for your wife in sickness and health—she's always been healthy enough in my opinion, fine girl, known her since was a little thing no higher than my knee, she won't trouble you with sickness much—and . . . er, everything else? Look after her like a husband should? See off wild animals if they come prowling? Providing she does what I told her . . . obeys you?" Gideon looked puzzled and took so much time considering his answer that John Baptist bellowed an impatient "Well?"

Caitlin whispered, "You have to say yes too. Just say yes, Gideon! Please! Or we're not married."

"Yes."

"Good. Henry, do you take Sophy for your wife? In sickness and health for the rest of her life, like I asked Caitlin? You heard it once already, we all heard it, no need to say the same."

"Je suppose. Oui," muttered Henri.

"He means yes," Sophia interjected.

"I heard him, missy, no need for you to do his talking. Sophia, do you marry Henry Marshallman? And the same parts about richer and poorer and sicker and better, until death do you part. Come along, young lady, be as quick with your own answer as you were with his. Are you taking Henry or not?"

"Yes. Yes, I will."

"And you, girl who ain't a slave no more—girl, what's your name?"

"Venus," interjected Sophia.

"Venus and . . . Who're you again?"

"Seth," said Seth very loudly.

"No need to shout! Have to know who it is I'm marryin' before God! You've already heard what I said, what a husband and wife promise to do, and seeing as you're free, I guess you can be husband and wife too. What do you say?"

"I say we be married together, to stay together and die together before they takes us away from each other," said Seth firmly, looking down at Venus. "And Susan our baby and nobody else's."

"Amen," said Venus softly. "Amen. Oh, Seth!"

"Well then, guess you're married as the rest. God be praised in heaven, you're all married men and wives! To each other, no confusion about who's bound in holy matrimony to who. Everyone knows. Let us pray." John Baptist hugged the Bible for dear life and, swaying harder, launched into a long meandering prayer that took in the rainy weather, Noah's Ark, good shepherds, good sheep, and children raised in the fear of the Lord. This led John Baptist off on a lusty new tangent of prayer, involving the marriage bed and the getting of the children. Toby snickered. Caitlin was blushing. Sophia, trying desperately to stifle her giggles, caught Henri's eye, and both bent their heads and shook with silent laughter. Malinda was wide-eyed at so much information.

"The broom! It's not done till they jump the broom!" Caitlin's father interrupted John Baptist midsentence. He fetched the broom from the corner. His youngest brother took the other end, and they held it up. "Come along, Caitlin, you and Gideon."

"Tad, it's waist high! Lower! We're not giants!"

There was another lively dispute about how high custom required it to be to make a marriage official in Wales, and then Caitlin held out her hand to Gideon. "Come on, or there'll be no peace. We have to jump together. It's to show that as husband and wife we'll always agree." Gideon nodded. Caitlin hitched up her skirts and slipped off the too-big high-heel slippers. "One, two, three!" and over they went, and the Caradocs stamped their feet and cheered noisily.

"Now you." Caitlin's father nodded at Henri.

"Of course!" said Sophia, gathering her skirts and taking Henri by the hand. They jumped. The Caradocs roared approval. *At least we'd be considered married in Wales,* thought Sophia.

Then Venus and Seth, Seth letting out a great whoop of joy as he leaped, and then spinning Venus round in his arms. The Caradocs roared again, stomped the floor, did an impromptu jig, and passed the jug around. Refreshed, the youngest Caradoc picked up his fiddle and launched into a Welsh love song. John Baptist returned to the jug and offered it to the three grooms. Gideon and Henri declined, though Seth was happy to accept, while Venus fed Susan, who had begun to fret.

Sophia opened the writing box and wrote out a marriage license for Venus and Seth. "You need a last name on the marriage license," she said. Venus and Seth looked at each other.

"Hadn't reckoned no other name," said Seth. "Slaves don't mostly have other names."

"But you're free now, Seth. Venus will be Mistress what?"

"Another name! I want a fine one for Venus and me and Susan. Finest name there is."

"Hmm." Sophia considered. "What about Venus and Seth Hanover? Back in England, that's . . . er . . . the king's . . . last name."

"Sounds fine." Neither could write, so first Venus, then Seth made their mark, and Sophia filled in their names, then signed John Baptist's name and promised herself that the first thing she would do at Wildwood would be to have a school and teach the freed slaves to read and write. Then she got up to help Caitlin and Saskia set out the food on the table. Caitlin tied an apron over her new dress and carved the ham with her father's hunting knife.

The men, except Henri and Gideon, went back to their fiddles—the occasion called for music—and their jug on the porch. Rufus had grown sentimental with drink and was trying to describe his and Molly's wedding day to his sons, who weren't listening. Toby and Jack kept creeping back to the table, trying to snatch nibbles of ham and bits of pastry off the tempting golden pie, but Rufus caught them and dragged them back to the porch by the scruff of their necks. "Your mother, God rest her soul, taught you your manners! Disgrace her memory, and I'll box your ears, I will."

"Ohhhh! Paaaa!" they whined, dying from hunger, but something in Rufus's manner kept them from trying it again.

Much later, in the afternoon, it stopped raining and the sun came out. The remains of the feast lay on the table, turkey carcasses picked clean and the raised pie just a remnant of crust in a puddle of melted meat jelly. The remainder of the ham had been wrapped in a piece of muslin and stored in the food cupboard. By then even the boys had eaten their fill and could only nibble a last *bara brith* spread with Caitlin's sweet butter. The fiddlers were snoring on the porch, and Malinda was asleep in a heap under the table.

Before sunset, the Caradocs, John Baptist, Rufus, Meshack, and Nott had woken and emptied the first jug. Caitlin's father staggered off to find another. Henri and Seth went to feed the animals, and Gideon had disappeared. Caitlin giggled and told Sophia she wasn't sure where he'd gone, but she'd warned Gideon about the Welsh custom of shivaree, making noise to disturb a married couple on their wedding night. Gideon laughed, said he didn't want that, and had gone looking for a place where no one could find them. Caitlin blushed, and Sophia laughed.

As evening drew on, Seth came back, but there was no sign of Henri. Sophia thought he must have gone looking for Thierry, who had left earlier in the day to avoid the ceremony and wedding breakfast, refusing to "stand up" with Henri. Then it dawned on her: Henri would have reasoned he'd left her with the marriage license, and she and the people with her were safe now. The two Frenchmen had seized their chance while everyone was drunk, stolen two of the Caradocs' horses, and made their escape. She would never see him again.

Sophia was surprised at her dismay, the sad, sinking feeling in the pit of her stomach. She hadn't realized how much she'd been looking forward to her wedding night, but it was clear Henri hadn't thought her worth staying for after all. She fought back the urge to cry—it would just upset Caitlin. She, Caitlin, Venus, and Saskia cleared the table, and afterward the women sat sipping muscadine wine, two of them waiting for their men to come back. Caitlin was happy and distracted, watching for Gideon. Venus was calmer but glowing, whispering over and over to Susan as she fed her, "Seth and me married, Susan. You our baby, Seth be your pa, you can forget any other pa 'cause I be Seth's wife! We the Hanover family now. We free and can't nobody sell us away."

Sophia, now technically Mistress de Marechal, was trying to reason her disappointment away. It was just as well that Henri had gone, she told herself, now she needn't torture herself any longer wondering when he would go. She and her companions would reach Wildwood with or without Henri. She told herself sternly that she had gotten what she wanted. Everything was fine. She had nothing to regret.

Her eyes stung with unshed tears.

The Caradoc brothers were playing again, this time a plaintive song Caitlin said was called "Suo Gran."

"A love song?" asked Sophia glumly.

"A Welsh lullaby," said Caitlin, and blushed. "It's supposed to mean children," she whispered to Sophia. "And here comes Gideon." She got up to join Gideon, who put his arm round Caitlin's shoulders, and Sophia watched them wander off until they were swallowed up in the dusk.

"Venus." Seth beckoned from the door, and Venus rose to join him, leaving Susan sleeping on Saskia's shoulder. They walked off hand in hand.

Sophia wandered out to the far end of the porch, staring into the gathering dusk, thinking at least she was spared having to spend her wedding night in the cabin, where drunken Caradocs and John Baptist were likely to lurch in any moment. She could cry now, though, and the first tear rolled down her cheek, when a voice said, "Madame de Marechal?"

She looked up, startled, and there was Henri looking pleased with himself. He held out his hand. What? He hadn't gone? Hard as she tried to stop it, Sophia's heart leaped. She swiped her hand across her wet cheeks, took his outstretched hand, and the two of them walked down toward the river. Henri pointed out the first stars. Behind them the Caradocs fiddled on, the music growing fainter as it followed them into the night. They could hear the rush of the mill. Fireflies lit tiny points of light around them, and bats flitted against the evening sky that was still a faint band of pink on the horizon. On they went until they were out of sight of the cabin and the wagons and the music was very faint. Henri stopped by a river birch and pulled back a sort of curtain hanging from its low branches—one of Caitlin's quilts. "Your *boudoir de campagne*, madame!"

Sophia ducked her head to look. "Oh, Henri! How charming!" So this was where Henri had been all that time! Sheltered under the branches was one of Caitlin's corn-husk mattresses, covered with more quilts. Outside, the river rushed and murmured in the dark, and Henri held the hanging quilt for Sophia to stoop and enter first, then he followed and drew her down onto the mattress.

"The cabin was out of the question. It shouldn't be too damp here. Well, madame, are we married?" he asked nuzzling her neck.

"*Oui*, monsieur," Sophia whispered and shivered as he began to undress her.

He undid her hair and then did other things he knew women liked, slowly and expertly, until she was murmuring his name and he knew she had abandoned any intention of keeping aloof from the business. Much later, as he fell asleep, he smiled with satisfaction in the dark, knowing himself back on familiar territory. Women were all the same. Who was master now? He had regained the upper hand, and he'd keep it until he left. It would teach her a lesson. He stretched pleasantly and fell asleep at once.

Sophia curled up against his back and listened to the rise and fall of Henri's breath. *Whatever happens later, I will always remember this night, and I will never, never regret it, immoral or not,* Sophia thought happily as she fell asleep beside him.

She woke as their little tent grew light. Her whole body ached in a pleasant, luxurious, well-used way, and she felt a rush of happiness recalling the previous night. In case there was more of the same this morning, she would have a wash before Henri woke up. Clutching a quilt about her, she emerged into the gray half-light, and the sound of birdcalls across the river blanketed with early morning mist.

She went to the riverbank, dropped the quilt on a rock, and then slipped quietly into the water beside it before she realized something was moving on the river, too big for a river bird. Instinct warned her to keep still. She crouched in the water by the rock with only her head above water and watched as a line of Indian canoes, carrying braves, women, children, and old people as well as their belongings paddled silently past, like ghosts in the mist. She rubbed her eyes. Then she clapped her hand over her mouth to stifle a shriek of surprise. There, in one of the canoes, was Cully! She waited until the last canoe disappeared, then wrapped herself in the quilt and hurried back to her boudoir.

Henri was just waking up. He stretched and smiled, as if he too were pleased with the way the night had gone. He rolled over. "Now, my ugly little monkey," he murmured without opening his eyes, "shall I remind you again who is your master? And if your master orders you to beg, then you will—"

"Henri, get up!"

Henri's eyes flew open. Sophia was not lying adoring and submissive by his side but hastily fastening her dress and giving orders. "Hurry! I just saw Indians on the river, a long line of canoes. They had Cully. Find Gideon."

Alarmed, Henri sat up and reached for his shirt. "A war party? How far away, Sophy? Have they attacked the ferry?" Surely the Caradocs were armed, but he heard no shots. Could the few of them hold off an all-out attack? Or more likely, the Caradocs and John the Baptist were too drunk from the night before to know if they were being attacked and had probably been murdered and scalped without resisting. "And what were you doing at the river?"

"Having a bath." Sophia was plaiting her hair with quick fingers. "I doubt it was a war party. They had women and children and, it looked like, their belongings. Maybe the Chickasaws attacked and they're escaping . . . though I don't think Cherokees would run away from anything. Gideon will know. But thank God, Cully's alive, and Gideon can go after him. What will the Indians want as a ransom?"

CHAPTER 20
AFTER THE WEDDINGS

July 1755

Unarmed, Sophia and Henri had cautiously made their way back through the trees to see if the trading post was still standing and the inhabitants alive. But there had been no attack, which was fortunate since the Caradocs and John Baptist were so poorly after the wedding festivities they couldn't have defended anything. Saskia cried to hear Cully was alive and wanted to run after the canoes herself, but Sophia persuaded her not to. Gideon would know how to find him and the best way to deal with the Indians who had kidnapped him. Saskia wouldn't be any use to Cully if she too were kidnapped or lost or killed.

Saskia was frantic at having to wait, but she had no choice. Gideon and Caitlin couldn't be found, and it was four days before they returned. Caitlin whispered to Sophia that she and Gideon had been in a camp Gideon had made in a cave, and blushed.

When Sophia told Gideon she had seen Cully, he agreed to go after the child and try to ransom him. He would try to get him back without a ransom of whiskey; he refused to bargain with poison even for the child's release. He left, calculating how to negotiate.

Venus and Seth disappeared with Susan so often that Saskia took out her frustration and anxiety about Cully by furiously upbraiding Venus for not doing her share of the work. Seth tried to intervene, and Saskia, who was on a knife edge of nerves, turned on him, and there was a heated argument until Nott came and calmed Saskia down. Nott shooed the others away, put his arms around Saskia and said she had to be patient a little longer, they'd get Cully back. He was sure of it. Saskia burst into tears.

Henri and Thierry urged the Caradocs on with the raft building, but the Caradoc brothers suffered so badly from the wedding celebrations that for days afterward, the raft building went very slowly indeed and, in Sophia's opinion, very inexpertly. She pointed out where parts kept falling off. John Baptist finally took himself off to his island in a subdued frame of mind.

Meanwhile there was a little excitement when travelers, several generations of the same extended family and their livestock, arrived at the trading post on a flotilla of overcrowded rafts, children tied with ropes to the side. They came ashore and bought gunpowder and cornmeal and a little bacon from Caitlin, who was efficiently minding the trading post while her father and uncles were at work on the rafts. They had two horses they were willing to trade for one of Sophia's cows, since their own cow had died. They weren't particularly good horses, but Sophia muttered to Henri they had better take them.

Her face puckered with distress, Malinda tugged on Sophia's skirt and pointed to the children tied to the raft. Sophia bent down and explained that those children were tied on to keep them from falling in the water and drowning. This didn't calm Malinda, so Sophia asked the women on the raft if the children could be untied to play, and for an afternoon, the riverbank at Caradoc Station rang with children's shrieks and laughter. All the children, even Toby and Jack, played blind man's bluff and hide-and-seek. Malinda joined in and opened her mouth with joy, though no sound came out.

"Cain't that one talk?" asked one of the settler children, pointing at Malinda. "She don't say nothing!"

"Malinda's too smart to talk," boasted Jack.

The settler children digested this. "Ain't never heard of that," said the oldest one.

Caitlin baked some sweet biscuits the children gobbled with tumblers of buttermilk while their mothers drank tea. Caitlin felt sorry for the women, who looked frightened and worn. She made corn pone and a huge pot of stew with the last of the previous autumn's potatoes and dried vegetables, and squirrels Thierry had killed that morning, and insisted everyone eat dinner. The next morning as the settlers prepared to leave, she gave the women a clay pot of honey and a basket of eggs.

"You been real kind. It's been happiness for the children and us. Wish we could stop here and get a homestead fine as yours, save us going all the way to Kentuckee. You reckon we'll make it there?" whispered one of the anxious women to Caitlin. "Bein' married to a half-blood, you got any idea where the Indians are?"

Caitlin said she didn't know. The woman didn't look like she wanted to get back on the raft, but her husband had tied her children on again, so she did.

With the three new rafts in various stages of completion, Caitlin and her father took stock of the goods Caitlin and Gideon would take with them to the new trading post, working out what to take on the rafts and what to leave on the wagons. Meshack and Nott would drive the wagons and livestock on the riverside trail and catch up when the rafts tied up for the night. They were not happy about this, fearing they would be easy prey for the Indians, but Sophia said they could each take a cow if they agreed. Still, there was so much to go on the rafts that Sophia was afraid they would get out into the river and sink. The thought of sinking terrified Saskia so much that she insisted she would go in the wagon with Nott when the time came.

Meanwhile week after week passed with no sign of Gideon. "He can't have been killed, can he, Sophy?" Caitlin asked again and again, eyes wide with apprehension. "Or tired of being married? He can't be tired of that, can he?" Sophia was sure Gideon would be back but sympathized with Caitlin's misery. Saskia alternated between wild hope Gideon would appear any minute with Cully and misery fearing he would not.

Sophia and Caitlin both found they hadn't much appetite. Sophia put it down to the heat, and Caitlin to moping. Then one morning Sophia went out to gather eggs and found Caitlin being sick behind the chicken house. Sophia, queasily gathering eggs she had begun to find revolting to eat, was promptly sick too. Both continued to be actively sick in the mornings. Finally Saskia said they must both be pregnant.

Caitlin touched her stomach reverently and whispered, "A baby! The lullaby worked!"

Oh no! thought Sophia in horror and begged Saskia and Caitlin to keep her condition secret and say nothing to Henri. Puzzled, they agreed, and Caitlin danced off to tell her father.

Hot muggy day succeeded hot muggy day, and close airless nights hummed with mosquitoes thriving on the now-sluggish river. Nauseous, bitten, and strangely sleepy all the time, Sophia thought she had never felt worse in her life, but her struggle to hide it went largely unnoticed because Thierry fell seriously ill with a high fever that left him too listless to move, vomiting, and, despite the suffocating heat, shivering with chills. Caitlin covered him with blankets and heated stones to put under them and tried medicinal teas she brewed from wild plants. Henri reassured Thierry he wouldn't leave without him.

"We'll be home in a few months, Thierry, I promise," he said over and over, wiping Thierry's brow with a damp cloth that was hot by the time he removed it from Thierry's forehead.

Caitlin's mood was easy to judge from her choice of songs—she alternated between lullabies and mournful love ballads. Seth, Nott, Meshack, and the boys weeded the vegetable garden and killed insects, and Rufus looked after the livestock. The men took it in turns to watch through the night, armed. All the former slaves were watchful and on edge, expecting slave catchers or the militia would come out of the woods sooner or later, and Rufus and his boys feared being hauled back to Williamsburg. The men made sure their weapons were loaded and to hand at all times. They were as anxious as Henri to be gone, and impatient for Gideon's return.

Venus begged a shawl from Sophia and tied Susan to her chest while she went about the household chores she shared with Saskia and Caitlin. Sophia busied herself with the sewing and mending for everyone, mainly because the work allowed her to sit down, and when she sat, she felt less nauseous and dizzy.

Caitlin questioned Venus relentlessly about what having a baby felt like, wanted a full description of every moment. How painful did it get? She listened wide-eyed while Venus dwelt on the part where the pain had been so terrible she'd been unable to do anything but scream. Sophia tried not to listen.

The rank smell of animal pelts curing on the porch increased Sophia's misery, and a need to escape yet another telling of Venus's suffering in childbirth drove her to seek refuge in the springhouse from the steamy heat and everyone and everything. There was a small bench and room for one person among the butter, cheese, and buttermilk, and it was damp but cool. She felt overwhelmed with melancholy, cried often, and read Lady Burnham's prayer book, hoping this would fortify her spirit. The sight of Lady Burnham's and her mother's handwriting on the flyleaf anchored her somehow, though she felt certain neither her mother, her father, nor Lady Burnham would approve of the situation in which she now found herself. Sophia knew she had to keep her mind on getting them all to Wildwood, but sometimes she felt too sick to care. She hoped she was doing her duty.

Whatever that duty was. It had been so easy to know one's duty in England, she thought, even if she hadn't always done it. But in Virginia it was frequently hard, if not impossible, to be certain what was right. While she tried to reason herself into a better frame of mind, Sophia absentmindedly nibbled handfuls of watercress that grew in the spring. It tasted cool and fresh, the only thing she could bear to eat.

It was nearly August before Gideon returned, but he brought Cully with him. Saskia, who had aged with worry and had dark circles under her eyes, screamed with joy when she saw her son, fell on her knees, and clutched Cully tightly, sobbing her thanks to Gideon.

Gideon's grim expression softened when Caitlin told him about the baby. Then he told them his news, what he had learned when he caught up with his tribe, why they had been traveling upriver, and how he had persuaded them to release Cully.

Two young braves from his own village who had gone looking for Chickasaw war parties had returned to the tribe with a fat bear they had killed, plus horses, quilts, meal, and a Negro child they had taken from whites camped along the river. When taunted for not returning with white scalps, the braves boasted they would ambush the whites again in a few days. There was no hurry, the whites were easy prey, children could scalp them. Now there was fresh meat, and they would feast and dance first. They would join in the ball game the young men played for days at a time. But after a few days feasting and dancing, the braves could no longer participate in the ball game. They could scarcely stand. They lay on their blankets, faces spotted and swollen; spots covered their bodies too. They shook with cold even as they grew hotter and hotter, and though the shamans and beloved men carried them to the river for the water cure, it did not end their fever. They died within a week.

Soon others in the tribe were ill as well, and they too began to die, not only children and women and old people but strong young warriors. The shamans looked and looked for the cause and decided that the spots had been caused by frogs, which were also spotted. The people had offended the frogs in some way. The cure was to go to water, where the frogs lived, and there they dipped the burning people in the river. They spat the juice of spotted plants over the heads of the sufferers. They even had the sufferers eat the roasted meat of frogs to counteract off the evil. Still, most died.

During this time, a war party of Creeks had raided the village and burned the council house, taken many captives and slaves, because many warriors were too debilitated to resist. The enemies had paraded them in triumph among their own people, though the warriors they had taken were too weak to torture and kill. Instead they would suffer the humiliation of becoming slaves with their women, but no matter how much they were beaten, they grew ill with fever and spots, could not walk, and died. Soon their captors were ill as well.

The wars and the taking of prisoners that brought the tribes in contact every spring continued, and the spotted sickness had spread like a raging fire through the native settlements, from one tribe to the next, killing Gideon's people and their enemies equally. In little more than one moon, the land echoed with laments for the dead, among them Gideon's grandmother and most of his village.

When none of the shamans' spells and treatments stopped the people from dying, an old beloved man had seen in a dream that the whites had brought this killing disease, and their horses and quilts and the black child stolen from them were cursed and unclean in some way. To lift the curse, he said, the people still living must kill the horses, leave their homes to be cleansed by the wind and rain, and return to the place where the horses had been stolen and burn the blankets and Cully there. The survivors took sorrowful leave of their dead, gathered their possessions, and, grieving, set out upriver as he directed.

"Spots? Oh, Gideon, it sounds as if they all had measles!" exclaimed Sophia. "The braves who took Cully must have caught measles from him, like Rufus and the boys did. Though so many people couldn't have died of measles. One hardly dies of measles."

Gideon looked at her. He did not believe the whites caused the spotted sickness, since they suffered from it themselves, but the whites had some power or spell to protect themselves and the Negroes from being killed by it. That was a great power, and the tribes would fear venturing onto land inhabited by people who possessed it.

He did not mention that he had reached Cully just in time. The Indians who had kidnapped him had died, and it had been decided that Cully was cursed and he must be burned as a sacrifice to appease the spirits. Only long negotiations with the remaining elders in the council of grandmothers, who decided the fate of prisoners and hostages, had prevented it. They reminded Gideon that his own grandmother was dead of the strange sickness that followed Negroes and whites. Did her spirit not cry out to him to avenge her? Was it not the duty of a clan member to avenge the death of another clan member? Was her spirit waiting for the child to be burned so that she and other spirits might be free to go to the Darkening Land? Had he spent so long away from his people that he was lost to his obligations?

Gideon had countered with an argument that it was better to keep Cully alive to work because so many of the young women responsible for planting and harvesting crops had died. The grandmothers discussed this practical point, but the shamans had said to burn him, and they did not like to act against the shamans' advice. Besides, the people had been forced to leave their fields of corn to wither and die unharvested. There would be no Green Corn Ceremony to mark the harvest, and the coming winter would be hard. They had nothing to eat, few warriors left to hunt. Cully would be an extra mouth to feed.

Gideon said that his grandmother's spirit had not told him to burn the child and had offered that as a ransom, he would bring ground corn from the trading post to feed them through the winter in exchange for Cully. The grandmothers deliberated again and again. Finally they agreed to accept the cornmeal and let Gideon take Cully back before the ransom was paid—and before any more evil could come from him. Neither the grandmothers nor Gideon doubted that Gideon would return with the cornmeal.

He considered whether he and Caitlin should change their plan for the trading post, but perhaps this bad thing was an omen that the travelers brought other evils with them, and if so, it was his duty to try and understand them, and perhaps he could learn what spells and incantations would work against them. He must go up to the flat rock overlooking the valley, where the spirits of his ancestors often came on the wind. He would make a sacrifice of tobacco in the fire and ask what he must do.

Gideon had other news to tell. Long hunters reported that the British, the French, and their Indian allies had been at war on the Ohio. Many people had died, including the English general Braddock. Colonel Washington had seen him buried, then had driven wagons over the grave so that it was lost to sight and could not be desecrated or dug up and eaten by wild animals.

That was how Henri learned that his report was worthless, that he and Thierry had nothing to guarantee their voyage home, and there would be no reward if and when he reached France again. He swore furiously in French, cursed Sophia to the Devil, and stormed off.

The next day Gideon kissed Caitlin, told her he would return as soon as he could and not to worry. He hitched two of the Caradocs' mules to the largest wagon, and without asking the Caradocs, loaded it with barrels of cornmeal and went back the way he had come. Caitlin wept as he drove away, and Sophia put her arm round Caitlin's shoulders. "We must try to be cheerful," she sighed.

CHAPTER 21
HOME TO WILDWOOD

Gideon had spent a fortnight in the council house negotiating with the grandmothers while Cully's life hung in the balance. Then once he and Cully returned, it had taken even longer to drive the ransom wagonload of ground corn back, as the tribe had moved on. By the time Gideon returned with an empty wagon at the end of August, Caitlin had talked the Caradoc men out of their anger that Gideon had ransomed Cully using their cornmeal. She knew Gideon had no sense of personal property; he said Cherokee shared what they had equally and were shocked that among the whites some had much and some had little. When the Caradoc men protested angrily that it wasn't their view of the world and they had worked hard enough for their goods, by God, Caitlin flew into a temper, stamped her foot, and shouted at them, "For shame! You promised before God to do right by others if you escaped hanging! What could be more right than rescuing Cully for his poor mother, in all the world?"

Caitlin in a temper was an unusual sight, but she could be quite fierce when roused. The Caradoc men capitulated.

It was harvest time, and Caitlin wouldn't set out for her new home until she had finished preserving and drying a good part of her vegetables and fruit. It wasn't until a hot morning in late September that she gathered her sun-wizened beans, tomatoes, sliced pumpkins, squash, peaches, and apples into sacks, leaving strict instructions about what was to be done with whatever was still ripening or drying. "Mind what you're about. Don't sack them up until they're really dried out or they'll be full of worms when you come to eat them," she ordered her uncles.

"They probably wouldn't notice. They'll eat anything," she muttered to Sophia, "but I don't like to think of them eating worms. I wish they'd wives to look after them. I don't know what they'll do without me."

Meshack, Nott, and Saskia set off in the wagons, driving the livestock. Nott said Cully could come with them, but Saskia insisted he go by raft. She tied him to the rail herself. The wagons disappeared down the trail, and Caitlin's uncles cast off the ropes and waved as the rafts were poled away from the landing into the current. Because Caitlin's father and Gideon had experience navigating the river, Caitlin's father steered the lead raft, with Gideon rowing on one side and Cully watching for fallen trees and rocks underwater. The other two rafts followed, with Caitlin's father shouting back to stay close behind; the river was deceptive with its currents and submerged hazards. Thierry steered the second as Henri and Toby rowed, then Seth the third with Rufus, Venus, and Jack rowing.

Caitlin waved until her uncles disappeared from view, then sat on a pile of quilts between her father and Gideon and stitched contentedly on a baby's dress from a basket of fabric scraps. Malinda sat by her side and played with the scraps, examining each piece of fabric minutely. She had a doll Meshack had made her from corncobs, with a wooden head, and when Caitlin finished up the baby's dress, Malinda held up the doll with some flowered calico and made a sewing motion. Caitlin understood. "Yes, we can make your baby a dress." Caitlin cut out a doll's dress, threaded a needle for Malinda, and showed her how to stitch the dress together with small, even stitches.

Malinda bit her lip and concentrated. Hours later, she proudly held up the finished dress, and Caitlin admired her sewing and helped work the dress over the doll's head. Malinda hugged her doll, stuck her thumb in her mouth, and fell asleep against Caitlin's knees.

Caitlin was surprised Malinda had made the dress so neatly, since she'd had to show Malinda how to make a stitch. Malinda was a quick learner. When something needed to be done right, Caitlin had got into the habit of asking Malinda to do it. She could be trusted to gather eggs without dropping them, closed the farmyard gate that the boys often forgot and left open, needed to be shown only once what was a weed that needed pulling and a vegetable that needed watering. Malinda pulled down the laundry hanging on the line when she saw it was dry and, without being told, folded it into neat, smooth piles, the way she'd watched Caitlin do it. She could be relied on to hack sugar off the hard loaves with a knife, gently, without injuring herself or anyone else. If the boys did that job, they invariably cut themselves and got blood on the sugar. She patted the newly churned butter into discs and salted them efficiently before wrapping them in muslin and taking them to the springhouse. Although Sophia insisted Malinda was her responsibility, Malinda saw herself as Caitlin's deputy, followed Caitlin everywhere she went, and copied what Caitlin did.

Gideon signaled back to the other boats when they had to veer to avoid obstructions. Because of the current, Henri found it was hard work keeping a raft on course while avoiding submerged rocks and trees that could rip the bottom out of the boat. Sophia tried to be helpful, sitting in front and acting as lookout. Henri was arguing in French with Thierry about how they could return to France. They doubted their welcome in La Nouvelle-Orléans now and would have to avoid the authorities. Thierry proposed they strike out for the port of Savannah in the east. Henri thought the English in Savannah were as sure to hang them for spies as the English in Williamsburg. Thierry thought there were Huguenot refugees in Savannah—perhaps they'd be safe if they could pass themselves off as Huguenots.

Wherever they went, the problem was they had no money to buy their passage home. How could they get money? Henri always said he would think of a plan, but so far there was no plan.

The constant arguments went round and round themselves like angry buzzing hornets. Trying to ignore the sound, Sophia took her pocket book from the housewife at her waist and studied the list of things the Williamsburg ladies had assured her she would need to order for the house. Then she began to sketch a garden. Drawing on her recollection of Mr. Barker's sketch of the walled garden at Wildwood, she drew in some shrubs, then a small fountain, a sundial, and a stone bench. Then she leaned against the raft's lean-to shelter and dozed off.

She woke to the sun angling low through the trees and the rafts tied to stumps on the bank. The cows were standing knee-deep in water, and the mules were grazing on whatever they could find. Henri wiped a forearm over his sweating brow and said, "Wake up, sleepyhead. If you and Caitlin build a fire, the smoke will drive these damned mosquitoes away. We'll stretch our legs, exercise the horses and mules before it gets dark. And I'll catch a fish for your dinner."

Sophia stretched and yawned and reached for her teapot and the silver tea canister with its small lock and key, which she kept carefully wrapped in a shawl. The English tea had long been drunk, but Caitlin had filled the tea caddy with a powder made from dried and pounded sumac berries that could be mixed with boiling water to make a sour and refreshing hot drink. It was one of the few things Sophia could stomach.

Henri picked her up, carried her through the water, and set her on the bank. Sophia thanked him with a kiss and went to help Caitlin with the fire. Caitlin had found a mass of blackberry vines laden with fruit, and while the copper pot of water slowly came to a boil for tea, she and Sophia and Malinda filled a bucket with ripe berries still warm from the sun and oozing juice. As dusk fell, the fire crackled, stones were heated beside it, and with purple-stained hands Caitlin and Sophia patted out flat cornmeal cakes to bake on them. Malinda wandered off to catch fireflies with Cully and Jack.

"I like being a married woman, don't you?" Caitlin said happily. "Everything's exciting. Just think, Gideon and me will have our own trading post! Tad's already calling it Vann Station—grand, isn't it! There's our own cabin waiting for us, and Tad and my uncles will visit and wonder at how nice I've made it with my quilts and all my pots. And then the baby will be there too, and I've got the cradle Tad made me when I was a baby to set in the corner. Gideon and I'll keep it full. I told Gideon I want so many children you can't see the floor. He said he does too."

Sophia looked into the future and saw nothing like this cheerful picture. Just herself and a baby she couldn't imagine very well and Malinda in the nursery. "Mmm, yes, of course. Well, I've been planning my garden as we came down the river. We can sit in it and watch our babies play." *Until I go home to England,* she thought. Would Caitlin miss her? Heavens, she would miss Caitlin!

Caitlin was saying something.

"What?"

"Sophy, you aren't listening!" Caitlin shook her head, amused. "I said you're a funny one. Fancy just sitting idle in a garden when there are vegetables needing to be tended!"

"Oh no, I didn't mean sitting in the kitchen garden! Not vegetables, they'll be planted somewhere else. Actually I was thinking of the flowers, you know, larkspur and mignonette and heliotrope."

"Don't be daft. You can't eat those!" Caitlin snorted with laughter. She patted her stomach. "Have you told Henri yet?"

"No. And don't say a word, Caitlin! You mustn't!"

Caitlin shook her head with disapproval. "I won't, but you'd think for all the world he'd realize; look how sick you are all the time." Caitlin had recovered her appetite, while almost any food looked and smelled disgusting to Sophia and made her feel miserably nauseous. But Henri hadn't noticed she barely ate anything and just picked a little at what was on her plate. "Is that all you're going to eat?" he would ask, reach for her plate, and finish off whatever was on it.

The men returned with fish. Caitlin expertly wove a lattice of wet sticks to cook them over the fire, and her father got out his penknife to clean them. Sophia watched fish guts spilling onto the ground and, just in time, heaved herself to her feet to go and throw up in the bushes.

A week later the flotilla emerged from the trees into a wider stretch of river flanked by rolling hills on either bank. Gideon pointed to a large shape in the distance—Frog Mountain, he called it. Sophia was squinting, trying to decide if it really looked like a frog, when she was almost thrown into the water as the raft hit something submerged and shuddered to a halt with an ominous grating noise. The other rafts tied up on the bank, and Gideon swam underneath to find the raft stuck fast on a sandbar. The bottom had parted, and it began to list. The men managed to dislodge the flatboat, though they made the damage worse in the process. They towed it to shore and began the tedious process of unloading and repairing it. The boards the raft was made from had split. This meant felling a tree and getting out the tools to plane new ones, and the tools were on the wagon with Meshack, so they had to wait.

When Meshack and Nott arrived, they set about finding pine trees and collecting resin from them, which Caitlin's father said had to be mixed with dung from the animals to seal the rafts. Thierry was impatiently heaving wood on the fire to heat the first batch of resin when

Caitlin's father shouted a warning to stop, not to build too large a fire, when the pot of resin ignited and shot a pillar of flame into the air. Thierry and Rufus cried out and leaped back, their hair and eyebrows badly singed. Caitlin's father shook his head. "Take warning, pitch loves fire. It only wants warming a little."

Four days later they were still camped on the bank, waiting for the resin-and-dung coating to dry. Sophia woke in unusually good spirits and realized that she no longer felt sick and dizzy. Miraculously, the constant fog of nausea had gone. She felt energetic and was impatient to reach her new home and begin putting her house in order. Ravenously hungry, she ate a large breakfast of corn cakes and honey and fish and suggested to Henri they saddle the horses and ride on ahead, if Gideon thought it would be safe. Gideon said every tribe in the valley believed there was a curse on the Grafton land, that it was inhabited now only by the dead. If Sophia, Henri, and Thierry did not fear the dead, he said, they would be safe.

"Why fear dead people, Gideon? They can't hurt us," exclaimed Sophia.

Gideon saw from their faces that they truly believed the dead disappeared and was struck as he often was by the ignorance of whites who did not experience the whole of living and dead and people and animals and sky and water but only in the small part of the existence they could see or the part they believed they owned. But he said nothing about that, just told them there was a path up Frog Mountain and if they followed it they would come to a rock with a man's profile and a flat top from which they could see the valley.

As he gave them directions, Gideon reflected uneasily that this was the way with whites' names, like Frog Mountain; they were a way of seizing it for themselves. When Gideon was a young man, the great branch forking off from the river to go through the valley and southwest toward the Darkening Land was called "the river that forks after the pass and disappears beyond the mountains" in Tsalagi. When the

Tsalagi named a place, it was information—"long grass where deer lick the salt," "cave where the bears sleep," "plain where the buffalo gather," "treacherous water with many fish in spring." The tribes hunted and fought across the land, built their towns, and planted their crops. But with the whites, their naming was a way of setting their hands on something. Taking hold for themselves alone.

And he knew that when the whites looked down on the valley for the first time, they would appropriate it for their own in this way.

Sophia's suggestion they ride ahead and see Wildwood appealed to Henri, who had grown bored with fishing and waiting, and to Thierry, who wanted to find some fresh meat. The three of them set off, Thierry with his musket and Henri with the pouch with the map and the deeds and the sketches of the house.

Sophia's hunter had recovered some of its former sprightliness, was eager for exercise, and pranced impatiently up the sun-dappled path through the trees, ahead of the two plodding horses ridden by Henri and Thierry.

Finally they caught up with Sophia. She had pulled up, and behind her they could see the broad, flat rock and the valley stretching below it. "Hurry!" she exclaimed excitedly. "The map."

They dismounted and took the map from its leather pouch, and she and Henri spread it on the rock and weighed it down with stones. They all took in the view. The valley swept out below them, with mountains on the other side and the river winding through the middle. Henri tried to orient the map with what was below them. "Now, if you look at the map, I think we've lined it up with the valley; see the river on the map, in line with that down there. Then that big bend, and that must be Gideon and Caitlin's cabin and trading post." He pointed to a cabin and a landing on the river, then tapped the place on the map.

Sophia looked at the map and traced the outline of the river to the edge of the map where it turned west. Then back at the valley.

"Yes, I can see where the river bends, but not the house. Mr. Barker sent the drawings of the house, so I know what it looks like, but didn't say where it was exactly. And the tobacco? Don't the fields down there look rather more like pastures with stumps?" The three of them peered, shading their eyes with their hands.

"By this time of year, the tobacco would have been cut. It's in the drying sheds," said Henri, finally. "Or perhaps already on its way to Yorktown or Savannah."

"Of course!" cried Sophia. "Let's find the house—I'm longing to see it. I wasn't able to send Mr. Barker word, so he'll be surprised to see us. I hope the servants can manage some dinner for us at short notice." She pointed to a cabin on a lower slope overlooking the river, surrounded by a cleared area. "Mr. Barker must have a tenant," said Sophia, "a sort of home farm. I see a man down there. He can direct us. It can't be far. Hidden by trees, probably."

Thierry went to untie their horses, and Henri pulled Sophia to her feet. They were rolling up the map when they heard a loud snuffling and grunting in the woods behind them, and a group of wild pigs trotted out. There was a large sow with vicious tusks, followed by her young. They stopped and snuffled. Henri shouted a warning—a sow with her young was dangerous—and a startled young pig let out a piercing squeal and scampered wildly toward Sophia's horse. The horse reared, neighing frantically, and nearly trampled it. The sow snorted and charged.

"Sanglier!" shouted Henri.

Thierry grabbed his musket, took aim, and fired, and the sow fell in its tracks just before it reached him. The rest of the sounder swerved and went crashing into the forest.

Thierry and Henri approached the sow to make sure it was dead and not merely wounded and able to gore them. When they were certain, they tied its legs together with vines and spent some time finding branches long and strong enough to serve as a litter to drag the carcass with them. "Fresh meat, at least," grunted Henri, struggling to fix the heavy pig on the litter while Thierry held on to the horses, who weren't keen on wild pigs, dead or alive.

Thierry grunted, "Your *manoir* is a *baugé*."

"What's a *baugé*?" asked Sophia.

"A wild pig mud wallow."

"La Rivière Baugé," quipped Henri, trying to balance the branch with the dead pig. They all remounted and rode down to the cleared patch of land, dragging their kill. The figure they had seen turned to watch as they approached. The man turned out to be an old Negro woman dressed in a man's clothes and shuffling along in men's boots, carrying a bucket of water.

She regarded the pig and its tusks warily. "It dead?" She put the bucket down and told them her name was Zaydie. An Englishman had bought her and six male slaves in Virginia, along with mules and farm tools, and brought them here on a raft with an overseer. The Englishman had ordered the male slaves to cut down trees, build a house and barn, plow a garden, plant an orchard, and plant tobacco for an owner who lived far away. He kept saying it all had to be done before the owner came or they'd all be sorry, and the overseer was a cruel man who drove them hard, but the slaves laughed at the Englishman behind his back. What he asked was impossible.

Zaydie told them the man had bought her cheap, to cook and keep house and tend the garden. She was too old for other work. Not that there'd been much house to tend to. Just the cabin. Indians had attacked them several times, killed two slaves, took their scalps, before the Englishman and the overseer drove them off with their guns. But the two white men had quarreled constantly. Several times a year, the Englishman would leave to go upriver to the trading post for his letters, and he'd bring back cornmeal and gunpowder and nails and other supplies. Later he'd come back with only jugs of spirits. The slaves heard the overseer, shouting that his wages had gone on whiskey. Finally the overseer took what little money remained and left, saying only a fool would think mountain land was good for tobacco. The Englishman, too drunk to stand up, had shaken his fist and watched him go. Then he became sick, just kept drinking his whiskey until there was none left. After that he was in a bad way, sometimes shouting, sometimes just sitting on the ground, shaking, wrapped in a blanket watching Zaydie tend to the chickens and dig the garden. Then he got worse and mostly he lay on his pallet till he died during the winter.

The other slaves had run away, but Zaydie thought she might as well stay. She was afraid of Indians, but she was too old to live in the swamp where the others were going. It was as close to being free as she was going to get. She had a few vegetables in the garden, she had an axe to chop firewood, and the cows and the chickens lived through the winter in the lean-to of a barn. She could live. Sophia asked faintly what the Englishman's name had been.

"Massa Barker."

"Are you certain it was Mr. Barker? Because Mr. Barker was my father, Lord Grafton's, agent, and the man you're describing sounds nothing like that!"

"Hunh." Zaydie squinted at Sophia. "He say Grafton sometime, when he drinkin'. Sometime when he drinkin' say somethin' 'bout his wife, how he wished he hadn't come back to Virginny." The old woman pointed. "He buried, back a'hind there. I dug the best I could, put some rocks on his grave, 'count of the animals. Had him some papers he fetched from the trading post, kep' on a table in there. After he die, I used me some to light the fire when kindling run low, but most left. He say I could have his clothes if he die, account a I took care of him. I wearin' them, don't have nothing else." Beyond that, Zaydie only shrugged when Sophia asked if there was another house.

"I ain't live nowhere but here. Don't know 'bout a other house."

"Perhaps this is the . . . the estate office," Sophia said. "I'll get the letters, then we'll find the house in the sketch." Henri helped her dismount, and she followed Zaydie through a door that hung crookedly.

Inside, the dark cabin stank of raw wood, ashes, sweat, and something rotting. Embers smoked in a large stone fireplace, and next to it was a pallet and some filthy blankets. A table made of pine planks that had warped held some cooking pots, rags, a few rusting farm implements, some pewter plates, pieces of wire. As her eyes adjusted to the gloom, Sophia saw that the room with the fireplace was the only part of the cabin with a roof. There were three other rooms in various stages of completion, as if the builders had begun in one direction, then changed their plan and started over several times. Zaydie pointed to a pile of papers that had been chewed by mice. "Them his papers." Then she shuffled back out the door. Sophia was shocked by the slovenly state of the office, but she would deal with that in due course. She gathered up the papers and pulled the only chair to the doorway for enough light to read them.

Outside, Henri and Thierry were arguing again in French, this time about whether they would go tomorrow or the next day. Sophia sighed and thought how well suited the French language was for bickering and indignant spluttering. She put the letters in order by date and began to read. Her father's handwriting brought tears to her eyes. "Dear Papa," she murmured, "when we spoke of Virginia, you never expected I would be here reading your letters."

She was sadly acquainted with the litany of borrowed money and interest and growing debt, but the last two letters revealed more than the solicitors had told her. The penultimate letter, from Lord Grafton's lawyers to Mr. Barker, written the last summer in Sussex when her father was still alive, made it clear Lord Grafton was unwilling and unable to remit further funds until the tobacco began to pay. He had borrowed against his English property to the hilt on the understanding the plantation would by now be yielding a substantial return, and he was too unwell at present to make any further arrangements.

But the final letter confirmed something worse. In it the solicitors protested that even Mr. Barker's confession that the house he had sketched for Lord Grafton had never been built would not sway them to release more funds to build it now. It was no use applying to them instead of Lord Grafton. Lord Grafton was too ill to be troubled at the moment, and if the solicitors had had their way, they would see Mr. Barker in Newgate Prison for fraud when he returned to England.

Several times Sophia put the letter down, exclaiming, "No, no! This cannot be!" Only to pick it up to read again. "Papa would never have allowed this to happen." She read the letters yet again, trying to see what she had misunderstood, certain that somewhere in the papers she would find evidence that at least one, if not two consignments of tobacco had shipped, as surely they had. Surely!

But Sophia could no longer deny the reality of her situation. No house had been built; no tobacco had been grown or shipped. Only a few slaves had been bought, not the workforce of dozens.

The lawyers' final letter also confirmed the true extent of the debt. The solicitors must have lied when they suggested she might live in the dower house. According to their last letter to Mr. Barker, the entire Grafton estate, including the dower house, would soon be in the hands of the bailiffs. The tenants for whom the solicitors had insisted she vacate the house most likely did not exist. They must have hoped she would act as she had, because her going to Virginia had merely saved them the trouble of evicting her.

She had indeed risked everything. Escaping Thomas had made her a murderess, had put the slaves' lives at risk, and had even led her to jeopardize her honor in a sham marriage. Sophia felt the earth give way beneath her. She felt dizzy, as if she were falling into a void. She sank her head in her hands. "Dearest Papa, the Grafton estate, gone! How? With your pride in the family, how could you permit such a thing to happen? Mr. Barker lied about everything, the tobacco, the house . . . but why did the solicitors advise all would be well if it has turned out so very badly? Surely they could have foreseen the risk . . ." Though it was a warm day, she was cold with fear as she contemplated her dilemma. She was destitute, with no home, and a baby coming. Henri would leave soon. She was responsible for everyone—the Negroes, the Drumhellers, Malinda. And the baby, of course. She saw Lavinia holding her newborn child, dead and covered with flies. Would that be her fate in a few months? Wildwood was in as bad a state as Lavinia and William's small holding.

She emerged from the cabin in a daze. Henri looked up from the wild pig. "Well, Sophy, we're nearly finished. We'll leave a piece for the old woman and give the rest to your cook at the *manoir*," said Henri, splattered in boar blood. "I need a bath before dinner."

Sophia clutched the doorjamb for support, her mouth open but unable at first to speak. Her fields of tobacco, her house, her barn and stable, the flower garden she had described to Caitlin, everything she had been sure of finding in Virginia did not exist.

"There's no cook, no bath, no dinner. No anything," she croaked. She waved her hand at the cabin. "My *manoir*? This is my *manoir*. Wildwood. This is my house. The orchard's there on the slope." She pointed to an unevenly built low rock wall that surrounded a field of weeds and a few spindly apple trees. "That's a well and the kitchen garden." She pointed to another patch of earth outlined in rocks that did nothing to stop a rabbit eating the remains of some vegetable planted in rows. "And there's the . . . the stable block . . ."—she pointed to the lean-to where a few chickens pecked about—". . . with the horses I promised."

She began to laugh hysterically. "Oh, there's *land*." She gestured toward the valley. "Land everywhere. But there's been no tobacco planted on it, and there's no money left. I've no idea what to do with *land* . . . Mr. Barker lied . . . the solicitors lied, my father lied." Sophia's laughter ended in a wild hiccup of distress, and she burst into tears. "Ruined! I can't go back to England. There's no house, only this hovel to live in. The baby and I will die!" she sobbed. "Like Lavinia."

Henri stared at her. "What are you saying? No house? No horses? How?" Then, "Baby? Whose baby?"

"Whose baby do you suppose, simpleton!" Sophia shrieked.

"You are . . . *enceinte*?"

Sophia choked and didn't deign to answer.

Henri reflected that nothing could be more possible. He had never known a woman quite so eager in bed. But Sophy in bed was one thing; a pregnant Sophy was something else. As the unwelcome news sank in, he swore and knew at once the best thing to do was for him and Thierry to mount their wretched horses and go without looking back. Run. Go anywhere. Leave this Englishwoman and her miserable patch of wilderness at the end of the earth, among the savages, with her hangers-on, the half-skinned boar, and the mumbling Negro woman.

Because if he didn't . . . even as he contemplated leaving, Henri felt an invisible trap closing round him. He was a Frenchman and, as a Frenchman, knew that family ties transcended every other consideration. Even though he was not a legitimate de Marechal son, the count had instilled in him that the ancient de Marechal name and blood were his, all the legacy he would have, but a legacy to be prized. "Everything can be bought except blood," his father had taught him.

While Henri might dispute whether his marriage ceremony was valid, his father would have insisted a de Marechal child was indisputably in gestation, legitimate or not. And it was likely to be a boy—the de Marechal children were usually boys. It would be Henri's paternal duty to take his son back to France, to the place he belonged. To abandon a de Marechal, however begotten, in uncivilized, English Virginia, among the English and the Indians and the Negroes, was unthinkable. That much was clear to him at once.

He put down his knife and calculated. In France he could raise the boy as his natural son, just as he had been. No, he would adopt the child as his heir, as soon as they reached France. A plan began to form in his mind. When he reached Louisiana, he would avoid the garrison and the authorities altogether and pass himself off as a Huguenot widower with a young son.

Only, money for their passage was the problem; Sophia had spent the last of her money on their keep at the Caradocs'. He'd have to find a way to get some money, enough for Thierry's passage as well. He would need more money in France to raise a child—he saw that this would be a much greater problem, but perhaps Madame de Pompadour would take pity and come to his assistance if he had a child with him.

He wiped his bloody hand on his trousers and put an arm around Sophia's shoulders. "Of course I won't leave you, Sophy. Land must always be good for something. We'll do something to make it pay."

He had no idea what. He knew how land was the basis of wealth in France, as in England, but he wasn't sure how to turn land to money in Virginia, unless it was tobacco. All he'd learned about growing tobacco was that it was a complicated process that needed many slaves. But he was Sophia's husband, and her land belonged to him now. He could make use of it as he wished. Perhaps he could sell it. Or some of it. He remembered the woman from the raft that had stopped at Caradoc Station who had said she wished they didn't have to go all the way to Kentuckee to find a homestead. Yes! He would clear and sell homesteads here in the valley. There were settlers who would buy them.

His conscience troubled him, a little. What would Sophia do when he'd sold her land and taken their son back to France?

He soothed his conscience by thinking he needn't sell all of it. Magnanimously, he decided that he wouldn't sell all of it. He would leave Sophia with a roof over her head and a garden.

"I'll think of something. *Courage*, Sophy."

He was rewarded with a tearstained smile. "Oh, Henri, how strong you are! What would I do without you?" she murmured. Henri felt guilty, briefly. He promised himself he would even give Sophia a small part of the money from the sales of the land, and felt his conscience relax completely. He went back to his pig butchering, leaving a bloody handprint on Sophia's shoulder.

Sophia thought to herself, *I can tell he was thinking and he has something up his sleeve. I can rely on him for a little while but not for long. Then it will all be up to me. I must think . . .*

She looked around her. Her predicament required her to take stock of her situation quickly because it would soon be winter, but for the moment she felt so overwhelmed she couldn't think where to begin. Like Henri she understood that land was wealth, although in an equally general way. She knew very well that the Grafton fortune had been based on land granted by William the Conqueror, that nearly all the great old fortunes in England were "landed," but she'd never stopped to consider the exact nature of the connection. She had only the vaguest knowledge of farming, mostly what she had gleaned from her months in Sussex, and even that was riding in lanes or looking over hedgerows at Grafton farm laborers working in the fields or herding sheep. She remembered the gardener and his instructions about growing her pink roses, but that wasn't likely to be any use in the present situation.

She sat back down on the chair she'd dragged to the door and put her head in her hands. They had barely survived the hardships of traveling through the wilderness in summer, nearly died of starvation before they reached the Caradocs. How would they survive the winter? There was little shelter and no food. She had kept going, sustained by the prospect that a working plantation and a good house were waiting for them. She was flummoxed by what she'd found. Instead of an establishment with a dairy, a cook, a poultry yard, a thriving kitchen garden, like in Sussex, there was a ruin of a cabin, an old slave, and a dead wild pig. She had no idea what to do.

But unless she wanted to die like poor Lavinia, she had to think of what to do next.

The more of them there were, the more likely they could survive, but two able-bodied men, Henri and Thierry, would leave, and the others might go any day. She'd already heard Meshack regretting that he had not gone to Florida when he had the chance; it would have been safer. He was afraid of the militia and slave-catcher patrols and might decide to go at any moment. Nott agreed with him that it would have been safer. He too seemed undecided about staying. If Nott went, Saskia, Venus, and Seth would probably go with him. Rufus worried he and his boys would be caught as well, if the patrols or slave catchers came; there was nothing to stop him from pushing on to Kentuckee with the boys. She thought about it. It was only her promise of land that had held them. Perhaps when they were actually marking out the plots they wanted, and she'd drawn up the deeds confirming their ownership, if she gave them all as much land as they wanted, if they started work on their cabins at once, perhaps the prospect of putting down roots would hold them. And if the militia or slave catchers came? Well, they could swear they belonged to Henri. And they were all armed. And she would shoot if she had to, she would shoot anyone.

The thought of shooting people was bracing. Sophia took heart and thought of the Caradocs. The Caradocs had made a good settlement at their station. If the able-bodied men stayed, perhaps they could do the same here. Caitlin and Gideon would have their trading post at the river bend, so it wasn't a complete wilderness.

What ought they to do first? Sophia calculated they would have to wait until spring to sow food crops and the tobacco seeds. Caitlin and Gideon would know. The half-built Wildwood would have to be made habitable. Caitlin's father knew how to build cabins, Gideon too. The barn would do for the livestock if it were repaired. They had their goods from the raft and the cows, a mule, three horses, and some chickens Caitlin had given her.

Zaydie watched the white people. Whatever they were shouting about or crying about or looking like they were ready to open their mouth and complain about, whatever was making the white woman talk to herself now, so long as it didn't concern her, Zaydie was indifferent.

So long as nobody tried to sell her again. If they did, she'd put a curse on them; she knew many good spells. On the other hand, it wouldn't hurt to make herself useful. She wanted to stay, not drag her old bones somewhere else. She hobbled over to the woman.

"You white folks leavin'?" she asked hopefully.

"No, we'll stay," said the white woman. "We're going to live here."

Zaydie digested this in silence. It wasn't good news. But they had a dead pig the two men had just finished cutting up, and they had to do something with it. That pig had the makings of some hams. She licked her lips. It had been a long time since she'd had any meat. She was hungry most of the time, and she knew how to cure hams. The thought of ham made her mouth water.

"You got a wild pig, and they's a smokehouse there, nothin' in it." She pointed to a hump of stones with a sort of chimney on top. The white woman looked like she was dreaming wide awake, just staring at the wild pig and the two men.

Zaydie wondered if the woman knew anything about curing ham. Because if they were going to make hams, they'd better do it before the meat spoiled in the warm weather. She would have been happy to watch whites eat rotten pork crawling with maggots, but it was more use telling them how to do it, because she liked ham and hoped they would give her some. She no longer had any teeth to chew it, but that didn't matter if it was cut up fine. Or she would just suck a piece for the taste.

"Could make ham. Got hick'ry up there." She pointed up the mountain. "Or sourwood, that good too," said Zaydie ingratiatingly. It wouldn't hurt to get off on a good foot with the new mistress. And now she was thinking about it, oh, she did want to taste ham again before she died!

"Make ham?"

Zaydie prompted "Got salt inside. Made it from the salt lick down yonder. Make you up a brine, brine that meat fast. It hot, maggots in it before you blink. Let it soak in the brine. Then you got to rub it hard with the wood ash. Wrap it up in a clean cloth, you got one. Seven days. Then got to smoke it. Smoke it there in the smokehouse. Lot a hick'ry trees. Hick'ry smoke make the best ham."

"How long?"

White woman finally taking an interest.

"Got to leave it a while. Few months. Almost till winter gone, but not quite."

The woman just looked at Zaydie. "Winter."

"'Less you ain't planning to eat nothing before summer." Zaydie was exasperated.

Then to Zaydie's surprise, the woman pulled herself upright, like she just woke up. She turned her head this way and that, looking around her at what was in front of them, instead of looking off into the faraway. She stood up, commenced to telling people to do this and that like she was used to telling people to do things.

Sophia was calculating the number of mouths to feed and what they had to eat. "We have to make hams with the boar, Henri. I'll stay here and see to it with Zaydie. She says she knows how. I'll cure the belly as well. Caitlin told me they always wait until the weather turns cold before they butcher a pig, because otherwise the flies lay eggs in the meat, but we can't wait. There's salt and wood ash here. Zaydie, you gather up the wood ash from the fireplace. There's a big pot inside. I'll start the fire and boil up the brine. While it's cooling, Henri, you fetch some hickory wood. Thierry, you ride back and ask Caitlin to give you some sacking for me to wrap the meat in while it brines. Then we'll put it in the smokehouse."

"Oui, mon general!" muttered Thierry, and rolled his eyes at Henri.

"Henri, you'll need to find the best way up from Gideon's landing, so by the time the rafts reach it, the men can drive the wagons up here."

We have the cows, she thought, *and some chickens, and Caitlin and Gideon have cornmeal and dried vegetables, but is that enough to feed everyone until summer when the crops are harvested?*

Sophia looked again at the pitiful vegetable garden, the scrawny chickens, and shivered. Lavinia's ghost flitted between the apple trees. "Go away," Sophia muttered at it. As she'd told Gideon, she refused to believe in ghosts.

A week later the wagons bumped slowly up the slope as the first chill of autumn set in. Zaydie got a fire going in the smokehouse and judged when the heat was slow and steady enough to hang the brined meat there. They all set to work, even Thierry, with feverish haste. Mr. Barker had left them some English tools—*At least some of Papa's money was well spent,* thought Sophia. With those and the tools Sophia had taken from Thomas, the men felled trees and stripped the branches from the logs. Seth, Nott, and Meshack planed logs for a barn and new cabins. Gideon and Caitlin's father knew how to build a cabin, notching logs and fitting them together. Caitlin's father showed Toby, Jack, and Cully how to carve and dress roof shingles from split cedar planks. The boys had blisters on their hands and wanted to stop, but Caitlin's father said he'd box their ears if they did. Malinda was put to work fetching buckets of water from a spring nearby to mix mud and piles of small sticks and twigs for chinking between the gaps in the logs. They all worked from sunrise until it grew too dark to see what they were doing, ate a supper of corn pone and whatever animals Thierry had killed and roasted on a spit over the fire, and fell into an exhausted sleep around the fireplace.

Sophia, who was anxious to make sure Seth and Meshack and Rufus and Nott stayed to work on her property, told them to walk her round their plots as soon as they marked them so she could draw up the deeds. The men could tell Henri wasn't interested and Seth, Nott, Rufus, and Meshack wasted no time marking off plots of land for their homesteads down by the river, hardly able to believe they would have their own farms and cabins. "Anybody come here and say it ain't mine, I got to be a slave again, I kill 'em," said Meshack.

"Amen," said Seth, driving markers in the ground with all his might. "Amen."

"I might take me a little more." Nott grinned, moving his markers as far as he dared.

Rufus chose a site away from everyone, the far southern end of the valley at the base of Little Frog Mountain, reasoning that the farther away he was, the less Miss Grafton—now Mrs. de Marechal—would be likely to object to how much he had taken. He'd been thinking of the boys, what he could leave to set them up in life, so he had staked out a big piece of land, far larger than that claimed by Nott, Seth, or Meshack, who whistled at his presumption. "But he white," said Seth scornfully, "can take what he like."

Rufus overheard him and suddenly was afraid that greed might be the undoing of what he wanted for the boys. He badly wanted the land, but Sophia was the grand lady of the plantation, and while she had said they could take as much as they could farm, he was in her power. Rufus didn't trust the gentry, and there was nothing to prevent her changing her mind and taking it back. She had promised to draw up proper deeds to the land she was giving away as soon as they showed her what piece of land each of them had chosen and walked her round each plot, so she could make a map showing the boundary. And even if she didn't object to the size of Rufus's plot, what if Henri did? He thought hard about it. He could mark out a smaller piece—he'd had his fill of disputes over land with Molly's brother, was still licking his wounds from his loss there. But there was a spring on the lower slope of Little Frog Mountain where the water tasted of iron. He was sure there was ore in the mountain. He was a blacksmith. He ached to own that slope.

During the day, as he planed logs, he wrestled with what he ought to do, weighing up the risks of Sophia refusing. At night he lay awake, tormented by the thought such a good piece of land was almost but not quite his.

Rufus decided that the best tactic with the gentry was to eat humble pie. He went to Sophia, who was bent over mixing a pile of chinking with her bare hands. He explained he had marked out a plot and would walk Sophia round it when she had a moment to spare but feared he might have taken too much land, he was sorry if he'd been greedy, he'd been thinking of the boys . . . he all but tugged his forelock obsequiously.

Sophia had straightened up from her mixing, weary and mud splattered and looking nothing like the grand lady of the plantation, and assured him that he should take what he could manage; land was the only way she could pay him and the boys for staying to work for her. In fact, Sophia didn't care how much Rufus took. There was far too much land to manage. He was to place markers round his landholding, and she'd make a deed showing what it was. Relieved, Rufus thanked her effusively and that evening daringly moved his markers even farther up the side of Little Frog Mountain, high above the spring with the iron water.

Henri was less eager to part with large parcels of land, but Sophia told him the sooner everyone had a stake in the land, the better. It would keep them from leaving. She used the deeds in Thomas de Bouldin's chest as a model and drew up deeds to all the homesteads, together with a crude plan of the land belonging to each one. This meant the former slaves needed a last name. Sophia asked if they wanted a royal name like Seth and Venus had, and after discussing it, Nott and Saskia, who decided they'd live together, agreed they liked Stuart, and Meshack chose Tudor, so Henri and Sophia had signed over the deeds to Meshack Tudor, Venus and Seth Hanover, and Saskia and Nott Stuart.

Meshack grinned as he took his.

Venus and Seth held their document proudly, Venus already planning her cabin.

"I guess we good as married now, Saskia," said Nott. "What you say to that? Saskia Stuart sound good to you? 'Cause it sound good to me."

"Hmm, we'll see," said Saskia. She patted her hair. "Don't you go losing that paper."

Rufus held the precious deed, signed by both Henri and Sophia de Marechal and sealed with Henri's signet ring pressed into a seal of candle wax, like it was the key to the heavenly kingdom. Unbelievably, the land, spring and all, was suddenly his, in return for which he was to spend so many days a year laboring in the de Marechals' fields.

After Sophia had drawn up the deed, Henri had specified how many days in which season before either of them would sign it. Henri was a harder person to negotiate with than Sophia, but in the end, Rufus would have agreed with any terms to own such a piece of land. He was incredulous. He'd had so little luck in his life; now here he was with a farm larger than the one he and Molly had had in Suffolk. After that, he walked down the valley whenever he could, marking out in the twilight where his cabin would be, where would be the best position for the barn. He had promised Molly an orchard . . . He dreamed at night of the homestead he would build. And perhaps, one day, a forge and a smithy like his father had had.

All the new landowners were anxious to build cabins before winter set in, but only Gideon and Caitlin's father had built cabins before. Henri agreed with Gideon that it would be most efficient if everyone worked together to build the cabins one by one. Henri put straws in a hat and let Malinda hold it while Meshack, Rufus, Nott, and Seth drew to see who got the first cabin. Rufus was the winner. Then Meshack, then Seth, then Nott. Sophia drew the shortest straw, so they'd repair Wildwood last.

The days were punctuated by the crash of felled trees and much grumbling about how much time each cabin was taking. Long rails were cut to fence a farmyard around the dilapidated barn. Logs were planed and notched to fit together, and Caitlin's father shook his head because they had no time to season the wood. The barn was repaired enough so it wouldn't collapse. Sophia, Caitlin, Venus, Saskia, and Zaydie helped strip the branches from felled trees, and when the notched logs were fitted together, they mixed mud and twigs and small rocks and packed it into the gaps between the logs. Their hands were red and raw from the wet mixture. Caitlin and Sophia grew larger and for decency wore aprons over the bodices they could no longer button. Caitlin giggled at her new roundness.

October became November. More trees were felled and notched, and one by one, two-room cabins were raised on the sites chosen by Rufus, Nott, Seth, and Meshack. Each had a large stone fireplace and chimney and a shingled roof covered in pine pitch. Finally the four half-built rooms of the original cabin were finished and roofed. The three boys' hands were callused and full of splinters from making so many shingles that had to be hammered into place with wooden pegs as they had no nails.

The new cabins in the valley stood empty as winter set in. Though all the settlers were eager to move into their own homes, to save firewood and share what little food there was, they decided to live crowded together at the Wildwood cabin, waiting until spring to move.

Sophia felt Lavinia's ghost hovering. "Go away!" Sophia told her and worked grimly, harder and harder.

The valley was a blaze of color with the changing leaves against a bright blue autumn sky, but what they noticed were the cold and the darker mornings. And their constant hunger. Gideon pointed at the slope above the flat rock shaped like a man's head and said there were caves where bears hibernated, and Thierry managed to shoot a young bear climbing up. They ate bear meat for a few days, and the women had bear grease to rub into their painful hands. Thierry preferred hunting to building, which he saw as peasants' work, and went farther and farther afield as fall drew on, looking for anything they could eat. Gideon told him the best way to snare and trap rabbits and pigeons, because larger game had disappeared.

At dusk, when it was too dark to continue the day's frantic building, Caitlin led the women and Malinda to gather chestnuts and fox grapes and ripe persimmons whose orange fruit were just visible in the fading light. These sessions were short because it quickly got cold and too dark to see much. There were a few persimmon puddings, and they stewed the grapes with some sorghum to preserve them. They planned to save the hams curing in the smokehouse for the lean days of January and February when Gideon warned there would be little to eat.

When the children were allowed to put down their tools and their shingles, they had to collect firewood. They complained of aches and pains, hunger and cold, and at night by the fire, Saskia took a needle from the sewing box and extracted splinters from their hands. Nott and Seth had the overseers' boots, but barefoot Meshack managed to fashion some shoes for himself and the three children out of bark and deer gut. Then he made some for Rufus, whose shoes were little more than flapping soles tied onto his feet.

With the cabins built, Sophia divided the spoils from Thomas's plantation so that each household possessed a small store of household items—a few pots and pans, pewter or china plates. She kept the teapot.

Caitlin had insisted Gideon bring her store of dried vegetables and fruit and cornmeal, and she stretched them into stews made with the occasional squirrel Thierry shot, but with so many hungry people, the stew was very thin. Then there was no meat at all because Thierry had another bout of his fever and lay shivering violently by the fireplace, wrapped in Henri's old cloak, unable to hunt for a fortnight. By the time he was well enough to go out, the game had disappeared.

Christmas came, and they were driven indoors by snow to huddle round the fireplace at Wildwood. The candles were used up, and they had only spitting pine knots and the fire for light. Caitlin's father took out his fiddle, and he and Caitlin sang "Shepherds Rejoice" and "Hark!

All Around the Welkin Rings" and every other carol they could think of in harmony. Sophia followed with "The boar's head in hand bear I, bedecked with bay and rosemary," that her father had remembered singing while at Oxford College, and Rufus and the boys tried to recall all the words to the "Cherry Tree Carol," which had been Molly's favorite. They sang these over and over until everyone knew the words. Malinda opened her mouth and pretended she was singing too until Jack tickled her and she collapsed in silent giggles.

Henri was the only one who didn't sing. He was sunk in gloom remembering the Reveillon feasts that followed late-night Mass on Christmas Eve.

They were so hungry they decided to eat the smoked wild pig for a Christmas feast, before it was ready. It was tough, had an odd taste, and made them sick. By the end of January, the last of the cornmeal and chestnut flour had gone, along with the grapes in sorghum. They killed and butchered the oldest horse, but it was mostly skin and bone. Saskia made soup with it, but it tasted vile. They ate it anyway.

They were starving again.

CHAPTER 22
THE STARVING WINTER

February 1756

There was nothing left to eat, and it was very cold, a cold they felt to their bones as they grew thinner. Constantly chopping wood for the fire sapped what little energy they had. Caitlin had practically no food left either. Gideon was accustomed to lean winters, but he tried to find small game, and sometimes he caught a fish for his pregnant wife. Caitlin wouldn't let him leave her and go upriver to her uncles for supplies. The sky turned gray, and it snowed and froze and thawed and snowed again.

When it stopped and a weak sun shone on the winter landscape, Thierry took the blunderbuss and rode up the mountain toward the flat rock where he'd killed the sow in the autumn. If there was any game, it would make tracks in the snow. He was hunched over, cold to his bones, to his very soul, half mad with the everlasting hunger, weak and aching in his joints from the last bout of the unpredictable fever that seized him from time to time. He hated this wilderness with all his heart, was unable to contemplate this miserable existence any longer if he did not find something to shoot for food. He had set out hoping to find a few squirrels, a wild turkey, or a possum, anything, but he had done this many times, finding nothing. He had headed for the flat rock, hoping against hope there might be another wild pig there. But when he reached it, there were no signs of wild pigs, just a bleak winter landscape in every direction, an eternity of mountains and black leafless trees stretching away into the east. He felt an irrational impulse to whip and whip his horse, to ride away and escape. But there was nowhere to go.

Letting the underfed horse pick its way, the two of them went aimlessly down into the next valley to the east, until finally his weary horse stumbled at every other step. Thierry dismounted and kept walking, leading the horse. He was too tired to think where he was going or why, driven only by the urge to get away. There was no game. He would go until he could no longer walk or stand, then lie down and give up.

In the next valley, they reached a clump of trees and a stream that was only partly frozen over, and the horse would go no farther. It was early afternoon, but the sun was low in the winter sky and there was a brisk wind. Thierry tethered the horse to let it drink and sank down with his back to a chestnut tree. He shouldn't have taken the blunderbuss; it was their most accurate weapon. The others would need it. If they didn't die before the game returned. His eyes started to close. He was cold and would be colder when night came. He hoped he would sleep and never wake up. Wild animals or buzzards would find him and the horse. He had no strength left to resist his fate. He envied his brother. François was lucky to have died, spared the terrible, everlasting hunger.

His eyes closed, and he became aware of a distant rustling sound, like whispers or dry leaves. The sound grew louder, then quieted, louder and quieted. Rhythmic, like the sea, and strangely peaceful. There was no sea for miles and miles; he would never see the sea again, any more than he would see France. He fancied it must be the sound of Death approaching stealthily. He supposed he ought to pray before he died. He wasn't religious, but he was French and a Catholic.

He saw his mother's face as she bent over him, teaching him to use his father's gift, the rosary the cardinal had commissioned for his son, made small to fit a child's hands. Its five decades had been small coral beads separated by larger beads of gold filigree, with a gold filigree cross. Where the beams of the cross met, a rock crystal held a tiny image of the crucified Christ, painted on ivory. Three years later he had been obliged to yield it to François, when his father had given him another fine rosary, of amber and silver, fit for a big boy, the cardinal had said, though it had never held the enchantment of the tiny picture under the rock crystal.

It was his first rosary with the rock crystal picture he held in his mind's eye as he began the "Ave Maria," struggling to remember the words. The wind blew, the noise grew louder again, and more insistent. *"Plenia gracia,"* he continued, a little louder, irritated by the noise. The horse whinnied. *"Dominus tecum . . ."* He tried to close his ears. Whatever it was, he was past caring. "*Salve Regína, Mater misericórdiæ; Vita dulcédo, et spes nostra, salve. Ad te . . .*"

The horse whinnied again, pulling at its tether with more energy than Thierry thought it had left in it. The whinnying drove the words out of his head. Painfully he hauled himself to his feet, midprayer. He untied the horse and began to undo the bridle. Maybe it was fear; maybe it sensed a mountain lion. He would let the horse take its chances; it could wander until it fell down or a mountain lion got it. He didn't care. The sound of the sea rose again in his ears.

Before he finished taking off the bridle, the horse pulled hard toward the sound, and since the bridle was only half off, it dragged him along. The horse trotted around the trees and tossed its head free, leaving Thierry holding the bridle. He blinked hard. The Devil was tormenting him with hallucinations.

Before him, like a cruel joke, lay a huge clearing. It had been a cornfield, and dead cornstalks rattled in the wind, dry ghosts. Almost food. Taunting him. Maybe this was hell. He reached out his hand and gripped one, then looked closer. There was a dried tassel waving. His hand, though numb with cold, felt something solid. It was a fat, desiccated ear of corn. He stared at it blankly, wondered if there might be another. He gripped a second stalk, then a third. More dried tassels. More desiccated ears of corn. He shut his eyes to banish the sight, he wanted to return to the comforting recollection of his mother in the warm firelight . . . but when he opened them, he was still gripping a cornstalk heavy with dried ears.

He looked around him, then took one step, then another into the cornfield, grasping wildly. There were dried ears of corn everywhere he looked. Slowly he realized the crop had been left unharvested. The field stretched out in front of him a long way, the dried stalks rustling and swaying, rustling and swaying as the wind blew, and he understood this was the noise he had mistaken for the sea. He went from stalk to stalk, finding the same hard, fat ears. He was surrounded by corn.

Behind him, the horse was noisily attacking a dried ear. Thierry let him eat a few, and then dragged him away before the starved horse got colic from filling its stomach too quickly. It was all he could do to resist gnawing a dried cob himself, but even in the extremis of hunger, he knew it had to be soaked and cooked before it could be eaten. He ripped off cob after cob and stuffed his pockets and shirt to take it back, then remounted his horse. Tomorrow they would come back with the wagons and harvest the corn.

He led the protesting horse back toward the way they had come. He turned and took a last dazed look at the cornfield to make certain it was really there; he had not imagined it nor the dried ears scratching against his bare skin, making his shirt bulky and uncomfortable so that he mounted awkwardly.

Then he froze. On the far edge of the cornfield, something was moving, a dark shape against the snow. All his hunter's senses were alert. Indians? A mountain lion? If so he'd have to stand his ground and shoot; his horse couldn't outrun a lion and probably not Indians. But even as he fumbled for his blunderbuss, he saw it wasn't slinking through the corn toward him; it was moving in a different direction, very slowly. The dark shape was followed by other dark shapes. He squinted. Wild pigs! They were eating the corn! He gazed, stupefied, with his mouth open, too weary and cold and famished and stunned by the discovery of the cornfield to believe the pigs were as real as his shirt was full of corn. He was too weak now to kill one and get it back to the settlement, but tomorrow or the next day, he and Henri would return with the mules and wagon.

They were saved.

He began to shout, to laugh, hysterically. *"Sanglier!"* he cried, over and over. "*Maize!* Food! Food! Oh, God, food!" Tears streamed down his face. In his weakened state, he was overcome, sank to his knees, unable to stand. "How?" Suddenly he realized he had been vouchsafed a miracle, by a God he had not believed in. He had been saying the rosary, and the Virgin had heard and sent boar and maize. The suddenness, the mercy of it! "Holy Mother of God, Virgin most pure . . . Holy Queen of Heaven. Mother of Mercies," he wept. "Ave Maria," he shouted wildly to the sky. "Ave Maria!"

"Ave Maria," echoed against the mountain. "Ave . . . ve . . . ve . . . ria . . . ria . . . ria." Filling the distance.

Finally Thierry pulled himself up. He remounted and urged his horse slowly back up the mountain, letting it set its own weary pace. At the top, he turned the horse around and looked back down at the cornfield, reluctant to leave it, even until the next day. Then as he looked west, the horizon was no longer gray but streaked with a brilliant sunset, red and gold and pink and orange, vivid as winter sunsets often are.

As he looked, the Virgin's image appeared for an instant, robed in the colors of the sunset, her hand raised in benediction, then disappeared.

Thierry rubbed his eyes. Had the Virgin really appeared to him? He had no doubt she had led him to the cornfield. He watched the bright winter sunset fade in the gathering dusk. Finally, he crossed himself and made a solemn vow. One day, he would return to the valley with the cornfield and the wild pigs and bring with him a priest and some holy relic or other venerable object. He would see a shrine consecrated to Our Lady as an act of thanksgiving for their miraculous deliverance. He would dedicate his life to that purpose.

CHAPTER 23
BIRTHS

March 1756

The settlers had finally dispersed to their own cabins and homesteads. Three days previously, Gideon had come with a supply of corn, pumpkin, and squash and bean seeds for the spring planting. He was ashamed that he and the other men were doing the work of women, but the planting could not be left to women who had no knowledge of it, which described Sophia, Saskia, and Venus. Caitlin did but was too large and near her time to be tramping the fields, planting things.

Vann Station and its landing were at the river bend between Frog and Little Frog Mountains. The cabin Gideon had built there was smaller than Wildwood but snug and comfortable and tidy, the chinks tightly packed with mud and twigs, cheerful with Caitlin's quilts, preserves, mirror, willow platter, and cooking pots. Caitlin had everything prepared for the baby, and Gideon was to bring her up to Wildwood when her time came.

Sophia and Caitlin had speculated nervously about which of them would have the first baby, and when Sophia saw Caitlin and Gideon climbing slowly up through the orchard, Caitlin holding on to Gideon's arm, she knew the answer. Unless, she thought, her baby came at the same time to keep Caitlin's baby company. The afternoon was sunny, and the little apple trees were putting out early blossoms that Caitlin stopped every few steps to admire.

As if she might never see them again, Lavinia's ghost murmured.

"Go away! You belong in your grave!" muttered Sophia, vehemently stamping her foot. She mustn't allow such thoughts. When the Vanns arrived, she greeted her friend with a happy smile. "Well, Caitlin, is it . . . ?"

Caitlin said, "I think. I'm not sure because I've not had a baby before. But it must come soon, mustn't it? I'm glad to see you, Sophy. I was too busy to come for ages. Now I've left Venus and Jack and Toby in charge in case a raft of settlers or long hunters come. I feel better when I'm with you, Sophy."

Sophia was glad to see her friend and eager to show Caitlin the improvements since her last visit. The kitchen had had a bread oven built into the stone chimney. The cabin was now watertight. The roof had been repaired with wooden shingles carved by the three boys, and a new porch had been built on the back side of the cabin with a view over the orchard and the valley to the area where Seth, Nott, Meshack, and Rufus had marked out their properties. All had moved into their cabins ahead of the work of the spring planting, taking the household possessions Sophia had divided up. From the porch, Sophia pointed the cabins out to Caitlin, saying what a comfort it was to see the smoke rising from their chimneys. It felt like a village.

Henri, Gideon, Seth, Rufus, Nott, and Meshack rode off to work out what crops would be planted where, and Thierry had gone in search of the buffalo herd Gideon had spotted at the end of the valley. They had eaten almost nothing but hominy and corn cakes and wild pork since Thierry had discovered the cornfield abandoned by Gideon's people the previous summer. And grateful though they were for that food, they were starved for a taste of something fresh. Gideon had told them where to find oniony ramps now coming up, and Zaydie and Malinda had brought back a basketful, and Sophia eyed them doubtfully. They smelled quite strong.

The two women had a rare moment of peace. Caitlin had brought some sassafras tea, and from a basket beneath the bed Sophia unpacked the porcelain teacups that had once belonged to Anne de Bouldin, in honor of Caitlin's visit. The two of them sat companionably on the wooden bench fixed to the side of the porch, with Malinda, as usual a silent little presence, sipping her tea. They often forgot about Malinda, who would play quietly with her doll for hours if no one thought to give her a chore or if Jack were not around. They stitched at baby clothes and talked of the best way to get light bread to rise, if they were ever so fortunate as to have some wheat flour again, and preserving blackberries in honey, if they found a beehive. They looked at the clouds gathering beyond the mountains and hoped the men wouldn't be caught in a storm.

Caitlin paused every so often, catching her breath and stopping her sewing. Finally she sent Malinda off to put the pot of water on to boil for more tea and said, "Sophy? Will you promise something?"

"Mmm?"

"If I die, will you promise to look after the baby? And Gideon too?"

"Don't speak of dying!"

"But women die of babies. Look at your own mother. Look at Malinda's. And you're the person in all the world I'd want to raise my child."

"Caitlin, don't! It will be all right."

"But in case it isn't, then . . . it makes it easier to say God's will be done . . . I was afraid, all of a sudden, because I'd never got to ask you . . . I wasn't afraid of dying before, when I first knew about the baby, just happy, but . . . now all I can think of is the baby and Gideon with no one to look after them in all the world. And that makes me afraid. I'll feel less afraid if you say yes. Please!"

"Of course I will, if Gideon will let me. I promise. And . . . and will you promise me the same?"

"Of course, if Henri agrees. Oh, Sophy." They clasped hands for an instant, a pact of life and death.

Then Caitlin had put her hand on her swollen belly and smiled nervously. "Good. Because I do think it's started coming. I've had this . . . this *tight* feeling since yesterday. It comes and goes. This morning it felt stronger. But it's not terrible, not yet. Venus says it gets terrible, and I have to put a knife under the bed to cut the pain in half."

"That's nonsense! I'll send Malinda to get Saskia."

Sophia was levering her own large self up from the bench when Caitlin cried, "Oh! Oh!" She winced, arching her back. Her eyes grew big, and she clutched Sophia's hands. "It was stronger that time! What'll happen now, Sophy? Will it be quick, like when calves are born? Or the pigs? What if the baby gets stuck? I've had to pull calves and piglets out with my hands when they wouldn't come, can that happen with women?"

"Neither of us knows exactly, but don't worry, Caitlin. Women have babies all the time. Saskia knows what to do. Maybe you ought to . . . to get ready . . . You're meant to be lying in bed when it happens." Sophia tried to be reassuring and calm as she helped Caitlin up, but the depths of her ignorance about childbirth were terrifying. She put Lavinia out of her mind. Lavinia wouldn't have died if Saskia had been there for the birth, and Saskia would be there for Caitlin. The birth would go well, she told herself.

Only it hadn't for her mother. Or Lavinia.

In her heart Sophia was afraid, for Caitlin and herself, and she knew this wasn't the time to show it. "Come and see how I've prepared," she said, pulling Caitlin to her feet. "It's all ready for you."

Two weeks earlier, Sophia had curtained off a corner of the de Marechal cabin so she and Caitlin could have their babies in something like privacy. Sophia's only experience of childbirth had been when Venus had Susan, and she was anxious about being seen in undignified agony. Henri and Thierry had moved a bed, and the horsehair mattress that normally rested on ropes crisscrossing the frame had been taken away, and Saskia had replaced it with a thick straw pallet. "Got to burn it after, 'count of the blood. Bad luck not to," Saskia had said, heaving the pallet in place. A wooden cradle waited expectantly in the corner, with a pretty little quilt Caitlin had stitched.

Malinda raced off to fetch Saskia, and Sophia helped Caitlin undress to her shift that pulled tight over her distended stomach, then covered her with a quilt and settled her as comfortably as she could on the straw pallet.

Caitlin giggled nervously. "In all the world, fancy lying in a bed in the afternoon! It isn't natural! Read me some psalms, won't you, to pass the time." Caitlin shifted herself up into a sitting position and resumed her sewing. "No need to be idle," she said. Sophia picked up Lady Burnham's prayer book and began to read, glancing at Caitlin every few lines. By the end of the afternoon, she could hear Caitlin catching her breath at intervals.

Saskia arrived and bustled in and out, getting what she would need for the birth, including a knife. Malinda sat silently in the corner, hugging her doll and looking at the knife with worried eyes. Malinda loved Caitlin, and Sophia knew Malinda ought not to be there. There was no place in the small cabin where Malinda could be out of the way or avoid hearing moans or, worse, screams. Venus had screamed horribly. Sophia didn't want Malinda to witness another birth just now, and Caitlin was beginning to grimace when the pains came, saying afterward, "That wasn't so bad." Sophia felt sure it would soon be worse.

Sophia wondered if she dared send a six-year-old by herself down to Venus at the trading post. But Malinda had a propensity to wander off by herself, usually to visit Meshack, to whom she had taken a liking. She always reappeared safely, and though Sophia had scolded her the first few times, everything else Malinda did suggested she had more sense than they gave her credit for. She didn't like to scold Malinda; it seemed cruel, so finally Sophia just let her go where she liked.

Sophia called Malinda over and took the child's face in her hands. "Malinda, you're going to have to go down to the trading post, by yourself. Venus is there. You need to go and help her with Susan, and she'll give you your dinner. You're a big, brave girl; you know the way, through the orchard. Go now, quickly, before it gets dark. Take your doll for company." Malinda nodded and tucked the doll under her arm efficiently. "You needn't be afraid." Malinda shook her head, looking solemn.

"And because you're such a good girl, you shall wear my shawl." Malinda broke into a smile of delight. She loved Sophia's fine India shawl with its colors and intricate pattern. She held still, looking pleased, while Sophia draped her shawl round and round her shoulders and over her head, tying it under her chin. "Lovely, darling. Off with you now!" Malinda trotted away. The fairy tale of the encounter of the little girl in a red hood with a wolf in the forest came unbidden to Sophia's mind, but they'd have to risk the wolf.

The breath-catching intervals grew more frequent, and Caitlin put down her sewing when it happened and began to say "Oh!" a little louder. By nightfall she stopped trying to sew.

"It's a little worse," she admitted, gasping. "Read the psalms to me again, Sophy. It helps to hear you. Do you think it will be long, Saskia?"

By the time it was dark, Caitlin was twisting the quilt in both hands. "'In sorrow shall she bring forth . . .'" Caitlin quoted in a quavering voice, then bit her lip and held her breath until the contraction passed. "That wasn't . . . so bad." She tried to smile, but her eyes said it was. Sophia held her hand and made soothing noises and said the baby would be there soon.

Midnight came, and Caitlin stopped saying it wasn't so bad. And the baby hadn't come soon. All night Saskia and Sophia took turns wiping her face with a damp cloth and holding her hand. Morning finally came, and a day that grew worse slowly passed, followed by a long, terrible night that was worse still. By the second morning, Caitlin's eyes were ringed with dark shadows, and the freckles stood out on her white face as she struggled and moaned. Sophia tried not to think about her promise to look after the baby in case it made Caitlin die.

Caitlin was in agony, grinding her teeth and crying with pain and exhaustion. Sophia thought it felt like the baby had been coming forever. She and Saskia hung over the bed. Between pains Saskia felt Caitlin's distended stomach with her hands and nodded, trying to be encouraging. "Be over soon." She had been saying that all afternoon, but it wasn't over; it was worse and worse. Caitlin was crying, screaming with each contraction. Bulky and awkward because she was due soon herself, Sophia leaned over to gently wipe Caitlin's face with a wet cloth.

Caitlin's blue eyes were fixed wide and pleading. "I can't, I can't do this any longer, oh Jesus! Oh merciful God, spare me any more! I'm going to die!" Caitlin gasped, tears running down her cheeks. "Where's Gideon? Please fetch Gideon, Sophy!"

"Cully's gone to look for him, but yes, you can do it, darling, please, you have to, just a little longer, Saskia says," murmured Sophia, smoothing Caitlin's damp hair. Really she wanted to run from the cabin that had been a torture chamber for two entire days . . . She told herself not to think that way, not with her own hour of trial nearly upon her. Zaydie hovered inside the curtain, muttering she saw "them" eyeing Caitlin and she wouldn't let "them" get past her.

"Stop it!" Sophia hissed at her. "Hasn't Cully found the men yet?" Her back ached, she was tired beyond endurance, and her terror that Caitlin might die was matched by the fear that Gideon wouldn't come back in time to say good-bye. She knew she ought to be praying for

Caitlin and the baby, but her mind was too numb to do more than form the words: "Please, God, please, God, bring Gideon in time."

Zaydie retreated, muttering about getting chicken feathers. It had rained constantly that spring, and now there was thunder and a flash of lightning and then rain pounding on the roof. At least it no longer leaked, thought Sophia, a small mercy in the circumstances.

Saskia, always uneasy when Cully was out of her sight, was worried about him out in the storm, alone. He had taken the steady old farm horse, but the valley was long, and the men could be anywhere; it could take forever for Cully to find them.

On the second night, Caitlin fell into a moment's sleep. Sophia went to the bucket of fresh water Zaydie had brought. She ladled some into a basin and wrung out the cloth for Caitlin's forehead, then splashed water on her own face while Saskia let go of Caitlin's wrists to flex her own hands and rub her eyes. Neither of them had eaten more than a few bites of cold corn cake or snatched more than a few moments' sleep for two days, and both women felt groggy and ready to drop to the floor.

Zaydie hobbled in with sumac tea, and Saskia and Sophia drank it gratefully, then both took advantage of the moment to close their eyes. Both fell asleep with their heads on their arms. They woke to see Zaydie bending over Caitlin and forcing a cup to her mouth, then shaking a handful of twigs and feathers over her while whispering fiercely. "Ain't lettin' the spirits take her," Zaydie muttered as Saskia and Sophia pulled her away.

Caitlin's eyes opened, and she arched her back against the pain and cried, "Here it comes! Why won't the baby come out? I can't bear it any longer! I'm going to die, I want Gideon! Please, Sophy! Fetch Gideon!"

She grabbed Sophia's hands and howled like an animal while Saskia massaged her stomach and then reached between her legs, urging, "Good! That's it, that's it, it coming! Coming now! Push, push!" Saskia shouted to be heard over another thundery spring storm that hammered the shingle roof and sent rain down the chimney, hissing into the fire.

Caitlin gasped and sobbed. "I can't, I can't! Sophy, your promise! Remember your promise . . . the baby . . . you promised . . . oh . . . Lord Jesus!"

"Never mind no promises, you got to push hard now!" Saskia ordered, grabbing Caitlin's wrists as Caitlin braced her feet against the footboard once more. She groaned and pushed and made a horrible unearthly sound, but suddenly Saskia was maneuvering something away from Caitlin, something Sophia saw was covered in blood and white slime. Saskia cut the cord and swiftly wiped its mouth and eyes, then gave it a gentle slap on the back. There was silence, then an infant's cries filled the room.

"A girl," said Saskia, holding the baby up. "A fine girl. Good, she cryin'." Saskia wiped the baby's face, wrapped her in the baby quilt, and laid the baby in the cradle. She turned back to Caitlin, massaged her stomach again, and her hands filled with something bloody and pulsating. "Help me with this. Get the knife."

Sophia felt the room spinning around her and shut her eyes, trying not to faint. When she finally opened them, Caitlin lay still on the bloodstained bed, her eyes closed in an unnaturally white face. Sophia looked round for Saskia, but Saskia wasn't there. "Caitlin?" Sophia squeezed Caitlin's hand, but there was no answering pressure. "Caitlin? Caitlin? Wake up! Oh, Caitlin, darling, wake up!" There was no response. "No! Caitlin! Wake up!" And Gideon hadn't come back in time to say good-bye . . . the only thing Caitlin had wanted at the end. Now she was dead.

Sophia began to cry. At the door Zaydie stood with her back to them, waving her dried things and feathers at the air. "They take a mother, take the baby too if they can, but I ain't lettin' no spirits in. Done be afeard. Grab holt of Caitlin, that baby too, till they gone. Git that baby, I say!" Too weary to think this was nonsense, Sophia leaned over and picked up the swaddled baby, then grasped Caitlin's limp hand.

Caitlin's face was whiter than Sophia thought a human face could be, but suddenly her eyelids fluttered open. "A girl, you said!" she whispered. "Praise the Lord! Let me see her."

"That good, you keep talking," said Saskia, slow and clumsy from tiredness, coming in with the basin of hot water and a rag. "I gets you washed, then you feed her."

The room smelled heavy and rank, of blood and perspiration. Sophia held the baby for Caitlin to see while Saskia washed Caitlin, got her into a clean unbuttoned shift, and somehow maneuvered the blood-soaked pallet from under her and replaced it with a fresh one. Then Saskia laid the baby in her arms, and Caitlin managed a small, exhausted smile at the baby's tiny fingers and her little pink mouth working as if she were trying to say, "Oh!"

The three exhausted women admired the baby in silence as the fire crackled and rain poured down on the roof. "What's her name?" asked Sophia, slipping her own finger into the baby's tiny hand, hardly able to believe this sweet baby had caused Caitlin's suffering.

"It's Rhiannon, like the Welsh heroine," Caitlin murmured, looking adoringly at her infant. "Rhiannon, wait till your pa sees you. And Tad! They'll say there's never been such a baby in all the world. A princess, you are! Oh, Sophy, I kept thinking I'd die, and I'd not be here to look after her! Never see her, even!"

She put Rhiannon to her breast and began humming, "Guide me, O thou great Jehovah." The baby sucked while the rain fell steadily on the new roof, and finally the new mother and Rhiannon fell asleep. Caitlin's face looked almost normal, pale but no longer deathly white. Sophia tucked the quilt round the arm holding Rhiannon so the baby couldn't fall, then slumped onto a chair.

"Praise be to God on high that's over!" she muttered. Caitlin's screams still rang in her ears, and she was drained with the shock of thinking Caitlin had died. There was a bundle of bloody sheets waiting to be boiled clean, the blood-soaked straw pallet needed burning, and her back ached as if it would snap in two. If this was what it took to bring a new life into the world, it was a wonder there were any people in it. She rubbed her stiff neck and shut her eyes. Sophia dreamed that Lavinia was watching from the corner of the room. Sophia struggled to tell her Malinda wasn't there when she was woken by a hand on her shoulder.

It was Zaydie. "You cryin' out at somethin', I knowed it was there, but cain't nothin' hurt her now. They gone. They want to take her, but I knowed the spell, and I run 'em off."

Sophia rubbed her eyes. "Thank you, Zaydie, I know. Thank you!" *I don't care if it was witchcraft, so long as Caitlin and the baby lived,* thought Sophia.

She rested her hand on top of Zaydie's. "Thank you!"

Zaydie glanced over at Caitlin and the baby and nodded. "They be fine," she repeated. Then she gave Sophia a piercing look. "You be fine too, Miss Sophy. It go easier for you than for her. Don't worry none." She gave Sophia a final pat on the shoulder before making a motion with her hands, as if she were shooing chickens ahead of her as she shuffled out the door.

Sophia picked up her prayer book, then put it down, thinking there was nothing in it that could have done what Zaydie and her feathers had done. Yet another thing that would have horrified Lady Burnham and her mother . . . Well, thought Sophia tiredly, this was Virginia, Lady Burnham and her mother were dead, and she was having to manage as best she could, even if it sent her soul to perdition.

The next day, Gideon returned with Cully, who was swaggeringly proud of having found the men despite the storm. Saskia tried to fuss over him, but Cully protested he was eight now and too old to get fussed over, men shouldn't get fussed over by their mothers. "Humph!

We see 'bout that later," muttered Saskia, who was too tired to argue at present.

Caitlin was propped up in bed, looking white and frail but happy. Gideon held his daughter and, after gazing at her a moment, whispered in her tiny ear that her Cherokee name would be Singing Wind Between the Mountains. Caitlin wished her father and uncles knew about Rhiannon, but when Gideon offered to make the trip upriver, Caitlin insisted they wait for a long hunter or a trader going that way to take word. She didn't want Gideon to leave her.

Sophia did the best she could with the meager supplies at her disposal to feed Caitlin something besides corn gruel. She made a broth made from a scrawny rabbit Thierry snared, saved a few precious eggs the hens laid, and beat them into a kind of eggnog with the little milk the cows were giving. She made tea from spice wood sweetened with the last scrapings of the honey.

They were hanging on as best they could until summer. The Caradoc uncles were to come with a mill wheel and help build a mill at the Vanns' trading post, but there would be nothing to grind until the new corn that had just been planted was harvested. They had been pleased to find three broken plows Mr. Barker had bought. Meshack and Rufus had managed to repair them, and the men had planted the rich bottom land with vegetables and sowed field after field of corn.

With the longer days and new grass in the pasture, the cows gave more milk, and a bull calf had survived the winter and was trotting about in his own fenced-off enclosure. Zaydie's chickens scratched about for worms and produced more eggs, then a few chicks. A hawk took most of the chicks before Henri and Thierry devised a shelter, but four were left.

After a week, Caitlin was better and insisted on returning to her own home. On a warm day, she and Gideon left with Rhiannon strapped to Gideon's back on a bark cradleboard. Gideon was glad no

Indian man could see him carrying a baby, but he thought Caitlin still looked frail, and very white.

Henri told Thierry he had a plan to get them home soon. He would clear land in the valley and sell it as homesteads to passing settlers. Thierry protested that clearing more land was a big job, and most settlers had little money. Henri shrugged and said some did. He neglected to mention to either Thierry or Sophia that he intended to take his son with them, or that their return would have to be postponed until the child was weaned. He hoped Sophia would see that it was to the child's advantage to be brought up in France after he was weaned, but this was not the time to tell her. Sophia's temper was volatile.

She alternated between growing anxiety about what lay ahead and envy of Caitlin being over it. Two weeks after Rhiannon's birth, Sophia felt like her pregnancy would never end. She was too bulky to stand long, so she sat and did everyone's mending. Sitting was uncomfortable too. She forced her bulk up from her chair at night and from her bed every morning, telling herself the baby was certain to be born today. She was irritable, heard herself snapping at Malinda, who seemed to be underfoot every time she moved. She sent Malinda down to Caitlin for a day, saying Malinda could help with Rhiannon. Malinda loved helping Caitlin and rocking the baby in her cradle, so she skipped off while Sophia was telling her to be careful.

Sophia decided the time had come to plant the tobacco seeds she had taken from Thomas. None of the whites knew how to grow tobacco, but Sophia knew that Seth, Nott, and Meshack did. She was unprepared for their flat refusal. To her astonishment and then fury, they declared nothing would make them plant tobacco like slaves. Sophia had pinned her every hope on tobacco, and she raged and wept, but the men insisted, "No, Miss Sophy. Won't do it."

Afterward Henri reasoned with her for a long time before she accepted that it took a large workforce to grow tobacco. They didn't have a large workforce, and if she wouldn't own slaves, she wouldn't have a great many workers and couldn't have tobacco, and in any case, what they needed more than tobacco was to grow enough food, for themselves and fodder for the animals. Argued into a corner, her hopes crushed, hugely pregnant, uncomfortable, irrational, and angry, Sophia burst into tears and shouted that she hated Henri, and the Negroes ought to give back her land. Henri took her by the shoulders and said very calmly that no one would give back the land, it was theirs now, and everyone here needed everyone else if they were to survive; this was Virginia, not England, and she was not milady. She would feel better when the baby was born.

Sophia lost the will to argue and gave up the tobacco. She thought wearily she didn't care, she didn't care about anything any more. Day after day she waited, but if anything happened, it was some sensations that came and went and then stopped. She tried to prepare herself in case she died. After watching Caitlin, that seemed all too likely. Her mother and Lavinia were in her mind every waking moment. Lady Burnham and probably her mother would have advised that prayer would fortify her. Trying to look ahead to the time when the birth would be behind her, she turned to the service for the churching of women after childbirth in her prayer book.

"O Almighty God, we give thee humble thanks for that thou hast vouchsafed to deliver this woman thy servant from the great pain and peril of childbirth."

She slammed the prayer book closed and hurled it across the room. She didn't feel like humble thanks and she didn't want to be reminded about pain and peril. She felt fat and ungainly and furious with everything and everyone. Whoever wrote that prayer had never been an apprehensive mother-to-be. The more she tried to forget the words "great pain and peril," the more vividly she recalled what Caitlin had gone through. Oddly, Caitlin seemed to have forgotten how terrible Rhiannon's birth had been. Sophia hadn't.

Malinda came home. After two days, Sophia sent her back down to the trading post for her own good and ordered her to stay until they sent word the baby had come.

Sophia could no longer sleep. She felt hot all the time. At night she was too uncomfortable to do anything but snatch short naps. She was easily waked by the cries of a night bird or Zaydie snoring in the next room.

When she felt a tightening around her abdomen one night shortly after they went to bed, she was so tired that she dozed off anyway, half sitting. Later she was woken by more tightening sensations. They came and went, closer and closer together, and grew a little stronger, but they were hardly unbearable, to her surprise and relief. Goodness, she thought, if this was all there was to it, she needn't send for Saskia till morning. She ignored them and dozed off again.

Suddenly she woke in the vise-like grip of a fierce sensation that left her unable to breathe. "Henri!" Sophia gasped and shook her soundly sleeping husband. "Henri! Fetch Saskia!"

Sophia shook him again, hard, and finally he groaned and said, "Why?"

"Why do you think I'm waking you in the middle of the night? Because it's . . . the . . . baby! Ohhhh!" Sophia gasped. "Ohhhh God! Get Saskia! Now!"

Groggily, Henri reached for the candle, couldn't find it, ran a hand through his hair, and swung his feet out of bed. He had been dreaming of France; he often dreamed he was back in France, and it was always disorienting to wake up in Virginia. He groped on the floor for his breeches and pulled them on in the dark. "Saskia, *bien sûr*, at once," he muttered, tripping on a footstool on his way out the door.

Behind him Sophia shrieked, "Hurry!"

Saskia had offered to sleep on a pallet on the floor of Sophia and Henri's cabin until the baby came, but at the time she'd offered, the cabin had been so crowded with Caitlin and Gideon, the baby, Thierry,

Malinda, and Zaydie, who insisted on sleeping in her old bed of rags by the fireplace, even though the men had built her a small, snug one-room cabin of her own a short distance away. Zaydie's cabin had a stone fireplace, a rope bed, and a good straw mattress. Meshack, who was skilled with his hands at almost anything, had made her a table and two chairs, and Caitlin had contributed a quilt. It looked quite cozy and comfortable, but Zaydie took a look and returned to her fireside nest of rags, saying she would think about it.

Malinda had stopped trying to sleep next to Sophia—after the wedding, Henri told her firmly that was his place—and tried to snuggle up with Zaydie, but Zaydie wasn't having it and made Malinda sleep off on a pallet by herself.

Now Henri stumbled over Malinda's empty pallet as he searched frantically for his boots in the dark, because it was spring and there were rattlesnakes and copper snakes everywhere, and he was terrified of being bitten. And he didn't want to step on Zaydie any more than on the snakes. Once asleep she was dead to the world until she chose to wake up. She threatened to lay a curse on anyone who shook her or tried to wake her before she was good and ready.

"The lantern, where is the lantern?" muttered Henri. "My boots!" There was a crash as his elbow hit the lantern.

"Henri, go now!" shrieked Sophia from the bedroom, a new note in her voice. "I need Saskia! At once! Ooooh! *Ooooh!*" she screamed. "Help me!"

There was an angry rumble from Zaydie's pallet. Henri ran out into the darkness barefoot.

Sophia tried to shout again, but she suddenly felt disoriented. Though the pain was terrible, she was somehow detached from what was happening to her body. She knew she was in the grip of some powerful force and the room slid away until it was only her and the pulsing sense of urgency that something was bearing down, bearing down, bearing down. She gasped for breath and struggled to sit up, to get hold of something to pull against. "Help me," she heard herself crying. "Help me!"

Then Zaydie was there above her, saying something Sophia couldn't hear, before another contraction took hold and overwhelmed her. From a long way away, she heard herself shouting, and a hand gripped hers, and a voice said, "It coming now . . ."

An hour later it was getting light when Henri came back with Saskia, who had had to get dressed and was panting from being rushed up the hill to the house. Zaydie met them at the bedroom door. "Be quiet. It over."

Henri's heart almost stopped beating—beyond Zaydie, Sophia lay motionless, her hair across the pillow. "Is she . . ." He couldn't ask.

"No, she ain't, no thanks to your slow feet. Take this here child," commanded Zaydie. "I got work to do." Only then did Henri notice she was holding a bundle in one arm. She gave it to him. The bundle felt impossibly light, and he peered into the wrapping to see if there was really a baby. "A girl," said Zaydie. "We needs water, Saskia," she ordered and turned away.

"Girl?" Henri exclaimed. He felt a sharp pang of disappointment. It should have been a son. De Marechals always had sons. A girl baby hardly counted as a de Marechal. He felt the bundle move, and he looked down, frowning. His first thought was that the baby's face looked squashed. Like a little frog. The baby opened her eyes. He was unprepared for her intense, solemn gaze, as if she looked into his soul and recognized him. He thought she was frowning back at him. As if she were just as disappointed as he was. After a minute, she screwed up her little frog face under its thatch of dark hair, opened her mouth in an *O*. Her mouth was very tiny and soft. He was gripped by a sudden, unexpected surge of emotion for this child he had fathered. His daughter! *"Bonjour, chérie. Je suis ton papa."* He blinked back tears. *"Ma belle petite!"*

"Sophy . . . a girl!" He glanced over at Sophy being fussed over by Saskia and Zaydie. "I . . ." Henri had intended to say he hadn't wanted a girl before, but now he realized that he did. But he couldn't speak for the lump in his throat. He had a daughter!

"I know. I named her Catherine after my mother. We'll call her Kitty."

The baby crossed her tiny wrists, little fingers splayed then curled, squirmed again, and shut her eyes. Perfection! "Kitty!" he whispered adoringly. He kissed her hair. It was very soft, like goose down. She was so little! She was his! His very own little de Marechal princess! He was in love.

Caitlin came in, panting. "Saskia sent Cully to get me. I intended to help, but look at you!" She kissed Sophia and admired the baby in Henri's arms, exclaiming, "Kitty! Except Rhiannon, there's not a prettier baby in all the world. What a fine head of hair already! And so quick!"

Sophia laughed weakly. "She was here so fast that Zaydie was just in time to catch her."

Kitty screwed up her face and made a squeaking noise, which Henri found enchanting. Then she took a deep breath and opened her mouth, her small face turned red, and she began to howl. "What's wrong? What must we do?" cried Henri. He clutched the baby tighter. She screamed louder.

"She hungry! Wants her mama feed her now. Let go that chile! Let go!" Henri reluctantly let Zaydie take the baby and give her to Sophia. When he did, his arms felt empty and incomplete without the warm, light, tiny bundle. He wanted it back.

Zaydie was helping Sophia maneuver the baby into the right position to feed, and Henri hovered by the bed, ready to hold her again after Sophia finished. He was standing so close he knocked her elbow and dislodged Kitty, who had just latched on to Sophia's nipple. Kitty wailed. Zaydie turned on Henri. "Git out! Men ain't no use in the birthing room."

"But I want . . ."

"No matter what you want! Git!" snapped Zaydie, and she shoved him out the door.

The sun was rising, and Henri went in search of Thierry to tell him the news. Thierry had been living in the barn since Caitlin gave birth, unable to face being in the cabin when another woman screamed for two nights running. Bursting with new fatherhood, Henri found him saddling their best horse. Before Henri could speak, Thierry said, "I know about the baby. I am glad it's born, but now, you will never leave Virginia. I must go back to France. There is something I must do, before it is too late for me as well." While Henri spluttered that of course it wasn't too late, of course he would go back to France, didn't he have a plan for them to go together? It was just that he had to take the child and . . .

Thierry shook his head and tightened his saddle. "I cannot wait. I made a solemn vow to the Virgin after I found the corn and must go home to fulfill it. I will go to La Nouvelle-Orléans now and work or beg, find the Jesuit mission and throw myself on their mercy—anything—and get passage to France."

"You? You made a vow? Thierry, what do you take me for?" muttered Henri, stunned and angry. "How can you abandon me here? Is this your friendship?"

"I swear that I am your friend. One day I will return to keep my vow, and then, perhaps, you will be ready to go with me. Until then, *au revoir, mon ami*." Thierry embraced Henri quickly, swung up into the saddle, and rode away without a backward glance.

"You'll be back by next week," Henri shouted at the departing figure. *"Je m'en fous!"* he swore angrily. "A vision? You? Ha!"

Malinda watched all this from a corner of the barn. She had decided to come back from the trading post, following Caitlin from a distance so she couldn't be seen and sent back. Henri didn't notice her. Malinda thought she would wait here a little longer before going into the house.

She stuck her thumb in her mouth, hugged her doll, and thought about the old Indian she had just seen when she'd come through the orchard. He'd been there before, then he'd gone. He was dressed like a white man, but she knew he wasn't. He hadn't seen her. Most people didn't when she came and went; she was small and very quiet. She was also very observant. He was watching the valley where the Negroes lived.

She didn't like him.

The Indian's name was Dayugidaski. Translated into English, it meant Slave Catcher.

CHAPTER 24

MESHACK

He'd come here to the valley against his better judgment, not wanting to be separated from Nott and Seth. There'd been so many separations—slave traders appeared on the plantation, watched the slaves work, appraised the women, inspected the children, and made their choice of those to be bound or shackled and led away, never to be seen again. Like his two daughters one time. His son the next. Their mother had been selected another time, but she foiled the traders and ran to the barn and hung herself before they could take her too.

He'd regretted not going to the Spanish in Florida. He'd known in his bones eventually they would find him and the others here. He'd told Zaydie, who agreed they always did come. She'd promised to say spells, to ask the spirits to tell them how many and when, but it was Malinda who warned him they were here.

Malinda had come to his cabin one afternoon while he was devising a new chicken coop that he hoped would keep the chickens in and the foxes and hawks out. She appeared soundlessly like she always did, just waiting until someone noticed her. Her habit of doing this gave everyone a turn, and Meshack had jumped and sworn as he hammered his thumb. He sucked his hand and said, "Child, you spook folks! You need me to make you a new head for your baby?" Malinda had the habit of nervously twisting the wooden head of her doll until it came off, and each time she did, Meshack would make a big show of dismay, cluck over the poor doll with no head, and make her a new one with a different face, hair, and expression. Eventually she would twist that off too.

But this time Malinda shook her head, held up her doll to show the last head was still on, and beckoned Meshack inside the cabin.

The child wasn't right; what did she want in the cabin? Meshack shrugged and humored her like he always did, following her in and waiting for his eyes to adjust to the gloom after the brightness outside. "You hungry? Got some cold cornpone, you want it."

Malinda shook her head. She was standing to the side of the door, pointing at it. "Why you pointin' at where you just come in? Door open, I see that."

Malinda shook her head and pointed to the door again and raised her pointing finger.

"Up? Up where? On the roof? What is it? Something wrong? Did a shingle blow off?"

Malinda pointed at the roof, shook her head, and pointed in the direction of Wildwood. "Somebody up yonder?"

Malinda nodded.

"Miss Sophia?" She shook her head and pointed again. "Mist' Henri?" Another headshake.

Malinda paused, then cupped her hands around an imaginary round thing, then took a pretend bite. She pointed up again.

"You want a apple? Apple trees? Why you pointin' at them? Apples ain't ready yet. They little and green now, make you sick."

Malinda put her hand on her brow as if shading her eyes, stretched her neck, and looked as if searching. "Lookin' for somethin' in the apple trees? You lose somethin'? What you want, child? What game you playin'? Ain't got all day!" She looked at him, pointed, and clapped her hand to her brow again, looking past him, narrowing her eyes.

"Don't know what you want," sighed Meshack, "but can't play no games now. I busy. Got to finish this coop. Fox done took two chickens last night. He come back for more."

Malinda dropped her hand and stamped her feet in frustration. She took a deep breath and tugged Meshack's right arm up with both hands. She grabbed his hand and curled his fingers into a fist so only the index finger was straight. She pulled it toward the door, staying away from the opening, then swung it in the direction of the orchard. Then she dropped it and pointed to the same place. Then she turned to face Meshack and adopted her searching pose, staring straight at him. Then she pointed at him. Earnestly she repeated the performance, and Meshack tried to understand her.

"You pointing at the orchard, yes?"

Malinda nodded, put her hand over her brow again, and narrowed her eyes. Then pointed at him. She held his gaze steadily and didn't smile.

He understood this was no game. Malinda wanted to tell him something.

"Somebody in the orchard? Watchin' us down here?"

She nodded hard.

Meshack felt a cold tremor of fear. There was only one reason somebody would be watching a runaway slave and not coming straight to get him. That was because the watcher was the half-blood known as Slave Catcher, who had tracked him and Seth and Nott and Venus and Saskia here because there was a reward. With Cully, that made six slaves, and six slaves meant a big reward, six criminal slaves an even bigger one, because they had burned down Massa's house and barn and killed the overseers.

Slave Catcher was notorious, a figure of fear among slaves. He boasted he could track anybody or anything, man, woman, child, or animal. Slave Catcher had time and supplies, cunning and patience on his side, and he always caught any runaway he was set to catch, even venturing into the swamps if the reward was big enough. They said he was successful because he had a special power, could get inside the mind of any runaway slave and figure out where he'd gone.

If a gang of slaves absconded, too many for him to take alone, he would guide the militia to them. Slave Catcher had grown rich from his work; they said he now owned fifty slaves himself and a large piece of land. Meshack knew what happened to captured runaways—at best they were whipped; usually they had the tendon in their heel slashed to cripple them or were branded. At worst they were sold to the owners of the lead mines, sold to the West Indies, and runaways who'd done it repeatedly were castrated or hung to teach other slaves a lesson.

Meshack had no intention of being caught. He might die, but he wouldn't be taken back. But he had to think of a plan.

He knelt down so his face was level with Malinda's. She regarded him as solemnly as a little owl. "Malinda, you got to listen to me. It's a bad man watchin'. Stay away from the orchard, don't let him see you, don't talk to him. You're a good girl to tell me, but it be better you don't tell anyone else," he said earnestly. "So this our secret. I take care of it. And you go back to Miss Sophy now, you stay in her sight, you hear me? You do, you be safe. I cain't take you myself 'cause he watchin'. He know by now how you go in and out all the cabins, nobody ever take you back. I take you back, he'll figure you told me. That how he thinks. But you safe. He don't want you."

She pointed at him, her small face puckered with anxiety, and he understood her question. "Meshack be safe too, don't worry none, but I got to figure it out. Man you saw is smart."

Malinda nodded.

"But I smarter," said Meshack, hoping it was true. "Thank you, child," he said, and stood up. "You a good girl to come and tell Meshack. You best not go back through the orchard." She gave him a scornful look that said, "I *know that*!" so clearly he had to smile. "Go on now."

He watched her run off to the de Marechals' by a longer way and remembered how Malinda had held up her doll outside, waving it around like she was making a show, then come inside the cabin to give him the message. So the watcher in the orchard would think she wanted her toy mended. Then she hadn't stood right in front of the door when she pointed, because the watcher might have seen her and known she was warning him. Meshack shook his head and muttered, "That little one smart as a whip. Don't talk, but smarter than most folks. They just don't see it."

Since then, he'd slept in the daytime, a few hours here and there, hiding in the bushes down by the river, and waited through the nights, listening to the cicadas. He had told Seth and Nott and Venus and Saskia they'd been tracked, and Seth and Nott wanted to take their families and run, but Zaydie had warned them Slave Catcher would have brought other men with him; even Slave Catcher wouldn't try to take six runaways alone. They would come in the night, take him and then the others by surprise, while they were asleep. Zaydie had known many runaways, had tried and failed to get up the courage to run herself, had watched what happened. All the slaves were made to watch the punishments.

Thanks to Slave Catcher, the patrollers and the militia usually caught runaways. With Slave Catcher tracking, they would follow runaways till they tired, patrollers and the militia biding their time. Runaways were dangerous when they were fresh and rested and desperate.

Meshack was prepared; in fact, he'd prepared for this as soon as his cabin was built, not knowing how much warning he'd have when the time came or how many there would be. Knowing they would come soon, if not tonight, he waited till dark to make the final preparations.

The straw pallet made a man-size shape in the bed. He covered it with a bearskin. He hated to sacrifice the skin, but it couldn't be helped. He tied the shutters over the windows together with deer gut, too tight to open. He put ash logs on the fire. They weren't seasoned yet, but ash burned fine and steady even when it was green. He got the fire crackling away, giving off perhaps more heat than most people want on a summer night. The flickering light made the shadows jump, made the figure on the bed look like it was breathing.

He had dried pinecones banked around the walls, pine needles everywhere. Cully had helped him collect baskets and baskets of them, puzzled that Meshack wanted so many, but Meshack told him he was making something. Meshack was always making something, from shoes to shingle pegs to a spit that turned itself. He was good at thinking of things and then working out how to make them.

He took the pot of resin from the corner where he'd been keeping it, and set it on the hearth to warm, but not too close to the flames. He took a long plaited lariat of deer gut from a bucket of water and tied it round the handle of the pot, and set the pot on a stool he'd made, exactly the right height and the right distance to spill over into the fire. He had calculated this over and over, had practiced how it would work, but the timing was crucial.

Leaving the door a little way open, he slipped out of his cabin, uncoiling the wet lariat in a straight line as he went. Another plaited lariat attached to a bar propped up on a latch was coiled by the door, and he picked the end of that up too and trailed it beside the first one in a straight line to the vegetable patch at the side of the cabin.

Five days after Malinda had warned him, he sensed them coming. Meshack flattened himself between the spreading leaves of two rows of squash he had watered well at sunset. The big leaves were still heavy with water. He put his ear to the ground to be sure. Yes, he could hear the horses faintly above the cicadas, feel the vibrations of their hooves. He waited, holding a lariat in each hand.

Venus and Seth and Susan, Saskia, Nott, and Cully were hiding; they'd gone up the narrow path to the bear cave where they'd left muskets and food. The cave smelled bad, but Gideon had said no bears would be there until it was time to hibernate. Seth and Nott had wanted to stay and help Meshack, but he refused, said they had families to protect. All he'd tell them was he had a plan. He wouldn't say what it was.

Seth and Nott discussed it and agreed with Meshack that if he were killed, they were safer in the bear cave than they would be if they tried running from Slave Catcher. Out in the open, they would be tracked and hunted down easily. In the cave, Slave Catcher and anyone with him would have to go in after them. The cave entrance wasn't big, and they would have to go in one by one. Inside, the cave grew bigger as it went deeper into the mountain, opening up into caverns too big for the militia to smoke them out. There were hiding places from which they could ambush pursuers. Meshack even devised some traps and snares to lay inside the opening.

Meshack hadn't said anything to the de Marechals, Rufus, or the Vanns. He preferred to rely on himself alone.

He had taken the precaution of hiding his few possessions, his table and chairs and tools, in his barn, along with ten gold-rimmed porcelain plates painted with roses Sophia had given him when sharing out the china. Their delicacy had beguiled him; he had traced the roses in admiration of the petals, the tiny thorns, the subtle colors. "Look more like flowers than most flowers does," Meshack said appreciatively. Sophia had agreed they were beautiful; Meissen, she called them. The plates were the finest of the things she had brought from Thomas's house. He'd been touching the pink glaze to see if it would feel soft, then instinctively he'd withdrawn his hand from the white folks' china. "Them thorns is sharp," he said. Joking.

Sophia had said she hadn't noticed the thorns, and if Meshack had, he must keep the plates, that whoever had painted the plates would have wanted the person who appreciated the thorns to have them. He was very proud of those plates; it made him happy to look at them. He'd carved a set of horn spoons and forks to go with them. He never used the china to eat from, it was too fine, but the ownership of such handsome things gave him immense satisfaction. Owning them proved he was no longer a slave.

It was a moonless night, full of the usual noises of cicadas and night birds in the trees and wild animals in the distance. The men and horses were waiting, and from his prone position, he could just make out the dark shadows moving toward him from the orchard. He counted five of them. His cabin was the first they would reach.

At the bottom of the orchard, they stopped, getting their bearings.

They didn't speak, but dismounted some distance away and walked quietly toward the cabin. Meshack's night vision was keen. He made out that three had guns, one had coiled ropes, and the last one was laden with something that clinked. Metal chains and shackles. It would be done quietly, sleepers waking to find themselves gagged and bound and then chained. Meshack was sweating. They reached the cabin and made signals to each other—they had done this many times. *Go in, take him while he's sleeping; he's the biggest. Gagged, he can't rouse the others. We'll get 'em all.*

One by one they stepped inside. Only the man with the chains and shackles waited outside. Meshack knew he was Slave Catcher.

Meshack counted to three, took a deep breath, and tugged the lariat in his right hand. He ducked his head, held his breath, and waited. But nothing happened. He tugged harder. Then he gave a mighty jerk of the lariat. Inside the cabin there was a clunk as a large cauldron full of warm pine resin tipped onto the floor by the fire, spilling to form a big pool that ran into the fire and across the floor into the piles of pine needles, followed by an exclamation, "Nigger ain't in the bed!" then "Fire's blazed up all a sudden, smells like pitch!" then a loud "Hell, git out!" from inside the cabin as Meshack tugged the second lariat and the cabin door closed hard and the heavy wooden bar slammed down into a wedge, barring the door from outside. He had worked and worked, perfecting everything, weighting the long wooden bar to fall and wedge itself tight. It couldn't be opened from inside.

There were shouts and curses, and the spilled resin ignited. A pillar of flame shot up through the chimney, and the floor and stores of dry pine needles and cones caught at once. A red glow showed through a gap in the chinking. There were screams and the thud of desperate efforts to open it from inside, but Meshack had designed a slot for the bar to slam into, and the lariat he had pulled taut helped keep it there. The man outside had dropped the chain and leg iron and was struggling to unjam the bar as the screams grew louder.

Then as Slave Catcher shoved and heaved, Meshack let the lariat go slack so finally Slave Catcher succeeded in raising the bar and wrenching the door open. There was an angry roar as, fed by the fresh air, the flames that engulfed the whole cabin swallowed him. Meshack was hit by a fierce blast of heat that scorched his face and lungs made him duck his head under the wet squash leaves, and when he looked up through his fingers, there were, briefly, figures silhouetted in the open door of the flaming cabin. They staggered and jerked like puppets, then crumpled to their knees, and their cries now drowned out by those of Slave Catcher. His arms flailed as he tried to beat out the flames and get away, but he couldn't find a direction. Blinded and burning, he turned and turned, finally stumbling over the chains that tangled in his feet, and fell into Meshack's yard.

Meshack lay facedown and endured searing heat on his back as the cabin burned. There was a terrible stench of incinerated human flesh. When the flames finally died down and the heat lessened, he rose from his hiding place and approached the blackened figure on the ground. Slave Catcher was alive, but he wouldn't be for long. His face was almost melted off the bones by the fire; his teeth were bared in a rictus of agony, and he made unearthly choking, whimpering sounds. Meshack made no move to help him, just stared back. "I free now," said

Meshack conversationally. "So I'll keep you company a while. Wished those slaves you caught and brung back was all here now." He sat down to wait. Slave Catcher's eyelids were burned away, so he stared straight at Meshack. He made more noises from time to time, horrible ones, and died slowly.

The cabin was a smoldering pile of logs in the gray predawn light when Meshack stood and stretched. He fetched the shovel and the sack he'd kept handy. He would shovel what was left of Slave Catcher and his henchmen into the sack and bury it deep in the forest, away from the fields. Didn't want what was left of them being plowed up. Didn't want their damned ashes polluting his fields. He'd bury the shackles and chains and their evil with them.

He wasn't sure how to explain their horses or the saddles, but he would think of something. There were five horses, several muskets, and a little money even in one of the saddlebags, along with jerky. He threw the jerky into the sack with the remains. The bones were only partly burned, and the skulls had hardly burned at all. After a minute, he threw in the money as well, then the saddlebags. It was all evil, all except the horses. One for each household. Horses couldn't be evil.

He shoveled, thinking how he would explain what happened. The de Marechals and the Vanns would be horrified that his cabin had burned down, would ask with concern what had happened. He'd have to look sorry about the accident, say he'd been re-laying the floor, intending to seal it with pitch, when the pot of resin he was using had been too near the fire; next thing he knew it was ablaze. He'd say it was a lucky thing he'd had his plates and table and chairs in the barn while he did the work—he didn't want Sophia to grieve thinking those fine things had been destroyed in the fire.

He'd rebuild his cabin a little farther away. He didn't mind. He'd make it bigger. He would even make improvements. He couldn't stop smiling. It looked like he'd be living here a while longer.

CHAPTER 25
THE HOUSEHOLDERS

September 1756

Venus and Saskia watched Cully playing with one-year-old Susan, who was shrieking with delight at the way he swung her around. She adored Cully. "I'm spectin' again," said Venus. "Gettin' big." She patted her stomach. "I know it's gon' be another girl."

"Hunh, you can't know till it's born."

"Don't know how I know, but I do."

"You always sayin' you know this and that!" muttered Saskia. "Didn't know that Slave Catcher coming for us."

"I know what I see. Can't know more than that. I see girls and me and Seth in the cabin. Settin' round the table Seth made. All talkin' at once."

"If you see things, you see Thomas in those two?" asked Saskia, looking at Cully and Susan. "I try not to see it, but you think Cully take after his father?" She sighed. "I wish he didn't, but I wouldn't take nothin' for my Cully, however he look. He a good boy."

"Way he is, it's like Thomas had no part in him, Saskia. Handsome like himself, not like old Thomas. Susan don't resemble Thomas at all either, far as I can see."

"No, she don't. She a pretty child. You got her away from Thomas in time, that's the important thing. See how she laughin', playin' with her brother. Neither one got any idea."

"Oh, Saskia, when I think what happened, what he done, what might have happen to Susan . . ."

"Don't think, child. Never think about it. You safe now. Safe as you can be."

"Almost wasn't, when Slave Catcher come."

Saskia nodded. "What I can't figure is how come he took so long? Place burned down, we been gone a year, then they come lookin'. Why didn't Thomas send him sooner?"

"'Cause wasn't Thomas sent him, that's why."

"Now, who else gon' send Slave Catcher?"

"Don't know who exactly, maybe the sheriff or the patrollers, somebody white find everything burned up, overseers dead, us slaves gone. But wasn't Thomas. He already dead."

"Hunh, what you talkin' about? Wish he was, but Thomas ain't dead."

"He is too." Venus paused a minute. She had seen it clear as anything, Thomas's face a strange purple color for a white person, lying in the street. She knew it wasn't just wishing. He was dead. But Saskia didn't believe Venus "knew" things. Maybe Saskia was right, Venus thought, maybe she didn't. Maybe it was all in her head. She tried to "know" something else, but all she saw were baby girls.

"Seth hope he have a boy this time," she said, challenging her own prediction of girls.

"And Nott want whatever chillum he can get. Nothin' yet," said Saskia. She grinned. "But he workin' on it good."

"I bet he is, too." Venus giggled.

"He building two more rooms on the cabin, at the back there, now he finish the porch. Say he be ready when they come." They were sitting on Saskia's porch steps, and Saskia patted the step proudly. They didn't sag. Nott was a good builder. Careful. Seth did things more rushed, and they didn't always last.

"You got a nice view down to the river," said Venus. "Peaceful."

"Nott gets up early, goes fishin'. He loves a fried fish for breakfast."

Cully was limping toward them with a grinning Susan on his shoulder. "This one wore me out!"

"Got to get along," said Venus, rising to her feet, holding out her arms to take Susan. "Cow to milk, chickens to feed."

"Dinner to get," said Saskia standing too.

"The child's mending. And I got to finish her quilt 'fore it turns cold."

"Butter to churn."

"Seth say tomatoes ready, need dryin'. I say he build me something to dry them on so I can."

"Cucumbers needs picklin'. Nott picked me five baskets. So I told him, he like pickles so much, he can bring me some more salt from the marsh."

"Can't draw breath. Be blackberry time soon, then got preserves to put up, take all day. And then I . . ."

"Woo-hoo-hoo!" Cully was laughing so hard he had to put Susan down and slap his sides. "Hoo-wee! You saying who got to do what, way you talkin', both sound like you bragging 'bout work, seein' who got the mos' work to do, like it a race! *Ooooh, I got to make pickles! Ooooh, I got to dig the garden!*" he mimicked in a falsetto voice. "Hoo-hoo-hoo!"

His mother and Venus turned to stare at him. Of course they were bragging. This conversation was always part of the visit. And this conversation could not have taken place if they were still slaves, had no cabins, no garden, no cows or chickens or husbands or babies or time to devote to anything but domestic tasks for themselves and their families, scared every minute they'd be sold away. This was their riches. Cully didn't realize this conversation wasn't about work; it was about freedom. It wouldn't have taken place if they still belonged to Thomas.

CHAPTER 26
THE BLACKBERRY PICNIC

September 1766

The September afternoon of the annual occasion Cully had named the Blackberry Picnic was perfect, hot in the sun with just a welcome touch of autumn cool in the air, as the settlers climbed the path up Frog Mountain to their picnic spot in the broad clearing behind the flat rock that looked out over the valley. The men were laden with baskets and jugs, and the women's arms were full of quilts. Susan Hanover, Kitty de Marechal, and Kitty's younger brothers, Francis and Georgie, had wooden buckets, while their younger sister, two-year-old Charlotte, insisted on carrying her own small basket. Rhiannon had a large Cherokee woven basket that had been traded for some cornmeal and ammunition, which she would get her little brothers, Bryn and Cadfael, to help her fill. Nineteen-year-old Jack carried Malinda's bucket for her and held her hand, and strapping Toby, who at twenty-two had joined the men, walked with his father and Meshack and carried a jug of cider. Cully limped along, cheerfully shooing the younger Hanover girls ahead of him.

Sophia and Venus and Caitlin and Saskia had put on fresh caps and removed their aprons, and each, in unconscious gestures born out of an instinctive female desire to look nice for a special occasion, had smoothed her skirt and patted her darned kerchief into place before leaving her cabin.

Blackberries grew abundantly all over the mountains, and the children were sent to pick them regularly, just as they were sent to gather the wild strawberries and ramps in spring, and the pawpaws, persimmons, walnuts, beech, and hickory nuts in the autumn. But the Blackberry Picnic was different. It had become the closest thing to a holiday the settlers had, a celebration after the corn and wheat had been harvested and vegetables and fruit gathered and sliced to dry in the sun. After weeks of hasty meals of corn bread and buttermilk and vegetables eaten quickly in order to get on with the harvest, the women prepared their best food. The baskets contained venison pies and beaten biscuits flavored with thin slivers of ham, fresh cream cheese, peaches, and muscadine grapes, a kind of gingerbread flavored with pulverized spice-wood bark, and little cakes speckled with the ends of last year's dried fruit. Meshack would bring whiskey and Rufus hard cider, and Sophia would take her tea things in a carefully packed basket.

The quilts were spread out, the men made a fire, and when one of the children had fetched her a pail of water from a nearby spring, Sophia set a pot to boil for tea while she and the other women dressed salads from their kitchen gardens and set them out with the other food, fending off the children, who all complained they were too hungry to pick berries. Finally the children were given a cake each and told sternly not to come back until their buckets were full. The children were always warned not to eat too many while they were picking, but it was a useless warning. They would stuff themselves with blackberries, then eat a large picnic supper, and complain of stomachaches at bedtime.

After the children picked until the buckets were full and earned their dinner, they savored the picnic, each woman praising the lightness of another's pastry, the crumb of the beaten biscuits, the sharpness of the cream cheese, the way Caitlin always managed to arrange fruit in a pretty pile on a bed of grape leaves in the center of the quilt where the food was set out.

Then the children went to play blind man's bluff and tag, and the adults settled down to a rare moment of ease, with their tea or cider or brandy, a brief respite marking the end of weeks of backbreaking labor and tomorrow's renewed cycle of unending chores. It felt luxurious to do nothing, and they stretched out comfortably on the quilts. They reminisced about their early days in the valley and watched the sun dipping toward the horizon a little earlier than it had the week before.

"Charlotte, come look at the sunset," said Sophia, reaching for her youngest child. Charlotte was too young to pick berries on account of the prickly thorns, but she had been playing quietly behind Sophia's back. "Look, darling, at all the pretty colors. There's pink, there."

"Pink," said Charlotte, crawling onto her mother's lap.

"Lavender."

"Lav'ner," said Charlotte.

"Blue."

"Blue!" said Charlotte gleefully, holding up arms purple to the elbows with blackberry juice. "Like me!"

"Oh no! Charlotte, whatever have you done?"

"Wash clothes!" She held a crumpled blue thing in her fist. Behind her, a bucket of blackberries had been reduced to soup.

"My handkerchief! Oh, Charlotte, that's why you were so quiet. You played washing in the blackberries Kitty gathered! She'll be so cross. That was naughty." At least the handkerchief had been clean.

"Notty!" Charlotte agreed happily. "Notty!"

Kitty saw Charlotte waving her purple hands and ran over from the game of tag to investigate her bucket. "Charlotte's got into the berries I picked. They're all squashed!" Kitty shrieked.

"I know. Never mind, Kitty dear. I'll make cordial. I'd have to press the juice out anyway, and Charlotte's saved me the trouble."

"Oh, Mother, you always take Charlotte's part!" grumbled Kitty, stamping her foot. "Papa," she appealed to her father, hoping he would scold Charlotte. "Mother let Charlotte . . ."

"Here, Kitty, your mother made peach fritters." Henri held out a basket. "Take them all, share them out with your brothers and Cully and the others."

Kitty wavered. "But Charlotte will—"

"She got into your berries before I saw her, but there's really no harm done," said Sophia soothingly. "Don't scowl, Kitty. Your face might set in that expression. And do look at the sunset for a minute. You can't be cross when that's so beautiful. Yes, take the fritters."

Partly mollified, Kitty stomped off in Cully's direction with the fritters.

Sophia returned to her contemplation of the fading colors. "This is where Papa and I first saw Wildwood," she told Charlotte, who was too young to know the story yet, though all the other children did. "Right here from this rock with your papa and Thierry. Thierry named the river the Bowjay and shot a wild pig. Bang!" she exclaimed into Charlotte's neck, and Charlotte giggled and squirmed out of her embrace to run after Georgie and Francis.

Henri was propped up on an elbow by Sophia's side, finishing the last venison pie. "I wonder if Thierry ever made his way back to France to keep his mysterious vow," he said.

"Thierry wouldn't recognize it now," said Sophia. There were murmurs of agreement from the Hanovers and the Stuarts and Meshack and Caitlin. Gideon said nothing.

Sophia leaned back on her arms and looked up at Henri. "I was just thinking of the Harvest Home in Sussex. The people who worked on the estate were given a holiday every year after the harvest was finished. There was a service at the church and a dinner at tables in the barn. The men would carry a roast beef around the room, and everyone danced in the evening."

"We did something like that at my father's *manoir*. At the grape harvest Thierry and François and I were usually sent to the country to help. There was a great wine making that went on for days, and when it was done, tables were set up in the orchard for the workers and their families, and food was sent from the castle." He sighed. Memories of France made him melancholy. The dream of taking Kitty to France and then returning for his sons once Kitty was established in a suitable convent school resurfaced periodically, together with a sense of guilt that he had so far failed to find a means of doing so.

Despite this, Henri shared the sense of accomplishment that bound them all as they looked at the sunset and the glow it cast over the valley below. These Blackberry Picnics satisfied something in each of them, to look down and take stock of what they'd achieved, an opportunity to mark their dominion over the wilderness.

They rarely saw buffalo and panthers any longer, animals that had once trampled the crops and preyed on the cattle. Deer and bears and wild pigs were still a plentiful source of meat, though so many trees had been felled that in much of the valley, their habitat had been pushed back to the base of the mountains.

The small, hastily built log cabin shelters strung along the valley the first year now had added rooms and covered porches. They had windows of greased paper, and shutters and doors that fit. They were surrounded by split-rail fences, separated by fields and broad pastures where trees had been cut down, stumps burned, where more land was put into planting every year and cows and mules grazed.

Sophia and Henri's cabin, Wildwood, on the slope of Frog Mountain was the largest, with a fine porch running the back length of the cabin, looking west across the valley. Mr. Barker's original tumble-down building with its unfinished rooms now had two stories, with four rooms on both levels, two on either side of a large central hall-way upstairs and down. It smelled of pine boards, and upstairs the girls shared a bedroom, the boys shared another, and the other two rooms were used for storing dried fruit and vegetables and sacks of flour and cornmeal. The stone fireplace in the kitchen was large enough to roast a haunch of venison or a whole pig, with a special spit turned by weights that Meshack had devised and made with iron from the iron ore Rufus discovered on Little Frog Mountain. Below the kitchen was a small stone cellar where cabbages and apples were laid in straw to keep through the winter months.

Seth had built a bread oven to Saskia's directions next to the fire-place in each cabin, and the women agreed the scent of bread baking made a cabin smell like a home. At the side of Wildwood, Sophia had planted salad and wild herbs, with paths of crushed stone in attractive patterns like the herbiary in Sussex, her small defiant gesture against the wilderness. She had insisted on planting another just like it for Caitlin behind the Vanns' cabin next to their one-room trading post, Vann Station.

If the de Marechal cabin was the largest, the Vann cabin was the coziest and most cheerful; the Hanover cabin the noisiest and most crowded; the Stuart cabin the neatest; Meshack Tudor's the most inter-esting, fitted out with useful contraptions of his inventing; and the Drumheller cabin far and away the worst. Unlike the others, Rufus had never improved on the original structure of what he always referred to as his cottage. It provided an adequate shelter but a chaotic home for him-self and the boys, still just two rooms and a fireplace. Inside, the three of them existed amid a disordered jumble of clothes, unwashed cooking pots, and pewter plates that the dogs licked clean, so the Drumhellers rarely saw the need to wash or scour them after use.

But it would have been a mistake to gauge the Drumhellers' fortunes by the state of the cabin. Rufus had made efforts elsewhere. He had built an approximation of a Suffolk timber-framed barn with a cowshed at one end and a granary at the other. He had fashioned a dovecote like the one on their old farm in Suffolk. He had planted apple trees, and his small orchard was home to a noisy flock of geese, thanks to a goose and a gander some settlers had exchanged for shoeing their horses three years earlier. Rufus had dug a pond for the geese and his cows. All of this, including his cottage, was enclosed by a low stone wall painstakingly built from mountain rocks to resemble the flint walls of Suffolk. The effect, from a distance, was impressive.

With the de Marechals at one end of the valley and the Drumhellers at the other, Meshack, Nott, and Seth had clustered their cabins in the middle. Seth had added two more rooms to accommodate his growing family. Eleven-year-old Susan now had five boisterous younger sisters. Saskia and Nott's cabin was next to it, and the children went from one cabin to the other at will. Meshack lived alone in his second cabin, and Cully often took refuge with him from the six girls and their mothers. Sometimes Seth and Nott joined him to get a little peace and quiet, and all four would sip Meshack's whiskey late into the night.

All the households had a woodpile stacked nearby, a crib barn with bins of dried cobs and cornstalks for the livestock, and a farmyard with a fence. After the first year of hunger, there were barrels of sauerkraut pickling in brine behind each cabin, a cellar where vegetables and preserves could be stored, and buffalo robes and quilts on the rope beds with their corncob mattresses. Food was plentiful enough that each kitchen had a cupboard, with tiny holes bored in the wooden doors, to keep the flies away from what wasn't eaten. All the cabins had springs or streams close by for water and a small shady springhouse for buttermilk and cheese and clabber. Each had a small stone smokehouse, and their pigs were driven into the forest to fatten on acorns and chestnuts in the fall, then smoked from killing time in December until late spring, when they were rubbed with wood ash and hung from the side of the chimney. Chickens pecked around vegetable gardens.

The valley soil was good; crops had grown well every year. After the first terrible winter, the specter of starvation had receded. In the flat bottom land, plowed fields stretched in every direction, yielding pumpkins, beans, potatoes, turnips, cabbages, squash, and tomatoes; and beyond, areas were cleared, but not planted yet, where tree stumps still had to be burned away.

There was a gristmill now to grind their corn and wheat. As promised, Caitlin's uncles had come down the river to help Gideon with the millstone and to help Meshack with the design of the mill wheel. The mill had been located along a creek half a mile from the Vanns' cabin and trading post. Along with the night sounds of owls and the barking deer and the scream of wild boar, the splash of the mill wheel as it turned made a rhythmic *thwap*, *thwap* in the valley on still nights.

River traffic had increased, and Gideon and the Caradoc uncles had built a bigger landing and jetty at Vann Station on the river's bend west. A large storeroom had been added on to the side of the Vanns' cabin to keep the flour, cornmeal, bacon, and smoked fish they produced, along with gunpowder, bolts of fabric, iron pans, and other goods sent along from Caradoc Station that Caitlin sold or traded. Gideon had built a ferry to carry long hunters and fur traders and those settlers coming by wagon to the buffalo trail on the opposite bank that skirted the land Henri hoped to sell. That trail went directly overland across the western part of the valley, still part of Wildwood Plantation, through the mountains of Indian country to Kentuckee, a shorter route but, because of Indians and now brigands, more dangerous than the river.

They knew where to gather wild strawberries in spring, wild black cherries in June, and blackberries, beechnuts, chestnuts, walnuts, hickory nuts, and persimmons in the fall. They smoked haunches of venison and wild pigs over smoldering hickory, as well as some of the large catches of river fish they landed once they learned to use Cherokee nets. They'd planted fields of wheat and corn and sorghum, and the women had wheat flour for cakes and light bread and *bara brith* on special occasions. There was sorghum syrup for sweetening and dipping bread, and Caitlin also had some to sell or trade along with her barrels of wheat flour.

Malinda continued to go about by herself silently and had never told anyone about the Indian in the orchard. He had never come back after Meshack's cabin burned, but Meshack had been very cheerful and not minded about his cabin. He had set about rebuilding another cabin in what he told her was a better place, closer to his spring. He'd sung loudly as he worked. He'd made his new cabin bigger, with a room on the side where Meshack kept his tools and a big table for making things.

The first thing he had made in this workroom was a doll family for Malinda, a mother, father, girl, and smaller boy, with fine carved heads, corn silk hair he had stained dark with walnut juice, and jointed wooden limbs that moved. He had begged some calico and a needle and sewing cotton from Caitlin's supply at her store and, to Caitlin's astonishment, made clothes for them and even fashioned small shoes out of bark. Malinda insisted on taking these dolls with her everywhere, so Sophia had sewed four large pockets onto her apron to carry them. Malinda no longer twisted dolls' heads off.

Sometimes if Henri had a possum or squirrels to spare after hunting, sixteen-year-old Malinda would saddle a horse and cross the valley to Little Frog Mountain, dolls in her apron, and let herself into the Drumhellers' cabin. She would sweep and air the cabin and leave a stew simmering on the fire for the Drumhellers to find when they finished the day's work. Sometimes they found a line of drying clothes as well. Malinda did a boiled wash if she thought clothes and bedding needed it. Malinda still didn't talk to anyone, even Sophia, but Jack continued to tease her, and she smiled and laughed soundlessly when he did.

Malinda had a way of looking after Meshack too, though she knew better than to do too much or to fool around in his house, washing clothes and sweeping. Unlike the Drumheller men, Meshack kept everything meticulously neat and clean. But Malinda knew he was fond of fried pies. Especially peach and wild plum. Malinda made fine fried pies. She would soak dried fruit and make dough Sophia had showed her how to mix, then drop the plump filled pastry half-moons in boiling grease until they rose to the top, crisp and golden and a little bit charred. She knew just the moment to remove them.

When they'd cooled, she'd sprinkle them with a little honey if there was some or sometimes a little salt if there wasn't, to bring out the sweetness, and take a basketful to leave on Meshack's porch.

Before the drama with Charlotte and Kitty's blackberry bucket, Henri had been explaining to Sophia how he intended to get on with his long-held plan to sell land to settlers. "Now that the harvest is done, I've a mind to start again, and this time I'll finish. I'll start over there, where there's room for two homesteads." He pointed to the opposite side of the river. "More settlers are coming through. If I could just get enough land cleared and build a cabin. I think there's room for at least two."

"Mmm," murmured Sophia. She had heard about Henri's plan for years—but while she would have fought like a mother bear if he had truly tried to take her cubs away to France, she had ceased to worry that he would try. Several times after the harvest, Henri revived his project, only to lose heart by the time cold weather set in. It was too big a job for one person, and Henri, who was easily discouraged at the best of times, would give up.

Though all the settlers helped with the sowing and harvest in each other's fields or pitched in with repairs or larger jobs on each other's homes and properties, the other men had been unwilling to help Henri with his undertaking. While they liked Henri, they didn't quite trust him, though none of them could have said why that was so. In any case they all had their own farms and fields and livestock to tend and were busy. After several false starts, Henri's plan had lapsed into something he often spoke of but did little to advance.

The idea of selling land to settlers made the former slaves deeply uneasy. Nott, Meshack, and Seth feared slave-owning newcomers who might query their free status and lay claim to their land. Slaves couldn't own property. Though Sophia and Henri tried to reassure them the manumission papers and deeds meant they were not slaves and their land was theirs, the Negroes' experience had taught them life was precarious, freedom precious and uncertain, and that little that white people said or did could be trusted absolutely. And even if a few white people could be trusted, most couldn't. Whether out of habit or courtesy or a nagging fear they might one day be held in bondage again, they made fine distinctions in how they addressed the whites. They still called Sophia and Henri Miss Sophy and Mist' Henri. They called Caitlin Miss Caitlin, but Gideon was Gideon and Rufus was Rufus, not Mist' Rufus. And that was fine. But they didn't want more white people in the valley.

As for Rufus, he was unwilling to help Henri with his project because Rufus was busy with an enterprise of his own. And in fact, it was Rufus's success in the various enterprises he undertook that had lately sparked something competitive in Henri. One of these was Rufus's hard cider business.

Below the de Marechal cabin, the apple trees had thrived after Seth and Rufus dug in manure and pruned them the first spring, and the following year, Caitlin had added to the orchard by planting some peach seedlings her father brought her from upriver. They yielded a bigger crop each year. Everyone took what fruit they wanted, and dried peach and apple pies were a mainstay of their winter meals. The orchard belonged to everyone; it would never have occurred to Sophia or Henri to claim it as theirs, though no one would have paid any attention if they had tried.

But with help from Meshack, Rufus had made a cider press and would crush apples into cider for anyone who'd let him keep a jug or two for himself. He had a special way of fermenting it and turning it into a powerful brandy-like drink. He made quite a profit selling it to long hunters and settlers coming down the river who stopped at the Vanns' trading post.

But his endeavors didn't stop there. Rufus, who had moved his boundary markers up the heavily wooded side of Little Frog Mountain the first autumn, had discovered that, as he suspected, there was a seam of iron ore near his spring. The surrounding woods were a good source of charcoal. After the crops were planted that first spring, Rufus, the village blacksmith's son, determined that he would have a forge. He had set to work collecting rocks to build the chimney, only to discover the area around the spring was infested with rattlesnakes. He killed all he could, skinned them, and took the skins down to the trading post to try and sell them to Gideon, to make hatbands and whips.

Gideon told him he was a fool to kill the snakes, the snakes had always been in that area of Little Frog Mountain, the Indians called it Rattlesnake Springs, and when Rufus said it didn't belong to the snakes now, it belonged to him and he'd get rid of them, Gideon warned him against it. Rattlesnakes belonged to the god of thunder, and they were a clan. To kill one was a wrongful act that, like the killing of an Indian clan member, required blood revenge by taking the life of the killer or one of the killer's clan. Whoever killed one rattlesnake would soon see others. For every dead snake, more would come to take its place, to lie in wait for the killer and surround him with glistening eyes and darting tongues so the killer would be confused and lost in the woods forever.

Gideon advised Rufus to leave the iron ore, but Rufus was hell bent on having his forge, so Gideon gave him some roots, saying if Rufus was bitten he should chew a little of the root and rub the rest on the bite, preferably with some wet tobacco. But he knew that Rufus was making enemies of the snakes and they would take their revenge.

In spite of snakes Rufus managed to build his stone furnace with a forge and a smithy. Loud noise and thrashing the underbrush with a pole would drive the snakes away for a time, but they kept coming back, drawn to nest by the warmth of the chimney. He kept the roots and tobacco Gideon had given him in a pouch at his waist at all times, and hung more of the snakeroot on a nail at the smithy door.

As a blacksmith he soon made himself indispensable to the other settlers, and to long hunters and travelers with horses and mules that needed shoeing, and to the packhorse caravans that sometimes came on the buffalo trail. Leaving the farming mostly to Toby and Jack, Rufus repaired tools and plows, crafted rakes and hoes, pots, axes, nails, and hammers and had copied the spit that Meshack designed for Sophia that turned meat using weights. He fashioned barrel hoops. There was a great demand for barrel hoops. He began imprinting a crude coiled snake and an *RS* for Rattlesnake Springs on each piece of ironware. Toby helped man the bellows for his father when he wasn't needed in the fields. He'd shot up into a strapping young man with a thatch of brown hair, stronger and taller than his father, with a deliberate unhurried manner. He could swing a powerful hammer and was good with the horses. Jack was undersized, wiry, and quick, with a cheerful grin, with no interest in the forge itself, but very persuasive when trying to convince travelers or even Caitlin to buy one of his father's hoes or pots.

Meshack was fascinated by the forge and the process of turning iron into something and often worked with Rufus to learn blacksmithing, how to make horseshoes, pots, nails, and tools, which they sold or traded at Vann Station or even sent up to the Caradocs' trading post. The more Meshack learned, the more helpful he knew he was, and he bargained for a larger share of the profits than Rufus wanted or intended to pay him. In this way Rufus and Meshack entered into a cantankerous partnership whose terms were constantly being renegotiated by one or the other. Each had acquired a small hoard of coins and Virginia scrip from their enterprise.

In competition with Rufus's apple brandy, Meshack made whiskey. After consulting Caitlin's father, he'd planted a big field of sorghum behind his cabin. When he was ready to harvest it, he asked Sophia if he might have the use of her big copper pot and promised to pay her for it when he could. He used it to make a still from his memory of how the Caradocs' worked. After a period of trial and error distilling whiskey, which involved testing his product on Seth, Nott, and Rufus with often unfortunate consequences in the beginning, he arrived at a formula for distilled corn mash sweetened with sorghum that tasted much smoother than the whiskey made by the Caradocs.

This guaranteed a brisk trade with fur traders and long hunters and the occasional drivers of packhorse trains, when they wanted a change from Rufus's powerful but rough apple brandy. Sometimes someone asked him who his owner was, and Meshack would fix the questioner with a hard stare and say, "Nobody owns me. I's a free man. You wouldn't get no whiskey if I wasn't free, understand me?" Meshack was a big man, strong from felling trees. He had a hard stare. If he decided not to sell his whiskey, he wouldn't sell it. He'd gained a reputation as a big crazy free nigger prone to picking up anyone who irritated him with too many questions and tossing them in the river.

Generally people saw no reason to argue with Meshack. Long hunters and fur traders weren't usually landowners, so they didn't own slaves. They weren't bothered by a free nigger who sold a fine whiskey. Meshack had been proud the day he'd gone to pay Sophia for her copper pan, chuckling to himself as he handed her the coins.

As Meshack passed around his whiskey at the Blackberry Picnic, Rufus aggressively urged people to try his new batch of apple brandy instead, bragging that the fur traders preferred it to Meshack's whiskey, and described the quantity of the ore he was mining to Seth and Nott. Henri watched Kitty depart with the peach fritters and resume a shrieking game of tag-you're-it in her patched dress and bare feet. "Sophy, Kitty's growing up. She's taller."

"She has. I've had to let down her skirts." Sophia nodded.

Around her, Caitlin and Venus and Saskia were packing up their baskets and shouting for their children. They wanted to get down the path before dark fell. The buckets of berries were assigned to the older children to carry, the adults hoisted their baskets, and the procession began down the slope.

"Lightning bugs is out," the children shouted, handed their buckets to the nearest adult, and raced to catch the little glowing pinpricks of light, whooping as they went.

"Don't forget, you've each part of a poem to memorize and recite to me at school tomorrow," Sophia called after them. She hoped they were listening. She had painstakingly written a poem for each on a piece of slate using sandstone, because now that the harvest was done and the children weren't needed in the fields, her school would be resumed.

"We know," the children called back.

Sophia had realized her plan to have a school soon after Kitty was born. She concentrated on the adults first, but her success there had been limited. Rufus declined lessons, saying he could read and write and figure as well as he needed to. Their second winter in the valley, when everyone was driven indoors by a long spell of cold weather, she managed to teach Saskia, Venus, Meshack, Seth, and Nott to do sums and write a legible hand and to read well enough to read the deeds to their properties and Caitlin's Bible, which she borrowed for the purpose because there was no other reading material.

The former slaves read the Bible with little enthusiasm. They had been forced to hear Anne de Bouldin read it to them every Sunday, explaining how the Old Testament proved Negroes had bestial natures and were meant to be slaves to serve the whites. Sophia said there were different stories, like Moses and the Israelites crossing the Red Sea out of slavery in Egypt, and managed to pique their interest somewhat when she compared the escaping Israelites to their own escape from Thomas. The part where the Red Sea parted for the Jews and then closed over the pursuing Egyptian army struck a chord, but by then it was warmer weather and time for the spring plowing and sowing, and with so much work to be done the adults had little time or inclination for more reading practice or lessons.

She had managed to hang on to the children for two hours every morning unless it was harvest time. She hurried through her morning chores to be able to act as teacher, setting her bread dough to rise before dawn, interrupting lessons to pound it down or pat it into loaves for a final rise before baking it. They would do arithmetic first. Then she would sit with her mending or sewing and listen to them read aloud or recite a piece or Bible verse she had given them to write out on their slates and memorize. Sophia remembered what a trying pupil she had been when young and, determined to give the children as much of an education as possible in the circumstances, was a strict teacher. To the children's chagrin, mistakes were not allowed. If they failed to do their arithmetic correctly they had to do it over with extra sums. If they were lazy about memorizing and recited their assigned poem or Bible verse incorrectly, they had to copy out the verse or poem ten times on their slates, a task they all hated. They grumbled and complained and balked, but Sophia held as firm as her old governess who was unmoved by Sophia's tantrums. The children gradually learned it was better to do their lessons right the first time.

Until they were too old to attend school with the younger children, Cully, Toby, and Jack had sat at one end of the long wooden table known as the eating table, because there was a smaller wooden cooking table next to the bread oven. Malinda always insisted on sitting next to Jack and would elbow Cully or Toby out of the way if necessary. Jack seemed able to understand Malinda even though she never spoke. The two of them would have entire conversations made of quick gestures and glances and pointing. He was her mouthpiece, understood if she had a question or a thought she wanted to express, and would tell Sophia what it was. Malinda was quick, and Sophia could tell from the look in her eyes if she understood something or not. She nearly always did.

Kitty and Rhiannon and Susan sat together on one side of the table, giggling among themselves or, later, shushing the younger ones on the other. From the time they joined the school, Susan kept a watchful and bossy eye on her half sisters, Patsy, Polly, and Pearlie. A younger sister, Pen, was still toddling around after Venus, and the youngest sister, Peach, was a fat baby still in her cradle.

Susan liked authority and made sure her little sisters remembered who was in charge. In lessons she kept up a running commentary, sounding like her mother: "Patsy, sit still; no, hold the writing stone this way. Polly, stop kicking Patsy. No, Pearlie, you don't need another drink of water, leave the bucket be. Patsy, *stop* it or I smack you good!" But she was responsible for an eleven-year-old, could be counted on not to let them wander into poison oak, fall in the river, eat poison berries, or be chased by Rufus's geese.

Rhiannon Vann looked after her little brothers—Bryn, six, and Cadfael, five—more sedately, leaning over to make sure they did their sums correctly. The three Vann children resembled Gideon, with his dark hair, dark level brows, and reserved temperament. Rhiannon was a rather intense child, Bryn was the liveliest of the three, and Cadfael had his mother's sweet nature and was willing to play patiently with Charlotte, who adored him.

Francis and Georgie de Marechal were a little younger than the Vann boys and less well behaved. Sophia had persuaded them that school would make them grow up quickly like Jack, whom they regarded with absolute hero worship because he made them slingshots and let them practice carving sticks with his penknife when Sophia wasn't looking. They sat across from their big sister, Kitty, at the end opposite the older boys and Malinda, swinging their legs and kicking each other under the table while their mother devised learning games along the lines of "who knows the most words that begin with *A*" to hold their attention.

Charlotte was too young for any kind of lesson, an imp with silky white-blond hair and blue-green eyes who toddled around the room getting into trouble and chewing whatever she could reach. She had learned to climb with surprising agility as soon as she could walk, and there were regular crashing noises followed by wails because Charlotte had climbed a piece of furniture and fallen. Lessons were punctuated by one or another of the children crying that Charlotte was eating a fistful of the bread dough set to rise, was gnawing a shoe, had got hold of Henri's hunting knife and was chewing the sheath, was waving a nail about, was about to eat a clump of dirt tracked in on the children's boots, or had opened the canister of dried sumac tea and was gleefully throwing red powder everywhere. Charlotte seemed so much more energetic and naughty than her siblings, Sophia often thought wearily as she hauled the child away from yet another dangerous or poisonous or messy adventure. Then Charlotte would put a hand on Sophia's cheek and croon "Muvver. I notty girl!" and Sophia would melt.

Compared with her brown-haired, brown-eyed sisters and brothers, Charlotte was a changeling. Henri told the others the French fairies had brought her from far away, where Papa's home was, a beautiful castle deep in a forest inhabited by unicorns and knights with magic swords and princesses asleep in towers, just like in the fairy tales their mother told them.

"I want to see unicorns! Papa?" Kitty wheedled each time he mentioned it. "Why aren't there unicorns in our forest?"

"Unicorns are magic and beautiful and can only live in France. In Virginia people would not understand what unicorns are for. They would make them into hams."

Between kneading her bread, mending, laundry, soap and candle making, her kitchen garden, and keeping Charlotte out of trouble,

Sophia fought a valiant battle to broaden the children's education. Having taught them to read and write, she devised lessons from her prayer book, verses she copied from Caitlin's Bible, an old almanac she had found in the barn that had belonged to Mr. Barker, and what she could remember of her own geography lessons. She told the children fairy stories and Greek and Roman myths, and as much English history as she could remember—the Wars of the Roses, Tudors and the civil war and the beheading of Mary Queen of Scots, a gory story that the children relished.

She had tried to teach the older boys Latin but couldn't remember past the second declension and gave up, much to their relief. Henri was uninterested in teaching the children Latin or anything else on a regular basis, though he sometimes taught Kitty French phrases and words. But when the weather was bad so that Henri wanted an excuse to stay indoors, he found that he could remember fairy tales from La Fontaine's *Contes* of his own childhood.

"Have you heard the story of 'The Fox and the Grapes'? 'Death and the Woodman'?" he would ask, and act them out in a mixture of French and English. The children acquired a small French vocabulary as a result, though no grammar. Sophia taught them the rudiments of music by teaching them to sing English ballads she remembered, and every Christmas they continued to sing the carols they had sung on that occasion their bleak first year to forget their hunger. When Caitlin's father or uncles paid a visit to the trading post they would play their fiddles for the children to sing along to Caitlin's hymns or the energetic "Blow, Ye Winds, Blow" that had them all stamping their feet to the chorus. If she could get hold of paper and paints, she planned to teach the girls wildflower painting one day. She decided not to bother with Italian, which she didn't remember very well.

When she ran out of inspiration, the children never tired of hearing the description of her presentation at St. James's Palace. Sophia would plumb her imagination to conjure up the scene at court in terms they could understand, because they had no concept of grandeur or ceremony. She no longer possessed her blue-and-silver ball gown to show them—it had been an early casualty of the wilderness when some small animal or other had chewed its way into the trunk where it was stored and shredded the gown and its silver threads into a nest.

But she described the width of the ladies' dresses, the jewels, the fans with pictures painted on the ivory, the men's swords and hats, how Princess Amelia looked sitting on her throne, how she herself had curtseyed. She mimicked King George, a grumpy little man with a German accent she could not understand. "Boetry! Boets? Bainting? Bainters? Vat are dey?" Sophia would exclaim, frowning down her nose. "And do you write boetry, Miss Grafton?" she would growl playfully at Charlotte.

"Noooo!" Charlotte would giggle, shaking her head.

"And my skirt was *this* wide." Sophia would demonstrate. "And so heavy it could knock a man over. All the ladies had to go through the doors sideways, like this." The older boys had heard this account too many times to be amused, but the girls and younger children found these stories very funny, and they would beg her to reenact over and over again how she had curtseyed and knelt and been kissed by the princess, curtseyed three more times before backing away from the king, how her knees had buckled from the weight of her dress and all the curtseying.

Kitty and Rhiannon and Susan made a giggly game of going through doors sideways, shrieking, "Oh la, my gown! It knocked him down!" It wasn't long before Patsy, Polly, and Pearlie were copying them, and an exasperated Venus was demanding to know why her daughters wouldn't walk straight through any door.

I don't dare mention the bourdaloue, Sophia thought.

CHAPTER 27
NEWS FROM AFAR

1767

Despite a dozen years at Wildwood, Henri and Sophia managed to convey to their children that "home" was elsewhere, and the de Marechal children had always been slightly confused about whether "home" meant France or England. It depended on whether their mother or father was talking. When they were small they had learned there were celestial beings called kings and queens in distant places called England and France, rather like the place called heaven that Caitlin told them about or Gideon's Darkening Land.

Meanwhile, thanks to Henri, Kitty formed an idea of France as a fairytale place of great forests, unicorns, and castles, inextricably linked with convent schools and a French husband. Everyone in this magical place spoke a language her father was trying to drum into her head. This language was the secret spell that would gain her entrance.

On the one hand, this sounded interesting, and she adored her father, so she tried her hardest to learn the strange sounding words. On the other hand, he said it would mean leaving Rhiannon and Susan and Cully and sailing away across the ocean. This filled her with dismay.

"Papa keeps saying I'm French and I will live in France one day, but I don't want to go," she whispered to her mother. "Must I? I'd rather stay here, Mother."

"I shouldn't worry, darling," said Sophia. The homestead building on the western bank of the river, which Henri had sworn enthusiastically he would resume at the last Blackberry Picnic, had ground to a halt in a wet winter.

Sophia, who spent more time with the children than Henri did, redoubled her efforts to implant the idea of England as the motherland. She described London, the pleasure gardens, the carriages, the theaters, Cheapside, the royal palaces, and the Grafton estate in Sussex, the gardens, the village school and its children, the dairy, the sheep, and the mysterious white horse carved in the chalk cliff. She told them the stories of Hugh de Graftonne and William the Conqueror, castles, and English smugglers and their tunnels and the excise men who tried to catch them. She told them about Robin Hood and King Arthur and his Knights of the Round Table.

She told them about Lady Burnham and made Susan, Kitty, Rhiannon, and Malinda sew samplers with the words "Duty before Inclination" with their names and their ages. Kitty's was the worst because she hated sewing and always managed to escape the task whenever she appealed to her father. Sophia made her do it over again, which sent Kitty into a fury of sulking.

Sophia found it harder and harder to think of new things to teach, but she managed to acquire a shelf of oddly assorted reading material, contributed by the Caradocs and the Vanns, as travelers traded whatever items they could spare for goods they needed from the trading post, and on rare occasions this happened to be a book. Or part of a book.

Thus Sophia had acquired a book of sermons missing some pages, part of a romance called *Love's Intrigues*, and an improving tome, *An Inquiry into the Better Preventing of Clandestine Marriages*. It was complete, and only the first few pages had been cut, suggesting it had not held the interest of the previous owner for long. It did not hold the children's interest either, and Sophia gave up trying to make them read from it. There were the first twenty pages of something called *The Garden of Cyrus* by Sir Thomas Browne, which Sophia feared at first was a double entendre for something racy. Instead it proved to be a dense, incomprehensible work about nature.

Of all the settlers, it was Gideon who sent reading material her way. He had been taught to read by the Scottish trapper who had been his father, and after his father had gone away into the wilderness, his mother had impressed on him that the whites' method of making paper speak was magic worth knowing. He had a great respect for books and showed Sophia a book he had been given by Caitlin's father. It had been traded to the Caradocs by a party of Chickasaws when Caitlin was a child. It was rather fine and had a gilt-tooled leather cover with a cross in gilt on it. Caitlin's father had assumed it was a Bible and took it in exchange for some blankets and whiskey. When the Indians had gone, he discovered the book's parchment pages had brown stains and were written in Spanish, though in a neat, clear, and legible hand.

Disappointed with his unreadable bargain, he had given it to Gideon. Gideon, unlike Caitlin's father, was deeply curious about what it contained. The following year a slave catcher from Florida came by the trading post with a Spanish runaway in chains. The trader intended to resell him in Savannah. The Caradoc brothers detained the slave trader for a fortnight as he was very fond of whiskey and cards and had plenty of money to enjoy both.

The slave spent this time shackled in the barn. In return for his teaching Gideon the rudiments of Spanish, Gideon sawed off his chains, and the slave escaped for the second time. By the time the trader had sobered up enough to hunt him again, the slave had disappeared and Gideon could read Spanish well enough to understand the book was very old and described things he knew, the valley and the river and the flat rock shaped like a man's head. This seemed like some kind of omen. When he had time to spare in the evenings, Gideon opened his book and laboriously translated a paragraph or two.

Sophia would make the children take turns reading aloud to the class, which she believed would help their grammar and vocabulary, but the books were rather dull for children. Then she discovered that the most useful reading material came from old newspapers. Sometimes the Caradocs obtained part of one, usually a crumpled or torn *Virginia Gazette* or the *Boston News-Letter* from passing travelers. These newspapers were also used to wrap loaves of sugar or to pack or wrap other goods at the trading posts. Caitlin got in the habit of saving them for Sophia. They were always out of date by months or even years, which meant that news could be out of sequence, and a story or an article would break off because the rest of the page was missing, but they were greatly prized all the same. In a limited and out-of-date way, they kept the settlers abreast of news of the world beyond their valley.

Sophia had the children take turns reading them out loud from beginning to end: notices of arriving and departing ships; announcements of the arrival of consignments of goods, from haberdashery to medicine to glass and tools from England or rum and sugar from the Caribbean; notices that gentlemen desirous of Madeira might place their orders in expectation of the arrival of a certain ship; advertisements offering the services of milliners newly arrived from England and acquainted with the latest fashions in bonnets, or doctors with the latest treatments for any ailment; court cases; news from Boston and New

York; excerpts from the *London Chronicle*; and news from Europe, all more interesting to the children than reading the prayer book out loud.

At first she had stopped the children from reading the notices of crimes committed or advertisements for runaway slaves and indentured servants, as well as the whippings, punishments, and rewards when runaways were captured, but Saskia took her to task. "They got to know what happen," said Saskia. "Might not happen they livin' here, but it sho' happen everywheres else. Got to learn. How else they know to watch out for patrollers, know they free and not slaves, red they free papers, protect theyselves?" So the children read everything, even the notices of hangings and the last words spoken by the condemned.

Listening to them read, Sophia also gleaned news of the world beyond the valley.

In 1762 she learned while Jack was reading aloud that the grumpy old king, George II, had died in 1760 and that the coronation of his grandson, now George III, and his bride, Princess Charlotte of Mecklenburg-Strelitz, had taken place in September of 1761 at Westminster Abbey. She made the children stand and repeat "God Save the King." And occasionally the children read out a nugget of particularly interesting information.

Two years later Susan unfolded an old sheet of newsprint and read out:

> *"Death Notice, de Bouldin, Thomas, Burgess, late of Bouldin Hundreds Plantation in Amelia County on Friday the tenth, instant of a Fit of apoplexy when attending the sitting of the General Assembly in Williamsburg. Born in Sussex near Hove in England 28 November 1698. His wife being lately deceased and having no relatives, he was buried at the church of Bruton Parish.*

"TO BE SOLD at Publick Auction to the highest bidders at the late Dwelling House of Thomas de Bouldin, deceased, in Amelia on Friday, July 16 at Bouldin Hundreds Plantation all the Land, the late Dwelling House, all Household Goods, Plate, and Books, also Horses, Cows, and Negroes. Six Months' credit being allowed the purchaser giving bond. Persons that have any demands against the said Estate are desired to make them known on the day of sale."

Sophia startled Susan by crying, "What is the year of that paper?"

"1755," said Susan after a moment. She counted on her fingers. "When Mama and Seth ran away with you."

The news took Sophia's breath away. So Thomas had been dead for twelve years!

Later Sophia read and reread the death notice. Even after so many years, her nagging fear that one day Thomas and his henchmen would come was lifted from her shoulders and the relief was almost overwhelming. She hurried off to Venus and Saskia.

"Praise God!" said Saskia. "Susan told me."

"*I* told you!" said Venus. "I know before that. Way back, when Susan a little chile playin' with Cully, I saw it. I told you."

Months later Susan read from another sheet:

"LATELY DISCOVERED. We have an account a vile crime was committed at the plantation of Thomas de Bouldin, Burgess, lately deceased. The Alarm being raised when the house and outbuildings were discovered burned to the ground with all Household goods destroyed, the slaves and livestock gone. The cremated remains of two bodies were discovered in the ashes of the house, but whether they be the bodies of the overseer or an English lady believed to be Thomas de Bouldin's

> *ward is uncertain. There is reason to fear an Act of Felony by the slaves, now presumed to be at large or likely gone to the Dismal Swamp. Any Person or Persons that will secure and contrive intelligence thereof or convey to the Sheriff all or any of the above-mentioned slaves shall, according to the service, etcetera, have an immediate AMPLE REWARD . . . the names of the slaves are . . ."*

Here the paper had been torn off.

"Mother?" said Kitty. Sophia realized all the children were staring at her. "Are you sick? You look so strange."

"It's nothing, Kitty. Nothing." They thought she was dead. It was unsettling to be thought dead, and she dismissed school early. "Get along with you. Enough lessons for this morning. The vegetables won't weed themselves."

"Charlotte, give Mother a hug." Charlotte sprang into Sophia's arms. She danced Charlotte around the room and felt better. It didn't matter; she had Charlotte.

Sophia loved all her children, but Kitty was spoiled by Henri, whom she resembled, and otherwise trailed after Cully and the boys. Francis and Georgie, being sons, also claimed his attention. Henri was never more charming than when he had his three eldest children about him. They doted on Papa. Sophia said he was like the Pied Piper; the three of them trailed behind him whenever they could, Georgie's little fat legs running to keep up until Henri swept him up and sat him on his shoulders.

That left Charlotte as hers. Charlotte played hide-and-seek in the piles of clothes waiting to be boiled, shrieking with laughter when she was found. "Up," she would demand, raising her arms whenever Sophia sat down. "Tell story." Or "Singing!" Charlotte loved nursery rhymes and singing, and Sophia would put down her mending and sing lullabies and hymns. For all her mischief, Charlotte was a sunny, affectionate, snuggling child. Charlotte went on Sophia's hip to feed the chickens and gather eggs and kept her company in the kitchen while Sophia cooked or mended or boiled washing or churned butter. Charlotte adored her mother. She would hold out her arms and crow with happiness on seeing Sophia each morning, would kiss Susan or Rhiannon or Kitty if they picked her up. She would crouch down, fascinated to watch the boys playing with the spinning tops Meshack made them, but above all she loved the chickens that came clucking up to be fed. Throwing them scraps and corn from a bucket became Charlotte's task every morning and evening. They were smaller than cows and mules and pigs, just her size. "Oh, my chickens! Oh, my little chickens!" she would coo happily as they pecked around her feet.

Despite these happy moments with her favorite child, Sophia was succumbing to a growing unease, as if a summer thunderstorm were gathering over the valley. She tried to ward off the feeling, to count her blessings. Even though Thierry had gone, Henri had not managed to take Kitty and follow him. Though life was hard work from dawn to dusk, there was plenty of food. Her children were healthy; all the children were. There had been a terrifying interval the previous summer when all the children had come down with scarlet fever after playing with traveler children whose raft had stopped at the trading post. After the raft had gone, the children began to complain of excruciating sore throats, then one by one they had developed such high fevers that their mothers had watched by the children's beds through long, hot, anxious nights, laying cool cloths on their brows and praying their children wouldn't die.

Still, an unnamed worry would not be reasoned away. Her apprehension fixed itself on Charlotte. By day she scolded herself for nonsense; Charlotte was healthy and cheerful as a little lark. But if Sophia woke in the night, the unwelcome litany of ills and accidents that could harm the child went round and round in her head. She grew weepy over trifles and for as long as possible pushed to the back of her mind the knowledge that she was always oversensitive and anxious in the early stages of pregnancy. Finally she could no longer avoid the truth. She wasn't being silly, she was pregnant again, and it frightened her to realize how much she wished that she were not. She hadn't fully recovered from Charlotte's birth, hadn't felt right inside since. What would happen if she had another baby so soon? The thought of leaving Charlotte motherless was agony. And added to this was a growing threat from the Indians.

In the years following the measles epidemic, Indians had avoided Frog Mountain and what the settlers and even the river people and long hunters now called the Bowjay Valley, lest the curse of the whites' disease still clung to it. But beyond the valley, Indians were everywhere. Some traded furs and salt at the trading posts dotted along the river and brought their corn to be ground at the Caradocs' mill, but relations with the Indians were increasingly uneasy. Caitlin's uncles and raft people stopping at the Vanns' trading post brought terrifying news of raids on homesteads to the north and east, with settlers tomahawked or taken prisoner and cabins and barns burned. A river fort had been overrun, and the soldiers and settlers who had fled to it for protection had all been massacred.

Caitlin said Gideon had met Indians returning now to the mountains and valleys where they'd lived, angry to find long hunters killing and trapping more and more game and settlers fencing in land. A party of Cherokee from one of the other clans including women and young children had come to the Vanns' trading post. Caitlin had showed the women blankets and cooking pots while their men unloaded a pile of deer hides. Gideon greeted them and asked where they were going and if they were hunting or at war. The men said they were following the buffalo, they needed hides for the winter in their new town. They admired the iron pots and plows Rufus and Meshack had made and said they'd be back with deer and beaver hides to trade for axes and gunpowder and cornmeal.

Gideon soon discovered that these Cherokee had come from the east, two valleys beyond the one with the abandoned cornfield Thierry had found during the Starving Winter. He rode off to investigate at the time of the First New Moon Festival. He found new clearings with houses of saplings and mud and bark and a council house and knew that after the festival they would plant their crops. As he expected, braves soon reappeared in their old hunting grounds in the Bowjay Valley, looking for the buffalo that were no longer there, the bears on Frog Mountain, the deer that were drawn to the salt marsh beyond Rufus's homestead, and the plentiful fish in the river. He had seen them hunting again in the settlers' farthest new-planted fields, where there had once been forest, and setting their fishing nets in the river, though the Indians managed to keep out of the settlers' sights.

They came for the salt as well. Like the settlers, they came and boiled up the water from a salty spring and let it evaporate. Caitlin did this too and sold this salt at the trading post. Everyone needed salt. Rufus insisted that the salt marshes were his, but Caitlin just said mildly, "For all the world, Rufus, you can't use up the salt yourself!" and none of the other settlers took any notice of Rufus's angry protests.

Gideon knew that Rufus's possessiveness about the salt was an indication of trouble to come. The settlers thought the land was theirs; the Indians thought the land was just the land. He tried hard to see how hostilities could be prevented, but he had lived so long away from his own people he sensed his gift of knowing was slipping away from him. He looked at his children and wondered if any of his gifts had gone to live in them. Sometimes he thought Rhiannon had inherited some of them, but she was young and he couldn't be sure. But he knew that if she had, that would be another source of trouble. With Caitlin.

CHAPTER 28
STORMS IN THE VALLEY

1768

Though all three of his children resembled Gideon in looks, only Rhiannon resembled him in mind and heart. Cadfael and Bryn were happy, boisterous children whom Caitlin called "my dumplings" until they protested they were too old to be called that. Gideon knew that his boys would never be trained in the necessary ways of a brave. Among the Cherokee it was not the father who taught boys to be men and braves, but the mother's brothers. With Bryn and Cadfael, the only male relatives to help with their upbringing were Caitlin's father and uncles, who would teach them about the gristmill and the trading post and, unless Gideon stopped them, how to make whiskey. But Rhiannon was a serious child who would be silent for a long time while she thought about something, unlike her friends Susan and pert Kitty.

Rhiannon's introspection struck Caitlin as odd behavior in a twelve-year-old, but Gideon knew she was silent because she was trying to hear and comprehend things in the Indian way. He told her it took time to learn this, and was surprised but gratified that his daughter's Cherokee blood was strong.

Rhiannon began to insist she be called by her Cherokee name, Singing Wind. This exasperated Caitlin, who refused to call her daughter anything but Rhiannon. But she saw Rhiannon was changing and grieved over it. She was no longer the child who listened raptly while Caitlin told her Welsh fairy tales or taught her to sing hymns in harmony as the two of them stirred puddings and kneaded bread or picked over dried grapes for *bara brith*. She now preferred the fields to the old companionable times in the kitchen with her mother. She told Caitlin that Cherokee women, not men, worked in the fields.

Caitlin was angry when Gideon encouraged Rhiannon's odd behavior, but Gideon knew that it was not he who encouraged it, but his daughter who must be who she must be. If she must be taught, he must teach her. He would know in time whether she had a true gift or whether she was merely dutiful. At times she was a young girl giggling with her friends Susan and Kitty, but more and more he began to think Rhiannon was different, that she saw the world as he did.

He took her on long walks and taught her Cherokee and how to observe everything around her. He explained that her grandmother had been able to interpret dreams and was a respected, beloved woman of the Wolf Clan—protectors of the people—and that a child took its clan from the mother, and that among the Cherokee clan loyalty was everything. Rhiannon memorized the seven clans—Wolf, Long Hair, Blue, Paint, Deer, Wild Potato, and Bird—and when she asked to what clan she belonged, it pained him to say she belonged to none, because Caitlin had no clan.

He told her of the Darkening Land and how the spirits cried out to their clan to avenge them, that a clan member was obliged to do this by killing the perpetrator or one of his family.

Rhiannon listened intently while her father explained about the upper world and its connection with fire, and the lower world connected with water, and the center world, which was where they were now. He told her there were spirits in everything. Every bird and animal and fish and stone. Rhiannon nodded and Gideon saw these were things she already knew.

He told her the stories of the Thunder Beings that lived in cliffs and mountains, of the Four Directions and the significance of the number seven, that the river was the Long Man and sacred, how there was good and evil, and how his mother, her grandmother, had interpreted dreams. He warned her sternly that it was forbidden for her to marry within her father's clan. "I won't!" she promised.

He saw more and more indications she might have her grandmother's gift and, again, was secretly gratified, though he knew it was best not to say anything of this to Caitlin. Without her father's prompting, Rhiannon was fascinated by dreams, her own and others'. She knew that dreams were important and their message must be understood. Gideon would test her from time to time, saying, "I had a dream that a tree fell, though there was no wind" or "I dreamed of the river rising around the council house" or "I dreamed a fox barked." Rhiannon would think about her answer, then give a thoughtful interpretation.

Bryn and Cadfael had Cherokee names too. Bryn was Redbird and Cadfael was Hill Climber, but Gideon saw no sign that either of them knew what lay beyond the world they could see, the people they knew, the things that were before them. They saw the valley and the mountains and the river and the sky with Caradoc eyes, but not the upper world and lower world. They did not sense the spirits of people and animals, whether living or dead.

In the nights when Gideon walked by the river, he sensed figures slipping away at his approach. No one greeted him. He was not afraid and would never stop anyone from hunting, but he felt separate from them now, the tribes who had come back. He pondered the way he had been born between the world of the Tsalagi and the whites. He had resolved it by slipping between them, just as he lived among the whites and walked at night among the shadows and spirits and people. But what would Rhiannon do? He went up the mountain to sit on the rock shaped like a man's head, straining to understand the message in the wind, to see omens. Because he knew it was just not buffalo and deer and bears and fish that drew his tribe back to this place; it was their dead crying out to them from the Darkening Land, visiting them in dreams, reminding them it was their duty to return and avenge their deaths, though that made no sense to Gideon now.

How to answer these cries? He could not see how the deaths caused by this sickness could be avenged. Or against whom. He doubted the illness that had killed his people was in the power of the whites. Sickness was caused by evil or offended spirits or by witchcraft or wizardry that he doubted the whites possessed. Sickness could be cured with the help of spirits who had a countervailing power or a spell or magic, helped by fire from the upper world and water from the lower one. Again, he doubted the whites had the necessary spells or magic to summon spirits, and why would spirits help the whites?

At first he thought the whites held a secret power against the sickness, like the shamans kept the powerful crystal stolen from the head of the Uktena, the creature who could fly at night in the shape of fire to drink blood. Yet whites suffered as well from the spotted sickness Sophia and Caitlin and Saskia called measles. Sophia had told him sometimes even whites died of it. At first he thought it was a matter of stealing the power from the whites. But the more he saw of the whites, the less he believed they possessed or understood such a power. They had no magic other than their books.

He hoped to persuade his tribe that it would be more cunning to befriend them and obtain the secrets of their power by stealth and patience. He wanted to prevent bloodshed if he could—he was sure it would lead to more bloodshed on a scale his people could not foresee.

But the dead from the Darkening Land could not be hushed. They filled the air, lamenting their parting from their families; they were lonely. He heard them, and he knew the Indians heard them, that their dead visited them in dreams and would not be quieted until something was done.

There had been no attacks on the valley settlers, but there was ominous news from elsewhere, and like Sophia, he was worried. A convoy of flatboats brought rumors that spring war parties of Creeks and Cherokee had been spotted at the shoals. The men were armed, and settlers were nervous everywhere on the frontier. Caitlin's father sent word that a packhorse caravan of white traders traveling the river path toward Caradoc Station had been attacked, their goods taken, and most traders scalped, and only a wounded few survivors had reached Caitlin's father. Caitlin was alarmed for her father and uncles.

Gideon knew that the same caravan had raped two Indian girls bathing in the river and left them for dead. He had told a horrified Caitlin trouble would come of it, and Caitlin wept for the Indian girls and said the men in the caravan should be hanged.

In her trading post Caitlin listened as a fur trader described a settlement to the north that had been attacked and burned by Creeks. The men and women had all been killed, save for one woman survivor driven to despair and madness by the loss of her family. She now lived locked away in a jail cell in a fortified outpost because no one knew what else to do with her. There were no children's bodies, so they had probably been taken as prisoners, as slaves, or, as the raft people said now happened often, to trade for ransom. Usually guns and whiskey. Which made life more dangerous for the settlers, he said. Gideon said some of the children would have been taken to replace the Indian dead, some as slaves. While he understood the logic of this, he said there would have to be negotiations, a treaty, to prevent an endless war of attrition with the whites.

Caitlin had never feared Indians; how could she, married to Gideon? Now her determination that Rhiannon must not become more

Cherokee hardened. Her daughter must not become the enemy, she told Gideon.

Gideon felt the tension in his home. Caitlin made Rhiannon memorize Bible verses and Welsh hymns and was angry when her daughter slipped away to walk with her father instead. "Your name is Rhiannon, not Singing Wind," she would call after them, angry at them both. Then Caitlin would weep because she had become a nag and a scold and hardly recognized herself.

A campaign with many white soldiers launched a series of attacks on the tribes to the east, regardless of whether they were hostile. There had been bloody battles leaving many dead. Cherokee and Creek towns had been burned, canoes and livestock destroyed, warriors taken prisoner, the wounded killed, and the survivors, including women, children, and old people, had been driven into the mountains, without food or shelter as the winter began. Rhiannon told her mother fiercely she hoped the soldiers would be killed.

Indians were a constant presence in the valley. In March, during one of her silent peregrinations while the Drumhellers were at work in their fields, Malinda had seen an Indian kill two geese at Rufus's pond. The Indian saw her but slung the geese over his back and walked away into the woods. Toby spotted Cherokee fishing nets in the river, and Rufus tore them apart. After that the men went armed when working in the fields, and Toby, Jack, and Cully took turns standing guard.

Meshack's horse was stolen, and Meshack devised traps that could imprison a man's foot in a kind of iron claw. He and Seth and Nott primed them in their barns before they went to bed at night. They were careful to step around the traps themselves—Meshack had fashioned a powerful spring, and Seth, usually an easygoing father, threatened to whip any of his girls if they so much as set foot in the barn.

Two Indian boys were caught in this way in Seth's barn. Meshack came to free the mechanism and release their legs, which were so badly mangled the bones showed. The boys were obviously in agony, but they made no sound, no whimper, just stared at Meshack and Seth with implacable hate. He and Seth went to seek Gideon's help about what to do next, thinking the boys were too badly injured to escape, but when the three men returned to the barn, the boys had gone and there was blood everywhere.

Gideon inspected the bloody claws of the trap and shook his head. The boys had been stealing horses to prove they were ready to be braves. Seth retorted that the trap proved they weren't. Meshack silently dismantled the traps. Gideon knew that if the boys died revenge would be taken on Seth or his family. He advised Seth to be watchful.

The violence came closer. An Indian village three valleys away was attacked by white militia in March, the animals killed, and the people driven into their homes, which were then set alight. The men were away hunting, so the dead were women and children and old people.

On a pleasant afternoon at the end of April, Caitlin was hanging the quilts to air outside the trading post in the sunshine. Seeing a raft approaching, she hung the last two quilts and went to the landing to greet the travelers. But to her surprise, the raft swung this way and that on the current. Oddly no one seemed to be poling. Finally she called Gideon, and he watched with her for a minute as it drifted erratically, turned sideways, and swung into the landing with a bang. As the two of them walked toward it, Caitlin said, "There's something inside, heaped up. It must have come untied . . ." She shrieked, "Oh, Gideon! Oh, God in heaven!"

Its cargo was a tangled bloody mass of mutilated corpses, some scalped soldiers, women, and, this time, children. One of them was a small boy who reminded her of Cadfael, lying with his feet turned in, in the arms of a young woman in an apron, who stared sightlessly past him at the sky.

They buried the terrible cargo in the land below the orchard. Gideon told Caitlin the children must not go to school and ordered Rhiannon to keep Bryn and Cadfael in sight and to stay close to the cabin and the trading post. He told Seth and Venus not to send the girls up for lessons with Sophia and, in case of an attack, to take refuge with Meshack.

All that summer, war songs echoed among the mountains, the sound carried to the settlers on the warm summer nights. They no longer dared hold their Blackberry Picnic. Gideon warned it would be too dangerous.

Sophia greased her pistol and their muskets with bear grease. Henri fumed helplessly that he had not managed to take Kitty away from danger sooner. He went to count his stash of currency he kept hidden in the barn, trying to calculate the values of coins, shillings and pence, colonial specie, and Spanish dollars that made up his hoard, but he knew it was insufficient for two passages back to France or to live on when they arrived. He renewed his efforts to clear the land west of the river, but even if he managed to save enough, the limited news that reached the Bowjay Valley said there was still war between Britain and France and now Spain. Henri knew that would make the Atlantic crossing more dangerous. He cursed himself for not going sooner.

But money in any form—coins, Virginia scrip, English currency—was hard to come by. They bartered and traded for most of what they needed. Only the occasional raft travelers possessed any currency, and if they spent, it usually went on cornmeal and bacon or tools purchased from Caitlin, who kept a close eye on their receipts. Most of Henri's coins had been won from the visiting Caradoc brothers in card and dice games, and even then Henri lost almost as much as he won. Thanks to the trading post, Gideon had the most money, but he refused to play cards or gamble. He was indifferent to money, leaving it all to Caitlin to deal with as she saw fit. Caitlin was far too canny to wager or loan the profits of the trading post; she or her father always had some scheme in mind to improve the post or buy stock.

Meshack had money, more than Henri realized, but said he had no head for gambling. The one time Henri had talked Meshack into a card game, Meshack had put a jug of whiskey on the table and stayed sober while Henri got drunk. Meshack had won all the money Henri wagered.

That left Rufus, who also had savings thanks to his forge and smithy, but Rufus wouldn't risk his earnings gambling, saying it belonged to his boys. Henri tried to badger and trick Rufus into wagers and card games, and when he continued to refuse, Henri swore Rufus was a whining, mean, ill-begotten peasant.

Relations between the two men grew hostile.

In June Gideon appeared with a worried look to tell Sophia that Rufus had seen more Indians openly hunting in his growing wheat. They had been chasing three white-tailed deer, and Rufus was so furious to see his laboriously planted crop trampled he'd fired his musket to scare them off and hit one of the deer without killing it, and the other two had gotten away. The braves were angry. They had always hunted deer in the valley. The wounded deer was thrashing and bleeding, and the Indians had whooped and taunted Rufus for being a bad shot and a weakling. Raging, Rufus fired at them indiscriminately and didn't know if he'd killed or wounded anyone. He hoped he had.

If he'd killed one or a wounded brave died, Gideon said grimly, the settlers would soon know.

Sophia was kneading bread at the time Gideon told her about Rufus and the Indians who mocked him. She gave the dough a hard thump and sighed wearily. Why did men have to squabble like children? Why did even a deer have to be a bone of contention? Why couldn't the Indians hunt somewhere other than Rufus's planted field? There were deer everywhere. Why couldn't Henri leave Rufus in peace with the money he'd earned rather than irritating Rufus so much that the two men now refused to work in each other's fields? And now Henri was talking again about taking Kitty to France. And there were Indians, and they might be attacked, and Rufus was jeopardizing all their safety.

Men! Sophia thumped the bread as hard as she could, over and over, because she couldn't decide whether Kitty ought to go to France or not if the opportunity presented itself. She picked up the ball of dough and slammed it down with all her might and asked Gideon about Caitlin. Caitlin, she knew, was unhappy; she had unburdened herself to Sophia about Rhiannon. Sophia had thought she had looked terrible when Caitlin last climbed the hill for a visit, with dark circles under her eyes, her former blooming complexion gray and wan. But it wasn't just Rhiannon, though Sophia longed to shake the girl and say, "Look at your mother! Treat her gently!"

After Cadfael, Caitlin had buried three perfect, stillborn baby boys, one after the other, in the little graveyard below the orchard. "The Lord giveth and taketh away," Caitlin had whispered each time the little pine coffin that had taken Meshack such a short time to make was lowered into a small grave. She had clung to Sophia's hand, her face a mask of grief. "For all the world I mustn't repine, Sophy, if it pleased God to take them. God's will be done. I have Rhiannon and the boys." But it had been a long time since her children or Gideon had heard her singing.

Gideon said Caitlin was expecting another baby late in the autumn. Sophia bit her lip and concentrated on her bread. The news made her uneasy. Caitlin's births were long and hard. Was Caitlin frightened? As frightened as she herself was at the prospect of having another baby without Zaydie.

Zaydie had died soon after Cadfael's birth six years earlier. The birth had been hard, as it always was with Caitlin, and Saskia, Sophia, and Zaydie had all been exhausted when it was over. The old woman had lain down on her pallet by the fire that night, said she was too tired to cross over to the little cabin Henri had built her, that babies wore her out, that she was tired and wouldn't be getting up again. Sophia had thought Zaydie was cross over something. Zaydie was often cross, and she would let everyone know why when she felt like telling them. Her sleeping in her old position next to the fire was a statement of something, and Sophia and Henri debated in whispers what it might be. But the next morning, Zaydie was cold and dead.

They had buried her below the orchard, with a marker of soft mountain sandstone, carving her name and a quote from Proverbs, "She is clothed in strength and dignity," chosen by Caitlin. Sophia wondered whether Zaydie would have wanted a Bible verse or whether it would just have been another thing that irritated her.

Afterward Sophia feared Zaydie's death left her and Caitlin with no protection against the perils of childbirth. When she had been pregnant with Georgie and then Charlotte, the nagging worry she felt by day swelled into the kind of anxiety that kept her awake at night. She was more terrified with every baby that she would die like her mother and leave her own children motherless and in the uncertain care of Henri.

One warm spring night before Georgie's birth, there had been a full moon that cast everything in a bright silvery light or deep shadows. The baby had been kicking vigorously, and Sophia had been too uncomfortable to sleep. So she had lain awake and finally given in to the fancies that fill the mind of a wakeful woman in the middle of a moonlit night. She had risen quietly, put on her shoes, and made her way down through the orchard to Zaydie's grave. She had picked a branch of apple blossom on her way, and sinking heavily to her knees, she laid it on Zaydie's grave and asked for her help.

Her pains had begun next morning, and by afternoon she was sitting up in bed, clean and brushed, with Georgie in her arms being admired by Caitlin. When pregnant with Charlotte two years later, she accused herself of being silly and superstitious and didn't repeat her nighttime expedition.

Up till then Sophia's births had been easier than Caitlin's, and she had recovered easily. But Charlotte's birth had been different, long and terrible, with the baby coming out eventually feet first. She was uneasy at the prospect of another baby so soon, and Caitlin was pregnant too. She had been afraid with each of Caitlin's babies that Caitlin might die, but for the first time she faced the possibility she might as well. And if she and Caitlin both died, what would happen to all the children?

Sophia knew Henri too well to rely on him completely. He had always talked openly of returning to France, and while she doubted he would ever manage to do it, if circumstances allowed, she believed he was capable of taking Kitty with the best intentions of returning for the other children. However, once in France, Henri might be unable to do so, despite his best intentions. And if her other children were left motherless, what would happen?

As evening fell, Sophia fed the children and checked that they had clean hands and faces before bed. She settled before the fire with the mending, waiting for Henri to return from his homestead building, which, to her surprise, actually seemed to be progressing.

When Henri came in, she told him about the new baby. "A companion for Charlotte. The boys are always fighting with each other, and Kitty and Rhiannon and Susan are inseparable, so she'll have someone of her own to mother. Caitlin's expecting too."

Henri muttered, "Ah good," and said, "I too have some news. Terrible news."

"What?" asked Sophia in alarm. She had forborne to say that her own news was terrible.

"Last year some long hunters trading muskrat furs at the Vanns' said Louisiana was Spanish. I told them that was impossible, it was French. Today more long hunters arrived and swore it was true, they'd just come from Louisiana territory. Spanish are everywhere in La Nouvelle-Orléans. Louisiana in the hands of the enemy! La Nouvelle-Orléans, Spanish!" He struck the table a hard blow with his fist. "Even then I did not believe it was possible. But the Vanns had a copy of the *Virginia Gazette*, a year old. A treaty ended the war years ago, and France ceded its territory in Louisiana to Spain. Secretly. Now a Spanish governor has come, and the French colonists refuse to recognize Spanish rule. There's talk of an uprising."

"Oh?" Sophia concentrated on her sewing. *Injured French pride,* she thought.

Henri stared moodily into the fire. Finally he told her that he had abandoned any plan of sailing from Yorktown or Charleston. He'd planned to seek the French governor's help in La Nouvelle-Orléans. It was fourteen years since his failed spying mission, and he hoped his part in it would be forgotten and the governor would help the son and granddaughter of the Marquis de Marechal. And possibly even Francis and Georgie, though Henri wondered if it wouldn't be best if he returned for them when they were older.

Sophia was startled. So his plan had been closer to fruition than she had realized. What would be best for Kitty and eventually for the boys? Kitty was twelve and, Sophia feared, something of a hoyden. Was it the only chance Kitty would have to return to Europe and a life in what Sophia still regarded as civilization? She didn't want Kitty to end up a worn-out settler's wife, like the women they saw on the rafts. Was it her duty to encourage Henri? She had never thought so before, but watching her children grow up, Sophia just didn't know. She felt imprisoned by these thoughts that went round and round in her head. She mustn't be selfish and deny her children opportunities, but for the moment she couldn't help feeling grateful the Spanish takeover of La Nouvelle-Orléans resolved the dilemma. She had enough on her mind.

CHAPTER 29
MAGDALENA

December 1768

It was so cold the river had frozen along the banks, but the men had gone downriver to fetch a load of beaver pelts from an Indian trader, leaving Toby to get on with reshoeing horses and Cully and Jack mending harnesses and fishing nets. Sophia had looked so ill during her pregnancy that Caitlin decided to keep her company while the men were away. After acting as Venus's right hand and lording it over her younger sisters, thirteen-year-old Susan was as efficient and bossy as Venus and could be left to mind the trading post. Caitlin made a syllabub to give Sophia strength and set out with it and her children, including the five-month-old baby, Anwyn, whom they called Annie, strapped to her back in Indian fashion, just as it began to snow. Caitlin had almost turned back because the path up through the orchard turned slippery in bad weather but fortunately she hadn't. She arrived anticipating a cozy visit, but a frightened Kitty greeted her at the door and threw her arms round Caitlin.

"Oh, Aunt Caitlin! Thank heaven you're here! Mother's pains started, and she's bleeding, and she says the baby's not due to be born yet and I . . . I . . . don't know what to do!" Caitlin swiftly took charge, helped Sophia into bed, and ordered the older girls to keep the younger children away from her room.

"I'll help you," said Kitty bravely.

"No, help Malinda with the younger ones. I can manage."

"No, I'm going to stay and help Mother. I'll change places with Rhiannon," insisted Kitty.

"No," said Caitlin.

"It's *my* mother," said Kitty desperately. "I want to be there, in case . . ."

Caitlin gave in, and in the terrible night that followed, Kitty proved steadier and calmer than Caitlin expected, and Caitlin was glad of her help.

Malinda and Rhiannon had kept the five children in the kitchen, feeding them and making up pallets for them to sleep on. Rhiannon told them Cherokee stories about the Uktena to distract them, but the children were uneasy, aware something wasn't right behind the closed door where Sophia lay. Rhiannon tried to appear calm, though she wasn't, and Malinda looked terrified, and sometimes a tear trickled down her cheek. The younger children were on edge, unable to sleep. "Muvver!" Charlotte wept as Sophia's muffled cries came from the bedroom.

Toby came up in the wintry dawn to shoe the de Marechals' horses, and Rhiannon made him hot tea and shook her head when he asked what was wrong, why the children were so quiet.

Finally the baby was born, and Caitlin said, "It's a girl, Sophy." The baby was very small and lay very still. "You should name her quickly."

Sophia opened her eyes and said, "She's dead?"

"No, but . . . name her quickly."

"Am I going to die too? I am . . . surrounded by darkness," Sophia whispered.

"Oh, don't speak of it, Sophy, not in all the world!"

"Caitlin, we both know I might. So in case I do but the baby lives, I want you . . . christen the baby . . . godfather . . . look after her."

They hadn't had godparents for any of the other children, but Sophia clutched Caitlin's hand and whispered urgently, "Henri will take Kitty and the boys . . . to France . . . if he can. I need to know . . . if she lives . . . not alone . . . a godfather in his place . . . Magdalena. Her name is Magdalena. My own godmother's name. A sister to look after will be . . . a . . . comfort . . . to . . . Charlotte."

"I'll look after her . . . all your children, Sophy. We promised each other that we would if . . . if . . ." Caitlin couldn't say it and began to cry.

Sophia murmured, "Darling, I know you are more than a godmother, but . . . you may have another child, and . . . you too may . . . these things are uncertain."

"But the men are gone. Only Toby in the barn, shoeing the horses."

"He was a good boy. He'll be a good man."

Caitlin sent Kitty running. "Get Toby!"

Toby heard Kitty crying his name as she ran across the barnyard. He put down a horseshoe as Kitty burst into the barn where he was shoeing a horse for her father. "Toby!" sobbed Kitty. "You have to come now!" She was hiccupping with distress, trying to catch her breath.

Toby put down the horseshoe and reached for his musket. "What's the matter, Kitty? Indians?"

"No. It's Mother. The baby's come early and Papa's not here and Saskia's too sick to come and Caitlin sent . . . sent me to fetch you . . . she thinks Mother and . . . and the baby will die and . . . and Mother wants . . . wants the baby to be baptized. Godfather . . . she needs a godfather, and there's no one else . . . Hurry, Toby! It's a girl . . ." Kitty burst into tears. "I don't want Mother to die!"

Outside a fierce wind threw sleet in their faces, and the ground was white and slippery from an earlier snow flurry, and the winter afternoon was already dark. There was no chance Henri and the other men could make it back in such bad weather. Inside the cabin where a large fire roared in the kitchen fireplace, it was hot. Rhiannon and Malinda cried as they prepared to feed the younger children gathered around the hearth.

"You go on, Kitty. Help Mother. We can manage," murmured Rhiannon. In the back bedroom, there was another fire and the extravagance of two candles. Caitlin was bending over the bed, doing things for Sophia, who lay very white and still, in shadow, her brown hair across the pillow, with streaks of gray showing. There was a small swaddled bundle by Sophia's side, and Sophia's eyes were shut. Kitty whispered, "Mother?" Caitlin's face was set, and her lips were moving in prayer. Caitlin shook her head slightly in answer to Kitty's question. Sophia wasn't dead. Yet.

Now Caitlin asked Toby, "You'll stand godfather? It means you promise to look after the baby if she has no mother or father . . ." He nodded.

"The prayer book just there on the shelf . . . *Ministrations of Private Baptism* . . . ," whispered Sophia. "Water on Magdalena's head . . . just a little." She gave a faint smile. "Not in the river as you Dissenters do it. Church of England's way . . ."

Kitty fetched the bucket and dipper.

Toby asked, "What do I . . ."

Caitlin handed him the bundled-up baby. "Hold her. I'll read."

Caitlin opened the prayer book with shaking hands. Sophia didn't look like she would live, and Caitlin could die herself with another baby. Who knew what Henri would take it into his head to do. Poor Sophia, thought Caitlin, fiercely grateful for Gideon's steady ways. It was unthinkable, but if Sophia died and Henri left and anything happened to Caitlin, Toby might be left in charge of the baby.

Thinking how precarious were the lives of motherless children, Caitlin stumbled through the words of the Anglican baptism service. They wet the baby's head and wiped the water off at once, saying her name, Magdalena. The baby cried weakly but only a little and stopped.

Toby was surprised by the baby's smallness; her tiny hands reminded him of mouse paws. Kitty swiped her eyes with the back of her hand, and suddenly Toby felt tears rolling down his own face. "Magdalena," he said. He knew Caitlin and Sophia expected her to die. Perhaps if she realized now she had been baptized with her own name, she could be called back into the world. "Magdalena," he said a little louder and thought of the way bellows blew fire into life, thought maybe his strength could blow the flame of this small life the same way. He thought the baby needed to hear her name spoken.

Caitlin was directing Kitty on what to do for Sophia. Toby sat down by the fire and held the baby, saying her name over and over, telling her about the forge and the bellows and how a great fire could be coaxed out of a little flickering flame.

When Caitlin took the baby from him to see if Sophia could feed her, Magdalena stirred a little, and to Caitlin's surprise, she latched on to the nipple and sucked, if not vigorously, well enough. But Sophia had lost a great deal of blood and was in a bad way. She kept falling asleep or fainting, Caitlin wasn't sure which. She wished Henri would come back, she wished Saskia was there, she wished she knew what to do next.

She did the best she could, then realized twelve-year-old Kitty was ashen-faced with exhaustion. "Kitty, you're tired, child. You and Toby go eat something." When they left, Caitlin opened her dress and started to feed Magdalena. Annie was grizzling in the corner, but she was healthy—Annie could wait. She would feed Annie afterward. After a few minutes, Magdalena fell asleep. Caitlin checked she was breathing and wrapped her in a quilt and laid her next to Sophia. Then she checked to make sure Sophia was breathing—Sophia was alarmingly white. Then she picked up Annie and fed her, and prayed, "Dear God, neither Sophy nor I can do this many more times. What in all the world will happen to our children if we both die?"

Sophia was very ill and too weak to get out of bed for a long time after the birth, but she lived. With Caitlin nursing Magdalena, and Kitty keeping a vigil lest the baby grow cold or wet, Magdalena lived as well. Venus came up to help at intervals, and they could hardly keep Toby away; he seemed to be at the door every five minutes, offering to hold the baby, and in the end Caitlin and Kitty were grateful for his help and even said it was Toby who kept the baby alive. He would insist on picking Magdalena up and would walk up and down with her, talking to her the whole time, while Caitlin and Kitty saw to the other children. Caitlin stayed up at Wildwood to help feed Magdalena for the first weeks, then took her brood home and climbed up through the orchard twice a day to nurse her until Sophia could manage.

Charlotte had finally been allowed in to see her mother, days after the birth. Caitlin put her finger to her lips and whispered that Sophia was sleeping. She beckoned Charlotte over and showed her the baby in her arms. Charlotte stared at Magdalena.

"What's that?"

"It's your baby sister," said Caitlin.

"What's a baby sister?"

"Well, let's see. You know, the chicks you love are baby chickens. This is a baby person."

"It should live in the chicken house, not with Mother."

"No, it . . . she . . . lives in the house. With us. With you."

"Does it say 'cheep, cheep'?"

Sophia opened her eyes and smiled faintly at Charlotte. "Not yet, darling."

"Can I feed her? Like I feed the chickens?"

Caitlin smiled too. "My love, she's a baby, not a chicken. She doesn't peck on the ground. She's your little sister. Like you're Kitty's little sister. Kitty's older and bigger than you. Now you're older and bigger than Magdalena, so you must learn to look after her, just like you look after the little chickens."

"Oh." Charlotte thought for a minute. "No. I like little chickens. Don't want a baby sister."

"Well, stroke her head. She feels soft as a little chicken, doesn't she? And she's sleeping now, but her eyes are open when she's awake."

Charlotte reached out a finger and touched Magdalena's hair.

Sophia saw Charlotte's expression and knew it was the expression of a child weighing up advantages and disadvantages. Sophia could tell Charlotte was deciding that if she was older than this baby sister, then Charlotte could order her around like Kitty ordered her.

Charlotte finally smiled at Magdalena in a proprietary way. "Oh, my little baby!" she cooed to the sleeping Magdalena in the same voice she used to the chickens. "Oh, my little baby sister!"

CHAPTER 30
A WEDDING IN THE VALLEY

Late October 1771

Sophia had been up even earlier than usual, and there had been a rushed breakfast so her yawning children could finish their chores and get ready. There was to be a wedding, arranged at short notice, and Sophia had felt an overwhelming urge to get her children in order for once, with baths and the best clothes they could muster. This was a monumental task, but the two younger sisters didn't share their mother's sense of urgency. It was Charlotte and Magdalena's morning task to feed the chickens and collect the eggs, but Charlotte whispered, "First let's sit in the porch swing and watch the sun come up and be a big persimmon," and the two little girls swung gently as the sky grew light. "Now listen, Magdalena," ordered seven-year-old Charlotte, who never missed a chance to exercise her authority and who today felt the special occasion warranted repeating Sophia's instructions to her two-year-old sister. "Mother says that today you have to be very, very good, Magdalena."

"Why?" asked Magdalena, who was always good and worshipped Charlotte, who knew everything.

"Because Malinda and Jack are getting married," said Charlotte. "And it's 'portant."

"Why is it 'portant?" asked Magdalena earnestly.

"Because there's a parson come on a raft and . . . and . . . because we have new dresses and Aunt Caitlin made a pie this big"—she held out her arms—"and Kitty and Rhiannon and Susan went to pick flowers and . . . and Malinda had a bath!"

"Why?"

"Because . . . Mother said everyone's having a bath. Even us. She wants us to smell sweet. Besides, you have to have a bath and smell sweet when it's a wedding. Everyone knows that," Charlotte pronounced with an air of finality.

"Even Toby? Is he having a bath?"

"Well, Toby's a boy . . . but probably. They're all having a bath at Uncle Rufus's. Mother said we'll have a bath after Kitty and Francis and Georgie. Georgie and Francis are having theirs first. Mother says they're the dirtiest. Then it will be our turn."

"Why?"

"For goodness' sake, Magdalena! Stop talking and look at the big persimmon. It's a persimmon big as the world. Then we'll feed the chickens."

Magdalena put her head on Charlotte's shoulder. "I'm afraid of the red chicken. It doesn't like it when I take the eggs. It bites my hand."

"I won't let it hurt you," promised Charlotte. "I'll stamp my foot and scare it off." She was in charge of the chickens.

"Charlotte, I know a secret."

"What secret? How?"

Magdalena savored the moment—she rarely knew something her sister didn't. "Guess what?"

"What?" demanded Charlotte.

Magdalena whispered, "We have new hair ribbons. I heard Mother say. When she was sewing our dresses."

Malinda and Jack were getting married at very short notice thanks to the unexpected arrival of a young parson on a convoy of three rafts en route to Kentuckee. The whole settlement had thrown themselves into the hasty preparations for the wedding. Down at the trading post, the wedding dress was being made with lightning speed. Caitlin and Saskia and Venus had stitched frantically to make a wedding dress for Malinda from a new bolt of pink-and-white calico. Seth and Nott had butchered one of the hogs, filled their stone-lined fire pit with hickory and apple wood, and began a hog roast as soon as the logs had burned down.

"We got two days to get this done," said Saskia to Venus and Caitlin as they sewed and pinned furiously.

Up at Wildwood, Sophia was busy too. She cut down the last of her English morning dresses, the red-and-white one she'd been married in, to make her daughters new frocks. The girls' clothes were terribly patched and shabby.

She had also made an English dessert called a trifle to be part of the wedding breakfast. The trifle was a labor of love, a difficult confection of cake, preserves, custard, and cream that Mrs. Betts had once taught Sophia to make. It had been put to set in a handsome blue-and-yellow Chinese bowl she had brought from Thomas de Bouldin's house and kept, a bowl that, like the trifle recipe, was used only on the most special occasions. The children had dared each other to stick a finger in and taste it. "How could they!" cried Sophia when she discovered the many finger-shaped holes bored in the cream. She seized a wooden spoon and smoothed them over.

She set a large pot of water to heat on the fire—it would take hours of heating water to bathe everyone—found a fresh cake of soap, and mustered all her spare pieces of sacking for the bathers to dry themselves. Then she surveyed her grubby, guilty brood and told them they were a band of ruffians and said it was a pity there was no time to wring their necks. And if they weren't clean, she said sternly, and if there was *one more* finger hole in the trifle, they would have to stay home from the wedding and miss Uncle Tad.

There had been space on the raft that had brought the parson, and Caitlin's father had seized the chance to deliver a dozen bolts of fabric and pay his daughter and her family a visit, to the joy of all the children in the settlement, who were far more excited about his arrival than any wedding. All the children in the valley called him Uncle Tad. He always had something interesting to give them, like spinning tops and slingshots. He played his violin and led them dancing a jig to wherever the fancy took him and then gave them barley sugar. He had an endless fund of stories of giants and ghosts and princesses and knights in armor and horses that rode on the wind.

"I'm sorry about the trifle, Mother," said Charlotte meekly. Most of the finger holes had been Charlotte-sized finger holes.

The parson, Cotton Mather Merriman, was on his way west to preach the gospel in Kentuckee, an undertaking funded by the widowed aunt who accompanied him, but was willing to stay and marry Malinda and Jack if the boatman and the other traveling passengers were agreeable to a few days' delay. The boatman said, "I say we wait, Katy." The boatman's wife took the pipe out of her mouth and said she was willing. The other passengers, three trappers and a thin-faced girl with lank hair named Mattie who was the boatman's orphaned niece, were in no particular hurry and declared themselves in favor of the change of plan.

However, the parson's aunt, Mrs. Sunshill, a large lady with a loud voice, had been against it. The settlement in Kentuckee where they were bound was Scotch Irish, a flock urgently in need of a shepherd to lead them in the paths of righteousness, chastity, and sobriety as soon as possible. There was a prodigious amount of drunkenness and fornication taking place among them, judging by the number of babies being born to those who were neither married nor concerned about not being so, and there was no time to be lost.

The boatman protested it was a wedding, but she wore him down, and he reluctantly agreed to leave as planned. But next morning when the hour for departure came, the air was full of the aromatic smoke of a hog roasting over a slow hickory fire. They would stay for the wedding, said the boatman firmly.

Rufus sat by the pit with a bucket of apple vinegar and a ladle to baste the pig. By his side was a basket of wooden beakers and a jug of his hard cider. He offered it to everyone passing, including the parson and his aunt and the girl Mattie, whom the parson's aunt had taken rather forcibly under her wing and obliged to walk with her and her nephew.

The travelers and the boatman and his wife accepted eagerly. Mattie couldn't decide—she was the sort of girl who hovered perpetually between "maybe I will" and "maybe I won't," whatever the question, before saying perhaps she would have just a taste. Mrs. Sunshill declined emphatically, but the parson was willing. He drank deeply, twice, pronounced it excellent, and, emboldened by alcohol, turned to his aunt and quoted St. Paul, saying it was better for the young people to marry than to burn and that he felt a positive call to do his Christian duty and stay and marry the young people and prevent . . . er . . . fornication. It was not a word he could utter comfortably. He blushed, and Mattie blushed too and looked away quite hard at something in the distance, pretending she hadn't heard. The parson expounded on his duty as a clergyman. If he was on the way to prevent fornication in Kentuckee, he had no less of a duty to prevent it here.

His aunt rumbled discontentedly but couldn't disagree. Anxious to be seen putting the delay to good use, the parson walked off, carrying his Bible under his arm to plant himself in the path of individual settlers with an "Oh, sinner! Pause a moment and think of the hereafter. Mend your evil ways while there's still time! Yield not to the Devil! Hear the word of the Lord!" before reading out scripture verses at random and following up with an impromptu homily of his own, good practice for future sermons.

"I wish he'd get out from under my feet," muttered Saskia, at intervals as she and Venus and Caitlin hurried back and forth with their meal preparations and sewing between their usual chores.

For the parson, clad in decent if hot clerical black broadcloth, this afternoon's wedding was the first occasion on which he would appear in an official capacity. Cotton Mather Merriman was nervous and afraid he might stutter. To practice he had read the wedding service several times to check that he needn't mention fornication.

He was growing warm from walking briskly to waylay this person and that in the heat, and on top of that, he was very hungry.

His turns about the trading post yard in search of sinners for his Bible verses took him back and forth past the kitchen, where he was drawn to the open kitchen door like a moth to the flame, mesmerized by the preparations for the wedding breakfast. Watched over by Venus and Caitlin, Susan and Rhiannon took turns basting several wild turkeys that were browning on a spit turned by a chain and weights, their juices dripping delectably down their golden sides. There was a ham, golden and brushed with honey. There was a roast possum, decoratively hanging by its tail from a branch. Caitlin had worked all night to make her raised game pie and *bara brith*, now hidden under muslin to keep off the flies.

The girls had gathered a large basket of muscadine grapes along with vines and greenery, and there was a large pawpaw pudding, cooling. There was a bowl of cream cheese, pitchers of buttermilk, and jugs of blackberry cordial, and Meshack had brought a jug of his finest whiskey.

The parson wandered back to the barrel of hard cider. "Weddings are thirsty work," he confided to Rufus.

His wooden cup was refilled, but the parson was not to get off lightly.

"I recall the day I married my dear wife, Molly, God rest her soul . . ." The occasion had made Rufus sentimental. He had a listener, and he was determined to make the most of it, though he was obliged to refresh the parson's cup several times in the course of a long recitation.

Up at Wildwood, Sophia had avoided the parson and his Bible and was fully occupied in making her children look nice, clean, and brushed at the same time. She herself had had a long, delicious soak the night before, and after breakfast was cleared away, she began the daunting task of scrubbing the boys thoroughly first, ears, fingernails, and necks. "Mother," protested Francis through the soaping, "you're washing us away—there'll be nothing left!"

She handed them a piece of sacking. "Put your clean breeches on, sit on the porch, and do not move!"

"But we're still wet!"

"You'll soon dry."

Kitty helped empty the bathwater. "Ugh, Mother, it's black!"

"I know, let's not put it on the herb garden."

Sophia refilled the bath with fresh hot water and threw in some sprigs of bog myrtle to scent it for the girls. Kitty first, then Charlotte, then Magdalena last. Then she washed their hair in a bucket of rainwater and combed it out to dry. Sophia sprinkled them and herself with rose water she'd made from wild roses, and the girls climbed gingerly into fresh undergarments and their new dresses. The flowered muslin that Sophia had kept for best had been rarely worn and so had lasted well. "That was my wedding dress," said Sophia to Charlotte, tugging a flounce here and patting a seam smooth there.

"When you were married, did you have to have a bath, Mother?"

"Yes, Magdalena, I did."

"It's the law, Magdalena," said Charlotte sternly.

Sophia produced the new hair ribbons, a gift from Caitlin. There was red for Kitty, blue for Charlotte, and green for Magdalena, and Sophia brushed and tied their hair back with a bow.

When the boys were dressed, she lined her children up. "I want to admire you." She smiled proudly. Clean, they were vulnerable and young and sweet, even her two rowdy boys. Now if she could just keep them clean and in order until the wedding was done.

"Do we look nice, Mother?" asked Charlotte earnestly.

"Oh, my darlings, there's never been a handsomer family!" Sophia exclaimed. The children were proud and self-conscious—they were rarely dressed up and admired.

"Don't forget the trifle, Mother!" exclaimed Kitty.

Sophia smoothed her skirt, told the children not to stir, and went to the springhouse for the repaired trifle.

Armed with the trifle bowl and five clean, momentarily subdued children, Sophia led her family down the orchard path to the trading post.

There she found Caitlin bustling around putting the finishing touches on the wedding feast, and Malinda in a corner while Saskia and Venus sewed the final seams, giving her contradictory instructions to turn this way or that or hold still. The large, bossy woman from the raft had joined them, introduced herself as Mrs. Sunshill, and claimed the credit for persuading her nephew, the parson, to accept a call she had heard on his behalf to go as a missionary among the settlers in Kentuckee. Saskia rolled her eyes at Caitlin.

In the middle of it all, Malinda looked radiant. Her curly hair was piled on her head with the help of some new hairpins from Caitlin, her eyes danced, her cheeks were pink. She caught Sophia's eye and smiled, revealing perfect little white teeth.

"Doesn't she look pretty, Mother!" exclaimed Kitty. "Look, there's Jack, peeking in the door." Jack winked at Malinda, and Malinda blew him a kiss.

"Get out!" Mrs. Sunshill went to shoo him away.

"You look very pretty yourself, Kitty dear," said Sophia. At fifteen, she had grown as tall as her mother during the past summer, and her figure had filled out. She had Sophia's expressive brown eyes, a fine complexion, a slender waist, and a mass of auburn hair. Her eyes sparkled. "Really, Mother?"

"Really." Sophia smiled. "And your new dress is very becoming."

"Oh, I think so too!" exclaimed Kitty happily. She kept walking back and forth past the corner where Caitlin's mirror with the crack in it was propped, to see her reflection. Susan skipped in and claimed Kitty. "Come on, Kitty, stop looking at yourself . . ." She whispered something that sounded like "wait till you see the parson," and the two girls went off giggling.

She'll be sixteen next year, thought Sophia, watching them wistfully. She'd done the best she could with lessons, but had she taught Kitty anything serious about duty and inclination, beyond the botched sampler? Kitty seemed to do as she pleased much of the time, following Cully about everywhere.

Kitty was as lively as quicksilver, kind to her younger sisters and brothers, but she was mischievously irreverent and ready to laugh at anything and leave her chores undone when she thought no one would reprimand her. *Just like Henri!* thought Sophia with exasperation, often finding it easiest to do Kitty's undone chores herself. Arguments with Kitty were protracted, as Kitty was quick to justify whatever it was she had done or not done because there was something more urgent and pleasant she had to do, and these disputes always left Sophia feeling obscurely bested. But Kitty had grown pretty in the last year. It had suddenly begun to worry Sophia that the long hunters and fur traders were looking at Kitty with new eyes, and they were by and large a rough lot. And no matter how Venus and Sophia ordered them to stop it, Kitty and Susan flirted with them, for fun. Would Kitty acquire some decorum in France? And would France improve Kitty's marriage prospects? Sophia recalled the elaborate preparations for her own presentation at court to signal the fact she was ready to be married, her father's machinations afterward to find her a suitable husband, and then Lady Burnham's lectures when Sophia laughingly rejected all her father's choices. What could be done for Kitty in Virginia? What if Kitty decided to fancy herself in love with a fur trader? Where was Kitty to find a suitable husband? Sophia thought she understood her father and Lady Burnham better with every year that passed.

Sophia went to help Caitlin with the ham. "I hope that one day Kitty has a daughter just like herself," Sophia said. Then she realized Caitlin wasn't her usual calm self. In fact, she was hacking at the ham with her knife as if she wanted to kill it.

"Let me. You've worked so hard on the wedding, you must be tired," said Sophia, taking the knife Caitlin was stabbing into the ham. "I just realized Kitty is growing up. She's willful and exasperating, and I daresay just like I was at that age. It's probably too late to do anything about her."

Caitlin sighed and relinquished the knife. "Rhiannon too. Oh, Sophy, how does it happen so quickly? One minute babies, you're rocking them to sleep in front of the fire, their little heads tucked under your chin, the next they're tall as their mothers and disagreeing with everything you say. And one day they'll be gone with their husbands. I wasn't much older when I married Gideon, but I hate to think of Rhiannon getting married at that age, maybe going west to Kentuckee like so many do. It seems like the saddest thing in all the world, how short a time you have with children."

"Caitlin, don't make us both cry! And speaking of children, I need your advice. If by some miracle Henri managed to sell homesteads and got enough money to take Kitty to France, ought Kitty to go? I was against it always, but then I never believed he could get the money to take her. Now I'm afraid he might. He's actually been working very hard clearing the land and is now talking about building cabins. Maybe a year or so in a convent school would do wonders." Sophia sighed. "Henri thinks the people he knows at court or his father's friends really would befriend the boys, and the ladies take Kitty under their wing. It might be her only chance to meet a husband who isn't a settler or a trader or a buffalo hunter . . ."

"Or an Indian," said Caitlin bitterly.

Sophia put down the knife and stared at her friend. "Caitlin, whatever's the matter? You love Gideon!"

"I do, and there's not another man in all the world I'd have married. But Rhiannon . . . is too like him. She . . . doesn't want to be like me."

"Yes, she is like Gideon, I grant you, but—"

The two mothers were interrupted by a dark form planting itself between them and a voice saying, "Woe to sinners on the day of judgment! Pause a moment! Where will you be when the Rapture comes? Caught up to meet God in the air? Or left behind, wishing you had spared a thought . . . hic! . . . for your immortal . . . hic!"

They looked up to see a young man in black clothes, rather red in the face and perspiring, with a Bible in one hand and the other pointing rhetorically skyward. He gave another loud hiccup, and his face grew even redder. "I beg your pardon, goody de Mar'shell . . ."

Sophia drew herself up and gave the young man such an icy stare that he quailed. She would not be addressed as goodwife no matter how backward Virginia was. "You, sir, must be the parson," she said icily. "How obliging of you to interrupt your journey. Might I inquire, what branch of the faith ordained you?"

"Brother Merriman, Cotton Mather Merriman, a Covenanter, naturally, at your service, I just . . . my duty . . ." Here he hiccupped again, and Sophia smelled apple brandy. Caitlin wrinkled her nose and turned back to her ham.

Sophia spotted Kitty and Susan behind the swaying parson, now swaying themselves and pretending to have the hiccups too. *Oh dear,* thought Sophia. "Please excuse me." She abandoned the parson and went to deal with the girls.

"Stop that! It's rude!" Sophia ordered.

The two girls raced outside, snickering "fornication" between hiccups. For a moment Sophia longed for Henri to take Kitty to France tomorrow.

The parson gazed wistfully at the ham, but Caitlin flapped her hands at him and said, "Not yet!" and he wandered away unsteadily.

"We should have the wedding before Tad and Rufus give the parson any more cider," muttered Caitlin, wiping her knife. "I'll call the children." Sophia called down to the landing, where the boys were showing Charlotte and Magdalena and Peach how to skip stones on the river.

Mrs. Sunshill, who had been shifted aside every time she tried to insinuate herself to show the women how to do things a better way, was giving Mattie a full account of her wedding to her late husband, starting at the beginning. "They do things with more decorum in New Hampshire. It wasn't until we'd courted for three years that Mr. Sunshill proposed through the courting stick in my parents' parlor . . ."

"Mother, Malinda wants you." Kitty beckoned urgently from the corner. "There's a seam open all down the side of her bodice, and she doesn't trust me to sew it."

Malinda was standing on a chair where Saskia and Venus had left her, saying they'd be back in a minute, pointing to a gaping seam up the side of the bodice but afraid to move because of the pins. "Oh, Malinda! I'll see to it." Sophia began to stitch it up, removing pins as she went.

Jack was at the door again. "Hurry up, Malinda, the parson's in his cups. Pa says he'd better marry us while he still can. Come on!" He held out his hand to help her down.

"Wait!" Sophia snipped the last thread, and Jack put his hands on Malinda's slim waist and lifted her down. They smiled into each other's eyes.

"You're beautiful," said Jack with a catch in his voice. Malinda did look beautiful. The dress was a becoming blue that set off the pink in her cheeks, and her hair was tumbling down from its pins just a little. He pinned it back. Malinda stroked Jack's cheek.

"Plenty of time for spooning later. If you want to get married, come along now. Parson won't last much longer!" said Rufus from the door and hurried his son and Malinda to the door of Caitlin's storeroom, now disguised with honeysuckle and trumpet creeper and woodbine for the occasion. Sophia said someone had to give the bride away, did she want Henri or Gideon? Malinda pointed at Meshack.

Jack hurried to Brother Merriman's side. Everyone was there—Saskia and Nott and Cully, who was now taller than Nott, Caitlin and her father and Gideon and Bryn and Rhiannon and Venus and her daughters with Seth and the boatman and his wife, Katy, who had put on a bonnet and shawl for the occasion, and Mrs. Sunshill and the boatman's niece, Mattie. The trappers were at the back against the wall, trying to stand in a respectful way. All three had a plug of tobacco wadded into their cheeks and were desperate to spit.

Cotton Mather Merriman was being propped up by Henri and Toby, and when he saw the groom, he began the wedding at once, asking if Jack were willing to be married to . . . Jack stopped him. Malinda wanted to walk in slowly. At the door, Malinda smoothed her dress, put her hand on Meshack's arm, and smiled up at him. Meshack patted her hand but kept his face stern. If he tried to smile back, he thought he'd cry; his heart was on the verge of breaking with love for this sweet child who'd been like his own daughter. Malinda squeezed his arm to let him know she understood.

Sophia thought what a good man Meshack was. He'd been kind with all the children, mending toys and fishing rods, Malinda's doll that had had the head twisted off a score of times. He'd understood Malinda couldn't help it. He'd taught Cully carpentry, and Cully had surprised Saskia with a fine oak table and six chairs with well-turned legs. Meshack wouldn't let Cully cut corners, and Cully had lost his temper many times but always came back, because he was anxious to give his mother a fine present. Meshack never got mad, just carried on where he'd been when Cully stamped off.

Then she counted the children standing at the front . . . Charlotte's little shining head with her braids down her back, Magdalena, Peach, Annie, and Cadfael.

Meshack handed Malinda to Jack and stepped back.

The apple brandy had made Brother Merriman eloquent. After asking Malinda and Jack each if they covenanted to be married to the other, and they said they did, the trappers had assumed it was over and were relieved they could go outside and spit. To their dismay, Brother Merriman launched into prayer. He prayed for an interminably long time, with long contemplative silences between thoughts, as if he was composing a sermon on marriage as he went. And indeed Brother Merriman felt the spirit take hold, however intermittently, and give his eloquence wings. As he warmed to his topic, his repeated references to "fornication," which marriage was ordained by God to prevent, had Mrs. Sunshill harrumphing. Sophia and Caitlin and Venus exchanged startled looks. "What he saying! What kind of talk is that in front of the children!" exclaimed Saskia in a voice heavy with disapproval, turning a wrathful eye on Mrs. Sunshill.

"What's fornication?" Annie asked her brother Cadfael in a loud voice.

One of the trappers snickered and choked on his tobacco wad. Caitlin, who knew Annie would ask a question over and over, louder each time, until she got an answer, reached out and pulled Annie back between her and Gideon and bent down to whisper. Kitty, Susan, and even Rhiannon got the giggles again so badly that the four youngest children exploded too. Sophia leaned over, tapped Charlotte's shoulder, and pointed to the door. "Out!" Charlotte, then Cadfael, Magdalena, and Peach scurried away. Brother Merriman continued his praying, oblivious. Annie squirmed, wanting to run too, but Caitlin held on to her.

Brother Merriman finally pronounced Malinda and Jack married. Caitlin's father went for the broom, and Sophia went to find the younger children, to give them a piece of her mind and a lecture about manners before they ate. Otherwise they'd grow up like Kitty. But they weren't in the kitchen. They weren't in the cabin either. They weren't at the river landing skipping stones, and they weren't in the barn. She called and called them, but there was no answer. Of all times for them to go off hiding! Where could they have got to?

Sophia was running now all the places they could be, calling their names, calling Charlotte. Little by little she grew afraid, even as she reasoned fear away—they couldn't have fallen off the landing, there was a wooden railing around the landing, Caitlin had insisted Gideon put it there, and even if they had, the children could all swim, even Charlotte and Peach—Cully had taught them all in the shallows on hot summer afternoons.

Sophia hurried toward the orchard. They must be in the orchard; they'd gone to climb a tree . . . but they weren't. She called and called.

She ran as fast as she could back to the Vanns' cabin, where Caitlin's father had begun playing his fiddle. She screamed to be heard over it, "The children are gone! Magdalena and Charlotte." She gasped as Henri caught her. "Peach and . . . Cadfael . . ."

"What you mean, gone?" said Venus. "Can't be gone. I saw them through the door after you said go outside for being noisy. They goin' toward the landing. The four of them's together. Must be hidin'. They can't all four be gone!"

"But they are! Or I can't find them. We have to . . . have to find them," Sophia choked. "Charlotte! Oh God, Charlotte!"

Everyone, even the trappers and Mrs. Sunshill, Malinda and Jack, went searching and calling, first at the landing where Gideon said their bodies would surely have been if they'd drowned; the river was running low after the summer, and the current was sluggish. He swam under the landing to look. Then they searched the orchard all the way up to the de Marechals', then across the valley to and all the way up Little Frog Mountain to Rufus's forge. Caitlin was white-faced and frantic, Venus and Seth and their girls shouting Peach's name. The wedding feast was forgotten. The sun set and night fell, and in the dark, they called and called the children.

By dawn everyone was haggard, drained, and hoarse, and there was no sign of the four children. Peach's sisters and Kitty were crying, and Rhiannon walked off by herself to sit on the landing where the children had last been.

The adults slumped on the porch of the Vanns' cabin, exhausted, Caitlin and Sophia and Venus bereft and speechless with shock. Their children must have fallen into the river and drowned; it was the only explanation.

Sophia and Caitlin silently put their arms round each other, beyond words or tears. Rhiannon came back and tugged her father's arm. "Come with me," she whispered. "I don't think they're dead. Something else happened. I don't know how to tell Mother." Out of hearing distance of the cabin, she turned to her father and said urgently, "I think they've been taken. I went down to the landing, and the big catfish that swims there came and told me they were playing on the landing when the canoes came. They've been kidnapped. The catfish told me, Father, but I'm afraid the others won't believe me. Mother won't believe me. She looks like someone killed her."

"I believe you. Did the catfish say where? Or who took them?"

"It was Creeks, and they went downriver. Can you get them back?"

"Singing Wind, I will try," said Gideon grimly. If they'd been taken by canoe, the kidnappers would be far away by now. And they would sell the children. But they were alive.

Later he went up to his rock and sacrificed tobacco and some beads, asking the catfish spirits of the river to help him find his son and the other children. But Gideon realized the spirits did not speak to him as they used to. They told him that his daughter must go to live among the Cherokee and learn to use her gift so they could speak to her. All he knew when he went home was that Cadfael would become a brave before he saw him again.

Someday. Caitlin couldn't bear that now. He would say nothing to her of Rhiannon and the catfish. Yet.

CHAPTER 31
MOURNING

1771–1772

After that first horrible night Sophia shed no more tears. It was as if she no longer inhabited her shell of a body. Henri and Caitlin and Venus and Seth and all the children grieved, but Sophia grew quiet and went about her daily tasks mechanically and in silence.

In the aftermath of the children's abduction, Brother Merriman firmly declined to go on to Kentuckee, telling his aunt that God had called him to stay with the valley settlers to help them bear their cross. Mrs. Sunshill found it hard to accept that the Almighty had neglected to consult her in the matter. She reminded her nephew forcefully that it was she who had brought him this far for the express purpose of leading a large flock to righteousness in Kentuckee, and he was duty bound to go on to Kentuckee. She protested so long and so loudly in the face of her nephew's intransigence that Rufus finally suggested she remain a while longer herself, to set an example of Christian patience and submission to God's will.

Mrs. Sunshill had at length been persuaded—her nephew was adamant about staying, and it was hard to argue against a call from God even though she made it plain to everyone that the Almighty ought to have spoken to her too. She was not especially eager to go on to Kentuckee alone with only the trappers for company. She had been unable to persuade Mattie to accompany her, even when she hinted there might be a young man in Kentuckee in need of a wife. For a wan girl with lank hair and not much to say for herself, Mattie stood surprisingly firm against the formidable widow Sunshill. She wished to go back with the boatman and Aunt Katy, and that was that.

Brother Merriman persuaded his aunt to purchase a small piece of land from Henri. He planned to first build himself a cabin and then a church. Since this would take him some time, Brother Merriman took up residence in the small cabin next to Wildwood that had been built for Zaydie, empty since her death. There he had attempted to bring Sophia to a submission to God's will, an acknowledgment of her own sinful nature, and an acceptance that the loss of her child was God's judgment on her sin. Sophia refused to speak to him. Further to his dismay, his host Henri raised his Catholicism like a blunt shield whenever Brother Merriman confronted him, intending to preach and pray him into righteousness and out of the error of his idolatrous ways.

Mrs. Sunshill didn't quite dare move in with him, feeling somewhat quelled by Sophia's icy demeanor. Instead she had stayed for a time in Caitlin's storeroom, sleeping on a pallet on the floor and spending her days with her nephew. She was a bustler by nature and busied herself tidying and cleaning and cooking in the small cabin until Brother Merriman was nearly driven out of his mind. Nor could she step across to pass the day with Sophia when there was nothing more for her to do for her nephew. Mrs. Sunshill quickly understood that it would be advisable to leave Sophia alone. Drawing on the Grafton hauteur and an intense dislike of Brother Merriman's interference, Sophia had managed a look that froze Mrs. Sunshill's blood in the middle of her one ill-advised condolence about the loss of Charlotte and equally ill-timed advice about the duty of Christians to meekly accept the scourges Divine Providence sent. Mrs. Sunshill had retreated in defeat.

Then Mrs. Sunshill learned Malinda was pregnant, and had been pregnant on her wedding day. After that, to Malinda's dismay and irritation, Mrs. Sunshill found excuses to spend her days at Rufus's cabin, where she lectured Malinda unmercifully about the divine punishments awaiting those guilty of lewd behavior. Instead of going up to make herself useful in her nephew's small abode, at Rufus's cabin she insisted on cooking and rearranging the table and chairs, airing the bedclothes and the mattresses even when Malinda had just seen to it, and scrubbing the pots Malinda had just scoured. She ejected the dogs and bossed Toby unmercifully. She had to be dragged from the birthing room—Saskia and Caitlin understood the pleading look in Malinda's eyes meant "Make that woman go!" and Venus folded her arms and shoved Mrs. Sunshill out the door, saying, "We call you when we needs you."

Afterward Mrs. Sunshill disapproved of the way Malinda managed her baby, Little Molly, named after Jack and Toby's mother. Mrs. Sunshill would frown and shake her head because Malinda picked up Little Molly at every whimper. Mrs. Sunshill harrumphed it was the Devil in the child and she shouldn't be coddled. When Malinda's back was turned, she would snatch up the just-swaddled baby to swaddle it differently. Malinda took to making furious faces at Mrs. Sunshill behind her back. It made Jack laugh, but Malinda was caught sticking her tongue out and flapping her hands with her thumb in her ears, and Mrs. Sunshill flew into a fury.

Jack was soon motivated to build a new home for him and Malinda and Little Molly, and a new four-room cabin was duly built, shouting distance away from Rufus. It had a bar across the door so it could be barred from the inside. Unable to gain access, Mrs. Sunshill continued to bustle and make herself useful at Rufus's cabin while the men were busy in the fields and at the forge. She cooked and swept and scoured, boiled laundry, and mended whatever needed it, which was practically everything. She killed the mice that until now had lived comfortably in the bottom of the cupboard. With every week that passed, the cabin became cleaner and tidier, and it became clearer that dislodging Mrs. Sunshill would prove difficult.

"Pa, you've got to make her go!" pleaded Toby.

In the spring Rufus was "spoken to" by the Brother Merriman about the impropriety of a single female and a single man being so much under the same roof without a chaperone. Rufus saw the writing on the wall and, to his sons' dismay, told the parson he would marry the widow Sunshill, if she was willing. Brother Merriman delivered the message and hastened back with word that she was. No one had the heart for a wedding celebration after the kidnappings at Jack and Malinda's wedding. The wedding was a very quiet affair, conducted by Brother Merriman in front of Rufus's fireplace, with Toby, Jack, and Malinda as witnesses, and a ham dinner afterward. Then Rufus and the new Mrs. Drumheller, somewhat sheepishly, retired together for the night.

Afterward they called each other Mrs. Drumheller and Mr. Drumheller, never Patience and Rufus. Rufus gave his new wife a sturdy mare for a wedding present so that Mrs. Drumheller could go down the valley to visit her nephew more easily and set his new cabin to rights.

When Henri told her this news, hoping to rouse some interest, Sophia had shrugged and said she hoped that Patience Drumheller would not pay her a wedding visit at Wildwood. "I can't bear the woman," she insisted. But Sophia couldn't bear anyone. She hated herself because she had sent the children outside. She hated everyone who wasn't Charlotte—even Henri and her other children. Months passed, and she and Caitlin avoided each other. Sophia felt indifference to everything and everyone seeping like cold poison through her heart.

CHAPTER 32

ABIDING SORROW

1772

In the year that followed the kidnapping, word reached the valley of skirmishes and battles over land between the Indians and settlers everywhere. The kidnapping had hardened the settlers' feelings against all Indians, not just toward those who had taken the children. For yet another year, they were afraid to have the Blackberry Picnic, lest they be attacked.

Gideon had set out after the kidnapped children with four horses, one for each child as a ransom, but the horses had slowed him down, and it was some time before he located the party of Creeks who had kidnapped them. He returned to three anxious mothers with only the two youngest, Magdalena and Peach. Cadfael and Charlotte were gone. The Creeks had traded the child with moonlight hair to Cherokee traveling south on the migration trail, and the boy had been taken for adoption by a woman whose sons had all been killed in battles with white soldiers. Venus and her daughters cried and hugged Peach and said she wasn't allowed out of their sight again, ever. Caitlin had fallen in a faint when he'd come back without Cadfael. Sophia, who had clung to the hope Gideon would bring Charlotte, felt like she'd been turned to stone.

Sophia was hollow eyed and sleepless, barely able to go through the motions of life every day. She would stand motionless at her work, forgetting her broom or her cooking until food burned, unable to complete a line of sewing. She was gray at the temples. Kitty took over in the house and weeded the neglected herb garden in tears.

Caitlin and Sophia were separated, not united, in sorrow. They were thankful Magdalena and Peach were back, and even Sophia's all-encompassing hate ebbed for a moment, but both mothers lay wide-eyed and sleepless in their cabins in the night, reliving the afternoon of Malinda's wedding, Caitlin wishing she'd pulled Cadfael back with Annie, Sophia bitterly regretting sending the four children out of the wedding. When they could no longer lie quietly, grief drove them from bed to pace outside on their porches. Their hearts followed their kidnapped children through the dark and down the river, to wherever they might be now, crying for their mothers and home.

Caitlin's face grew lined, her blue eyes faded with grief. Sophia still felt Charlotte's baby weight on her hip as she went about her tasks, the toddler demanding, "Up! Tell story." Sophia heard Charlotte ordering Magdalena about, Sophia's little deputy, repeating what Sophia said.

Stifled with grief, Sophia abandoned her school.

Their husbands and other children suffered. Magdalena, who adored Charlotte, was bereft. She hardly ate and didn't talk much. The chickens made her cry, and Sophia turned the chore of feeding them, cleaning the henhouse, and gathering eggs over to the boys. Kitty watched her mother grow thin and tried to make her eat, covered her shoulders with a shawl when it grew chilly, and cried in secret when Sophia was short-tempered with her. Georgie and Francis grumbled about extra chores, but Kitty shushed them with a new sharpness of misery in her voice.

Henri threw himself into hard work, clearing land and building cabins on the west side of the river until he was almost too tired to row himself back. This time he was driven, determined to finish. He decided to build a jetty on the opposite bank so any purchasers were within rowing distance of the trading post, or if they were of an enterprising frame of mind, they could make a ferry. He longed for France.

At the Vanns', Bryn and Annie understood only that sorrow had settled on their mother's shoulders. She no longer played games with them or laughed or told them stories from the Bible or sang them to sleep. The Vann children grew anxious and uncertain, and Annie cried at nothing.

Venus still had nightmares over Peach's disappearance. Seth was forever checking on his six children, wanting to know where each of them was every minute of the day, insisting they had to stick together, until Polly protested they couldn't get on with their other chores if they had to come running every time Seth called them to be counted. Pearlie, the sassiest of the Hanover girls, chipped in, "Pa, leave us be! Mama gets mad if we don't finish our chores. They's five of us! If they try to get us, we'll screech like Uncle Rufus's geese do. Like this, *sqwawaw-wawk*!" Polly and Pen and Patsy and even Peach joined in the goose noises, drowning out Seth, who shouted at them to be quiet, they made his ears hurt.

"Ain't none of 'em exactly quiet," Venus told him later. "I their mother, and what's a mother gon' do but worry every living minute, but you a man and their pa, and you got to stop worryin' and think a something sensible. They all together is worse than geese. I know, been listenin' to 'em ever since they draw breath. And they loud. But if you worried, you get a musket for Polly. She can keep watch. She a good shot, and she got better sense than Patsy, sense enough not to shoot her sisters anyway. Susan a good shot too, but she can't be looking after the others all the time. I need Susan to help me."

After that Polly watched with a flintlock pistol bought from the trading post while Patsy, Pearlie, Pen, and Peach worked. This led to friction—the ones who worked were nervous Polly would shoot them by mistake, and Patsy was cross that she hadn't been given the gun, as she was the eldest. They argued loudly about whether standing guard meant Polly didn't have to work as hard as the others.

Midsummer approached. Saskia was relieved Cully wasn't likely to be kidnapped again. He could take care of himself, despite his limp. He was a tall young man of twenty-three, strong from working in the fields and helping Toby and Rufus and Meshack at the forge. His mixed parentage was obvious—his dark hair was tinged with yellow, and his skin and eyes were light brown. His features were a younger and finer version of fleshy, red-faced Thomas de Bouldin.

Cully was restless.

He would go up to Wildwood often to chop wood, see Kitty, and tease her like he'd always done, but it seemed like the light had gone out of Kitty. Desperate to cheer her up, he asked Meshack to help him make Kitty a present. Meshack thought for a minute, then said girls sewed so they must like sewing boxes. Meshack showed him how to carve it from a nice piece of cedar and how to burn Kitty's name into it with a hot poker. It had sections for Kitty's cotton thread and needles and pins and scissors. Neither Meshack nor Cully knew that Kitty avoided sewing whenever possible.

"Oh, Cully," Kitty exclaimed when he brought it and said he'd made it for her. "How beautiful! It makes me feel . . . so . . . so . . . happy!" She burst into tears, and Cully put his arms round her. Kitty felt his heart beating against hers and stopped crying. Then she lifted her head to smile. "Thank you," she whispered, "for the box."

They looked into each other's eyes, and then Cully kissed her. He'd never done that before. Kitty finally pulled away, feeling there was the possibility of happiness after all. “Oh, Cully,” she whispered. If he’d just kiss her again . . .

Cully put one arm back around her shoulders and pulled her to his side. “It’s a going-away present. I come to tell you I’m goin’ to La Nouvelle-Orléans,” he said.

Kitty’s face fell. “When?”

“Tomorrow morning. Just for a while. Fur traders I’m goin’ with, they say it’s a good place to make money, ’specially for good carpenters. I know what Meshack taught me.”

“But La Nouvelle-Orléans is so far! Will you come back?”

“I’ll come back if I have to swim up the river. Don’t worry none. Mama worried enough for everybody. Promise me you’ll keep her company for me?”

Kitty nodded, too sad to speak.

Cully left the next day with the traders on a flatboat going down to La Nouvelle-Orléans. Kitty waved good-bye and felt completely empty inside. He took the paper certifying Cully Stuart was a free Negro with him. Saskia was terrified he’d be seized as a slave and sold regardless. Cully repeated what the fur traders told him—La Nouvelle-Orléans was full of free blacks and mulattos. Nothing like Virginia. Saskia was dubious. You couldn’t trust what “they” said. She meant white people.

Summer passed, and Cully didn’t come back.

In late September Saskia made what was now for her a laborious climb up through the orchard to visit Sophia, not caring whether Sophia wanted to be visited or not. It would soon be a year since the kidnapping, and Sophia and Caitlin had hardly seen or spoken to each other. Saskia brought her specialty, a basket of beaten biscuits still warm from the oven, buttered, with a little slice of ham inside and covered with a clean white cloth. Sophia exerted herself to make tea, and though she had lost all interest in food, somehow ate six of the biscuits before she realized it.

Saskia didn't talk about Charlotte or the day of Malinda and Jack's wedding. She talked, as she would have done on any visit, about Cully. She allowed to Sophia that much as she loved Cully, she wished he didn't resemble such an evil man as his father.

"Cully has your heart, and that's the part that matters, Saskia," Sophia said. It had been a long time since she'd thought of saying something like that, made an effort for another person.

"Maybe he got some of Nott's heart too, just livin' under the same roof," said Saskia. "I hope so. Nott a good, good man. Wouldn't have had him we hadn't 'scaped with you that time, Miss Sophy. I ain't forgetting that. You helped me have Nott and keep my boy, have my home. You think on that a little, Miss Sophy. When you got time."

Sophia reached out and put her hand on Saskia's.

Saskia sighed. "But Cully, I wish Cully find somebody to marry, build them a cabin. I like to have some grandchildren round me. Nott say they can have that piece of corner land. Has a spring and a shade tree. I keep hopin' maybe a black gal he'll like will come down the river. But Cully, he ain't waitin' for that. Gone off to La Nouvelle-Orléans." Just thinking about Cully made her short of breath, her heart pounding in her chest.

"I know," said Sophia. "I hope he comes home soon."

"With Cully gone, Kitty been a comfort to me," Saskia remarked, and she stood to say good-bye. "Some days I don't see too good. Kitty come every day, help me watch the river, see if he comin' home yet. She a good girl," said Saskia. "Take after her mama. A fine child to have, don't want to forget you have her, and those three other fine children. All need their mama like they always did. Henri too."

Saskia pretended not to see first one tear, then another roll down Sophia's cheeks. It was time she cried, thought Saskia, let the sorrow out before it killed her and everyone around her. She patted Sophia's shoulder and set off home.

The visit to Sophia took its toll. Saskia was exhausted by the time she got home. She was heavier than ever and sometimes breathless and wheezing, with dark circles under her eyes. Nott had made her a rocking chair, and though she had heaved herself up to go and deliver Malinda's baby, that too had tired her badly. Ever since Little Molly's birth, she spent a large part of the day in her chair. She had taken to smoking Nott's pipe while she rocked gently back and forth. She'd positioned her chair just right so she could watch the river and the place where the river trail emerged from the trees south of the landing, to get the first sight of Cully when he came back.

"Maybe he's found him a wife, bringin' her back with him," she told Nott, trying to look on the bright side. "Take time to get everything ready to go."

"Be fine if he did," Nott agreed. "'Specially if it a nice fat wife, like you. Fat women the prettiest." He chuckled.

"Get along, Nott!"

Cully still didn't come back. The leaves were turning, and it was getting cool at night. Saskia sat on her porch with a quilt over her knees. Susan or Kitty or Rhiannon came to the Stuarts' cabin every few days with a pot or a covered plate. "Mama made you this stew," or "I made these apple pies myself, and Mother says we can't eat but so many," or "Got some biscuits and fresh buttermilk here!"

Caitlin came with strawberry leaf tea and was shocked at the state of Saskia's undone washing. She built up the fire, shaved yellow soap into the pot, boiled everything she could get her hands on, and hung it where the autumn sun could dry it. Nott got it down that afternoon when he came from the fields. "Which way you fold this?" he demanded, almost buried under armfuls of dry laundry.

"Put it down, Nott, I do it," said Saskia wearily. She hardly had the strength to lift her arms. Nott went off to milk the cows.

When he came back, Saskia was slumped across the laundry. "Saskia?" Nott pulled the laundry away and shook her shoulder, gently at first, then harder and harder. There was no response. "You just sleepin', you got to wake up now!" he begged. "Saskia, wake up. Say you ain't died on me, Saskia! Say you ain't died on me," he cried frantically over and over, until it sank in that Saskia wouldn't wake up again. He slumped to his knees beside the rocking chair. "You die, what I do now? What I do, Saskia?" He was still kneeling with his arms around Saskia's shoulders, wailing Saskia's name, when Susan came with some bean soup.

"Oh no! No," she cried. "Oh, Nott! I'll get Ma and Caitlin. Oh, poor Cully! Not even here!" Susan ran off into the dusk.

Finally Nott heard the women coming and wiped his eyes with his sleeve. "Gettin' dark, Saskia. Gettin' dark."

First thing the next day, Meshack brushed his clothes, put on his hat, and found Brother Merriman working in the patch of land Henri had sold him. "We needs a funeral. Saskia's dead."

Cotton Mather Merriman straightened up and removed his hat. "I'm grieved to hear that all Saskia's earthly labor is over," he said, resting on his shovel. He had never conducted a funeral, and he tried to think what must be done. His time at Yale had consisted of much Bible study, divinity, Latin, and Hebrew but had not prepared him in any practical way to comfort a distressed old man with grief etched deep in his face.

"Don't want no talk of sinners and hellfire neither."

Brother Merriman was acquiring sense. Slowly perhaps, but still, good sense is welcome however it arrives. In his case, Saskia had given good sense a helping hand. Brother Merriman's sermons had been so grim and gloomy that people got tired of listening. Everyone but Patience Drumheller avoided him. Finally Saskia had told the despondent, lonely young man, "Can catch more flies with honey than you do with vinegar. You got any honey to sweeten up those sermons?"

Brother Merriman thought a minute. "No," he said sadly, "just a Bible. And a *Bay Psalm Book*."

"What's that?"

"A hymn book, for singing the psalms. No music, mind you, nothing ungodly like that. Just singing."

"Humph! You a singing man?"

"Not by myself. But my sister used to sing with me, and—"

"You get a girl to sing with you, and you sing, people might listen. Then you can go on preachin', but not too much. Got to know when to stop."

Saskia had walked off, and later asked Kitty and Rhiannon and Susan and her sisters if they'd help Brother Merriman, but they snickered and refused. The only girl to greet the idea with any enthusiasm was the boatman's niece, Mattie, when her uncle's riverboat happened to be stopping at the trading post.

So with a little practice, Mattie and Brother Merriman sang psalms on the landing on Sundays whenever Mattie's uncle happened to be passing. At first Caitlin was the only one to join in, singing in harmony, but gradually the others did as well. It was a novelty and, to Caitlin at least, a comfort. Brother Merriman and Mattie would lead the singing, Brother Merriman calling out a line and everyone singing it back. There would be an interval in the middle while he preached a short sermon before ending with more singing. It was something to do.

Brother Merriman grew cautiously hopeful that there were souls that could yet be snatched from the hellfire.

Now when Meshack told him there would be no mention of hellfire at the funeral, Brother Merriman nodded in agreement. "No, not for Saskia."

He thought back to the funerals of his younger days and what was wanted. "There must be psalms," he said out loud, "and a procession to the grave. A eulogy, where we remember Saskia's good works. Hymns, Saskia liked the singing. And a meal afterward. Come in, and we'll discuss how it should be." He indicated his cabin. "We'll need a coffin," he was saying as he led Meshack inside.

"Can do that," said Meshack, his voice heavy with sorrow. "I can do that."

Meshack worked all night by candlelight and pine knots and, by next morning, had a fine cedar coffin ready. A tearful Nott came to help him carry it back to Nott's cabin, where Saskia had been laid out on the oak table Cully had made for her. Venus and Caitlin had washed the body, dressed Saskia, and wrapped her in her best shawl. They and Rhiannon and Kitty and Susan and Malinda had watched all night by Saskia's side.

At Wildwood, Kitty had told her mother. When Sophia looked at her with her usual uncomprehending gaze, Kitty shrieked, "Saskia's dead, Mother. Dead! Dead! Dead! And it seems you are too!"

Henri had shaken Kitty hard and told her to stop, but Kitty shrieked on until her father dragged her out of the house to scream in the orchard.

Sophia was staring into the fire when Henri and Kitty went to bed. At dawn Sophia had wound herself very tightly in her shawl, as if it would hold her together, and come down to the Stuarts' cabin with a pan of beaten biscuits with ham. Sophia had used up all her wheat flour and pounded and pounded the biscuit dough hard as she could, far past the point even beaten biscuit required, until woken by the noise, Henri came in and took the mallet out of her hands and she had sobbed in his arms.

Midmorning at Nott and Saskia's, Meshack put a hand on Nott's shoulder. "Nott. It's time."

"I know." Nott's eyes were red. "I just hopin' maybe . . ."

"Cully not back today, Nott," said Meshack. "I know that what you waitin' for, but the boy be back when he back. He can't know."

"It would grieve Saskia he ain't here," said Nott. "She doted on that boy." But he finally nodded, and Henri, Rufus, Seth, and Toby counted to three and picked up the coffin. They took a minute to settle it on their shoulders and made their way out of the house, maneuvering carefully through the doorway then past Saskia's empty rocking chair on the porch and down the porch steps.

Brother Merriman, clutching his Bible, led the way. Outside it was a beautiful day, the sun shining, with a crisp, cool breeze, but the sun was hot, and there was the usual glorious display of fall leaves. It struck everyone as incongruous, but they were glad of the hot sun on their shoulders. Everyone walked quietly behind the coffin as they made their way to the grave Toby and Jack had dug in the cemetery below the orchard. Instead of a single eulogy, one by one the women whose children Saskia had delivered gave her thanks, except for Malinda, who kissed her hand and laid it on the coffin. Then all the children who had drawn their first breath in Saskia's hands copied Malinda, with Malinda helping Little Molly touch her chubby hand to her lips and pat the coffin.

The coffin was lowered into the ground, and Brother Merriman was drawing breath to launch into one of his lengthy sermon prayers when Caitlin nudged him. "Don't. Just don't. Proverbs thirty-one," she whispered. "Just read that. Nothing else." Brother Merriman opened his Bible to Proverbs:

> *Who can find a virtuous woman? for her price is far above rubies.*
> *The heart of her husband doth safely trust in her, so that he shall have no need of spoil.*
> *She will do him good and not evil all the days of her life . . .*

"That Saskia," said Nott. There was a murmur of agreement that it was.

Her husband is known in the gates, when he sitteth among the elders of the land . . .

"He is for sure," said Meshack, "for sure." He put an arm around Nott's shoulders.

She openeth her mouth with wisdom; and in her tongue is the law of kindness . . .
Her children arise up, and call her blessed; her husband also, and he praiseth her.
Many daughters have done virtuously, but thou excellest them all.
Favour is deceitful, and beauty is vain: but a woman that feareth the Lord, she shall be praised.
Give her of the fruit of her hands; and let her own works praise her in the gates.

It all sounded so like Saskia that for a moment it was as if she were there with them.

"Rest in peace. Amen," murmured Sophia, then Caitlin, then the rest echoed it. "Amen."

Brother Merriman allowed a moment's silence, and everyone present looked toward the river, in case Cully was coming at last.

Finally Brother Merriman signaled to Jack and Toby to start shoveling earth. The first shovelful landed on the coffin with a thud, and Nott fell to his knees with a howl of grief as Meshack, Venus, Seth, and their girls closed in a circle round him, trying to lift him up as he continued to sob until the burial was done.

No one wanted to sing.

"Come on now, Nott," said Venus. "We go eat a little somethin'. She wouldn't like it you hungry."

Patience Drumheller had unexpectedly taken the lead in the matter of the funeral feast at their cabin. Caitlin admitted that for once the woman's bustle proved useful. Malinda helped her set out plates of cold meat, hot corn bread, and baked apples while Kitty and Susan looked after Little Molly and the younger children. Meshack brought a jug of his whiskey, though on this occasion it had no uplifting effect.

By the time they left the Drumhellers', many eyes were still red. Outside the afternoon had turned gray and raw, and the brightly colored leaves looked duller. A subdued Susan, Kitty, and Rhiannon were the last to leave, after helping Patience and Malinda put the kitchen to rights. Going across the valley in the dusk, Susan burst out, "I wish Cully hadn't gone away! Cully should have been here!"

"Yes," said Rhiannon. "Saskia was always wishing Cully was home."

There was a sharp intake of breath from Kitty. "I wish Cully was home too," she said passionately. "I wish it with all my heart!"

Susan turned her head to look at Kitty, surprised at the tone. "What a terrible day," said Kitty dejectedly.

The three walked in silence until Kitty changed the subject.

"Rhiannon, I heard that someone left a deer carcass at your door, that your mother woke up first and found it. Papa says it means a brave wants to marry you. Are you getting married to a brave?"

"Married!" exclaimed Susan.

"I don't know," said Rhiannon, kicking at leaves. "Mother was angry about the deer. I think Father had left one at her door before they were married." She sighed. "Mother never used to get angry, but after Cadfael . . ."

Kitty sighed too. She had been relieved to see her mother moving about, exerting herself to make ham biscuits. Trying. Now Kitty permitted herself to feel angry with Sophia. "I miss Charlotte too, so do

Magdalena and the boys, but Mother forgot she has other children," she said bitterly. "I kept trying to make Mother remember, trying to be as good as possible, but I told Saskia I couldn't. I think it was Saskia who made her remember."

"Perhaps Saskia could have made our mothers friends again," said Rhiannon tentatively.

"Oh, Rhiannon!" said Kitty sadly. "If only she had!"

CHAPTER 33
TO QUICKEN THE FALTERING SPIRIT

1773

Sophia began to grasp at little things after Saskia's death, began to try. By the fire at night, she resumed teaching Magdalena and the boys, while Kitty read to herself if there was any scrap of anything to read. Henri would take up his pipe of tobacco and share any interesting news: whether anything had been heard of Cully, that he had spotted an eagle, how well the new crops were doing, or that Rufus had killed another nest of rattlesnakes next to the forge. Sophia would show some interest, ask questions, nod at the answers, but all this effort tired her, and sometimes, five minutes later, she forgot what Henri had said.

Henri thought it was as if Sophia was waking from a sleep, and he found it necessary to repeat things that he had told her before, such as the fact that he had finally completed his homesteads. He had cleared and fenced in pastures and marked out fields and built two cabins, one large of four rooms and one small of two. Now he needed buyers.

"Oh. Yes. Someone's bound to come."

Sophia was rousing herself more and more, listening again, and he talked to her at length. Lately his talk had been of the Vanns. "A bear carcass was left at Gideon's door last week. Rhiannon has a suitor." If anything was likely to arouse Sophia's interest, it would be that, he thought.

Kitty put down a half-sheet of the *Virginia Gazette*.

"What?" Sophia did look up at this. "No! She's Kitty's age."

"Eighteen," said Kitty loudly. "Almost. If anyone can be troubled to remember."

"I remember when she was born just before you," sighed Sophia. "How did she become acquainted with the brave who left it?" *And what does Caitlin make of this news?* she wondered, but didn't ask.

"Gideon was trying to prevent a war," Henri began.

"He has so far," Kitty interjected, "and Rhiannon was helping."

"Hush, Kitty, your mother asked when Rhiannon met the brave."

"Oh, *that* was before Saskia died," said Kitty.

"You knew?" demanded Sophia. "And you didn't mention it?"

"Of course I *mentioned* it, Mother," said Kitty, rolling her eyes.

There had been no point mentioning anything to her mother for a very long time. Sophia had taken no interest in anything.

"His name is Two Bears."

"Two Bears?"

"Mother! I told you but you took no notice!"

Kitty's tone irritated Sophia. To be irritated was a distraction from sorrow. Sophia wondered what else had happened without her noticing in the preceding months. "Kindly tell me again, Kitty!"

"You remember, Mother, when Indians stole two cows and some chickens from Seth? A horse went missing from our barn, and Rufus's geese were disappearing? Meshack's still was raided, and two barrels of his whiskey stolen? Brother Merriman's new cabin at the end of the valley was burned to the ground and he said it was Indians? No? Never mind . . ."

"Oh . . . did it? Poor man," said Sophia without much conviction.

"He's nicer than he used to be, Mother. I think it's because of the boatman's niece."

"Who?"

"Mattie. Her name is Mattie. I knew she liked Brother Merriman, because she helps him with his singing, and you'd think Brother Merriman would notice the way she looks at him and fall in love, but he's always being, I don't know, parson-like, as if he never thought at all about getting married or fornica—"

"What?"

"So Susan and I . . . helped him along."

"Did you indeed?" Sophia's eyes were focused on Kitty for the first time in ages. "Pray, *how* did the two of you do that?"

"Last time she came through with her aunt and uncle, Susan and I braided her hair nicely, and we lent her some ribbons, and I had some lavender water you'd made."

Sophia had made lavender water as usual, mindlessly, after Charlotte was gone.

"Susan and I doused Mattie with it and dragged her on a walk to where we knew Brother Merriman was working in his cornfield. And," Kitty paused.

"And then what?" Sophia asked suspiciously, suddenly alert for whatever mischief Kitty and Susan might have conceived.

"Oh, we just happened to walk past. We had planned it out and dared Mattie to faint so Brother Merriman would rush over and carry her to the shade and see how nice she looked and finally fall in love. But then when we got there in sight of Brother Merriman, Mattie didn't want to faint, so . . ."

"So you and Susan . . . ?"

"It was really Susan's idea, Mother. Mattie's getting older, and we had to do *something*. She's dreadfully afraid of spiders. So Susan had said in case Mattie was shy about fainting—she is *quite* shy, Mother—Susan had secretly caught a lot of spiders in her handkerchief and quick as anything dropped them down the neck of Mattie's dress. Of course Mattie screamed and screamed and tore her bodice open to get the spiders out, and Brother Merriman heard and came running to see what was the matter. Susan and I screamed and screamed too, that Mattie was having one of her turns and needed to be held down in the shade till it passed, or otherwise she'd tear all her clothes off. Brother Merriman picked Mattie up and obligingly carried her under a tree, which was hard work because Mattie was kicking and screaming, and he was holding her down when Susan and I ran away."

Kitty saw the look on her mother's face. "But it turned out well, Mother. Mattie and Brother Merriman are engaged now. Mattie's gone back with her aunt and uncle to get her wedding clothes."

"Let us return to Rhiannon's brave. Two Feet?"

"Two *Bears*, Mother." Kitty tried hard not to grind her teeth.

Henri took up the story as Gideon had told it to him. "It was Rufus's fault. With all the other trouble about the stolen horse and the whiskey and so on, Rufus was angry. He began patrolling the salt marsh, dousing the fires the squaws had made to boil the water. He broke their pots, and whenever he saw a woman, he would lash out with his whip. But they kept coming back, and Rufus had no qualms about firing his musket to scare them off, even when women had their children along. And then he killed one of the squaws."

Sophia gasped. "Oh no!"

Henri continued with his story. Rufus claimed to Gideon that he only fired over their heads, but muskets were unreliable. He had hit and killed a young woman and wounded the baby on her back. From the landing Gideon heard shots in the salt marsh and thought sure that Rufus had fired at Indians making salt. He found Rufus standing over the body of a young woman about seventeen, her long black braid soaked in blood and half her face gone. When he saw Gideon coming, Rufus unstrapped the bark papoose with a baby from her back before it drowned in the marsh. Gideon thought the baby was dead too, but it choked and began to wail. It had been grazed by the bullet.

Gideon was furious. He recognized the woman, Bright Star, a shaman's daughter. Gideon had attended her wedding feast two years ago. He thought Rufus would have left the baby to die if he hadn't come. Gideon warned Rufus that now Jack and Malinda and Little Molly, might be killed in revenge. Rufus swore the savages shouldn't have what was his and he'd like to kill them all.

Gideon told him it was likely to be the other way around. Rufus finally agreed to let the Indian women make salt, but Gideon told him the damage had been done.

Gideon took pots and knives and axes from the trading post storeroom when he rode back with the body of the young woman. Rhiannon went with him, the baby in its sling on her back. Caitlin had doctored and bandaged the baby as best she could, but Rhiannon was already on her horse when Caitlin learned Gideon intended to take their daughter to return Bright Star's body and the baby.

"Not Rhiannon! Oh, Gideon, they'll keep her! No! I can't lose her too! I'll go with you." Caitlin had been wild.

"Caitlin, Singing Wind must go with me. It's the only way I can prevent something worse happening to everyone," said Gideon, and Henri had seen Caitlin sobbing and screaming, running after them as they rode away.

When Gideon and Rhiannon reached their destination two valleys to the east, he delivered the young woman's body. He gave the baby to its wailing grandmother. Bright Star's husband wanted to burn the settlement to avenge her. The shaman prevented him, saying they would have a life for a life but must consider how this should be done, whether Rufus or one of his sons should be killed. Gideon and

Rhiannon stayed for the period of mourning and waited for the shaman's decision. Gideon knew any negotiations to save the Drumhellers could not be rushed.

In the days of negotiations that followed, the council discussed whether any restitution could be made or whether only another death would avenge Bright Star.

Gideon negotiated patiently, trying to restore relations between the Indians and the settlers. It was nearing the time for the corn harvest, and the tribe was less interested in war for the moment. Gideon said his own son had been abducted, along with the daughter of another white settler. The council heard him out, then pointed out they had already helped Gideon recover the other two children that had been taken. Gideon reminded them that there were two more children who had never been recovered, one of them his own son.

In the course of the negotiations, he had become aware that a tall young brave named Two Bears from the Paint Clan was eyeing Rhiannon. Rhiannon was studiously taking no notice of him, which of course meant she was very aware of his presence whenever he was near.

Rhiannon spent time with the grandmothers, who at first treated her roughly. But Gideon told them about the catfish and the dreams, and they recalled Gideon's mother, a beloved woman, and began to look at Rhiannon with interest. Her gravity and respect pleased them. Though she had no clan, they began to refer to her by her Cherokee name, Singing Wind. Two Bears's grandmother was one of the council that decided that to avenge Bright Star, Rhiannon must remain with them.

Gideon said that would depend on whether, as his mother's granddaughter, she could be adopted into a clan, but this required discussion and consideration and would not happen soon. Meanwhile they would go home.

It was following their return home that the first deer carcass had been left at the Vanns' door, and the message was unmistakable. Two Bears wanted to marry Rhiannon. Caitlin was beside herself. Gideon tried to explain that he had taken Rhiannon with him because he had believed that if the grandmothers accepted her for Gideon's mother's sake, there would be no blood revenge for the murder of Shining Star.

"And now," Henri finished the story, "Caitlin is furious with Gideon, furious with Rufus, who caused the crisis, furious with Rhiannon, who insists on being called Singing Wind and won't answer if Caitlin calls her Rhiannon, and more than anyone is furious with Two Bears."

"Of course she is," said Sophia, thinking, *Poor Caitlin.*

"Caitlin was sixteen when she married Gideon," Henri said.

"Yes," said Sophia. "I remember." How happy Caitlin had been then.

"You should visit her, Sophy. Caitlin's in trouble. You haven't been down to the trading post since Saskia's funeral."

"No . . . I . . . I've just had work to do here, Henri. I've no time to go gadding about." Sophia had become reluctant to do anything that obliged her to see Caitlin or Venus. She felt raw. A hug from one of them would break her entirely. And Saskia, who would have known if it wasn't a good time to hug, was gone.

"Sophy, you must."

She wanted to refuse but knew he was right. She thought of Lady Burnham and realized she hadn't thought of her godmother in a long time. She was beginning to understand she had thought of very little. It was her duty to visit Caitlin. "It's horrible. It all reminds me of that Greek story, the one about Agamemnon, I think it was, who sacrificed his daughter so the Greeks would have a fair wind to sail away to the Trojan War. Yes, I'll go tomorrow." She tried to remember the blood-soaked story. Hadn't Agamemnon's wife, Clytemnestra, avenged her daughter by killing Agamemnon when he returned from Troy? She understood that.

"Good, because there's more news and another reason you should go to the trading post to see Caitlin. Some people have come up from La Nouvelle-Orléans on the trail," said Henri.

"Only hunters or buffalo skinners or one of those packhorse caravans, I suppose."

"No, a man and a woman and a child."

"Oh. How pleasant it would be to meet travelers who don't chew tobacco and spit on the floor, for a change," murmured Sophia. "Are they French? Or Spanish?" she asked, trying to take an interest.

"No, I don't think so. You'll see them tomorrow if you go. It's a man and a younger woman with a child. His widowed daughter. They want a homestead and say they have Spanish dollars." He rubbed his hands excitedly. "I told them I've some cleared land with a cabin I'm willing to sell, and the man wants to see it. I think they are happy to find cleared land. Neither of them looks like they know which end of an axe to hold, much less how to fell trees or build a cabin.

"I'll take them across the river on Gideon's ferry to see it, but it might help persuade them if you and Caitlin were friends with the woman. I'm curious to know what you make of them. I think they might be Gypsies."

"Gypsies!"

"The man said *Gitanos*. That's Spanish for *Gypsies*. They've come from La Nouvelle-Orléans, and it's Spanish now, remember?"

This roused Sophia's interest enough for her to say, "I'd like to meet them. I went off with Gypsies once."

"You, Mother?" exclaimed Kitty.

"Mmm, yes. In Spain. I remember dancing in a tavern to music, and everyone was clapping. I'm ashamed to say I bit the footman who came looking for me, and he told me later the Gypsies were picking pockets while I was dancing on a table."

Kitty looked so shocked that it lifted Sophia's spirits enough to say, "I'll visit Caitlin tomorrow. I need thread."

The next afternoon when Sophia pushed open the door of the trading post, Caitlin was wrapped in an apron, scrubbing shelves in her storeroom. "Caitlin? I . . . I needed . . . thread," Sophia said as if were hard to remember what thread was. She was shaking.

"Sophy! In all the world!" Caitlin exclaimed. She wiped her hands on her apron and welcomed Sophia with a cautious hug. After she found the reel of thread Sophia wanted, the two women walked into Caitlin's kitchen as they had done so many times before. Settled at the table, they avoided looking into each other's eyes, each fearing to see her own grief in the mirror of the other's eyes in an infinite reflection of the loss of their children. They discussed the weather, the crops, the tea, and finally the newcomers.

Caitlin had seen them before any of the other settlers.

Just after dawn Caitlin had been fetching buttermilk from her springhouse for breakfast when she saw that strangers had come in the night. A closed wooden carriage on red wheels, painted in a bright design of birds and flowers, stood on the riverbank not far from the trading post. She saw mules and four horses had been tethered to graze nearby, then a man appeared and led them to the river to drink. Afterward he fed them and built a fire. A young woman emerged with a pot and a tripod and began to prepare their breakfast.

Later that morning, the young woman came into the trading post. She had bought meal and eggs and salt meat and even buttermilk, since Caitlin had some to spare. She had paid with a Spanish dollar, and when Caitlin protested it was too much for what she had bought and she had nothing in the way of change, the young woman said that it didn't matter, that she would buy whatever she needed until the dollar was used up. Caitlin had never had a Spanish dollar, and the newcomer was strange in her looks in a way but interesting too. Caitlin asked her to have some tea, and the woman had smiled and happily accepted.

"Henri said she's a Gypsy. How intriguing! What's she like?" asked Sophia.

"Oh, Sophy, I don't know. I've seen nothing like her in all the world. I'll ask her to come have tea, and you can see for yourself." And before Sophia could protest she didn't want to meet anyone, Caitlin was out the door and calling. "Rosalia? Rosalia?" Sophia was preparing to slip away when Caitlin was back with a young woman holding the hand of a little girl.

Sophia had expected a woman like those she saw heading west with their husbands on the flatboats, but the young woman before her was nothing like that. She was a creature of sound and vivid colors. She was very beautiful, slender, and olive skinned. Her eyes were dark, not black but dark blue, with sweeping lashes and heavy brows. She had a mass of curling dark hair wrapped in a curiously patterned silk scarf, coiled round and round her head, an arrangement that set off her long graceful neck and her strong profile. She wore embroidered skirts, a blue blouse, many bracelets on each arm, rings on all her fingers, and little gold wires, strung with bells, round her ankles. The bells and the bracelets jingled as she walked.

Caitlin said, "Rosalia Chiaramonte and Stefania." Mother and daughter had the same tentative smile.

"Stefania, what a pretty name," said Sophia.

In the days that followed, the man exercised their horses and Rosalia went about her daily tasks. She fascinated men and women alike. Walking, bending over her campfire to stir a pot, carrying her laundry to the river, her comings and goings were accompanied by a musical jingling sound and a faint swaying of her hips. And Stefania was a source of wonder to Annie and the Hanover girls. A rather exotic child, she had her mother's olive skin and dark curly hair, the same dark-blue eyes fringed with long lashes. She wore a short embroidered dress and little gold rings in her ears and conversed in a language no one else could understand, though Henri thought it was an Italian dialect.

Rosalia's father was considerably older, with silver hair, a face turned almost black by the sun, and a hardy, weathered look. His attire was as exotic as his daughter's. He had baggy breeches, over which he wore knee-high leather boots that might once have been scarlet or purple, a dark shirt, a cap with a silken tassel, and a waistcoat embroidered with a large-headed bird of many colors. He would point to the bird on his chest, nod, and flash strong white teeth in a smile and say, "Kingfisher! Good fortune, no?"

Thus Tamás Morgades came to be known as the Kingfisher, and his widowed daughter Rosalia Chiaramonte as the Kingfisher's daughter. They had come from La Nouvelle-Orléans, traveling up the Mississippi to the Tinassi, and from there up the river to the Bowjay Valley. They said they were traveling entertainers, that Tamás was a musician and Rosalia danced. They were tired of traveling and looking for a place to settle, for the child.

Rosalia seemed anxious to make friends, as much for Stefania as for herself, and was always willing to pause and chat if Caitlin wasn't too busy. She found an excuse to go to the trading post every day, where Stefania was gradually coaxed to play by four-year-old Annie Vann. Rosalia explained to Caitlin that wherever there were people to be an audience, they would stop and perform, but there had been fewer and fewer settlements along the Mississippi, almost none at all on the Tinassi. Caitlin said shyly that she had danced reels to her father's violin, and she couldn't help wondering what a dancing woman alone might do, without a partner. "Like this," said Rosalia, throwing up her arms and beginning to stamp her feet. She suddenly seemed taller and full of authority.

"I never in all the world!" exclaimed Caitlin as Rosalia whirled to a stop. "I wish Sophy and Venus could see you!"

"If you permit me, I will dance for the women—but only the women—in your storeroom, where the men cannot spy on us."

It was arranged for the next day, and Caitlin sent Annie off to tell Venus and Patience Drumheller and Malinda, while Caitlin put on her sunbonnet and went up through the orchard to invite Sophia. She was happy to have an invitation to deliver as an excuse. They had been like sisters until the last two years and sorrow had driven them apart. Caitlin longed to heal the rift.

To make her peace with both Sophia and Gideon was now everything to Caitlin. Gideon had finally told her that he believed Cadfael and Charlotte were alive, and the chances of getting them back depended on keeping good relations with the Indians. He hadn't wanted to tell her when she was raw with grief after Cadfael was taken, and Gideon warned her against telling Sophia now, until he knew more. Heartened by this news, Caitlin was trying to reconcile herself to Rhiannon voluntarily going to live with the tribe two valleys away. "Not forever," Gideon said patiently over and over, "but just for a time, to learn."

Caitlin didn't like it, but she wasn't made for dissention in her family, and her strong-minded daughter was determined to go. But there was the worrying matter of Two Bears. Rhiannon actually seemed to like him! Caitlin looked forward to being able to confide in Sophia again and ask what she ought to do. It was a comforting prospect, like old times when Rhiannon and Kitty were small and they could discuss how to deal with croup and teething.

CHAPTER 34

A NEW FRIEND

Spring 1773

The next afternoon the women gathered in the storeroom, all thinking guiltily of the chores that were being left undone, but curious. Rhiannon, Kitty, and Susan had been admitted on the understanding there would be no silliness. The younger children, including Stefania, who liked Annie enough to be lured away from her mother, were led off to be amused by Henri in his best Pied Piper mode. He had a supply of sorghum taffy that Caitlin made for the trading post and would take the children fishing. Only Little Molly, not yet walking, was allowed to stay, sitting on Malinda's lap. Space had been cleared in the center of the room. Rosalia didn't appear at first, but beyond the door there were sounds of a swish of skirts, then a jingle of bells, then, louder, something snapping an irregular staccato beat. Speaking over these sounds, Rosalia entered, explaining that normally her father would play his accordion or violin to attract attention—snap, snap, snap-snap-snap went the clicking thing in her hand—but today—snap, snap, snap—she would just stamp the rhythm with her feet. There was a crescendo of snapping, a whirl, and she stopped. The silence felt abrupt and startling.

Rosalia began to saunter in a circle round the room. When people were drawn by the Kingfisher's music, Rosalia said, she would promise to dance once enough coins had been thrown into the small brass pot at his feet. Until then, she said, she would pace, back and forth in front of him. Like this. The staccato clicking began again, and Rosalia began to walk up and down the storeroom, hips swaying, shoulders twisting, slowly untying the scarf while casting glances over her shoulder until she could shake her long mass of dark curls free. Flashing a look at her audience, she lifted her chin and cried, *"Taliari!"* The meaning was clear: "Behold!"

She struck a pose with her arms just a little behind her, and whatever she held in her hands began to clack-clack a new rhythm in time with her feet.

"Brazen!" exclaimed Patience Drumheller. "Dancing like a temptress . . . the Devil's lure . . . Not fit for pure young girls to be watching . . . If Brother Merriman knew, he'd . . ."

Venus, who had never taken to the second Mrs. Drumheller, told her to be quiet.

All the other women were fascinated, and wild horses couldn't have dragged the pure young girls away. Kitty, Rhiannon, and Susan watched openmouthed as Rosalia began to dance, slowly at first, then faster and harder. Gradually Rosalia's presence filled the room, casting a spell over all the women. She danced with her whole body, her posture erect, her arms graceful and decisive, her thrown-back head and her neck arched, her eyes blazing, and her feet striking the wooden floor with force in counterpoint to the now incessant, insistent clacking noise.

This was no minuet or quadrille or allemande, dances of grace and order, pretty steps, and swaying skirt. This was dancing to command life and death, thought Sophia, the war dance of a woman going into battle against grief and suffering and betrayal. Clytemnestra dancing over Agamemnon's body because he had killed her daughter. Watching, Sophia felt something like courage restored to her heart. She glanced at Caitlin and saw Caitlin felt the same.

When Rosalia had danced herself breathless, she finally stopped, leaving her audience under a spell. It was the most interesting thing any of them had ever seen. Sophia herself thanked Rosalia. "I hope one of the homesteads pleases you and your father," she said.

"If he takes it, I hope you will bring your little girl and visit us," Rosalia replied.

"Yes, of course," exclaimed Sophia, who had not wanted to visit anyone for a long time.

In the week that followed, Henri rowed the Kingfisher and his daughter across the river to show them the land he had cleared. The Kingfisher seemed reluctant at first, but finally chose the larger of the two cabins and then haggled so cleverly over the price that, before he realized it, Henri had agreed to build a springhouse and to throw two chickens and a young heifer into the bargain. But Henri's dismay at being outnegotiated was outweighed by the fact the Kingfisher had Spanish dollars to pay for the land. And Sophia and Magdalena seemed to like Rosalia. Both talked of nothing else.

The Kingfisher managed to get his painted wooden carriage across the river on Gideon's ferry, and Gideon was impressed that Tamás had coaxed the mules and horses into the water with him to swim across.

"The horses and mules, they like me." The Kingfisher flashed one of his white smiles.

While dripping Tamás led the animals to their new pasture, Rosalia set about establishing her little family in their new home. Across the river, Sophia watched from the porch up at Wildwood as the bright flash of Rosalia's dress went in and out of the new cabin. A few days afterward, as Henri was preparing to go to cross the river to mark out a third homestead and site for a cabin, Sophia cried, "Wait, I'll go with you."

"What?"

"It's proper, Henri, to pay the first call on a new neighbor. I shall wait on Rosalia."

Sophia had not "paid a call" let alone so much as thought of "waiting" on anyone since leaving Williamsburg, and she could not account for thinking in such polite terms now. But she put on a fresh cap and took some scraped spice-wood-bark tea, a basket of new eggs, and a pat of butter, and Henri rowed them across the river.

Tamás went off with Henri, saying he might need to buy more land, he hoped to have more horses in time, and Henri could show him what other land he was willing to sell. Rosalia welcomed her first visitor as graciously as if the cabin had been a palace. She made tea, and the two women sat down at a small table with benches on either side. Both sat with the straight backs that said posture had been a part of their training.

There was an exchange of pleasantries, a hope on Sophia's part that Rosalia would find herself happy in her new home. They commented on the fine weather. Rosalia inquired about Sophia's methods of educating her children. They discovered that while Sophia had been fond of painting wildflowers as a girl, Rosalia preferred sketching landscapes.

Sophia was puzzled. This was a different Rosalia from the one who had danced with flashing eyes a few days earlier. It was as if she were taking tea with the Hawkhurst sisters. Sophia, who had not for many years given a moment's thought to whether or not someone was well-bred, thought Rosalia appeared far too well bred for a dancing girl. In fact she appeared to have been brought up in a similar way to Sophia—aside from comparing their girlish sketching, there had been mentions of "my nurse" and music lessons. Rosalia substituted an Italian word, not a Spanish one, when she could not think of the English term. Sophia had not spoken Italian in years, but she found she could manage if the conversation slipped a little way into Italian. There was something friendly in their understanding of each other in this way. They talked easily.

"You are *sympática*," Rosalia sighed.

But what struck Sophia most as they talked lightly of this and that topic was that deep in Rosalia's eyes Sophia saw that Rosalia had a great grief of her own. She supposed it was because she was a widow. But there was an odd sense of kinship.

They were discussing the scenery when Henri and Tamás returned, talking about the fields still for sale. "And tell me, please, are there caves here?" Rosalia asked, turning to the men.

"Are you fond of caves, signora?" said Henri.

"They . . . interest me."

"Yes, there are many."

Rosalia said gravely that caves were a great curiosity.

"Come, I'll show you." Henri led Rosalia to the porch and pointed across the river and up the mountain. "That's our cabin, Wildwood, and then way up and to the right, near the top of the mountain, are some bushes, yes? Behind them you can just see the mouth of the cave, a big, dark hole. It's empty now since it's summer, but bears hibernate there in winter."

"Like guardians," said Rosalia thoughtfully. She gave Henri a dazzling smile. "I would love to see a bear cave. Perhaps"—she turned to Sophia—"you know this cave? I told you, Sophia, about my landscapes. I have not sketched for a while, and a bear cave—what an interesting subject. I would happily spend an afternoon there with my pencil and paper. We could take your Magdalena and Stefania and a picnic?"

"I have much to do at home," Sophia said abruptly, noticing the dazzling smile accorded Henri.

Sophia's sudden coolness was not lost on Rosalia.

Startled, Henri looked from one woman to the other. Sophia a little jealous? He thought that was a good sign.

The tone of Sophia's voice made Rosalia bite her lip and turn away from Henri. She put her hand on Sophia's arm. "I would like to be friends," she said urgently. "I need a friend to advise me. And Stefania, she likes Magdalena. It is lonely for her without other children. Please, let's go to the bear cave, just the four of us . . ."

"Henri seems anxious to show it to you himself," muttered Sophia.

"Sophia, my heart is my husband's whether he is alive or dead."

"Your father said you were a widow."

"Neither Tamás nor I are what we seem," said Rosalia. "Come, let us see the bear cave together, and I will tell you. For the first time I feel safe here and I have something I must do. I will tell you why if you have time. And then I will show you."

Sophia couldn't help herself. Intrigued, she agreed.

As Henri rowed them back across the river, Sophia said, "Tamás is not Rosalia's father."

"Oh?" grunted Henri, pulling at the oars. "Did she tell you?"

"No, I could tell. He is a peasant. She is not. I think Rosalia is . . . like I was."

"When you were what?"

"When I was the Honorable Miss Grafton."

CHAPTER 35

THE GODDESS OF MANY CROWNS

Summer 1773

Sophia had left Kitty to finish the rest of the morning chores. She had risen very early and picked a basket of wild strawberries. She had skimmed off a small pitcher of cream after Kitty milked the cows and baked muffins and boiled eggs in their shells and put the food in a larger basket with a tinderbox and her teapot wrapped in a quilt they could spread on the ground. She told Kitty she and Magdalena were going to show Rosalia the bear cave.

"How pleasant, Mother," said Kitty. It was a hopeful sign that Sophia was bestirring herself. Though Sophia had seemed to be slowly improving since Saskia's funeral, she was taking much more of an interest in life since the dancing woman's arrival.

Henri had rowed across to fetch Rosalia and Stefania, and as the three of them climbed up through the orchard, the two little girls waved happily when they saw each other. Sophia could see that Henri was much taken with beautiful Rosalia but saw no sign that Rosalia was taken with him.

Rosalia too was carrying a large basket. "*Scaccia.* It's a kind of flat bread, with cheese inside. I hope you will like it." Her cheeks were pink from the climb.

Henri reluctantly went off to deal with some fencing and a lost cow, and the two women and their daughters began climbing up a narrow path to the cave. The little girls played hide-and-seek and picked wild-flowers while Sophia and Rosalia put down their baskets and Sophia led Rosalia through the narrow entrance into the cave, pointing out how much bigger it was inside.

"This will do," said Rosalia.

"Do for what?"

"Come back outside. I don't like to leave Stefania for long, and I will tell you my story while we eat. Then you will understand that you need not worry about Henri with me, and that we can be friends."

"How mysterious you are, Rosalia." Sophia spread the quilt and lit a small fire to boil water for tea.

Rosalia sighed and opened her basket. "Where to begin?" she murmured as she prepared bread for the children with tomatoes and salt. "But it will be a relief to speak of it."

"Yes, do," said Sophia, peeling boiled eggs. She found she was really quite interested. And hungry.

"You should know first I am not from Spain but from Sicily, though Sicily is under Spanish control. Tamás is a *Gitano*, a Gypsy. I am not. He is not my father, though I would have been blessed to have such a father instead of my own. I'm here because my dearest husband ordered me to save our child—I was pregnant when I last saw him. I could do nothing to save him too. That is my sorrow. We have come as far as we can, Stefania and I, a hard journey made worse by the baggage of a heavy and grieving heart. In this valley where Tamás has settled us, we have surely reached earth's end, but we are at last in an English colony, and for the first time in years, I feel safe.

"We fled the Inquisition, Stefania and I. Do you know what that is?"

Sophia thought hard, then nodded. "Yes, I remember it from my lessons when I was a schoolgirl."

"In Sicily, the faith is oppressive as the heat of summer, heavy as gilded ceilings in the cathedral, suffocating as incense, as omnipresent as the shrines that line the street and the holy images above the doors to the houses. They say there is no Inquisition in La Nouvelle-Orléans, but it is Spanish now, and who can be certain it will not come?

"In Palermo, in our summer palazzo in the mountains, throughout Sicily, wherever the eyes turn, they see a church, a cathedral, a monastery, a convent, a shrine, a holy image, constant reminders that God hovers, all-seeing and wrathful, to punish the unfaithful, smite the heretics. Here in this English colony, there are no churches or monasteries, no convents, no Jesuits. The air is lighter for it. One can breathe.

"There is an Inquisition prison in Palermo, a fearsome place as forbidding as the frown of God, from which few of those taken through its gates return. They say the walls of the cells are covered with drawings, with names, with pleas to the Virgin and Santa Rosalia. 'Oh, Santa Rosalia, who saved Palermo from the plague in 1624, deliver me from the tortures of this place.' I am tormented thinking my husband, Stefano, must have added his name to the list of prisoners beneath it. I bear the saint's name. I too prayed to Santa Rosalia, but she turned from me, did not answer my supplication. As I will tell you, I sought help elsewhere.

"The settlers here, Caitlin and Venus and the Drumhellers, they are not Catholic, and therefore not Christians at all. The church would call this a heathen land. Here, there are no listening ears, no prying eyes, no whispers, no churches, no shrines, no Inquisition.

Here, I feel the absence of an angry, terrifying God, as if a burden is lifted from my shoulders. Coming from a land where the mountains rise hard and rocky and unforgiving, with steep, narrow roads, rocks, and sheer precipices, I could never have imagined these endless, green, undulating mountains that rise and fall and rise and fall, blue with distance until they disappear into the horizon. They are as infinite as the sea we have crossed, and the sight of them soothes me. For the first time, I believe that I can live content and at peace and raise my child.

"I was married to the man I loved, only slightly against my father's wishes. But when I became pregnant, I believed my father was reconciled at last to my marriage, had forgiven me my love for Stefano, because the Chiaramonte line would bear a shoot. Even though the child would bear Stefano's name, Albanisi—a daughter bears that of her father for life. Married I am still a Chiaramonte, and my father is not a man to concede importance to any name but ours. In his eyes, a daughter of the family belongs to the family always, and his daughter's child would belong to the Chiaramonte, not the Albanisi, who were not even noble. In his eyes our nobility entitles us to everything, whatever the law or reality. To his mind the Chiaramontes are as powerful as they had been in the old days when they vanquished Moors and determined the choice of popes.

"Even though our palaces were crumbling and the rents from the estates were less every year, my father clung to his belief in his right to power and riches and land and influence. This made him ruthless, I knew, but still, he was my father, and he had consented to my marriage, though I saw he was sometimes angry, sometimes envious, that the Albanisi were far wealthier than he. I was in disfavor. Then suddenly he invited us to come to our family's summer palace in the mountains.

"I had persuaded Stefano that we should accept his invitation. On the coast the heat in summer is unbearable, and the coming child was an olive branch. Stefano laughed and agreed that he supposed he could put up with my father's rudeness for the sake of my comfort.

"When we arrived, there was a warm welcome. My old apartments had been freshly painted and filled with silk cushions. There was sweet syrup on glasses of shaved ice from the mountains, my brothers were full of Palermo gossip, and my father managed to be unusually civil to Stefano. For a time it was like the old carefree summers of my childhood.

"Then Stefano agreed to go back to Palermo at the urgent request of my father and brothers to transact some important business. The Albanisi were a merchant class, and Stefano had a gift for this—he is courteous and painstaking, and no detail escapes him. He is liked and respected by the other merchants. When Stefano left, he kissed me and put his hand on my belly, saying good-bye to us both. The child kicked in response, and we laughed, and Stefano set off with his old manservant, Michele, who was complaining bitterly about leaving the mountains.

"One sleepy afternoon the next week, I was resting on the terrace when Michele suddenly appeared in the garden below. He put his finger to his lips, signaling me to say nothing. He had come to tell me Stefano had been arrested in Palermo and taken to the Inquisition prison. There was an accusation of heresy, that the Albanisi were secret Jews. Michele did not know who had denounced Stefano, but I suspected my father at once. It was to oblige him that Stefano had braved the heat of the city. My brothers had let it slip that our father had gambled away yet more of the Chiaramonte land, regretted giving me such a large dowry, that Stefano was wealthy enough to have taken me without it.

"I knew how devious my father was, how unpredictable. As Michele spoke I could see my father was craftily arranging things for his advantage. Though the Inquisition confiscated the property of heretics, my father had connections—if he had denounced Stefano, some of the

Albanisi fortune would come into his hands. I was already back under his roof, and as good as a prisoner. Stefano's child would be his for the taking. A daughter is in the hands of her father and brothers. They would be jailers for me and the baby. And I would never see Stefano again.

"Michele gave me a purse of Neapolitan piastra, saying it was all Stefano had been able to lay hands on before he was taken away. Stefano wished me to leave at once.

"'Leave?' My distress at the news of Stefano's imprisonment was so great I could scarcely breathe. 'I will not abandon him!'

"'It is too dangerous for you to return to the Albanisi palace, even if you were allowed to leave your father's house. My master wishes you to go to America. It is far enough away to be safe. His cousin lives there, in Louisiana. He will care for you and the child. This is the direction, his cousin's house, in La Nouvelle-Orléans.' Michele pressed a folded paper into my hands.

"I protested, but Michele silenced me. 'He says that if God and Santa Rosalia help him escape, he will know where to find you.'

"'But America!'

"'My master said that he knew what your reaction would be, but he begs you will go. It is not safe to remain at your father's. My master cares for nothing but your well-being, lady. He implores you, begs you, commands you, go for his sake. If he is relieved of worry for you, he can concentrate on freeing himself. Go and he will find you. He wished me to say, lady, that you are resourceful and will find the courage to undertake the journey. Grant him the comfort of knowing you and the child are gone. He has little enough comfort.'

"Little enough comfort! I shuddered. His words touched too lightly on hell. Oh, Santa Rosalia . . .

"'God keep your master, Michele. I will do as he wishes.'

"'Then I will return for you later tonight, take a mountain path I know, and at the bottom I will have donkeys and food and a peasant woman's cloak for you for the journey to Palermo. You must take nothing with you that would make them think you had fled. They would follow and soon overtake you. They must believe you met with an accident, lady. Tear a strap on your sandal and leave it by the great ravine below the olive grove. Leave a piece of your gown on the thorns. Women with child are sometimes light-headed—ask your maid if she has a remedy.' Imagining the accident I was to feign, a headlong fall into the deep, rocky chasm, I felt my stomach turn. Was this the fate my father and brothers had in mind for me once the baby was born?

"'Until tonight. God keep you and your child, lady,' he replied, slipping away through the garden.

"I felt as if an earthquake had struck, but shocked and terrified as I was, I knew that if I was to go, I must go at once. By luck, my father and brothers were hunting, spending a few days at the *refugio* in the mountains, killing wolves, boar, and wildcats by day and at night sporting with whatever unfortunate peasant girl had taken their liking.

"It would take half a day for a messenger to reach them with news I had met with an accident, less for them to return. If I left tonight, I had perhaps a day's advantage.

"I thought Michele's plan over. He was right. If my father suspected I had run away, he would announce a large reward to anyone who would bring me back, and I would soon be found and dragged home. But if there had been an accident and I had fallen into the ravine, it was too deep and wild to search easily. Searching would delay them a little longer, but I must find a way to take some of my jewels at least, I must have something to bargain or sell if I was not to starve. The piastra might look like a small fortune to a peasant like Michele, but would they take me to La Nouvelle-Orléans?

"I began to set the scene. I rose from the couch and called to my maid to say that I would walk a little, it was the only thing that eased the cramp in my legs. She said her mother had suffered from the cramp in her pregnancies and that walking and prayers to St. Agatha had been the best means of relieving them. I waved away the offer of her arm, saying I was not yet so large that I was unable to walk through the olive grove. I gave the girl orders to prepare a bath and fresh clothes for my return.

"I hoped these tasks would divert her attention from me, and pretended not to hear her grumbles about the carrying of hot water in this weather.

"Now, Sophia, comes the important part. I walked down to the olive grove, picking a branch laden with young green olives. At the bottom, out of sight of the palace, I went to the place I had found as a child, an entrance to a small cave hidden by myrtle bushes. I had heard the faint drip of water and saw worn, overgrown steps green with moss on the edges that had been cut into the side of the cave. I was thirsty and curious, and I stepped carefully down into the cave, into the silence and damp of an ancient, ruined sanctuary. As my eyes adjusted to the dim light, I saw there was an alabaster basin that held the dripping water, an altar, and on it the fragments of a small statue.

"It was a figure of a woman with heavy waving hair, parted in the middle beneath a distinctive crown. I knew what it was at once. Do you know the story of Demeter and Persephone?"

Sophia nodded. "Of course. The goddess whose daughter was stolen by the god of the underworld."

"Christian though we are in Sicily, every Sicilian knows of Demeter, the Greek goddess of grain and agriculture, mother of Persephone, whom we call Kore. When the Greeks conquered Sicily, Demeter's cult was powerful there. The old beliefs still linger among the peasants, that Demeter's grief for her abducted daughter brought winter, that her joy when Kore was restored to her for six months brought the spring and summer and renewed life to the dark earth. Demeter, the Goddess of

Many Crowns, the people called her. Protector of life. And she is those things, just as she ever was.

"Greeks and the Romans built as many temples and shrines to Demeter and Kore in Sicily as there are now churches and shrines and altars to Our Lady and the saints. There are still small shrines and sanctuaries in out-of-the-way places, and after I found it, I visited often. I prayed to Demeter as a child, daring in my heresy, and I turned to her in her sanctuary now in desperation. I sensed the little shrine was there because many women in trouble must have been there before me."

How odd, Sophia thought, *to meet someone who speaks of Greek myth as if it is real.* "But go on, Rosalia."

"This time it was harder to manage the narrow steps, but I did. I took a sip of water from the spring, then took from their hiding place behind the crumbling altar the four little terracotta votive figures I had discovered there in an alcove.

"Unlike the statue of Demeter, they were almost intact. One carried a blossom, one a vase, one a torch, and one a small pig whose hind legs had broken off. I set them on the altar, knelt, and placed the olive branch before them as an offering. The Virgin, the saints of the church to whom I had prayed and prayed, had not answered my prayers for my husband. So I sought Demeter's help and pleaded, 'I, who will be a mother soon, beseech your aid. Help me, great Demeter, Goddess of Many Crowns, who sought her child in hell. As you succeeded in bringing her from the embrace of Hades, help me to save my child. Help me, oh, Kore, who returns each year to make your mother and the earth rejoice. And help Stefano, her father.'

"The figures' blank eyes stared past mine. The sound of the water's steady drip, drip in the silence held me in the goddess's presence, as if she listened. I prayed again, reminding the goddess of her ancient greatness and implored her to waken and use her power again for Stefano, our child, and me. Stefano had ordered me to leave Sicily and undertake a dangerous journey to a place I did not know. What must I do?

"I closed my eyes and concentrated on the sound of water dripping into the ancient basin. I waited. Then, in the sound of the water, the goddess spoke. She bid me go and take the votive figures with me. The journey was dangerous and long, but they would protect me. When I reached the journey's end, I must find a safe place for them and dedicate it as a sanctuary to the eternal Demeter and her beloved daughter.

"'I thank you and I obey,' I answered, and carefully wrapped the figures in a fold of my skirt, which I then held bunched up the way one keeps a hem out of the dust. *If one of the servants sees me, that is how it will appear.* It was necessary to remember always there are watching eyes. I climbed out of the cave and back up to the palace, holding the figures carefully.

"Back in my room, with the shadows lengthening across the garden, I wrapped each figure in a scarf and made a bundle that was padded with another so they would not break even if I fell. I put the bundle under my pillow as the maid came with my bathwater and rose petals to scent it.

"After my bath I asked her to fasten the straps on my most delicate sandals of kid with thin jeweled straps. I laughed that I could no longer bend over enough to do it. While she did it, I sat at my dressing table, playing with my rings. I held up my bedecked hands, saying some rings fit, pointing out others that would not slide over my swollen fingers. I told her I wished to rest quietly in bed all the following day, if I could do so without the cramp, and I would permit her a holiday to visit her sister in the next village. She was dubious about leaving me, but I urged her to go at once, as soon as she had brought my supper, so that she could reach the village before dark. I had a fancy for fruit and almond cakes and perhaps a glass of sweet wine. Especially the wine, even though it made me dizzy. She was to bring me a large glass.

"The girl obeyed, quickly brought back a little bread and oil, cheese, grapes, and a plate of almond pastries, along with a goblet of strong dark-gold wine. She murmured that I should take care not to walk about after drinking it. I was still trying my rings, and I told her to go before it was dark. She thanked me and ran off. I ate, emptied the wine onto the ground, then tied the bundle to my chest above my swollen belly and waited for Michele.

"He appeared after dark with a stout pair of peasant sandals. I gave Michele the jeweled ones I wore and laced on the ones he'd brought. He wrenched one of the jeweled straps apart, held out his hand to me for the other, and looked askance at my rings.

"'They will know you did not fall but ran away!'

"'No, Michele, my maid will be asked what I was doing when she last saw me. She will say I had a fancy for trying on my jewelry. And that I often walked in the olive grove to ease a cramp in my leg. I ordered her to bring me a glass of strong wine, and she said I must take care lest it make me unsteady on my feet. It will appear that I fell while walking to ease the cramp in my legs, and the rings will be in the ravine with me. No one will imagine a woman so large with child, and inebriated, would attempt a mountain path in the dark.' Michele muttered something about a woman's cunning, that Stefano had been right to trust me."

"What happened? Weren't you frightened?" asked Sophia.

"And so we left. Of course I was terrified. We paused at the ravine and dropped the broken sandal on the edge. Michele tossed the other one a long way down, where it would still be visible. Then he tore pieces from my skirt, threw the scraps so they fell over the edge.

"'Come,' he said. 'It is dark, but we peasants who do not ride in fine carriages can walk this path blindfolded. It is steep and narrow, but I know every twist and turn.'

"Michele went ahead of me so that I could place my hand on his shoulder and be guided. It was steep, and I was glad of the support and the stout peasant sandals. Though I stumbled and slid several times, Michele caught me, and we made it safely to the bottom of the mountain before dawn. He gave a low whistle, and a cart with a mule drove up with his son. He helped me in and told me the rest of the plan. I would leave Palermo that morning in a fishing boat for Naples.

"'In Palermo I must—'

"'No, lady, you will not go to the prison. My master forbids it.'

"'But I can bribe the jailers to speak to him for a moment.'

"'No, lady, you cannot lest you are arrested too.'

"I put my head down and finally began to weep.

"A week later I was in Naples, waiting for the ship that would take me to America and Stefano's cousin in Louisiana. I had sold my least valuable ring for enough to pay my passage and hidden the others with my little statues to avoid being robbed. Waiting for the day the ship would sail, I had gone from one church to another, hiding in the shadows to sleep a little or falling asleep on my knees at Mass. I was approached twice by a sacristan, but I put on a peasant's accent and said on the priest's advice I was offering continual prayers for my husband who was sick with a wasting disease. I spent my piastra on bread and fruit and prayed that my father believed I had fallen into the ravine.

"Finally the appointed day came for the ship to sail, and a crowd of us were herded on board like goats. I was so eager to be gone I told myself this must be endured if I was to escape. I guarded my little statues carefully. Though now large with child, as a single woman, I began to be the object of unwanted attention from some male fellow passengers, until a kind older man and his wife protected me.

"We soon fell into conversation and were companions for the rest of the voyage, which eased the terrible discomforts of it. I learned they were Tamás and Maria Morgades, Spanish *Gitanos*, persecuted for their habit of wandering about the country. *Gitanos* were accused of thievery and sedition, and there had been an edict that forbade *Gitanos* to marry among themselves, as was their custom, or to travel. Tamás and his wife, Maria, were cousins. They had been arrested on the road between Seville and Madrid and put into a camp where they were forced to work in a noble's fields, mistreated, and beaten. Though the edict had been revoked, the experience convinced them Spain was not safe for *Gitanos,* and they were seeking a new life in America. Though the ship was bound for La Nouvelle-Orléans, their destination was Virginia, where they had heard people took great pride in their horses. Although they believed the distance between La Nouvelle-Orléans and Virginia was great, they were in the habit of traveling, and this presented no difficulties.

"I decided I could trust them, and anyway, we were far out to sea. I told them my story. They said I should come with them, but I insisted I must go to the cousin in La Nouvelle-Orléans. Then one night my pains began, and next day, Stefania was born. Maria delivered her, and though it was very terrible at the time, by some miracle all was well.

"When we arrived in La Nouvelle-Orléans, I took the dirty scrap of paper Stefano had bribed a guard to give Michele and set out to find the cousin's house. I was surprised to arrive at a large house with a balcony, but when the door was answered by a servant, I learned that Stefano's cousin had just died of a fever in one of the epidemics that visit this city. The slave butler said the house and all the cousin's 'people' were to be sold, unless the new owner of the house wanted to keep the house slaves. I said I hoped that would be the case, and that the new owners were kind. The poor slave feared he would be parted from his wife, who was a cook, and his children, who served in the dining room and worked in the stables.

"I returned to Tamás and Maria in despair, and they urged me to come with them. I was afraid to be alone and decided to go with them. I had no other friends and didn't know what else to do. They refused to think of going by sea from La Nouvelle-Orléans to Williamsburg. Being *Gitanos* they were sick of ocean travel and said it was their habit to travel overland freely and live again in the open air as they had done in Spain, making their living along the way by entertainment and horse trading. They had made inquiries and discovered a route they planned to take, following the Mississippi and Tinassi Rivers into Virginia.

"I sold my remaining rings for Spanish dollars because Tamás had said it was the soundest currency in America. Then I returned to the cousin's house and told the butler I was obliged to leave La Nouvelle-Orléans in order to stay with my friends. We would travel to Williamsburg, going overland along the river. I gave the butler a purse of dollars and said that I had been separated from his master's cousin, my husband, Stefano Albanisi. I expected my husband to seek me here at his cousin's house. The butler must tell him to follow me to Virginia. It was a hopeless plan but the only one I could think of." Rosalia sighed. "I did not know then how vast the wilderness is."

"I know," said Sophia, remembering her own journey.

"I sold another ring and insisted Tamás take the money—Stefania and I would not be a drain on the couple's generosity.

"Tamás was a musician and could stir the blood making his fiddle weep or sing with joy. Graceful Maria would dress in her brightly colored skirts and many bracelets and step forward, clicking her shells made of chestnut wood to perform a dance that started slowly, like a snake uncoiling as the tempo of her feet and heels and the clicking shells grew faster and faster until all the world was in one stamping, gyrating woman full of power and emotion. It was impossible to think of anything else while Maria danced. Tamás often put down his fiddle to clap in time to her feet. It was thrilling to watch, and it left both the audience and Maria exhausted.

"They took pleasure in their music and dancing and the money they made in this way, but I discovered Tamás had far more money, all in Spanish dollars, than I expected for one who traveled in such miserable conditions belowdecks as we had done on the ship from Naples.

"Tamás purchased a small closed carriage that he, Maria, and I painted in a bright design with red wheels, together with a string of horses and two mules. Tamás rubbed his hands and said he'd gotten a good bargain from the Irishman who'd sold them. Maria laughed and said no one knew horses better than Tamás.

"So we set off, and I watched Maria dance, thinking how I wished I could do that. Finally Maria said she was growing too old to dance as she used to, she grew breathless easily, and would gladly have me dance in her place if I wished to learn. It was harder than I expected, and I saw my first efforts were feeble compared to hers. Maria could hold twenty or thirty people spellbound by the emotion she expressed when she danced. She said I danced like a woman thinking of when to feed the baby.

"The passion, Maria said over and over, must come from the heart, the soul, from love that was not simpering and weak but white-hot and raw, from hate, from terror even. She taught me to keep the rhythm with the shells, to hold my head boldly up, to move my feet with decision and purpose, to plant them like a command. 'Dance the Devil and all his host under your feet.' And little by little I improved, grew bolder. I practiced and practiced, and Maria would clap her hands to keep the rhythm. Stefania would watch from her makeshift cradle under a tree or propped on the driver's seat of the carriage.

"Tamás and Maria were happy to be traveling again but found the weather uncomfortable. It was a damp heat along the Mississippi, and we were tormented by mosquitoes and gnats and midges and did not travel fast. We stopped along the way wherever there were settlements and taverns and small towns. Tamás sold horses and acquired new ones, and this business took him days and sometimes weeks. Maria would make the most of our long stops, doing laundry and scrubbing her cooking pots and airing the bedding in the carriage. Stefania passed her first birthday.

"I noticed Maria began to seem unwell. She would cough and complain of being feverish at night. She aged, was often tired, could dance less and less, and when she did, the fire had gone out of her dancing, as if the flame of her existence was burning low. Tamás muttered she had had consumption in the prison camp but had recovered when they left it, after he said a novena. What was he to do, he asked me helplessly. I did not know.

"Maria begged me to dance in her place more and more often, and though I had no confidence anyone would want to watch, I could not refuse after their kindness. Before Stefania's second birthday, all the dancing had fallen to me. Before her third, Maria was dead, buried beneath a live oak tree in sight of the river. Tamás was bereft, weeping like a child. We camped a long time near Maria's grave before Tamás had the heart to go on. He had grown much older with sorrow very quickly. He had become a father to me, and I was glad he was not alone. Stefania and I did our best to take care of him. Stefania loved the horses—that helped. Tamás promised to teach her how to talk to them.

"I could not help thinking, what if Tamás also died? Stefania and I cannot live a traveling life in a painted carriage alone. I needed a home. I had long ago abandoned any hope that Stefano could follow me or that he was even alive. Sometimes hope is unbearable. If I am to draw breath and live for Stefania, I decided I must put my old life behind me and make the best of this new one, as well as I can. I will never be other than Stefano's wife.

"The country along the Mississippi, then the Tinassi grew wilder, the forests thicker. There were few settlers, though we saw hunters and trappers and fur traders. We saw Indians from time to time, and though we had heard terrible stories of scalpings and kidnappings, when we met them, they were interested in our carriage and treated us kindly with great hospitality in their villages.

"I did not think Tamás would settle before we reached Williamsburg, but the morning after we arrived in this valley, he asked the man at the trading post if there was land available. That was Henri, and now we have a home. The people are amiable enough, and those I thought were slaves are not, but landowners like the rest. You all live as simply as the peasants do at home, and I like all the women very much. But I think I must take care when dealing with the men here, Sophia."

Sophia blushed.

"Tamás scolded me for flirting with Henri over the bear cave, and you thought so too. But I wasn't. I only needed to know where it was. I have no wish to flirt or even to think of another man.

"I've asked you to come and hear my story, hoping it would make you my friend. I have the goddess and her votive figures in my basket. I want to make her shrine in the cave. Will you help me?"

Sophia felt slightly dazzled by this exotic story, but Rosalia had told it so compellingly that Sophia said, "Of course. Let me light those pine knots so we can see."

The little girls had fallen asleep on the quilt. "First let's carry the children just inside the entrance," said Rosalia. They put their shawls over the sleeping children, lit their pine knots, and stood up to explore. In the cool darkness of the cave, their spluttering torches cast great dancing shadows on the walls that grew higher the farther in they went.

"If bears hibernate here, I must find a place where they can't reach the figures," said Rosalia.

"Hmm," said Sophia. Then, "Look!" She held up the pine knot. "Just look, Rosalia, how splendid!" Their light danced over magnificent formations of rocks and columns that looked like frozen water and rocks of many colors.

"The farther we go, the more beautiful it becomes," whispered Rosalia.

Sophia said, "Look up there. It's another level, a sort of alcove." She pointed higher in the cave wall. Too high for bears but for people too. "How will we reach it with no ladder?"

"Yes, what a pity . . . Wait! Look, Sophy! It's as if someone carved a step in the cave wall, now another, and there's another. How can that be, do you suppose?"

Skeptical, Sophia held her pine knot up, and there were steplike indentations, slanted at an angle as if worn by many feet. "Indians? It must have been Indians."

They climbed up barefoot for a better purchase on the narrow steps, placing their feet carefully. When they reached it, the alcove was a shallow cave inside the cave, high enough to stand. Rosalia held her torch up and said, "Look, marking on the walls. I think . . ."

What happened next was startling. The setting sun's rays began to penetrate the cave through the entrance, making the pillars of rock sparkle and shimmer with crystals. The sun's rays gradually lit up the alcove walls, and pictures appeared of a man with the head of a bird, winged animals, and a deer with a swollen belly. And these foremost drawings were overlaid on other drawings on the rock wall, heads of animals and birds and men and what were surely pregnant women, receding into the distance on the cave wall to fill the cave with life.

Then Rosalia cried out, "Look!" On the wall above their heads was a handprint.

"Why is that there?" murmured Sophia. It was white against red, so clear it could have just been made. Something drew her to raise her own hand and place it against the white palm. And then she saw above it were more faint outlines of other hands, as if a lost race of people had made a sign of their presence before saying farewell.

Rosalia held her hand against another print until the sun moved and the rays no longer illuminated the wall. The hands faded and disappeared. Rosalia shivered. "This is an ancient place. This is where the shrine belongs." She placed the votive figures on a low outcrop of rock under the hand and welcomed the Goddess of Many Crowns and her daughter, Kore, to their sanctuary.

Sophia had never been religious; if anything, she had inherited her father's skepticism. But she paid lip service to her Anglican tradition. Now, waiting for Rosalia to finish her odd pagan ritual, she was caught up in the strangeness of the moment. Rosalia's dancing had fortified her, and now today's experience in the cave soothed her heart. She hoped she could hold on to the feeling.

The children woke and chattered happily like little birds in their different languages and didn't notice their mothers were silent as Sophia and Rosalia packed up the picnic things and they began the walk back down. From the slope they could see Henri waiting by the landing, looking up Frog Mountain. They waved to him.

"I love this valley," exclaimed Rosalia. "The sunsets are beautiful."

"Yes," said Sophia, who hadn't noticed sunsets in a long time. "Glorious." And it was.

They walked carefully down the steep path. "Henri will row you back across the river," said Sophia. "I'm so glad you've come, Rosalia."

CHAPTER 36
CULLY

1774

Cully was back. Kitty knew he was there, knew he'd been back a week and was still grieving for his mother, shocked to learn she had died. He'd stayed out of sight, nursing his grief, helping Nott, and tending her grave, and Kitty couldn't decide whether to seek him out or not. Both would cause her pain. Kitty bided her time.

Finally he went to see Susan, where Venus alternated between hugging and tears and berating him for staying away.

Susan had been angry with him when he finally appeared at the Hanovers'.

"I couldn't get back till now," he said.

"What you talking about, Cully! You went, you can come back. Ought to be 'shamed of yourself," snapped Susan.

When he got free from Venus's embrace, and then the clamoring of the smaller girls, who all wanted a hug, Cully said, "Let's go find Kitty."

Susan said she was minding the trading post most days, said how tall he'd got, and all three went down to the landing.

Kitty and Susan and Cully sat on the landing as they had so many times when they were children. The girls were swinging bare feet in the water, and at last Cully took off his shoes and stockings and wet his feet too. Susan let him know she was still mad at him for staying away. Kitty looked like she couldn't decide whether she was mad or not, something careful in her eyes when she glanced at him.

"I couldn't come back, not right away. I'll tell you why but don't tell anybody, you got to swear you won't." Both girls nodded, Kitty taking a little longer than Susan.

Cully watched the water rippling through Kitty's toes.

"La Nouvelle-Orléans a fine place. It's big, streets up and down. Big fine houses and canals. All full of people. People everywhere. Like an anthill full of ants. It used to be French, like Mist' Henri is French. They speak French like he can. Now it Spanish, people talk Spanish too. You hear it all when you in the street, can't understand it no more than can understand birds, but it's got a pretty sound. They have slaves but lot of free blacks too. They got Creoles, people all mixed up with black and white and Spanish and French."

The water reflected afternoon sunlight off Cully's gold skin. He had a mustache now and wore his hair long and tied back with a black ribbon. He had on a white shirt with full sleeves and linen breeches, and his long legs, bare from the knee down, were covered in drops of water. The girls had their skirts pulled up to their knees. Under the water, Kitty's feet were pale beside Susan's and Cully's.

"They've got a big port there, ships from all over. From some islands down south where the Spanish are too, they get sugar and rum and tobacco. They need workers on the quay, and I worked for nearly a year, saved my money, bought me a wagon and a mule, was hauling barrels and things and making more money when I got attacked by three men. They were rough fellows, and strong. Tied me up, a-saying

I was a runaway. I said I had my paper saying I was free, but they took it and tore it up. They sold me to a slave trader."

Susan and Kitty gasped together. "Oh, Cully!"

"Well . . . I fought but you can't fight hard when you're in shackles. They threw me in a cage and left me there for two weeks. Time I got let out, I was too weak to fight anybody."

Kitty put her hand on his arm.

"They sold me to a plantation owner, and I thought it would be the death of me, working in those hot fields. Then one day the plow broke, and the overseer was threatening to kill the slave that done it, and I said don't kill him, I could mend it, I'd worked iron before, with Rufus."

"What happened?"

"It got me out of the fields. After a while I'm making this and mending that, the plantation owner started to trust me. He said I had to have better food, my own cabin, found out I could read and write, but he said that was between us. But he had me writing his accounts. He finally said he'd let me get married, said he had a pretty girl in mind."

"Oh?" said Kitty, looking away. "Was she pretty?"

"Pretty enough to have three of his children."

"What happened?"

"I said I was happy to marry her. He grinned, said his wife was happy too, so happy he wanted me to have some money for a new suit to get married in. He winked and gave me some dollars. I had the tailor make me this"—he pointed to his shirt and breeches—"but there was a storm with a lot of wind the night before the wedding, roofs blowing off the slave quarters, a tree down on my owner's house, the barn ripped open, and the horses running loose, and I ran away. And here I am." He smiled at Kitty. "Glad to be here. But I miss Mama. Nobody to cook for me, care if I'm alive or dead."

He looked at Kitty, who hadn't exactly smiled at him for coming back.

"Pitiful," muttered Susan. "I guess you can eat with us if you want to. Uncle Nott does most days."

"That would be fine," said Cully, looking at Kitty. Kitty looked at Cully.

"Kitty, don't let your white skin get freckles in this sun," said Susan ominously.

"Tell me what's happened while I was gone."

"Rhiannon got married to a brave named Two Bears," said Kitty. "She lives two valleys over with the Indians, who've adopted her as one of them. She has a baby. Caitlin's there now, which is why I'm looking after the trading post. She didn't want Rhiannon to marry Two Bears and carried on something terrible, made Gideon promise he'd take her whenever she wanted to go visit."

"We have some Gypsies living over there." Susan pointed across the river to a cabin with a painted wagon in front of it. "Tamás and Rosalia and Rosalia's little girl, Stefania."

"They bought one of Papa's homesteads. Then some fields behind it," said Kitty. "Papa made a lot of money."

"I see a lot of horses," said Cully. "Look like he has a racetrack."

"Tamás buys and sells horses. Papa says he's a true Gypsy, knows a good horse and can bargain the Devil into a corner for it," said Kitty.

"Meshack's got trouble with his rheumatism," said Susan. "Seth got bitten by a rattlesnake at Rufus's forge. He's been bitten a lot, and that time he almost died."

"Malinda's expecting another baby," said Kitty.

"Patience Drumheller is expecting too!" Kitty and Susan exploded with laughter. "And we thought she was too old!"

"Her nephew, the parson, is still here. He married Mattie, the girl who was the boatman's niece. Mattie kept coming here on the flatboat with her aunt and uncle, and Susan and I, we helped him see Mattie's pretty and . . . um . . . the boatman took him aside and asked what the parson's intentions were, and the parson got all flustered, and the boatman said for God's sake just marry the girl. We heard him, didn't we, Susan? So Mattie went off to get her wedding clothes—well, she did after we helped her to attract his attention and propose—and they did." Susan giggled.

"Parson Merriman is building a church. Mother still dislikes him. She threatened to shoot him if he didn't leave her alone after Charlotte was taken." Kitty sighed. "Magdalena and I often talk about whether Charlotte and Cadfael are still alive. Rhiannon thinks they are. She has visions or something. She's become very odd. But you'd think we'd know by now if they were. Gideon tried and tried to get word of them. But Mother's better, almost like she was before."

"Toby keeps talking about tea tax and the sons of something," said Susan.

"Sons of Liberty," said Kitty. "Papa says they're rabble. Mother says it's treason and they'll all be hanged. Whenever we get any bits of newspaper, there's always something about the tea or the tax or the Sons of Liberty."

"Rufus likes them," said Susan.

"Do you want to see something interesting up in the bear cave?" asked Kitty.

"What's interesting about the cave? We've been up there lots," yawned Susan. "And it smells."

"Can't tell you, you have to see it. At sunset."

They heard Venus calling Susan. "Got to go help Mama with the supper. You comin', Cully?"

"I'll be there for supper, if that's all right. I want to see whatever Kitty wants to show me."

They stood up, and Kitty and Susan shook their skirts out. Susan looked from Kitty to Cully, then turned on her heel and walked away.

"What's up there?" asked Cully as they walked up the path.

"Something Stefania showed us. Her mother put something in the bear cave. You'll see," said Kitty, stepping nimbly ahead of him. "I might go away myself, you know. Papa's been talking for years about taking me back to France, and now with all the land he's sold Tamás, he says we can go soon. He wants to get me married there. Mother says she'd rather I married an Englishman, but she doesn't object to Papa taking me. Papa keeps pointing out I won't meet either kind of husband if I stay here. I'll end up an old maid or married to a fur trader."

"Hunh!" said Cully "And what kind of husband do you want?"

Kitty stopped and turned to face him. "I want you! You know I do, ever since you kissed me, before you went away. I did for the last two years. I was mad at you for staying away, and I would have been madder if you'd married that other woman. I might have shot you, now that I think about it. With Mother's little pistol."

"I know, Kitty. Don't think I don't. I told you I'd come home to you, when I left," said Cully. "Wasn't a day go by I didn't think about Mama grievin', think about you, would I ever get back."

"What I need to know, Cully, is should I go to France?"

"No!" Cully almost shouted.

Kitty's eyes filled with tears. "Then what? I want to marry *somebody*!"

"This," said Cully, and he put his arms around her. They needed to try the kiss again. And soon, after such a long separation, they wanted more. Later in the bear cave, up in the alcove Cully rolled onto his bare back and said, "My, my, that was some homecoming surprise. You been keeping a quilt up here just in case I come back?"

The relief and joy Kitty felt were so intense she could hardly bear it.

"I put it up here when I heard you'd come home. I don't know why. It wasn't ladylike." Kitty said drowsily into his shoulder, thinking how good Cully's skin smelled.

Cully shifted so he could get his arm around her. He traced a line from her chin to her navel. "You grown up," he said.

"After this I'm grown up, I guess." She sighed and sat up.

He pulled her back down to the quilt. "I'm glad I'm home," he said.

"Don't go away again, Cully," she said later. "Please. I can't stand it."

"I won't. But we got to think what to do," said Cully, turning on his back. And then, "Oh glory, will you look at that!" The rays of the setting sun filled the alcove. "There's pictures! Animals, and up there, hands! I see hands! Who done all that?"

"I know, that's what I wanted to show you. Don't know who did it, Mother says it must have been Indians. She and Stefania's mother found it."

Cully shook his head in wonder. "It's like they saying hello. Or goodbye. Or something. Makes you shiver, don't it."

"Yes," whispered Kitty.

CHAPTER 37

THE PAINTER OF PORTRAITS

June 1774

Secondus Conway was a small man, of indeterminate age, wiry but well-worn in appearance. His hands, however, were at odds with the rest of him. They should have been knotted and callused, but they were fine, with long, slender fingers. Not at all the hands of a man as weathered by life as the rest of Secondus appeared to have been. But he took great care of his hands. An itinerant artist, he was obliged to travel whatever the weather, so he rubbed them with bear grease to keep them supple and wrapped them in rags against the cold. Wherever he found himself of an evening—and Secondus thought of himself as tossed on the waves and tides of his commissions, whether this meant a plantation drawing room, a rough tavern, or a lodging in the corner of a bare little cabin—he sought out a place where he could hold his hands to the fire, caging a little whiskey if it was available and sassafras or sumac tea if it was not. Bundles of brushes and paints by his feet, he would bow and introduce himself as "a painter of portarits" obliged to travel far and wide in the service of art.

As he told anyone who would listen, it was normally the master or mistress whose portrait he was engaged to paint. But according to Secondus, when they saw the result, he was never allowed to depart until every last member of the family had had a portrait taken as well, from aged granny down to the last, smallest infant. If the cost was an issue—and here Secondus would wave his hand dismissively—why, there was even a saving to be had when all were painted together in a group.

But his specialty, he would eventually reveal, his "fortee" so to speak, were the children. Living children and those little angels who had died, God rest the pure little souls. He had taken the likeness of many a child as it lay in its coffin, eyes closed in a waxy little face, so it lived again on the canvas. But his talents extended further than that, because he was able to paint a child already dead and buried, just from the mother's description. And the wonderful thing was, the mother always agreed these portraits were as like her child as like could be. "It was a *mentomori*," he would murmur with respectful sympathy, "of a little angel in the eternal bloom of its youth and innocence."

Secondus was never slow to invoke the names of his former patrons, nor quick to run out of conversation. He was a talker. Given an opening, he would begin a litany of his distinguished clients and the plantations whose hospitality he had enjoyed—Carters, Fairfaxes, Custises, Byrds, and Fitzhughs featured large in his distinguished clientele. Nomini Hall, Carters Grove, Westover, and Berkeley were places with which he was intimately acquainted. He could describe the rooms, the fine furniture, the habits of the household, their musical tastes, and even enumerate the dishes served at dinner. "Your Virginia ladies, your educated gentlemen, now *there's* refinement. When my labors were done and the finished portarit stood before them, they would gaze and admire, too moved for speech, you might say. Often they would wipe tears from their eyes, beg me to tarry with them longer. They were hungry, you see, for culture, to hear my stories of the salons of Europe where artists gathered as persons of importance and were treated with deference. They sighed when I described museums in Italy and France, the paintings, the porcelain and ivory, the precious *objets* gathered from all over the world.

"And when they begged, of course, I would oblige my kind friends—a painter of portarits must always be friendly and obliging to his patrons—but at the same time, I would insist on departing when my work was done. 'Grateful am I for your kind words and gracious hospitality to mine humble self. But art is my master,' I say, kindly but firmly, with a little regretful shake of my head, 'and art calls me on. I must take my leave of you.' Then the head of the family would shake my hand, with manly emotion as he pressed remuneration into it, while the lady of the house would plead with tears in her eyes for me to remain just one more night. But in vain. Always in vain. I must away."

What had lured such a successful artist from his charmed circle of wealthy and adoring patrons in the Tidewater to the rougher territory of the Bowjay River was the one topic on which Secondus refused to elaborate. He hinted, naming no names, that there had been what some might call a misunderstanding in the matter of a young married lady with dark eyes, a most unfortunate misunderstanding, as it led to satisfaction being demanded by her jealous husband. His account of the matter always ended with the "polishing of the dueling pistols" and the precipitate flight, before the pistols could be used, of an artistic soul ill-suited to violence and whose art happened to be calling particularly insistently just at that moment.

The call came from some distance away, in the southern part of the colony, where he had heard that an English lady lived in a grand house in rustic surroundings. It was a tragic story; Secondus had wept when he heard it. The lady's angelic little daughter had been stolen by Indians at a young age, and never recovered. Though he could not put his hand on his heart and say he'd exactly been sent for, Secondus was making his way to Wildwood Plantation.

Secondus traveled with some pretensions to elegance and style, with two mules. He rode one and led the other, which was laden with his paints and brushes and rolls of canvas, and what he called his "portomanto" containing his clothes. At first glance these seemed surprisingly fine for an itinerant painter. There were breeches and waistcoats and coats with deep cuffs. There was a good deal of gold braid, much velvet, damask, and English linen, though on closer inspection, most of the finery had seen better days, being worn and dirty, with buttons hanging by a thread or missing altogether, and, for the most part, they fitted him badly, as if the garments had been made for other, larger men who had discarded them.

He also traveled with a large jug of spirits, which he topped up at every opportunity with whatever drink was at hand. The resulting mixture was a murky, foul-smelling brew, some ten years in the making without a pause for washing the jug and starting afresh. Should he find himself in male company, where courtesy dictated a man share his refreshment—usually not an overly particular gathering in that part of the world—Secondus's jug usually enjoyed the rare distinction of being rejected on the strength of its powerful smell. Only Secondus could bear to drink what was in it.

"A man who is too particular is a thirsty man," he would remark, before holding his breath and downing a good swallow.

A June summer night found Secondus on board a flatboat with his mules, and his jug newly topped up with whatever had been at hand before he went on board. Secondus was in a nervous state of mind. Being unable to swim, he feared and distrusted water, and the prospect of a journey down the river had been agony. It seemed to Secondus that they traveled very fast—once or twice they passed travelers on land at alarming speed.

"White settlers call that a buffalo trail, Indians call it their Great Path," the boatman told him, nodding toward the bank. "Sometimes see war parties on it, have to head into the current and pole like the Devil. Don't want to be scalped." Secondus clutched his jug for comfort, taking only the occasional surreptitious nip to keep his courage up when the boatman wasn't looking. By the time they reached Caradoc Station, even Secondus was running out of conversation, and the jug's contents were seriously depleted.

Until the Caradocs' trading post, Secondus had been the only passenger. There he had his jug topped up with restoring Welsh whiskey before he, the boatman, the boatman's wife, Katy, and several grizzled buffalo hunters, who were going on the flatboat, passed the night on the trading post floor, sheltered from a torrential rain that hammered the roof until dawn.

The next morning the boatman and Katy flung aboard some supplies, and Katy took charge of a pouch of letters bound for the settlers at Vanns' Station down the river. Secondus learned there was something particularly dangerous called the shoals still ahead of them to be got past without sinking and drowning and that Indians had been seen in war paint.

He watched nervously as the boatman pulled up the gangplank of boards from a rickety landing, and Katy clenched her pipe between her teeth and cast off the ropes that had tied them to a post half in, half out of the water. As they moved away from the shore, Secondus hugged his jug, calculating how best to stretch its contents to the length of the journey, which the boatman said would be eight days, give or take. Normally Secondus only broached his jug in the dark—when no one could see—but he spent the day contemplating the dangers ahead, and by late afternoon he needed a reassuring nip.

He became aware the boatman and the buffalo hunters were eyeing him expectantly. "Here," demanded the biggest buffalo hunter.

There was nothing to be done but hand over the jug, though Secondus was confident it would be returned as full as when it left his hands. But to Secondus's horror neither the buffalo hunters nor the boatman refused it. Deprived now of some part of his only source of comfort, Secondus sought reassurance from the boatman, asking if the shoals were truly as dangerous as the Welshmen had described them.

The boatman rolled his eyes, and even the buffalo hunters looked a little less easy than before. "Two of them Caradocs, wives and children, all except the girl, was lost in the shoals. I 'spect you heard, them shoals are the Devil's trap for souls, they has to stay drowning for all eternity. Drowning's a hard death too."

The buffalo hunters shook their heads. The biggest one muttered, "D'ruther have a knife in my guts any day, rather'n drown."

Secondus nodded uncertain agreement. He couldn't say he fancied either prospect.

The boatman steered out into the current. Secondus could see that after the heavy rain of the previous night, the water was now running a little faster than before. "You're in luck, brother, that I knows how to give the Devil the slip," said the boatman.

Katy rolled her eyes and retreated to the lean-to that was the boatman's quarters, to smoke her pipe in peace.

"Aye, we hit them shoals yonder a ways. It looks easy enough here, just carried along on the current like a passenger pigeon on the breeze, but that's when the river's most treacherous. Drown there and the Devil's waitin', he'll have your soul before it can rise up to heaven. Folks who drowns there has to stay forever. Only time the Devil lets a soul go is when it grabs another one down to take its place. Devil plays the fiddle, merry as you please, makes it look like the drowned folks is smiling, laughing, like they's dancin' and eatin' on gold plates.

"You hear fiddle music, take warning. Dead folks feastin' an' drinkin' and dancing down there'll be raising up their arms. Callin' your name. And you lean over a little to look, before you know it, cold, wet hands grab you. Cold, wet arms of the dead pull you under. Your breath comes short and your chest fills up with water, choking the breath out of you, only slow like, and you want to get away, but your sins are weights on your feet as you go down, down, down, where the Devil is reachin' for you with his claws out. No saving you then, in this world or the next. Even Indians are scared of that stretch of water, and ain't much scares Indians."

Secondus shivered. As he would tell the story later, he felt the cold, wet hand of a drowned man on his neck. "Is there anything the living can do?" Secondus asked, clutching the jug.

"It's all in the captain's hands," said the captain, holding out his hand for the jug. Secondus thought it best to give it to him. The captain drank and passed the jug to the buffalo hunters, who also drank deeply before handing it back to Secondus.

Then they heard faint music.

"That sound—wouldn't be a fiddle now, would it?" quavered Secondus.

By now he deeply regretted this expedition to Wildwood. But his commissions in Virginia had dried up—people could only use so many portraits, and besides, plantation owners and their wives visited each other. Once they'd had a chance to compare the ones they'd commissioned with ones he'd done for others, there had been unfavorable comments about how similar the portraits were, some going so far as to accuse Secondus of having a stock of heads, ready painted. Somehow word had spread, and he'd been obliged to go farther afield in search of clients.

"Perhaps we should ask the saints to help hold the rudder steady," Secondus suggested. "Say a prayer." He took a long pull and tried to remember a prayer before handing the jug back to the boatman again, who drank before passing it to the buffalo hunters.

"Prayer's not as much help as you'd think," said the boatman, clutching the rudder for support as he swayed, sending the boat directly toward some rocks on the shore. One of the buffalo hunters managed to shout a warning. And just in time the boatman pushed and the bow swung away from disaster. But the fiddle music seemed to be following them. Secondus could hear it clear as anything, and as tuneful. He even recognized the song.

"'Merrily Danced the Quaker's Wife,'" he hiccupped. "Not what you'd imagine the Devil would . . ."

A buffalo hunter scratched his head. "Naw! Sounds more like 'Hunt the Squirrel.'"

"No, it ain't! He playin' 'Soldiers' Joy'!" bellowed his companion.

"Damned music's making me dizzy!" muttered the boatman. "Devil's trick to confuse folks, playing one thing to my ears, 'nother thing to his. We got to sing. Try and drown him out. Devil hates singing."

Secondus's jug made the rounds again. The fiddling grew ominously louder. Secondus began the only song that came to mind, "Maid in the Pump Room." The others joined in even though no one knew all the words. The main thing was to sing as loud as possible, roared the boatman, you were safe if you couldn't hear the Devil.

They sang and they sang. Then from time to time they fell silent, to refresh themselves from the jug and to listen. Had they drowned out the Devil yet? Sung him away?

But no, the Devil was a tireless fiddler. Fiddle music was all around them now, sometimes louder, sometimes softer, but there was no getting away from it. They sang and they sang, more hoarsely now, and interrupted from time to time when a buffalo hunter bellowed, "Steer, you fool!" as one bank or another swung toward them.

But the fiddle music went maniacally on and on. The Devil might have been playing one tune, and he might have been playing another. Secondus no longer cared. He was helpless to do anything but clutch at the side of the raft, unable in his terror to remember a single prayer, although he felt it would be a particularly good time to pray. When

Secondus looked up, the evening sky was spinning above them, whirling and whirling. The stars were a blur. He had some idea they had abandoned singing and were now desperately trying now to shout the Devil away. He wanted to ask if that would work, but couldn't get the words out. The boatman was swaying on his feet, shouting too. It wasn't helping, because Secondus still heard the music. A jig. He saw the Devil dancing toward them on his cloven hooves.

"Mother of God . . ." Secondus tried to get his jug to his lips, but his hand and his arm and his mouth seemed no longer to be connected.

Feeling very far away, he watched the curtain across the door of the lean-to jerk aside, and the boatman's wife stepped out. "What in the name of God are you shouting at?" Then, "The bank, the bank, you fool! Them's rocks!" she screamed, and moving fast for so large a woman, she grabbed the tiller from her husband. She heaved it, and just in time the raft swung away from the shore, though there was a grating sound as it scraped over something underwater.

"Devil's under the boat! Them's his claws! Help me! Help me, Jesus!"

The boatman's wife swore and leaned hard on the pole. The keelboat lurched off the rock, and the buffalo hunters were flung back.

"The Devil," sobbed the buffalo hunters from a now-supine position. "He's a-coming from below . . . clawin' his way in." The boatman had collapsed onto his knees. "See him, Katy!" he groaned, and pointed. "There in the dark, getting closer and closer, one big red-and-yellow eye."

Secondus had lost the power of speech, but he could still see, and in the darkness there was definitely a big red-and-yellow eye. He could smell smoke. He was going to Hell . . .

Katy shouted to be heard. She was a big woman, and she was heard. "You're all drunk as possums!"

"Katy, Devil's fiddlin'. We're doomed!"

His wife screamed, "Ain't no Devil playin' a fiddle! Ain't no doom neither. I got me one passel of drunk fools here on the river hearin' another passel of drunk fools over there fiddling by a fire on the bank there. Sounds like they trying to play 'Rufty Tufty,' but they keep losin' the tune. And it ain't the Devil fiddlin'. If it were, he'd play it right! And you steerin' around in circles the whole time like you got no more sense 'n a garfish, and now the boat's hit a rock and looks like a hole in the bottom. I don't know what you been drinking, but this here looks responsible to me."

Katy picked up the jug and shook it hard. It made a sloshing noise. She sniffed inside and coughed. "Wheeeeuw!" She tossed it overboard.

Secondus watched it fly into the air, heard the splash. He gave a terrible howl of anguish, loud and unearthly, from the bottom of a soul poised on the verge of the bottomless and everlasting abyss, that echoed across the water to the merrymakers on the bank. It stopped the music. There were wails from the riverbank.

"Devil's risin' out the water!"

"Coming after us!" someone cried.

"Run!"

"Ain't no Devil, you halfwit fools!" came from Katy in a sort of roar, but very, very faint and far away now. Secondus realized he was sinking under the water, for her to sound so far away; the water was closing around his ears. He whimpered a vow that if his feet only touched dry land, he would never again go on water. Then everything went dark and quiet.

Secondus had come to in such a bad way he knew himself in hell. It was a week before he realized he was lying on a pallet in a room crammed with barrels and sacks and bolts of cloth. At first he had thought he was going to die, but a nice woman named Mrs. Vann fed him restoring broth and milk toast and a terrible drink she called spice-wood tea. She insisted they had no strong drink and added firmly that she wouldn't give it to him if she had, not for all the world. Within a fortnight, he felt he was past the worst and was beginning to get his bearings again, telling Caitlin his stories of the grand houses and the portraits he had painted of their inhabitants. They had many interesting discussions, Secondus thought, though Caitlin rolled her eyes when she repeated the stories to Gideon.

"But what are we to do, Gideon, in all the world? He refuses to go on water again, and we can't send him off on the trail. He'd never last by himself. I don't think he's strong," she protested when Gideon suggested that now that he was better, they should send Secondus on his way. Secondus had managed to eavesdrop on these conversations—the storeroom opening onto the kitchen made this easy—and understood Mrs. Vann's husband would rather he left. Gideon suggested he board the next raft that had room for one more. Gideon would even pay the boatman. Pay him double if necessary.

"Oh, Gideon," Caitlin laughed. "I'll see to it."

Secondus crept back to his pallet. He felt betrayed by Mrs. Vann. He was unable to think of another boat trip without horror, and this was a great incentive to find local employment for his talents. He still had his donkeys, his paints and brushes, and a few canvases. He would no longer delay seeking out Wildwood, where the titled English lady lived. He had a little knowledge of grand English ladies and had formed the impression they were, in their own estimation at least, almost beings from the celestial stars. He hoped the mistress of Wildwood would not be so grand she looked down her nose at one who served Art.

Caitlin encouraged him to go, rather desperate by now to get rid of her visitor, saying that she was sure the de Marechals would find him a diverting company, and diversion would not come amiss because they had lost a child taken by the Indians—here Caitlin's voice trembled a little—and perhaps they would even commission a portrait of their eldest daughter who was very pretty, and who might soon leave with her father to live in France.

This was promising, and Secondus observed de Marechal was a mellifluous name that bespoke culture and refinement and the need for portraits.

A good first impression was important. "Madame!" he would say, with his best bow. "Your service!" But in the course of his travels, Secondus had shrewdly observed that artists like himself were a novelty to the plantation gentry, and were even expected to look a little out of the ordinary, to cut a flamboyant figure, though he had discovered that noteworthy flamboyance was harder to achieve in Virginia, where men's dress tended to the extreme. He opened his "portomanto" and examined his clothes, selecting the least shabby and most colorful garments to hang in the sun for an airing. Mrs. Vann obliged with a bucket of hot water and a piece of her strong yellow soap, for which Secondus thanked her profusely. He washed, brushed his hair, cleaned his fingernails with his penknife, and managed to shave, although rather badly, with his rusty razor. He took his leave, paying Caitlin the most lavish compliments he could devise, extolling her virtues, her hospitality, and her broth, called her his Good Samaritaness, and obtained directions to Wildwood. He promised that once he was settled with a commission, he would return and do his humble best to repay her kindness with a portrait of Caitlin and her children.

Feeling hopeful because he had discovered there were several more ladies with children or babies to approach in search of commissions, Secondus loaded his donkeys and set off along the river road, then turned up to climb through the orchard, prepared to rest his eyes on the kind of mansion that cried out for portraits. He decided he would try and persuade all the family to have their likeness taken, not just their pretty daughter. And he felt sure they would want a memento of their little kidnapped angel. Mrs. Vann had warned him not to mention the child because Mrs. de Marechal was still grieving, but Secondus had had much experience with grieving mothers, and he knew what the circumstances called for.

One commission would lead to another. And another. Everything would be all right here, he felt it in his bones.

He emerged from the orchard to see before him not the grand house of his imagination, but another log cabin, bigger than the Vanns', with two stories and a sort of verandah at the back that seemed to be sagging.

A middle-aged man was cleaning a gun.

"Ah, monsieur, the master of the house." Secondus called and doffed his hat at once, lest the man be the sort of suspicious settler who fired at strangers without a by-your-leave. "Good day to you. I hope I find you and your family well?"

"What the Devil," exclaimed Henri who had been intent on his gun and was unprepared to see a small figure in shabby velvet and gold braid emerging from the orchard to greet him.

This was an unpromising start, but Secondus refused to be put off. He had nowhere to go, and he continued to the porch where Henri sat, to introduce himself and his purpose, eloquent, lyrical, and persuasive by turns, urging Henri to commission a family portrait.

"Are *you* an artist?" Henri asked dubiously.

"I am. Mrs. Vann suggested that I . . ."

"I'll fetch my wife."

Sophia was in the kitchen, kneading bread. "Sophy, the odd little man Caitlin looked after has come up, he says she sent him and he's trying to persuade me to commission a family portrait."

"How curious," said Sophia and, wiping her hands on her apron, followed Henri to the door.

"He is persistent. You must send him away."

Secondus bowed. "Your service, madame."

"Sir." Sophia took in the velvet suit and the hopeful expression. Even the donkeys had a pleading expression, she thought. She sighed. "My husband has explained the reason for your call but, naturally, your terms will be high, sir," Sophia began, "and we cannot—"

"Dear madame, not so high as all that," Secondus was quick to point out.

"Sir, whatever your terms, they will be beyond us," Sophia said firmly.

Despair welled in Secondus's heart—where was he to go? His eyes filled with tears.

Sophia looked at the donkeys again. Her heart misgave her. "But perhaps," she wavered, "if you're willing to work for food and lodging, we have a place you could live."

"Oh, I am!" Secondus nodded. He was in no position to reject the offer of anything so long as he did not have to travel on the river again.

Sophia led the way to a small cabin, explaining that it had been built for a slave named Zaydie who had died, and Secondus felt a frisson of fear when he cautiously poked his head through the door to see inside. An artistic soul was sensitive to its surroundings and he felt a definite presence. Would the dead slave haunt him? Then he thought about the river and his vow never to leave dry land. He swallowed hard and stepped into the cabin. Better a dead slave than the Devil, wild beasts, or scalping Indians.

"Ah, dear madame, rustic bliss!" enthused Secondus.

Secondus had expected a more elevated establishment, but he had somehow negotiated a portrait of the mother and the four children, in return for his board and lodging, and that was something. He intended to paint as slowly as possible and comforted himself that even though the lady had no pretensions to an English title after all, the de Marechal name hinted at glory or at least the distinction of being French and civilized.

At his first supper with the family, Secondus ate heartily of venison stew that was far better than he expected and surreptitiously studied his subjects. He was preparing for a tearful private tête-à-tête with the mother first, to get a description of the missing child to work it into his composition when Henri startled him by saying Secondus should do no such thing. He was to paint Monsieur and Madame de Marechal and the four children only.

"Of course," said Secondus. The missing child haunted him, but it was for the patron to command.

Over the next weeks, Secondus grouped the mother and her children in different ways and took his time making sketches. The eldest daughter was a very beautiful girl of eighteen, who had a glow of what Secondus felt sure was love about her. The two tall teenage sons were handsome, lively boys who sparred cheerfully with their older sister and seemed at ease with their father and teased their younger sister, a melancholy child of six, Magdalena. It was to be his surprise that he would paint Henri into the "portarit," as Henri refused to sit still and pose, And he would work out where best to put little lost Charlotte. That was to be a surprise too.

He would let no one see the portrait until he finished, and he worked as slowly as possible. He found that of all the family, Magdalena was the only one willing to tell him the story of her kidnapped sister, to describe what she had looked like, so he let her talk.

Weeks became a month, one month became two, and two months became three. His composition developed. Secondus made himself comfortable in the cabin. The dead slave didn't bother him, although sometimes at night he thought he could hear an elderly woman mumbling complaints at the fireplace.

Sophia and Henri and the children were now intrigued by the portrait. Sophia confessed to Henri she had become quite eager to see it.

Christmas was approaching, and Secondus announced he would perform the great unveiling on Christmas Day. He worked late into the night on Christmas Eve while the others were singing carols and next morning he viewed the result with satisfaction.

After dinner, just as the candles were lit, Secondus asked the family to sit. They sat.

He carried in his largest canvas, with the back turned toward its audience. He asked them to shut their eyes, and turned it around. He told them softly he had a gift, to open their eyes and behold it.

There was silence, then a collective intake of breath. Then Kitty cried, "No!" Magdalena clapped her hand to her mouth, the boys stared, Henri swore. Sophia went white, gave a moan, and fainted.

It was a rather fine portrait of most of them. Henri and Sophia in the middle, the boys on Henri's right hand, and Magdalena and Kitty on Sophia's left. And in the middle was a child with moonlight hair and blue-green eyes holding Magdalena's hand. There was a chicken just visible in each corner. Oddly the painted face of Sophia looked as if it were marked by a bad case of smallpox. On closer inspection, the pockmarks were tears, and in each tear was a tiny version of a child with moonlight hair.

"Make him take it away," Kitty hissed at her father, chafing her mother's wrists. "Mother was so much better! Now he's sent her back into a state. You must make him and the portrait go!"

"Where?"

"Let him . . . take it to one of those cabins you built across the river. But get him and his donkeys and his paints away. Now!" Kitty sounded exactly like imperious Sophia in her younger days, and Henri did as she told him. Somehow he and the boys gathered a bewildered Secondus and his belongings and paints and brushes and donkeys and "porto-manto" and the portrait down to the landing. Gideon agreed to row Secondus and his goods over first thing in the morning and resigned himself to another night of Secondus in the storeroom. "I'll take him early," he said to Caitlin as they were going to bed.

And next morning before he was even awake, Secondus found himself again in a boat crossing water, bewildered as to what had happened. He had painted the child with silvery hair exactly how she ought to look. That was his gift; everyone said he did paint dead children accurately, though he did not know how he did this. Perhaps the lady objected to the chickens. *That must be it,* he thought miserably.

CHAPTER 38
AN AFTERSHOCK

Twelfth Night 1775

In the aftermath of Christmas, Sophia felt low and sad in a way she had not for several years. The wretched portrait had revived the tragedy of Charlotte and opened every wound in Sophia's heart. Sophia looked haggard, Henri was short-tempered even with Kitty. Francis and George went hunting, Magdalena was moping, and Kitty hadn't wanted any breakfast again.

Breathing hard after the steep climb through the orchard, Caitlin came up to visit Sophia when she heard what had happened, and to apologize for having sent Secondus to Wildwood. She reported that Secondus was ensconced in the smaller cabin across the river. He was prostrated, still in a state from his enforced boat ride and reeling from the de Marechals' reception of his great work. His mules had promptly escaped and got into Rosalia's yard. Rosalia and Tamás felt sorry for Secondus. Tamás had put Secondus's mules in the paddock with his own animals and fed them. Rosalia had taken Secondus soup and corn bread and listened to a distraught account of the portrait debacle.

On Twelfth Night, Sophia made a great effort to restore the family equilibrium. She larded a wild turkey the boys had shot, and roasted it with sweet potatoes. She made a cake and applesauce from her store of dried apples. When they were gathered round the table, they discussed rumors of a rebellion across the colonies. Sophia thought the king would send troops to crush it quickly.

Finally the atmosphere mellowed in the aftermath of a good dinner. Toasts were drunk to the king and the New Year with some of Meshack's whiskey. Sophia, Kitty, and Magdalena watered theirs.

Henri stood and said he had an announcement. His family looked at him expectantly. "In March, Kitty and I are going to La Nouvelle-Orléans, and we'll sail to France. Kitty, you must prepare." Henri smiled. "The boys will follow us next year—"

Kitty looked at him in shock. "No! Papa, I don't want to!"

"What do you mean, Kitty? I've worked for this for years. You want to go, of course you want to go! Of course you will go!"

"Henri," Sophia said in warning, standing to gather the plates. There was no point trying to corner Kitty; she was too stubborn. "Let me talk with Kitty, and I'm sure that—"

Kitty stood to help her mother. "No, Papa, I won't go!"

"What?" Henri was simply incredulous. "I'm telling you, you will go if I have to drag you by your hair every step of the way down the trail. You are going to France!" he insisted.

"Papa, I want to stay here." Her lip was trembling.

"No! You may not stay here. You will not defy your parents! You will obey! Why are you behaving like this?" Henri roared at his favorite child.

"Because . . . I'm going to marry Cully!"

"What? *Cully?* Never, never, never. You will marry a Frenchman and have French children!"

"Papa, I'm going to have a baby. Cully's baby."

Sophia stared at her daughter, openmouthed, too shocked to say anything. Then there was a crash, pewter plates went tumbling onto the floor as Sophia fainted for the second time in a fortnight.

CHAPTER 39
THE RAID

1779

For four years Sophia and Caitlin had listened in dismay to the accounts that reached them of growing unrest in the colonies. There were shocking stories: officials had been hung in effigy, the colonial assemblies in each colony were passing resolutions against England, the Sons of Liberty rampaged, and Governor Dunmore had first threatened to arm the slaves and then fled back to England with his wife and child. The British had sent troops. Then suddenly the colonies were at war, actually at war, with England.

Something called the Continental Army had been formed, and men were rushing to join it to fight the British. Sophia was astonished to learn the Continental Army was commanded by the Colonel Washington she'd once danced with in Williamsburg. Later there were accounts of terrible battles and new worries about which tribes were allied with the British and likely to attack settlers, then of bitter fighting between the American forces and the British. George and Francis liked the idea of soldiering but argued about whether to fight with the Continental Army or join the loyalist regiment they'd heard had formed in North Carolina.

Sophia felt outraged by the disloyalty of the king's subjects and bewildered by it all. "This is unthinkable!" she exclaimed over and over to Caitlin and Rosalia.

Two years into the war with England, Toby and Jack had gone to enlist with Washington after reading an account of the battle in a newspaper that came their way. They were excited at the prospect of being soldiers. Rufus thought of the London judge those many years ago who had nearly hung him and the boys and begged them to kill some Englishmen in his name. Exasperated, Sophia tried to talk them out of going, saying they would be sorry when they were hung for treason. She thought the world was coming apart. How could they rebel against their king?

Malinda wept. Caitlin sent Bryn to her father and uncles. The Caradoc men were all getting old and infirm and needed help. Bryn was very fond of his grandfather who taught him to play the fiddle, and liked the idea of managing Caradoc Station. Caitlin hoped that would keep him sufficiently occupied to prevent his going off to war too. Bryn sheepishly announced he and Peach Hanover wanted to get married so Peach could go with him, and Caitlin encouraged him because she thought it was one more thing that would keep Bryn from the war. The Caradocs' brush with near execution in their criminal days had left Caitlin with no love for the English authorities, but she agreed with Sophy that the Continentals sounded like rabble, tarring and feathering their opponents and besieging the English in Boston until the city became a hell hole.

Kitty was thankful Cully had no interest in fighting anyone; he said they could all shoot each other for all he cared. Cully and Kitty had been married by Parson Merriman and had named the baby, born five months after the wedding, Henry, hoping to placate Henri. They lived in Saskia's old cabin. Nott had gone to live with Meshack, saying babies kept him awake at night. Cully had added two more rooms, and Sophia had planted one of her ornamental herb gardens by the side. Sophia doted on little Henry, and she and Caitlin spent all their spare time sewing blankets and quilts and little clothes for their grandchildren. Rhiannon, as Caitlin pointedly persisted in calling her daughter, seemed happy enough. Caitlin never came round to actually approving her daughter's marriage but conceded Two Bears was always courteous to his mother-in-law, and Rhiannon seemed to enjoy a certain status among the tribe, thanks to her ability to interpret dreams and, on rare occasions, speak with animals. Caitlin rolled her eyes when she reported this to Sophia. "In all the world, Sophy, it's not possible to talk with animals. Oh, why does Rhiannon say such things!"

But what worried Caitlin now, more than her recalcitrant daughter, were reports that both the English and the Americans were making alliances with the Indian tribes to attack their opponents. There had been massacres of civilians and the same old stories of burned homesteads, scalped and mutilated bodies, destroyed crops, pillaging and rape, only this time the atrocities were part of a war between whites. Many colonists, like the Vanns and the de Marechals and Cully and Kitty wanted no part of the hostilities.

Tamás grew worried about his horses. The Continentals were requisitioning horses and food, and he had found another cave with a spring deep in the mountains where he'd built a corral in case he needed to hide his animals. Rosalia obtained rifles and ammunition and taught nine-year-old Stefania to shoot. All the households were armed. Occasionally deserters from both sides made a furtive appearance. The women gave them food and bandaged the injured and were relieved when they'd move on again.

Brother Merriman tended his fields and held Bible readings and hymn singings in his new church. Caitlin visited Mattie to keep her company and sometimes persuaded Malinda or Kitty to join her. Patience attended every Sunday service with her son Zebulon on her knee. She'd chosen the name with a pin and an open Bible.

Gideon told Caitlin that Rhiannon was expecting another child, but skirmishes between Indians and opposing Continentals and Tories made it too dangerous to visit Rhiannon for the time being. Caitlin fretted miserably.

The Continental currency was worthless, and counterfeit money was everywhere. Caitlin refused to take any paper currency and would only accept coins or barter. Upriver at Caradoc Station, Bryn was doing the same.

Magdalena, who had been fond of climbing trees and fishing and even wearing her brothers' old trousers and hats to ride the horses, grew taller. Kitty suddenly noticed and said, "Why, Lena, if you ever get out of those awful breeches, I do believe you're going to be prettier than me!"

Magdalena was stunned. This from *Kitty*?

In August Rosalia proposed a gathering to take their minds off the war that seemed to be hovering round them so menacingly. It was Ferragosto, Assumption Day in Sicily. They would have a picnic, and afterward Tamás would play his fiddle and everyone could dance. Stefania was wildly excited and helped her mother improvise Sicilian sweets and little cakes from dried fruit and honey.

The prospect lifted the spirits of everyone. They hadn't held the Blackberry Picnic for several years and everyone felt oppressed by news of the fighting. Caitlin agreed to make one of her raised pies and sent Gideon to shoot passenger pigeons and a deer. Henri and Seth decided to butcher a hog to roast, and Venus made a cake. Rosalia made a rich sauce from tomatoes, onions, wild garlic, and lard, and deep-fried little cornmeal cakes with cheese inside to dip in it. Rufus rowed over with a jug of fermented cider from the previous autumn, though Patience strongly disapproved of the drink and made him take a jug of blackberry shrub for the ladies and children. Meshack brought whiskey. Rufus and Seth between them said they would bring Nott, who had to be helped everywhere now, as he was increasingly unsteady on his feet and was going blind. Susan took her sisters to find vines and flowers and the first muscadine grapes for the tables Rosalia was setting up outside. Susan put some de-thorned dog roses in her hair and wondered if Francis and George would think she looked pretty. Especially Francis.

Sophia said she was feeling tired, and Kitty offered to stay with her, but Sophia said no, Kitty should take Henry and go with her father and Cully. She'd wait until the boys came in from their chores and they would row her over later. She would much rather not go anywhere she would meet Secondus. She saw him when she went to visit Rosalia, who had been kind to him, but the poor man with his worn and ragged finery and his wretched "mentomori" had fanned the embers of her grief back into life, and each time she saw him, he insisted on apologizing, which made it much worse. But of course it would offend Rosalia if she stayed away. *Duty before inclination,* thought Sophia wryly.

Sophia banked the fire and thought how unusual it was to have the cabin to herself and quiet except for its own creaky noises. It was funny how she'd never noticed how loud they were. Francis and George were taking their time, but it didn't matter. She was in no hurry to see Secondus, and it was peaceful to sit by herself for a little while.

She picked up her sewing basket. Was that an owl already? It was early for owls. They usually heard owls later, in the autumn. But no, there was another owl, answering.

Perhaps it meant the winter would be exceptionally cold or something, if the owls were hooting out of season. While she waited, she stitched at a shirt she was making for little Henry, who outgrew things so quickly. How strange, to think that little Henry was Thomas's grandson as well as her own. What a string of events since she left Thomas's house with his slaves and Henri. Nothing had gone as she had once planned, nothing whatsoever. She had not grown tobacco or grown rich. She had not returned to England. She had somehow absorbed the loss of her favorite child—grief had not killed her after all, though she had longed for it at the time. She had been shocked to the core to learn Kitty was expecting Cully's child, but she supposed it had turned out for the best. Kitty was happy.

I'm an old woman of forty-four, she thought, smiling to herself. *I've ceased to manage everything as I once did.* She shut her eyes and rested her head on her arms and fell asleep. Someone was calling, "Mother, Mother."

"Francis? Is that you?" Waking from her nap, Sophia was disoriented. She never dropped off before bedtime. It was so peaceful to be left alone with her thoughts. Then she remembered she was waiting for Francis and George, who would row her across the river to the party. There was a noise at the door, a scrabbling sound.

She rose to open it though she wondered why the boys didn't just come in, and then Francis stumbled through the door and fell onto the floor, an arrow through his side and another in his back. "Mother," he tried to say, and died. Sophia screamed. Behind him George lay in the yard, and she saw Indians and heard cries of "Kill the Tories." Something was on fire, she smelled smoke then spotted a familiar face . . . Sophia tried to scream his name, but an arrow felled her before she could.

It had grown dark, and from across the river, Tamás's fiddle was playing a jig. Henri supposed Sophia had decided she couldn't bear Secondus after all. Susan was disappointed Francis and George hadn't come. Supper had been eaten, and the children and adults one and all were dancing. There was a blazing campfire, and it took some time to realize there was also something burning on the side of Frog Mountain.

They stopped dancing and froze.

"Wildwood!" exclaimed Caitlin. "It's Wildwood! Henri, Gideon, *hurry!*" but Gideon was already running to his canoe, with Cully close behind and both leaped in and were paddling furiously.

"A raid, there must have been a raid!" Everyone rushed to their canoes.

"Mother!" screamed Kitty.

Sophia opened her eyes. She was in bed, and something hurt terribly. She smelled scorched hair, felt the tight bandage around her chest. George lay on the bed beside her, his head bloody and his shoulder bandaged. Kitty was asleep on the chair.

"What happened?" murmured Sophia.

Kitty woke and touched her hand. "Mother, you were in a raid. The Indians attacked. Do you remember? I'm afraid Francis is dead. George had an arrow in his shoulder. It narrowly missed his heart, but Venus and Caitlin think he'll be all right. Cully found you. Your hair had just caught on fire. You've bled a lot, and you must rest." Kitty's face was ashen and tearstained.

Sophia wondered why Kitty's voice was coming from a long way away. Magdalena was there, and Henri, and Sophia thought she saw Two Bears. No, she *had* seen Two Bears, and she tried to tell them.

"Mother recognized Two Bears . . . Rhiannon's husband . . . reward for Two Bears, Caitlin begged us not to send for the militia . . . her grandchildren . . . Sophy? Sophy!" It was a man's voice. Henri. The voices faded. There was a child with silvery hair. Sophia went toward her, but the child went farther and farther away.

Farther and farther. Sophia tried to follow, but she could not. "Charlotte," she called. "Charlotte . . . wait."

CHAPTER 40

THE HESSIAN WIDOW

October 1783

It was the first morning there had been a hard frost, and the autumn sun wasn't yet up when a yawning Magdalena left her corn cakes baking in last night's ashes, wrapped her shawl tight round her shoulders, and went to fetch a pat of butter from the springhouse. Then she picked a sprig of witch hazel and went down through the orchard to lay it on her mother's grave. She let her hand rest on the headstone a moment. "Mother," she whispered. Sophia had been dead for four years, but Magdalena still laid something on her mother's grave first thing most days. Sometimes she found blossoms Kitty or Henri or Georgie or his wife, Annie, Caitlin's daughter, had left too.

Climbing back up to the cabin, she was startled by a movement as something came out of the woods into the orchard. Peering through the gray light, she could see it was rooting for windfall apples the wasps had left. Most likely a boar; they loved apples. Fresh meat! Clutching her shawl and her butter, she quickened her step to fetch Papa's musket.

A strange sobbing noise stopped her. Magdalena looked again. About the size of a wild pig, it was a human shape on all fours scrabbling in the orchard grass, pausing only to stuff something into its mouth as if nothing else existed in the world but hunger and rotting fruit. Magdalena crept closer until she could see it was a woman in the remnants of a ragged dress, hair tangled with twigs like a battered bird's nest, and fear deep in her eyes when she looked. The wild woman froze in place with an apple in her hand and just stared as if she had seen a creature from another world.

Magdalena put her butter down. She slipped the shawl from her shoulders and approached carefully. "You are safe here," she murmured. "Poor thing! It's all right." She held out the shawl, but the woman just stared at her wildly, her breath ragged, then looked around, deciding where to bolt. Magdalena stopped in her tracks, as careful as if she were soothing a frightened animal. She crooned over and over that no one would hurt her. The woman continued eating her apple, one eye on Magdalena, who came closer step by careful step until she could drape the shawl round the woman's shoulders. "Come in and warm yourself. Eat something," said Magdalena, holding out her hand. "Come." She beckoned the woman, who stood and clutched the shawl tightly around herself with crossed hands, still holding the apple, quiet now, staring and still wary.

"Come with me," said Magdalena again, pointing to the cabin. The smell of wood smoke and bacon on the cold air meant Papa was up. He always started their fire in the morning and set the bacon hissing and spitting in the skillet. "Come with me. Breakfast."

She beckoned, and the woman followed a few steps behind, looking nervous and ready to run. Magdalena coaxed her into the cabin, and the woman jumped when Henri exclaimed, "What?"

Magdalena gave him a warning look and shook her head. She led the strange woman to her own chair next to the fire, plumped the patchwork cushion invitingly, and sat her down. The woman looked around nervously, then sank into the chair with a sigh. She blinked at Henri but said nothing. Magdalena hurried to the fireplace, deftly turned the bacon and set the skillet to the side so it didn't burn, and mixed corn cakes. The woman slowly held up her hands, either in disbelief or for warmth. They were large and raw. She was tall and gaunt and could have been anything between twenty and forty.

When the corn cakes were done. Magdalena filled three plates, put butter and then a spoon of honey from the crock on top of them, added bacon, and gave the largest plate to the woman, and another to Henri. The woman fell on the meal like a starving dog. Magdalena ate, watching the woman from the corner of her eye. Shoving the last crumbs into her mouth with her fingers, the woman mumbled, *"Danken Sie Gott!"* and *"Danken!"*

"I am Magdalena," said Magdalena, pointing to herself, gathering their empty plates. "Magdalena de Marechal." She pointed at her father. "Henri de Marechal." She pointed at the woman.

"Magdalena," the woman repeated in a hoarse voice. "Magdalena." She pointed to herself. "Rosenhauer. Anna."

"My husband, Robert, is a doctor, but he's gone to visit a sick old man who lives across the river."

"Doktor?"

Magdalena nodded and poured boiling water to make sassafras tea. *"Danke,"* Anna said, holding her cup tightly, and though it was hot by the fire, she began to shake as if she were cold, until her teeth clattered on the rim of her cup. First one tear, then another coursed down her cheeks and just dripped onto her chest and lap.

Magdalena took a handkerchief from her pocket and handed it to the woman. "I don't know where you came from, but you can stay with us."

"Sie konnen blei," muttered Henri. Anna looked surprised to hear him speak German, but Magdalena was also astonished. She never knew whether Henri would speak at all. Since her mother died, her father could sink into himself for days. Magdalena sometimes thought that must be why she had married Robert so quickly, so she could have someone to talk to.

"Ask her if she's Moravian, Papa." There were Moravians over the mountains, east in Carolina. She pointed. But Anna understood what she was asking. She swiped her hand across her wet cheeks and shook her head. "*Nein.* Hesse-Cassel."

Henri looked up from his plate of corn cakes. "Hesse-Cassel? She must have been married to one of the Hessians the British hired to fight. Their wives and families go where the army goes. They look after the men, draw half rations, they say."

"Hesse-Cassel!" Anna repeated over and over, nodding and pointing to herself. *"Frau. Kinder,"* she whispered, shaking her head. *"Kinder . . . mein Mann . . . gestor."*

"She was married. She has children. Had children. They're probably all dead. It's no life for women and children, following their men and their damned army," said Henri, rising stiffly to take their horses to be reshod by Toby the blacksmith. His rheumatism was getting worse now the autumn cold was settling into his bones.

When Toby heard Magdalena had found a Hessian woman in the orchard and taken her in, he spat and snarled that he had killed plenty of the Hessian dogs. Their red coats made good targets. Maybe he had killed her husband among them and she had come for revenge. He laughed harshly at his own joke. He hated the Hessian mercenaries even more than he hated the British and all American loyalists. The Hessians were more savage wild dog than human, murdering the wounded as they lay begging for mercy and water, plundering corpses, looting and burning and raping their way through the Carolinas with even less restraint than the British.

And there had been Hessians at Kings Mountain. That was where Toby had been wounded, hit in the shoulder and knocked to the ground. As he lay, a Hessian had come out of the mist, stood over him, and fired his musket into Toby's leg, just above the knee. He had laughed when Toby screamed in agony, then fixed his bayonet. It was Jack who saved Toby. Jack saw his brother fall on the slope above, saw the Hessian approach and fire at Toby's leg, with his bayonet raised to deliver the kill, and leaped up to charge the Hessian, stabbing his own bayonet deep into the Hessian's red-coated stomach and twisting it. As the man fell to his knees, Jack grabbed Toby, who was screaming with pain as his leg gushed blood, and dragged him through a hail of musket fire and smoke down to the field hospital. He poured the army surgeon's whiskey into Toby's throat and held his brother down while a Whig doctor performed an amputation with a bloody saw.

Toby should have died from loss of blood and shock, but the Drumhellers were tough. As an old man who walked with a limp, Rufus still worked his fields and his forge, and early in the war, Jack had somehow survived the smallpox that killed more soldiers than the enemy before General Washington ordered his troops inoculated.

Toby now had a wooden stump to balance on while he shoed horses and made whiskey from corn his father grew. He sold the whiskey from a lean-to beside his smithy, and his earnings filled a wooden box he had carved. He had a lined face and broad shoulders and little to say to anyone except his father and brother. He tended the cows and horses and pigs while his father and brother worked the Drumheller land at the farthest end of the valley.

Field by field, Rufus had acquired a spreading farm on the periphery of the Grafton patent, buying land from Henri, who would sell anything for ready money. Rufus came to own so much land that he had to hire such laborers as he could find—mostly drifting war veterans—to work for him. Between the crops and the livestock and the whiskey and the crude wagons and the keelboats Jack built from the timber felled when fields were cleared for planting corn, the Drumhellers had prospered. The original log cabin had been extended again and again to accommodate Jack, Jack's plump wife, Malinda, and their five children and chaos, children's laughter, and whatever Malinda had simmering on the fire—stews, preserves, or the laundry pot.

Toby preferred to sleep in his filthy lean-to with his money box.

Before the war, Toby had a soft spot for Magdalena. He had been twenty-seven when they called him to act as godfather at the hurried christening they held for the puny baby girl, fearing she would die. She hadn't died, and as she grew up, Toby felt proprietorial, especially after the Indians kidnapped her sister. Magdalena had adored Charlotte and grieved so much she stopped eating. Toby taught her to ride and fish and skip a smooth stone in the river, how to climb a tree, calm a horse before shoeing, ease honey from a beehive without getting stung.

Before Toby and Jack rode off to fight the British, Toby had carved Magdalena a farewell present, a honey spoon whose long handle was carved with flowers and a bee at its end. All through the war, he had carried his last sight of her with him—a barefoot hoyden of eleven with brown curls who resembled the portrait of her mother painted by Secondus Conway. If you ignored the things that looked like pockmarks on Sophia's face. After Sophia was killed in the raid, Henri had insisted on bringing the painting back to hang above the fireplace at Wildwood.

Magdalena had waved good-bye until Toby and Jack disappeared behind the mountain. The war had changed everything. He came back with one leg gone, a crutch, and a bitter heart, to find Magdalena sixteen and married to Robert Walker, a veteran army physician who had come through on his way to Kentuckee and met Magdalena, bought land from Henri, and stayed.

And now she'd taken in a filthy Hessian's woman. Robert had gone to La Nouvelle-Orléans to collect some medical equipment, and when he returned, Toby was sure he'd send the Hessian bitch packing.

But when he returned, Robert didn't. He treated her for worms and made up some salve for her sores. He looked at her crooked arm and told Magdalena later that it had been broken but never set and there was nothing he could do now. "Of course she can stay with us, Maggie," he said, before she even asked, reading the question in her eyes.

Anna couldn't have missed Toby's dislike. He spat at her when she came near until Magdalena caught him at it and berated Toby soundly, threatening never to speak to him again if he behaved so cruelly. After that Toby contented himself with seething and glowering.

Magdalena gave the woman some of her mother's clothes, though it cost her a struggle. She missed her mother desperately. She felt she'd had her heart torn out twice, once with Charlotte and once with Sophia. But this poor woman had suffered too. She fed her and spoke softly, because Anna would jump in fright at any sudden noise. But what to do with Anna? Robert agreed it would be best if she had something to occupy her.

She took her to see Kitty and her children. Kitty was surprised but cordial. Malinda held out both hands to Anna. Caitlin, who could hardly see any longer, said she'd done the right thing. Patience looked askance, but she looked askance at everyone but Zebulon, who was quite a horrid, smug child.

Rosalia had buried Tamás the previous year, and was still sad and rather lonely herself. When Magdalena coaxed a nervous Anna in a canoe and rowed her across to visit Rosalia, Rosalia welcomed Anna into her kitchen, where she was giving Stefania a lesson in Italian, baking bread, and boiling jam. Within minutes, Rosalia had an idea. Secondus still lived in the smallest homestead cabin and had come to be fed at Rosalia's table every day until he could no longer walk the distance. Poor Secondus was very isolated and did nothing but paint and sketch. The cabin was very messy, and Rosalia couldn't keep him and his paints and canvases in order. Perhaps Anna would come and live at Rosalia's and look after Secondus? Tamás's room was empty. While Secondus wasn't actually elderly, Rosalia understood there had been many years of heavy drinking, and Secondus needed someone to look after him. She showed Anna to a small bedroom at the back of her cabin, with its own fireplace, a rope bed, and a bright quilt made from Rosalia's old dancing skirts. Anna fell to her knees and kissed Rosalia's hands before Rosalia could stop her.

Toby was pleased the Hessian was on the other side of the river.

Within eight months, Anna had filled out a little, and her haunted look had lessened. She was impressed to be looking after an artist and bustled around Secondus's cabin, cleaning and tidying and cooking, always ready to admire anything Secondus did. She was also a good listener, going "Ah!" respectfully at intervals while Secondus talked incessantly. She didn't understand enough English to realize if he repeated the same stories over and over, but she seemed pleased he spoke to her. Secondus began to see Anna as an unusually discerning female.

Summer had come, and all the settlers were wary. There were Indians on the river trail, there one minute and gone the next, migrating or war, but there had been no more attacks on the settlement. But as Magdalena went about her daily chores, between the barn and the house and the chicken house and her mother's herb garden that she carefully tended, she told Robert she saw little movements now and then, and she was sure someone was watching her.

Magdalena was in the orchard getting a basket of peaches to make a pie for supper when she sensed someone there. She looked up and a few feet away an Indian woman dressed in deerskin was gazing back at her. Magdalena was so startled she dropped the peaches and cried out. She stared, unable to believe her eyes.

The Indian woman had moonlight hair and blue-green eyes and a baby strapped to her back. A bright-eyed child clutched her hand. The woman stared back at Magdalena and finally asked, "Are you my sister Magdalena?"

Magdalena's eyes filled with tears. "It can't be," she whispered when she could finally speak. "Charlotte? After all this time? Alive? You are alive after all?" She could scarcely get the words out.

"Yes," said the Indian woman.

Magdalena walked up to her, reached out her hands, and gently touched Charlotte's cheek.

"Oh, Charlotte! To see you again! I never thought . . . We all missed you so! We tried to ransom you. Mother believed you were dead. If you were alive, why did you not come before now? Why not send us word? If only Mother was alive!" She burst into tears. "Charlotte!" She reached out to embrace the stranger.

"My name is Winter Moon," her sister said, laying her cheek against Magdalena's.

"But you've come back! That's all that matters! And with your children! Let me prepare Papa first, or the shock will—"

"No, do not tell him."

"*What?* Charlotte, you're home now, and—"

"No, I'm not staying. Our tribe is going south on the river trail. I married a brave, and I have my children. I cannot leave them. I was adopted and raised by the Indians and have become one of them. I can live no other way now. I don't even wish to. But I hoped to see Mother again, and have always felt a great longing to see you, Magdalena. I missed you so for many years."

Magdalena tried to wipe her eyes, but the tears would not stop. "Oh, Charlotte, if you knew how we suffered when you were taken. Mother worst of all. She changed, Charlotte. And then she was killed in a raid. Francis died too. George was wounded but he survived."

"Yes," sighed Charlotte. "I know. The British believed this part of Virginia was full of rebel Americans, and the Americans thought it was full of British loyalists. The tribes were persuaded to attack so many. Our braves, my husband among them, have fought hard for the British."

"Rhiannon Vann married a Cherokee from her father's tribe who fought for the Americans," said Magdalena bitterly. "Two Bears. They were allies of the Americans, and ordered to attack Tories like Mother. Mother recognized him, and then she . . . she died of her injuries . . . It was horrible. Caitlin Vann, Mother's dearest friend, cut off her ties with her daughter Rhiannon, refused to see her ever again. Caitlin's husband rode away to reason with Rhiannon, persuade her to divorce Two Bears and return home with her children, but Gideon disappeared, and we've not seen Rhiannon again. They say Gideon's gone to live in the mountains, to make his campfires and have his visions, that he has learned to fly like an eagle. So many terrible things, Charlotte."

Charlotte smiled sadly. "There will be war and sorrow and blood revenge for many years for these things. I cannot come back. Good-bye, Magdalena."

"No, Charlotte, please, don't go, you can't go, not yet . . ." But Charlotte had slipped away silently into the trees. "Don't go!" cried Magdalena. There was so much she wanted to know, so much to tell Charlotte. Magdalena rubbed her eyes. Had she been dreaming? No, she had lost her sister twice.

Magdalena could tell no one except Robert, who understood why she could say nothing to Henri. But Charlotte's brief appearance weighed heavily on Magdalena. Hoping to cheer his wife up, Robert told her to put on her shawl and bonnet, they would visit Rosalia and Stefania. There was a new rope ferry she ought to see, and he wanted to try it. Down at the landing, Anna was waiting with some meal she had purchased from Caitlin. They were preparing to push off when Caitlin called from her doorway they should wait a moment, that there was another passenger who had fallen asleep in the corner while waiting for enough passengers to assemble for the crossing. "Who is he?" asked Magdalena. "Does he want Secondus?"

Looking sightlessly into the distance, Caitlin smiled a strange smile. "You'll see."

A middle-aged gentleman with a beard came hurrying out, settling his hat and adjusting his coat. Magdalena regarded the stranger curiously. She knew that the war had left many people damaged in mind, and she thought the man was behaving as if he too were damaged.

"I wonder what he wants on the other bank," whispered Magdalena. "There's only Secondus and Rosalia and Stefania. Perhaps he wants to buy land from Papa, or a horse from Rosalia." She glanced at the man and raised her eyebrows at Anna. Anna shrugged. She had no idea who he was.

To their surprise the strange man followed the Walkers and Anna to Rosalia's. When they reached her gate, Rosalia was feeding her chickens, and she looked up at them. "Thank you, Anna. And come in, Magdalena dear. Stefania will be so happy to see you, and I've just made a . . ."

Rosalia stopped midsentence. She turned deathly pale and clapped her hands to her mouth. The stranger bowed slightly. Rosalia's lips moved, but at first no sound came out. "It cannot be," she whispered finally. "Pardon me, sir . . . excuse my foolishness, you resemble my . . . husband, but you cannot be . . . Stefano. You are older than I remember him, but you have his eyes . . . but it cannot be. Are you a ghost?" she cried. "Have you found me, or do I dream it?" She reached a hand to stroke his cheek. The man's face was working oddly as if he were trying to speak but could not. "Oh, Stefano, you feel real. Or I am dying?"

Rosalia began to laugh and sob, and the man she called Stefano put his arms around her. "Shh, the Inquisition are gone, banished from Sicily. I was set free, and I reached La Nouvelle-Orléans two years ago, and the servants at my cousin's house said you had gone north to Virginia. I'd almost given up hope of finding you. But I have found you at last, my Rosalia. At last."

CHAPTER 41
THE EVANGELIST

June 1790

He was a long-faced man, no longer young, in a threadbare black coat somewhat ripped at the back, as if someone had picked him up like a kitten by the scruff and thrown him. He had a large hat and broken shoes and had walked out of the forest and knocked on the door of the first cabin he reached. He asked the stout Negro woman who answered if her master and mistress would give him food in return for work. Venus drew herself up and snapped that she was a free woman, it was her house, and she would give food to whomever she pleased. Or not.

The man apologized. He found the distinctions in this part of the world confusing. He was tired and thirsty; if she had no work for him, might he ask a dipper of water?

Venus relented. She pointed to the bucket and dipper beside the door. Since Seth's death there were many small jobs that required doing. She listed them to the man. Shingles off the roof, she said. A bucket leaking, she said. Her vegetable patch could do with weeding and a good hoeing before she planted it. Door coming off its leather hinges.

"I am a good worker. I can do these things."

She nodded him inside. "Then I got stew." He removed his hat, rendered speechless by the word *stew*.

Venus sat him at her table. The man stroked the wood with his fingers, appreciating the workmanship and the polishing with beeswax. "Well made," he said.

"My husband"—Venus lingered on the word—"my husband made it for me, after we was married. Built this cabin, made this furniture." She gestured proudly round her kitchen at the chairs and the wooden chests, the large dresser where she kept plates and teacups.

She stirred a pot and waited for him to say something about slaves and marriage. "This is very fine," said the visitor. "Such work, strong and serviceable. Handsome in the eyes of God and goodly for the use of man."

Venus thought about it for a minute. It was a strange way to talk, but she liked the respectful tone in which the visitor said "handsome" and "serviceable" to describe the things Seth had made. She put as much stew on his dish as it would hold.

He stared at the generous dinner Venus set before him, then watched as she served herself, not quite so much. "Please, don't let me have more than my share. I mustn't deprive thee."

"I got more in the pot, could feed the whole valley if I had to," Venus boasted. She did own fields and the cows, chickens, and pigs. Her bacon was the best cured in the valley—she'd gotten the right combination of hickory to apple wood for the smoke cure. The butter she churned was sweeter than her daughters'. His lip trembled when she put corn cakes and butter and a dish of last summer's mayhaw confit on the table. He closed his eyes, inhaled deeply, bowed his head, and said grace.

Venus said, "Amen, you can eat now."

He nodded and began, not falling on the food as Venus had expected—the man was clearly hungry—but slowly. An intense look of concentration, then contentment replaced the pinched expression. He ate a corn cake with butter, savoring it. He said the stew was delicious. He took small bites, but it disappeared quickly all the same. Without asking, Venus refilled his dish. "I am greedy, but I thank thee," he whispered. "I haven't eaten for . . . days."

"Have another," said Venus, pushing the corn cakes toward him. "Butter it while it's hot." Color was coming back into his face, a little. Some strange people came on the river these days, she thought.

What was his name?

"Forgive me. Iddo Fox. And you?"

"Venus Hanover."

"Pleased to make your acquaintance, Mrs. Hanover." Venus still liked the sound of *Mrs. Hanover* in her ears.

"Where you come from, Mr. Fox?" she asked.

"From Pennsylvania. I'm a Dissenter."

"Hunh. You look white to me."

"No, a Quaker." He sighed and regarded a torn sleeve with dismay. "I've been in some difficulties on account of it. We don't hold with armies and wars and killing, and we do not believe slavery is right. Some Friends and I came to Virginia, to speak against it. Alas"—he shrugged—"the planters there depend on slavery, and we are not well received. We have been beaten and hounded, throughout the colony. But the Lord tempers the wind to the shorn lamb." He finished his stew. "Is your husband here?"

"No," said Venus. "He died. Before the war. He free too. Was working at this forge up on that mountain there." She pointed to Little Frog Mountain. "Rattlesnakes just loved it round the forge, don't know why, but they come out the woods to that spot. Indian who run the trading post told him and Rufus, the man owned the forge, not to kill rattlesnakes 'cause they'll get you back, but Rufus do what he want, he hate snakes, kill every one he can find. Still, snakes, snakes, and more snakes come there. Seth got bit twice, took some root the Indian give him as a cure. Third time he by himself, disturbed a whole nest, they found him there next morning, all swole up and dead. Brought him home. We buried him." She started to cry. "Buried him the best we could, but best burying in the world, it don't bring nobody back to life. And what happen? Nobody seen a snake at the forge since." She dried her eyes, then teared up again.

Iddo Fox got to work soon after, and Venus thought he was a little like Seth, careful and painstaking. She admired a repair, saying he'd done it well. Iddo Fox smiled. "The laborer is worthy of his hire."

It was getting dark when Iddo Fox gathered his coat and put on his hat. "I thank thee again for a fine meal, Mrs. Hanover."

"It's dark now! Where you going in the dark?"

"I will sleep in the woods . . . I've done it many times . . ."

"No, you won't. You'll sleep here in front of the fire. I got plenty of quilts."

"Mrs. Hanover!"

"Oh, get on! I'm a grandmother, almost sixty. And by the looks of it, you ain't much younger. I got no more sin of that kind left in me. And there's more jobs need doing."

"I don't think I should—"

"Give me that coat. I'll mend it. And for breakfast. I got ham."

Iddo Fox became known in the valley as "the man doing jobs for Venus." Her daughters were scandalized their mother was sharing her home with a man, but they couldn't make her change her mind. "Maybe I'm lonesome. You all gone with your husbands and children. I'm here by myself." This brought a flurry of protest she should come live with this one or that one, until Susan, Patsy, Polly, Pen, Pearlie, and Peach were all shouting, arguing who could look after Mama best. Peach especially. Wanting to have the last word, Peach said she'd come by every day to check to see that her mother wasn't being taken advantage of. She shook her finger at Iddo Fox and her mother too.

"Stop that!" Venus could still outshout her children. "I ain't leavin' my own good house. I'm staying here and so's Mr. Fox. This his lodging. He boarding here. Boardinghouse is respectable."

So they had to put up with it.

Brother Merriman came to remonstrate over the arrangement, lest despite the age of the parties they might be tempted into his favorite sin, fornication. He discovered that Mr. Fox was a Quaker and expressed a good deal of puritan outrage, including his opinion that Quakers weren't Christians at all and Iddo Fox ought to be whipped out of the valley.

Brother Merriman left the Hanover cabin almost thrown through the door by Venus.

Iddo Fox stayed put. Venus thought it was a comfort to have a man to look after and feed, and Iddo was company but quiet, which was nice for a change. Both of them settled into an easy routine together, as if they were an old married couple, sitting comfortably together by the fire at night talking of this and that if they had anything to say, and if not, they enjoyed a companionable silence while Venus sewed and Iddo smoked his pipe.

Along with his other jobs for Venus, Iddo fetched things from the trading post when Venus needed them. He would bring back news—whether Caitlin was well or not; that her son Bryn was getting married; that Brother Merriman's wife, Mattie, was expecting again; that Brother Merriman had asked to marry Secondus and Anna.

"What?" exclaimed Venus. "That crazy old man who paints things? Gettin' married?"

Iddo Fox chuckled as he filled his pipe. "Thee is surprised. It was Rosalia's idea, I hear."

And then there was more news. From the woods to the south, four strangers, three Jesuits in robes led by a man of military bearing, all mounted on good horses with fine saddles and a baggage train of mules appeared. Iddo had seen them at the trading post, and the military leader pointed this way and that, as if orienting himself. Then he led the procession up through the orchard to Frog Mountain to Wildwood.

Later Iddo had discovered what had happened next from Caitlin's daughter Annie who was married to George de Marechal.

Cully had greeted the strangers and the leader had swept off his hat. "Is Henri de Marechal still alive?"

"My wife's father," said Cully. "Pa?" he called through the door. "There's someone asking for you." An old man shuffled out.

"Henri?" said the stranger. "Don't you know me?"

Henri peered at the strangers. They were speaking French. Why was that, he wondered. "My sight isn't what it was. Who are you?"

"Don't you recognize me, old friend? It's Thierry. On the day your daughter Kitty was born, I left and promised I would be back. And now after many years, I have kept my promise."

"Eh?" said Henri. "Did you go to France?"

"I went back to France for a time, then nearly died fighting with Lafayette in your war, and after that I nearly died at the guillotine. But the mercy of God kept me alive to keep a vow. Do you remember the Starving Winter, Henri? The Virgin led me to the cornfield abandoned by the Indians, and we were saved."

Henri had looked bewildered. He was bewildered.

"Thierry?" Henri struggled to remember who Thierry might be. Sophia would know. He must ask her.

"I have brought a precious reliquary with a bone of St. Eustache, who was out hunting and saw a stag with an image of the cross in its horns. I, too, was hunting and had a miracle. Come with us, Henri, my cousin will find a place to consecrate and say Mass. How long since you have heard Mass, eh?"

The stranger was still speaking French. People didn't speak French anymore, Henri thought, but he felt himself transported to another place, something to do with stags and hunting lodges. He turned to Cully. "What do they want?" he asked.

There were a lot of people and dogs everywhere. He thought it was Sophia on the porch . . . it looked like Sophia, but the mulatto man was calling her Kitty. Whoever she was, she was telling the strangers something, they were dismounting, and the woman had been joined by another woman she called Annie. Who was Annie? Someone was saying there was room for them to stay tonight, please come in and make themselves comfortable, and someone else said they would take Henri with them the next day. *Demain.*

Demain, muttered Henri, and he went back inside to his seat by the fire. People crowded into the room around him. "Papa, you shouldn't be riding a long way," said a man who had the woman called Annie by his side. Henri heard someone roaring that he damned well would go if he pleased. He thought it might be he who was roaring but couldn't be sure. Was George the man with Annie?

There was dinner and everyone talking at once. Then it was morning. People were bustling, everyone talking at once. It must be a hunt. Dogs were everywhere.

The woman he thought was Sophia came in from the porch. "What's this about Papa riding with you, Thierry? Papa, you get dizzy. You mustn't. You're not well enough."

"Nonsense," said Henri testily. He asked for a horse to be saddled, and when Robert remonstrated, he flew into a fury and said he'd do it himself.

"Let me saddle the old cob," Robert muttered to Magdalena. "Safest thing to do."

Henri mounted with a hint of his old vigor. Robert and Kitty and George and the woman called Annie watched him go.

As Henri rode with the others, he was glad to be out of the cabin, glad to be hunting. He felt younger now that he was riding. His horse seemed to fly up Frog Mountain and then down the other side. He lost track of time. It seemed that things were drifting, unreal; on they went, the five of them. They dismounted at the edge of a field. He knew why but couldn't remember. He was tired suddenly, with a heaviness in his limbs. Someone helped him and said, "Steady." Then they were kneeling, and he must have fallen asleep. He opened his eyes with an effort and saw the priest was placing a golden box in a niche above a rock. The priest was speaking, though Henri could not hear him well. The sound came and went. He caught an occasional Latin phrase.

He looked for Thierry. He had so much to say to Thierry and François. It had been a long time. But he was kneeling, all of them were. His knees hurt. He was tired. He closed his eyes and woke as someone thrust a wafer into his mouth. He tried to open his mouth wider to receive it. But the wafer was too big. Everything was sinking, sinking. He looked at the golden box, and it disappeared into the soundless darkness that filled his mind as he slumped forward.

CHAPTER 42

ADELINA MAURY

September 1833

Sign above the Slipping Creek Mission:

"TO MAKE THE WHOLE TRIBE ENGLISH IN THEIR LANGUAGE, CIVILIZED IN THEIR HABITS, AND CHRISTIAN IN THEIR RELIGION."

Dearest Ma, Papa, and Sisters,

We have reached the mission at last! I have finished unpacking my trunk, washed my traveling clothes, packed away my traveling bonnet on a top shelf, and have laid out my good serviceable everyday bonnet, a fresh cotton dress, and clean apron, ready for tomorrow when I shall at last bend my neck to my freely chosen yoke to begin the Lord's work bringing the good news to the Indian children and laboring to awaken their heathen spirits to the mercy of God Almighty and Our Savior Jesus. The evening is still bright enough to write. I have prepared as well as I can for my first day's teaching and may now feel justified in indulging myself with the pleasure of giving you an account of our journey and to reassure you of my safe arrival at my new home.

This place is not half so wild and unsettled as you feared it would be. I understand there was a very colorful titled English lady to whom the land was granted by an English king many years ago. There is now a thriving town, Grafton, with a large trading post that does a brisk business with the flatboats on the river and the parties of settlers and traders who pass continuously. Our mission sits at the end of a wide valley on a kind of low ridge between Frog Mountain and Little Frog Mountain. In the valley there are homesteads on either side of the river. The settlers are English and Welsh, I am told, though there have been Italians and Germans among them. The mission is on land gifted by the Hanover family to the mission board, and it is rather a wonder, but the Hanovers, a large and important family here, are descended from freed slaves! Indeed there are several such families, though there had been much intermarriage between all the people in the valley, another wonder as I do not think it possible that any degree of intermarriage would take place elsewhere!

I hope there will be someone traveling north to take this letter so it may reach you sooner than if I have to wait to send it with the bag of letters that goes twice a year.

But I must give you an account of our arrival. We received a most kind welcome from the other missionaries yesterday. There were prayers of thanksgiving for our safe journey, and much rejoicing over the trunks of goods we brought. A good, hot dinner of roast venison, vegetables, and pies had been prepared by the ladies, of which we ate heartily, though I think the ladies here do not have Ma's light hand with pastry.

It will not surprise you to learn both venison and pie disagree with Mrs. Whitaker's stomach.

After dinner and prayers, Mrs. Whitaker and I were much refreshed by a bath in a creek behind the mission, although it was modestly taken in our petticoats. Mrs. Whittaker disliked the tucks on mine. I think I have never met with a sourer disposition than Mrs. Whittaker's. Were the Rapture to take place tomorrow, she would be certain to frown at some part of it.

But I must tell you of our journey, which sometimes felt longer and harder because of Mrs. Whittaker's presence as a traveling companion. I will begin with that heartrending moment two months ago, when Pa loaded my trunk into Reverend Whitaker's wagon before sunrise and I kissed you all good-bye. As he helped me in, I prayed to the Lord for strength and had to keep my Bible clutched tight in my hands to stop myself gathering up my skirts and jumping down to run back home. The wheels made a mournful sound as we rolled away down the drive, and for a moment I fancied I was on my way to the guillotine like the poor French queen Marie Antoinette, instead of setting out to do the Lord's work, which ought always to be done with a joyful heart. When we passed the Hendersons' fields and gate, I kept my head low. I didn't want Mrs. Whitaker to see the tears rolling down my cheeks under the traveling bonnet Sister Margaret had trimmed specially. Mrs. Whittaker is ever watchful to chide and would have been sure to give me a sharp lecture.

I tell you of my sadness in leaving not to distress you, but to say that I have battled in spirit to overcome my weakness in repining a course that was my own choice and no other's. I may have given way to tears under the cover of the darkness that morning, but I resolved to maintain a cheerful appearance, at least, during the hot, weary days of traveling ahead. Indeed there is something about a change of scene that must lift even the heaviest of spirits. Within weeks the landscape changed from the flat fields of Maryland to rolling hills in Virginia, like bald heads. The world is so large! The forest grew thick around us, and then we reached the river. Reverend Whitaker said that we would embark on a flatboat to travel almost the rest of the way.

At the landing, which was very muddy, there was a great bustle. We were to travel in a flotilla of flatboats, rafts, and bark canoes for safety from Indian attack, and most of these vessels had one or two men with long rifles. The Whitakers and I and a few other passengers crowded together on a rough wooden platform that was raised a little above the mud as a sort of wharf, though a rather shaky one, to wait. For nearly half a day, we had to wait in the broiling sun while the rafts were loaded with numerous families hoping to stake a claim to land to the south, as well as their household goods, sheep, cattle, horses, and even pigs, chickens, plows and bags of seed, hoes, and spinning wheels.

The slaves stacked a shipment of molasses and whiskey and guns for the trading post at our destination. The casks of whiskey gave off a vile smell, as no doubt will the men who drink it. As the whiskey and guns were loaded, we were entertained—though that is not quite the right word—by many tales, loudly told, of the drunken shootings that always followed such deliveries. Mrs. Whitaker's mouth pursed tighter and tighter, and for the first time I felt a little sympathy for her. She must be anxious about the rough place to which we are going. I am anxious myself but will trust in the Lord to lead us safely through any valley of the shadow. Or across the water. Deep water makes me nervous.

As our flotilla prepared to depart there was a cry of "Wait!" Hastening toward the landing came a wagon carrying a delegation of solemn, bearded gentlemen from the mission board. Their ladies had prepared a large box of useful things to equip us—Bibles, nails, large cooking pots for the school, sewing cases, and bolts of serviceable calico for modest new dresses for the Indian girls. Just in time. The wharf slaves were ordered to carry it on board. The solemn gentlemen were surprised to find I was so young, and one remarked he had not expected a fine elegant miss to be appointed a teacher. Elegant, Ma! And said in such a tone of voice! Is that what they call the brown woolsey dress that you made for me, serviceable boots, and a clean handkerchief? I bit my lip in order not to retort that my parents taught us sisters that clean and tidy female dress and appearance were signs of inward cleanliness of spirit and tidiness of heart.

I turned away from his censure. The river was brown and sluggish-looking, and I peered in to see if any fish were visible. The captain saw me and snorted that dangerous currents ran underneath the surface and careless young ladies who leaned too far over the water to look at their reflections often fell in and were sucked under and drowned. When I started back and said I wasn't looking at myself but for fish, he laughed heartily. Mrs. Whitaker looked reproving as always, although whether it was at me for leaning, the captain for laughing, or the river for flowing I could not tell. Mrs. Whitaker disapproves of me generally—and especially disapproves of my having red hair, which is so hard to keep tidy, as you know, willful curls escape no matter how tightly I pull it into its bun. She also looked sourly at the bonnet Margaret trimmed with mallard feathers as well as at the bottle of lavender water you gave me for the journey, which I have found most refreshing. She looked askance at my little volume of Shakespeare's sonnets, which I take from my pocket to while away the time when we are obliged to stop to exercise the horses, and I expect would disapprove of the supply of clean stockings, handkerchiefs, and underthings dear Ma packed in my carpetbag.

Mrs. Whitaker constantly reminded me that being eighteen, I could expect not to have any authority among the native girls. Reverend Whitaker is kinder but rather abstracted. It was unfortunate not to have more congenial companions, but I decided I must bear it and them.

We settled ourselves with our baskets and parcels as best we could in the tiny cabin-like shelter allocated to us, our trunks and the mission's box squeezed in almost on top of us. We turned the mission box into a sort of seat.

Then we cast off and were soon in the middle of the river. The afternoon was so warm and close, and I was pressed so uncomfortably against Reverend Whitaker, that I went to the rail for the fresh air. The riverbank was slipping past faster than I expected, and since the sun on the water was so hot, I took off my bonnet to catch the breeze. My hair tumbled out of its pins, and I shook it loose before gathering it up again. I saw the captain watching in a way that made me uncomfortable. "Missionaries, eh? I know of places other than the mission would be pleased to have such as you under their roofs. Men'd pay well for that hair."

The Whitakers heard the last of this. "Put your bonnet on at once," Mrs. Whitaker hissed. I obeyed. Then she turned to her husband and commanded, "Reverend Whitaker, a prayer for our undertaking, if you please." I sighed but bowed my head, closed my eyes, and folded my hands. Reverend Whitaker prays in his great booming voice at great length about everything that springs to mind. I wonder that the Lord doesn't grow weary of listening, or give him a divine revelation about brevity. For the next week or so, we prayed our way down the river, though fortunately on deck because of the heat, where I peeked continually through my fingers to see what might be happening on the other boats or the banks.

As you can imagine, our progress was noisy, because the animals did not like being tethered on one spot day after day, and there was much lowing and squealing and squawking. The farmyard smells were rather overpowering in the sun. Occasionally a child fell overboard to the alarm of its parents if not to the captain. Fortunately all such children had no more than a dunking, as they had been fished out by the Indians manning the bark canoes, but the captain insisted afterward that they be tied to the rail.

There was a great shouting banter kept up between the guards with rifles across the flotilla, about the rapids and shoals that awaited us farther down the river, a very dangerous stretch, I understood, which had to be carefully navigated, where many rafts have sunk, and this has given rise to a superstition that a spirit known as the Snatcher of Souls lurks there, who plays the fiddle, and they say there is a vast host of the drowned who sing and dance and feast below the water to entice travelers above to join them and to lure travelers to their death. If this happens, their souls belong to the Snatcher.

But the brown river remained calm, the weather sunny, and the nights warm. The men caught fish for our dinner most days. But even cooked, the fish tastes of mud. I ate it because I am very hungry.

The landscape changed as we went south and west. The riverbanks grew steeper and more heavily forested, and rising in the distance were mountains. Behind the laurels and beeches, the men said an Indian road or warriors' path runs along the river, and travelers who could not afford passage on the river and merchants with long strings of mules sometimes risked it. As our guards called back and forth to each other, their voices were sharper. They were constantly on the alert for any attack. Sometimes, they said, Indians were friendly, and sometimes not.

We saw buffalo drinking, and several times the whole flotilla has halted while a hunting party went in search of fresh meat—bear or venison or buffalo to replenish our food supply. The wild meat was tough but better than muddy fish.

After nearly three weeks on the river, our supplies of cornmeal were gone and everyone was hungry. Some of the ladies picked blackberries when we pulled into the bank for the night. I joined the party, as Mrs. Whitaker never ceases to remind me the Devil finds work for idle hands. She meant my writing of this letter. But berrying is a task I enjoy, so I obeyed her cheerfully. I am very fond of blackberries, which I suppose the Lord has sent as a sort of manna to give us heart in the wilderness.

That night they said that the trading post was around the next bend on the river, and that we would reach it early the next day. The captain said that I should give this letter to one of the boats going in the direction from which we had come, and that in this way, letters are generally passed on back and forth along the river. At the landing where we embarked, the men from the mission board come regularly to see if any letters have arrived from the mission in this manner, and they duly pass any such on to families of their missionaries and teachers.

I pray this will eventually find its way to you and send much love to you all, begging you will believe me strong in heart and in the love of our Lord, and always your loving daughter and sister,

Adelina Maury

Slipping Creek Mission
Cherokee Lands
March 16, 1835

Dearest Ma, Papa, and Sisters,

I hope this finds you all well, as I am. After a year and a half, I have an opportunity to send a long letter! The mission board warned us we would suffer separation from our families in order to do the Lord's work among the Indians, and I confess I have missed you all greatly, but Jesus may test us but never fails us in our hour of need. In this place of mountains and rivers and rocks and forests, all untamed and rushing, where urgent and rough nature daily threatens to overwhelm the clearing where our mission sits, we feel quite frail, and overwhelmed.

As for William Henderson . . . Cousin Mary was William's choice. I assure you I have subdued all fond recollections that may have remained in my heart until I can truthfully say that I wish him and Cousin Mary joy of their union. I have willingly submitted to the different path God intended me to follow. I doubt William would even recognize me now, a sober spinster who has given over idle thoughts of ribbons and waltzes. I hope Sister Hezzia has worn my pink muslin dress to great advantage—with her coloring, it suited her better than me. Perhaps she is engaged? Is she blushing as you read this out loud? Oh, Hezzi, if only I were there to see. But I run on. The messenger who kindly offered to take my letters north says he will wait for an answer so that he can bring me a letter from you on his return. My description of this messenger must serve as his introduction. His name is Major Caradoc Vann. He is a man of about forty, the grandson of Miss Caitlin, the lady who started the trading post.

He has served in the army, is recently come home. It transpires that he owns the trading post on the river after the death of his father. There is frequent intermarriage between the Cherokee and the white people, and they say the major's grandfather was the product of such a union, and what people call a "half-blood," but really, no one knows for sure to what degree he is or is not an Indian. But the major is a man of few words on that or any other matter, and he has not said. He is clean shaven, which makes him resemble an Indian more than anything, as the Cherokee men have no facial hair. His features are strong, and his hair is straight and dark, though his eyes are gray. In the dress common in these parts, a woodsman's hunting shirt of deerskin and rough woolen trousers, he could be one or the other.

Major Vann is a rather thoughtful man, whose presence is not exactly frightening but, you will agree,

I am sure when you meet him, commands respect. And I am glad you will meet him. He made the offer in the politest way. There was nothing particular or insinuating about his manner, as there usually is in the manners of the rough men here toward ladies, especially those of a man named Zebulon Drumheller, who is also a descendant of some of the first settlers. In his somber way, Major Vann is a true gentleman most courteous and obliging to all females. I am ashamed to think he sensed how homesick I was here at first and witnessed my struggle against repining. That battle has long been won, I assure you, which is why I can write of it cheerfully.

Major Vann's niece, a dear little girl of six named Dora, the daughter of the major's cousin Jesse (his English name; I cannot pronounce his Cherokee one!), is one of my pupils. She is one of the cleverest and sweetest children imaginable, quick to learn her lessons and prayers and a great favorite of mine. It is thanks to her that the major has offered to deliver my letter. He is traveling to Washington this month, and when Dora told him my family was far away, he called after school one day to say that a detour to you in Maryland will take him only a little out if his way if I had any letters he could deliver. I accepted gratefully and sat down at once to write this. Major Vann's business in Washington is something to do with an agreement between the Cherokee and the government over ownership of Cherokee lands. The Indians rarely own land individually in parcels or farms, it is simply owned by all, and they hunt and grow crops where it is best to do so. This seemed to me to demonstrate a truly Christian spirit of sharing, but there are many new settlers here who are desirous of laying claim to great parcels of land for themselves. There is talk of the government paying the Cherokees for their land and assisting them to take up lands farther west, beyond the Mississippi. But looking down the valley from the mission, the valley is a patchwork of homesteads, Indian, white, half-blood, and of course the Indians do not wish to go. It is very wrong and greedy of the new settlers to speak of forcing them to go, and I pray that God will bless Major Vann's endeavors to prevent that.

But the front and back of this paper are nearly full. I will leave you to read it and to believe me ever, dear Ma and Papa and Sisters, your loving daughter and sister.

Adelina Maury

Slipping Creek Mission
Cherokee Lands
March 1837

Dearest Ma, Pa, and Sisters,

Major Vann has returned from another trip to Washington, bringing with him your kind letter of permission and blessing on our engagement. I have been on tenterhooks ever since his proposal at Christmas, knowing my heart was entirely his, yet insisting to him that I could not give him an answer without your sanction. Now my heart is so filled with joy after saying yes I can scarcely think, can scarcely write but to assure you over and over that I love him and must subdue my thoughts enough to thank God, who has drawn me to this place and to him. I am crying and laughing so that I cannot tell which. We shall be married at summer's end, after the harvest. Oh, Ma and Pa, Hezzi and Margaret, was ever a girl as happy as I am?

Your loving daughter,
Adelina Maury

CHAPTER 43
DANCING RABBIT

May 1837

High on the bluff, the path that wound up to the ridge forked imperceptibly beneath a jutting stone. It was just wide enough for an animal or a human foot, and invisible to anyone who did not know it was there, which was most people. It turned steeply up between two rock walls into bushes. Behind the bushes, in the cliff was the narrow opening of a cave. The Cherokee called it Breathing Rock because it was like the mouth of the mountain. In summer a breeze blew out of the cave, and in winter air was sucked in.

Inside, the cave widened and vaulted into two rooms. The only sound came from water dripping into a rock basin. When a fire was lit in the cave, the light glittered on seams of quartz in the rocks, and higher up, the walls were blackened by smoke from other, older fires. The light also picked up shards of bone and flat, pointed stones with a narrow groove on side, broken clay pots, and half-buried Spanish coins.

Eight-year-old Dancing Rabbit and her great-grandmother, her two young aunts who were newly married and missing their husbands, her mother, and her younger brother and a little sister who could barely walk had been there for weeks, ever since their neighbor, the white man Drumheller, who pastured his cattle on the lower slopes of the mountain, came to offer Dancing Rabbit's father money for their land by the river. By then he and Dancing Rabbit's mother and great-grandmother and aunts had already plowed the black soil, and the corn and beans and squash that Dancing Rabbit helped plant were poking up tiny green shoots. "Come on, Jesse," the man had pleaded as her father turned his back. "We been neighbors for years, can't nobody say I didn't try to pay you for your livestock, you know you got to leave it behind anyway, and what you done to improve the land, your fences and all; use the money to get yourself set up in the west territory the government's giving you. Buy some new cattle and chickens. They got good land waiting for you there, and you can . . ." Dancing Rabbit's father had stalked off.

It wasn't the first time Drumheller had come to their cabin tucked away in a cove by the river, offering money, always brusquely refused. Dancing Rabbit overheard her parents' whispered conversations afterward. "They want us to give up our land . . . to go west . . . where darkness lives and the wind of death blows . . . John Ross refused . . . but the treaty was signed . . . Elias Boudinot . . . Major Ridge . . . Stand Watie . . . agreed. Betrayers . . . hide here and bide our time . . . everything will be all right in the end. They cannot force us . . ."

"They say soldiers will come . . . a new stockade by the river . . ."

Dancing Rabbit's great-grandmother listened, impassive and contemptuous of the white people's greed and lying ways. Dancing Rabbit wondered why they said at school that her great-grandmother's name had once been Rhiannon and she had lived among the whites. Her great-grandmother was Singing Wind, a beloved woman and powerful. The old woman muttered a death sentence on Watie and Ridge and Boudinot for binding the Cherokee to removal without their consent.

She told Dancing Rabbit, these three should be taken alive and tortured, long and slowly according to the old ways, before being burned at the stake.

Dancing Rabbit's father refused to go. "This is our land. I will die here. Anyway, I don't want you traveling," he said. Her mother's stomach was swollen like the full moon, and Dancing Rabbit knew that meant there would soon be another baby in the corner of the cabin where the children slept rolled in quilts.

Dancing Rabbit had seen her mother touch her father's face. "Be careful," and then her father would slip away again at dawn to tend the crops and see to the chickens and horses or to notch the ears of new calves. He wouldn't return until late, when the white men were sure to be drunk or sleeping. The weather had been exceptionally good this year. He described how the beans were flowering already, the first little squashes had appeared on the vines, and the maize had shot up in record time and was now taller than Dancing Rabbit.

Her great-grandmother didn't like their enforced seclusion at a busy time of year. She fretted that her grandson-in-law had no business in the fields, that hoeing and weeding and keeping the birds and cattle away were women's work. She muttered about men who ought to be hunting and weren't, how there would be no jerky to dry in the fireplace, no bear grease through the lean months of winter. She refused to call her granddaughter's husband Jesse. She referred to him by his Cherokee name.

In the cave they had blankets, water from the spring in the rocks, and a supply of dried corn and jerky. Sometimes her father brought fresh meat or fish from the river. After a while her two young aunts had slipped away in the night to find their husbands and had not returned. Her great-grandmother complained of their shameful behavior in going. It was for a man to come to his wife, at her mother's house.

Dancing Rabbit's great-grandmother used their enforced idleness to tell Dancing Rabbit and her little brother and sister about the old ways of "the people" and the seven clans. This knowledge was important, she said. They must remember and pass it on to their own children and grandchildren. She made the children recite it back to her: the names of the seven clans—the clan was the most important family. Sons and daughters belonged to their mother's clan from birth to death. Dancing Rabbit, her sister, and brother were of the Wolf Clan like her mother and grandmother and aunts. Their father was a Deer, like his mother, brothers, and sisters. They must not marry within their own Wolf Clan; it was forbidden for any but a member of the Wolf Clan to kill a wolf. She taught them the ancient law of blood revenge, that a clan was obliged to avenge the killing of one of its members, whether accidental or not. The blood of the victim cried out to his or her relations until the killer or a member of the killer's clan was slain or a substitute was offered and accepted for adoption in the victim's place. Until the matter was settled one way or another, the spirit of the dead could not pass on to the Darkening Land.

"Shh, Grandmother!" said Dancing Rabbit's mother, lying on a pile of skins. "Our people agreed years ago to abolish this law."

Dancing Rabbit's great-grandmother spat contemptuously into the fire. Dancing Rabbit could see the resentment and disappointment in her heart that this was so. "They should not have agreed to this," she said in a low voice to Dancing Rabbit. "The council of grandfathers agreed because they thought it bought them the patience and forbearance of the whites. An advantage, they believed. The council of grandmothers would have cared nothing for the white man's advantage."

Her great-grandmother described to the wide-eyed children how the Cherokee girls were the most beautiful, the women the strongest and most graceful, the grandmothers the wisest, most beautiful women of the tribe, how the Cherokee braves were the greatest warriors of all, and how they withdrew from the tribe to purify and paint themselves before a battle, their war songs and victory shouts and death chants, their victories over the Creeks and Choctaw, how Cherokee warriors never showed fear even at the moment of death, the power of the wise council of grandmothers to decide whether to give captives to the women to torture and kill or to pardon them to use them as slaves, or even adopt captives. She sang songs about the Uktena, who had the body of a snake, wings of a bird, and antlers of a deer and lurked to paralyze the unwary and kill them with its breath, to prevent them from seizing the crystal in the middle of its head. Anyone who succeeded in snatching the crystal obtained extraordinary powers.

Her great-grandmother recited the same things over and over until Dancing Rabbit grew bored. She knew it all by heart. She missed their home, her friends at the mission school, her lessons, and especially her teacher, Miss Maury, who had curly red hair that was wound tightly into a bun at the nape of her neck each morning. By midday her hair had escaped in wisps and tendrils, which Miss Maury would try and try to repin. Afternoon lessons were punctuated by the sound of falling hairpins, and the children would wait for the moment Miss Maury gave up and let down her hair that caught the light and looked as if it were on fire. This hair fascinated the children, who giggled and pointed, and Miss Maury laughed with them and shrugged. She also had very blue eyes that seemed wide with surprise even when nothing surprising had happened. The eyes reminded Dancing Rabbit that her great-grandmother had blue eyes too. Miss Maury had explained that Dancing Rabbit's Christian name was really Dora and showed her how to write it in the white people's script. Miss Maury was astounded how easily Dora learned her lessons and praised her for her neat writing and correct figuring, her ability to memorize hymns and Bible verses.

At the beginning of the year, Miss Maury had told the children that the mission board had donated a copy of the Bible to be given to the child who had memorized the most Bible verses by the end of the year. Dancing Rabbit was determined to be the one called up to receive it at the prize giving on the last day of school. She imagined over and over how it would be; her parents and great-grandmother and all the different clan members who sent their children to the mission school would clap with approval and admiration as Dora Bonney of the Wolf Clan was called up before everyone.

All the elders, except for Dancing Rabbit's great-grandmother, said the school was a good thing, that the children must be heedful, learn well, and bring credit to the tribe and their clans. Bored now without her lessons and her daily scripture verse to memorize, and missing Miss Maury, Dancing Rabbit teased her mother to let them go home so she could return to school, but her mother refused. Dancing Rabbit's great-grandmother, who never called her Dora, said sharply that they should never have allowed the school on tribal land.

The next time her father came, he reported soldiers had come to build a stockade by the river. He had forbidden the children to go near the entrance of the cave where they could at least sit in the sunlight and look at the forest. Now they must stay far back in the cave. He told them he heard the Uktena outside, hungry and waiting.

At first Dancing Rabbit obeyed and kept far back from the entrance in case the Uktena stuck its head inside looking for them. But the Uktena kept out of sight, and Dancing Rabbit was tired of the cave and no longer wanted to play with the odd-shaped shells, the stones with a small creature trapped inside, or the sharp flints her great-grandmother said were old spear points that had killed many enemies. The cave was dark and stank of bear, and the water that trickled down the rocks tasted strongly of iron. They had been in the dark and cold for weeks.

Nor did her mother want to play. For days all her mother wanted to do was lie quietly in her blanket by their small fire, until today when she had begun breathing hard, with sharp little gasps every so often. Dancing Rabbit hovered until her great-grandmother told her to make herself useful and collect a gourd of water. Then her great-grandmother took some slippery elm bark and touch-me-not stems from her pouch, and she pounded them into a paste. She mixed the paste with a little of the water, then sprinkled it over Dancing Rabbit's mother, chanting softly and touching the mixture to her mother's lips to make the baby appear quickly.

While her great-grandmother hovered chanting and crooning over her mother, Dancing Rabbit scowled. She wanted a drink from the sacred spring at the bottom of the mountain, where she knew the wild strawberries would be ripe and sweet and scented in the sun. She was tired of being cooped up! She crept to the entrance and peered out, looking for the Uktena. She didn't see it anywhere; maybe it had gone away. Outside the sunshine was dazzling and hot, and the birds called her to come outside too. A white-tailed deer and her fawn were feeding on the slope in the spring sunshine, the fawn's tail twitching merrily. "Come!" it called and bounded off a few feet.

Checking that her great-grandmother's back was turned, Dancing Rabbit seized her chance and sprang free from the cave into the hot sun. The doe and her fawn bolted.

Inside the cave, Dancing Rabbit's mother cried out and, despite her great-grandmother's protests, heaved herself up. Scrambling down the slope to the path leading off toward the spring, Dancing Rabbit looked back, happy to see her mother coming after her, playing the chase game they both loved.

The little girl skipped and looked back, shouting for her mother to hurry and they would find strawberries before the Uktena ate them all. Usually her mother could run like the wind, but not now. She slid heavily down the path, her calico skirts snagging on the bushes and clutching at saplings to slow her, calling for Dancing Rabbit to come back at once. But Dancing Rabbit was very thirsty now, and she could hear the trickle of the spring, so she pretended not to hear.

She was kneeling to scoop up a drink when she heard her mother's sharp cry. Turning, she saw that white men on horses followed by a wagon were approaching. One of the men was Mr. Drumheller; the others were strangers. One of the strangers whipped his horse and rode straight up the hill at Dancing Rabbit's mother. He cut her off before she could reach Dancing Rabbit, and reining in sharply, he leaned down to give her a hard blow across her face. Dancing Rabbit saw her mother stumble and fall heavily down the slope and lie still. Dancing Rabbit froze and watched the rest of the men dismount and walk to where her mother lay.

"Well . . . we found Jesse's family. Not at their homestead, the children not at school, I knew they had to be here somewheres. Sure enough, they musta been hidin' in a cave somewhere up there."

"Little one's over there getting a drink. Get her first. Indian kids are slippery." The tall white man who had hit her mother strode toward her, swinging a length of rope in his hand. He grabbed the child hard by the arm and jerked her to her feet. She fought back at once, sinking her sharp little teeth into his hand as hard as she could. He swore and grabbed her by the hair until she let go, then gave her a slap that made her ears ring. "Indian brat!" he snarled, lifting his hand again. "We just taught your pa a lesson, teach you one too. Shoulda killed the whole damned tribe years ago when they had the chance. Sooner you people are gone the better." He hit her again.

Dancing Rabbit's nose began to bleed, and she saw stars. It was her first taste of violence. Cherokee children were never hit. The man let go of her to unwind his rope, and Dancing Rabbit fell to the ground. Something made her lie there quietly. "My people are warriors." She repeated her great-grandmother's words in Cherokee under her breath. She told herself she felt no pain from the blows.

"Come on, Silas, she's just a kid. Leave her and her mother till we get the others. They ain't going nowhere. The old lady and other children won't be far away."

"Let her be," agreed the man named Drumheller. He was the one who had tried to give her father money. Now Drumheller knelt where her mother had fallen in the dirt. "Nancy," he said, "come on, you know you got to go. They got Jesse this morning, didn't treat him too good neither, but it was his own fault. He pitched into three of them with his hoe, lucky they didn't shoot him outright. After you folks are all accounted for, they'll bring everybody's household stuff on the wagons. So you won't lose nothing." He tried pulling Dancing Rabbit's mother up by her arm, but she was heavy and groaning, and she didn't get up, no matter how hard he pulled.

"We tried to pay for his improvements, even though we don't have to, strictly speaking; can't nobody said we didn't try to do right by you. But you're going." Dancing Rabbit's mother gave a shrill unearthly cry of pain and arched her back. The tall white man drew back. "I didn't hurt her," he said. The others stared. "We wasn't supposed to hurt nobody, just bring 'em in. But Nancy here's got a baby coming." He stood and stepped back, taking off his hat and wiping a forearm across his brow. He was uncertain, out of his depth.

Dancing Rabbit's mother screamed again, with all her strength so that it echoed, so that it disconcerted the men, who looked at each other and shrugged. Dancing Rabbit ran to her mother's side. White people were so ignorant. She knew pain wasn't the cause of her mother's screaming; it was to warn the others still hiding in the cave not to come out. Dancing Rabbit felt something wet on her knees. When she looked down to see why, red was seeping slowly through her mother's calico skirts to stain her own deerskin one. Her mother's scream rose again, and Dancing Rabbit could feel her mother's hand crushing her own small one to give her courage. Then her mother was panting for breath like a wounded deer, her eyes wide and rolling back in her head, and a sudden scent of hot, now dark red blood filled Dancing Rabbit's nostrils. Dancing Rabbit felt dizzy but turned her head and stared defiantly up at the white men. *Never show fear before an enemy.*

"Got to get them on the boat, that's our orders. They don't go willing, we tie 'em up and take 'em."

"You can't tie Nancy up now! What good's that gonna do? They didn't say nothin' about women havin' babies . . ."

Dancing Rabbit's mother moaned loudly, arched her back again, and shut her eyes.

"Looks like there'll be two less to move soon," said Drumheller, not wanting to touch Nancy. Both of his wives had died giving birth, and he had nothing personal against Jesse or his family, but they were mixed bloods, and now that the treaty had been signed, the law said they had to leave and go west with the others. This morning he and the other boys were just doing their duty. Upholding the law.

On the ground, Dancing Rabbit's mother began to shiver as the red crept farther from under her body. Drumheller saw and stepped back even farther. Childbirth was women's business, and like most men, he was squeamish about woman blood.

"Little one's not going anywhere. Let's go find the others. Old woman can deal with this mess. She'll have her herbs and stuff, birth the baby in the wagon. Nancy'll be all right. Indian women are tough. Wagon's here. Let's get the others. They're up there." He pointed up the hill.

The men disappeared through the trees. Dancing Rabbit's knees grew wetter. Her mother was whispering, and she leaned close to hear. Dancing Rabbit's mother's breathing was ragged and uneven. Her eyes opened and took in Dancing Rabbit's bloody face and swelling nose.

"Do not be afraid, Daughter, but listen and obey me. Leave me and run, hide from them quickly," she gasped. "Hide well so they cannot take you away. My spirit will not go to the Darkening World yet. I will stay to guide and protect you . . ." She groaned again. "Dancing Rabbit," she whispered, her eyes full of love and death. "Hide until they are gone, then find your kinsman Gideon Wolfpaw. He is Great-Grandmother's father. He went into the mountain to live many years ago, and he is there still. They say he can fly with the eagles. Tell him," she said, closing her eyes tight again against whatever pain was inside of her, "his daughter Singing Wind's granddaughter sent you, that I leave you with him to be guardians of our land and to avenge this evil done to your people. Go." She released Dancing Rabbit's hand, pointed feebly to a sheer rock cliff where scraggly bushes grew, enough for a small person to find a foothold. She gave her daughter a push. "Go before they return . . . go, and my spirit will find you."

There were shouts above. "Got 'em!"

Minutes later the white men were crashing back down through the trees, the one named Drumheller dragging Dancing Rabbit's gray-haired great-grandmother with her hands tied behind her and Dancing Rabbit's little brother and sister trussed and dragged roughly in the dirt. The old woman spat at the man dragging her. "Easy, Granny, or I'll leave Nancy behind where she's lying," he threatened, angry. "You wouldn't want me doing that, now would you?"

Dancing Rabbit's great-grandmother began to chant a curse on the white men in Cherokee and spat again. She was little and gray and bent, but she kicked out sideways, and the man dragging the two children fell. "Damn you, old witch. Call yourself Singing Wind, but you're just crazy Rhiannon Vann. Your pa up there?" He jerked his head up at the mountain. "They say Gideon is still alive up there but can't nobody find him. He ain't helping you none, is he, Rhiannon?"

Her great-grandmother kicked out again, and this time the man fell harder.

He swore and got to his feet, slapped her great-grandmother, who staggered, then kicked him again. He hit her hard enough to knock her down, but the old woman clung to his foot, shrieking wildly, struggling with the men who busied themselves restraining her with a rope. In a fierce whisper, Dancing Rabbit's mother gasped, "She's making it possible for you to run, Daughter! While they aren't looking. Go!" and pushed her away. Now Dancing Rabbit obeyed, disappearing into the bushes as swiftly and silently as a small animal. Ten minutes later she was high above the cave, hidden in a tree. She caught her breath and looked down.

The white men had brought the wagon and turned it around. She watched them lift her mother's bulky form into the wagon and throw her great-grandmother in afterward. She heard her little brother and sister, too young to know better than to cry, wailing as they were thrown after her and landing with a hard thump. She could see Drumheller saying something and pointing up the slope. The other men shook their heads and pointed toward the river. "Bobcat'll get her if she don't come out now. He'll claw her to pieces, eat her alive," one shouted up at the mountain. "Bobcat . . . bobcat . . . bobcat," his voice echoed. "Claw . . . claw . . . claw . . . alive . . . live . . . live . . ."

They waited to see if this had any effect. Then the driver cracked his whip, and the wagon lurched back down the narrow road, disappearing behind the trees. When it emerged at the foot of the mountain, it turned toward the river landing. A thin echo of her great-grandmother's voice raised in a death chant carried back to Dancing Rabbit, who knew this was her great-grandmother's farewell. Craning through a gap in the branches, Dancing Rabbit could see the river landing below, crowded with people. She watched until the wagon carrying her family emerged from the trees and reached it. Two men came off a raft to carry her mother. She thought her father was one of them but couldn't really be sure. He was limping. Too late she understood why he had made them hide, though she did not understand why the white men were doing this.

More white men with guns kicked and pushed a last few stragglers up the gangplank, and with the soldiers standing by with their rifles at the ready, the raft was poled slowly away from the bank.

Dancing Rabbit's heart lurched with hope. A lone figure with fiery hair was running distractedly up and down the landing, waving her handkerchief, calling the names of her pupils from the mission. Her keening cries of "Polly, Daniel, Dora . . ." came on the wind. Miss Maury waved and shouted and finally seemed to give up. The men with guns took no notice of her. Finally Miss Maury sank to her knees on the quay. Dancing Rabbit knew that meant she was praying. When Miss Maury prayed, Dancing Rabbit had learned that meant Miss Maury was talking to God, and she must kneel quietly by Miss Maury's side and open her heart to Jesus, who loved children. Miss Maury said God and the Lord Jesus could do anything and that Christians should put their whole trust in them to help in times of trouble. The Lord Jesus heard prayers, especially those of children.

Dancing Rabbit decided the best thing was to pray too. She and her whole family had been baptized in the creek behind the mission church, and although she was in a tree up the cliff and could not kneel down, she bowed her head and squeezed her eyes shut tight and said the Lord's Prayer that Miss Maury had taught them.

But when she looked up, neither God nor the Lord Jesus had been listening, because they hadn't turned the raft around and led everyone back to the shore. Instead the boat was moving farther away, catching the current. She said the Lord's Prayer over and over, as loud as she could, but the boat kept moving downstream, getting smaller.

The air around Dancing Rabbit swelled with sorrow and disbelief. Down below her were cabins and barns, empty now, their inhabitants being carried away. And the fields where the beans and squash were already up, so fine had the weather been, so fertile the soil. It was a favorite saying of her father's that a Cherokee never farmed poor land. The fields with their new crops were empty!

It was time for the Lord Jesus to come down from the sky, now, and turn the boat around so the people could go home. Expecting this to happen any minute, Dancing Rabbit watched the raft disappear round a bend in the river. She watched throughout the day so she would know when it came back, and then she watched the sun disappear into the western darkness where the boat had gone. As the sun set, abandoned cows in the valley lowed miserably to be milked, and she watched the stars come out, heard dogs barking for their owners. She climbed down from her perch and huddled at the base of the tree and fell asleep waiting for her mother's spirit to come.

The next morning when she woke, the world felt empty. Miss Maury had lied; the Lord Jesus had no power over white men. Her mother had not come. Dancing Rabbit decided this must be because she had not obeyed her mother's order to find Gideon Wolfpaw. She looked up at the cliff rising above her. It looked impossible to climb. She considered the few scrubby plants and crevasses for a long time to see what offered a purchase. She was light-headed from hunger but would have to find a way up it somehow. Her mother's spirit was waiting until Dancing Rabbit had obeyed.

In the old days, warriors went days without eating, her great-grandmother had told her. They did not feel hunger any more than they felt pain. Dancing Rabbit must be like the warriors. The empty, faint feeling did not matter. She must climb the cliff and learn from Gideon Wolfpaw the old ways that made the people powerful. One day when she had learned enough, she would become a beloved woman herself. She would hunt the Uktena, steal the jewel from its forehead, and turn herself into an eagle. Then she would fly down among the white settlers and pluck out their eyes with her beak, rip their crops from the earth with her talons, and spit in their wells to poison their water so that when a white person drank, he would sicken and die. She would kill their children, put an end to the accursed race until there was not a single white person left to mourn what had been.

Then she would fly above the earth into the Darkening Land until she found her people. They would see the eagle wheeling triumphantly above them and greet her with joy. And when they had all gathered, she would fly ahead of them, leading them back to the place where the sun dwelt, leading them home.

This she swore to her mother's spirit.

Dancing Rabbit clutched a root and began to pull herself up the cliff.

ACKNOWLEDGMENTS

Writing a manuscript is one thing, producing a book quite another. The people who have turned *The Valley* into an actual book have been, one and all, fantastic to work with, and I am grateful for their support, professionalism, and determination to transform what I wrote into the best possible book. I was fortunate to work with all of them, and any success this book may enjoy reflects on everyone involved.

First, I would like to thank my wonderful agent, Jane Dystel, at Dystel & Goderich Literary Management for her support, patience, and friendship. Jane is the agent every author dreams of having, for her professionalism, her sound advice, and her talent for understanding how an author works best. In my case this meant, for the most part, leaving me to get on with it, even while my rashly optimistic deadlines passed us by. Jane remained calm, always available if I needed her, ready with a gentle nudge at all the right times and the reminder that "It takes as long as it takes" when I began to despair of ever putting my characters into their graves and bringing the story to a close.

I am also grateful to Miriam Goderich at Dystel & Goderich, who deals so efficiently and swiftly with contracts and who, once again, brought her invaluable editorial expertise to bear on a first draft. I appreciate her suggestions and support.

Amazon Publishing, as always, is a joy to work with, focused on turning out the best possible book and hugely supportive of their authors. I owe special thanks to Tara Parsons, former editorial director at Amazon Publishing, for her extraordinary patience and whose unflagging enthusiasm and support convinced me from the first that my book was in good hands. I'm also grateful for her helpful editorial input and judgment. Finally, I ought to mention that Tara's ability to resolve any issue with charm and speed in a conference call is truly impressive.

Thanks are due to Jodi Warshaw, senior editor at Amazon Publishing, for her constant support and engagement and the kind of professionalism that makes the publishing process appear effortlessly smooth, from an author's perspective at least. It has been a pleasure to work with her.

Also at Amazon, I would like to thank the wonderful author team, especially Gabriella Van den Heuvel, who is always quick to respond to any query I might have.

It was my good luck to work again with developmental editor Charlotte Herscher. She deals brilliantly and insightfully with lengthy manuscripts and is blessed with a rare ability to understand an author's intentions and go straight to the heart of a book. Her sure touch transforms a manuscript, and I trust her judgment implicitly.

I appreciate the hard work done by copy editor Laura Petrella, who copyedited with skill, humor, and an eagle eye. It is slightly shaming for an author to realize how necessary a copy editor is, especially as, after many years living in England, said author's spelling has become stuck in a sort of no-man's-land between British English and American. Laura performed an expert job on a very long manuscript.

I want to express my appreciation to cover designer Shasti O'Leary-Soudant, who kindly put up with my many suggestions and developed the elusive "perfect" image for the cover. It catches the spirit of the book and is just exactly right.

Finally, my family never fails to amaze me with their generous, unflagging support of my writing. Special thanks are due to my husband, Roger Low, who puts up with my distracted concentration on other eras, imaginary people, and complicated timelines, not to mention very late dinners, with love, good humor, and better crisis management skills than I possess. He does not find comments like "My mind is too full and it hurts" anything out of the ordinary, and he understands my need to work in the sort of quiet, private space that Virginia Woolf called "a room of her own" and he calls "lockdown."

Given that so much of my day is spent absorbed in a fictional world of my own devising, I'm unfailingly grateful that beyond my study, Roger, Cass, Michelle, Niels, Jonny, and our darling grandchildren, Bo, Poppy, and Jake, are there to remind me that real life is just that, real. They are my greatest fans and proudest, least critical supporters. Everything I write, I write for them.

—Helen Bryan

ABOUT THE AUTHOR

Photo © 2016 Cassell Bryan-Low

Helen Bryan is a Virginia native who grew up in Tennessee. After graduating from Barnard College, she moved to England, where she studied law and was a barrister for ten years before devoting herself to writing full-time.

A member of the Inner Temple, Bryan is the author of four previous books: the World War II novel *War Brides*; the historical novel *The Sisterhood*; the biography *Martha Washington: First Lady of Liberty*, which won an Award of Merit from the Colonial Dames of America; and the legal handbook *Planning Applications and Appeals*. *The Valley* is the first in a planned trilogy based on her childhood stories of ancestors who settled in Virginia and Maryland before Tennessee became a state.

Bryan resides in London with her family.